DIAL PRESS, INC.
461 - 4th AVENUE
NEW YORK 16, N.Y.

GREAT
ENGLISH SHORT
NOVELS

GREAT
ENGLISH SHORT
NOVELS

EDITED AND WITH AN INTRODUCTION
BY CYRIL CONNOLLY

A PERMANENT LIBRARY BOOK

THE DIAL PRESS   NEW YORK 1953

Acknowledgments

THE SECRET SHARER by Joseph Conrad reprinted by permission of J. M. Dent & Sons, Ltd., London.

THE FARCICAL HISTORY OF RICHARD GREENOW by Aldous Huxley reprinted from LIMBO, by permission of Harper and Brothers, and Chatto and Windus, London.

BETWEEN THE ACTS by Virginia Woolf, copyright, 1941, by Harcourt, Brace and Company, Inc. Reprinted by permission of Harcourt, Brace and Company, and Leonard Woolf.

DESIGNED BY WILLIAM R. MEINHARDT

MANUFACTURED IN THE UNITED STATES OF AMERICA BY

THE HADDON CRAFTSMEN, INC., SCRANTON, PENNA.

Contents

Introduction

THE GREAT SHORT NOVEL is not an English form. We have no word like *nouvelle* or *novella* or *conte*, we have neither *Candide* nor *Adolphe* nor *The Aspern Papers* nor *The Great Gatsby*. We have *Rasselas* which is insupportable, *Vathek* which was written in French and *Wuthering Heights* and *Persuasion* which are both on the long side. Does such a form exist in England or do we but possess short stories which at a certain climax of verbosity are designated novels, like *The House with the Green Shutters* which I read "in its first form was only 20,000 words long but this was elaborated to 80,000, when the book was published." The reading public, abetted by the publisher was—and is—the villain, a public which required three-volume novels to read aloud in the winter evenings and now demands 100,000 words to obtain value for money. Yet some very short novels have enjoyed a popular success: *The Loved One*; *Olivia*; *The Young Visiters*; *Lady into Fox*; *Gentlemen Prefer Blondes*.

Until the Eighteenth Century the English had a perfect art form of this length: it was the play. The Elizabethan and Restoration dramatists ran to about seventy pages and I was much tempted fraudulently to present *Love for Love* or *The Revenger's Tragedy* as a classical example. But there is a profound dissimilarity between a story which is intended to be read aloud and the play which is meant to be acted: they are like a teapot and a coffeepot, similar but not interchangeable. The difference lies in what is called 'theatre.' And so I have left out plays and made an investigation of what happened to this imaginary form after 1700 when the drama was no longer there to fill it.

The Eighteenth Century witnessed the rise of the English novelists, of Defoe, Fielding, Richardson, Smollett and Sterne. They are long-winded writers and I find their few short books intolerably bright and affected. *Jonathan Wild* is a sadistic firework, the *Sentimental Journey* too mannered and whimsical. All my favorite novels possess both intelligence and simplicity; there is no combination I admire more, especially when one can also detect imagination in the use of words. When we arrive at the Victorian novelists we find them as little conscious as their predecessors of the novel's aesthetic possibilities. They are both prolix and prolific. Dickens and Thackeray favour digressions and in a short novel there is no room for them. Thus *Denis Duval* is short only because it is unfinished and suffers, like everything Thackeray wrote, from his glittering uneasy manner. If we are looking for great short novels, then, we shall have to go out into the byways for them. Is the search justified? To answer this we must return to a consideration of the form.

What is a book? The object as we know it derives from the papyrus roll, from 15 to 30 feet long, written without breaks on only one side, and this roll gradually gave way, in the Christian era, to the Codex or papyrus book.

These books were short (the average length being one of Thucydides), and the ancient book, whether on papyrus or vellum, was a small and precious object. The short book is the perpetuation of the *Encheiridion* or small portable volume which, like the *Odes* of Horace or *The Imitation of Christ*, can go everywhere with us. It has nothing to do with the huge folios of the seventeenth-century library. Now for those with normal eyesight these short books run to about 150 pages and we can say that the form is determined by what can be staunchly bound, yet fit into the sleeve or the pocket and be read without a magnifying glass. In this length of 40,000 to 50,000 words only a certain amount can be said, even as on a canvas of small dimensions only a few kinds of picture can be painted. This is especially true of fiction, and it is almost an

viii

axiom that, in such a length, there is room only to develop two or three characters, and that if there be many more, they are seldom brought out, but represent humours or ideas, like people in a cartoon. The simplest composition will explore but one character, after which will come the love story that makes use of two, or the triangle drama where there are three; or there can be two characters and a narrator: but the utmost limit will be four and then there will scarcely be room for all to develop interlocking relationship; and to be changed by time and each other. Thus in *Adolphe* or *Sylvie* we have a love story recounted by a narrator and in *Candide* we have a hero and a procession of characters who represent ideas and are not fully drawn. In a play like *Othello* we find a triangle drama which is truly exploited except that Desdemona does not mature like the other two principals. The essence, in fact, of these short novels for which we are looking must be a character who is changing, or who is involved with two or even three others whose lives are being altered by interaction or by spiritual experiences which deepen them, so that the reader who begins the book on the surface is led inward by a subterranean passage. When we can find an imaginary experience which enriches our understanding of existence and which involves two or three people, not a whole society, and when we can detect signs of pressure and elimination—in fact intensity —surrounding that experience, then we can be sure that we have come upon an excellent short novel.

The simplest of such forms which involve but one character is the straight biography or autobiography and we must look about for examples of these which betray the presence of the magic trio—style, growth, intensity (style being that mixture of intelligence, simplicity and the imaginative use of words for which we have so pronounced a craving). Fortunately there is one. Johnson's *Life of Savage* has been accounted the best short biography in English, it is remarkable to our purpose for three reasons. The style is without the polished effort noticeable in his *Rasselas*, it is ponderous yet agile and unaffected, being kept in hand by Johnson's affection for his subject; then it may be said to reveal growth and intensity, for as Savage progresses from injustice to injustice, from poverty to ease and back, we watch his character forming and his relationship with Johnson increasing in intimacy and understanding, until the stern moralist has learnt to forgive—and to plead for our forgiveness.

We come now to the simplest form of fiction. *Castle Rackrent* is an imaginary biography, in this case of a family. It belongs to the end of the Eighteenth Century and had an influence on Scott and afterwards on Turgeniev who was encouraged by it to take his country gentlemen and peasants as his model. It was one of the first of the family chronicles and certainly the first to put the Irish on the scene. All Anglo-Irish literature has descended from it down to Somerville and Ross and Miss Elizabeth Bowen. The reader must honour it as a prototype and remember that the jokes, though not always subtle, occur here for the first time.

Another simple type of the short novel is the adventure story, in which a narrator describes some thrilling sequence of events. Buchan's *Thirty-nine Steps*, Falkner's *Moonfleet*, Erskine Childers' *Riddle of the Sands*, and innumerable stories by Stevenson, Hardy, Conrad, Kipling, and Maugham fit into this category. Push the adventure over into the macabre and we get the *Roman Noir*—the *Castle of Otranto*, *Dracula*, *The Monk* and many others. I have chosen one which is on the borderline of the supernatural; Sheridan Le Fanu's *Room in the Dragon Volant* because the author clearly intended it for a short novel and divided it into chapters and because I much enjoy the Anglo-Parisian scene and the period of which he writes so freshly and carelessly. Published in 1872, *In a Glass Darkly* (from which it is taken) seems happily ignorant of all developments in the art of fiction over half a century; the style is as archaic and un-self-conscious as a suite of Early Victorian mahogany in a station hotel.

So much for the simple unicellular varieties. We now reach

a section which I have called the 'Expanding Psyche' because it is no longer straight fiction; if there be a narrator, he is not by the end the same simple fellow as at the beginning; the characters act upon each other; the author burrows under ground. The narrator of *Castle Rackrent* or *The Room in the Dragon Volant* is simply telling a story, in *Cousin Phillis* or *The Secret Sharer* he grows up with the telling. *Cousin Phillis* is a love story built round the impact of modern industrial civilisation (the railway) on the old slow deep patterns of an agricultural community; both are given their due, but Phillis and her father are inevitably defeated by the narrator and his new-fangled friend. If all four characters were equally developed this would be a perfect short novel, but only the father and daughter are fully realised and we are left with an admirable Victorian 'genre' painting.

The Lifted Veil seems to me that rare thing, a horror story which is horrible. George Eliot is not only a most gifted writer but the possessor of a first-rate mind. One can understand Henry James's passionate admiration for her and see how such a psychological story must have influenced him. I believe it to be as correct a picture of 'second sight,' or one kind of schizophrenic delusion as can be found in Nerval or Poe. For a time I considered capping it with Stevenson's *Doctor Jekyll and Mr. Hyde*, a progenitor, with its romantic London background, of Sherlock Holmes and Dorian Gray. However, since the phrase 'Jekyll and Hyde' has passed into the language, none can read the tale without being aware of the solution. The *Farcical History of Richard Greenow*, a similar story by Aldous Huxley, also fails in the ending, for cases of dual possession which lead to suicide seem to beg the question. But I have included it for its wit and charming period flavour. There were also other candidates for a love story, such as, David Garnett's *Lady into Fox*, *Sailor's Return*, and *Man in the Zoo*. The first two are written in an archaic style, *tours de force*, examples of de-sophistication written to satisfy a sophisticated audience and therefore not quite great, even as *Man in* the Zoo suffers from an unreal heroine. Hardy's *Adventures of a Milkmaid* is another triangle drama of great charm which tails away into facetiousness. Conrad's stories suffer from the unreality of his opening scenes, particularly in the dialogue, and it is hard to find one where he comes quickly to the point. *Typhoon* is, I think, a model of its kind, but I have included the less familiar *The Secret Sharer* because it is all story and no padding and haunts the reader with its obsessional undertones.

We come now to the limits of the form. Meredith's *Case of General Ople* is a love story depicted with the brush of a Chinese painter instead of words. The suburban scene is irridescent with silent laughter. Peacock's *Nightmare Abbey* (1818) is a comedy of manners, a key book of the anti-romantic movement which manages to satirise Coleridge, Shelley and Byron with a dig at Wordsworth. This short novel is very like a play and seems at first to be introducing half a dozen major characters but on examination it will be found that several represent ideas and are but simulacra of humanity; the essential situation is another triangle. The conflict of ideas here represented has, however, never subsided. People who have been disillusioned by the Russian Revolution behave just like people who were disillusioned by the French Revolution; existentialists enjoy their pessimism as much as transcendentalists like Mr. Flosky, and the forces of normality like Mr. Hilary are still driven on to a position of epicurean common sense which is seldom conducive to works of art. *Gryll Grange* is Peacock's best book, also his longest, and his humanism has there had time to mellow and fortify itself; but *Nightmare Abbey* is gay, crisp and youthful and underneath the ridicule the Romantics are present in all their mutinous youth and glory.

Hazlitt's *Liber Amoris* is a love story in depth. We see the affair in three dimensions; as dialogue, as comments in the narrator's *Journal Intime*, as letters passing from him to a friend and even more objectively in the friend's reply. It is one of the strangest and subtlest books in English, long obscured by Victorian moral indignation.

One would like to have been able to end with some brilliant discovery that might make the fortune of an unknown author, but in this I have not been successful. The last entry I feel, should also be the most intricate in form and should carry the short novel a stage further and suggest to the reader its latent possibilities.

For this purpose I first chose Ford Madox Ford's *Good Soldier* which seemed a beautiful version of the 'mixed double,' but it is really a long novel, a short book ruined by the addition of extra characters and by the fear of omission. A look at Virginia Woolf's *Mrs. Dalloway* made me quickly recoil when suddenly I remembered her posthumous novel *Between the Acts* which received so little attention when it appeared in the gloomiest moment of the war. Here is a short novel which is also an allegory, where the complete and adult power of Virginia Woolf is at its best, and whose theme, as it were, sums up all the others. Finished, though unrevised, it has the importance of a great writer's last words and the poignancy of her backward glance on the England that in 1939 was passing away. I have not been able to crack the code and solve the allegory and that, with a work of art, is as it should be. I have given what hints I can and perhaps one of those who read this book will penetrate the sibyl's last mysterious cry.

So there they are; a biography, an imaginary biography, an adventure story; four types of psychological thriller—and an idyll on allegory, an analytical love story and a comedy of manners. So rich is our literature that, even according to this strict formula, one could easily choose eleven more. And yet the perfect work of art seems wanting. I do not see *Hamlet* or *Phèdre* or the *Georgics* among them. So that still remains to be written. There is still room, there is still time for a writer to take four characters and fit them into a perfect composition, so that each affects each and not a word is wasted. I see it as a string quartet, or as one of Goya's tapestries, of youth beside the water, but I cannot find it in words, nor can I even find a triangle drama in which all three characters seem equally real —so *Gatsby* or *The Spoils of Poynton* must remain without peers—unless this anthology may help someone to surpass them.

1. *The Simplest Forms*

Life of Richard Savage

1744

SAMUEL JOHNSON

As A young man in about 1739 Johnson had met Savage at the offices of the Gentleman's Magazine. Both were very poor but Savage was already well established as a hack and had been responsible for procuring scandalous information on his fellow writers which Pope required for his Dunciad. Like the country mouse with his city mentor, Johnson fell at once under the spell of the more sophisticated and experienced poet and it was probably his youthful admiration and generosity and his unqualified acceptance of Savage's version of himself which spared him the vengeance of this difficult and dangerous paranoiac. According to this version Savage was the natural son of the Countess of Macclesfield and her lover, Richard Savage Earl Rivers, who acknowledged the child by becoming his godfather; his godmother was a Mrs. Lloyd. By this open confession of his wife's adultery Lord Macclesfield obtained a divorce. She kept her fortune and afterwards married a Colonel Brett, and the child was adopted by a baker's wife called Portlock whom he assumed to be his real mother until he went through her papers at her death and found letters from Mrs. Brett's mother, Lady Mason. On his deathbed Lord Rivers had demanded news of his son to whom he wished to leave six thousand pounds, but he had been told by Lady Macclesfield that the boy was dead. She also prevented Savage from ever claiming a legacy from his devoted godmother Mrs. Lloyd, meanly apprenticed him to a cobbler and basely attempted to have him transported to the American colonies. She refused all further communication with him and this unnatural cruelty which deprived him of his birthright and of a mother's love was the source of his misfortune and the explanation of his conduct. Savage either believed this story implicitly, or had deceived himself into believing it, or merely used it to impose

5

on the credulity of others, but in any case it is not wholly true. Lord Rivers' will was made some time before his death and if Mrs. Lloyd had indeed bequeathed a sum of money to Savage none could have prevented him from claiming it. There is no legal proof of her existence. The child of Lord Macclesfield was baptized Richard Smith and no Mrs. Lloyd was godmother. The reasoning is decisive as Croker summed it up. "If Savage were what he represented himself to be nothing could have prevented him his recovering his legacy." Boswell believed that Lady Macclesfield's child did indeed die young and that Savage was the son of the shoemaker under whose wife's care the child had been placed. (He is here confusing the shoemaker with Portlock the baker.) "The talents of Savage," wrote Boswell, "and the mingled fire, rudeness, pride, meanness and ferocity of his character concur in making it credible that he was fit to plan and carry on an ambitious and daring scheme of imposture." While the world still "vibrates in a state of uncertainty as to the truth" one may make a guess that Savage had sufficient information about this distressing episode in Mrs. Brett's life to make her unwilling to go to law about it, and even to persuade her nephew, Lord Tyrconnel, to accept him as a relative for a period as the price of his silence (this period was probably before his trial, not afterwards as Johnson dates it).

On the other hand his failure ever to produce the evidence of his claim, such as the letters to his nurse, or to ask the court for his legacy, appears conclusive. Mrs. Brett, who always called him an impostor, incidentally appears to have been a charming woman, "well known in all the polite circles." Looking out from her window one day she had seen a very handsome man being assaulted for debt by bailiffs, she had called him in, paid his debt and married him. It was Colonel Brett. "Mrs. Brett came into a room one day in her own house and found the Colonel and her maid both fast asleep in two chairs. She tied a white handkerchief round her husband's neck, which was a sufficient proof that she had discovered his intrigue but she never at any time took notice of it to him."

6

The appeal Savage makes to us is that of the typical literary scallywag, a precursor of the French Bohemian writers of the Nineteenth Century. We can assume that at this moment a Savage in New York is getting a second advance from a different publisher on a book he has not written, while another in London is taking his friends or patron's treasures off to the pawn shop and drinking up the proceeds. He is the persecuted persecutor, in whom envy and revenge and frustrated talent masquerade as independence, although he can prove the best of company in the rare moments when the world grants him the living which he is convinced it owes him. When both too poor for a bed, he and Johnson would walk the streets all night singing or shouting patriotic slogans. As an author Savage is remembered by one line, from The Bastard,

> "He lives to build, not boast, a generous race
> No tenth transmitter of a foolish face!"

I like also his letter to his erstwhile patron, Lord Tyrconnel, whom he once addressed, "with the highest gratitude and veneration"; it begins, "Right Honourable Brute and Booby" and concludes, "I defy and despise you. I am, Your determined adversary, R.S."

Johnson wrote the life of Savage largely at one all-night sitting. He received fifteen guineas and it was an immediate success, giving "pleasure as a work of art where the original could only excite disgust." Sir Joshua Reynolds discovered the anonymous pamphlet in Devonshire and began it against a chimney piece, reading it straight through until his arm was entirely numb—and time has not diminished this property.

The appeal Savage makes to us is that of the typical literary scallywag, a precursor of the French Bohemian writers of the Nineteenth Century. We can assume that at this moment a Savage in New York is getting a second advance from a different publisher on a book he has not written, while another in London is taking his friends or patron's treasures off to the pawn shop and drinking up the proceeds. He is the persecuted persecutor, in whom envy and revenge and frustrated talent masquerade as independence; although he can prove the best of company in the rare moments when the world grants him the living which he is convinced it owes him. When both too poor for a bed, he and Johnson would walk the streets all night singing or shouting patriotic slogans. As an author Savage is remembered by one line, from 'The Bastard.'

"He lives to build, not boast, a generous race;
No tenth transmitter of a foolish face."

I like also his letter to his erstwhile patron, Lord Tyrconnel, whom he once addressed, "with the highest gratitude and veneration", it begins, "Right Honourable Brute and Booby", and concludes, "I defy and despise you. I am Your determined adversary, R.S."

Johnson wrote the life of Savage largely at one all-night sitting. He received fifteen guineas and it was an immediate success, giving "pleasure as a work of art where the original could only excite disgust." Sir Joshua Reynolds discovered the anonymous pamphlet in Devonshire and began it against a chimney-piece, reading it straight through until his arm was cramped, numb—and time has not diminished this property.

GREAT ENGLISH SHORT NOVELS

Life of Richard Savage

SAMUEL JOHNSON

I T HAS BEEN observed in all ages, that the advantages of nature or of fortune have contributed very little to the promotion of happiness; and that those whom the splendour of their rank, or the extent of their capacity, have placed upon the summit of human life, have not often given any just occasion to envy in those who look up to them from a lower station; whether it be that apparent superiority incites great designs, and great designs are naturally liable to fatal miscarriages; or that the general lot of mankind is misery, and the misfortunes of those, whose eminence drew upon them an universal attention, have been more carefully recorded, because they were more generally observed, and have in reality been only more conspicuous than those of others, not more frequent, or more severe.

That affluence and power, advantages extrinsic and adventitious, and therefore easily separable from those by whom they are possessed, should very often flatter the mind with expectations of felicity which they cannot give, raises no astonishment; but it seems rational to hope, that intellectual greatness should produce better effects; that minds qualified for great attainments should first endeavour their own benefit; and that they, who are most able to teach others the way to happiness, should with most certainty follow it themselves. But this expectation, however plausible, has been very frequently disappointed. The heroes of literary as well as civil history have been very often no less remarkable for what they have suffered, than for what they have achieved; and volumes have been written only to enumerate the miseries of the learned, and relate their unhappy lives and untimely deaths.

To these mournful narratives, I am about to add the Life of RICHARD SAVAGE, a man whose writings entitle him to an eminent rank in the classes of learning, and whose misfortunes claim a degree of compassion, not always due to the unhappy, as they were often the consequences of the crimes of others, rather than his own.

In the year 1697, Anne Countess of Macclesfield, having lived some time upon very uneasy terms with her husband, thought a public confession of adultery the most obvious and expeditious method of obtaining her liberty; and therefore declared, that the child, with which she was then great, was begotten by the Earl Rivers. This, as may be imagined, made her husband no less desirous of a separation than herself, and he prosecuted his design in the most effectual manner; for he applied not to the ecclesiastical courts for a divorce, but to the parliament for an act, by which his marriage might be dissolved, the nuptial contract annulled, and the children of his wife illegitimated. This act, after the usual deliberation, he obtained, though without the approbation of some, who considered marriage as an affair only cognizable by ecclesiastical judges; and on March 3rd was separated from his wife, whose fortune, which was very great, was repaid her, and who having, as well as her husband, the liberty of making another choice, she in a short time married to Colonel Brett.

While the Earl of Macclesfield was prosecuting this affair, his wife was, on the 10th of January, 1697-8, delivered of a son; and the Earl Rivers, by appearing to consider him as his own, left none any reason to doubt of the sincerity of her declaration; for he was his godfather, and gave him his own name, which was by his direction inserted in the register of St. Andrew's parish in Holborn, but unfortunately left him to the care of his mother, whom, as she was now set free from her husband, he probably imagined likely to treat with great tenderness the child that had contributed to so pleasing an event. It is not indeed easy to discover what motives could be found to overbalance that natural affection of a parent, or what interest could be promoted by neglect or cruelty. The dread of shame or of poverty, by which some wretches have been incited to abandon or to murder their children, cannot be supposed to have affected a woman who had proclaimed her crimes and solicited reproach, and on whom the clemency of the legislature had undeservedly bestowed a fortune, which would have been very little diminished by the expenses which the care of her child could have brought upon her. It was therefore not likely that she would be wicked without temptation; that she would look upon her son from his birth with a kind of resentment and abhorrence; and, instead of supporting, assisting, and defending him, delight to see him struggling with misery, or that she would take every opportunity of aggravating his misfortunes, and obstructing his resources, and with an implacable and restless cruelty continue her persecution from the first hour of his life to the last. But whatever were her motives, no sooner was her son born, than she discovered a resolution of disowning him; and in a very short time removed him from her sight, by committing him to the care of a poor woman, whom she directed to educate him as her own, and enjoined never to inform him of his true parents.

Such was the beginning of the life of Richard Savage. Born with a legal claim to honour and to affluence, he was in two months illegitimated by the parliament, and disowned by his mother, doomed to poverty and obscurity, and launched upon the ocean of life, only that he might be swallowed by its quicksands, or dashed upon its rocks. His mother could not indeed infect others with the same cruelty. As it was impossible to avoid the inquiries which the curiosity or tenderness of her relations made after her child, she was obliged to give some account of the measures she had taken; and her mother, the Lady Mason, whether in approbation of her design, or to prevent more criminal contrivances, engaged to transact with the nurse, to pay her for her care, and to superintend the education of the child.

In this charitable office she was assisted by his godmother, Mrs. Lloyd,* who, while she lived, always looked upon him with that tenderness which the barbarity of his mother made peculiarly necessary; but her death, which happened in his tenth year, was

---

* The illegitimate child of Lady Macclesfield was registered as Richard Smith; no Mrs. Lloyd was godmother and no identifiable Mrs. Lloyd is known from registers to exist. (*Ed.*)

another of the misfortunes of his childhood; for though she kindly endeavoured to alleviate his loss by a legacy of three hundred pounds, yet, as he had none to prosecute his claim, to shelter him from oppression, or call in law to the assistance of justice, her will was eluded by the executors, and no part of the money was ever paid. He was, however, not yet wholly abandoned. The Lady Mason still continued her care, and directed him to be placed at a small grammar school near St. Alban's, where he was called by the name of his nurse, without the least intimation that he had a claim to any other. Here he was initiated in literature, and passed through several of the classes, with what rapidity or with what applause cannot now be known. As he always spoke with respect of his master, it is probable that the mean rank, in which he then appeared, did not hinder his genius from being distinguished, or his industry from being rewarded; and if in so low a state he obtained distinction and rewards, it is not likely that they were gained but by genius and industry.

It is very reasonable to conjecture, that his application was equal to his abilities, because his improvement was more than proportioned to the opportunities which he enjoyed; nor can it be doubted, that if his earliest productions had been preserved, like those of happier students, we might in some have found vigorous sallies of that sprightly humour which distinguishes The Author to be Let, and in others strong touches of that imagination which painted the solemn scenes of The Wanderer.

While he was thus cultivating his genius, his father, the Earl of Rivers, was seized with a distemper, which in a short time put an end to his life. He had frequently inquired after his son, and had always been amused with fallacious and evasive answers; but, being now in his own opinion on his death-bed, he thought it his duty to provide for him among his other natural children, and therefore demanded a positive account of him, with an importunity not to be diverted or denied. His mother, who could no longer refuse an answer, determined at least to give such as should cut him off for ever from that happiness which competence affords, and therefore declared that he was dead; which is perhaps the first instance of a lie invented by a mother to deprive her son of a provision which was designed him by another, and which she could not expect herself, though he should lose it. This was therefore an act of wickedness which could not be defeated, because it could not be suspected; the earl did not imagine there could exist in a human form a mother that would ruin her son without enriching herself, and therefore bestowed upon some other person six thousand pounds, which he had in his will bequeathed to Savage.

The same cruelty which incited his mother to intercept this provision which had been intended him, prompted her in a short time to another project, a project worthy of such a disposition. She endeavoured to rid herself from the danger of being at any time made known to him, by sending him secretly to the American Plantations. By whose kindness this scheme was counteracted, or by whose interposition she was induced to lay aside her design, I know not; it is not improbable that the Lady Mason might persuade or compel her to desist, or perhaps she could not easily find accomplices wicked enough to concur in so cruel an action; for it may be conceived, that those, who had by a long gradation of guilt hardened their hearts against the sense of common wickedness, would yet be shocked at the design of a mother to expose her son to slavery and want, to expose him without interest, and without provocation; and Savage might on this occasion find protectors and advocates among those who had long traded in crimes, and whom compassion had never touched before.

Being hindered, by whatever means, from banishing him into another country, she formed soon after a scheme for burying him in poverty and obscurity in his own; and that his station of life, if not the place of his residence, might keep him for ever at a distance from her, she ordered him to be placed with a shoemaker in Holborn, that, after the usual time of trial, he might become his apprentice.

It is generally reported, that this project was for some time successful, and that Savage was employed at the awl longer than he was willing to confess; nor was it perhaps any great advantage to him, that an unexpected discovery determined him to quit his occupation.

About this time his nurse, who had always treated him as her own son, died; and it was natural for him to take care of those effects which by her death were, as he imagined, become his own: he therefore went to her house, opened her boxes, and examined her papers, among which he found some letters written to her by

13

the Lady Mason, which informed him of his birth, and the reasons for which it was concealed. He was no longer satisfied with the employment which had been allotted him, but thought he had a right to share the affluence of his mother; and therefore without scruple applied to her as her son, and made use of every art to awaken her tenderness, and attract her regard. But neither his letters, nor the interposition of those friends which his merit or his distress procured him, made any impression on her mind. She still resolved to neglect, though she could no longer disown him. It was to no purpose that he frequently solicited her to admit him to see her; she avoided him with the most vigilant precaution, and ordered him to be excluded from her house, by whomsoever he might be introduced, and what reason soever he might give for entering it.

Savage was at the same time so touched with the discovery of his real mother, that it was his frequent practice to walk in the dark evenings for several hours before her door, in hopes of seeing her as she might come by accident to the window, or cross her apartment with a candle in her hand. But all his assiduity and tenderness were without effect, for he could neither soften her heart nor open her hand, and was reduced to the utmost miseries of want, while he was endeavouring to awaken the affection of a mother. He was therefore obliged to seek some other means of support; and, having no profession, became by necessity an author.

At this time the attention of the literary world was engrossed by the Bangorian controversy, which filled the press with pamphlets, and the coffee-houses with disputants. Of this subject, as most popular, he made choice for his first attempt, and, without any other knowledge of the question than he had casually collected from conversation, published a poem against the bishop. What was the success or merit of this performance, I know not; it was probably lost among the innumerable pamphlets to which that dispute gave occasion. Mr. Savage was himself in a little time ashamed of it, and endeavoured to suppress it, by destroying all the copies that he could collect. He then attempted a more gainful kind of writing, and in his eighteenth year offered to the stage a comedy borrowed from a Spanish plot, which was refused by the players, and was therefore given by him to Mr. Bullock, who, having more interest, made some slight alterations, and brought it upon the stage, under the title of *Woman's a Riddle*, but allowed the unhappy author no part of the profit.

Not discouraged, however, at his repulse, he wrote two years afterwards *Love in a Veil*, another comedy, borrowed likewise from the Spanish, but with little better success than before: for though it was received and acted, yet it appeared so late in the year, that the author obtained no other advantage from it, than the acquaintance of Sir Richard Steele, and Mr. Wilks, by whom he was pitied, caressed, and relieved.

Sir Richard Steele, having declared in his favour with all the ardour of benevolence which constituted his character, promoted his interest with the utmost zeal, related his misfortunes, applauded his merit, took all the opportunities of recommending him, and asserted, that "the inhumanity of his mother had given him a right to find every good man his father." Nor was Mr. Savage admitted to his acquaintance only, but to his confidence, of which he sometimes related an instance too extraordinary to be omitted, as it affords a very just idea of his patron's character. He was once desired by Sir Richard, with an air of the utmost importance, to come very early to his house the next morning. Mr. Savage came as he had promised, found the chariot at the door, and Sir Richard waiting for him, and ready to go out. What was intended, and whither they were to go, Savage could not conjecture, and was not willing to inquire; but immediately seated himself with Sir Richard. The coachman was ordered to drive, and they hurried with the utmost expedition to Hyde Park Corner, where they stopped at a petty tavern, and retired to a private room. Sir Richard then informed him, that he intended to publish a pamphlet, and that he had desired him to come thither that he might write for him. He soon sat down to the work. Sir Richard dictated, and Savage wrote, till the dinner that had been ordered was put upon the table. Savage was surprised at the meanness of the entertainment, and after some hesitation ventured to ask for wine, which Sir Richard, not without reluctance, ordered to be brought. Then they finished their dinner, and proceeded in their pamphlet, which they concluded in the afternoon.

Mr. Savage then imagined his task over, and expected that Sir Richard would call for the reckoning, and return home; but his expectations deceived him, for Sir Richard told him that he was without money, and that the pamphlet must be sold before the dinner could be paid for; and Savage was therefore obliged to go and offer their new production to sale for two guineas, which with some difficulty he obtained. Sir Richard then returned home, having retired that day only to avoid his creditors, and composed the pamphlet only to discharge his reckoning.

Mr. Savage related another fact equally uncommon, which, though it has no relation to his life, ought to be preserved. Sir Richard Steele having one day invited to his house a great number of persons of the first quality, they were surprised at the number of liveries which surrounded the table; and after dinner, when wine and mirth had set them free from the observation of a rigid ceremony, one of them inquired of Sir Richard, how such an expensive train of domestics could be consistent with his fortune. Sir Richard very frankly confessed, that they were fellows of whom he would very willingly be rid. And being then asked why he did not discharge them, declared that they were bailiffs, who had introduced themselves with an execution, and whom, since he could not send them away, he had thought it convenient to embellish with liveries, that they might do him credit while they stayed. His friends were diverted with the expedient, and by paying the debt, discharged their attendance, having obliged Sir Richard to promise that they should never again find him graced with a retinue of the same kind.

Under such a tutor Mr. Savage was not likely to learn prudence or frugality; and perhaps many of the misfortunes which the want of those virtues brought upon him in the following parts of his life, might be justly imputed to so unimproving an example. Nor did the kindness of Sir Richard end in common favours. He proposed to have established him in some settled scheme of life, and to have contracted a kind of alliance with him, by marrying him to a natural daughter, on whom he intended to bestow a thousand pounds. But though he was always lavish of future bounties, he conducted his affairs in such a manner, that he was very seldom able to keep his promises, or execute his own intentions: and, as he was never able to raise the sum which he had offered, the marriage was delayed. In the meantime he was officiously informed that Mr. Savage had ridiculed him; by which he was so much exasperated, that he withdrew the allowance which he had paid him, and never afterwards admitted him to his house.

It is not indeed unlikely that Savage might by his imprudence expose himself to the malice of a tale-bearer; for his patron had many follies, which as his discernment easily discovered, his imagination might sometimes incite him to mention too ludicrously. A little knowledge of the world is sufficient to discover that such weakness is very common, and that there are few who do not sometimes, in the wantonness of thoughtless mirth, or the heat of transient resentment, speak of their friends and benefactors with levity and contempt, though in their cooler moments they want neither sense of their kindness, nor reverence for their virtue; the fault therefore of Mr. Savage was rather negligence than ingratitude. But Sir Richard must likewise be acquitted of severity, for who is there that can patiently bear contempt from one whom he has relieved and supported, whose establishment he has laboured, and whose interest he has promoted?

He was now again abandoned to fortune without any other friend than Mr. Wilks; a man, who, whatever were his abilities or skill as an actor, deserves at least to be remembered for his virtues, which are not often to be found in the world, and perhaps less often in his profession than in others. To be humane, generous, and candid, is a very high degree of merit in any case; but those qualifications deserve still greater praise, when they are found in that condition which makes almost every other man, for whatever reason, contemptuous, insolent, petulant, selfish, and brutal.

As Mr. Wilks was one of those to whom calamity seldom complained without relief, he naturally took an unfortunate wit into his protection, and not only assisted him in any casual distresses, but continued an equal and steady kindness to the time of his death. By this interposition Mr. Savage once obtained from his mother fifty pounds, and a promise of one hundred and fifty more; but it was the fate of this unhappy man, that few promises of any advantage to him were performed. His mother was infected, among others, with the general madness of the South Sea traffic; and having been disappointed in her expectations, refused to pay what perhaps nothing but the prospect of sudden affluence prompted her to promise.

Being thus obliged to depend upon the friendship of Mr. Wilks, he was consequently an assiduous frequenter of the theatres; and in a short time the amusements of the stage took such possession of his mind, that he never was absent from a play in several years. This constant attendance naturally procured him the acquaintance of the players, and, among others, of Mrs. Oldfield, who was so much pleased with his conversation, and touched with his misfortunes, that she allowed him a settled pension of fifty pounds a year, which was during her life regularly paid. That this act of generosity may receive its due praise, and that the good actions of Mrs. Oldfield may not be sullied by her general character, it is proper to mention that Mr. Savage often declared, in the strongest terms, that he never saw her alone, or in any other place than behind the scenes.

At her death he endeavoured to show his gratitude in the most decent manner, by wearing mourning as for a mother; but did not celebrate her in elegies, because he knew that too great a profusion of praise would only have revived those faults which his natural equity did not allow him to think less, because they were committed by one who favoured him: but of which, though his virtue would not endeavour to palliate them, his gratitude would not suffer him to prolong the memory or diffuse the censure.

In his *Wanderer*, he has indeed taken an opportunity of mentioning her; but celebrates her not for her virtue but her beauty, an excellence which none ever denied her; this is the only encomium with which he has rewarded her liberality, and perhaps he has even in this been too lavish of his praise. He seems to have thought, that never to mention his benefactress would have an appearance of ingratitude, though to have dedicated any particular performance to her memory would have only betrayed an officious partiality, and that, without exalting her character, would have depressed his own. He had sometimes, by the kindness of Mr. Wilks, the advantage of a benefit, on which occasions he often received uncommon marks of regard and compassion; and was once told by the Duke of Dorset, that it was just to consider him as an injured nobleman, and that in his opinion the nobility ought to think themselves obliged, without solicitation, to take every opportunity of supporting him by their countenance and patronage. But he had generally the mortification to hear that the whole interest of his mother was employed to frustrate his applications, and that she bring his play upon the stage in the summer, when the chief actors had retired, and the rest were in possession of the house for their own advantage. Among these, Mr. Savage was admitted to play the part of Sir Thomas Overbury, by which he gained no great reputation, the theatre being a province for which nature seems not to have designed him; for neither his voice, look, nor gesture were such as were expected on the stage; and he was so much ashamed of having been reduced to appear as a player, that he always blotted out his name from the list when a copy of his tragedy was to be shown to his friends.

In the publication of his performance he was more successful, for the rays of genius that glimmered in it, that glimmered through all the mists which poverty and Cibber had been able to spread over it, procured him the notice and esteem of many persons eminent for their rank, their virtue, and their wit. Of this play, acted, printed, and dedicated, the accumulated profits arose to a hundred pounds, which he thought at that time a very large sum, having been never master of so much before.

In the dedication, for which he received ten guineas, there is nothing remarkable The preface contains a very liberal encomium on the blooming excellence of Mr. Theophilus Cibber, which Mr. Savage could not in the latter part of his life see his friends about to read without snatching the play out of their hands. The generosity of Mr. Hill did not end on this occasion; for afterwards, when Mr. Savage's necessities returned, he encouraged a subscription to a *Miscellany of Poems* in a very extraordinary manner, by publishing his story in the *Plain Dealer*, with some affecting lines, which he asserts to have been written by Mr. Savage upon the treatment received by him from his mother, but of which he was himself the author, as Mr. Savage afterwards declared. These lines, and the paper in which they were inserted, had a very powerful effect upon all but his mother, whom, by making her cruelty more public, they only hardened in her aversion.

Mr. Hill not only promoted the subscription to the *Miscellany*, but furnished likewise the greatest part of the poems of which it is composed, and particularly *The Happy Man*, which he published as a specimen.

The subscriptions of those whom these papers should influence to patronise merit in distress, without any other solicitation, were directed to be left at Button's coffee-house; and Mr. Savage going thither a few days afterwards, without expectation of any effect from his proposal, found, to his surprise, seventy guineas, which had been sent him in consequence of the compassion excited by Mr. Hill's pathetic representation.

To this *Miscellany* he wrote a preface, in which he gives an account of his mother's cruelty in a very uncommon strain of humour, and with a gaiety of imagination, which the success of his subscription probably produced. The dedication is addressed to the Lady Mary Wortley Montagu, whom he flatters without reserve, and, to confess the truth, with very little art. The same observation may be extended to all his dedications: his compliments are constrained and violent, heaped together without the grace of order, or the decency of introduction: he seems to have written his panegyrics for the perusal only of his patrons, and to imagine that he had no other task than to pamper them with praises, however gross, and that flattery would make its way to the heart, without the assistance of elegance or invention.

Soon afterwards, the death of the king furnished a general subject for a poetical contest, in which Mr. Savage engaged, and is allowed to have carried the prize of honour from his competitors: but I know not whether he gained by his performance any other advantage than the increase of his reputation: though it must certainly have been with farther views that he prevailed upon himself to attempt a species of writing, of which all the topics had been long before exhausted, and which was made at once difficult by the multitudes that had failed in it, and those that had succeeded.

He was now advancing in reputation, and though frequently involved in very distressful perplexities, appeared however to be gaining upon mankind, when both his fame and his life were endangered by an event, of which it is not yet determined whether it ought to be mentioned as a crime or a calamity.

On the 20th of November, 1727, Mr. Savage came from Richmond, where he then lodged, that he might pursue his studies with less interruption, with an intent to discharge another lodging which he had in Westminster; and accidentally meeting two gentlemen, his acquaintances, whose names were Merchant and Gregory, he went in with them to a neighboring coffee-house, and sat drinking till it was late, it being in no time of Mr. Savage's life any part of his character to be the first of the company that desired to separate. He would willingly have gone to bed in the same house; but there was not room for the whole company, and therefore they agreed to ramble about the streets, and divert themselves with such amusements as should offer themselves till morning. In this walk they happened unluckily to discover a light in Robinson's coffee-house, near Charing-cross, and therefore went in. Merchant with some rudeness demanded a room, and was told that there was a good fire in the next parlour, which the company were about to leave, being then paying their reckoning. Merchant, not satisfied with this answer, rushed into the room, and was followed by his companions. He then petulantly placed himself between the company and the fire, and soon after kicked down the table. This produced a quarrel, swords were drawn on both sides, and one Mr. James Sinclair was killed. Savage, having likewise wounded a maid that held him, forced his way with Merchant out of the house; but being intimidated and confused, without resolution either to fly or stay, they were taken in a back-court by one of the company, and some soldiers, whom he had called to his assistance. Being secured and guarded that night, they were in the morning carried before three justices, who committed them to the Gatehouse, from whence, upon the death of Mr. Sinclair, which happened the same day, they were removed in the night to Newgate, where they were, however, treated with some distinction, exempted from the ignominy of chains, and confined, not among the common criminals, but in the Press-yard.

When the day of trial came, the court was crowded in a very unusual manner; and the public appeared to interest itself as in a cause of general concern. The witnesses against Mr. Savage and his friends were, the woman who kept the house, which was a house of ill-fame, and her maid, the men who were in the room with Mr. Sinclair, and a woman of the town, who had been drinking with them, and with whom one of them had been seen in bed. They swore in general, that Merchant gave the provocation, which Savage and Gregory drew their swords to justify; that Savage drew first, and that he stabbed Sinclair when he was not in a posture of defence, or while Gregory commanded his sword; that after he had given the thrust he turned pale, and would have retired, but the maid clung round him, and one of the company endeavoured to detain him, from whom he broke, by cutting the maid on the head, but was afterwards taken in a court. There was some difference in their depositions; one did not see Savage give the wound, another saw it given when Sinclair held his point towards the ground; and the woman of the town asserted, that she did not see Sinclair's sword at all: this difference, however, was very far from amounting to inconsistency; but it was sufficient to show, that the hurry of the dispute was such, that it was not easy to discover the truth with relation to particular circumstances, and that therefore some deductions were to be made from the credibility of the testimonies.

Sinclair had declared several times before his death, that he received his wound from Savage: nor did Savage at his trial deny the fact, but endeavoured partly to extenuate it, by urging the suddenness of the whole action, and the impossibility of any ill design, or premeditated malice; and partly to justify it by the necessity of self-defence, and the hazard of his own life, if he had lost that opportunity of giving the thrust: he observed, that neither reason nor law obliged a man to wait for the blow which was threatened, and which, if he should suffer it, he might never be able to return; that it was allowable to prevent an assault, and to preserve life by taking away that of the adversary by whom it was endangered. With regard to the violence with which he endeavoured to escape, he declared, that it was not his design to fly from justice, or decline a trial, but to avoid the expenses and severities of a prison; and that he intended to appear at the bar without compulsion.

This defence, which took up more than an hour, was heard by the multitude that thronged the court with the most attentive and respectful silence: those who thought he ought not to be acquitted, owned that applause could not be refused him; and those who before pitied his misfortunes, now reverenced his abilities. The witnesses which appeared against him were proved to be persons of characters which did not entitle them to much credit; a common strumpet, a woman by whom strumpets were entertained, a man by whom they were supported: and the character of Savage was by several persons of distinction asserted to be that of a modest inoffensive man, not inclined to broils or to insolence, and who had, to that time, been only known for his misfortunes and his wit. Had his audience been his judges, he had undoubtedly been acquitted:

but Mr. Page, who was then upon the bench, treated him with his usual insolence and severity, and when he had summed up the evidence, endeavoured to exasperate the jury; as Mr. Savage used to relate it, with this eloquent harangue:—

"Gentlemen of the jury, you are to consider that Mr. Savage is a very great man, a much greater man than you or I, gentlemen of the jury; that he wears very fine clothes, much finer clothes than you or I, gentlemen of the jury; that he has abundance of money in his pockets, much more money than you or I, gentlemen of the jury; but, gentlemen of the jury, is it not a very hard case, gentlemen of the jury, that Mr. Savage should therefore kill you or me, gentlemen of the jury?"

Mr. Savage, hearing his defence thus misrepresented, and the men who were to decide his fate incited against him by invidious comparisons, resolutely asserted, that his cause was not candidly explained, and began to recapitulate what he had before said with regard to his condition, and the necessity of endeavouring to escape the expenses of imprisonment; but the judge having ordered him to be silent, and repeated his orders without effect, commanded that he should be taken from the bar by force.

The jury then heard the opinion of the judge, that good characters were of no weight against positive evidence, though they might turn the scale where it was doubtful; and that though, when two men attack each other, the death of either is only manslaughter; but where one is the aggressor, as in the case before them, and, in pursuance of his first attack, kills the other, the law supposes the action, however sudden, to be malicious. They then deliberated upon their verdict, and determined that Mr. Savage and Mr. Gregory were guilty of murder; and that Mr. Merchant, who had no sword, only of manslaughter.

Thus ended this memorable trial, which lasted eight hours. Mr. Savage and Mr. Gregory were conducted back to prison, where they were more closely confined, and loaded with irons of fifty pounds weight: four days afterwards they were sent back to the court to receive sentence; on which occasion Mr. Savage made, as far as it could be retained in memory, the following speech:—

"It is now, my lord, too late to offer anything by way of defence or vindication; nor can we expect from your lordships, in this court, but the sentence which the law requires you, as judges, to pronounce against men of our calamitous condition. But we are also persuaded, that as mere men, and out of this seat of rigorous justice, you are susceptive of the tender passions, and too humane not to commiserate the unhappy situation of those, whom the law sometimes perhaps—exacts—from you to pronounce upon. No doubt you distinguish between offences which arise out of premeditation, and a disposition habituated to vice or immorality, and transgressions, which are the unhappy and unforeseen effects of casual absence of reason, and sudden impulse of passion: we therefore hope you will contribute all you can to an extension of that mercy, which the gentlemen of the jury have been pleased to show to Mr. Merchant, who (allowing facts as sworn against us by the evidence) has led us into this our calamity. I hope this will not be construed as if we meant to reflect upon that gentleman, or remove anything from us upon him, or that we repine the more at our fate, because he has no participation of it: No, my lord! For my part, I declare nothing could more soften my grief, than to be without any companion in so great a misfortune."

Mr. Savage had now no hopes of life, but from the mercy of the crown, which was very earnestly solicited by his friends, and which, with whatever difficulty the story may obtain belief, was obstructed only by his mother.

To prejudice the queen against him, she made use of an incident, which was omitted in the order of time, that it might be mentioned together with the purpose which it was made to serve. Mr. Savage, when he had discovered his birth, had an incessant desire to speak to his mother, who always avoided him in public, and refused him admission into her house. One evening walking, as it was his custom, in the street that she inhabited, he saw the door of her house by accident open; he entered it, and, finding no person in the passage to hinder him, went up stairs to salute her. She discovered him before he entered the chamber, alarmed the family with the most distressful outcries, and, when she had by her screams gathered them about her, ordered them to drive out of the house that villain, who had forced himself in upon her, and endeavoured to murder her. Savage, who had attempted with the most submissive tenderness to soften her rage, hearing her utter so detestable an accusation, thought it prudent to retire; and, I believe, never attempted afterwards to speak to her.

But, shocked as he was with her falsehood and her cruelty, he imagined that she intended no other use of her lie, than to set herself free from his embraces and solicitations, and was very far from suspecting that she would treasure it in her memory as an instrument of future wickedness, or that she would endeavour for this fictitious assault to deprive him of his life. But when the queen was solicited for his pardon, and informed of the severe treatment which he had suffered from his judge, she answered, that, however unjustifiable might be the manner of his trial, or whatever exten-uation the action for which he was condemned might admit, she could not think that man a proper object of the king's mercy, who had been capable of entering his mother's house in the night, with an intent to murder her.

By whom this atrocious calumny had been transmitted to the queen; whether she that invented had the front to relate it; whether she found any one weak enough to credit it, or corrupt enough to concur with her in her hateful design; I know not: but methods had been taken to persuade the queen so strongly of the truth of it, that she for a long time refused to hear any one of those who petitioned for his life.

Thus had Savage perished by the evidence of a bawd, a strumpet, and his mother, had not justice and compassion procured him an advocate of rank too great to be rejected unheard, and of virtue too eminent to be heard without being believed. His merit and his calamities happened to reach the ear of the Countess of Hertford, who engaged in his support with all the tenderness that is excited by pity, and all the zeal which is kindled by generosity; and, de-manding an audience of the queen, laid before her the whole series of his mother's cruelty, exposed the improbability of an accusation by which he was charged with an intent to commit a murder that could produce no advantage, and soon convinced her how little his former conduct could deserve to be mentioned as a reason for extraordinary severity.

The interposition of this lady was so successful, that he was soon after admitted to bail, and, on the 9th of March, 1728, pleaded the king's pardon.

It is natural to inquire upon what motives his mother could persecute him in a manner so outrageous and implacable; for what reason she could employ all the arts of malice, and all the snares of

GREAT ENGLISH SHORT NOVELS

calumny, to take away the life of her own son, of a son who never injured her, who was never supported by her expense, nor obstructed any prospect of pleasure or advantage: why she would endeavour to destroy him by a lie—a lie which could not gain credit, but must vanish of itself at the first moment of examination, and of which only this can be said to make it probable, that it may be observed from her conduct, that the most execrable crimes are sometimes committed without apparent temptation.

This mother is still [1744] alive, and may perhaps even yet, though her malice was so often defeated, enjoy the pleasure of reflecting, that the life, which she often endeavoured to destroy, was at last shortened by her maternal offices; that though she could not transport her son to the plantations, bury him in the shop of a mechanic, or hasten the hand of the public executioner, she has yet had the satisfaction of embittering all his hours, and forcing him into exigencies that hurried on his death. It is by no means necessary to aggravate the enormity of this woman's conduct, by placing it in opposition to that of the Countess of Hertford; no one can fail to observe how much more amiable it is to relieve than to oppress, and to rescue innocence from destruction, than to destroy without an injury.

Mr. Savage, during his imprisonment, his trial, and the time in which he lay under sentence of death, behaved with great firmness and equality of mind, and confirmed by his fortitude the esteem of those who before admired him for his abilities. The peculiar circumstances of his life were made more generally known by a short account, which was then published, and of which several thousands were in a few weeks dispersed over the nation; and the compassion of mankind operated so powerfully in his favour, that he was enabled, by frequent presents, not only to support himself, but to assist Mr. Gregory in prison; and when he was pardoned and released, he found the number of his friends not lessened.

The nature of the act for which he had been tried was in itself doubtful; of the evidences which appeared against him, the character of the man was not unexceptionable, that of the woman notoriously infamous; she, whose testimony chiefly influenced the jury to condemn him, afterwards retracted her assertions. He always himself denied that he was drunk, as had been generally reported. Mr. Gregory, who is now (1744) collector of Antigua, is said to declare him far less criminal than he was imagined, even by some who favoured him; and Page himself afterwards confessed, that he had treated him with uncommon rigour. When all these particulars are rated together, perhaps the memory of Savage may not be much sullied by his trial. Some time after he obtained his liberty, he met in the street the woman who had sworn with so much malignity against him. She informed him that she was in distress, and, with a degree of confidence not easily attainable, desired him to relieve her. He, instead of insulting her misery, and taking pleasure in the calamities of one who had brought his life into danger, reproved her gently for her perjury; and changing the only guinea that he had, divided it equally between her and himself. This is an action which in some ages would have made a saint, and perhaps in others a hero, and which, without any hyperbolical encomiums, must be allowed to be an instance of uncommon generosity, an act of complicated virtue; by which he at once relieved the poor, corrected the vicious, and forgave an enemy; by which he at once remitted the strongest provocations, and exercised the most ardent charity.

Compassion was indeed the distinguishing quality of Savage: he never appeared inclined to take advantage of weakness, to attack the defenceless, or to press upon the falling: whoever was distressed, was certain at least of his good wishes; and when he could give no assistance to extricate them from misfortunes, he endeavoured to soothe them by sympathy and tenderness. But when his heart was not softened by the sight of misery, he was sometimes obstinate in his resentment, and did not quickly lose the remembrance of an injury. He always continued to speak with anger of the insolence and partiality of Page, and a short time before his death revenged it by a satire.

It is natural to inquire in what terms Mr. Savage spoke of this fatal action, when the danger was over, and he was under no necessity of using any art to set his conduct in the fairest light. He was not willing to dwell upon it; and, if he transiently mentioned it, appeared neither to consider himself as a murderer, nor as a man wholly free from the guilt of blood. How much and how long he regretted it, appeared in a poem which he published many years afterwards. On occasion of a copy of verses, in which the failings of good men are recounted, and in which the author had endeavoured to illustrate his position, that "the best may sometimes deviate from virtue," by an instance of murder committed by Savage in the heat of wine, Savage remarked, that it was no very just representation of a good man, to suppose him liable to drunkenness, and disposed in his riots to cut throats.

He was now indeed at liberty, but was, as before, without any other support than accidental favours and uncertain patronage afforded him; sources by which he was sometimes very liberally supplied, and which at other times were suddenly stopped; so that he spent his life between want and plenty; or, what was yet worse, between beggary and extravagance; for, as whatever he received was the gift of chance, which might as well favour him at one time as another, he was tempted to squander what he had, because he always hoped to be immediately supplied. Another cause of his profusion was the absurd kindness of his friends, who at once rewarded and enjoyed his abilities, by treating him at taverns, and habituating him to pleasures which he could not afford to enjoy, and which he was not able to deny himself, though he purchased the luxury of a single night by the anguish of cold and hunger for a week.

The experience of these inconveniences determined him to endeavour after some settled income, which, having long found submission and entreaties fruitless, he attempted to extort from his mother by rougher methods. He had now, as he acknowledged, lost that tenderness for her, which the whole series of her cruelty had not been able wholly to repress, till he found, by the efforts which she made for his destruction, that she was not content with refusing to assist him, and being neutral in his struggles with poverty, but was ready to snatch every opportunity of adding to his misfortunes; and that she was now to be considered as an enemy implacably malicious, whom nothing but his blood could satisfy. He therefore threatened to harass her with lampoons, and to publish a copious narrative of her conduct, unless she consented to purchase an exemption from infamy, by allowing him a pension.

This expedient proved successful. Whether shame still survived, though virtue was extinct, or whether her relations had more delicacy than herself, and imagined that some of the darts which satire might point at her would glance upon them; Lord Tyrconnel, whatever were his motives, upon his promise to lay aside his design of exposing the cruelty of his mother, received him into his family, treated him as his equal, and engaged to allow him a pension of two hundred pounds a year. This was the golden part of Mr. Savage's life; and for some time he had no reason to complain of fortune; his appearance was splendid, his expenses large, and his acquaintance extensive. He was courted by all who endeavoured to be thought men of genius, and caressed by all who valued themselves upon a refined taste. To admire Mr. Savage was a proof of discernment; and to be acquainted with him was a title to poetical reputation. His presence was sufficient to make any place of public entertainment popular; and his approbation and example constituted the fashion. So powerful is genius, when it is invested with the glitter of affluence! Men willingly pay to fortune that regard which they owe to merit, and are pleased when they have an opportunity at once of gratifying their vanity, and practising their duty.

This interval of prosperity furnished him with opportunities of enlarging his knowledge of human nature, by contemplating life from its highest gradations to its lowest; and, had he afterwards applied to dramatic poetry, he would perhaps not have had many superiors; for, as he never suffered any scene to pass before his eyes without notice, he had treasured in his mind all the different combinations of passions, and the innumerable mixtures of vice and virtue, which distinguished one character from another; and, as his conception was strong, his expressions were clear, he easily received impressions from objects, and very forcibly transmitted them to others. Of his exact observations on human life he has left a proof, which would do honour to the greatest names, in a small pamphlet, called *The Author to be Let*, where he introduces Iscariot Hackney, a prostitute scribbler, giving an account of his birth, his education, his disposition and morals, habits of life, and maxims of conduct. In the introduction are related many secret histories of the petty writers of that time, but sometimes mixed with ungenerous reflections on their birth, their circumstances, or those of their relations; nor can it be denied, that some passages are such as Iscariot Hackney might himself have produced. He was accused likewise of living in an appearance of friendship with some whom he satirised, and of making use of the confidence which he gained by a seeming kindness, to discover failings and expose them:

31

it must be confessed, that Mr. Savage's esteem was no very certain possession, and that he would lampoon at one time those whom he had praised at another.

It may be alleged, that the same man may change his principles; and that he, who was once deservedly commended, may be afterwards satirised with equal justice; or, that the poet was dazzled with the appearance of virtue, and found the man whom he had celebrated, when he had an opportunity of examining him more narrowly, unworthy of the panegyric which he had too hastily bestowed; and that, as a false satire ought to be recanted, for the sake of him whose reputation may be injured, false praise ought likewise to be obviated, lest the distinction between vice and virtue should be lost, lest a bad man should be trusted upon the credit of his encomiast, or lest others should endeavour to obtain like praises by the same means. But though these excuses may be often plausible, and sometimes just, they are very seldom satisfactory to mankind; and the writer, who is not constant to his subject, quickly sinks into contempt, his satire loses its force, and his panegyric its value; and he is only considered at one time as a flatterer, and a calumniator at another. To avoid these imputations, it is only necessary to follow the rules of virtue, and to preserve an unvaried regard to truth. For though it is undoubtedly possible that a man, however cautious, may be sometimes deceived by an artful appearance of virtue, or by false evidences of guilt, such errors will not be frequent; and it will be allowed, that the name of an author would never have been made contemptible, had no man ever said what he did not think, or misled others but when he was himself deceived.

The Author to be Let was first published in a single pamphlet, and afterwards inserted in a collection of pieces relating to the *Dunciad*, which were addressed by Mr. Savage to the Earl of Middlesex, in a dedication which he was prevailed upon to sign, though he did not write it, and in which there are some positions, that the true author would perhaps not have published under his own name, and on which Mr. Savage afterwards reflected with no great satisfaction: the enumeration of the bad effects of the uncontrolled freedom of the press, and the assertion that the "liberties taken by the writers of journals with their superiors were exorbitant and unjustifiable," very ill became men, who have themselves not always shown the exactest regard to the laws of subordination in their writings, and who have often satirised those that at least thought themselves their superiors, as they were eminent for their hereditary rank, and employed in the highest offices of the kingdom. But this is only an instance of that partiality which almost every man indulges with regard to himself: the liberty of the press is a blessing when we are inclined to write against others, and a calamity when we find ourselves overborne by the multitude of our assailants; as the power of the crown is always thought too great by those who suffer by its influence, and too little by those in whose favour it is exerted; and a standing army is generally accounted necessary by those who command, and dangerous and oppressive by those who support it.

Mr. Savage was likewise very far from believing, that the letters annexed to each species of bad poets in the *Bathos* were, as he was directed to assert, "set down at random"; for when he was charged by one of his friends with putting his name to such an improbability, he had no other answer to make than that "he did not think of it"; and his friend had too much tenderness to reply, that next to the crime of writing contrary to what he thought, was that of writing without thinking.

After having remarked what is false in this dedication, it is proper that I observe the impartiality which I recommend, by declaring what Savage asserted; that the account of the circumstances which attended the publication of the *Dunciad*, however strange and improbable, was exactly true.

The publication of this piece at this time raised Mr. Savage a great number of enemies among those that were attacked by Mr. Pope, with whom he was considered as a kind of confederate, and whom he was suspected of supplying with private intelligence and secret incidents; so that the ignominy of an informer was added to the terror of a satirist. That he was not altogether free from literary hypocrisy, and that he sometimes spoke one thing and wrote another, cannot be denied; because he himself confessed, that, when he lived with great familiarity with Dennis, he wrote an epigram against him.

Mr. Savage, however, set all the malice of all the pigmy writers at defiance, and thought the friendship of Mr. Pope cheaply purchased by being exposed to their censure and their hatred; nor had

33

he any reason to repent of the preference, for he found Mr. Pope a steady and unalienable friend almost to the end of his life.

About this time, notwithstanding his avowed neutrality with regard to party, he published a panegyric on Sir Robert Walpole, for which he was rewarded by him with twenty guineas, a sum not very large, if either the excellence of the performance, or the affluence of the patron, be considered; but greater than he afterwards obtained from a person of yet higher rank, and more desirous in appearance of being distinguished as a patron of literature.

As he was very far from approving the conduct of Sir Robert Walpole, and in conversation mentioned him sometimes with acrimony, and generally with contempt; as he was one of those who were always zealous in their assertions of the justice of the late opposition, jealous of the rights of the people, and alarmed by the long-continued triumph of the court; it was natural to ask him what could induce him to employ his poetry in praise of that man who was, in his opinion, an enemy to liberty, and an oppressor of his country? He alleged that he was then dependent upon the Lord Tyrconnel, who was an implicit follower of the ministry: and that, being enjoined by him, not without menaces, to write in praise of the leader, he had not resolution sufficient to sacrifice the pleasure of affluence to that of integrity.

On this, and on many other occasions, he was ready to lament the misery of living at the tables of other men, which was his fate from the beginning to the end of his life; for I know not whether he ever had, for three months together, a settled habitation, in which he could claim a right of residence.

To this unhappy state it is just to impute much of the inconsistency of his conduct; for though a readiness to comply with the inclinations of others was no part of his natural character, yet he was sometimes obliged to relax his obstinacy, and submit his own judgment, and even his virtue, to the government of those by whom he was supported: so that, if his miseries were sometimes the consequences of his faults, he ought not yet to be wholly excluded from compassion, because his faults were very often the effects of his misfortunes.

In this gay period of his life, while he was surrounded by affluence and pleasure, he published The Wanderer, a moral poem, of which the design is comprised in these lines:

> I fly all public care, all venal strife,
> To try the still, compared with active, life;
> To prove, by these, the sons of men may owe
> The fruits of bliss to bursting clouds of woe;
> That ev'n calamity, by thought refined,
> Inspirits and adorns the thinking mind.

And more distinctly in the following passage:—

> By woe, the soul to daring action swells;
> By woe, in plaintless patience it excels:
> From patience prudent, clear experience springs,
> And traces knowledge through the course of things.
> Thence hope is form'd, thence fortitude, success,
> Renown:—whate'er men covet and caress.

This performance was always considered by himself as his masterpiece; and Mr. Pope, when he asked his opinion of it, told him, that he read it once over, and was not displeased with it; that it gave him more pleasure at the second perusal, and delighted him still more at the third.

It has been generally objected to *The Wanderer*, that the disposition of the parts is irregular; that the design is obscure, and the plan perplexed; that the images, however beautiful, succeed each other without order; and that the whole performance is not so much a regular fabric, as a heap of shining materials thrown together by accident, which strikes rather with the solemn magnificence of a stupendous ruin, than the elegant grandeur of a finished pile. This criticism is universal, and therefore it is reasonable to believe it at least in a degree just; but Mr. Savage was always of a contrary opinion, and thought his drift could only be missed by negligence or stupidity, and that the whole plan was regular, and the parts distinct. It was never denied to abound with strong representations of nature, and just observations upon life; and it may easily be observed, that most of his pictures have an evident tendency to illustrate his first great position, "that good is the consequence of evil." The sun that burns up the mountains, fructifies the vales; the deluge that rushes down the broken rocks with dreadful impetuosity, is separated into purling brooks; and the rage of the hurricane purifies the air.

Even in this poem he has not been able to forbear one touch upon the cruelty of his mother, which, though remarkably delicate and tender, is a proof how deep an impression it had upon his mind. This must be at least acknowledged, which ought to be thought equivalent to many other excellences, that this poem can promote no other purposes than those of virtue, and that it is written with a very strong sense of the efficacy of religion. But my province is rather to give the history of Mr. Savage's performances than to display their beauties, or to obviate the criticisms which they have occasioned; and therefore I shall not dwell upon the particular passages which deserve applause: I shall neither show the excellence of his descriptions, nor expatiate on the terrific portrait of suicide, nor point out the artful touches, by which he has distinguished the intellectual features of the rebels, who suffer death in his last canto. It is, however, proper to observe, that Mr. Savage always declared the characters wholly fictitious, and without the least allusion to any real persons or actions.

From a poem so diligently laboured, and so successfully finished, it might be reasonably expected that he should have gained considerable advantage; nor can it, without some degree of indignation and concern, be told, that he sold the copy for ten guineas, of which he afterwards returned two, that the two last sheets of the work might be reprinted, of which he had in his absence entrusted the correction to a friend, who was too indolent to perform it with accuracy.

A superstitious regard to the correction of his sheets was one of Mr. Savage's peculiarities: he often altered, revised, recurred to his first reading or punctuation, and again adopted the alteration; he was dubious and irresolute without end, as on a question of the last importance, and at last was seldom satisfied: the intrusion or omission of a comma was sufficient to discompose him, and he would lament an error of a single letter as a heavy calamity. In one of his letters relating to an impresson of some verses, he remarks, that he had, with regard to the correction of the proof, "a spell upon him"; and indeed the anxiety with which he dwelt upon the minutest and most trifling niceties, deserved no other name than that of fascination. That he sold so valuable a performance for so small a price, was not to be imputed either to necessity, by which the learned and ingenious are often obliged to submit to very hard conditions; or to avarice, by which the booksellers are frequently incited to oppress that genius by which they are supported; but to that intemperate desire of pleasure, and habitual slavery to his passions, which involved him in many perplexities. He happened at that time to be engaged in the pursuit of some trifling gratification, and, being without money for the present occasion, sold his poem to the first bidder, and perhaps for the first price that was proposed, and would probably have been content with less, if less had been offered him.

This poem was addressed to the Lord Tyrconnel, not only in the first lines, but in a formal dedication filled with the highest strains of panegyric, and the warmest professions of gratitude, but by no means remarkable for delicacy of connexion or elegance of style. These praises in a short time he found himself inclined to retract, being discarded by the man on whom he had bestowed them, and whom he then immediately discovered not to have deserved them. Of this quarrel, which every day made more bitter, Lord Tyrconnel and Mr. Savage assigned very different reasons, which might perhaps all in reality concur, though they were not all convenient to be alleged by either party. Lord Tyrconnel affirmed, that it was the constant practice of Mr. Savage to enter a tavern with any company that proposed it, drink the most expensive wines with great profusion, and when the reckoning was demanded, to be without money: if, as it often happened, his company were willing to defray his part, the affair ended without any ill consequences; but if they were refractory, and expected that the wine should be paid for by him that drank it, his method of composition was, to take them with him to his own apartment, assume the government of the house, and order the butler in an imperious manner to set the best wine in the cellar before his company, who often drank till they forgot the respect due to the house in which they were entertained, indulged themselves in the utmost extravagance of merriment, practised the most licentious frolics, and committed all the outrages of drunkenness. Nor was this the only charge which Lord Tyrconnel brought against him: Having given him a collection of valuable books, stamped with his own arms, he had the mortification to see them in a short time exposed to sale upon the stalls, it being usual with Mr. Savage, when he wanted a small sum, to take his books to the pawnbroker.

Whoever was acquainted with Mr. Savage easily credited both these accusations: for having been obliged, from his first entrance into the world, to subsist upon expedients, affluence was not able to exalt him above them; and so much was he delighted with wine and conversation, and so long had he been accustomed to live by chance, that he would at any time go to the tavern without scruple, and trust for the reckoning to the liberality of his company, and frequently of company to whom he was very little known. This conduct indeed very seldom drew upon him those inconveniences that might be feared by any other person; for his conversation was so entertaining, and his address so pleasing, that few thought the pleasure which they received from him dearly purchased, by paying for his wine. It was his peculiar happiness, that he scarcely ever found a stranger, whom he did not leave a friend; but it must likewise be added, that he had not often a friend long, without obliging him to become a stranger.

Mr. Savage, on the other hand, declared, that Lord Tyrconnel quarrelled with him, because he would not subtract from his own luxury and extravagance what he had promised to allow him, and that his resentment was only a plea for the violation of his promise. He asserted, that he had done nothing that ought to exclude him from that subsistence which he thought not so much a favour as a debt, since it was offered him upon conditons which he had never broken; and that his only fault was, that he could not be supported with nothing. He acknowledged, that Lord Tyrconnel often exhorted him to regulate his method of life, and not to spend all his nights in taverns, and that he appeared desirous that he would pass those hours with him, which he so freely bestowed upon others. This demand Mr. Savage considered as a censure of his conduct, which he could never patiently bear, and which, in the latter and cooler parts of his life was so offensive to him, that he declared it as his resolution, "to spurn that friend who should pretend to dictate to him"; and it is not likely, that in his earlier years he received admonitions with more calmness. He was likewise inclined to resent such expectations, as tending to infringe his liberty, of which he was very jealous, when it was necessary to the gratification of his passions; and declared, that the request was still more unreasonable, as the company to which he was to have been confined was insupportably disagreeable. This assertion affords another instance of that inconsistency of his writings with his conversation, which was so often to be observed. He forgot how lavishly he had, in his dedication to *The Wanderer*, extolled the delicacy and penetration, the humanity and generosity, the candour and politeness of the man, whom, when he no longer loved him, he declared to be a wretch without understanding, without good nature, and without justice; of whose name he thought himself obliged to leave no trace in any future edition of his writings; and accordingly blotted it out of that copy of *The Wanderer* which was in his hands.

During his continuance with the Lord Tyrconnel, he wrote *The Triumph of Health and Mirth*, on the recovery of Lady Tyrconnel from a languishing illness. This performance is remarkable, not only for the gaiety of the ideas, and the melody of the numbers, but for the agreeable fiction upon which it is formed. Mirth overwhelmed with sorrow, for the sickness of her favourite, takes a flight in quest of her sister Health, whom she finds reclined upon the brow of a lofty mountain, amidst the fragrance of perpetual spring, with the breezes of the morning sporting about her. Being solicited by her sister Mirth, she readily promises her assistance, flies away in a cloud, and impregnates the waters of Bath with new virtues, by which the sickness of Belinda is relieved. As the reputation of his abilities, the particular circumstances of his birth and life, the splendour of his appearance, and the distinction which was for some time paid him by Lord Tyrconnel, entitled him to familiarity with persons of higher rank than those to whose conversation he had been before admitted; he did not fail to gratify that curiosity, which induced him to take a nearer view of those whom their birth, their employments, or their fortunes, necessarily placed at a distance from the greatest part of mankind, and to examine whether their merit was magnified or diminished by the medium through which it was contemplated; whether the splendour with which they dazzled their admirers was inherent in themselves, or only reflected on them by the objects that surrounded them; and whether great men were selected for high stations, or high stations made great men.

For this purpose he took all opportunities of conversing familiarly with those who were most conspicuous at that time for their power or their influence; he watched their looser moments, and examined their domestic behavior, with that acuteness which nature had given him, and which the uncommon variety of his life had contributed to increase, and that inquisitiveness which must always be produced in a vigorous mind, by an absolute freedom from all pressing or domestic engagements. His discernment was quick, and therefore he soon found in every person, and in every affair, something that deserved attention; he was supported by others, without any care for himself, and was therefore at leisure to pursue his observations. More circumstances to constitute a critic on human life could not easily concur; nor indeed could any man, who assumed from accidental advantages more praise than he could justly claim from his real merit, admit any acquaintance more dangerous than that of Savage; of whom likewise it must be confessed, that abilities really exalted above the common level, or virtue refined from passion, or proof against corruption, could not easily find an abler judge, or a warmer advocate.

What was the result of Mr. Savage's inquiry, though he was not much accustomed to conceal his discoveries, it may not be entirely safe to relate, because the persons whose characters he criticised are powerful; and power and resentment are seldom strangers; nor would it perhaps be wholly just, because what he asserted in conversation might, though true in general, be heightened by some momentary ardour of imagination, and, as it can be delivered only from memory, may be imperfectly represented; so that the picture at first aggravated, and then unskilfully copied, may be justly suspected to retain no great resemblance of the original.

It may, however, be observed, that he did not appear to have formed very elevated ideas of those to whom the administration of affairs, or the conduct of parties, has been intrusted; who have been considered as the advocates of the crown, or the guardians of the people; and who have obtained the most implicit confidence, and the loudest applauses. Of one particular person, who has been at one time so popular as to be generally esteemed, and at another so formidable as to be universally detested, he observed, that his acquisitions had been small, or that his capacity was narrow, and that the whole range of his mind was from obscenity to politics, and from politics to obscenity.

But the opportunity of indulging his speculations on great characters was now at an end. He was banished from the table of Lord

Tyrconnel, and turned again adrift upon the world, without prospect of finding quickly any other harbour. As prudence was not one of the virtues by which he was distinguished, he made no provision against a misfortune like this. And though it is not to be imagined but that the separation must for some time have been preceded by coldness, peevishness, or neglect, though it was undoubtedly the consequence of accumulated provocations on both sides; yet every one that knew Savage will readily believe that to him it was sudden as a stroke of thunder; that, though he might have transiently suspected it, he had never suffered any thought so unpleasing to sink into his mind, but that he had driven it away by amusements or dreams of future felicity and affluence, and had never taken any measures by which he might prevent a precipitation from plenty to indigence. This quarrel and separation, and the difficulties to which Mr. Savage was exposed by them, were soon known both to his friends and enemies; nor was it long before he perceived, from the behavior of both, how much is added to the lustre of genius by the ornaments of wealth. His condition did not appear to excite much compassion; for he had not been always careful to use the advantages he enjoyed with that moderation which ought to have been with more than usual caution preserved by him, who knew, if he had reflected, that he was only a dependent on the bounty of another, whom he could expect to support him no longer than he endeavoured to preserve his favour by complying with his inclinations, and whom he nevertheless set at defiance, and was continually irritating by negligence or encroachments.

Examples need not be sought at any great distance to prove, that superiority of fortune has a natural tendency to kindle pride, and that pride seldom fails to exert itself in contempt and insult; and if this is often the effect of hereditary wealth, and of honours enjoyed only by the merits of others, it is some extenuation of any indecent triumphs to which this unhappy man may have been betrayed, that his prosperity was heightened by the force of novelty, and made more intoxicating by a sense of the misery in which he had so long languished, and perhaps of the insults which he had formerly borne, and which he might now think himself entitled to revenge. It is too common for those who have unjustly suffered pain, to inflict it likewise in their turn with the same injustice, and to imagine that they have a right to treat others as they have themselves been treated.

That Mr. Savage was too much elevated by any good fortune, is generally known; and some passages of his Introduction to *The Author to be Let* sufficiently show, that he did not wholly refrain from such satire, as he afterwards thought very unjust when he was exposed to it himself; for, when he was afterwards ridiculed in the character of a distressed poet, he very easily discovered, that distress was not a proper subject for merriment, or topic of invective. He was then able to discern, that if misery be the effect of virtue, it ought to be reverenced; if of ill fortune, to be pitied; and if of vice, not to be insulted, because it is perhaps itself a punishment adequate to the crime by which it was produced. And the humanity of that man can deserve no panegyric, who is capable of reproaching a criminal in the hands of the executioner. But these reflections, though they readily occurred to him in the first and last parts of his life, were, I am afraid, for a long time forgotten; at least they were, like many other maxims, treasured up in his mind rather for show than use, and operated very little upon his conduct, however elegantly he might sometimes explain, or however forcibly he might inculcate them. His degradation, therefore, from the condition which he had enjoyed with such wanton thoughtlessness, was considered by many as an occasion of triumph. Those who had before paid their court to him without success, soon returned the contempt which they had suffered; and they who had received favours from him, for of such favours as he could bestow he was very liberal, did not always remember them. So much more certain are the effects of resentment than of gratitude: it is not only to many more pleasing to recollect those faults which place others below them, than those virtues by which they are themselves comparatively depressed: but it is likewise more easy to neglect than to recompense: and though there are few who will practise a laborious virtue, there will never be wanting multitudes that will indulge in easy vice.

Savage, however, was very little disturbed at the marks of contempt which his ill fortune brought upon him from those whom he never esteemed, and with whom he never considered himself as levelled by any calamities: and though it was not without some uneasiness that he saw some, whose friendship he valued, change their behavior, he yet observed their coldness without much emotion, considered them as the slaves of fortune, and the worshippers of prosperity, and was more inclined to despise them than to lament himself.

It does not appear that after this return of his wants, he found mankind equally favourable to him, as at his first appearance in the world. His story, though in reality not less melancholy, was less affecting, because it was no longer new; it therefore procured him no new friends; and those that had formerly relieved him thought they might now consign him to others. He was now likewise considered by many rather as criminal than as unhappy; for the friends of Lord Tyrconnel, and of his mother, were sufficiently industrious to publish his weaknesses, which were indeed very numerous; and nothing was forgotten that might make him either hateful or ridiculous. It cannot but be imagined, that such representations of his faults must make great numbers less sensible of his distress; many who had only an opportunity to hear one part, made no scruple to propagate the account which they received; many assisted their circulation from malice or revenge; and perhaps many pretended to credit them, that they might with a better grace withdraw their regard, or withhold their assistance.

Savage, however, was not one of those who suffered himself to be injured without resistance, nor was less diligent in exposing the faults of Lord Tyrconnel, over whom he obtained at least this advantage, that he drove him first to the practice of outrage and violence; for he was so much provoked by the wit and virulence of Savage, that he came with a number of attendants, that did no honour to his courage, to beat him at a coffee-house. But it happened that he had left the place a few minutes; and his lordship had, without danger, the pleasure of boasting how he would have treated him. Mr. Savage went next day to repay his visit at his own house; but was prevailed on, by his domestics, to retire without insisting on seeing him.

Lord Tyrconnel was accused by Mr. Savage of some actions which scarcely any provocation will be thought sufficient to justify, such as seizing what he had in his lodgings, and other instances of wanton cruelty, by which he increased the distress of Savage, without any advantage to himself.

These mutual accusations were retorted on both sides, for many years, with the utmost degree of virulence and rage; and time seemed rather to augment than diminish their resentment. That the anger of Mr. Savage should be kept alive, is not strange, because he felt every day the consequences of the quarrel; but it might reasonably have been hoped, that Lord Tyrconnel might have relented, and at length have forgot those provocations, which, however they might have once inflamed him, had not in reality much hurt him. The spirit of Mr. Savage indeed never suffered him to solicit a reconciliation; he returned reproach for reproach, and insult for insult; his superiority of wit supplied the disadvantages of his fortune, and enabled him to form a party, and prejudice great numbers in his favour. But though this might be some gratification of his vanity, it afforded very little relief to his necessities; and he was frequently reduced to uncommon hardships, of which, however, he never made any mean or importunate complaints, being formed rather to bear misery with fortitude, than enjoy prosperity with moderation.

He now thought himself again at liberty to expose the cruelty of his mother; and therefore, I believe, about this time, published *The Bastard*, a poem remarkable for the vivacious sallies of thought in the beginning, where he makes a pompous enumeration of the imaginary advantages of base birth; and the pathetic sentiments at the end, where he recounts the real calamities which he suffered by the crime of his parents. The vigour and spirit of the verses, the peculiar circumstances of the author, the novelty of the subject, and the notoriety of the story to which the allusions are made, procured this performance a very favourable reception; great numbers were immediately dispersed, and editions were multiplied with unusual rapidity.

One circumstance attended the publication which Savage used to relate with great satisfaction. His mother, to whom the poem was with "due reverence" inscribed, happened then to be at Bath, where she could not conveniently retire from censure, or conceal herself from observation; and no sooner did the reputation of the poem begin to spread, than she heard it repeated in all places of concourse; nor could she enter the assembly-rooms, or cross the walks, without being saluted with some lines from *The Bastard*.

This was perhaps the first time that she ever discovered a sense of shame, and on this occasion the power of wit was very conspicuous; the wretch who had, without scruple, proclaimed herself an adultress, and who had first endeavoured to starve her son, then to transport him, and afterwards to hang him, was not able to bear the representation of her own conduct; but fled from reproach, though she felt no pain from guilt, and left Bath in the utmost haste, to shelter herself among the crowds of London. Thus Savage had the satisfaction of finding, that, though he could not reform his mother, he could punish her, and that he did not always suffer alone.

The pleasure which he received from this increase of his poetical reputation was sufficient for some time to overbalance the miseries of want, which this performance did not much alleviate; for it was sold for a very trivial sum to a bookseller, who, though the success was so uncommon that five impressions were sold, of which many were undoubtedly very numerous, had not generosity sufficient to admit the unhappy writer to any part of the profit. The sale of this poem was always mentioned by Mr. Savage with the utmost elevation of heart, and referred to by him as an incontestable proof of a general acknowledgment of his abilities. It was indeed the only production of which he could justly boast a general reception. But, though he did not lose the opportunity which success gave him of setting a high rate on his abilities, but paid due deference to the suffrages of mankind when they were given in his favour, he did not suffer his esteem of himself to depend upon others, nor found anything sacred in the voice of the people when they were inclined to censure him; he then readily showed the folly of expecting that the public should judge right, observed how slowly poetical merit had often forced its way into the world; he contented himself with the applause of men of judgment, and was somewhat disposed to exclude all those from the character of men of judgment who did not applaud him. But he was at other times more favourable to mankind than to think them blind to the beauties of his works, and imputed the slowness of their sale to other causes; either they were published at a time when the town was empty, or when the attention of the public was engrossed by some struggle in the parliament, or some other object of general concern; or they were by the neglect of the publisher not diligently dispersed, or by his avarice not advertised with sufficient frequency.

45

Address, or industry, or liberality, was always wanting; and the blame was laid rather on any person than the author.

By arts like these, arts which every man practises in some degree, and to which too much of the little tranquillity of life is to be ascribed, Savage was always able to live at peace with himself. Had he indeed only made use of these expedients to alleviate the loss or want of fortune or reputation, or any other advantages which it is not in a man's power to bestow upon himself, they might have been justly mentioned as instances of a philosophical mind, and very properly proposed to the imitation of multitudes, who, for want of diverting their imaginations with the same dexterity, languish under afflictions which might be easily removed.

It were doubtless to be wished, that truth and reason were universally prevalent; that everything were esteemed according to its real value; and that men would secure themselves from being disappointed, in their endeavours after happiness, by placing it only in virtue, which is always to be obtained; but, if adventitious and foreign pleasures must be pursued, it would be perhaps of some benefit, since that pursuit must frequently be fruitless, if the practice of Savage could be taught, that folly might be an antidote to folly, and one fallacy be obviated by another. But the danger of this pleasing intoxication must not be concealed; nor indeed can any one, after having observed the life of Savage, need to be cautioned against it. By imputing none of his miseries to himself, he continued to act upon the same principles, and to follow the same path; was never made wiser by his sufferings, nor preserved by one misfortune from falling into another. He proceeded throughout his life to tread the same steps on the same circle; always applauding his past conduct, or at least forgetting it, to amuse himself with phantoms of happiness, which were dancing before him; and willingly turned his eyes from the light of reason, when it would have discovered the illusion, and shown him, what he never wished to see, his real state. He is even accused, after having lulled his imagination with those ideal opiates, of having tried the same experiment upon his conscience; and, having accustomed himself to impute all deviations from the right to foreign causes, it is certain that he was upon every occasion too easily reconciled to himself; and that he appeared very little to regret those practices which had impaired his reputation. The reigning error of his life was, that he mistook the love for the practice of virtue, and was indeed not so much a good man, as the friend of goodness.

This at least must be allowed him, that he always preserved a strong sense of the dignity, the beauty, and the necessity, of virtue; and that he never contributed deliberately to spread corruption amongst mankind. His actions, which were generally precipitate, were often blameable; but his writings, being the production of study, uniformly tended to the exaltation of the mind, and the propagation of morality and piety. These writings may improve mankind, when his failings shall be forgotten; and therefore he must be considered, upon the whole, as a benefactor to the world; nor can his personal example do any hurt, since whoever hears of his faults will hear of the miseries which they brought upon him, and which would deserve less pity, had not his condition been such as made his faults pardonable. He may be considered as a child exposed to all the temptations of indigence, at an age when resolution was not yet strengthened by conviction, nor virtue confirmed by habit; a circumstance which, in his *Bastard*, he laments in a very affecting manner:

> No Mother's care
> Shielded my infant innocence with prayer;
> No Father's guardian hand my youth maintain'd,
> Call'd forth my virtues, or from vice restrain'd.

The Bastard, however it might provoke or mortify his mother, could not be expected to melt her to compassion, so that he was still under the same want of the necessaries of life; and he therefore exerted all the interest which his wit, or his birth, or his misfortunes, could procure, to obtain, upon the death of Eusden, the place of Poet Laureat, and prosecuted his application with so much diligence, that the king publicly declared it his intention to bestow it upon him; but such was the fate of Savage, that even the king when he intended his advantage, was disappointed in his schemes; for the Lord Chamberlain, who has the disposal of the laurel, as one of the appendages of his office, either did not know the king's design, or did not approve it, or thought the nomination of the Laureat an encroachment upon his rights, and therefore bestowed the laurel upon Colley Cibber.

Mr. Savage, thus disappointed, took a resolution of applying to the queen, that, having once given him life, she would enable him to support it, and therefore published a short poem on her birthday, to which he gave the odd title of "Volunteer Laureat." The event of this essay he has himself related in the following letter, which he prefixed to the poem, when he afterwards reprinted it in *The Gentleman's Magazine*, whence I have copied it entire, as this was one of the few attempts in which Mr. Savage succeeded.

"Mr. Urban,—In your Magazine for February you published the last 'Volunteer Laureat,' written on a very melancholy occasion, the death of the royal patroness of arts and literature in general, and of the author of that poem in particular; I now send you the first that Mr. Savage wrote under that title.—This gentleman, notwithstanding a very considerable interest, being, on the death of Mr. Eusden, disappointed of the Laureat's place, wrote the following verses; which were no sooner published, but the late queen sent to a bookseller for them. The author had not at that time a friend either to get him introduced, or his poem presented at court; yet, such was the unspeakable goodness of that princess, that, notwithstanding this act of ceremony was wanting, in a few days after publication, Mr. Savage received a Bank-bill of fifty pounds, and a gracious message from her Majesty, by the Lord North and Guilford, to this effect: 'That her Majesty was highly pleased with the verses; that she took particularly kind his lines there relating to the king; that he had permission to write annually on the same subject; and that he should yearly receive the like present, till something better (which was her Majesty's intention) could be done for him.' After this he was permitted to present one of his annual poems to her Majesty, had the honour of kissing her hand, and met with the most gracious reception.   "Yours, &c."

Such was the performance, and such its reception; a reception, which, though by no means unkind, was yet not in the highest degree generous; to chain down the genius of a writer to an annual panegyric, showed in the queen too much desire of hearing her own praises, and a greater regard to herself than to him on whom her bounty was conferred. It was a kind of avaricious generosity, by which flattery was rather purchased than genius rewarded.

Mrs. Oldfield had formerly given him the same allowance with much more heroic intention: she had no other view than to enable him to prosecute his studies, and to set himself above the want of assistance, and was contented with doing good without stipulating for encomiums.

Mr. Savage, however, was not at liberty to make exceptions, but was ravished with the favours which he had received, and probably yet more with those which he was promised: he considered himself now as a favourite of the queen, and did not doubt but a few annual poems would establish him in some profitable employment. He therefore assumed the title of "Volunteer Laureat," not without some reprehensions from Cibber, who informed him, that the title of "Laureat" was a mark of honour conferred by the king, from whom all honour is derived, and which therefore no man has a right to bestow upon himself; and added, that he might with equal propriety style himself a Volunteer Lord or Volunteer Baronet. It cannot be denied that the remark was just; but Savage did not think any title, which was conferred upon Mr. Cibber, so honourable as that the usurpation of it could be imputed to him as an instance of very exorbitant vanity, and therefore continued to write under the same title, and received every year the same reward. He did not appear to consider these encomiums as tests of his abilities, or as anything more than annual hints to the queen of her promise, or acts of ceremony, by the performance of which he was entitled to his pension, and therefore did not labour them with great diligence, or print more than fifty each year, except that for some of the last years he regularly inserted them in *The Gentleman's Magazine*, by which they were dispersed over the kingdom.

Of some of them he had himself so low an opinion, that he intended to omit them in the collection of poems for which he printed proposals, and solicited subscriptions; nor can it seem strange, that, being confined to the same subject, he should be at some times indolent, and at others unsuccessful; that he should sometimes delay a disagreeable task till it was too late to perform it well; or that he should sometimes repeat the same sentiment on the same occasion, or at others be misled by an attempt after novelty to forced conceptions and far-fetched images. He wrote indeed with a double intention, which supplied him with some variety; for his business was to praise the queen for the favours

49

which he had received, and to complain to her of the delay of those which she had promised: in some of his pieces, therefore, gratitude is predominant, and in some discontent; in some, he represents himself as happy in her patronage; and, in others, as disconsolate to find himself neglected. Her promise, like other promises made to this unfortunate man, was never performed, though he took sufficient care that it should not be forgotten. The publication of his Volunteer Laureat procured him no other reward than a regular remittance of fifty pounds. He was not so depressed by his disappointments as to neglect any opportunity that was offered of advancing his interest. When the Princess Anne was married, he wrote a poem upon her departure, only, as he declared, "because it was expected from him," and he was not willing to bar his own prospects by any appearance of neglect. He never mentioned any advantage gained by this poem, or any regard that was paid to it; and therefore it is likely that it was considered at court as an act of duty, to which he was obliged by his dependence, and which it was therefore not necessary to reward by any new favour: or perhaps the queen really intended his advancement, and therefore thought it superfluous to lavish presents upon a man whom she intended to establish for life.

About this time not only his hopes were in danger of being frustrated, but his pension likewise of being obstructed, by an accidental calumny. The writer of *The Daily Courant*, a paper then published under the direction of the ministry, charged him with a crime, which, though very great in itself, would have been remarkably invidious in him, and might very justly have incensed the queen against him. He was accused by name of influencing elections against the court, by appearing at the head of a tory mob; nor did the accuser fail to aggravate his crime, by representing it as the effect of the most atrocious ingratitude, and a kind of rebellion against the queen, who had first preserved him from an infamous death, and afterwards distinguished him by her favour, and supported him by her charity. The charge, as it was open and confident, was likewise by good fortune very particular. The place of the transaction was mentioned, and the whole series of the rioter's conduct related. This exactness made Mr. Savage's vindication easy; for he never had in his life seen the place which was declared to be the scene of his wickedness, nor ever had been present in any town when its representatives were chosen. This answer he therefore made haste to publish, with all the circumstances necessary to make it credible; and very reasonably demanded, that the accusation should be retracted in the same paper, that he might no longer suffer the imputation of sedition and ingratitude. This demand was likewise pressed by him in a private letter to the author of the paper, who, either trusting to the protection of those whose defense he had undertaken, or having entertained some personal malice against Mr. Savage, or fearing lest, by retracting so confident an assertion, he should impair the credit of his paper, refused to give him that satisfaction. Mr. Savage therefore thought it necessary, to his own vindication, to prosecute him in the King's Bench; but as he did not find any ill effects from the accusation, having sufficiently cleared his innocence, he thought any farther procedure would have the appearance of revenge; and therefore willingly dropped it. He saw soon afterwards a process commenced in the same court against himself, on an information in which he was accused of writing and publishing an obscene pamphlet.

It was always Mr. Savage's desire to be distinguished; and, when any controversy became popular, he never wanted some reason for engaging in it with great ardour, and appearing at the head of the party which he had chosen. As he was never celebrated for his prudence, he had no sooner taken his side, and informed himself of the chief topics of the dispute, than he took all opportunities of asserting and propagating his principles, without much regard to his own interest, or any other visible design than that of drawing upon himself the attention of mankind.

The dispute between the Bishop of London and the chancellor is well known to have been for some time the chief topic of political conversation; and therefore Mr. Savage, in pursuance of his character, endeavoured to become conspicuous among the controvertists with which every coffee-house was filled on that occasion. He was an indefatigable opposer of all the claims of ecclesiastical power, though he did not know on what they were founded; and was therefore no friend to the Bishop of London. But he had another reason for appearing as a warm advocate for Dr. Rundle; for he was the friend of Mr. Foster and Mr. Thomson, who were the friends of Mr. Savage.

Thus remote was his interest in the question, which, however, as he imagined, concerned him so nearly, that it was not sufficient to harangue and dispute, but necessary likewise to write upon it. He therefore engaged with great ardour in a new poem, called by him, *The Progress of a Divine*; in which he conducts a profligate priest, by all the gradations of wickedness, from a poor curacy in the country to the highest preferments of the Church; and describes, with that humour which was natural to him, and that knowledge which was extended to all the diversities of human life, his behaviour in every station; and insinuates, that this priest, thus accomplished, found at last a patron in the Bishop of London. When he was asked, by one of his friends, on what pretence he could charge the bishop with such an action, he had no more to say than that he had only inverted the accusation; and that he thought it reasonable to believe, that he who obstructed the rise of a good man without reason, would for bad reasons promote the exaltation of a villain. The clergy were universally provoked by this satire; and Savage, who, as was his constant practice, had set his name to his performance, was censured in *The Weekly Miscellany* with severity, which he did not seem inclined to forget.

But return of invective was not thought a sufficient punishment. The Court of King's Bench was therefore moved against him; and he was obliged to return an answer to a charge of obscenity. It was urged, in his defence, that obscenity was criminal when it was intended to promote the practice of vice; but that Mr. Savage had only introduced obscene ideas, with the view of exposing them to detestation, and of amending the age by showing the deformity of wickedness. This plea was admitted; and Sir Philip Yorke, who then presided in that court, dismissed the information, with encomiums upon the purity and excellence of Mr. Savage's writings. The prosecution, however, answered in some measure the purpose of those by whom it was set on foot; for Mr. Savage was so far intimidated by it, that, when the edition of his poem was sold, he did not venture to reprint it; so that it was in a short time forgotten, or forgotten by all but those whom it offended. It is said that some endeavours were used to incense the queen against him: but he found advocates to obviate at least part of their effect; for, though he was never advanced, he still continued to receive his pension.

This poem drew more infamy upon him than any incident of his life; and, as his conduct cannot be vindicated, it is proper to secure his memory from reproach, by informing those whom he made his enemies, that he never intended to repeat the provocation; and that, though whenever he thought he had any reason to complain of the clergy, he used to threaten them with a new edition of *The Progress of a Divine*, it was his calm and settled resolution to suppress it for ever.

He once intended to have made a better reparation for the folly or injustice with which he might be charged, by writing another poem, called *The Progress of a Free-thinker*, whom he intended to lead through all the stages of vice and folly, to convert him from virtue to wickedness, and from religion to infidelity, by all the modish sophistry used for that purpose; and at last to dismiss him by his own hand into the other world. That he did not execute this design is a real loss of mankind; for he was too well acquainted with all the scenes of debauchery to have failed in his representations of them, and too zealous for virtue not to have represented them in such a manner as should expose them either to ridicule or detestation. But this plan was like others, formed and laid aside, till the vigour of his imagination was spent, and the effervescence of invention had subsided; but soon gave way to some other design, which pleased by its novelty for a while, and then was neglected like the former.

He was still in his usual exigencies, having no certain support but the pension allowed him by the queen, which, though it might have kept an exact economist from want, was very far from being sufficient for Mr. Savage, who had never been accustomed to dismiss any of his appetites without the gratification which they solicited, and whom nothing but want of money withheld from partaking of every pleasure that fell within his view. His conduct with regard to his pension was very particular. No sooner had he changed the bill than he vanished from the sight of all his acquaintance, and lay for some time out of the reach of all the inquiries that friendship or curiosity could make after him. At length he appeared again penniless as before, but never informed even those whom he seemed to regard most where he had been; nor was his retreat ever discovered. This was his constant practice during the whole time that he received the pension from the queen: he regularly disappeared and returned. He, indeed, affirmed that he retired to study, and that the money supported him in solitude for many months; but his friends declared that the short time in which it was spent sufficiently confuted his own account of his conduct.

His politeness and his wit still raised him friends, who were desirous of setting him at length free from that indigence by which he had been hitherto oppressed; and therefore solicited Sir Robert Walpole in his favour with so much earnestness, that they obtained a promise of the next place that should become vacant, not exceeding two hundred pounds a year. This promise was made with an uncommon declaration, "that it was not the promise of a minister to a petitioner, but of a friend to his friend."

Mr. Savage now concluded himself set at ease for ever, and, as he observes in a poem written on that incident of his life, trusted and was trusted; but soon found that his confidence was ill grounded, and this friendly promise was not inviolable. He spent a long time in solicitations, and at last despaired and desisted. He did not indeed deny that he had given the minister some reason to believe that he should not strengthen his own interest by advancing him, for he had taken care to distinguish himself in coffee-houses as an advocate for the ministry of the last years of Queen Anne, and was always ready to justify the conduct, and exalt the character, of Lord Bolingbroke, whom he mentions with great regard in an *Epistle upon Authors*, which he wrote about that time, but was too wise to publish, and of which only some fragments have appeared, inserted by him in the Magazine after his retirement.

To despair was not, however, the character of Savage; when one patronage failed, he had recourse to another. The Prince was now extremely popular, and had very liberally rewarded the merit of some writers whom Mr. Savage did not think superior to himself, and therefore he resolved to address a poem to him. For this purpose he made choice of a subject which could regard only persons of the highest rank and greatest affluence, and which was therefore proper for a poem intended to procure the patronage of a prince; and having retired for some time to Richmond, that he might prosecute his design in full tranquillity, without the temptations of pleasure, or the solicitations of creditors, by which his meditations were in equal danger of being disconcerted, he produced a poem On Public Spirit, with regard to Public Works.

The plan of this poem is very extensive, and comprises a multitude of topics, each of which might furnish matter sufficient for a long performance, and of which some have already employed more eminent writers; but as he was perhaps not fully acquainted with the whole extent of his own design, and was writing to obtain a supply of wants too pressing to admit of long or accurate inquiries, he passes negligently over many public works, which, even in his own opinion, deserved to be more elaborately treated.

But, though he may sometimes disappoint his reader by transient touches upon these subjects, which have often been considered, and therefore naturally raise expectations, he must be allowed amply to compensate his omissions, by expatiating, in the conclusion of his work, upon a kind of beneficence not yet celebrated by any eminent poet, though it now appears more susceptible of embellishments, more adapted to exalt the ideas, and affect the passions, than many of those which have hitherto been thought most worthy of the ornament of verse. The settlement of colonies in uninhabited countries, the establishment of those in security, whose misfortunes have made their own country no longer pleasing or safe, the acquisition of property without injury to any, the appropriation of the waste and luxuriant bounties of nature, and the enjoyment of those gifts which Heaven has scattered upon regions uncultivated and unoccupied, cannot be considered without giving rise to a great number of pleasing ideas, and bewildering the imagination in delightful prospects; and, therefore, whatever speculations they may produce in those who have confined themselves to political studies, naturally fixed the attention, and excited the applause, of a poet. The politician, when he considers men driven into other countries for shelter, and obliged to retire to forests and deserts, and pass their lives, and fix their posterity, in the remotest corners of the world, to avoid those hardships which they suffer or fear in their native place, may very properly inquire, why the legislature does not provide a remedy for these miseries, rather than encourage an escape from them. He may conclude that the flight of every honest man is a loss to the community;

that those who are unhappy without guilt ought to be relieved; and the life, which is overburthened by accidental calamities, set at ease by the care of the public; and that those, who have by misconduct forfeited their claim to favour, ought rather to be made useful to the society which they have injured, than be driven from it. But the poet is employed in a more pleasing undertaking than that of proposing laws which, however just or expedient, will never be made; or endeavouring to reduce to rational schemes of government societies which were formed by chance, and are conducted by the private passions of those who preside in them. He guides the unhappy fugitive, from want and persecution, to plenty, quiet, and security, and seats him in scenes of peaceful solitude, and undisturbed repose.

Savage has not forgotten, amidst the pleasing sentiments which this prospect of retirement suggested to him, to censure those crimes which have been generally committed by the discoverers of new regions, and to expose the enormous wickedness of making war upon barbarous nations because they cannot resist, and of invading countries because they are fruitful; of extending navigation only to propagate vice, and of visiting distant lands only to lay them waste. He has asserted the natural equality of mankind, and endeavoured to suppress that pride which inclines men to imagine that right is the consequence of power. His description of the various miseries which force men to seek for refuge in distant countries, affords another instance of his proficiency in the important and extensive study of human life; and the tenderness with which he recounts them, another proof of his humanity and benevolence.

It is observable that the close of this poem discovers a change which experience had made in Mr. Savage's opinions. In a poem written by him in his youth, and published in his *Miscellanies*, he declares his contempt of the contracted views and narrow prospects of the middle state of life, and declares his resolution either to tower like the cedar, or be trampled like the shrub; but in this poem, though addressed to a prince, he mentions this state of life as comprising those who ought most to attract reward, those who merit most the confidence of power, and the familiarity of greatness, and, accidentally mentioning this passage to one of his friends, declared, that in his opinion all the virtue of mankind was comprehended in that state.

In describing villas and gardens, he did not omit to condemn that absurd custom which prevails among the English, of permitting servants to receive money from strangers for the entertainment that they receive, and therefore inserted in his poem these lines:

> But what the flow'ring pride of gardens rare,
> However royal, or however fair,
> If gates, which to excess should still give way
> Ope but, like Peter's paradise, for pay;
> If perquisited varlets frequent stand,
> And each new walk must a new tax demand;
> What foreign eye but with contempt surveys?
> What Muse shall from oblivion snatch their praise?

But before the publication of his performance he recollected, that the queen allowed her garden and cave at Richmond to be shown for money; and that she so openly countenanced the practice, that she had bestowed the privilege of showing them as a place of profit on a man, whose merit she valued herself upon rewarding, though she gave him only the liberty of disgracing his country. He therefore thought, with more prudence than was often exerted by him, that the publication of these lines might be officiously represented as an insult upon the queen, to whom he owed his life and his subsistence; and that the propriety of his observation would be no security against the censures which the unseasonableness of it might draw upon him; he therefore suppressed the passage in the first edition, but after the queen's death thought the same caution no longer necessary, and restored it to the proper place. The poem was, therefore, published without any political faults, and inscribed to the prince; but Mr. Savage, having no friend upon whom he could prevail to present it to him, had no other method of attracting his observation than the publication of frequent advertisements, and therefore received no reward from his patron, however generous on other occasions. This disappointment he never mentioned without indignation, being by some means or other confident that the prince was not ignorant of his address to him; and insinuated, that if any advances in popularity could have been made by distinguishing him, he had not written without notice, or without reward. He was once inclined to have presented his poem in person, and sent to the printer for a copy with that design; but either his opinion changed, or his resolution deserted him, and he continued to resent neglect without attempting to force himself into regard. Nor was the public much more favourable than his patron; for only seventy-two were sold, though the performance was much commended by some whose judgment in that kind of writing is generally allowed. But Savage easily reconciled himself to mankind without imputing any defect to his work, by observing that his poem was unluckily published two days after the prorogation of the parliament, and by consequence at a time when all those who could be expected to regard it were in the hurry of preparing for their departure, or engaged in taking leave of others upon their dismission from public affairs. It must be however allowed, in justification of the public, that this performance is not the most excellent of Mr. Savage's works; and that, though it cannot be denied to contain many striking sentiments, majestic lines, and just observations, it is in general not sufficiently polished in the language, or enlivened in the imagery, or digested in the plan. Thus his poem contributed nothing to the alleviation of his poverty, which was such as very few could have supported with equal patience; but to which, it must likewise be confessed, that few would have been exposed who received punctually fifty pounds a year; a salary which, though by no means equal to the demands of vanity and luxury, is yet found sufficient to support families above want, and was undoubtedly more than the necessities of life require.

But no sooner had he received his pension, than he withdrew to his darling privacy, from which he returned in a short time to his former distress, and for some part of the year generally lived by chance, eating only when he was invited to the tables of his acquaintances, from which the meanness of his dress often excluded him, when the politeness and variety of his conversation would have been thought a sufficient recompense for his entertainment. He lodged as much by accident as he dined, and passed the night sometimes in mean houses which are set open at night to any casual wanderers, sometimes in cellars, among the riot and

filth of the meanest and most profligate of the rabble; and sometimes, when he had not money to support even the expenses of
these receptacles, walked about the streets till he was weary, and
lay down in the summer upon the bulk, or in the winter, with
his associates in poverty, among the ashes of a glass-house.

In this manner were passed those days and those nights which
nature had enabled him to have enjoyed in elevated speculations,
useful studies, or pleasing conversation. On a bulk, in a cellar,
or in a glass-house, among thieves and beggars, was to be found
the author of *The Wanderer*, the man of exalted sentiments,
extensive views, and curious observations; the man whose remarks
on life might have assisted the statesman, whose ideas of virtue
might have enlightened the moralists, whose eloquence might have
influenced senates, and whose delicacy might have polished courts.
It cannot but be imagined that such necessities might sometimes force him upon disreputable practices; and it is probable
that these lines in *The Wanderer* were occasioned by his reflections on his own conduct:

> Though misery leads to happiness, and truth,
> Unequal to the load this languid youth,
> (O, let none censure, if, untried by grief,
> If, amidst woe, untempted by relief),
> He stoop'd reluctant to low arts of shame,
> Which then, ev'n then, he scorned, and blush'd to name.

Whoever was acquainted with him was certain to be solicited
for small sums, which the frequency of the request made in time
considerable; and he was therefore quickly shunned by those who
were become familiar enough to be trusted with his necessities;
but his rambling manner of life, and constant appearance at houses
of public resort, always procured him a new succession of friends,
whose kindness had not been exhausted by repeated requests; so
that he was seldom absolutely without resources, but had in his
utmost exigencies this comfort, that he always imagined himself
sure of speedy relief. It was observed, that he always asked favours
of this kind without the least submission or apparent consciousness of dependence, and that he did not seem to look upon a
compliance with his request as an obligation that deserved any
extraordinary acknowledgments; but a refusal was resented by

59

him as an affront, or complained of as an injury; nor did he readily reconcile himself to those who either denied to lend, or give him afterwards any intimation that they expected to be repaid. He was sometimes so far compassionated by those who knew both his merit and distresses, that they received him into their families, but they soon discovered him to be a very incommodious inmate; for, being always accustomed to an irregular manner of life, he could not confine himself to any stated hours, or pay any regard to the rules of a family, but would prolong his conversation till midnight, without considering that business might require his friend's application in the morning; and, when he had persuaded himself to retire to bed, was not, without equal difficulty, called up to dinner: it was therefore impossible to pay him any distinction without the entire subversion of all economy, a kind of establishment which, however he went, he always appeared ambitious to overthrow. It must, therefore, be acknowledged, in justification of mankind, that it was not always by the negligence or coldness of his friends that Savage was distressed, but because it was in reality very difficult to preserve him long in a state of ease. To supply him with money was a hopeless attempt; for no sooner did he see himself master of a sum sufficient to set him free from care for a day, than he became profuse and luxurious. When once he had entered a tavern, or engaged in a scheme of pleasure, he never retired till want of money obliged him to some new expedient. If he was entertained in a family, nothing was any longer to be regarded there but amusement and jollity; wherever Savage entered, he immediately expected that order and business should fly before him, that all should thenceforward be left to hazard, and that no dull principle of domestic management should be opposed to his inclination, or intrude upon his gaiety. His distresses, however afflictive, never dejected him; in his lowest state he wanted not spirit to assert the natural dignity of wit, and was always ready to repress that insolence which the superiority of fortune incited, and to trample on that reputation which rose upon any other basis than that of merit: he never admitted any gross familiarities, or submitted to be treated otherwise than as an equal. Once, when he was without lodging, meat, or clothes, one of his friends, a man indeed not remarkable for moderation in his prosperity, left a message, that he desired to see him about nine in the morning. Savage knew that his intention was to assist him; but was very much disgusted that he should presume to prescribe the hour of his attendance, and, I believe, refused to visit him, and rejected his kindness.

The same invincible temper, whether firmness or obstinacy, appeared in his conduct to the Lord Tyrconnel, from whom he very frequently demanded, that the allowance which was once paid him should be restored; but with whom he never appeared to entertain for a moment the thought of soliciting a reconciliation, and whom he treated at once with all the haughtiness of superiority, and all the bitterness of resentment. He wrote to him, not in a style of supplication or respect, but of reproach, menace, and contempt; and appeared determined, if he ever regained his allowance, to hold it only by the right of conquest.

As many more can discover that a man is richer than that he is wiser than themselves, superiority of understanding is not so readily acknowledged as that of fortune; nor is that haughtiness, which the consciousness of great abilities incites, borne with the same submission as the tyranny of affluence; and therefore Savage, by asserting his claim to deference and regard, and by treating those with contempt, whom better fortune animated to rebel against him, did not fail to raise a great number of enemies in the different classes of mankind. Those who thought themselves raised above him by the advantages of riches, hated him because they found no protection from the petulance of his wit. Those who were esteemed for their writings feared him as a critic, and maligned him as a rival, and almost all the smaller wits were his professed enemies.

Among these Mr. Miller so far indulged his resentment as to introduce him in a farce, and direct him to be personated on the stage, in a dress like that which he then wore; a mean insult, which only insinuated that Savage had but one coat, and which was therefore despised by him rather than resented; for, though he wrote a lampoon against Miller, he never printed it: and as no other person ought to prosecute that revenge from which the person who was injured desisted, I shall not preserve what Mr. Savage suppressed; of which the publication would indeed have been a punishment too severe for so impotent an assault.

The great hardships of poverty were to Savage not the want of lodging or food, but the neglect and contempt which it drew upon him. He complained that, as his affairs grew desperate, he found his reputation for capacity visibly decline; that his opinion in questions of criticism was no longer regarded when his coat was out of fashion; and that those who, in the interval of his prosperity, were always encouraging him to great undertakings by encomiums on his genius and assurances of success, now received any mention of his designs with coldness, thought that the subjects on which he proposed to write were very difficult, and were ready to inform him, that the event of a poem was uncertain, that an author ought to employ much time in the consideration of his plan, and not presume to sit down to write in consequence of a few cursory ideas, and a superficial knowledge; difficulties were started on all sides, and he was no longer qualified for any performance but "The Volunteer Laureat."

Yet even this kind of contempt never depressed him; for he always preserved a steady confidence in his own capacity, and believed nothing above his reach which he should at any time earnestly endeavour to attain. He formed schemes of the same kind with regard to knowledge and to fortune, and flattered himself with advances to be made in science, as with riches, to be enjoyed in some distant period of his life. For the acquisition of knowledge he was indeed much better qualified than for that of riches; for he was naturally inquisitive, and desirous of the conversation of those from whom any information was to be obtained, but by no means solicitous to improve those opportunities that were sometimes offered of raising his fortune; and he was remarkably retentive of his ideas, which, when once he was in possession of them, rarely forsook him; a quality which could never be communicated to his money.

While he was thus wearing out his life in expectation that the queen would some time recollect her promise, he had recourse to the usual practice of writers, and published proposals for printing his works by subscription, to which he was encouraged by the success of many who had not a better right to the favour of the public; but, whatever was the reason, he did not find the world equally inclined to favour him; and he observed, with some discontent, that, though he offered his works at half a guinea, he was able to procure but a small number in comparison with those who subscribed twice as much to Duck. Nor was it without indignation that he saw his proposals neglected by the queen, who patronised Mr. Duck's with uncommon ardour, and incited a competition, among those who attended the court, who should most promote his interest, and who should first offer a subscription. This was a distinction to which Mr. Savage made no scruple of asserting, that his birth, his misfortunes, and his genius, gave a fairer title, than could be pleaded by him on whom it was conferred.

Savage's applications were, however, not universally unsuccessful; for some of the nobility countenanced his design, encouraged his proposals, and subscribed with great liberality. He related of the Duke of Chandos particularly, that, upon receiving his proposals, he sent him ten guineas. But the money which his subscriptions afforded him was not less volatile than that which he received from his other schemes; whenever a subscription was paid him, he went to a tavern; and, as money so collected is necessarily received in small sums, he never was able to send his poems to the press, but for many years continued his solicitation, and squandered whatever he obtained.

The project of printing his works was frequently revived; and, as his proposals grew obsolete, new ones were printed with fresher dates. To form schemes for the publication was one of his favourite amusements; nor was he ever more at ease than when, with any friend who readily fell in with his schemes, he was adjusting the print, forming the advertisements, and regulating the dispersion of his new edition, which he really intended some time to publish, and which, as long as experience had shown him the impossibility of printing the volume together, he at last determined to divide into weekly or monthly numbers, that the profits of the first might supply the expenses of the next.

Thus he spent his time in mean expedients and tormenting suspense, living for the greatest part in fear of prosecutions from his creditors, and consequently skulking in obscure parts of the town, of which he was no stranger to the remotest corners. But wherever he came, his address secured him friends, whom his necessities soon alienated; so that he had, perhaps, a more numerous acquaintance than any man ever before attained, there being scarcely any person eminent on any account to whom he was not known, or whose character he was not in some degree able to delineate. To the acquisition of this extensive acquaintance every circumstance of his life contributed. He excelled in the arts of conversation, and therefore willingly practiced them. He had seldom any home, or even a lodging in which he could be private; and therefore was driven into public-houses for the common conveniences of life and supports of nature. He was always ready to comply with every invitation, having no employment to withhold him, and often no money to provide for himself; and by dining with one company, he never failed of obtaining an introduction into another.

Thus dissipated was his life, and thus casual his subsistence; yet did not the distraction of his views hinder him from reflection, nor the uncertainty of his condition depress his gaiety. When he had wandered about without any fortunate adventure by which he was led into a tavern, he sometimes retired into the fields, and was able to employ his mind in study, to amuse it with pleasing imaginations; and seldom appeared to be melancholy, but when some sudden misfortune had just fallen upon him, and even then in a few moments he would disentangle himself from his perplexity, adopt the subject of conversation, and apply his mind wholly to the objects that others presented to it. This life, unhappy as it may be already imagined, was yet embittered, in 1738, with new calamities. The death of the queen deprived him of all the prospects of preferment with which he so long entertained his imagination; and, as Sir Robert Walpole had before given him reason to believe that he never intended the performance of his promise, he was now abandoned again to fortune. He was, however, at that time supported by a friend; and as it was not his custom to look out for distant calamities, or to feel any other pain than that which forced itself upon his senses, he was not much afflicted at his loss, and perhaps comforted himself that his pension would be now continued without the annual tribute of a panegyric. Another expectation contributed likewise to support him; he had taken a resolution to write a second tragedy upon the story of Sir Thomas Overbury, in which he preserved a few lines of his former play, but made a total alteration of the plan, added new incidents, and introduced new characters; so that it was a new tragedy, not a revival of the former.

Many of his friends blamed him for not making choice of another subject; but, in vindication of himself, he asserted, that it was not easy to find a better; and that he thought it his interest to extinguish the memory of the first tragedy, which he could only do by writing one less defective upon the same story; by which he should entirely defeat the artifice of the booksellers, who, after the death of any author of reputation, are always industrious to swell his works, by uniting his worst productions with his best. In the execution of this scheme, however, he proceeded but slowly, and probably only employed himself upon it when he could find no other amusement; but he pleased himself with counting the profits, and perhaps imagined, that the theatrical reputation which he was about to acquire, would be equivalent to all that he had lost by the death of his patroness. He did not, in confidence of his approaching riches, neglect the measures proper to secure the continuance of his pension, though some of his favourers thought him culpable for omitting to write on her death; but on her birthday next year, he gave a proof of the solidity of his judgment, and the power of his genius. He knew that the track of elegy had been so long beaten, that it was impossible to travel in it without treading in the footsteps of those who had gone before him; and that therefore it was necessary, that he might distinguish himself from the herd of encomiasts, to find out some new walk of funeral panegyric. This difficult task he performed in such a manner, that his poem may be justly ranked among the best pieces that the death of princes has produced. By transferring the mention of her death to her birthday, he has formed a happy combination of topics, which any other man would have thought it very difficult to connect in one view, but which he has united in such a manner, that the relation between them appears natural; and it may be justly said, that what no other man would have thought on, it now appears scarcely possible for any man to miss.

The beauty of this peculiar combination of images is so masterly, that it is sufficient to set this poem above censure; and therefore it is not necessary to mention many other delicate touches which may be found in it, and which would deservedly be admired in any other performance. To these proofs of his genius may be added, from the same poem, an instance of his prudence, an excellence for which he was not so often distinguished; he does not forget to remind the king, in the most delicate and artful manner, of continuing his pension.

With regard to the success of his address, he was for some time in suspense, but was in no great degree solicitous about it; and continued his labour upon his new tragedy with great tranquillity, till the friend who had for a considerable time supported him, removing his family to another place, took occasion to dismiss him. It then became necessary to inquire more diligently what was determined in his affair, having reason to suspect that no great favour was intended him, because he had not received his pension at the usual time.

It is said, that he did not take those methods of retrieving his interest, which were most likely to succeed; and some of those who were employed in the Exchequer, cautioned him against too much violence in his proceedings; but Mr. Savage, who seldom regulated his conduct by the advice of others, gave way to his passion, and demanded of Sir Robert Walpole, at his levee, the reason of the distinction that was made between him and the other pensioners of the queen, with a degree of roughness which perhaps determined him to withdraw what had been only delayed.

Whatever was the crime of which he was accused or suspected, and whatever influence was employed against him, he received soon after an account that took from him all hopes of regaining his pension; and he had now no prospect of subsistence but from his play, and he knew no way of living for the time required to finish it.

So peculiar were the misfortunes of this man, deprived of an estate and title by a particular law, exposed and abandoned by a mother, defrauded by a mother of a fortune which his father had allotted him, he entered the world without a friend; and though his abilities forced themselves into esteem and reputation, he was never able to obtain any real advantage, and whatever prospects arose, were always intercepted as he began to approach them. The king's intentions in his favor were frustrated; his dedication to the prince, whose generosity on every other occasion was eminent, procured him no reward; Sir Robert Walpole, who valued himself upon keeping his promise to others, broke it to him without regret; and the bounty of the queen was, after her death, withdrawn from him, and from him only.

Such were his misfortunes, which yet he bore, not only with decency, but with cheerfulness; nor was his gaiety clouded even by his last disappointments, though he was in a short time reduced to the lowest degree of distress, and often wanted both lodging and food. At this time he gave another instance of the insurmountable obstinacy of his spirit: his clothes were worn out; and he received notice, that at a coffee-house some clothes and linen were left for him: the person who sent them did not, I believe, inform him to whom he was to be obliged, that he might spare the perplexity of acknowledging the benefit; but though the offer was so far generous, it was made with some neglect of ceremonies, which Mr. Savage so much resented, that he refused the present, and declined to enter the house till the clothes that had been designed for him were taken away.

His distress was now publicly known, and his friends, therefore, thought it proper to concert some measures for his relief; and one of them [Pope] wrote a letter to him, in which he expressed his concern "for the miserable withdrawing of his pension"; and gave him hopes, that in a short time he should find himself supplied with a competence, "without any dependence on those little creatures which we are pleased to call the Great." The scheme proposed for this happy and independent subsistence was, that he should retire into Wales, and receive an allowance of fifty pounds a year, to be raised by a subscription, on which he was to live privately in a cheap place, without aspiring any more to affluence, or having any farther care of reputation. This offer Mr. Savage gladly accepted, though with intentions very different from those of his friends; for they proposed that he should continue an exile from London for ever, and spend all the remaining part of his life at Swansea; but he designed only to take the opportunity, which their scheme offered him, of retreating for a short time, that he might prepare his play for the stage, and his other works for the press, and then to return to London to exhibit his tragedy, and live upon the profits of his own labour. With regard to his works, he proposed very great improvements, which would have required much time, or great application; and, when he had finished them, he designed to do justice to his subscribers, by publishing them according to his proposals. As he was ready to entertain himself with future pleasures, he had planned out a scheme of life for the country, of which he had no knowledge but from pastorals and songs. He imagined that he should be transported to scenes of flowery felicity, like those which one poet has reflected to another; and had projected a perpetual round of innocent pleasures, of which he suspected no interruption from pride, or ignorance, or brutality. With these expectations he was so enchanted, that when he was once gently reproached by a friend for submitting to live upon a subscription, and advised rather by a resolute exertion of his abilities to support himself, he could not bear to debar himself from the happiness which was to be found in the calm of a cottage, or lose the opportunity of listening, without intermission, to the melody of the nightingale, which he believed was to be heard from every bramble, and which he did not fail to mention as a very important part of the happiness of a country life.

While this scheme was ripening, his friends directed him to take a lodging in the liberties of the Fleet, that he might be secure from his creditors, and sent him every Monday a guinea, which he commonly spent before the next morning, and trusted, after his usual manner, the remaining part of the week to the bounty of fortune.

He now began very sensibly to feel the miseries of dependence. Those by whom he was to be supported, began to prescribe to him with an air of authority, which he knew not how decently to resent, nor patiently to bear; and he soon discovered, from the conduct of most of his subscribers, that he was yet in the hands of "little creatures." Of the insolence that he was obliged to suffer, he gave many instances, of which none appeared to raise his indignation to a greater height, than the method which was taken of furnishing him with clothes. Instead of consulting him, and allowing him to send a tailor his orders for what they thought proper to allow him, they proposed to send for a tailor to take his measure, and then to consult how they should equip him. This treatment was not very delicate, nor was it such as Savage's humanity would have suggested to him on a like occasion; but it had scarcely deserved mention, had it not, by affecting him in an uncommon degree, shown the peculiarity of his character. Upon hearing the design that was formed, he came to the lodging of a friend with the most violent agonies of rage; and, being asked what it could be that gave him such disturbance, he replied with the utmost vehemence of indignation, "That they had sent for a tailor to measure him."

How the affair ended was never inquired, for fear of renewing his uneasiness. It is probable that, upon recollection, he submitted with a good grace to what he could not avoid, and that he discovered no resentment where he had no power. He was, however, not humbled to implicit and universal compliance; for, when the gentleman, who had first informed him of the design to support him by a subscription, attempted to procure a reconciliation with the Lord Tyrconnel, he could by no means be prevailed upon to comply with the measures that were proposed.

A letter was written for him to Sir William Lemon, to prevail upon him to interpose his good offices with Lord Tyrconnel, in which he solicited Sir William's assistance "for a man who really needed it as much as any man could well do"; and informed him, that he was retiring "for ever to a place where he should no more trouble his relations, friends, or enemies"; he confessed, that his passion had betrayed him to some conduct, with regard to Lord Tyrconnel, for which he could not but heartily ask his pardon; and as he imagined Lord Tyrconnel's passion might be yet so high, that he would not "receive a letter from him," begged that Sir William would endeavour to soften him; and expressed his hopes that he would comply with this request, and that "so small a relation would not harden his heart against him."

That any man should presume to dictate a letter to him, was not very agreeable to Mr. Savage; and therefore he was, before he had opened it, not much inclined to approve it. But when he read it, he found it contained sentiments entirely opposite to his own, and, as he asserted, to the truth; and therefore, instead of copying it, wrote his friend a letter full of masculine resentment and warm expostulations. He very justly observed, that the style was too supplicatory, and the representation too abject, and that he ought at least to have made him complain with "the dignity of a gentleman in distress." He declared that he would not write the paragraph in which he was to ask Lord Tyrconnel's pardon; for, "he despised his pardon, and therefore could not heartily, and would not hypocritically, ask it." He remarked that his friend made a very unreasonable distinction between himself and him; for, says he, "when you mention men of high rank in your own character," they are "those little creatures whom we are pleased to call the Great"; but when you address them "in mine," no servility is sufficiently humble. He then with propriety explained the ill consequences which might be expected from such a letter, which his relations would print in their own defence, and which would for ever be produced as a full answer to all that he should allege against them; for he always intended to publish a minute account of the treatment which he had received. It is to be remembered, to the honour of the gentleman by whom this letter was drawn up, that he yielded to Mr. Savage's reasons, and agreed that it ought to be suppressed.

After many alterations and delays, a subscription was at length raised, which did not amount to fifty pounds a year, though twenty were paid by one gentleman; such was the generosity of mankind, that what had been done by a player without solicitation, could not now be effected by application and interest; and Savage had a great number to court and to obey for a pension less than that which Mrs. Oldfield paid him without exacting any servilities. Mr. Savage, however, was satisfied, and willing to retire, and was convinced that the allowance, though scanty, would be more than sufficient for him, being now determined to commence a rigid economist, and to live according to the exact rules of frugality; for nothing was in his opinion more contemptible than a man, who, when he knew his income, exceeded it; and yet he confessed, that instances of such folly were too common, and lamented that some men were not to be trusted with their own money.

Full of these salutary resolutions, he left London in July, 1739, having taken leave with great tenderness of his friends, and parted from the author of this narrative with tears in his eyes. He was furnished with fifteen guineas, and informed, that they would be sufficient, not only for the expense of his journey, but for his support in Wales for some time; and that there remained but little more of the first collection. He promised a strict adherence to his maxims of parsimony, and went away in the stage-coach; nor did his friends expect to hear from him till he informed them of his arrival at Swansea. But when they least expected, arrived a letter dated the fourteenth day after his departure, in which he sent them word, that he was yet upon the road, and without money; and that he therefore could not proceed without a remittance.

They then sent him the money that was in their hands, with which he was enabled to reach Bristol, from whence he was to go to Swansea by water.

At Bristol he found an embargo laid upon the shipping, so that he could not immediately obtain a passage; and being therefore obliged to stay there some time, he with his usual felicity ingratiated himself with many of the principal inhabitants, was invited to their houses, distinguished at their public feasts, and treated with a regard that gratified his vanity, and therefore easily engaged his affection.

He began very early after his retirement to complain of the conduct of his friends in London, and irritated many of them so much by his letters, that they withdrew, however honourably, their contributions; and it is believed, that little more was paid him than the twenty pounds a year, which were allowed him by the gentleman who proposed the subscription.

After some stay at Bristol he retired to Swansea, the place originally proposed for his residence, where he lived about a year, very much dissatisfied with the diminution of his salary; but contracted, as in other places, acquaintance with those who were most distinguished in that country, among whom he has celebrated Mr. Powel and Mrs. Jones, by some verses which he inserted in *The Gentleman's Magazine*. Here he completed his tragedy, of which two acts were wanting when he left London; and was desirous of coming to town, to bring it upon the stage. The design was very warmly opposed; and he was advised, by his chief benefactor, to put it into the hands of Mr. Thomson and Mr. Mallet, that it might be fitted for the stage, and to allow his friends to receive the profits, out of which an annual pension should be paid him.

This proposal he rejected with the utmost contempt. He was by no means convinced that the judgment of those, to whom he was required to submit, was superior to his own. He was now determined, as he expressed it, to be "no longer kept in leading-strings," and had no elevated idea of "his bounty, who proposed to pension him out of the profits of his own labours."

He attempted in Wales to promote a subscription for his works, and had once hopes of success; but in a short time afterwards formed a resolution of leaving that part of the country, to which he thought it not reasonable to be confined, for the gratification of those, who, having promised him a liberal income, had no sooner banished him to a remote corner, than they reduced his allowance to a salary scarcely equal to the necessities of life. His resentment of this treatment, which, in his own opinion at least, he had not deserved, was such, that he broke off all correspondence with most of his contributors, and appeared to consider them as persecutors and oppressors; and in the latter part of his life declared, that their conduct toward him since his departure from London "had been perfidiousness improving on perfidiousness, and inhumanity on inhumanity."

It is not to be supposed, that the necessities of Mr. Savage did not sometimes incite him to satirical exaggerations of the behaviour of those by whom he thought himself reduced to them. But it must be granted, that the diminution of his allowance was a great hardship, and that those who withdrew their subscription from a man, who, upon the faith of their promise, had gone into a kind of banishment, and abandoned all those by whom he had been before relieved in his distresses, will find it no easy task to vindicate their conduct. It may be alleged, and perhaps justly, that he was petulant and contemptuous; that he more frequently reproached his subscribers for not giving him more, than thanked them for what he received; but it is to be remembered, that his conduct, and this is the worst charge that can be drawn up against him, did them no real injury, and that it therefore ought rather to have been pitied than resented; at least, the resentment it might provoke ought to have been generous and manly; epithets which his conduct will hardly deserve that starves the man whom he has persuaded to put himself into his power.

It might have been reasonably demanded by Savage, that they should, before they had taken away what they promised, have replaced him in his former state, that they should have taken no advantages from the situation to which the appearance of their kindness had reduced him, and that he should have been recalled to London before he was abandoned. He might justly represent, that he ought to have been considered as a lion in the toils, and demand to be released before the dogs should be loosed upon him. He endeavoured, indeed, to release himself, and, with an intent to return to London, went to Bristol, where a repetition of the kindness which he had formerly found, invited him to stay. He was not only caressed and treated, but had a collection made for him of about thirty pounds, with which it had been happy if he had immediately departed for London; but his negligence did not suffer him to consider, that such proofs of kindness were not often to be expected, and that this ardour of benevolence was in a great degree the effect of novelty, and might, probably, be every day less; and therefore he took no care to improve the happy time, but was encouraged by one favour to hope for another, till at length generosity was exhausted, and officiousness wearied.

Another part of his misconduct was the practice of prolonging his visits to unseasonable hours, and disconcerting all the families into which he was admitted. This was an error in a place of commerce, which all the charms of his conversation could not compensate; for what trader would purchase such airy satisfaction by the loss of solid gain, which must be the consequence of midnight merriment, as those hours which were gained at night were generally lost in the morning? Thus Mr. Savage, after the curiosity of the inhabitants was gratified, found the number of his friends daily decreasing, perhaps without suspecting for what reason their conduct was altered; for he still continued to harass, with his nocturnal intrusions, those that yet countenanced him, and admitted him to their houses.

But he did not spend all the time of his residence at Bristol in visits or at taverns, for he sometimes returned to his studies, and began several considerable designs. When he felt an inclination to write, he always retired from the knowledge of his friends, and lay hid in an obscure part of the suburbs, till he found himself again desirous of company, to which it is likely that intervals of absence made him more welcome. He was always full of his design of returning to London, to bring his tragedy upon the stage; but, having neglected to depart with the money that was raised for him, he could not afterwards procure a sum sufficient to defray the expenses of his journey; nor perhaps would a fresh supply have had any other effect than, by putting immediate pleasures into his power, to have driven the thoughts of his journey out of his mind. While he was thus spending the day in contriving a scheme for the morrow, distress stole upon him by imperceptible degrees. His conduct had already wearied some of those who were at first enamoured of his conversation; but he might, perhaps, still have

73

devolved to others, whom he might have entertained with equal success, had not the decay of his clothes made it no longer consistent with their vanity to admit him to their tables, or to associate with him in public places. He now began to find every man from home at whose house he called; and was therefore no longer able to procure the necessaries of life, but wandered about the town, slighted and neglected, in quest of a dinner, which he did not always obtain.

To complete his misery, he was pursued by the officers for small debts which he had contracted; and was therefore obliged to withdraw from the small number of friends from whom he had still reason to hope for favours. His custom was to lie in bed the greatest part of the day, and to get out in the dark with the utmost privacy, and, after having paid his visit, return again before morning to his lodging, which was in the garret of an obscure inn. Being thus excluded on one hand, and confined on the other, he suffered the utmost extremities of poverty, and often fasted so long that he was seized with faintness, and had lost his appetite, not being able to bear the smell of meat till the action of his stomach was restored by a cordial. In this distress, he received a remittance of five pounds from London, with which he provided himself a decent coat, and determined to go to London, but unhappily spent his money at a favourite tavern. Thus was he again confined to Bristol, where he was every day hunted by bailiffs. In this exigence he once more found a friend, who sheltered him in his house, though at the usual inconveniences with which his company was attended; for he could neither be persuaded to go to bed in the night nor to rise in the day.

It is observable, that in these various scenes of misery he was always disengaged and cheerful: he at some times pursued his studies, and at others continued or enlarged his epistolary correspondence; nor was he ever so far dejected as to endeavour to procure an increase of his allowance by any other methods than accusations and reproaches.

He had now no longer any hopes of assistance from his friends at Bristol, who as merchants, and by consequence sufficiently studious of profit, cannot be supposed to have looked with much compassion upon negligence and extravagance, or to think any excellence equivalent to a fault of such consequence as neglect of economy. It is natural to imagine, that many of those, who would have relieved his real wants, were discouraged from the exertion of their benevolence by observation of the use which was made of their favours, and conviction that relief would be only momentary, and that the same necessity would quickly return.

At last he quitted the house of his friend, and returned to his lodgings at the inn, still intending to set out in a few days for London; but on the 10th of January, 1742-3, having been at supper with two of his friends, he was at his return to his lodgings arrested for a debt of about eight pounds, which he owed at a coffee-house, and conducted to the house of a sheriff's officer. The account which he gives of this misfortune, in a letter to one of the gentlemen with whom he had supped, is too remarkable to be omitted.

"It was not a little unfortunate for me, that I spent yesterday's evening with you; because the hour hindered me from entering on my new lodging; however, I have now got one, but such an one as I believe nobody would choose.

"I was arrested at the suit of Mrs. Read, just as I was going up stairs to bed, at Mr. Bowyer's; but taken in so private a manner, that I believe nobody at the White Lion is apprised of it; though I let the officers know the strength, or rather weakness, of my pocket, yet they treated me with the utmost civility; and even when they conducted me to confinement, it was in such a manner, that I verily believe I could have escaped, which I would rather be ruined than have done, notwithstanding the whole amount of my finances was but threepence halfpenny.

"In the first place, I must insist, that you will industriously conceal this from Mrs. S——s, because I would not have her good-nature suffer that pain, which, I know, she would be apt to feel on this occasion.

"Next, I conjure you, dear Sir, by all the ties of friendship, by no means to have one uneasy thought on my account; but to have the same pleasantry of countenance, and unruffled serenity of mind, which (God be praised!) I have in this, and have had in a much severer calamity. Furthermore, I charge you, if you value my friendship as truly as I do yours, not to utter, or even harbour, the least resentment against Mrs. Read. I believe she has ruined me, but I freely forgive her; and (though I will never more have any intimacy with her) I would, at a due distance, rather do her an act of good, than ill-will. Lastly (pardon the expression) I absolutely command you not to offer me any pecuniary assistance, nor to attempt getting me any from any one of your friends. At another time, or on any other occasion, you may, dear friend, be well assured, I would rather write to you in the submissive style of a request, than that of a peremptory command.

"However, that my truly valuable friend may not think I am too proud to ask a favour, let me entreat you to let me have your boy to attend me for this day, not only for the sake of saving me the expense of porters, but for the delivery of some letters to people whose names I would not have known to strangers.

"The civil treatment I have thus far met from those whose prisoner I am, makes me thankful to the Almighty, that though he has thought fit to visit me (on my birth-night) with affliction, yet (such is his great goodness!) my affliction is not without alleviating circumstances. I murmur not; but am all resignation to the divine will. As to the world, I hope that I shall be endued by Heaven with that presence of mind, that serene dignity in misfortune, that constitutes the character of a true nobleman; a dignity far beyond that of coronets; a nobility arising from the just principles of philosophy, refined and exalted by those of Christianity."

He continued five days at the officer's, in hopes that he should be able to procure bail, and avoid the necessity of going to prison. The state in which he passed his time, and the treatment which he received, are very justly expressed by him in a letter which he wrote to a friend: "The whole day," says he, "has been employed in various people's filling my head with their foolish chimerical systems, which has obliged me coolly (as far as nature will admit) to digest, and accommodate myself to every different person's way of thinking; hurried from one wild system to another, till it has quite made a chaos of my imagination, and nothing done— promised—disappointed—ordered to send, every hour, from one part of the town to the other."

When his friends, who had hitherto caressed and applauded, found that to give bail and pay the debt was the same, they all refused to preserve him from a prison at the expense of eight pounds: and therefore, after having been for some time at the officer's house "at an immense expense," as he observes in his letter, he was at length removed to Newgate. This expense he was enabled to support by the generosity of Mr. Nash at Bath, who, upon receiving from him an account of his condition, immediately sent him five guineas, and promised to promote his subscription at Bath with all his interest.

By his removal to Newgate, he obtained at least a freedom from suspense, and rest from the disturbing vicissitudes of hope and disappointment: he now found that his friends were only companions, who were willing to share his gaiety, but not to partake of his misfortunes; and therefore he no longer expected any assistance from them. It must, however, be observed of one gentleman, that he offered to release him by paying the debt: but that Mr. Savage would not consent, I suppose, because he thought he had before been too burthensome to him. He was offered by some of his friends that a collection should be made for his enlargement; but he "treated the proposal," and declared "he should again treat it, with disdain. As to writing any mendicant letters, he had too high a spirit, and determined only to write to some ministers of state, to try to regain his pension."

He continued to complain of those that had sent him into the country, and objected to them, that he had "lost the profits of his play, which had been finished three years"; and in another letter declares his resolution to publish a pamphlet, that the world might know how "he had been used."

This pamphlet was never written; for he in a very short time recovered his usual tranquillity, and cheerfully applied himself to more inoffensive studies. He indeed steadily declared, that he was promised a yearly allowance of fifty pounds, and never received half the sum; but he seemed to resign himself to that as well as to other misfortunes, and lose the remembrance of it in his amusements and employments. The cheerfulness with which he bore his confinement appears from the following letter, which he wrote January the 30th, to one of his friends in London.

"I now write to you from my confinement in Newgate, where I have been ever since Monday last was se'nnight, and where I enjoy myself with much more tranquillity than I have known for upwards of a twelvemonth past; having a room entirely to myself, and pursuing the amusements of my poetical studies, uninterrupted, and agreeable to my mind. I thank the Almighty, I am now all collected in myself; and, though my person is in confinement, my mind can expatiate on ample and useful subjects with all the freedom imaginable. I am now more conversant with the Nine than ever, and if, instead of a Newgate bird, I may be allowed to be a bird of the Muses, I assure you, Sir, I sing very freely in my cage; sometimes indeed in the plaintive notes of the nightingale; but at others, in the cheerful strains of the lark."

In another letter he observes, that he ranges from one subject to another, without confining himself to any particular task; and that he was employed one week upon one attempt, and the next upon another.

Surely the fortitude of this man deserves, at least, to be mentioned with applause; and, whatever faults may he imputed to him, the virtue of suffering well cannot be denied him. The two powers which, in the opinion of Epictetus, constituted a wise man, are those of bearing and forbearing, which it cannot indeed be affirmed to have been equally possessed by Savage; and indeed the want of one obliged him very frequently to practise the other. He was treated by Mr. Dagge, the keeper of the prison, with great humanity; was supported by him at his own table, without any certainty of a recompense; had a room to himself, to which he could at any time retire from all disturbance; was allowed to stand at the door of the prison, and sometimes taken out into the fields; so that he suffered fewer hardships in prison than he had been accustomed to undergo in the greatest part of his life.

The keeper did not confine his benevolence to a gentle execution of his office, but made some overtures to the creditor for his release, though without effect; and continued, during the whole time of his imprisonment, to treat him with the utmost tenderness and civility.

Virtue is undoubtedly most laudable in that state which makes it most difficult; and therefore the humanity of a gaoler certainly deserves this public attestation; and the man, whose heart has not been hardened by such an employment, may be justly proposed as a pattern of benevolence. If an inscription was once engraved "to the honest toll-gatherer," less honours ought not to be paid "to the tender gaoler."

Mr. Savage very frequently received visits, and sometimes presents, from his acquaintances: but they did not amount to a subsistence, for the greater part of which he was indebted to the generosity of this keeper; but these favours, however they might endear to him the particular persons from whom he received them, were very far from impressing upon his mind any advantageous ideas of the people of Bristol, and therefore he thought he could not more properly employ himself in prison, than in writing a poem called *London and Bristol Delineated*.

When he had brought this poem to its present state, which, without considering the chasm, is not perfect, he wrote to London an account of his design, and informed his friend, that he was determined to print it with his name; but enjoined him not to communicate his intention to his Bristol acquaintance. The gentleman, surprised at his resolution, endeavoured to persuade him from publishing it, at least from prefixing his name; and declared that he could not reconcile the injunction of secrecy with his resolution to own it at its first appearance. To this Mr. Savage returned an answer agreeable to his character, in the following terms:—

"I received yours this morning; and not without a little surprise at the contents. To answer a question with a question, you ask me concerning London and Bristol, why will I add *delineated*? Why did Mr. Woolaston add the same word to his *Religion of Nature*? I suppose that it was his will and pleasure to add it in his case: and it is mine to do so in my own. You are pleased to tell me, that you understand not why secrecy is enjoined, and yet I intend to set my name to it. My answer is,—I have my private reasons, which I am not obliged to explain to anyone. You doubt my friend Mr. S—— would not approve of it. And what is it to me whether he does or not? Do you imagine that Mr. S—— is to dictate to me? If any man who calls himself my friend should assume such an air, I would spurn at his friendship with contempt. You say, I seem to think so by not letting him know it. And suppose I do, what then? Perhaps I can give reasons for that disapprobation, very foreign from what you would imagine. You go on in saying, Suppose I should not put my name to it. My answer is, that I will not suppose any such thing, being determined to the contrary: neither, Sir, would I have you suppose, that I applied to you for want of another press: nor would I have you imagine, that I owe Mr. S—— obligations which I do not."

Such was his imprudence, and such his obstinate adherence to his own resolutions, however absurd! A prisoner! supported by charity! and, whatever insults he might have received during the latter part of his stay at Bristol, once caressed, esteemed, and presented with a liberal collection, he could forget on a sudden his danger and his obligations, to gratify the petulance of his wit, or the eagerness of his resentment, and publish a satire, by which he might reasonably expect that he should alienate those who then supported him, and provoke those whom he could neither resist nor escape.

This resolution, from the execution of which it is probable that only his death could have hindered him, is sufficient to show, how much he disregarded all considerations that opposed his present passions, and how readily he hazarded all future advantages for any immediate gratifications. Whatever was his predominant inclination, neither hope nor fear hindered him from complying with it; nor had opposition any other effect than to heighten his ardour, and irritate his vehemence.

This performance was however laid aside, while he was employed in soliciting assistance from several great persons; and one interruption succeeding another, hindered him from supplying the chasm, and perhaps from retouching the other parts, which he can hardly be imagined to have finished in his own opinion; for it is very unequal, and some of the lines are rather inserted to rhyme to others, than to support or improve the sense; but the first and last parts are worked up with great spirit and elegance.

His time was spent in the prison for the most part in study, or in receiving visits; but sometimes he descended to lower amusements, and diverted himself in the kitchen with the conversation of the criminals; for it was not pleasing to him to be much without company; and, though he was very capable of a judicious choice, he was often contented with the first that offered; for this he was sometimes reproved by his friends, who found him surrounded with felons; but the reproof was on that, as on other occasions, thrown away; he continued to gratify himself, and to set very little value on the opinion of others. But here, as in every other scene of his life, he made use of such opportunities as occurred of benefiting those who were more miserable than himself, and was always ready to perform any office of humanity to his fellow-prisoners.

He had now ceased from corresponding with any of his subscribers except one, who yet continued to remit him the twenty pounds a year which he had promised him, and by whom it was expected that he would have been in a very short time enlarged, because he had directed the keeper to inquire after the state of his debts. However, he took care to enter his name according to the forms of the court, that the creditor might be obliged to make him some allowance, if he was continued a prisoner, and, when on that occasion he appeared in the hall, was treated with very unusual respect. But the resentment of the city was afterwards raised by some accounts that had been spread of the satire; and he was informed that some of the merchants intended to pay the allowance which the law required, and to detain him a prisoner at their own expense. This he treated as an empty menace; and perhaps might have hastened the publication, only to show how much he was superior to their insults, had not all his schemes been suddenly destroyed.

When he had been six months in prison, he received from one of his friends, in whose kindness he had the greatest confidence, and on whose assistance he chiefly depended, a letter, that contained a charge of very atrocious ingratitude, drawn up in such terms as sudden resentment dictated. Henley, in one of his advertisements, had mentioned "Pope's treatment of Savage." This was supposed by Pope to be the consequence of a complaint made by Savage to Henley, and was therefore mentioned by him with much resentment. Mr. Savage returned a very solemn protestation of his innocence, but however appeared much disturbed at the accusation. Some days afterwards he was seized with a pain in his back and side, which, as it was not violent, was not suspected to be dangerous; but growing daily more languid and dejected, on the 25th of July he confined himself to his room, and a fever seized his spirits. The symptoms grew every day more formidable, but his condition did not enable him to procure any assistance. The last time that the keeper saw him was on July the 31st, 1743; when Savage, seeing him at his bedside, said, with an uncommon earnestness, "I have something to say to you, sir": but, after a pause, moved his hand in a melancholy manner; and, finding himself unable to recollect what he was going to communicate, said, " 'Tis gone!" The keeper soon after left him; and the next morning he died. He was buried in the churchyard of St. Peter, at the expense of the keeper.

Such were the life and death of Richard Savage, a man equally distinguished by his virtues and vices; and at once remarkable for his weaknesses and abilities. He was of a middle stature, of a thin habit of body, a long visage, coarse features, and melancholy aspect; of a grave and manly deportment, a solemn dignity of mien, but which, upon a nearer acquaintance, softened into an engaging easiness of manners. His walk was slow, and his voice tremulous and mournful. He was easily excited to smiles, but very seldom provoked to laughter. His mind was in an uncommon degree vigorous and active. His judgment was accurate, his apprehension quick, and his memory so tenacious, that he was frequently observed to know what he had learned from others, in a short time, better than those by whom he was informed; and could frequently recollect incidents with all their combination of circumstances, which few would have regarded at the present time, but which the quickness of his apprehension impressed upon him. He had the art of escaping from his own reflections, and accommodating himself to every new scene.

To this quality is to be imputed the extent of his knowledge, compared with the small time which he spent in visible endeavours to acquire it. He mingled in cursory conversation with the same steadiness of attention as others apply to a lecture; and amidst the appearance of thoughtless gaiety lost no new idea that was started, nor any hint that could be improved. He had therefore made in coffee-houses the same proficiency as others in their closets; and it is remarkable, that the writings of a man of little education and little reading have an air of learning scarcely to be found in any other performances, but which perhaps as often obscures as embellishes them.

His judgment was eminently exact both with regard to writings and to men. The knowledge of life was indeed his chief attainment; and it is not without some satisfaction, that I can produce the suffrage of Savage in favour of human nature, of which he never appeared to entertain such odious ideas as some who perhaps had neither his judgment nor experience, have published, either in ostentation of their sagacity, vindication of their crimes, or gratification of their malice.

His method of life particularly qualified him for conversation, of which he knew how to practise all the graces. He was never vehement or loud, but at once modest and easy, open and respectful; his language was vivacious or elegant, and equally happy upon grave and humorous subjects. He was generally censured for not knowing when to retire; but that was not the defect of his judgment, but of his fortune: when he left his company, he used frequently to spend the remaining part of the night in the street, or at least was abandoned to gloomy reflections, which it is not strange that he delayed as long as he could; and sometimes forgot that he gave others pain to avoid it himself.

It cannot be said, that he made use of his abilities for the direction of his own conduct; an irregular and dissipated manner of life had made him the slave of every passion that happened to be excited by the presence of its object, and that slavery to his passions reciprocally produced a life irregular and dissipated. He was not master of his own motions, nor could promise anything for the next day.

With regard to his economy, nothing can be added to the relation of his life. He appeared to think himself born to be supported by others, and dispensed from all necessity of providing for himself; he therefore never prosecuted any scheme of advantage, nor endeavoured even to secure the profits which his writings might have afforded him. His temper was, in consequence of the dominion of his passions, uncertain and capricious; he was easily engaged, and easily disgusted; but he is accused of retaining his hatred more tenaciously than his benevolence. He was compassionate both by nature and principle, and always ready to perform offices of humanity; but when he was provoked (and very small offences were sufficient to provoke him), he would prosecute his revenge with the utmost acrimony till his passion had subsided.

His friendship was therefore of little value; for though he was zealous in the support or vindication of those whom he loved, yet it was always dangerous to trust him, because he considered himself as discharged by the first quarrel from all ties of honour and gratitude; and would betray those secrets which in the warmth of confidence had been imparted to him. This practice drew upon him an universal accusation of ingratitude; nor can it be denied that he was very ready to set himself free from the load of an obligation; for he could not bear to conceive himself in a state of dependence, his pride being equally powerful with his other passions, and appearing in the form of insolence at one time, and of vanity at another. Vanity, the most innocent species of pride, was most frequently predominant: he could not easily leave off, when he had once begun to mention himself or his works; nor ever read his verses without stealing his eyes from the page, to discover in the faces of his audience, how they were affected with any favourite passage.

A kinder name than that of vanity ought to be given to the delicacy with which he was always careful to separate his own merit from every other man's, and to reject that praise to which he had no claim. He did not forget, in mentioning his performances, to mark every line that had been suggested or amended; and was so accurate, as to relate that he owed three words in The Wanderer to the advice of his friends. His veracity was questioned, but with little reason; his accounts, though not indeed always the same, were generally consistent. When he loved any man, he suppressed all his faults; and, when he had been offended by him, concealed all his virtues: but his characters were generally true, so far as he proceeded; though it cannot be denied, that his partiality might have sometimes the effect of falsehood.

In cases indifferent, he was zealous for virtue, truth, and justice: he knew very well the necessity of goodness to the present and future happiness of mankind; nor is there perhaps, any writer, who has less endeavoured to please by flattering the appetites, or perverting the judgment.

As an author, therefore, and he now ceases to influence mankind in any other character, if one piece which he had resolved to suppress be excepted, he has very little to fear from the strictest moral or religious censure. And though he may not be altogether secure against the objections of the critic, it must however be acknowledged, that his works are the productions of a genius truly poetical; and, what many writers who have been more lavishly applauded, cannot boast, that they have an original air, which has no resemblance of any foregoing writer, that the versification and sentiments have a cast peculiar to themselves, which no man can imitate with success, because what was nature in Savage would in another be affectation. It must be confessed, that his descriptions are striking, his images animated, his fictions justly imagined, and his allegories artfully pursued; that his diction is elevated, though sometimes forced, and his numbers sonorous and majestic, though frequently sluggish and encumbered. Of his style, the general fault is harshness, and its general excellence is dignity; of his sentiments, the prevailing beauty is simplicity, and uniformity the prevailing defect.

For his life, or for his writings, none, who candidly consider his fortune, will think an apology either necessary or difficult. If he was not always sufficiently instructed in his subject, his knowledge was at least greater than could have been attained by others in the same state. If his works were sometimes unfinished, accuracy cannot reasonably be expected from a man oppressed with want, which he has no hope of relieving but by a speedy publication. The insolence and resentment of which he is accused were not easily to be avoided by a great mind, irritated by perpetual hardships, and constrained hourly to return the spurns of contempt, and repress the insolence of prosperity; and vanity surely may be readily pardoned in him, to whom life afforded no other comforts than barren praises, and the consciousness of deserving them.

Those are no proper judges of his conduct, who have slumbered away their time on the down of plenty; nor will any wise man easily presume to say, "Had I been in Savage's condition, I should have lived or written better than Savage."

This relation will not be wholly without its use, if those, who languish under any part of his sufferings, shall be enabled to fortify their patience, by reflecting that they feel only those afflictions from which the abilities of Savage did not exempt him; or those who, in confidence of superior capacities or attainments, disregard the common maxims of life, shall be reminded that nothing will supply the want of prudence; and that negligence and irregularity, long continued, will make knowledge useless, wit ridiculous and genius contemptible.

Castle Rackrent

1801

MARIA EDGEWORTH

No COMMENT on Maria Edgeworth is possible without a description of her father. He was an enlightened Eighteenth-Century despot, a Rousseau-phile who had four wives and from nineteen to twenty-two children. "Masterful, versatile, brilliant, enlightened, he stands as a type of the 'Superior Being' "; he was an inventor, and a politician, an educationalist and a philosopher, and, when he inherited the family estate at Edgeworthstown, an excellent landlord. Byron found him a "boisterous bore," his voice could carry for a mile and Castle Rackrent is one of his daughter's only two romances not to be revised or edited by him. She was born in 1767 and accompanied her father to Ireland in 1782 where she remained occupied in family, estate and household duties until her death in 1849 aged eighty-two. Castle Rackrent was her first book, of importance as a regional novel and family chronicle and as the first authentic picture of the Irish. "Without being so presumptuous as to hope to emulate the rich humour, pathetic tenderness and admirable taste which pervade the works of my accomplished friend," wrote Scott in his preface to Waverley, "I felt that something might be attempted for my own country of the same kind with that which she has so fortunately achieved for Ireland." Turgeniev also mentioned "he was an unconscious disciple of Miss Edgeworth in setting out on his literary career."

A great part of Maria Edgeworth's work is ruined by Victorian moralising; there is always something wooden about edification and her favourite theme—the regeneration of young men when they return from cold and formal England to Irish warmth and reality—is spoiled by over-emphasis. Ennui and The Absentee are perhaps the most personal of her books and both deal with this subject. I prefer the shorter Castle

Rackrent because there is no room in it for moralising; we rush down the torrent of family history in a flimsy canoe listening to the stories of their ancestors which the Edgeworths heard from their old bailiff when they returned to claim their inheritance. Those who have had any experience of pride and debt will recognise the frivolity of despair with which extravagant elder sons, or even whole families, plunge to their ruin.

The Edgeworth lands, we are grateful to learn, were well administered by Maria's father and brought in about three thousand pounds a year. Miss Thackeray, daughter of the novelist, near the close of the century paid a visit to Maria's nephew. "We saw the corner by the fire where Maria wrote; we saw her table with its pretty curves standing in its place in the deep casements. Miss Edgeworth's own room is a tiny little room above looking out on a back garden. What a strange fellow-feeling with the past it gave one to stand staring at the old books with their paper-backs and old-fashioned covers, at the grey boards, which were the liveries of literature in those early days; at the first editions with their inscriptions in the author's handwriting or Maria's pretty calligraphy. Other relics there are of course—her silver ink-stand, the little table her father left her—but none which touched one so vividly." She describes Maria from a picture "as having a spritely French appearance, with a marked nose of the retroussé order." Scott records her as being small and fairy-like, while a drawing by Slater pictures her as having something of the melting sensuousness, though accompanied by high principles, of the Byronic heroine. She never married. Among her nephews was the poet Beddoes.

Castle Rackrent first appeared anonymously and the authoress leapt into fame a year later with the second edition.

Castle Rackrent

MARIA EDGEWORTH

Monday Morning.[1]

Having, OUT OF friendship for the family, upon whose estate praised be Heaven! I and mine have lived rent-free time out of mind, voluntarily undertaken to publish the Memoirs of the Rackrent Family, I think it my duty to say a few words, in the first place, concerning myself. My real name is Thady Quirk, though in the family I have always been known by no other than "Honest Thady," afterward, in the time of Sir Murtagh, deceased, I remember to hear them calling me "Old Thady," and now I've come to "Poor Thady"; for I wear a long greatcoat[2] winter and

[1] See Glossary, p. 152.

[2] The cloak, or mantle, as described by Thady, is of high antiquity. Spenser, in his View of the State of Ireland, proves that it is not, as some have imagined, peculiarly derived from the Scythians, but that "most nations of the world anciently used the mantle; for the Jews used it, as you may read of Elias's mantle, etc.; the Chaldees also used it, as you may read in Diodorus; the Egyptians likewise used it, as you may read in Herodotus, and may be gathered by the description of Berenice in the Greek Commentary upon Callimachus; the Greeks also used it anciently, as appeared by Venus's mantle lined with stars, though afterward they changed the form thereof into their cloaks, called Pallai, as some of the Irish also use; and the ancient Latins and Romans used it, as you may read in Virgil, who was a great antiquary, that Evander, when Æneas came to him at his feast, did entertain and feast him sitting on the ground, and lying on mantles: insomuch that he useth the very word mantile for a mantle—

'Humi mantilia sternunt:'

so that it seemeth that the mantle was a general habit to most nations, and not proper to the Scythians only."

Spenser knew the convenience of the said mantle, as housing, bedding, and clothing:

"Iren. Because the commodity doth not countervail the discommodity; for

91

summer, which is very handy, as I never put my arms into the sleeves; they are as good as new, though come Holantide next I've had it these seven years: it holds on by a single button round my neck, cloak fashion. To look at me, you would hardly think "Poor Thady" was the father of Attorney Quirk; he is a high gentleman, and never minds what poor Thady says, and having better than fifteen hundred a year, landed estate, looks down upon honest Thady; but I wash my hands of his doings, and as I have lived so will I die, true and loyal to the family. The family of the Rackrents is, I am proud to say, one of the most ancient in the kingdom. Everybody knows this is not the old family name, which was O'Shaughlin, related to the kings of Ireland—but that was before my time. My grandfather was driver to the great Sir Patrick O'Shaughlin, and I heard him, when I was a boy, telling how the Castle Rackrent estate came to Sir Patrick; Sir Tallyhoo Rackrent was cousin-german to him, and had a fine estate of his own, only never a gate upon it, it being his maxim that a car was the best gate. Poor gentleman! he lost a fine hunter and his life, at last, by it, all in one day's hunt. But I ought to bless that day, for the estate came straight into the family, upon one condition, which Sir Patrick O'Shaughlin at the time took sadly to heart, they say, but thought better of it afterwards, seeing how large a stake depended upon it: that he should, by Act of Parliament, take and bear the surname and arms of Rackrent.

Now it was that the world was to see what was in Sir Patrick. On coming into the estate he gave the finest entertainment ever was heard of in the country; not a man could stand after supper but Sir Patrick himself, who could sit out the best man in Ireland, let alone the three kingdoms itself.[1] He had his house, from one

---

the inconveniences which thereby do arise are much more many; for it is a fit house for an outlaw, a meet bed for a rebel, and an apt cloak for a thief. First, the outlaw being, for his many crimes and villainies, banished from the towns and houses of honest men, and wandering in waste places, far from danger of law, maketh his mantle his house, and under it coureth himself from the wrath of Heaven, from the offence of the earth, and from the sight of men. When it raineth, it is his pent-house; when it bloweth, it is his tent; when it freezeth, it is his tabernacle. In summer he can wear it loose; in winter he can wrap it close; at all times he can use it; never heavy, never cumbersome. Likewise for a rebel it is as serviceable; for in this war that he maketh (if at least it deserves the name of war), when he still flieth from his foe, and lurketh in the *thick woods* (this should be *black bogs*) and straight passages, waiting for advantages, it is his bed, yea, and almost his household stuff."

[1] See Glossary, p. 153.

year's end to another, as full of company as ever it could hold, and fuller; for rather than be left out of the parties at Castle Rackrent, many gentlemen, and those men of the first consequence and landed estates in the country—such as the O'Neills of Ballynagrotty, and the Moneygawls of Mount Juliet's Town, and O'Shannons of New Town Tullyhog—made it their choice, often and often, when there was no room to be had for love nor money, in long winter nights, to sleep in the chicken-house, which Sir Patrick had fitted up for the purpose of accommodating his friends and the public in general, who honoured him with their company unexpectedly at Castle Rackrent; and this went on I can't tell you how long. The whole country rang with his praises!—Long life to him! I'm sure I love to look upon his picture, now opposite to me; though I never saw him, he must have been a portly gentleman—his neck something short, and remarkable for the largest pimple on his nose, which, by his particular desire, is still extant in his picture, said to be a striking likeness, though taken when young. He is said also to be the inventor of raspberry whisky, which is very likely, as nobody has ever appeared to dispute it with him, and as there still exists a broken punch-bowl at Castle Rackrent, in the garret, with an inscription to that effect—a great curiosity. A few days before his death he was very merry; it being his honour's birthday, he called my grandfather in—God bless him!—to drink the company's health, and filled a bumper himself, but could not carry it to his head, on account of the great shake in his hand; on this he cast his joke, saying, "What would my poor father say to me if he was to pop out of the grave, and see me now? I remember when I was a little boy, the first bumper of claret he gave me after dinner, how he praised me for carrying it so steady to my mouth. Here's my thanks to him—a bumper toast." Then he fell to singing the favourite song he learned from his father—for the last time, poor gentleman—he sung it that night as loud and as hearty as ever, with a chorus:

He that goes to bed, and goes to bed sober,
Falls as the leaves do, falls as the leaves do, and dies in October;
But he that goes to bed, and goes to bed mellow,
Lives as he ought to do, lives as he ought to do, and dies an honest
    fellow.

Sir Patrick died that night: just as the company rose to drink his health with three cheers, he fell down in a sort of fit, and was carried off; they sat it out, and were surprised, on inquiry in the morning, to find that it was all over with poor Sir Patrick. Never did any gentleman live and die more beloved in the country by rich and poor. His funeral was such a one as was never known before or since in the county! All the gentlemen in the three counties were at it; far and near, how they flocked! my great-grandfather said, that to see all the women, even in their red cloaks, you would have taken them for the army drawn out. Then such a fine whillaluh![1] you might have heard it to the farthest end of the county, and happy the man who could get but a sight of the hearse! But who'd have thought it? Just as all was going on right, through his own town they were passing, when the body was seized for debt—a rescue was apprehended from the mob; but the heir, who attended the funeral, was against that, for fear of consequences, seeing that those villains who came to serve acted under the disguise of the law: so, to be sure, the law must take its course, and little gain had the creditors for their pains. First and foremost, they had the curses of the country: and Sir Murtagh Rackrent, the new heir, in the next place, on account of this affront to the body, refused to pay a shilling of the debts, in which he was countenanced by all the best gentlemen of property, and others of his acquaintance; Sir Murtagh alleging in all companies that he all along meant to pay his father's debts of honour, but the moment the law was taken of him, there was an end to honour to be sure. It was whispered (but none but the enemies of the family believe it) that this was all a sham seizure to get quit of the debts which he had bound himself to pay in honour.

It's a long time ago, there's no saying how it was, but this for certain, the new man did not take at all after the old gentleman; the cellars were never filled after his death, and no open house, or anything as it used to be; the tenants even were sent away without their whisky.[2] I was ashamed myself, and knew not what to say for the honour of the family; but I made the best of a bad case, and laid it all at my lady's door, for I did not like her anyhow, nor anybody else; she was of the family of the Skinflints, and a widow;

[1] See Glossary, p. 153.
[2] See Glossary, p. 155.

it was a strange match for Sir Murtagh; the people in the country thought he demeaned himself greatly,[1] but I said nothing: I knew how it was. Sir Murtagh was a great lawyer, and looked to the great Skinflint estate; there, however, he overshot himself; for though one of the co-heiresses, he was never the better for her, for she outlived him many's the long day—he could not see that to be sure when he married her. I must say for her, she made him the best of wives, being a very notable, stirring woman, and looking close to everything. But I always suspected she had Scotch blood in her veins; anything else I could have looked over in her, from a regard to the family. She was a strict observer, for self and servants, of Lent, and all fast-days, but not holidays. One of the maids having fainted three times the last day of Lent, to keep soul and body together, we put a morsel of roast beef into her mouth, which came from Sir Murtagh's dinner, who never fasted, not he; but somehow or other it unfortunately reached my lady's ears, and the priest of the parish had a complaint made of it the next day, and the poor girl was forced, as soon as she could walk, to do penance for it, before she could get any peace or absolution, in the house or out of it. However, my lady was very charitable in her own way. She had a charity school for poor children, where they were taught to read and write gratis, and where they were kept well to spinning gratis for my lady in return; for she had always heaps of duty yarn from the tenants, and got all her household linen out of the estate from first to last; for after the spinning, the weavers on the estate took it in hand for nothing, because of the looms my lady's interest could get from the Linen Board to distribute gratis. Then there was a bleach-yard near us, and the tenant dare refuse my lady nothing, for fear of a lawsuit Sir Murtagh kept hanging over him about the watercourse. With these ways of managing, 'tis surprising how cheap my lady got things done, and how proud she was of it. Her table the same way, kept for next to nothing; duty fowls, and duty turkeys, and duty geese,[2] came as fast as we could eat 'em, for my lady kept a sharp look-out, and knew to a tub of butter everything the tenants had, all round. They knew her way, and what with fear of driving for rent and Sir Murtagh's lawsuits, they were kept in such good order, they never thought of

[1] See Glossary, p. 155.
[2] See Glossary, p. 155.

coming near Castle Rackrent without a present of something or other—nothing too much or too little for my lady—eggs, honey, butter, meal, fish, game, grouse, and herrings, fresh or salt, all went for something. As for their young pigs, we had them, and the best bacon and hams they could make up, with all young chickens in spring; but they were a set of poor wretches, and we had nothing but misfortunes with them, always breaking and running away. This, Sir Murtagh and my lady said, was all their former landlord Sir Patrick's fault, who let 'em all get the half-year's rent into arrear; there was something in that to be sure. But Sir Murtagh was as much the contrary way; for let alone making English tenants[1] of them, every soul, he was always driving and driving, and pounding and pounding, and canting[2] and canting, and replevying and replevying, and he made a good living of trespassing cattle; there was always some tenant's pig, or horse, or cow, or calf, or goose, trespassing, which was so great a gain to Sir Murtagh, that he did not like to hear me talk of repairing fences. Then his heriots and duty-work[3] brought him in something, his turf was cut, his potatoes set and dug, his hay brought home, and, in short, all the work about his house done for nothing; for in all our leases there were strict clauses heavy with penalties, which Sir Murtagh knew well how to enforce; so many days' duty-work of man and horse, from every tenant, he was to have, and had, every year; and when a man vexed him, why, the finest day he could pitch on, when the cratur was getting in his own harvest, or thatching his cabin, Sir Murtagh made it a principle to call upon him and his horse; so he taught 'em all, as he said, to know the law of landlord and tenant. As for law, I believe no man, dead or alive, ever loved it so well as Sir Murtagh. He had once sixteen suits pending at a time, and I never saw him so much himself: roads, lanes, bogs, wells, ponds, eel-wires, orchards, trees, tithes, vagrants, gravelpits, sandpits, dung-hills, and nuisances, everything upon the face of the earth furnished him good matter for a suit. He used to boast that he had a lawsuit for every letter in the alphabet. How I used to wonder to see Sir Murtagh in the midst of the papers in his office! Why, he could hardly turn about for them. I made bold to shrug my shoul-

[1] See Glossary, p. 155.
[2] See Glossary, p. 155.
[3] See Glossary, p. 155.

ders once in his presence, and thanked my stars I was not born a gentleman to so much toil and trouble; but Sir Murtagh took me up short with his old proverb, "Learning is better than house or land." Out of forty-nine suits which he had, he never lost one but seventeen[1]; the rest he gained with costs, double costs, treble costs sometimes; but even that did not pay. He was a very learned man in the law, and had the character of it; but how it was I can't tell, these suits that he carried cost him a power of money: in the end he sold some hundreds a year of the family estate; but he was a very learned man in the law, and I know nothing of the matter, except having a great regard for the family; and I could not help grieving when he sent me to post up notices of the sale of the fee simple of the lands and appurtenances of Timoleague.

"I know, honest Thady," says he, to comfort me, "what I'm about better than you do; I'm only selling to get the ready money wanting to carry on my suit with spirit with the Nugents of Carrickashaughlin."

He was very sanguine about that suit with the Nugents of Carrickashaughlin. He could have gained it, they say, for certain, had it pleased Heaven to have spared him to us, and it would have been at the least a plump two thousand a year in his way; but things were ordered otherwise—for the best to be sure. He dug up a fairy-mount[2] against my advice, and had no luck afterwards. Though a learned man in the law, he was a little too incredulous in other matters. I warned him that I heard the very Banshee[3] that my grandfather heard under Sir Patrick's window a few days before his death. But Sir Murtagh thought nothing of the Banshee,

[1] See Glossary, p. 156.

[2] These fairy-mounts are called ant-hills in England. They are held in high reverence by the common people in Ireland. A gentleman, who in laying out his lawn had occasion to level one of these hillocks, could not prevail upon any of his labourers to begin the ominous work. He was obliged to take a *loy* from one of their reluctant hands, and began the attack himself. The labourers agreed that the vengeance of the fairies would fall upon the head of the presumptuous mortal who first disturbed them in their retreat. See Glossary, p. 156.

[3] The Banshee is a species of aristocratic fairy, who, in the shape of a little hideous old woman, has been known to appear, and heard to sing in a mournful supernatural voice under the windows of great houses, to warn the family that some of them are soon to die. In the last century every great family in Ireland had a Banshee, who attended regularly; but latterly their visits and songs have been discontinued.

nor of his cough, with a spitting of blood, brought on, I understand, by catching cold in attending the courts, and overstraining his chest with making himself heard in one of his favourite causes. He was a great speaker with a powerful voice; but his last speech was not in the courts at all. He and my lady, though both of the same way of thinking in some things, and though she was as good a wife and great economist as you could see, and he the best of husbands, as to looking into his affairs, and making money for his family; yet I don't know how it was, they had a great deal of sparring and jarring between them. My lady had her privy purse; and she had her weed ashes,[1] and her sealing money[2] upon the signing of all the leases, with something to buy gloves besides; and, besides, again often took money from the tenants, if offered properly, to speak for them to Sir Murtagh about abatements and renewals. Now the weed ashes and the glove money he allowed her clear perquisites; though once when he saw her in a new gown saved out of the weed ashes, he told her to my face (for he could say a sharp thing) that she should not put on her weeds before her husband's death. But in a dispute about an abatement my lady would have the last word, and Sir Murtagh grew mad[3]; I was within hearing of the door, and now I wish I had made bold to step in. He spoke so loud, the whole kitchen was out on the stairs.[4] All on a sudden he stopped, and my lady too. Something has surely happened, thought I; and so it was, for Sir Murtagh in his passion broke a blood-vessel, and all the law in the land could do nothing in that case. My lady sent for five physicians, but Sir Murtagh died, and was buried. She had a fine jointure settled upon her, and took herself away, to the great joy of the tenantry. I never said anything one way or the other whilst she was part of the family, but got up to see her go at three o'clock in the morning.

"It's a fine morning, honest Thady," says she; "good-bye to ye." And into the carriage she stepped, without a word more, good or bad, or even half-a-crown; but I made my bow, and stood to see her safe out of sight for the sake of the family.

Then we were all bustle in the house, which made me keep out

[1] See Glossary, p. 158.
[2] See Glossary, p. 158.
[3] See Glossary, p. 158.
[4] See Glossary, p. 158.

of the way, for I walk slow and hate a bustle; but the house was all hurry-skurry, preparing for my new master. Sir Murtagh, I forgot to notice, had no childer[1]; so the Rackrent estate went to his younger brother, a young dashing officer, who came amongst us before I knew for the life of me whereabouts I was, in a gig or some of them things, with another spark along with him, and led horses, and servants, and dogs, and scarce a place to put any Christian of them into; for my late lady had sent all the feather-beds off before her, and blankets and household linen, down to the very knife-cloths, on the cars to Dublin, which were all her own, lawfully paid for out of her own money. So the house was quite bare, and my young master, the moment ever he set foot in it out of his gig, thought all those things must come of themselves, I believe, for he never looked after anything at all, but harum-scarum called for everything as if we were conjurors, or he in a public-house. For my part, I could not bestir myself anyhow; I had been so much used to my late master and mistress, all was upside down with me, and the new servants in the servants' hall were quite out of my way; I had nobody to talk to, and if it had not been for my pipe and tobacco, should, I verily believe, have broke my heart for poor Sir Murtagh.

But one morning my new master caught a glimpse of me as I was looking at his horse's heels, in hopes of a word from him. "And is that old Thady?" says he, as he got into his gig: I loved him from that day to this, his voice was so like the family; and he threw me a guinea out of his waistcoat-pocket, as he drew up the reins with the other hand, his horse rearing too; I thought I never set my eyes on a finer figure of a man, quite another sort from Sir Murtagh, though withal, *to me*, a family likeness. A fine life we should have led, had he stayed amongst us, God bless him! He valued a guinea as little as any man: money to him was no more than dirt, and his gentleman and groom, and all belonging to him, the same; but the sporting season over, he grew tired of the place, and having got down a great architect for the house, and an improver for the grounds, and seen their plans and elevations, he fixed a day for settling with the tenants, but went off in a whirlwind to town, just as some of them came into the yard in the morning. A circular

[1] *Childer:* this is the manner in which many of Thady's rank, and others in Ireland, formerly pronounced the word *children.*

letter came next post from the new agent, with news that the master was sailed for England, and he must remit £500 to Bath for his use before a fortnight was at an end; bad news still for the poor tenants, no change still for the better with them. Sir Kit Rackrent, my young master, left all to the agent; and though he had the spirit of a prince, and lived away to the honour of his country abroad, which I was proud to hear of, what were we the better for that at home? The agent was one of your middlemen,[1] who grind the face of the poor, and can never bear a man with a hat upon his head: he ferreted the tenants out of their lives; not a week without a call for money, drafts upon drafts from Sir Kit; but I laid it all to the fault of the agent; for, says I, what can Sir Kit do with so much cash, and he a single man? But still it went. Rents must be all paid up to the day, and afore; no allowance for improving tenants, no consideration for those who had built upon their farms: no sooner was a lease out, but the land was advertised to the highest bidder; all the old tenants turned out, when they spent their substance in the hope and trust of a renewal from the landlord. All was now let at the highest penny to a parcel of poor wretches, who meant to run away, and did so, after taking two crops out of the ground. Then fining down the year's rent came into fashion[2]—anything for the ready penny; and with all this and presents to the agent and the driver,[3] there was no such thing as

[1] *Middlemen.*—There was a class of men, termed middlemen, in Ireland, who took large farms on long leases from gentlemen of landed property, and let the land again in small portions to the poor, as under-tenants, at exorbitant rents. The head landlord, as he was called, seldom saw his under-tenants; but if he could not get the middleman to pay him his rent punctually, he *went to his land, and drove the land for his rent;* that is to say, he sent his steward, or bailiff, or driver, to the land to seize the cattle, hay, corn, flax, oats, or potatoes, belonging to the under-tenants, and proceeded to sell these for his rents. It sometimes happened that these unfortunate tenants paid their rent twice over, once to the *middleman,* and once to the *head landlord.*

The characteristics of a middleman were servility to his superiors and tyranny towards his inferiors: the poor detested this race of beings. In speaking to them, however, they always used the most abject language, and the most humble tone and posture—"*Please your honour; and please your honour's honour,*" they knew must be repeated as a charm at the beginning and end of every equivocating, exculpatory, or supplicatory sentence; and they were much more alert in doffing their caps to those new men than to those of what they call *good old families.* A witty carpenter once termed these middlemen *journeymen gentlemen.*

[2] See Glossary, p. 158.
[3] See Glossary, p. 158.

standing it. I said nothing, for I had a regard for the family; but I walked about thinking if his honour Sir Kit knew all this, it would go hard with him but he'd see us righted; not that I had anything for my own share to complain of, for the agent was always very civil to me when he came down into the country, and took a great deal of notice of my son Jason. Jason Quirk, though he be my son, I must say was a good scholar from his birth, and a very 'cute lad: I thought to make him a priest,[1] but he did better for himself; seeing how he was as good a clerk as any in the county, the agent gave him his rent accounts to copy, which he did first of all for the pleasure of obliging the gentleman, and would take nothing at all for his trouble, but was always proud to serve the family. By and by a good farm bounding us to the east fell into his honour's hands, and my son put in a proposal for it: why shouldn't he, as well as another? The proposals all went over to the master at the Bath, who knowing no more of the land than the child unborn, only having once been out a-grousing on it before he went to England; and the value of lands, as the agent informed him, falling every year in Ireland, his honour wrote over in all haste a bit of letter, saying he left it all to the agent, and that he must let it as well as he could—to the best bidder, to be sure—and send him over £200 by return of post: with this the agent gave me a hint, and I spoke a good word for my son, and gave out in the country that nobody need bid against us. So his proposal was just the thing, and he a good tenant; and he got a promise of an abatement in the rent after the first year, for advancing the half-year's rent at signing the lease, which was wanting to complete the agent's £200 by the return of the post, with all which my master wrote back he was well satisfied. About this time we learnt from the agent, as a great secret, how the money went so fast, and the reason of the thick coming of the master's drafts: he was a little too fond of play; and Bath, they say, was no place for no young man of his fortune, where there were so many of his own countrymen, too, hunting him up and down, day and night, who had nothing to lose. At last, at Christmas, the agent wrote over to stop the drafts, for he could raise no more money on bond or mortgage, or from the tenants, or anyhow, nor had he any more to lend himself, and desired at the same time to decline the agency for the

[1] See Glossary, p. 158.

future, wishing Sir Kit his health and happiness, and the compliments of the season, for I saw the letter before ever it was sealed, when my son copied it. When the answer came there was a new turn in affairs, and the agent was turned out; and my son Jason, who had corresponded privately with his honour occasionally on business, was forthwith desired by his honour to take the accounts into his own hands, and look them over, till further orders. It was a very spirited letter to be sure: Sir Kit sent his service, and the compliments of the season, in return to the agent, and he would fight him with pleasure to-morrow, or any day, for sending him such a letter, if he was born a gentleman, which he was sorry (for both their sakes) to find (too late) he was not. Then, in a private postscript, he condescended to tell us that all would be speedily settled to his satisfaction, and we should turn over a new leaf, for he was going to be married in a fortnight to the grandest heiress in England, and had only immediate occasion at present for £200, as he would not choose to touch his lady's fortune for travelling expenses home to Castle Rackrent, where he intended to be, wind and weather permitting, early in the next month; and desired fires, and the house to be painted, and the new building to go on as fast as possible, for the reception of him and his lady before that time; with several words besides in the letter, which we could not make out because, God bless him! he wrote in such a flurry. My heart warmed to my new lady when I read this: I was almost afraid it was too good news to be true; but the girls fell to scouring, and it was well they did, for we soon saw his marriage in the paper, to a lady with I don't know how many tens of thousand pounds to her fortune: then I watched the postoffice for his landing; and the news came to my son of his and the bride being in Dublin, and on the way home to Castle Rackrent. We had bonfires all over the country, expecting him down the next day, and we had his coming of age still to celebrate, which he had not time to do properly before he left the country; therefore, a great ball was expected, and great doings upon his coming, as it were, fresh to take possession of his ancestors' estate. I never shall forget the day he came home; we had waited and waited all day long till eleven o'clock at night, and I was thinking of sending the boy to lock the gates, and giving them up for that night, when there came the carriages thundering up to the great hall door. I got the first

sight of the bride; for when the carriage door opened, just as she
had her foot on the steps, I held the flam[1] full in her face to light
her, at which she shut her eyes, but I had a full view of the rest of
her, and greatly shocked I was, for by that light she was little
better than a blackamoor, and seemed crippled; but that was only
sitting so long in the chariot.

"You're kindly welcome to Castle Rackrent, my lady," says I
(recollecting who she was). "Did your honour hear of the bonfires?"

His honour spoke never a word, nor so much as handed her up
the steps—he looked to me no more like himself than nothing at
all; I know I took him for the skeleton of his honour. I was not
sure what to say next to one or t'other, but seeing she was a
stranger in a foreign country, I thought it but right to speak cheerful to her; so I went back again to the bonfires.

"My lady," says I, as she crossed the hall, "there would have
been fifty times as many; but for fear of the horses, and frightening
your ladyship, Jason and I forbid them, please your honour."

With that she looked at me a little bewildered.

"Will I have a fire lighted in the state-room to-night?" was the
next question I put to her, but never a word she answered; so I
concluded she could not speak a word of English, and was from
foreign parts. The short and the long of it was, I couldn't tell what
to make of her; so I left her to herself, and went straight down to
the servants' hall to learn something for certain about her. Sir
Kit's own man was tired, but the groom set him a-talking at last,
and we had it all out before ever I closed my eyes that night. The
bride might well be a great fortune—she was a *Jewish* by all
accounts, who are famous for their great riches. I had never seen
any of that tribe or nation before, and could only gather that she
spoke a strange kind of English of her own, that she could not
abide pork or sausages, and went neither to church or mass. Mercy
upon his honour's poor soul, thought I; what will become of him
and his, and all of us, with his heretic blackamoor at the head of
the Castle Rackrent estate? I never slept a wink all night for thinking of it; but before the servants I put my pipe in my mouth, and
kept my mind to myself, for I had a great regard for the family;
and after this, when strange gentlemen's servants came to the

[1] See Glossary, p. 158.

house, and would begin to talk about the bride, I took care to put
the best foot foremost, and passed her for a nabob in the kitchen,
which accounted for her dark complexion and everything.

The very morning after they came home, however, I saw plain
enough how things were between Sir Kit and my lady, though they
were walking together arm in arm after breakfast, looking at the
new building and the improvements.

"Old Thady," said my master, just as he used to do, "how do
you do?"

"Very well, I thank your honour's honour," said I; but I saw
he was not well pleased, and my heart was in my mouth as I
walked along after him.

"Is the large room damp, Thady?" said his honour.

"Oh damp, your honour! how should it be but as dry as a bone,"
says I, "after all the fires we have kept in it day and night? It's
the barrack-room[1] your honour's talking on."

"And what is a barrack-room, pray, my dear?" were the first
words I ever heard out of my lady's lips.

"No matter, my dear," said he, and went on talking to me,
ashamed-like I should witness her ignorance. To be sure, to hear
her talk one might have taken her for an innocent,[2] for it was,
"What's this, Sir Kit? and what's that, Sir Kit?" all the way we
went. To be sure, Sir Kit had enough to do to answer her.

"And what do you call that, Sir Kit?" said she; "that—that
looks like a pile of black bricks, pray, Sir Kit?"

"My turf-stack, my dear," said my master, and bit his lip.

Where have you lived, my lady, all your life, not to know a turf-
stack when you see it? thought I; but I said nothing. Then by and
by she takes out her glass, and begins spying over the country.

"And what's all that black swamp out yonder, Sir Kit?" says she.

"My bog, my dear," says he, and went on whistling.

"It's a very ugly prospect, my dear," says she.

"You don't see it, my dear," says he, "for we've planted it out;
when the trees grow up in summertime——" says he.

"Where are the trees," said she, "my dear?" still looking through
her glass.

[1] See Glossary, p. 158.
[2] See Glossary, p. 158.

"You are blind, my dear," says he; "what are these under your eyes?"

"These shrubs?" said she.

"Trees," said he.

"Maybe they are what you call trees in Ireland, my dear," said she; "but they are not a yard high, are they?"

"They were planted out but last year, my lady," says I, to soften matters between them, for I saw she was going the way to make his honour mad with her: "they are very well grown for their age, and you'll not see the bog of Allyballycarricko'shaughlin at-all-at-all through the skreen, when once the leaves come out. But, my lady, you must not quarrel with any part or parcel of Allyballycarrick-o'shaughlin, for you don't know how many hundred years that same bit of bog has been in the family; we would not part with the bog of Allyballycarricko'shaughlin upon no account at all; it cost the late Sir Murtagh two hundred good pounds to defend his title to it and boundaries against the O'Learys, who cut a road through it."

Now one would have thought this would have been hint enough for my lady, but she fell to laughing like one out of their right mind, and made me say the name of the bog over, for her to get it by heart, a dozen times; then she must ask me how to spell it, and what was the meaning of it in English—Sir Kit standing by whistling all the while. I verily believed she laid the corner-stone of all her future misfortunes at that very instant; but I said no more, only looked at Sir Kit.

There were no balls, no dinners, no doings; the country was all disappointed—Sir Kit's gentleman said in a whisper to me, it was all my lady's own fault, because she was so obstinate about the cross.

"What cross?" says I; "is it about her being a heretic?"

"Oh, no such matter," says he; "my master does not mind her heresies, but her diamond cross—it's worth I can't tell you how much, and she has thousands of English pounds concealed in diamonds about her, which she as good as promised to give up to my master before he married; but now she won't part with any of them, and she must take the consequences."

Her honeymoon, at least her Irish honeymoon, was scarcely well over, when his honour one morning said to me, "Thady, buy me

105

a pig!" and then the sausages were ordered, and here was the first open breaking-out of my lady's troubles. My lady came down herself into the kitchen to speak to the cook about the sausages, and desired never to see them more at her table. Now my master had ordered them, and my lady knew that. The cook took my lady's part, because she never came down into the kitchen, and was young and innocent in housekeeping, which raised her pity; besides, said she, at her own table, surely my lady should order and disorder what she pleases. But the cook soon changed her note, for my master made it a principle to have the sausages, and swore at her for a Jew herself, till he drove her fairly out of the kitchen; then, for fear of her place, and because he threatened that my lady should give her no discharge without the sausages, she gave up, and from that day forward always sausages, or bacon, or pig-meat in some shape or other, went up to table; upon which my lady shut herself up in her own room, and my master said she might stay there, with an oath: and to make sure of her, he turned the key in the door, and kept it ever after in his pocket. We none of us ever saw or heard her speak for seven years after that[1]: he carried her dinner himself.

[1] This part of the history of the Rackrent family can scarcely be thought credible; but in justice to honest Thady, it is hoped the reader will recollect the history of the celebrated Lady Cathcart's conjugal imprisonment. The editor was acquainted with Colonel M'Guire, Lady Cathcart's husband; he has lately seen and questioned the maid-servant who lived with Colonel M'Guire during the time of Lady Cathcart's imprisonment. Her ladyship was locked up in her own house for many years, during which period her husband was visited by the neighbouring gentry, and it was his regular custom at dinner to send his compliments to Lady Cathcart, informing her that the company had the honour to drink her ladyship's health, and begging to know whether there was anything at table that she would like to eat? The answer was always, "Lady Cathcart's compliments, and she has everything she wants." An instance of honesty in a poor Irishwoman deserves to be recorded. Lady Cathcart had some remarkably fine diamonds, which she had concealed from her husband, and which she was anxious to get out of the house, lest he should discover them. She had neither servant nor friend to whom she could entrust them, but she had observed a poor beggar woman, who used to come to the house; she spoke to her from the window of the room in which she was confined; the woman promised to do what she desired, and Lady Cathcart threw a parcel containing the jewels to her. The poor woman carried them to the person to whom they were directed, and several years afterwards, when Lady Cathcart recovered her liberty, she received her diamonds safely.

At Colonel M'Guire's death her ladyship was released. The editor, within this year, saw the gentleman who accompanied her to England after her husband's death. When she first was told of his death she imagined that the

Then his honour had a great deal of company to dine with him, and balls in the house, and was as gay and gallant, and as much himself as before he was married; and at dinner he always drank my Lady Rackrent's good health and so did the company, and he sent out always a servant with his compliments to my Lady Rackrent, and the company was drinking her ladyship's health, and begged to know if there was anything at table he might send her, and the man came back, after the sham errand, with my Lady Rackrent's compliments, and she was very much obliged to Sir Kit—she did not wish for anything, but drank the company's health. The country, to be sure, talked and wondered at my lady's being shut up, but nobody chose to interfere or ask any impertinent questions, for they knew my master was a man very apt to give a short answer himself, and likely to call a man out for it afterwards: he was a famous shot, had killed his man before he came of age, and nobody scarce dared look at him whilst at Bath. Sir Kit's character was so well known in the country that he lived in peace and quietness everafter, and was a great favourite with the ladies, especially when in process of time, in the fifth year of her confinement, my Lady Rackrent fell ill and took entirely to her bed, and he gave out that she was now skin and bone, and could not last through the winter. In this he had two physicians' opinions to back him (for now he called in two physicians for her), and tried all his arts to get the diamond cross from her on her death-bed, and to get her to make a will in his favour of her separate possessions; but there she was too tough for him. He used to swear at her behind her back after kneeling to her face, and call her in the presence of his gentlemen his stiff-necked Israelite, though before he married her that same gentleman told me he used to call her (how he could bring it out, I don't know) "my pretty Jessica!" To be sure it must have been hard for her

---

news was not true, and that it was told only with an intention of deceiving her. At his death she had scarcely clothes sufficient to cover her; she wore a red wig, looked scared, and her understanding seemed stupefied; she said that she scarcely knew one human creature from another; her imprisonment lasted above twenty years. These circumstances may appear strange to an English reader; but there is no danger in the present times that any individual should exercise such tyranny as Colonel M'Guire's with impunity, the power being now all in the hands of Government, and there being no possibility of obtaining from Parliament an Act of indemnity for any cruelties.

to guess what sort of a husband he reckoned to make her. When she was lying, to all expectation, on her deathbed of a broken heart, I could not but pity her, though she was a Jewish, and considering too it was no fault of hers to be taken with my master, so young as she was at the Bath, and so fine a gentleman as Sir Kit was when he courted her; and considering too, after all they had heard and seen of him as a husband, there were now no less than three ladies in our county talked of for his second wife, all at daggers drawn with each other, as his gentleman swore, at the balls, for Sir Kit for their partner—I could not but think them bewitched, but they all reasoned with themselves that Sir Kit would make a good husband to any Christian but a Jewish, I suppose, and especially as he was now a reformed rake; and it was not known how my lady's fortune was settled in her will, nor how the Castle Rackrent estate was all mortgaged, and bonds out against him, for he was never cured of his gaming tricks; but that was the only fault he had, God bless him!

My lady had a sort of fit, and it was given out that she was dead, by mistake: this brought things to a sad crisis for my poor master. One of the three ladies showed his letters to her brother, and claimed his promises, whilst another did the same. I don't mention names. Sir Kit, in his defense, said he would meet any man who dared to question his conduct; and as to the ladies, they must settle it amongst them who was to be his second, and his third, and his fourth, whilst his first was still alive, to his mortification and theirs. Upon this, as upon all former occasions, he had the voice of the country with him, on account of the great spirit and propriety he acted with. He met and shot the first lady's brother: the next day he called out the second, who had a wooden leg, and their place of meeting by appointment being in a new-ploughed field, the wooden-leg man stuck fast in it. Sir Kit, seeing his situation, with great candour fired his pistol over his head; upon which the seconds interposed, and convinced the parties there had been a slight misunderstanding between them: there-upon they shook hands cordially, and went home to dinner together. This gentleman, to show the world how they stood together, and by the advice of the friends of both parties, to re-establish his sister's injured reputation, went out with Sir Kit as his second, and carried his message next day to the last of his

adversaries: I never saw him in such fine spirits as that day he
went out—sure enough he was within ames-ace of getting quit
handsomely of all his enemies; but unluckily, after hitting the
toothpick out of his adversary's finger and thumb, he received a
ball in a vital part, and was brought home, in little better than an
hour after the affair, speechless on a hand-barrow to my lady.
We got the key out of his pocket the first thing we did, and my
son Jason ran to unlock the barrack-room, where my lady had
been shut up for seven years, to acquaint her with the fatal accident. The surprise bereaved her of her senses at first, nor would
she believe but we were putting some new trick upon her, to en-
trap her out of her jewels, for a great while, till Jason bethought
himself of taking her to the window, and showed her the men
bringing Sir Kit up the avenue upon the hand-barrow, which had
immediately the desired effect; for directly she burst into tears,
and pulling her cross from her bosom, she kissed it with as great
devotion as ever I witnessed, and lifting up her eyes to heaven,
uttered some ejaculation, which none present heard; but I take
the sense of it to be, she returned thanks for this unexpected interposition in her favour when she had least reason to expect it.
My master was greatly lamented: there was no life in him when
we lifted him off the barrow, so he was laid out immediately,
and "waked" the same night. The country was all in an uproar
about him, and not a soul but cried shame upon his murderer,
who would have been hanged surely, if he could have been
brought to his trial, whilst the gentlemen in the country were
up about it; but he very prudently withdrew himself to the Continent before the affair was made public. As for the young lady
who was the immediate cause of the fatal accident, however innocently, she could never show her head after at the balls in the
county or any place; and by the advice of her friends and physicians, she was ordered soon after to Bath, where it was expected,
if anywhere on this side of the grave, she would meet with the
recovery of her health and lost peace of mind. As a proof of his
great popularity, I need only add that there was a song made
upon my master's untimely death in the newspapers, which was
in everybody's mouth, singing up and down through the country,
even down to the mountains, only three days after his unhappy

exit. He was also greatly bemoaned at the Curragh,[1] where his cattle were well known; and all who had taken up his bets were particularly inconsolable for his loss to society. His stud sold at the cant[2] at the greatest price ever known in the county; his favourite horses were chiefly disposed of amongst his particular friends, who would give any price for them for his sake; but no ready money was required by the new heir, who wished not to displease any of the gentlemen of the neighbourhood just upon his coming to settle amongst them; so a long credit was given where requisite, and the cash has never been gathered in from that day to this.

But to return to my lady. She got surprisingly well after my master's decease. No sooner was it known for certain that he was dead, than all the gentlemen within twenty miles of us came in a body, as it were, to set my lady at liberty, and to protest against her confinement, which they now for the first time understood was against her own consent. The ladies too were as attentive as possible, striving who should be foremost with their morning visits; and they that saw the diamonds spoke very handsomely of them, but thought it a pity they were not bestowed, if it had so pleased God, upon a lady who would have become them better. All these civilities wrought little with my lady, for she had taken an unaccountable prejudice against the country, and everything belonging to it, and was so partial to her native land, that after parting with the cook, which she did immediately upon my master's decease, I never knew her easy one instant, night or day, but when she was packing up to leave us. Had she meant to make any stay in Ireland, I stood a great chance of being a great favourite with her; for when she found I understood the weather-cock, she was always finding some pretence to be talking to me, and asking me which way the wind blew, and was it likely, did I think, to continue fair for England. But when I saw she had made up her mind to spend the rest of her days upon her own income and jewels in England, I considered her quite as a foreigner, and not at all any longer as part of the family. She gave no vails to the servants at Castle Rackrent at parting, notwithstanding the old proverb of "as rich as a Jew," which she,

[1] See Glossary, p. 159.
[2] See Glossary, p. 159.

being a Jewish, they built upon with reason. But from first to last she brought nothing but misfortunes amongst us; and if it had not been all along with her, his honour, Sir Kit, would have been now alive in all appearance. Her diamond cross was, they say, at the bottom of it all; and it was a shame for her, being his wife, not to show more duty, and to have given it up when he condescended to ask so often for such a bit of a trifle in his distresses, especially when he all along made it no secret he married for money. But we will not bestow another thought upon her. This much I thought it lay upon my conscience to say, in justice to my poor master's memory.

'Tis an ill wind that blows nobody no good: the same wind that took the Jew Lady Rackrent over to England brought over the new heir to Castle Rackrent.

Here let me pause for breath in my story, for though I had a great regard for every member of the family, yet without compare Sir Conolly, commonly called, for short, amongst his friends, Sir Condy Rackrent, was ever my great favourite, and, indeed, the most universally beloved man I had ever seen or heard of, not excepting his great ancestor Sir Patrick, to whose memory he, amongst other instances of generosity, erected a handsome marble stone in the church of Castle Rackrent, setting forth in large letters his age, birth, parentage, and many other virtues, concluding with the compliment so justly due, that "Sir Patrick Rackrent lived and died a monument of old Irish hospitality."

Continuation of the Memoirs of the
RACKRENT FAMILY

HISTORY OF SIR CONOLLY RACKRENT

SIR CONDY RACKRENT, by the grace of God heir-at-law to the Castle Rackrent estate, was a remote branch of the family. Born to little or no fortune of his own, he was bred to the bar, at which, having many friends to push him and no mean natural abilities of his own, he doubtless would in process of time, if he could have borne the drudgery of that study, have been rapidly made King's Counsel at the least; but things were disposed of otherwise, and he never went the circuit but twice, and then made no figure for want of a fee, and being unable to speak in public. He received his education chiefly in the college of Dublin, but before he came to years of discretion lived in the country, in a small but slated house within view of the end of the avenue. I remember him, bare footed and headed, running through the street of O'Shaughlin's Town, and playing at pitch-and-toss, ball, marbles, and what not, with the boys of the town, amongst whom my son Jason was a great favourite with him. As for me, he was ever my white-headed boy: often's the time, when I would call in at his father's, where I was always made welcome, he would slip down to me in the kitchen, and love to sit on my knee whilst I told him stories of the family and the blood from which he was sprung, and how he might look forward, if the then present man should die without childer, to being at the head of the Castle Rackrent estate. This was then spoke quite and clear at random to please the child, but it pleased Heaven to accomplish my prophecy afterwards, which gave him a great opinion of my judgment in business. He went to a little grammar-school with many others, and my son amongst the rest, who was in his class, and not a little useful to him in his book-learning, which he acknowledged with gratitude ever after. These rudiments of his education thus completed, he got a-horseback, to which exercise he was ever addicted, and used to gallop over the country while yet but a slip of a boy, under the care of Sir Kit's huntsman, who was very fond of him, and often lent him his gun, and took him out a-shooting under his own eye. By these means he became well acquainted and popular amongst the poor in the neighbourhood early, for there was not a cabin at which he had not stopped some morning or other, along with the huntsman, to drink a glass of burnt whisky out of an eggshell, to do him good and warm his heart and drive the cold out of his stomach. The old people always told him he was a great likeness of Sir Patrick, which made him first have an ambition to take after him, as far as his fortune should allow. He left us when of an age to enter the college, and there completed his education and nineteenth year, for as he was not born to an estate, his friends thought it incumbent on them to give him the best education which could be had for love or money, and a great deal of money consequently was spent upon him at College and Temple. He was very little altered for the worse by what he saw there of the great world, for when he came down into the country to pay us a visit, we thought him just the same man as ever—hand and glove with every one, and as far from high, though not without his own proper share of family pride, as any man ever you see. Latterly, seeing how Sir Kit and the Jewish lived together, and that there was no one between him and the Castle Rackrent estate, he neglected to apply to the law as much as was expected of him, and secretly many of the tenants and others advanced him cash upon his note of hand value received, promising bargains of leases and lawful interest, should he ever come into the estate. All this was kept a great secret for fear the present man, hearing of it, should take it into his head to take it ill of poor Condy, and so should cut him off for ever by levying a fine, and suffering a recovery to dock the entail.[1] Sir Murtagh would have been the man for that; but Sir Kit was too much taken up philandering to consider the law in this case, or any other. These practices I have mentioned to account for the state of his affairs—I mean Sir Condy's upon his coming into the Castle Rackrent estate. He could not command a penny of his first year's income, which, and keeping no accounts, and the great sight of company he did, with many other causes too numerous to mention, was the origin of his distresses. My son Jason, who was now established agent, and knew everything, explained matters out of the face to Sir Conolly, and made him sensible of his embarrassed situation. With a great nominal rent-roll, it was almost all paid away in interest; which being for convenience suffered to run on, soon doubled the principal, and Sir Condy was obliged to pass new bonds for the interest, now grown principal, and so on. Whilst this was going on, my son requiring to be paid for his trouble and many years' service in the family gratis, and Sir Condy not willing to take his affairs into his own hands, or to look them even in the face, he gave my son a bargain of some acres which fell out of lease at a reasonable rent. Jason set the land, as soon as his lease was sealed, to under-tenants, to make the rent, and got two hundred a year profit rent; which was

[1] See Glossary, p. 159.

little enough considering his long agency. He bought the land at twelve years' purchase two years afterwards, when Sir Condy was pushed for money on an execution, and was at the same time allowed for his improvements thereon. There was a sort of hunting-lodge upon the estate, convenient to my son Jason's land, which he had his eye upon about this time; and he was a little jealous of Sir Condy, who talked of setting it to a stranger who was just come into the country—Captain Moneygawl was the man. He was son and heir to the Moneygawls of Mount Juliet's Town, who had a great estate in the next county to ours; and my master was loth to disoblige the young gentleman, whose heart was set upon the Lodge; so he wrote him back that the Lodge was at his service, and if he would honour him with his company at Castle Rackrent, they could ride over together some morning and look at it before signing the lease. Accordingly, the captain came over to us, and he and Sir Condy grew the greatest friends ever you see, and were for ever out a-shooting or hunting together, and were very merry in the evenings; and Sir Condy was invited of course to Mount Juliet's Town; and the family intimacy that had been in Sir Patrick's time was now recollected, and nothing would serve Sir Condy but he must be three times a week at the least with his new friends, which grieved me, who knew, by the captain's groom and gentleman, how they talked of him at Mount Juliet's Town, making him quite as one may say, a laughing-stock and a butt for the whole company; but they were soon cured of that by an accident that surprised 'em not a little, as it did me. There was a bit of a scrawl found upon the waiting-maid of old Mr. Moneygawl's youngest daughter, Miss Isabella, that laid open the whole; and her father, they say, was like one out of his right mind, and swore it was the last thing he ever should have thought of, when he invited my master to his house, that his daughter should think of such a match. But their talk signified not a straw, for as Miss Isabella's maid reported, her young mistress was fallen over head and ears in love with Sir Condy from the first time that ever her brother brought him into the house to dinner. The servant who waited that day behind my master's chair was the first who knew it, as he says; though it's hard to believe him, for he did not tell it till a great while afterwards; but, however, it's likely enough, as the thing turned out, that he was not far out of the way, for towards the middle of dinner, as he says, they were talking of stage-plays, having a playhouse, and being great play-actors at Mount Juliet's Town; and Miss Isabella turns short to my master, and says:

"Have you seen the play-bill, Sir Condy?"

"No, I have not," said he.

"Then more shame for you," said the captain her brother, "not to know that my sister is to play Juliet tonight, who plays it better than any woman on or off the stage in all Ireland."

"I am very happy to hear it," said Sir Condy; and there the matter dropped for the present.

But Sir Condy all this time, and a great while afterwards, was at a terrible nonplus; for he had no liking, not he, to stage-plays, nor to Miss Isabella either—to his mind, as it came out over a bowl of whisky-punch at home, his little Judy M'Quirk, who was daughter to a sister's son of mine, was worth twenty of Miss Isabella. He had seen her often when he stopped at her father's cabin to drink whisky out of the eggshell, out hunting, before he came to the estate, and, as she gave out, was under something like a promise of marriage to her. Anyhow, I could not but pity my poor master, who was so bothered between them, and he an easy-hearted man, that could not disoblige nobody—God bless him! To be sure, it was not his place to behave ungenerous to Miss Isabella, who had disobliged all her relations for his sake, as he remarked; and then she was locked up in her chamber, and forbid to think of him any more, which raised his spirit, because his family was, as he observed, as good as theirs at any rate, and the Rackrents a suitable match for the Moneygawls any day in the year; all which was true enough. But it grieved me to see that, upon the strength of all this, Sir Condy was growing more in the mind to carry off Miss Isabella to Scotland, in spite of her relations, as she desired.

"It's all over with our poor Judy!" said I, with a heavy sigh, making bold to speak to him one night when he was a little cheerful, and standing in the servants' hall all alone with me, as was often his custom.

"Not at all," said he; "I never was fonder of Judy than at this present speaking; and to prove it to you," said he—and he took from my hand a halfpenny change that I had just got along with my tobacco—"and to prove it to you, Thady," says he, "it's a toss-up with me which I should marry this minute, her or Mr. Money-gawl of Mount Juliet's Town's daughter—so it is."

"Oh—boo! boo!"[1] says I, making light of it, to see what he would go on to next; "your honour's joking, to be sure; there's no compare between our poor Judy and Miss Isabella, who has a great fortune, they say."

"I'm not a man to mind a fortune, nor never was," said Sir Condy, proudly, "whatever her friends may say; and to make short of it," says he, "I'm come to a determination upon the spot." With that he swore such a terrible oath as made me cross myself. "And by this book," said he, snatching up my ballad-book, mistaking it for my prayer-book, which lay in the window,—"and by this book," says he, "and by all the books that ever were shut and opened, it's come to a toss-up with me, and I'll stand or fall by the toss; and so Thady, hand me over that pin[2] out of the ink-horn"; and he makes a cross on the smooth side of the halfpenny; "Judy M'Quirk," says he, "her mark."[3]

God bless him! his hand was a little unsteadied by all the whisky-punch he had taken, but it was plain to see his heart was for poor Judy. My heart was all as one as in my mouth when I saw the halfpenny up in the air, but I said nothing at all; and when it came down I was glad I had kept myself to myself, for to be sure now it was all over with poor Judy.

"Judy's out a luck," said I, striving to laugh.

"I'm out a luck," said he; and I never saw a man look so cast down: he took up the halfpenny off the flag, and walked away quite sober-like by the shock. Now, though as easy a man, you would think, as any in the wide world, there was no such thing

---

[1] *Boo! boo!*—an exclamation equivalent to *pshaw* or *nonsense*.

[2] *Pin*, read *pen*.—It formerly was vulgarly pronounced *pin* in Ireland.

[3] *Her mark.*—It was the custom in Ireland for those who could not write to make a cross to stand for their signature, as was formerly the practice of our English monarchs. The Editor inserts the facsimile of an Irish mark, which may hereafter be valuable to a judicious antiquary—

Her

Judy × M'Quirk,

Mark.

In bonds or notes signed in this manner a witness is requisite, as the name is frequently written by him or her.

as making him unsay one of these sort of vows,[1] which he had learned to reverence when young, as I well remember teaching him to toss up for bog-berries on my knee. So I saw the affair was as good as settled between him and Miss Isabella, and I had no more to say but to wish her joy, which I did the week afterwards, upon her return from Scotland with my poor master.

My new lady was young, as might be supposed of a lady that had been carried off by her own consent to Scotland; but I could only see her at first through her veil, which, from bashfulness or fashion, she kept over her face.

"And am I to walk through all this crowd of people, my dearest love?" said she to Sir Condy, meaning us servants and tenants, who had gathered at the back gate.

"My dear," said Sir Condy, "there's nothing for it but to walk, or to let me carry you as far as the house, for you see the back road is too narrow for a carriage, and the great piers have tumbled down across the front approach; so there's no driving the right way, by reason of the ruins."

"Plato, thou reasonest well!" said she, or words to that effect, which I could noways understand; and again, when her foot stumbled against a broken bit of a car-wheel, she cried out, "Angels and ministers of grace defend us!" Well, thought I, to be sure, if she's no Jewish, like the last, she is a mad woman for certain, which is as bad: it would have been as well for my poor master to have taken up with poor Judy, who is in her right mind anyhow.

She was dressed like a mad woman, moreover, more than like any one I ever saw afore or since, and I could not take my eyes off her, but still followed behind her; and her feathers on the top of her hat were broke going in at the low back door, and she pulled out her little bottle out of her pocket to smell when she found herself in the kitchen, and said, "I shall faint with the heat of this odious, odious place."

---

[1] Vows.—It has been maliciously and unjustly hinted that the lower classes of the people of Ireland pay but little regard to oaths; yet it is certain that some oaths or vows have great power over their minds. Sometimes they swear they will be revenged on some of their neighbours; this is an oath that they are never known to break. But, what is infinitely more extraordinary and unaccountable, they sometimes make and keep a vow against whisky; these vows are usually limited to a short time. A woman who has a drunken husband is most fortunate if she can prevail upon him to go to the priest, and make a vow against whisky for a year, or a month, or a week, or a day.

"My dear, it's only three steps across the kitchen, and there's a fine air if your veil was up," said Sir Condy; and with that threw back her veil, so that I had then a full sight of her face. She had not at all the colour of one going to faint, but a fine complexion of her own, as I then took it to be, though her maid told me after it was all put on; but even complexion and all taken in, she was no way, in point of good looks, to compare to poor Judy, and withal she had a quality toss with her; but maybe it was my overpartiality to Judy, into whose place I may say she stepped, that made me notice all this.

To do her justice, however, she was, when we came to know her better, very liberal in her housekeeping—nothing at all of the skinflint in her; she left everything to the housekeeper, and her own maid, Mrs. Jane, who went with her to Scotland, gave her the best of characters for generosity. She seldom, or ever wore a thing twice the same way, Mrs. Jane told us, and was always pulling her things to pieces and giving them away, never being used, in her father's house, to think of expense in anything; and she reckoned to be sure to go on the same way at Castle Rackrent; but when I came to inquire, I learned that her father was so mad with her for running off, after his locking her up and forbidding her to think any more of Sir Condy, that he would not give her a farthing; and it was lucky for her she had a few thousands of her own, which had been left to her by a good grandmother, and these were very convenient to begin with. My master and my lady set out in great style; they had the finest coach and chariot, and horses and liveries, and cut the greatest dash in the county, returning their wedding visits; and it was immediately reported that her father had undertaken to pay all my master's debts, and of course all his tradesmen gave him a new credit, and everything went on smack smooth, and I could not but admire my lady's spirit, and was proud to see Castle Rackrent again in all its glory. My lady had a fine taste for building, and furniture, and playhouses, and she turned everything topsy-turvy, and made the barrack-room into a theatre, as she called it, and she went on as if she had a mint of money at her elbow; and to be sure I thought she knew best, especially as Sir Condy said nothing to it one way or the other. All he asked—God bless him!—was· to live in peace and quietness, and have his bottle or his whisky-punch at night to himself. Now this was little enough, to be sure, for any gentleman; but my lady couldn't abide the smell of the whisky-punch.

"My dear," says he, "you liked it well enough before we were married, and why not now?"

"My dear," said she, "I never smelt it, or I assure you I should never have prevailed upon myself to marry you."

"My dear, I am sorry you did not smell it, but we can't help that now," returned my master, without putting himself in a passion, or going out of his way, but just fair and easy helped himself to another glass, and drank it off to her good health.

All this the butler told me, who was going backwards and forwards unnoticed with the jug, and hot water, and sugar, and all he thought wanting. Upon my master's swallowing the last glass of whisky-punch my lady burst into tears, calling him an ungrateful, base, barbarous wretch; and went off into a fit of hysterics, as I think Mrs. Jane called it, and my poor master was greatly frightened, this being the first thing of the kind he had seen; and he fell straight on his knees before her, and, like a good-hearted cratur as he was, ordered the whisky-punch out of the room, and bid 'em throw open all the windows, and cursed himself: and then my lady came to herself again, and when she saw him kneeling there, bid him get up, and not forswear himself any more, for that she was sure he did not love her, and never had. This we learned from Mrs. Jane, who was the only person left present at all this.

"My dear," returns my master, thinking, to be sure, of Judy, as well he might, "whoever told you so is an incendiary, and I'll have 'em turned out of the house this minute, if you'll only let me know which of them it was."

"Told me what?" said my lady, starting upright in her chair.

"Nothing at all, nothing at all," said my master, seeing he had overshot himself, and that my lady spoke at random; "but what you said just now, that I did not love you, Bella; who told you that?"

"My own sense," she said, and she put her handkerchief to her face, and leant back upon Mrs. Jane, and fell to sobbing as if her heart would break.

"Why now, Bella, this is very strange of you," said my poor master; "if nobody has told you nothing, what is it you are taking on for at this rate, and exposing yourself and me for this way?"

"Oh, say no more, say no more; every word you say kills me," cried my lady; and she ran on like one, as Mrs. Jane says, raving, "Oh, Sir Condy, Sir Condy! I that had hoped to find in you—"

"Why now, faith, this is a little too much; do, Bella, try to recollect yourself, my dear; am not I your husband, and of your own choosing, and is not that enough?"

"Oh, too much! too much!" cried my lady, wringing her hands.

"Why, my dear, come to your right senses, for the love of heaven. See, is not the whisky-punch, jug and bowl and all, gone out of the room long ago? What is it, in the wide world, you have to complain of?"

But still my lady sobbed and sobbed, and called herself the most wretched of women; and among other out-of-the-way provoking things, asked my master, was he fit company for her, and he drinking all night? This nettling him, which it was hard to do, he replied, that as to drinking all night, he was then as sober as she was herself, and that it was no matter how much a man drank, provided it did noways affect or stagger him: that as to being fit company for her, he thought himself of a family to be fit company for any lord or lady in the land; but that he never prevented her from seeing and keeping what company she pleased, and that he had done his best to make Castle Rackrent pleasing to her since her marriage, having always had the house full of visitors, and if her own relations were not amongst them, he said that was their own fault, and their pride's fault, of which he was sorry to find her ladyship had so unbecoming a share. So concluding, he took his candle and walked off to his room, and my lady was in her tantrums for three days after; and would have been so much longer, no doubt, but some of her friends, young ladies, and cousins, and second cousins, came to Castle Rackrent, by my poor master's express invitation, to see her, and she was in a hurry to get up, as Mrs. Jane called it, a play for them, and so got well, and was as finely dressed, and as happy to look at, as ever; and all the young ladies, who used to be in her room dressing of her, said in Mrs. Jane's hearing that my lady was the happiest bride ever they had seen, and that to be sure a love-match was the only thing for happiness, where the parties could any way afford it.

As to affording it, God knows it was little they knew of the matter; my lady's few thousands could not last for ever, especially the way she went on with them; and letters from tradesfolk came every post thick and threefold, with bills as long as my arm, of years' and years' standing. My son Jason had 'em all handed over to him, and the pressing letters were all unread by Sir Condy, who hated trouble, and could never be brought to hear talk of business, but still put it off and put it off, saying, "Settle it anyhow," or, "Bid 'em call again to-morrow," or, "Speak to me about it some other time." Now it was hard to find the right time to speak, for in the mornings he was a-bed, and in the evenings over his bottle, where no gentleman chooses to be disturbed. Things in a twelvemonth or so came to such a pass there was no making a shift to go on any longer, though we were all of us well enough used to live from hand to mouth at Castle Rackrent. One day, I remember, when there was a power of company, all sitting after dinner in the dusk, not to say dark, in the drawing-room, my lady having rung five times for candles, and none to go up, the housekeeper sent up the footman, who went to my mistress, and whispered behind her chair how it was.

"My lady," says he, "there are no candles in the house."

"Bless me," says she; "then take a horse and gallop off as fast as you can to Carrick O'Fungus, and get some."

"And in the meantime tell them to step into the playhouse, and try if there are not some bits left," added Sir Condy, who happened to be within hearing. The man was sent up again to my lady, to let her know there was no horse to go, but one that wanted a shoe.

"Go to Sir Condy then; I know nothing at all about the horses," said my lady; "why do you plague me with these things?" How it was settled, I really forget, but to the best of my remembrance, the boy was sent down to my son Jason's to borrow candles for the night. Another time, in the winter, and on a desperate cold day, there was no turf in for the parlour and above stairs, and scarce enough for the cook in the kitchen. The little gossoon[1] was sent off to the neighbours, to see and beg or borrow some, but none

---

[1] *Gossoon:* a little boy—from the French word garçon. In most Irish families there used to be a barefooted gossoon, who was slave to the cook and the butler, and who, in fact, without wages, did all the hard work of the house. Gossoons were always employed as messengers. The Editor has known a gossoon to go on foot, without shoes or stockings, fifty-one English miles between sunrise and sunset.

could he bring back with him for love or money; so, as needs must, we were forced to trouble Sir Condy—"Well, and if there's no turf to be had in the town or country, why, what signifies talking any more about it; can't ye go and cut down a tree?"

"Which tree, please, your honour?" I made bold to say.

"Any tree at all that's good to burn," said Sir Condy; "send off smart and get one down, and the fires lighted, before my lady gets up to breakfast, or the house will be too hot to hold us."

He was always very considerate in all things about my lady, and she wanted for nothing whilst he had it to give. Well, when things were tight with them about this time, my son Jason put in a word again about the Lodge, and made a genteel offer to lay down the purchase-money, to relieve Sir Condy's distresses. Now Sir Condy had it from the best authority that there were two writs come down to the sheriff against his person, and the sheriff, as ill-luck would have it, was no friend of his, and talked how he must do his duty, and how he would do it, if it was against the first man in the country, or even his own brother, let alone one who had voted against him at the last election, as Sir Condy had done. So Sir Condy was fain to take the purchase-money of the Lodge from my son Jason to settle matters; and sure enough it was a good bargain for both parties, for my son bought the fee-simple of a good house for him and his heirs for ever, for little or nothing, and by selling of it for that same my master saved himself from a gaol. Every way it turned out fortunate for Sir Condy, for before the money was all gone there came a general election, and he being so well beloved in the county, and one of the oldest families, no one had a better right to stand candidate for the vacancy; and he was called upon by all his friends, and the whole county I may say, to declare himself against the old member, who had little thought of a contest. My master did not relish the thoughts of a troublesome canvass, and all the ill-will he might bring upon himself by disturbing the peace of the county, besides the expense, which was no trifle; but all his friends called upon one another to subscribe, and they formed themselves into a committee, and wrote all his circular letters for him, and engaged all his agents, and did all the business unknown to him; and he was well pleased that it should be so at last, and my lady herself was very sanguine about the election; and there was open house kept night and day at Castle Rackrent, and I thought I never saw my lady look so well in her life as she did at that time. There were grand dinners, and all the gentlemen drinking success to Sir Condy till they were carried off; and then dances and balls, and the ladies all finishing with a raking pot of tea in the morning.[1] Indeed, it was well the company made it their choice to sit up all night, for there were not half beds enough for the sights of people that were in it, though there were shake-downs in the drawing-room always made up before sunrise for those that liked it. For my part, when I saw the doings that were going on, and the loads of claret that went down the throats of them that had no right to be asking for it, and the sights of meat that went up to table and never came down, besides what was carried off to one or t'other below stair, I couldn't but pity my poor master, who was to pay for all; but I said nothing, for fear of gaining myself ill-will. The day of election will come some time or other, says I to myself, and all will be over; and so it did, and a glorious day it was as any I ever had the happiness to see.

"Huzza! huzza! Sir Condy Rackrent for ever!" was the first thing I hears in the morning, and the same and nothing else all day, and not a soul sober only just when polling, enough to give their votes as became 'em, and to stand the browbeating of the lawyers, who came tight enough upon us; and many of our free-holders were knocked off, having never a freehold that they could safely swear to, and Sir Condy was not willing to have any man perjure himself for his sake, as was done on the other side, God knows; but no matter for that. Some of our friends were dumb-founded by the lawyers asking them: Had they ever been upon the ground where their freeholds lay? Now, Sir Condy being tender of the consciences of them that had not been on the ground, and so could not swear to a freehold when cross-examined by them lawyers, sent out for a couple of cleavesful of the sods of his farm of Gulteeshinnagh[2]; and as soon as the sods came into town, he

---

[1] See Glossary, p. 161.

[2] At St. Patrick's meeting, London, March, 1806, the Duke of Sussex said he had the honour of bearing an Irish title, and, with the permission of the company, he should tell them an anecdote of what he had experienced on his travels. When he was at Rome he went to visit an Irish seminary, and when they heard who it was, and that he had an Irish title, some of them asked him, "Please your Royal Highness, since you are an Irish peer, will you tell us if you ever trod upon Irish ground?" When he told them he had not, "Oh, then," said one of the Order, "you shall soon do so." They then spread some earth, which had been brought from Ireland, on a marble slab, and made him stand upon it.

set each man upon his sod, and so then, ever after, you know, they could fairly swear they had been upon the ground.[1] We gained the day by this piece of honesty.[2] I thought I should have died in the streets for joy when I seed my poor master chaired, and he bare-headed, and it raining as hard as it could pour; but all the crowds following him up and down, and he bowing and shaking hands with the whole town.

"Is that Sir Condy Rackrent in the chair?" says a stranger man in the crowd.

"The same," says I. "Who else should it be? God bless him!"

"And I take it, then, you belong to him?" says he.

"Not at all," says I; "but I live under him, and have done so these two hundred years and upwards, me and mine."

"It's lucky for you, then," rejoins he, "that he is where he is; for was he anywhere else but in the chair, this minute he'd be in a worse place; for I was sent down on purpose to put him up,[3] and here's my order for so doing in my pocket."

It was a writ that villain the wine merchant had marked against my poor master for some hundreds of an old debt, which it was a shame to be talking of at such a time as this.

"Put it in your pocket again, and think no more of it anyways for seven years to come, my honest friend," says I; "he's a member of Parliament now, praised be God, and such as you can't touch him: and if you'll take a fool's advice, I'd have you keep out of the way this day, or you'll run a good chance of getting your deserts amongst my master's friends, unless you choose to drink his health like everybody else."

"I've no objection to that in life," said he. So we went into one of the public-houses kept open for my master; and we had a great deal of talk about this thing and that. "And how is it," says he, "your master keeps on so well upon his legs? I heard say he was off Holantide twelvemonth past."

"Never was better or heartier in his life," said I.

"It's not that I'm after speaking of," said he; "but there was a great report of his being ruined."

"No matter," says I, "the sheriffs two years running were his

[1] This was actually done at an election in Ireland.
[2] See Glossary, p. 161.
[3] *To put him up*: to put him in gaol.

particular friends, and the sub-sheriffs were both of them gentlemen, and were properly spoken to; and so the writs lay snug with
them, and they, as I understand by my son Jason the custom in
them cases is, returned the writs as they came to them to those
that sent 'em—much good may it do them!—with a word in
Latin, that no such person as Sir Condy Rackrent, Bart., was to be
found in those parts."

"Oh, I understand all those ways better—no offence—than you,"
says he, laughing, and at the same time filling his glass to my
master's good health, which convinced me he was a warm friend
in his heart after all, though appearances were a little suspicious or
so at first. "To be sure," says he, still cutting his joke, "when a
man's over head and shoulders in debt, he may live the faster for
it, and the better if he goes the right way about it; or else how is
it so many live on so well, as we see every day, after they are
ruined?"

"How is it," says I, being a little merry at the time—"how is it
but just as you see the ducks in the chicken-yard, just after their
heads are cut off by the cook, running round and round faster than
when alive?"

At which conceit he fell a-laughing, and remarked he had never
had the happiness yet to see the chicken-yard at Castle Rackrent.

"It won't be long so, I hope," says I; "you'll be kindly welcome
there, as everybody is made by my master: there is not a freer-
spoken gentleman, or a better loved, high or low, in all Ireland."

And of what passed after this I'm not sensible, for we drank
Sir Condy's good health and the downfall of his enemies till we
could stand no longer ourselves. And little did I think at the time,
or till long after, how I was harbouring my poor master's greatest
of enemies myself. This fellow had the impudence, after coming
to see the chicken-yard, to get me to introduce him to my son
Jason; little more than the man that never was born did I guess
at his meaning by this visit: he gets him a correct list fairly drawn
out from my son Jason of all my master's debts, and goes straight
round to the creditors and buys them all up, which he did easy
enough, seeing the half of them never expected to see their money
out of Sir Condy's hands. Then, when this base-minded limb of
the law, as I afterwards detected him in being, grew to be sole
creditor over all, he takes him out a custodiam on all the denomina-

tions and sub-denominations, and even carton[1] and half-carton upon the estate; and not content with that, must have an execution against the master's goods and down to the furniture, though little worth, of Castle Rackrent itself. But this is a part of my story I'm not come to yet, and it's bad to be forestalling: ill news flies fast enough all the world over.

To go back to the day of the election, which I never think of but with pleasure and tears of gratitude for those good times: after the election was quite and clean over, there comes shoals of people from all parts, claiming to have obliged my master with their votes, and putting him in mind of promises which he could never remember himself to have made: one was to have a freehold for each of his four sons; another was to have a renewal of a lease; another an abatement; one came to be paid ten guineas for a pair of silver buckles sold my master on the hustings, which turned out to be no better than copper gilt; another had a long bill for oats, the half of which never went into the granary to my certain knowledge, and the other half was not fit for the cattle to touch; but the bargain was made the week before the election, and the coach and saddle-horses were got into order for the day, besides a vote fairly got by them oats; so no more reasoning on that head. But then there was no end to them that were telling Sir Condy he had engaged to make their sons excisemen, or high constables, or the like; and as for them that had bills to give in for liquor, and beds, and straw, and ribands, and horses, and post-chaises for the gentlemen free-holders that came from all parts and other counties to vote for my master, and were not, to be sure, to be at any charges, there was no standing against all these; and, worse than all, the gentlemen of my master's committee, who managed all for him, and talked how they'd bring him in without costing him a penny, and subscribed by hundreds very genteelly, forgot to pay their subscriptions, and had laid out in agents' and lawyers' fees and secret service money to the Lord knows how much; and my master could never ask one of them for their subscription you are sensible, nor for the price of a fine horse he had sold one of them; so it all was left at his door. He could never, God bless him again! I say, bring himself to ask a gentleman for money, despising such sort of conversation himself; but others, who were not gentlemen born, behaved

[1] See Glossary, p. 161.

126

very uncivil in pressing him at this very time, and all he could do to content 'em all was to take himself out of the way as fast as possible to Dublin, where my lady had taken a house fitting for him as a member of Parliament, to attend his duty in there all the winter. I was very lonely when the whole family was gone, and all the things they had ordered to go, and forgot, sent after them by the car. There was then a great silence in Castle Rackrent, and I went moping from room to room, hearing the doors clap for want of right locks, and the wind through the broken windows, that the glazier never would come to mend, and the rain coming through the roof and best ceilings all over the house for want of the slater, whose bill was not paid, besides our having no slates or shingles for that part of the old building which was shingled and burnt when the chimney took fire, and had been open to the weather ever since. I took myself to the servants' hall in the evening to smoke my pipe as usual, but missed the bit of talk we used to have there sadly, and ever after was content to stay in the kitchen and boil my little potatoes,[1] and put up my bed there, and every post-day I looked in the newspaper, but no news of my master in the House; he never spoke good or bad, but, as the butler wrote down word to my son Jason, was very ill-used by the Government about a place that was promised him and never given, after his supporting them against his conscience very honourably, and being greatly abused for it, which hurt him greatly, he having the name of a great patriot in the country before. The house and living in Dublin too were not to be had for nothing, and my son Jason said, "Sir Condy must soon be looking out for a new agent, for I've done my part, and can do no more. If my lady had the bank of Ireland to spend, it would go all in one winter, and Sir Condy would never gainsay her, though he does not care the rind of a lemon for her all the while."

Now I could not bear to hear Jason giving out after this manner against the family, and twenty people standing by in the street. Ever since he had lived at the Lodge of his own he looked down, howsomever, upon poor old Thady, and was grown quite a great gentleman, and had none of his relations near him; no wonder

---

[1] *My little potatoes.*—Thady does not mean by this expression that his potatoes were less than other people's, or less than the usual size. *Little* is here used only as an Italian diminutive, expressive of fondness.

he was no kinder to poor Sir Condy than to his own kith or kin.[1] In the spring it was the villain that got the list of the debts from him brought down the custodiam, Sir Condy still attending his duty in Parliament; and I could scarcely believe my own old eyes, or the spectacles with which I read it, when I was shown my son Jason's name joined in the custodiam; but he told me it was only for form's sake, and to make things easier than if all the land was under the power of a total stranger. Well, I did not know what to think; it was hard to be talking ill of my own, and I could not but grieve for my poor master's fine estate, all torn by these vultures of the law; so I said nothing, but just looked on to see how it would all end.

It was not till the month of June that he and my lady came down to the country. My master was pleased to take me aside with him to the brewhouse that same evening, to complain to me of my son and other matters, in which he said he was confident I had neither art nor part; he said a great deal more to me, to whom he had been fond to talk ever since he was my white-headed boy before he came to the estate; and all that he said about poor Judy I can never forget, but scorn to repeat. He did not say an unkind word of my lady, but wondered, as well he might, her relations would do nothing for him or her, and they in all this great distress. He did not take anything long to heart, let it be as it would, and had no more malice or thought of the like in him than a child that can't speak; this night it was all out of his head before he went to his bed. He took his jug of whisky-punch—my lady was grown quite easy about the whisky-punch by this time, and so I did suppose all was going on right betwixt them, till I learnt the truth through Mrs. Jane, who talked over the affairs to the housekeeper, and I within hearing. The night my master came home, thinking of nothing at all but just making merry, he drank his bumper toast "to the deserts of that old curmudgeon my father-in-law, and all enemies at Mount Juliet's Town." Now my lady was no longer in the mind she formerly was, and did noways relish hearing her own friends abused in her presence, she said.

"Then why don't they show themselves your friends," said my master, "and oblige me with the loan of the money I condescended,

[1] *Kith* and *kin*: family or relations. *Kin* from *kind*; *kith* from we know not what.

by your advice, my dear, to ask? It's now three posts since I sent off my letter, desiring in the postscript a speedy answer by the return of the post, and no account at all from them yet."

"I expect they'll write to me next post," says my lady, and that was all that passed then; but it was easy from this to guess there was a coolness betwixt them, and with good cause.

The next morning, being post-day, I sent off the gossoon early to the post-office, to see was there any letter likely to set matters to rights, and he brought back one with the proper post-mark upon it, sure enough, and I had no time to examine or make any conjecture more about it, for into the servants' hall pops Mrs. Jane with a blue bandbox in her hand, quite entirely mad.

"Dear ma'am, and what's the matter?" says I.

"Matter enough," says she; "don't you see my bandbox is wet through, and my best bonnet here spoiled, besides my lady's, and all by the rain coming in through that gallery window that you might have got mended if you'd had any sense, Thady, all the time we were in town in the winter?"

"Sure, I could not get the glazier, ma'am," says I.

"You might have stopped it up anyhow," says she.

"So I did, ma'am, to the best of my ability; one of the panes with the old pillow-case, and the other with a piece of the old stage green curtain. Sure I was as careful as possible all the time you were away, and not a drop of rain came in at that window of all the windows in the house, all winter, ma'am, when under my care; and now the family's come home, and it's summer-time, I never thought no more about it, to be sure; but dear, it's a pity to think of your bonnet, ma'am. But here's what will please you, ma'am—a letter from Mount Juliet's Town for my lady."

With that she snatches it from me without a word more, and runs up the back stairs to my mistress; I follows with a slate to make up the window. This window was in the long passage—or gallery, as my lady gave out orders to have it called—in the gallery leading to my master's bedchamber and hers. And when I went up with the slate, the door having no lock, and the bolt spoilt, was ajar after Mrs. Jane, and, as I was busy with the window, I heard all that was saying within.

"Well, what's in your letter, Bella, my dear?" says he: "you're a long time spelling it over."

"Won't you shave this morning, Sir Condy?" says she, and put the letter into her pocket.

"I shaved the day before yesterday," said he, "my dear, and that's not what I'm thinking of now; but anything to oblige you, and to have peace and quietness, my dear"—and presently I had a glimpse of him at the cracked glass over the chimney-piece, standing up shaving himself to please my lady. But she took no notice, but went on reading her book, and Mrs. Jane doing her hair behind.

"What is it you're reading there, my dear?—phoo, I've cut myself with this razor; the man's a cheat that sold it me, but I have not paid him for it yet. What is it you're reading there? Did you hear me asking you, my dear?"

"*The Sorrows of Werter*," replies my lady, as well as I could hear.

"I think more of the sorrows of Sir Condy," says my master, joking like. "What news from Mount Juliet's Town?"

"No news," says she, "but the old story over again; my friends all reproaching me still for what I can't help now."

"Is it for marrying me?" said my master, still shaving. "What signifies, as you say, talking of that, when it can't be help'd now?"

With that she heaved a great sigh that I heard plain enough in the passage.

"And did not you use me basely, Sir Condy," says she, "not to tell me you were ruined before I married you?"

"Tell you, my dear!" said he. "Did you ever ask me one word about it? And had not you friends enough of your own, that were telling you nothing else from morning to night, if you'd have listened to them slanders?"

"No slanders, nor are my friends slanderers; and I can't bear to hear them treated with disrespect as I do," says my lady, and took out her pocket-handerchief; "they are the best of friends, and if I had taken their advice—— But my father was wrong to lock me up, I own. That was the only unkind thing I can charge him with; for if he had not locked me up, I should never have had a serious thought of running away as I did."

"Well, my dear," said my master, "don't cry and make yourself uneasy about it now, when it's all over, and you have the man of your own choice, in spite of 'em all."

"I was too young, I know, to make a choice at the time you ran away with me, I'm sure," says my lady, and another sigh, which made my master, half-shaved as he was, turn round upon her in surprise.

"Why, Bella," says he, "you can't deny what you know as well as I do, that it was at your own particular desire, and that twice under your own hand and seal expressed, that I should carry you off as I did to Scotland, and marry you there."

"Well, say no more about it, Sir Condy," said my lady, pettish-like; "I was a child then, you know."

"And as far as I know, you're little better now, my dear Bella, to be talking in this manner to your husband's face; but I won't take it ill of you, for I know it's something in that letter you put into your pocket just now that has set you against me all on a sudden, and imposed upon your understanding."

"It's not so very easy as you think it, Sir Condy, to impose upon my understanding," said my lady.

"My dear," says he, "I have, and with reason, the best opinion of your understanding of any man now breathing; and you know I have never set my own in competition with it till now, my dear Bella," says he, taking her hand from her book as kind as could be—"till now, when I have the great advantage of being quite cool, and you not; so don't believe one word your friends say against your own Sir Condy, and lend me the letter out of your pocket, till I see what it is they can have to say."

"Take it then," says she; "and as you are quite cool, I hope it is a proper time to request you'll allow me to comply with the wishes of all my own friends, and return to live with my father and family, during the remainder of my wretched existence, at Mount Juliet's Town."

At this my poor master fell back a few paces, like one that had been shot.

"You're not serious, Bella," says he; "and could you find it in your heart to leave me this way in the very middle of my distresses, all alone?" But recollecting himself after his first surprise, and a moment's time for reflection, he said, with a great deal of consideration for my lady, "Well, Bella, my dear, I believe you are right; for what could you do at Castle Rackrent, and an execution against the goods coming down, and the furniture to be canted, and an auction in the house all next week? So you have my full consent to go, since that is your desire; only you must not think of my accompanying you, which I could not in honour do upon the terms I always have been, since our marriage, with your friends. Besides, I have business to transact at home; so in the meantime, if we are to have any breakfast this morning, let us go down and have it for the last time in peace and comfort, Bella."

Then as I heard my master coming to the passage door, I finished fastening up my slate against the broken pane; and when he came out I wiped down the window-seat with my wig,[1] and bade him a "good-morrow" as kindly as I could, seeing he was in trouble, though he strove and thought to hide it from me.

"This window is all racked and tattered," says I, "and it's what I'm striving to mend."

"It *is* all racked and tattered, plain enough," says he, "and never mind mending it, honest old Thady," says he; "it will do well enough for you and I, and that's all the company we shall have left in the house by and by."

"I'm sorry to see your honour so low this morning," says I; "but you'll be better after taking your breakfast."

"Step down to the servants' hall," said he, "and bring me up the pen and ink into the parlour, and get a sheet of paper from Mrs. Jane, for I have business that can't brook to be delayed; and come into the parlour with the pen and ink yourself, Thady, for I must have you to witness my signing a paper I have to execute in a hurry."

Well, while I was getting of the pen and ink-horn, and the sheet of paper, I ransacked my brains to think what could be the papers my poor master could have to execute in such a hurry, he that never thought of such a thing as doing business afore breakfast in the whole course of his life, for any man living; but this was for

[1] Wigs were formerly used instead of brooms in Ireland for sweeping or dusting tables, stairs, etc. The Editor doubted the fact till he saw a labourer of the old school sweep down a flight of stairs with his wig; he afterwards put it on his head again with the utmost composure, and said, "Oh, please your honour, it's never a bit the worse."

It must be acknowledged that these men are not in any danger of catching cold by taking off their wigs occasionally, because they usually have fine crops of hair growing under their wigs. The wigs are often yellow, and the hair which appears from beneath them black; the wigs are usually too small, and are raised up by the hair beneath, or by the ears of the wearers.

my lady, as I afterwards found, and the more genteel of him after all her treatment.

I was just witnessing the paper that he had scrawled over, and was shaking the ink out of my pen upon the carpet, when my lady came in to breakfast, and she started as if it had been a ghost; as well she might, when she saw Sir Condy writing at this unseasonable hour.

"That will do very well, Thady," says he to me, and took the paper I had signed to, without knowing what upon the earth it might be, out of my hands, and walked, folding it up, to my lady.

"You are concerned in this, my Lady Rackrent," said he, putting it into her hands; "and I beg you'll keep this memorandum safe, and show it to your friends the first thing you do when you get home; but put it in your pocket now, my dear, and let us eat our breakfast, in God's name."

"What is all this?" said my lady, opening the paper in great curiosity.

"It's only a bit of a memorandum of what I think becomes me to do whenever I am able," says my master; "you know my situation, tied hand and foot at the present time being, but that can't last always, and when I'm dead and gone the land will be to the good, Thady, you know; and take notice it's my intention your lady should have a clear five hundred a year jointure off the estate afore any of my debts are paid."

"Oh, please your honour," says I, "I can't expect to live to see that time, being now upwards of fourscore years of age, and you a young man, and likely to continue so, by the help of God."

I was vexed to see my lady so insensible too, for all she said was, "This is very genteel of you, Sir Condy. You need not wait any longer, Thady." So I just picked up the pen and ink that had tumbled on the floor, and heard my master finish with saying, "You behaved very genteel to me, my dear, when you threw all the little you had in your power along with yourself into my hands; and as I don't deny but what you may have had some things to complain of,"—to be sure he was thinking then of Judy, or of the whisky-punch, one or t'other, or both,—"and as I don't deny but you may have had something to complain of, my dear, it is but fair you should have something in the form of compensation to look forward to agreeably in future; besides, it's an act of justice to myself, that none of your friends, my dear, may ever have it to say against me, I married for money, and not for love."

"That is the last thing I should ever have thought of saying of you, Sir Condy," said my lady, looking very gracious.

"Then, my dear," said Sir Condy, "we shall part as good friends as we met; so all's right."

I was greatly rejoiced to hear this, and went out of the parlour to report it all to the kitchen. The next morning my lady and Mrs. Jane set out for Mount Juliet's Town in the jaunting-car. Many wondered at my lady's choosing to go away, considering all things, upon the jaunting-car, as if it was only a party of pleasure; but they did not know till I told them that the coach was all broke in the journey down, and no other vehicle but the car to be had. Besides, my lady's friends were to send their coach to meet her at the cross-roads; so it was all done very proper.

My poor master was in great trouble after my lady left us. The execution came down, and everything at Castle Rackrent was seized by the gripers, and my son Jason, to his shame be it spoken, amongst them. I wondered, for the life of me, how he could harden himself to do it; but then he had been studying the law, and had made himself Attorney Quirk; so he brought down at once a heap of accounts upon my master's head. To cash lent, and to ditto, and to ditto, and to ditto and oats, and bills paid at the milliner's and linen-draper's, and many dresses for the fancy balls in Dublin for my lady, and all the bills to the workmen and tradesmen for the scenery of the theatre, and the chandler's and grocer's bills, and tailor's, besides butcher's and baker's, and, worse than all, the old one of that base wine merchant's, that wanted to arrest my poor master for the amount on the election day, for which amount Sir Condy afterwards passed his note of hand, bearing lawful interest from the date thereof; and the interest and compound interest was now mounted to a terrible deal on many other notes and bonds for money borrowed, and there was, besides, hush-money to the sub-sheriffs, and sheets upon sheets of old and new attorney's bills, with heavy balances, "as per former account furnished," brought forward with interest thereon; then there was a powerful deal due to the Crown for sixteen years' arrear of quit-rent of the town-lands of Carrickashaughlin, with driver's fees, and a compliment to the receiver every year for letting the quit-rent run on to oblige Sir Condy, and Sir Kit, afore him. Then there were bills for spirits and ribands at the election time, and the gentlemen of the committee's accounts unsettled, and their subscription never gathered; and there were cows to be paid for, with the smith and farrier's bills to be set against the rent of the demesne, with calf and hay money; then there was all the servants' wages, since I don't know when, coming due to them, and sums advanced for them by my son Jason for clothes, and boots, and whips, and odd moneys for sundries expended by them in journeys to town and elsewhere, and pocket-money for the master continually, and messengers and postage before his being a Parliament man. I can't myself tell you what besides; but this I know, that when the evening came on the which Sir Condy had appointed to settle all with my son Jason, and when he comes into the parlour, and sees the sight of bills and load of papers all gathered on the great dining-table for him, he puts his hands before both his eyes, and cried out, "Merciful Jasus! what is it I see before me?" Then I sets an arm-chair at the table for him, and with a deal of difficulty he sits him down, and my son Jason hands him over the pen and ink to sign to this man's bill and t'other man's bill, all which he did without making the least objections. Indeed, to give him his due, I never seen a man more fair and honest, and easy in all his dealings, from first to last, as Sir Condy, or more willing to pay every man his own as far as he was able, which is as much as any one can do.

"Well," says he, joking like with Jason, "I wish we could settle it all with a stroke of my grey goose quill. What signifies making me wade through all this ocean of papers here; can't you now, who understand drawing out an account, debtor and creditor, just sit down here at the corner of the table and get it done out for me, that I may have a clear view of the balance, which is all I need be talking about, you know?"

"Very true, Sir Condy; nobody understands business better than yourself," says Jason.

"So I've a right to do, being born and bred to the bar," says Sir Condy. "Thady, do step out and see are they bringing in the things for the punch, for we've just done all we have to do for this evening."

I goes out accordingly, and when I came back Jason was pointing to the balance, which was a terrible sight to my poor master.

"Pooh! pooh! pooh!" says he. "Here's so many noughts they dazzle my eyes, so they do, and put me in mind of all I suffered larning of my numeration table, when I was a boy at the day-school along with you, Jason—units, tens, hundreds, tens of hundreds. Is the punch ready, Thady?" says he, seeing me.

"Immediately; the boy has the jug in his hand; it's coming up-stairs, please your honour, as fast as possible," says I, for I saw his honour was tired out of his life; but Jason, very short and cruel, cuts me off with—"Don't be talking of punch yet awhile; it's no time for punch yet a bit—units, tens, hundreds," goes he on, counting over the master's shoulder, units, tens, hundreds, thousands.

"A-a-ah! hold your hand," cries my master. "Where in this wide world am I to find hundreds, or units itself, let alone thousands?"

"The balance has been running on too long," says Jason, sticking to him as I could not have done at the time, if you'd have given both the Indies and Cork to boot; "the balance has been running on too long, and I'm distressed myself on your account, Sir Condy, for money, and the thing must be settled now on the spot, and the balance cleared off," says Jason.

"I'll thank you if you'll only show me how," says Sir Condy.

"There's but one way," says Jason, "and that's ready enough. When there's no cash, what can a gentleman do but go to the land?"

"How can you go to the land, and it under custodiam to your-self already?" says Sir Condy; "and another custodiam hanging over it? And no one at all can touch it, you know, but the custodees."

"Sure, can't you sell, though at a loss? Sure you can sell, and I've a purchaser ready for you," says Jason.

"Have you so?" says Sir Condy. "That's a great point gained. But there's a thing now beyond all, that perhaps you don't know yet, barring Thady has let you into the secret."

"Sarrah bit of a secret, or anything at all of the kind, has he learned from me these fifteen weeks come St. John's Eve," says I, "for we have scarce been upon speaking terms of late. But what is it your honour means of a secret?"

"Why, the secret of the little keepsake I gave my Lady Rack-rent the morning she left us, that she might not go back empty-handed to her friends."

"My Lady Rackrent, I'm sure, has baubles and keepsakes enough, as those bills on the table will show," says Jason; "but whatever it is," says he, taking up his pen, "we must add it to the balance, for to be sure it can't be paid for."

"No, nor can't till after my decease," says Sir Condy; "that's one good thing." Then colouring up a good deal, he tells Jason of the memorandum of the five hundred a year jointure he had settled upon my lady; at which Jason was indeed mad, and said a great deal in very high words, that it was using a gentleman who had the management of his affairs, and was, moreover, his principal creditor, extremely ill to do such a thing without consulting him, and against his knowledge and consent. To all which Sir Condy had nothing to reply, but that, upon his conscience, it was in a hurry and without a moment's thought on his part, and he was very sorry for it, but if it was to do over again he would do the same; and he appealed to me, and I was ready to give my evidence, if that would do, to the truth of all he said.

So Jason with much ado was brought to agree to a compromise.

"The purchaser that I have ready," says he, "will be much displeased, to be sure, at the encumbrance on the land, but I must see and manage him. Here's a deed ready drawn up; we have nothing to do but to put in the consideration money and our names to it."

"And how much am I going to sell?—the lands of O'Shaughlin's Town, and the lands of Gruneaghoolaghan, and the lands of Crookaghnawaturgh," says he, just reading to himself. "And—oh, murder, Jason! sure you won't put this in—the castle, stable, and appurtenances of Castle Rackrent?"

"Oh, murder!" says I, clapping my hands; "this is too bad, Jason."

"Why so?" said Jason. "When it's all, and a great deal more to the back of it, lawfully mine, was I to push for it."

"Look at him," says I, pointing to Sir Condy, who was just leaning back in his arm-chair, with his arms falling beside him like one stupefied; "is it you, Jason, that can stand in his presence, and recollect all he has been to us, and all we have been to him, and yet use him so at the last?"

"Who will you find to use him better? I ask you," said Jason; "if he can get a better purchaser, I'm content; I only offer to purchase, to make things easy, and oblige him; though I don't see what compliment I am under, if you come to that. I have never had, asked, or charged more than sixpence in the pound, receiver's fees, and where would he have got an agent for a penny less?"

"Oh, Jason! Jason! how will you stand to this in the face of the county, and all who know you?" says I; "and what will people think and say when they see you living here in Castle Rackrent, and the lawful owner turned out of the seat of his ancestors, without a cabin to put his head into, or so much as a potato to eat?"

Jason, whilst I was saying this, and a great deal more, made me signs, and winks, and frowns; but I took no heed, for I was grieved and sick at heart for my poor master, and couldn't but speak.

"Here's the punch," says Jason, for the door opened; "here's the punch!"

Hearing that, my master starts up in his chair, and recollects himself, and Jason uncorks the whisky.

"Set down the jug here," says he, making room for it beside the papers opposite to Sir Condy, but still not stirring the deed that was to make over all.

Well, I was in great hopes he had some touch of mercy about him when I saw him making the punch, and my master took a glass; but Jason put it back as he was going to fill again, saying: "No, Sir Condy, it shan't be said of me I got your signature to this deed when you were half-seas over: you know your name and handwriting in that condition would not, if brought before the courts, benefit me a straw; wherefore, let us settle all before we go deeper into the punch-bowl."

"Settle all as you will," said Sir Condy, clapping his hands to his ears; "but let me hear no more. I'm bothered to death this night."

"You've only to sign," said Jason, putting the pen to him.

"Take all, and be content," said my master. So he signed; and the man who brought in the punch witnessed it, for I was not able, but crying like a child; and besides, Jason said, which I was glad of, that I was no fit witness, being so old and doting. It was so bad with me, I could not taste a drop of the punch itself, though my master himself, God bless him! in the midst of his trouble, poured out a glass for me, and brought it up to my lips.

"Not a drop; I thank your honour's honour as much as if I took it, though." And I just set down the glass as it was, and went out, and when I got to the street door the neighbours' childer, who were playing at marbles there, seeing me in great trouble, left their play, and gathered about me to know what ailed me; and I told them all, for it was a great relief to me to speak to these poor childer, that seemed to have some natural feeling left in them; and when they were made sensible that Sir Condy was going to leave Castle Rackrent for good and all, they set up a whillaluh that could be heard to the farthest end of the street; and one— fine boy he was—that my master had given an apple to that morning, cried the loudest; but they all were the same sorry, for Sir Condy was greatly beloved amongst the childer, for letting them go a-nutting in the demesne, without saying a word to them, though my lady objected to them. The people in the town, who were the most of them standing at their doors, hearing the childer cry, would know the reason of it; and when the report was made known, the people one and all gathered in great anger against my son Jason, and terror at the notion of his coming to be landlord over them, and they cried, "No Jason! no Jason! Sir Condy! Sir Condy! Sir Condy Rackrent for ever!" And the mob grew so great and so loud, I was frightened, and made my way back to the house to warn my son to make his escape, or hide himself for fear of the consequences. Jason would not believe me till they came all round the house, and to the windows with great shouts. Then he grew quite pale, and asked Sir Condy what had he best do?

"I'll tell you what you had best do," said Sir Condy, who was laughing to see his fright; "finish your glass first, then let's go to the window and show ourselves, and I'll tell 'em—or you shall, if you please—that I'm going to the Lodge for change of air for my health, and by my own desire, for the rest of my days."

"Do so," said Jason, who never meant it should have been so, but could not refuse him the Lodge at this unseasonable time. Accordingly, Sir Condy threw up the sash and explained matters, and thanked all his friends, and bid them look in at the punch-bowl, and observe that Jason and he had been sitting over it very good friends; so the mob was content, and he sent them out some whisky to drink his health, and that was the last time his honour's health was ever drunk at Castle Rackrent.

The very next day, being too proud, as he said to me, to stay an hour longer in a house that did not belong to him, he sets off to the Lodge, and I along with him not many hours after. And there was great bemoaning through all O'Shaughlin's Town, which I stayed to witness, and gave my poor master a full account of when I got to the Lodge. He was very low, and in his bed, when I got there, and complained of a great pain about his heart; but I guessed it was only trouble and all the business, let alone vexation, he had gone through of late; and knowing the nature of him from a boy, I took my pipe, and whilst smoking it by the chimney began telling him how he was beloved and regretted in the county, and it did him a deal of good to hear it.

"Your honour has a great many friends yet that you don't know of, rich and poor, in the county," says I; "for as I was coming along the road I met two gentlemen in their own carriages, who asked after you, knowing me, and wanted to know where you was and all about you, and even how old I was. Think of that."

Then he wakened out of his doze, and began questioning me who the gentlemen were. And the next morning it came into my head to go, unknown to anybody, with my master's compliments, round to many of the gentlemen's houses, where he and my lady used to visit, and people that I knew were his great friends, and would go to Cork to serve him any day in the year, and I made bold to try to borrow a trifle of cash from them. They all treated me very civil for the most part, and asked a great many questions very kind about my lady and Sir Condy and all the family, and were greatly surprised to learn from me Castle Rackrent was sold, and my master at the Lodge for health; and they all pitied him greatly, and he had their good wishes, if that would do; but money was a thing they unfortunately had not any of them at this time to spare. I had my journey for my pains, and I, not used to walking, nor supple as formerly, was greatly tired, but had the satisfaction of telling my master, when I got to the Lodge, all the civil things said by high and low.

"Thady," says he, "all you've been telling me brings a strange thought into my head. I've a notion I shall not be long for this world anyhow, and I've a great fancy to see my own funeral afore I die." I was greatly shocked, at the first speaking, to hear him speak so light about his funeral, and he to all appearance in good health; but recollecting myself, answered:

"To be sure it would be as fine a sight as one could see," I dared to say, "and one I should be proud to witness," and I did not doubt his honour's would be as great a funeral as ever Sir Patrick O'Shaughlin's was, and such a one as that had never been known in the county afore or since. But I never thought he was in earnest about seeing his own funeral himself till the next day he returns to it again.

"Thady," says he, "as far as the wake[1] goes, sure I might without any great trouble have the satisfaction of seeing a bit of my own funeral."

"Well, since your honour's honour's so bent upon it," says I, not willing to cross him, and he in trouble, "we must see what we can do."

So he fell into a sort of sham disorder, which was easy done, as he kept his bed, and no one to see him; and I got my shister, who was an old woman very handy about the sick, and very skilful, to come up to the Lodge to nurse him; and we gave out, she knowing no better, that he was just at his latter end, and it answered beyond anything; and there was a great throng of people, men, women, and childer, and there being only two rooms at the Lodge, except what was locked up full of Jason's furniture and things, the house was soon as full and fuller than it could hold, and the heat, and smoke, and noise wonderful great; and standing amongst them that were near the bed, but not thinking at all of the dead, I was startled by the sound of my master's voice from under the great-coats that had been thrown all at top, and I went close up, no one noticing.

"Thady," says he, "I've had enough of this; I'm smothering, and can't hear a word of all they're saying of the deceased."

"God bless you, and lie still and quiet," says I, "a bit longer, for my shister's afraid of ghosts, and would die on the spot with fright was she to see you come to life all on a sudden this way without the least preparation."

So he lays him still, though well nigh stifled, and I made all haste to tell the secret of the joke, whispering to one and t'other, and there was a great surprise, but not so great as we had laid out it would. "And aren't we to have the pipes and tobacco, after

[1] A "wake" in England is a meeting avowedly for merriment; in Ireland it is a nocturnal meeting avowedly for the purpose of watching and bewailing the dead, but in reality for gossiping and debauchery. See Glossary, p. 162.

coming so far to-night?" said some; but they were all well enough pleased when his honour got up to drink with them, and sent for more spirits from a shebeen-house,[1] where they very civilly let him have it upon credit. So the night passed off very merrily, but to my mind Sir Condy was rather upon the sad order in the midst of it all, not finding there had been such a great talk about himself after his death as he had always expected to hear.

The next morning, when the house was cleared of them, and none but my shister and myself left in the kitchen with Sir Condy, one opens the door and walks in, and who should it be but Judy M'Quirk herself! I forgot to notice that she had been married long since, whilst young Captain Moneygawl lived at the Lodge, to the captain's huntsman, who after a whilst 'listed and left her, and was killed in the wars. Poor Judy fell off greatly in her good looks after her being married a year or two; and being smoke-dried in the cabin, and neglecting herself like, it was hard for Sir Condy himself to know her again till she spoke; but when she says, "It's Judy M'Quirk, please your honour; don't you remember her?"

"Oh, Judy, is it you?" says his honour. "Yes, sure, I remember you very well; but you're greatly altered, Judy."

"Sure it's time for me," says she. "And I think your honour, since I seen you last—but that's a great while ago—is altered too."

"And with reason, Judy," says Sir Condy, fetching a sort of a sigh. "But how's this, Judy?" he goes on. "I take it a little amiss of you that you were not at my wake last night."

"Ah, don't be being jealous of that," says she; "I didn't hear a sentence of your honour's wake till it was all over, or it would have gone hard with me but I would have been at it, sure; but I was forced to go ten miles up the country three days ago to a wedding of a relation of my own's, and didn't get home till after the wake was over. But," says she, "it won't be so, I hope, the next time,[2] please your honour."

"That we shall see, Judy," says his honour, "and maybe sooner than you think for, for I've been very unwell this while past, and don't reckon anyway I'm long for this world."

[1] "Shebeen-house," a hedge alehouse. Shebeen properly means weak, small-beer, taplash.

[2] At the coronation of one of our monarchs the King complained of the confusion which happened in the procession. The great officer who presided told his Majesty that "it should not be so next time."

At this Judy takes up the corner of her apron, and puts it first to one eye and then to t'other, being to all appearance in great trouble; and my shister put in her word, and bid his honour have a good heart, for she was sure it was only the gout that Sir Patrick used to have flying about him, and he ought to drink a glass or a bottle extraordinary to keep it out of his stomach; and he promised to take her advice, and sent out for more spirits immediately; and Judy made a sign to me, and I went over to the door to her, and she said, "I wonder to see Sir Condy so low: has he heard the news?"

"What news?" says I.

"Didn't ye hear it, then?" says she; "my Lady Rackrent that was is kilt[1] and lying for dead, and I don't doubt but it's all over with her by this time."

"Mercy on us all," says I; "how was it?"

"The jaunting-car it was that ran away with her," says Judy. "I was coming home that same time from Biddy M'Guggin's marriage, and a great crowd of people too upon the road, coming from the fair of Crookaghnawaturgh, and I sees a jaunting-car standing in the middle of the road, and with the two wheels off and all tattered. 'What's this?' says I. 'Didn't ye hear of it?' says they that were looking on; 'it's my Lady Rackrent's car, that was running away from her husband, and the horse took fright at a carrion that lay across the road, and so ran away with the jaunting-car, and my Lady Rackrent and her maid screaming, and the horse ran with them against a car that was coming from the fair with the boy asleep on it, and the lady's petticoat hanging out of the jaunting-car caught, and she was dragged I can't tell you how far upon the road, and it all broken up with the stones just going to be pounded, and one of the road-makers, with his sledge-hammer in his hand, stops the horse at the last; but my Lady Rackrent was all kilt and smashed,[2] and they lifted her into a cabin hard by,

[1] See Glossary, p. 162.

[2] *Kilt and smashed.*—Our author is not here guilty of an anti-climax. The mere English reader, from a similarity of sound between the words "kilt" and "killed," might be induced to suppose that their meanings are similar, yet they are not by any means in Ireland synonymous terms. Thus you may hear a man exclaim, "I'm kilt and murdered!" but he frequently means only that he has received a black eye or a slight contusion. "I'm kilt all over" means that he is in a worse state than being simply "kilt." Thus, "I'm kilt with the cold," is nothing to "I'm kilt all over with the rheumatism."

and the maid was found after where she had been thrown in the gripe of a ditch, her cap and bonnet all full of bog water, and they say my lady can't live anyway.' Thady, pray now is it true what I'm told for sartain, that Sir Condy has made over all to your son Jason?"

"All," says I.

"All entirely?" says she again.

"All entirely," says I.

"Then," says she, "that's a great shame; but don't be telling Jason what I say."

"And what is it you say?" cries Sir Condy, leaning over betwixt us, which made Judy start greatly. "I know the time when Judy M'Quirk would never have stayed so long talking at the door and I in the house."

"Oh!" says Judy, "for shame, Sir Condy; times are altered since then, and it's my Lady Rackrent you ought to be thinking of."

"And why should I be thinking of her, that's not thinking of me now?" says Sir Condy.

"No matter for that," says Judy, very properly; "it's time you should be thinking of her, if ever you mean to do it at all, for don't you know she's lying for death?"

"My Lady Rackrent!" says Sir Condy, in a surprise; "why it's but two days since we parted, as you very well know, Thady, in her full health and spirits, and she, and her maid along with her, going to Mount Juliet's Town on her jaunting-car."

"She'll never ride no more on her jaunting-car," said Judy, "for it has been the death of her, sure enough."

"And is she dead then?" says his honour.

"As good as dead, I hear," says Judy; "but there's Thady here as just learnt the whole truth of the story as I had it, and it's fitter he or anybody else should be telling it you than I, Sir Condy: I must be going home to the childer."

But he stops her, but rather from civility in him, as I could see very plainly, than anything else, for Judy was, as his honour remarked at her first coming in, greatly changed, and little likely, as far as I could see—though she did not seem to be clear of it herself—little likely to be my Lady Rackrent now, should there be a second toss-up to be made. But I told him the whole story out of the face, just as Judy had told it to me, and he sent off a messenger with his compliments to Mount Juliet's Town that evening, to learn the truth of the report, and Judy bid the boy that was going call in at Tim M'Enerney's shop in O'Shaughlin's Town and buy her a new shawl.

"Do so," said Sir Condy, "and tell Tim to take no money from you, for I must pay him for the shawl myself." At this my shister throws me over a look, and I says nothing, but turned the tobacco in my mouth, whilst Judy began making a many words about it, and saying how she could not be beholden for shawls to any gentleman. I left her there to consult with my shister, did she think there was anything in it, and my shister thought I was blind to be asking her the question, and I thought my shister must see more into it than I did, and recollecting all past times and everything, I changed my mind, and came over to her way of thinking, and we settled it that Judy was very like to be my Lady Rackrent after all, if a vacancy should have happened.

The next day, before his honour was up, somebody comes with a double knock at the door, and I was greatly surprised to see it was my son Jason.

"Jason, is it you?" said I; "what brings you to the Lodge?" says I. "Is it my Lady Rackrent? We know that already since yesterday."

"Maybe so," says he; "but I must see Sir Condy about it."

"You can't see him yet," says I; "sure he is not awake."

"What then," says he, "can't he be wakened, and I standing at the door?"

"I'll not be disturbing his honour for you, Jason," says I; "many's the hour you've waited in your time, and been proud to do it, till his honour was at leisure to speak to you. His honour," says I, raising my voice, at which his honour wakens of his own accord, and calls to me from the room to know who it was I was speaking to. Jason made no more ceremony, but follows me into the room.

"How are you, Sir Condy?" says he; "I'm happy to see you looking so well; I came up to know how you did to-day, and to see did you want for anything at the Lodge."

"Nothing at all, Mr. Jason, I thank you," says he; for his honour had his own share of pride, and did not choose, after all that had passed, to be beholden, I suppose, to my son; "but pray take a chair and be seated, Mr. Jason."

Jason sat him down upon the chest, for chair there was none, and after he had set there some time, and a silence on all sides,

"What news is there stirring in the country, Mr. Jason M'Quirk?" says Sir Condy, very easy, yet high like.

"None that's news to you, Sir Condy, I hear," says Jason. "I am sorry to hear of my Lady Rackrent's accident."

"I'm much obliged to you, and so is her ladyship, I'm sure," answered Sir Condy, still stiff; and there was another sort of a silence, which seemed to lie the heaviest on my son Jason.

"Sir Condy," says he at last, seeing Sir Condy disposing himself to go to sleep again, "Sir Condy, I daresay you recollect mentioning to me the little memorandum you gave to Lady Rackrent about the £500 a year jointure."

"Very true," said Sir Condy; "it is all in my recollection."

"But if my Lady Rackrent dies, there's an end of all jointure," says Jason.

"Of course," says Sir Condy.

"But it's not a matter of certainty that my Lady Rackrent won't recover," says Jason.

"Very true, sir," says my master.

"It's a fair speculation, then, for you to consider what the chance of jointure of those lands, when out of custodiam, will be to you."

"Just five hundred a year, I take it, without any speculation at all," said Sir Condy.

"That's supposing the life dropt, and the custodiam off, you know; begging your pardon, Sir Condy, who understands business, that is a wrong calculation."

"Very likely so," said Sir Condy; "but, Mr. Jason, if you have anything to say to me this morning about it, I'd be obliged to you to say it, for I had an indifferent night's rest last night, and wouldn't be sorry to sleep a little this morning."

"I have only three words to say, and those more of consequence to you, Sir Condy, than me. You are a little cool, I observe; but I hope you will not be offended at what I have brought here in my pocket," and he pulls out two long rolls, and showers down golden guineas upon the bed.

"What's this," said Sir Condy; "it's long since—" but his pride stops him.

"All these are your lawful property this minute, Sir Condy, if you please," said Jason.

"Not for nothing, I'm sure," said Sir Condy, and laughs a little. "Nothing for nothing, or I'm under a mistake with you, Jason."

"Oh, Sir Condy, we'll not be indulging ourselves in any unpleasant retrospects," says Jason; "it's my present intention to behave, as I'm sure you will, like a gentleman in this affair. Here's two hundred guineas, and a third I mean to add if you should think proper to make over to me all your right and title to those lands that you know of."

"I'll consider of it," said my master; and a great deal more, that I was tired listening to, was said by Jason, and all that, and the sight of the ready cash upon the bed, worked with his honour; and the short and the long of it was, Sir Condy gathered up the golden guineas, and tied them up in a handkerchief, and signed some paper Jason brought with him as usual, and there was an end of the business: Jason took himself away, and my master turned himself round and fell asleep again.

I soon found what had put Jason in such a hurry to conclude this business. The little gossoon we had sent off the day before with my master's compliments to Mount Juliet's Town, and to know how my lady did after her accident, was stopped early this morning, coming back with his answer through O'Shaughlin's Town, at Castle Rackrent, by my son Jason, and questioned of all he knew of my lady from the servant at Mount Juliet's Town; and the gossoon told him my Lady Rackrent was not expected to live over night; so Jason thought it high time to be moving to the Lodge, to make his bargain with my master about the jointure afore it should be too late, and afore the little gossoon should reach us with the news. My master was greatly vexed—that is, I may say, as much as ever I seen him—when he found how he had been taken in; but it was some comfort to have the ready cash for immediate consumption in the house, anyway.

And when Judy came up that evening, and brought the childer to see his honour, he unties the handkerchief, and—God bless him! whether it was little or much he had, 'twas all the same with him—he gives 'em all round guineas apiece.

"Hold up your head," says my shister to Judy, as Sir Condy was busy filling out a glass of punch for her eldest boy—"Hold up your head, Judy; for who knows but we may live to see you yet at the head of the Castle Rackrent estate?"

"Maybe so," says she, "but not the way you are thinking of."

I did not rightly understand which way Judy was looking when she made this speech till a while after.

"Why, Thady, you were telling me yesterday that Sir Condy had sold all entirely to Jason, and where then does all them guineas in the handkerchief come from?"

"They are the purchase-money of my lady's jointure," says I.

Judy looks a little bit puzzled at this. "A penny for your thoughts, Judy," says my shister; "hark, sure Sir Condy is drinking her health."

He was at the table in the room,[1] drinking with the exciseman and the gauger, who came up to see his honour, and we were standing over the fire in the kitchen.

"I don't much care is he drinking my health or not," says Judy; "and it is not Sir Condy I'm thinking of, with all your jokes, whatever he is of me."

"Sure you wouldn't refuse to be my Lady Rackrent, Judy, if you had the offer?" says I.

"But if I could do better!" says she.

"How better?" says I and my shister both at once.

"How better?" says she. "Why, what signifies it to be my Lady Rackrent and no castle? Sure what good is the car, and no horse to draw it?"

"And where will ye get the horse, Judy?" says I.

"Never mind that," says she; "maybe it is your own son Jason might find that."

"Jason!" says I; "don't be trusting to him, Judy. Sir Condy, as I have good reason to know, spoke well of you when Jason spoke very indifferently of you, Judy."

"No matter," says Judy; "it's often men speak the contrary just to what they think of us."

"And you the same way of them, no doubt," answered I. "Nay, don't be denying it, Judy, for I think the better of ye for it, and shouldn't be proud to call ye the daughter of a shister's son of mine, if I was to hear ye talk ungrateful, and anyway disrespectful of his honour."

[1] The room—the principal room in the house.

"What disrespect," says she, "to say I'd rather, if it was my luck, be the wife of another man?"

"You'll have no luck, mind my words, Judy," says I; and all I remembered about my poor master's goodness in tossing up for her afore he married at all came across me, and I had a choking in my throat that hindered me to say more.

"Better luck, anyhow, Thady," says she, "than to be like some folk, following the fortunes of them that have none left."

"Oh! King of Glory!" says I, "hear the pride and ungratitude of her, and he giving his last guineas but a minute ago to her childer, and she with the fine shawl on her he made her a present of but yesterday!"

"Oh, troth, Judy, you're wrong now," says my shister, looking at the shawl.

"And was not he wrong yesterday, then," says she, "to be telling me I was greatly altered, to affront me?"

"But, Judy," says I, "what is it brings you here then at all in the mind you are in; is it to make Jason think the better of you?"

"I'll tell you no more of my secrets, Thady," says she, "nor would have told you this much, had I taken you for such an unnatural fader as I find you are, not to wish your own son preferred to another."

"Oh, troth, you are wrong now, Thady," says my shister.

Well, I was never so put to it in my life: between these womens, and my son and my master, and all I felt and thought just now, I could not, upon my conscience, tell which was the wrong from the right. So I said not a word more, but was only glad his honour had not the luck to hear all Judy had been saying of him, for I reckoned it would have gone nigh to break his heart; not that I was of opinion he cared for her as much as she and my shister fancied, but the ungratitude of the whole from Judy might not plase him; and he could never stand the notion of not being well spoken of or beloved like behind his back. Fortunately for all parties concerned, he was so much elevated at this time, there was no danger of his understanding anything, even if it had reached his ears. There was a great horn at the Lodge, ever since my master and Captain Moneygawl was in together, that used to belong originally to the celebrated Sir Patrick, his ancestor; and his honour was fond often of telling the story that he learned from me when

149

a child, how Sir Patrick drank the full of this horn without stopping, and this was what no other man afore or since could without drawing breath. Now Sir Condy challenged the gauger, who seemed to think little of the horn, to swallow the contents, and had it filled to the brim with punch; and the gauger said it was what he could not do for nothing, but he'd hold Sir Condy a hundred guineas he'd do it.

"Done," says my master; "I'll lay you a hundred golden guineas to a tester[1] you don't."

"Done," says the gauger; and done and done's enough between two gentlemen. The gauger was cast, and my master won the bet, and thought he'd won a hundred guineas, but by the wording it was adjudged to be only a tester that was his due by the exciseman. It was all one to him; he was as well pleased, and I was glad to see him in such spirits again.

The gauger—bad luck to him!—was the man that next proposed to my master to try himself, could he take at a draught the contents of the great horn.

"Sir Patrick's horn!" said his honour; "hand it to me: I'll hold you your own bet over again I'll swallow it."

"Done," says the gauger; "I'll lay ye anything at all you do no such thing."

"A hundred guineas to sixpence I do," says he; "bring me the handkerchief." I was loth, knowing he meant the handkerchief with the gold in it, to bring it out in such company, and his honour not very able to reckon it. "Bring me the handkerchief, then, Thady," says he, and stamps with his foot; so with that I pulls it out of my greatcoat pocket, where I had put it for safety. Oh, how it grieved me to see the guineas counting upon the table, and they the last my master had! Says Sir Condy to me, "Your hand is steadier than mine to-night, old Thady, and that's a wonder; fill you the horn for me." And so, wishing his honour success, I did; but I filled it, little thinking of what would befall him. He swallows it down, and drops like one shot. We lifts him up, and he was speechless, and quite black in the face. We put him to bed,

[1] *Tester*: sixpence; from the French word *tête*, a head—a piece of silver stamped with a head, which in old French was called *un testion*, and which was about the value of an old English sixpence. "Tester" is used in Shakespeare.

and in a short time he wakened, raving with a fever on his brain. He was shocking either to see or hear.

"Judy! Judy! have you no touch of feeling? Won't you stay to help us nurse him?" says I to her, and she putting on her shawl to go out of the house.

"I'm frightened to see him," says she, "and wouldn't nor couldn't stay in it; and what use? He can't last till the morning." With that she ran off. There was none but my shister and myself left near him of all the many friends he had.

The fever came and went, and came and went, and lasted five days, and the sixth he was sensible for a few minutes, and said to me, knowing me very well, "I'm in a burning pain all withinside of me, Thady." I could not speak, but my shister asked him would he have this thing or t'other to do him good? "No," says he, "nothing will do me good no more," and he gave a terrible screech with the torture he was in; then again a minute's ease—"brought to this by drink," says he. "Where are all the friends?—where's Judy? Gone, hey? Ay, Sir Condy has been a fool all his days," said he; and there was the last word he spoke, and died. He had but a very poor funeral after all.

If you want to know any more, I'm not very well able to tell you; but my Lady Rackrent did not die, as was expected of her, but was only disfigured in the face ever after by the fall and bruises she got; and she and Jason, immediately after my poor master's death, set about going to law about that jointure; the memorandum not being on stamped paper, some say it is worth nothing, others again it may do; others say Jason won't have the lands at any rate; many wishes it so. For my part, I'm tired wishing for anything in this world, after all I've seen in it; but I'll say nothing—it would be a folly to be getting myself ill-will in my old age. Jason did not marry, nor think of marrying Judy, as I prophesied, and I am not sorry for it: who is? As for all I have here set down from memory and hearsay of the family, there's nothing but truth in it from beginning to end. That you may depend upon, for where's the use of telling lies about the things which everybody knows as well as I do?

The Editor could have readily made the catastrophe of Sir Condy's history more dramatic and more pathetic, if he thought it allowable to varnish the plain round tale of faithful Thady. He lays it before the English reader as a specimen of manners and characters which are perhaps unknown in England. Indeed, the domestic habits of no nation in Europe were less known to the English than those of their sister country, till within these few years.

Mr. Young's picture of Ireland, in his tour through that country, was the first faithful portrait of its inhabitants. All the features in the foregoing sketch were taken from the life, and they are characteristic of that mixture of quickness, simplicity, cunning, carelessness, dissipation, disinterestedness, shrewdness, and blunder, which, in different forms and with various success, has been brought upon the stage or delineated in novels.

It is a problem of difficult solution to determine whether a union will hasten or retard the amelioration of this country. The few gentlemen of education who now reside in this country will resort to England. They are few, but they are in nothing inferior to men of the same rank in Great Britain. The best that can happen will be the introduction of British manufacturers in their places.

Did the Warwickshire militia, who were chiefly artisans, teach the Irish to drink beer? or did they learn from the Irish to drink whisky?

GLOSSARY

Some friends, who have seen Thady's history since it has been printed, have suggested to the Editor, that many of the terms and idiomatic phrases, with which it abounds, could not be intelligible to the English reader without further explanation. The Editor has therefore furnished the following Glossary.

Page 91. Monday morning.—Thady begins his memoirs of the Rackrent Family by dating Monday morning, because no great undertaking can be auspiciously commenced in Ireland on any morning but Monday morning. "Oh, please God we live till Monday morning, we'll set the slater to mend the roof of the house. On Monday morning we'll fall to, and cut the turf. On Monday we'll see and begin mowing. On Monday morning, please your honour, we'll begin and dig the potatoes," etc.

All the intermediate days, between the making of such speeches and the ensuing Monday, are wasted: and when Monday morning comes, it is ten to one that the business is deferred to the next Monday morning. The Editor knew a gentleman, who, to counteract this prejudice, made his workmen and labourers begin all new pieces of work upon a Saturday.

Page 92. *Let alone the three kingdoms itself.*—*Let alone*, in this sentence, means *put out of consideration.* The phrase, *let alone*, which is now used as the imperative of a verb, may in time become a conjunction, and may exercise the ingenuity of some future etymologist. The celebrated Horne Tooke has proved most satisfactorily, that the conjunction *but* comes from the imperative of the Anglo-Saxon verb (*beoutan*) *to be out;* also, that *if* comes from *gif*, the imperative of the Anglo-Saxon verb which signifies *to give*, etc.

Page 94. *Whillaluh.*—Ullaloo, Gol, or lamentation over the dead—

> Magnoque ululante tumultu.—Virgil.

> Ululatibus omne
> Implevere nemus.—Ovid.

A full account of the Irish Gol, or Ullaloo, and of the Caoinan or Irish funeral song, with its first semichorus, second semichorus, full chorus of sighs and groans, together with the Irish words and music, may be found in the fourth volume of the *Transactions of the Royal Irish Academy.* For the advantage of lazy readers, who would rather read a page than walk a yard, and from compassion, not to say sympathy, with their infirmity, the Editor transcribes the following passages:

"The Irish have been always remarkable for their funeral lamentations; and this peculiarity has been noticed by almost every traveller who visited them; and it seems derived from their Celtic ancestors, the primæval inhabitants of this isle. . . .

"It has been affirmed of the Irish, that to cry was more natural to them than to any other nation, and at length the Irish cry became proverbial. . . .

"Cambrensis in the twelfth century says, the Irish then musically expressed their griefs; that is, they applied the musical art, in which they excelled all others, to the orderly celebration of funeral obsequies, by dividing the mourners into two bodies, each alternately singing their part, and the whole at times joining in full chorus. . . . The body of the deceased, dressed in grave clothes, and ornamented with flowers, was placed on a bier, or some elevated spot. The relations and keeners (*singing mourners*) ranged themselves in two divisions, one at the head, and the other at the feet of the corpse. The bards and croteries had before prepared the funeral Caoinan. The chief bard of the head chorus began by singing the first stanza, in a low, doleful tone, which was softly accompanied by the harp: at the conclusion, the foot semichorus began the lamentation, or Ullaloo, from the final note of the preceding stanza, in which they were answered by the head semichorus; then both united in one general chorus. The chorus of the first stanza being ended, the chief bard of the foot semichorus began the second Gol or lamentation, in which he was answered by that of the head; and then, as before, both united in the general full chorus. Thus alternately were the song and choruses performed during the night. The genealogy, rank, possessions, the virtues and vices of the dead were rehearsed, and a number of interrogations were addressed to the deceased; as, "Why did he die? If married, whether his wife was faithful to him, his sons dutiful, or good hunters or warriors? If a woman, whether her daughters were fair or chaste? If a young man, whether he had been crossed in love; or if the blue-eyed maids of Erin treated him with scorn?"

We are told, that formerly the feet (the metrical feet) of the Caoinan were much attended to; but on the decline of the Irish bards these feet were gradually neglected, and the Caoinan fell into a sort of slipshod metre amongst women. Each province had different Caoinans, or at least different imitations of the original. There was the Munster cry, the Ulster cry, etc. It became an extempore performance, and every set of keeners varied the melody according to their own fancy.

It is curious to observe how customs and ceremonies degenerate. The present Irish cry, or howl, cannot boast of such melody, nor is the funeral procession conducted with much dignity. The crowd of people who assemble at these funerals sometimes amounts to a thousand, often to four or five hundred. They gather as the bearers of the hearse proceed on their way, and when they pass through any village, or when they come near any houses, they begin to cry—Oh! Oh! Oh! Oh! Oh! Agh! Agh! raising their notes from the first *Oh!* to the last *Agh!* in a kind of mournful howl. This gives notice to the inhabitants of the village that a *funeral is passing*, and immediately they flock out to follow it. In the province of Munster it is a common thing for the women to follow a funeral, to join in the universal cry with all their might and main for some time, and then to turn and ask—"Arrah! who is it that's dead?—who is it we're crying for?" Even the poorest people have their own burying-places—that is, spots of ground in the churchyards where they say that their ancestors have been buried ever since the wars of Ireland; and if these burial-places are ten miles from the place where a man dies, his friends and neighbours take care to carry his corpse thither. Always one priest, often five or six priests, attend these funerals; each priest repeats a mass, for which he is paid, sometimes a shilling, sometimes half a crown, sometimes half a guinea, or a guinea, according to their circumstances, or, as they say, according to the *ability* of the deceased. After the burial of any very poor man, who has left a widow or children, the priest makes what is called a *collection* for the widow; he goes round to every person present, and each contributes sixpence or a shilling, or what they please. The reader will find in the note upon the word *Wake*, more particulars respecting the conclusion of the Irish funerals.

Certain old women, who cry particularly loud and well, are in great request, and, as a man said to the Editor, "Every one would wish and be proud to have such at his funeral, or at that of his friends." The lower Irish are wonderfully eager to attend the funerals of their friends and relations, and they make their relationships branch out to a great extent. The proof that a poor man has been well beloved during his life is his having a crowded funeral. To attend a neighbour's funeral is a cheap proof of humanity, but it does not, as some imagine, cost nothing. The time spent in attending funerals may be safely valued at half a million to the Irish nation; the Editor thinks that double that sum would not be too high an estimate. The habits of profligacy and drunkenness which are acquired at wakes are here put out of the question. When a labourer, a carpenter, or a smith, is not at his work, which frequently happens, ask where he is gone, and ten to one the answer is—"O, faith, please your honour, he couldn't do a stroke to-day, for he's gone to the funeral."

Even beggars, when they grow old, go about begging *for their own funerals*; that is, begging for money to buy a coffin, candles, pipes, and tobacco. For the use of the candles, pipes, and tobacco, see *Wake*.

Those who value customs in proportion to their antiquity, and nations in proportion to their adherence to ancient customs, will doubtless admire the Irish *Ullaloo*, and the Irish nation, for persevering in this usage from time immemorial. The Editor, however, has observed some alarming symptoms, which seem to prognosticate the declining taste for the Ullaloo in Ireland. In a comic theatrical entertainment, represented not long since on the Dublin stage, a chorus of old women was introduced, who set up the Irish howl round the relics of a physician, who is supposed to have fallen under the wooden sword of Harlequin. After the old women have continued their Ullaloo for a decent time, with all the necessary accompaniments of wringing their hands, wiping or rubbing their eyes with the corners of their gowns or aprons, etc., one of the mourners suddenly suspends her lamentable cries, and, turning to her neighbour, asks, "Arrah now, honey, who is it we're crying for?"

Page 94. The tenants were sent away without their whisky.—It is usual with some landlords to give their inferior tenants a glass of whisky when they pay their rents. Thady calls it *their* whisky; not that the whisky is actually the property of the tenants, but that it becomes their *right* after it has been often given to them. In this general mode of reasoning respecting *rights* the lower Irish are not singular, but they are peculiarly quick and tenacious in claiming these rights. "Last year your honour gave me some straw for the roof of my house and I expect your honour will be after doing the same this year." In this manner gifts are frequently turned into tributes. The high and low are not always dissimilar in their habits. It is said, that the Sublime Ottoman Porte is very apt to claim gifts as tributes: thus it is dangerous to send the Grand Seignor a fine horse on his birthday one year, lest on his next birthday he should expect a similar present, and should proceed to demonstrate the reasonableness of his expectations.

Page 95. He demeaned himself greatly—means, he lowered or disgraced himself much.

Page 95. Duty fowls, duty turkeys, and duty geese.—In many leases in Ireland, tenants were formerly bound to supply an inordinate quantity of poultry to their landlords. The Editor knew of thirty turkeys being reserved in one lease of a small farm.

Page 95. English tenants.—An English tenant does not mean a tenant who is an Englishman, but a tenant who pays his rent the day that it is due. It is a common prejudice in Ireland, amongst the poorer classes of people, to believe that all tenants in England pay their rents on the very day when they become due. An Irishman, when he goes to take a farm, if he wants to prove to his landlord that he is a substantial man, offers to become an *English tenant.* If a tenant disobliges his landlord by voting against him, or against his opinion, at an election, the tenant is immediately informed by the agent that he must become an *English tenant.* This threat does not imply that he is to change his language or his country, but that he must pay all the arrear of rent which he owes, and that he must thenceforward pay his rent on that day when it becomes due.

Page 96. Canting—does not mean talking or writing hypocritical nonsense, but selling substantially by auction.

Page 96. Duty work.—It was formerly common in Ireland to insert clauses in leases, binding tenants to furnish their landlords with labourers and horses for several days in the year. Much petty tyranny and oppression have resulted from this feudal custom. Whenever a poor man disobliged his landlord the agent sent to him for his duty work; and Thady does not exaggerate when he says, that the tenants were often called from their own work to do that of their landlord. Thus the very means of earning their rent were taken from them: whilst they were getting home their landlord's harvest, their own was often ruined, and yet their rents were expected to be paid as punctually as if their time had been at their own disposal. This appears the height of absurd injustice.

In Esthonia, amongst the poor Sclavonian race of peasant slaves, they pay tributes to their lords, not under the name of duty work, duty geese, duty turkeys, etc., but under the name of *righteousnesses*. The following ballad is a curious specimen of Esthonian poetry:—

> This is the cause that the country is ruined,
> And the straw of the thatch is eaten away,
> The gentry are come to live in the land—
> Chimneys between the village,
> And the proprietor upon the white floor!
> The sheep brings forth a lamb with a white forehead,
> This is paid to the lord for a *righteousness sheep*.
> The sow farrows pigs,
> They go to the spit of the lord.
> The hen lays eggs,
> They go into the lord's frying-pan.
> The cow drops a male calf,
> That goes into the lord's herd as a bull.
> The mare foals a horse foal,
> That must be for my lord's nag.
> The boor's wife has sons,
> They must go to look after my lord's poultry.

Page 97. *Out of forty-nine suits which he had, he never lost one but seventeen.*—Thady's language in this instance is a specimen of a mode of rhetoric common in Ireland. An astonishing assertion is made in the beginning of a sentence, which ceases to be in the least surprising, when you hear the qualifying explanation that follows. Thus a man who is in the last stage of staggering drunkenness will, if he can articulate, swear to you—"Upon his conscience now, and may he never stir from the spot alive if he is telling a lie, upon his conscience he has not tasted a drop of anything, good or bad, since morning at-all-at-all, but half a pint of whisky, please your honour."

Page 97. *Fairy-mounts—Barrows*. It is said that these high mounts were of great service to the natives of Ireland when Ireland was invaded by the Danes. Watch was always kept on them, and upon the approach of an enemy a fire was lighted to give notice to the next watch, and thus the intelligence was quickly communicated through the country. *Some years ago, the common people believed that these barrows were inhabited by fairies, or, as they called them, by the good people.* "Oh, troth, to the best of my belief, and to the best of my judgment and opinion," said an elderly man to the Editor, "it was only the old people that had nothing to do, and got together, and were telling stories about them fairies, but to the best of my judgment there's nothing in it. Only this I heard myself not very many years back from a decent kind of a man, a grazier, that, as he was coming just fair and easy (*quietly*) from the fair, with some cattle and sheep, that he had not sold, just at the church of——, at an angle of the road like, he was met by a good-looking man, who asked him where he was going? And he answered, 'Oh, far enough, I must be going all night.' 'No, that you mustn't nor won't (says the man), you'll sleep with me the night, and you'll want for nothing, nor your cattle nor sheep neither, nor your *beast* (horse); so come along with me.' With that the grazier *lit* (*alighted*) from his horse, and it was dark night; but presently he finds himself, he does not know in the wide world how, in a fine house, and plenty of everything to eat and drink; nothing at all wanting that he could wish for or think of. And he does not *mind* (*recollect* or *know*) how at last he falls asleep; and in the morning he finds himself lying, not in ever a bed or a house at all, but just in the angle of the road where first he met the strange man: there he finds himself lying on his back on the grass, and all his sheep feeding as quiet as ever all round about him, and his horse the same way, and the bridle of the beast over his wrist. And I asked him what he thought of it; and from first to last he could think of nothing, but for certain sure it must have been the fairies that entertained him so well. For there was no house to see anywhere nigh hand, or any building, or barn, or place at all, but only the church and the *mote* (*barrow*). There's another odd thing enough that they tell about this same church, that if any person's corpse, that had not a right to be buried in that churchyard, went to be burying there in it, no, not all the men, women, or childer in all Ireland could get the corpse anyway into the churchyard; but as they would be trying to go into the churchyard, their feet would seem to be going backwards instead of forwards; ay, continually backwards the whole funeral would seem to go; and they would never set foot with the corpse in the churchyard. Now they say that it is the fairies do all this; but it is my opinion it is all idle talk, and people are after being wiser now."

The country people in Ireland certainly *had* great admiration mixed with reverence, if not dread, of fairies. They believed that beneath these fairy-mounts were spacious subterraneous palaces, inhabited by *the good people*, who must not on any account be disturbed. When the wind raises a little eddy of dust upon the road, the poor people believe that it is raised by the fairies, that it is a sign that they are journeying from one of the fairies' mounts to another, and they say to the fairies, or to the dust as it passes, "God speed ye, gentlemen; God speed ye." This averts any evil that *the good people* might be inclined to do them. There are innumerable stories told of the friendly and unfriendly feats of these busy fairies; some of these tales are ludicrous, and some romantic enough for poetry. It is a pity that poets should lose such convenient, though diminutive machinery. By the bye, Parnell, who showed himself so deeply "skilled in faerie lore," was an Irishman; and though he has presented his fairies to the world in the ancient English dress of "Britain's isle, and Arthur's days," it is probable that his first acquaintance with them began in his native country.

Some remote origin for the most superstitious or romantic popular illusions or vulgar errors may often be discovered. In Ireland, the old churches and churchyards have been usually fixed upon as the scenes of wonders. Now antiquaries tell us, that near the ancient churches in that kingdom caves of various constructions have from time to time been discovered, which were formerly used as granaries or magazines by the ancient inhabitants, and as places to which they retreated in time of danger. There is (p. 84 of the R. I. A. *Transactions* for 1789) a particular account of a number of these artificial caves at the west end of the church of Killossy, in the county of Kildare. Under a rising ground, in a dry sandy soil, these subterraneous dwellings were found: they have pediment roofs, and they communicate with each other by small apertures. In the Brehon laws these are mentioned, and there are fines inflicted by those laws upon persons who steal from the subterraneous granaries. All these things show that there was a real foundation for the stories which were told of the appearance of lights, and of the sounds of voices, near these places. The persons who had property concealed there, very willingly countenanced every wonderful relation that tended to make these places objects of sacred awe or superstitious terror.

Page 98. *Weed ashes.*—By ancient usage in Ireland, all the weeds on a farm belonged to the farmer's wife, or to the wife of the squire who holds the ground in his own hands. The great demand for alkaline salts in bleaching rendered these ashes no inconsiderable perquisite.

Page 98. *Sealing money.*—Formerly it was the custom in Ireland for tenants to give the squire's lady from two to fifty guineas as a perquisite upon the sealing of their leases. The Editor not very long since knew of a baronet's lady accepting fifty guineas as sealing money, upon closing a bargain for a considerable farm.

Page 98. *Sir Murtagh grew mad*—Sir Murtagh grew angry.

Page 98. *The whole kitchen was out on the stairs*—means that all the inhabitants of the kitchen came out of the kitchen, and stood upon the stairs. These, and similar expressions, show how much the Irish are disposed to metaphor and amplification.

Page 100. *Fining down the year's rent.*—When an Irish gentleman, like Sir Kit Rackrent, has lived beyond his income, and finds himself distressed for ready money, tenants obligingly offer to take his land at a rent far below the value, and to pay him a small sum of money in hand, which they call fining down the yearly rent. The temptation of this ready cash often blinds the landlord to his future interest.

Page 100. *Driver.*—A man who is employed to drive tenants for rent; that is, to drive the cattle belonging to tenants to pound. The office of driver is by no means a sinecure.

Page 101. *I thought to make him a priest.*—It was customary amongst those of Thady's rank in Ireland, whenever they could get a little money, to send their sons abroad to St. Omer's, or to Spain, to be educated as priests. Now they are educated at Maynooth. The Editor has lately known a young lad, who began by being a post-boy, afterwards turn into a carpenter, then quit his plane and work-bench to study his *Humanities,* as he said, at the college of Maynooth; but after he had gone through his course of Humanities, he determined to be a soldier instead of a priest.

Page 103. *Flam.*—Short for flambeau.

Page 104. *Barrack-room.*—Formerly it was customary, in gentlemen's houses in Ireland, to fit up one large bedchamber with a number of beds for the reception of occasional visitors. These rooms were called Barrack-rooms.

Page 104. *An innocent*—in Ireland, means a simpleton, an idiot.

Page 110. *The Curragh*—is the Newmarket of Ireland.

Page 110. *The cant.*—The auction.

Page 113. *And so should cut him off for ever by levying a fine, and suffering a recovery to dock the entail.*—The English reader may perhaps be surprised at the extent of Thady's legal knowledge, and at the fluency with which he pours forth law-terms; but almost every poor man in Ireland, be he farmer, weaver, shopkeeper, or steward, is, besides his other occupations, occasionally a lawyer. The nature of processes, ejectments, custodiams, injunctions, replevins, etc., is perfectly known to them, and the terms as familiar to them as to any attorney. They all love law. It is a kind of lottery, in which every man, staking his own wit or cunning against his neighbour's property, feels that he has little to lose, and much to gain.

"I'll have the law of you, so I will!" is the saying of an Englishman who expects justice. "I'll have you before his honour," is the threat of an Irishman who hopes for partiality. Miserable is the life of a justice of the peace in Ireland the day after a fair, especially if he resides near a small town. The multitude of the *kilt* (*kilt* does not mean *killed*, but hurt) and wounded who come before his honour with black eyes or bloody heads is astonishing: but more astonishing is the number of those who, though they are scarcely able by daily labour to procure daily food, will nevertheless, without the least reluctance, waste six or seven hours of the day lounging in the yard or court of a justice of the peace, waiting to make some complaint about— nothing. It is impossible to convince them that *time is money*. They do not set any value upon their own time, and they think that others estimate theirs at less than nothing. Hence they make no scruple of telling a justice of the peace a story of an hour long about a *tester* (sixpence); and if he grows impatient, they attribute it to some secret prejudice which he entertains against them.

Their method is to get a story completely by heart, and to tell it, as they call it, *out of the face*, that is, from the beginning to the end, without interruption.

"Well, my good friend, I have seen you lounging about these three hours in the yard; what is your business?"

"Please your honour, it is that I want to speak one word to your honour."

"Speak then, but be quick. What is the matter?"

"The matter, please your honour, is nothing at-all-at-all, only just about the grazing of a horse, please your honour, that this man here sold me at the fair of Gurtishannon last Shrove fair, which lay down three times with myself, please your honour, and *kilt* me; not to be telling your honour of how, no later back than yesterday night, he lay down in the house there within, and all the childer standing round, and it was God's mercy he did not fall a-top of them, or into the fire to burn himself. So please your honour, to-day I took him back to this man, which owned him, and after a great deal to do, I got the mare again I *swopped* (exchanged) him for; but he won't pay the grazing of the horse for the time I had him, though he promised to pay the grazing in case the horse didn't answer; and he never did a day's work, good or bad, please your honour, all the time he was with me, and I had the doctor to him five times anyhow. And so, please your honour, it is what I expect your honour will stand my friend, for I'd sooner come to your honour for justice than to any other in all Ireland. And so I brought him here before your honour, and expect your honour will make him pay me the grazing, or tell me, can I process him for it at the next assizes, please your honour?"

The defendant now turning a quid of tobacco with his tongue into some secret cavern in his mouth, begins his defence with—

"Please your honour, under favour, and saving your honour's presence, there's not a word of truth in all this man has been saying from beginning to end, upon my conscience, and I wouldn't for the value of the horse itself, grazing and all, be after telling your honour a lie. For, please your honour, I have a dependence upon your honour that you'll do me justice, and not be listening to him or the like of him. Please your honour, it's what he has brought me before your honour, because he had a spite against me about some oats I sold your honour, which he was jealous of, and a shawl his wife got at my shister's shop there without, and never paid for; so I offered to set the shawl against the grazing, and give him a receipt in full of all demands, but he wouldn't out of spite, please your honour; so he brought me before your honour, expecting your honour was mad with me for cutting down the tree in the horse park, which was none of my doing, please your honour—ill-luck to them that went and belied me to your honour behind my back! So if your honour is pleasing, I'll tell you the whole truth about the horse that he swopped against my mare out of the face. Last Shrove fair I met this man, Jemmy Duffy, please your honour, just at the corner of the road, where the bridge is broken down, that your honour is to have the presentment for this year—long life to you for it! And he was at that time coming from the fair of Gurtishannon, and I the same way. 'How are you, Jemmy?' says I. 'Very well, I thank ye kindly, Bryan,' says he; 'shall we turn back to Paddy Salmon's and take a naggin of whisky to our better acquaintance?' 'I don't care if I did, Jemmy,' says I; 'only it is what I can't take the whisky, because I'm under an oath against it for a month.' Ever since, please your honour, the day your honour met me on the road, and observed to me I could hardly stand, I had taken so much; though upon my conscience your honour wronged me greatly that same time—ill-luck to them that belied me behind my back to your honour! Well, please your honour, as I was telling you, as he was taking the whisky, and we talking of one thing or t'other, he makes me an offer to swop his mare that he couldn't sell at the fair of Gurtishannon, because nobody would be troubled with the beast, please your honour, against my horse, and to oblige him I took the mare—sorrow take her! and him along with her! She kicked me a new car, that was worth three pounds ten, to tatters the first time I ever put her into it, and I expect your honour will make him pay me the price of the car, anyhow, before I pay the grazing, which I've no right to pay at-all-at-all, only to oblige him. But I leave it all to your honour; and the whole grazing he ought to be charging for the beast is but two and eightpence halfpenny, anyhow, please your honour. So I'll abide by what your honour says, good or bad. I'll leave it all to your honour."

I'll leave it all to your honour—literally means, I'll leave all the trouble to your honour.

The Editor knew a justice of the peace in Ireland who had such a dread of having it all left to his honour, that he frequently gave the complainants the sum about which they were disputing, to make peace between them, and to get rid of the trouble of hearing their stories out of the face. But he was soon cured of this method of buying off disputes, by the increasing multitude of those who, out of pure regard to his honour, came "to get justice from him, because they would sooner come before him than before any man in all Ireland."

Page 123. *A raking pot of tea.*—We should observe, this custom has long since been banished from the higher orders of Irish gentry. The mysteries of a raking pot of tea, like those of the Bona Dea, are supposed to be sacred to females; but now and then it has happened that some of the male species, who were either more audacious, or more highly favoured than the rest of their sex, have been admitted by stealth to these orgies. The time when the festive ceremony begins varies according to circumstances, but it is never earlier than twelve o'clock at night; the joys of a raking pot of tea depending on its being made in secret, and at an unseasonable hour. After a ball, when the more discreet part of the company has departed to rest, a few chosen female spirits, who have footed it till they can foot it no longer, and till the sleepy notes expire under the slurring hand of the musician, retire to a bedchamber, call the favourite maid, who alone is admitted, bid her *put down the kettle*, lock the door, and amidst as much giggling and scrambling as possible, they get round a tea-table, on which all manner of things are huddled together. Then begin mutual railleries and mutual confidences amongst the young ladies, and the faint scream and the loud laugh is heard, and the romping for letters and pocket-books begins, and gentlemen are called by their surnames, or by the general name of fellows! pleasant fellows! charming fellows! odious fellows! abominable fellows! and then all prudish decorums are forgotten, and then we might be convinced how much the satirical poet was mistaken when he said—

There is no woman where there's no reserve.

The merit of the original idea of a raking pot of tea evidently belongs to the washerwoman and the laundry-maid. But why should not we have *Low life above stairs* as well as *High life below stairs*?

Page 124. *We gained the day by this piece of honesty.*—In a dispute which occurred some years ago in Ireland, between Mr. E. and Mr. M., about the boundaries of a farm, an old tenant of Mr. M's cut a *sod* from Mr. M.'s land, and inserted it in a spot prepared for its reception in Mr. E.'s land; so nicely was it inserted, that no eye could detect the junction of the grass. The old man, who was to give his evidence as to the property, stood upon the inserted sod when the *viewers* came, and swore that the ground he then stood upon belonged to his landlord, Mr. M.

The Editor had flattered himself that the ingenious contrivance which Thady records, and the similar subterfuge of this old Irishman, in the dispute concerning boundaries, were instances of 'cuteness unparalleled in all but Irish story: an English friend, however, has just mortified the Editor's national vanity by an account of the following custom, which prevails in part of Shropshire. It is discreditable for women to appear abroad after the birth of their children till they have been *churched*. To avoid this reproach, and at the same time to enjoy the pleasure of gadding, whenever a woman goes abroad before she has been to church, she takes a tile from the roof of her house, and puts it upon her head: wearing this panoply all the time she pays her visits, her conscience is perfectly at ease; for she can afterwards safely declare to the clergyman, that she "has never been from under her own roof till she came to be churched."

Page 126. *Carton, and half-carton.*—Thady means cartron, and half-cartron. "According to the old record in the black book of Dublin, a *cantred* is said to contain 30 *villatas terras*, which are also called *quarters* of land (quarterons, *cartrons*); every one of which quarters must contain so much ground as will pasture 400 cows, and 17 plough-lands. A knight's fee was composed of 8 hydes, which amount to 160 acres, and that is generally deemed about a *plough-land*."

The Editor was favoured by a learned friend with the above extract, from a MS. of Lord Totness's in the Lambeth library.

Page 141. *Wake.*—A wake in England means a festival held upon the anniversary of the saint of the parish. At these wakes, rustic games, rustic conviviality, and rustic courtship, are pursued with all the ardour and all the appetite which accompany such pleasures as occur but seldom. In Ireland a wake is a midnight meeting, held professedly for the indulgence of holy sorrow, but usually it is converted into orgies of unholy joy. When an Irish man or woman of the lower order dies, the straw which composed the bed, whether it has been contained in a bag to form a mattress, or simply spread upon the earthen floor, is immediately taken out of the house, and burned before the cabin door, the family at the same time setting up the death howl. The ears and eyes of the neighbours being thus alarmed, they flock to the house of the deceased, and by their vociferous sympathy excite and at the same time soothe the sorrows of the family.

It is curious to observe how good and bad are mingled in human institutions. In countries which were thinly inhabited, this custom prevented private attempts against the lives of individuals, and formed a kind of coroner's inquest upon the body which had recently expired, and burning the straw upon which the sick man lay became a simple preservative against infection. At night the dead body is waked, that is to say, all the friends and neighbours of the deceased collect in a barn or stable, where the corpse is laid upon some boards, or an unhinged door, supported upon stools, the face exposed, the rest of the body covered with a white sheet. Round the body are stuck in brass candlesticks, which have been borrowed perhaps at five miles' distance, as many candles as the poor person can beg or borrow, observing always to have an odd number. Pipes and tobacco are first distributed, and then, according to the *ability* of the deceased, cakes and ale, and sometimes whisky, are *dealt* to the company—

> Deal on, deal on, my merry men all,
> Deal on your cakes and your wine,
> For whatever is dealt at her funeral to-day
> Shall be dealt to-morrow at mine.

After a fit of universal sorrow, and the comfort of a universal dram, the scandal of the neighbourhood, as in higher circles, occupies the company. The young lads and lasses romp with one another, and when the fathers and mothers are at last overcome with sleep and whisky (*vino et somno*), the youth become more enterprising, and are frequently successful. It is said that more matches are made at wakes than at weddings.

Page 143. *Kilt.*—This word frequently occurs in the preceding pages, where it means not *killed*, but much *hurt*. In Ireland, not only cowards, but the brave "die many times before their death."—There *killing is no murder*.

The Room in the Dragon Volant

1872

JOSEPH SHERIDAN LE FANU

JOSEPH SHERIDAN LE FANU was born in 1814, his father was a
dean in the Protestant Irish church whose mother was a sister
of Sheridan from whom he inherited the Sheridan family por-
traits. He was educated at Trinity College, Dublin and as an
undergraduate began to write for the Dublin University Magazine where all his novels appeared and which eventually became
his property. In 1839 he was called to the Bar but in the same
year he acquired a Dublin evening paper and gave up legal practice. Moderately successful as a journalist, editor and newspaper proprietor, it was not until 1863 that he became famous
as a writer of supernatural romances of which The House in
the Churchyard, Wylder's Hand, Checkmate and Uncle Silas
are the best known. In 1872, he published the volume of
stories In a Glass Darkly which includes that admirable ghost
story Green Tea, the forerunner of Freud's Id and Stevenson's
Doctor Jekyll and from which The Room in the Dragon
Volant is also taken. He died the following year.

Le Fanu's early novels and ballads were in the rollicking
style of Lover and Charles Lever or clearly influenced by Mrs.
Radcliffe. He did his best work in the last ten years of his life
when he discovered his own principal virtues, an understanding of the supernatural from a Swedenborgian basis and a
morbid sense of atmosphere. V. S. Pritchett writes of his style,
"Vigilance is a word that recurs in these stories and that defines
Le Fanu's cooler and finer mood. He had the gift of brevity,
the talent for the poetic sharpness and discipline of the short
tale. Where he knows the bounds of what he is writing, he has
an infallible eye for the essential things, the power of unim-
peachable definition. Faced by the uncanny subject, he rises
with the equanimity of the dompteur; he invites, he caresses,
he laughs, he cracks the whip. It is a sinister but gracious per-

165

formance." His books are beautifully constructed, as can be seen by a second reading of this story.

Le Fanu belongs so completely to the provincial atmosphere of Dublin that there is nothing Victorian in his work, it is pure Eighteenth Century in feeling, "A delicious, clean unfusty style that diffuses a pale amber light like bog-water." He is spared the bright self-consciousness of those who set out to make our flesh creep and who know all the tricks. In fact there is something wholesome, well-made and pleasing about The Room in the Dragon Volant, a fastidious gusto—as if he were saying (like the author of Moon Fleet, that other admirable short novel about the past), "Never mind about the thrills, the contraptions or even the horrors of catalepsy—that was the time!"

In appearance, Le Fanu was handsome and strong featured, with deep-set eyes and an air of melancholy, "the beau ideal of an Irish wit and scholar of the old school." After the death of his wife in 1858 he became more and more of a recluse and was nicknamed 'The Invisible Prince' for he seldom left his great Eighteenth-Century house in Merrion Square. Here according to his recent biographer Mr. Nelson Browne, "he wrote mostly in those chill silent hours between midnight and the first light of dawn, his imagination stimulated by the stillness of the great house, a stillness broken only by the faint crepitations of the dying fire and the mysterious knocks and cracks proceeding from the ponderous furniture of his bed-chamber. Propped up in bed, a copybook on his knee, he wrote by the light of the two candles burning on a side table. One candle would be extinguished while he dozed for an hour or so, and when he awoke about two o'clock in the morning he would make himself a strong cup of tea and resume work for a couple of hours. . . .

"For many years he had slept in the affliction of terrible dreams and nightmares of which one recurred with menacing persistency—in this vision he beheld one of those menacing houses he had so often described in his romances—a mansion so ruinous and tottering that it looked as if it might at any moment fall and bury the dreamer, helpless with terror. This dream was so terrifying that he often cried out in his sleep. He had mentioned the trouble to his doctor, who was treating him for a form of heart disease. When the end came the doctor looked into the terror-stricken eyes of the dead man, and said: 'I feared this—that house fell at last.' "

The Room in the Dragon Volant

JOSEPH SHERIDAN LE FANU

Prologue

THE CURIOUS CASE which I am about to place before you, is referred to, very pointedly, and more than once, in the extraordinary Essay upon the drugs of the Dark and the Middle Ages, from the pen of Doctor Hesselius.

This Essay he entitles *Mortis Imago*, and he, therein, discusses the *Vinum letiferum*, the *Beatifica*, the *Somnus Angelorum*, the *Hypnus Sagarum*, the *Aqua Thessalliæ*, and about twenty other infusions and distillations, well known to the sages of eight hundred years ago, and two of which are still, he alleges, known to the fraternity of thieves, and, among them, as police-office inquiries sometimes disclose to this day, in practical use.

The Essay, *Mortis Imago*, will occupy as nearly as I can, at present, calculate, two volumes, the ninth and tenth, of the collected papers of Doctor Martin Hesselius.

This Essay, I may remark, in conclusion, is very curiously enriched by citations, in great abundance, from mediæval verse and prose romance, some of the most valuable of which, strange to say, are Egyptian.

I have selected this particular statement from among many cases equally striking, but hardly, I think, so effective as mere narratives, in this irregular form of publication, it is simply as a story that I present it.

Chapter I

On the Road

IN THE EVENTFUL year, 1815, I was exactly three-and-twenty, and had just succeeded to a very large sum in consols, and other securities. The first fall of Napoleon had thrown the continent open to English excursionists, anxious, let us suppose, to improve their minds by foreign travel; and I—the slight check of the "hundred days" removed, by the genius of Wellington, on the field of Waterloo—was now added to the philosophic throng.

I was posting up to Paris from Bruxelles, following, I presume, the route that the allied army had pursued but a few weeks before —more carriages than you could believe were pursuing the same line. You could not look back or forward, without seeing into far perspective the clouds of dust which marked the line of the long series of vehicles. We were, perpetually, passing relays of return-horses, on their way, jaded and dusty, to the inns from which they had been taken. They were arduous times for those patient public servants. The whole world seemed posting up to Paris.

I ought to have noted it more particularly, but my head was so full of Paris and the future, that I passed the intervening scenery with little patience and less attention; I think, however, that it was about four miles to the frontier side of a rather picturesque little town, the name of which, as of many more important places through which I posted in my hurried journey, I forget, and about two hours before sunset, that we came up with a carriage in distress.

It was not quite an upset. But the two leaders were lying flat. The booted postillions had got down, and two servants who seemed very much at sea in such matters, were by way of assisting them. A pretty little bonnet and head were popped out of the window of the carriage in distress. Its *tournure*, and that of the shoulders that also appeared for a moment, was captivating: I resolved to play the part of a good Samaritan; stopped my chaise, jumped out, and with my servant lent a very willing hand in the emergency. Alas! the lady with the pretty bonnet, wore a very thick, black veil. I could see nothing but the pattern of the Bruxelles lace, as she drew back.

A lean old gentleman, almost at the same time, stuck his head out of the window. An invalid he seemed, for although the day was hot, he wore a black muffler which came up to his ears and nose, quite covering the lower part of his face, an arrangement which he disturbed by pulling it down for a moment, and poured forth a torrent of French thanks, as he uncovered his black wig, and gesticulated with grateful animation.

One of my very few accomplishments besides boxing, which was cultivated by all Englishmen at that time, was French; and I replied, I hope and believe, grammatically. Many bows being exchanged, the old gentleman's head went in again, and the demure, pretty little bonnet once more appeared.

The lady must have heard me speak to my servant, for she framed her little speech in such pretty, broken English, and in a voice so sweet, that I more than ever cursed the black veil that baulked my romantic curiosity.

The arms that were emblazoned on the panel were peculiar; I remember especially, one device, it was the figure of a stork, painted in carmine, upon what the heralds call a "field or." The bird was standing upon one leg, and in the other claw held a stone. This is, I believe, the emblem of vigilance. Its oddity struck me, and remained impressed upon my memory. There were supporters besides, but I forget what they were.

The courtly manners of these people, the style of their servants, the elegance of their travelling carriage, and the supporters to their arms, satisfied me that they were noble.

The lady, you may be sure, was not the less interesting on that account. What a fascination a title exercises upon the imagination! I do not mean on that of snobs or moral flunkies. Superiority of rank is a powerful and genuine influence in love. The idea of superior refinement is associated with it. The careless notice of the squire tells more upon the heart of the pretty milkmaid, than years of honest Dobbin's manly devotion, and so on and up. It is an unjust world!

But in this case there was something more. I was conscious of being good looking. I really believe I was; and there could be no mistake about my being nearly six feet high. Why need this lady have thanked me? Had not her husband, for such I assumed him to be, thanked me quite enough, and for both? I was instinctively aware that the lady was looking on me with no unwilling eyes; and, through her veil, I felt the power of her gaze.

She was now rolling away, with a train of dust behind her wheels, in the golden sunlight, and a wise young gentleman followed her with ardent eyes, and sighed profoundly as the distance increased.

I told the postillions on no account to pass the carriage, but to keep it steadily in view, and to pull up at whatever posting-house it should stop at. We were soon in the little town, and the carriage we followed drew up at the Belle Etoile, a comfortable old inn. They got out of the carriage and entered the house.

At a leisurely pace we followed. I got down, and mounted the steps listlessly, like a man quite apathetic and careless.

Audacious as I was, I did not care to inquire in what room I should find them. I peeped into the apartment to my right, and then into that on my left. My people were not there.

I ascended the stairs. A drawing-room door stood open. I entered with the most innocent air in the world. It was a spacious room, and, beside myself, contained but one living figure—a very pretty and lady-like one. There was the very bonnet with which I had fallen in love. The lady stood with her back towards me. I could not tell whether the envious veil was raised; she was reading a letter.

I stood for a minute in fixed attention, gazing upon her, in the vague hope that she might turn about, and give me an opportunity of seeing her features. She did not; but with a step or two she placed herself before a little cabriole-table, which stood against the wall, from which rose a tall mirror, in a tarnished frame.

I might, indeed, have mistaken it for a picture; for it now reflected a half-length portrait of a singularly beautiful woman.

She was looking down upon a letter which she held in her slender fingers, and in which she seemed absorbed.

The face was oval, melancholy, sweet. It had in it, nevertheless, a faint and undefinably sensual quality also. Nothing could exceed the delicacy of its features, or the brilliancy of its tints. The eyes, indeed, were lowered, so that I could not see their colour; nothing but their long lashes, and delicate eyebrows. She continued reading. She must have been deeply interested; I never saw a living form so motionless—I gazed on a tinted statue.

Being at that time blessed with long and keen vision, I saw this beautiful face with perfect distinctness. I saw even the blue veins that traced their wanderings on the whiteness of her full throat.

I ought to have retreated as noiselessly as I came in, before my presence was detected. But I was too much interested to move from the spot, for a few moments longer; and while they were passing, she raised her eyes. Those eyes were large, and of that hue which modern poets term "violet."

These splendid melancholy eyes were turned upon me from the glass, with a haughty stare, and hastily the lady lowered her black veil, and turned about.

I fancied that she hoped I had not seen her. I was watching every look and movement, the minutest, with an attention as intense as if an ordeal involving my life depended on them.

Chapter II

The Inn-Yard of the Belle Etoile

THE FACE WAS, indeed, one to fall in love with at first sight. Those sentiments that take such sudden possession of young men were now dominating my curiosity. My audacity faltered before her; and I felt that my presence in this room was probably an impertinence. This point she quickly settled, for the same very sweet voice I had heard before, now said coldly, and this time in French, "Monsieur cannot be aware that this apartment is not public." I bowed very low, faltered some apologies, and backed to the door.

I suppose I looked penitent and embarrassed. I certainly felt so; for the lady said, by way it seemed of softening matters, "I am happy, however, to have an opportunity of again thanking Monsieur for the assistance, so prompt and effectual, which he had the goodness to render us to-day."

It was more the altered tone in which it was spoken, than the speech itself that encouraged me. It was also true that she need not have recognised me; and even if she had, she certainly was not obliged to thank me over again.

All this was indescribably flattering, and all the more so that it followed so quickly on her slight reproof.

The tone in which she spoke had become low and timid, and I observed that she turned her head quickly towards a second door of the room, I fancied that the gentleman in the black wig, a jealous husband, perhaps, might reappear through it. Almost at the same moment, a voice at once reedy and nasal, was heard snarling some directions to a servant, and evidently approaching. It was the voice that had thanked me so profusely, from the carriage windows, about an hour before.

"Monsieur will have the goodness to retire," said the lady, in a tone that resembled entreaty, at the same time gently waving her hand towards the door through which I had entered. Bowing again very low, I stepped back, and closed the door.

I ran down the stairs, very much elated. I saw the host of the Belle Etoile which, as I said, was the sign and designation of my inn.

I described the apartment I had just quitted, said I liked it, and asked whether I could have it.

He was extremely troubled, but that apartment and the two adjoining rooms were engaged—

"By whom?"

"People of distinction."

"But who are they? They must have names, or titles."

"Undoubtedly, Monsieur, but such a stream is rolling into Paris, that we have ceased to inquire the names or titles of our guests— we designate them simply by the rooms they occupy."

"What stay do they make?"

"Even that, Monsieur, I cannot answer. It does not interest us. Our rooms, while this continues, can never be, for a moment, disengaged."

"I should have liked those rooms so much! Is one of them a sleeping apartment?"

"Yes, sir, and Monsieur will observe that people do not usually engage bedrooms, unless they mean to stay the night."

"Well, I can, I suppose, have some rooms, any, I don't care in what part of the house?"

"Certainly, Monsieur can have two apartments. They are the last at present disengaged."

I took them instantly.

It was plain these people meant to make a stay here; at least they would not go till morning. I began to feel that I was all but engaged in an adventure.

I took possession of my rooms, and looked out of the window, which I found commanded the inn-yard. Many horses were being liberated from the traces, hot and weary, and others fresh from the stables, being put to. A great many vehicles—some private carriages, others, like mine, of that public class, which is equivalent to our old English post-chaise, were standing on the pavement, waiting their turn for relays. Fussy servants were to-ing and fro-ing, and idle ones lounging or laughing, and the scene, on the whole, was animated and amusing.

Among these objects, I thought I recognised the travelling carriage, and one of the servants of the "persons of distinction" about whom I was, just then, so profoundly interested.

I therefore ran down the stairs, made my way to the back door; and so, behold me, in a moment, upon the uneven pavement, among all these sights and sounds which in such a place attend upon a period of extraordinary crush and traffic.

By this time the sun was near its setting, and threw its golden beams on the red brick chimneys of the offices, and made the two barrels, that figured as pigeon-houses, on the tops of poles, look as if they were on fire. Everything in this light becomes picturesque; and things interest us which, in the sober grey of morning, are dull enough.

After a little search, I lighted upon the very carriage, of which I was in quest. A servant was locking one of the doors, for it was made with the security of lock and key. I paused near, looking at the panel of the door.

"A very pretty device that red stork!" I observed, pointing to the shield on the door, "and no doubt indicates a distinguished family?"

The servant looked at me, for a moment, as he placed the little key in his pocket, and said with a slightly sarcastic bow and smile, "Monsieur is at liberty to conjecture."

Nothing daunted, I forthwith administered that laxative which, on occasion, acts so happily upon the tongue—I mean a "tip."

The servant looked at the Napoleon in his hand, and then, in my face, with a sincere expression of surprise.

"Monsieur is very generous!"

"Not worth mentioning—who are the lady and gentleman who came here, in this carriage, and whom, you may remember, I and my servant assisted to-day in an emergency, when their horses had come to the ground?"

"They are the Count, and the young lady we call the Countess—but I know not, she may be his daughter."

"Can you tell me where they live?"

"Upon my honour, Monsieur, I am unable—I know not."

"Not know where your master lives! Surely you know something more about him than his name?"

"Nothing worth relating, Monsieur; in fact, I was hired in Bruxelles, on the very day they started. Monsieur Picard, my fellow-servant, Monsieur the Comte's gentleman, he has been years in his service and knows everything; but he never speaks except to communicate an order. From him I have learned nothing. We are going to Paris, however, and there I shall speedily pick up all about them. At present I am as ignorant of all that as Monsieur himself."

"And where is Monsieur Picard?"

"He has gone to the cutler's to get his razors set. But I do not think he will tell anything."

This was a poor harvest for my golden sowing. The man, I think, spoke truth, and would honestly have betrayed the secrets of the family, if he had possessed any. I took my leave politely; and mounting the stairs, again I found myself once more in my room.

Forthwith I summoned my servant. Though I had brought him with me from England, he was a native of France—a useful fellow, sharp, bustling, and, of course, quite familiar with the ways and tricks of his countrymen.

"St. Clair, shut the door; come here. I can't rest till I have made out something about those people of rank who have got the apartments under mine. Here are fifteen francs; make out the servants we assisted to-day; have them to a *petit souper*, and come back and tell me their entire history. I have, this moment, seen one of them who knows nothing, and has communicated it. The other, whose name I forget, is the unknown nobleman's valet, and knows everything. Him you must pump. It is, of course, the venerable peer, and not the young lady who accompanies him, that interests me—you understand? Begone! fly! and return with all the details I sigh for, and every circumstance that can possibly interest me."

It was a commission which admirably suited the tastes and spirits of my worthy St. Clair, to whom, you will have observed, I had accustomed myself to talk with the peculiar familiarity which the old French comedy establishes between master and valet.

I am sure he laughed at me in secret; but nothing could be more polite and deferential.

With several wise looks, nods and shrugs, he withdrew; and looking down from my window, I saw him, with incredible quickness, enter the yard, where I soon lost sight of him among the carriages.

Chapter III

Death and Love Together Mated

WHEN THE DAY drags, when a man is solitary, and in a fever of impatience and suspense; when the minute-hand of his watch travels as slowly as the hour-hand used to do, and the hour-hand has lost all appreciable motion; when he yawns, and beats the devil's tattoo, and flattens his handsome nose against the window, and whistles tunes he hates, and, in short, does not know what to do with himself, it is deeply to be regretted that he cannot make a solemn dinner of three courses more than once in a day. The laws of matter, to which we are slaves, deny us that resource.

But in the times I speak of, supper was still a substantial meal, and its hour was approaching. This was consolatory. Three-quarters of an hour, however, still interposed. How was I to dispose of that interval?

I had two or three idle books, it is true, as travelling-companions; but there are many moods in which one cannot read. My novel lay with my rug and walking-stick on the sofa, and I did not care if the heroine and the hero were both drowned together in the water-barrel that I saw in the inn-yard under my window.

I took a turn or two up and down my room, and sighed, looking at myself in the glass, adjusted my great white "choker," folded and tied after Brummel, the immortal "Beau," put on a buff waistcoat and my blue swallow-tailed coat with gilt buttons; I deluged my pocket handkerchief with eau-de-Cologne (we had not then the variety of bouquets with which the genius of perfumery has since blessed us); I arranged my hair, on which I piqued myself, and which I loved to groom in those days. That dark-brown chevelure, with a natural curl, is now represented by a few dozen perfectly white hairs, and its place—a smooth, bald, pink head—knows it no more. But let us forget these mortifications. It was then rich, thick, and dark-brown. I was making a very careful toilet. I took my unexceptionable hat from its case, and placed it lightly on my wise head, as nearly as memory and practice enabled me to do so, at that very slight inclination which the immortal person I have mentioned was wont to give to his. A pair of light French gloves and a rather club-like knotted walking-stick, such as just then came into vogue, for a year or two again in England, in the phraseology of Sir Walter Scott's romances, "completed my equipment."

All this attention to effect, preparatory to a mere lounge in the yard, or on the steps of the Belle Etoile, was a simple act of devotion to the wonderful eyes which I had that evening beheld for the first time, and never, never could forget! In plain terms, it was all done in the vague, very vague hope that those eyes might behold the unexceptionable get-up of a melancholy slave, and retain the image, not altogether without secret approbation.

As I completed my preparations the light failed me; the last level streak of sunlight disappeared, and a fading twilight only remained. I sighed in unison with the pensive hour, and threw open the window, intending to look out for a moment before going downstairs. I perceived instantly that the window underneath mine was also open, for I heard two voices in conversation, although I could not distinguish what they were saying.

The male voice was peculiar; it was, as I told you, reedy and nasal. I knew it, of course, instantly. The answering voice spoke in those sweet tones which I recognised only too easily. The dialogue was only for a minute; the repulsive male voice laughed, I fancied, with a kind of devilish satire, and retired from the window, so that I almost ceased to hear it.

The other voice remained nearer the window, but not so near as at first.

It was not an altercation; there was evidently nothing the least exciting in the colloquy. What would I not have given that it had been a quarrel—a violent one—and I the redresser of wrongs, and the defender of insulted beauty! Alas! so far as I could pronounce upon the character of the tones I heard, they might be as tranquil a pair as any in existence. In a moment more the lady began to sing an odd little *chanson*. I need not remind you how much farther the voice is heard *singing* than speaking. I could distinguish the words. The voice was of that exquisitely sweet kind which is called, I believe, a semi-contralto; it had something pathetic, and something, I fancied, a little mocking in its tones. I venture a clumsy, but adequate translation of the words:

> "Death and Love, together mated,
> Watch and wait in ambuscade;
> At early morn, or else belated,
> They meet and mark the man or maid.

> "Burning sigh, or breath that freezes,
> Numbs or maddens man or maid;
> Death or Love the victim seizes,
> Breathing from their ambuscade."

"Enough, Madame!" said the old voice, with sudden severity. "We do not desire, I believe, to amuse the grooms and hostlers in the yard with our music."

The lady's voice laughed gaily.

"You desire to quarrel, Madame!" And the old man, I presume, shut down the window. Down it went, at all events, with a rattle that might easily have broken the glass.

Of all thin partitions, glass is the most effectual excluder of sound. I heard no more, not even the subdued hum of the colloquy.

What a charming voice this Countess had! How it melted, swelled, and trembled! How it moved, and even agitated me! What a pity that a hoarse old jackdaw should have power to crow down such a Philomel! "Alas! what a life it is!" I moralized, wisely. "That beautiful Countess, with the patience of an angel and the beauty of a Venus and the accomplishments of all the Muses, a slave! She knows perfectly who occupies the apartments over hers; she heard me raise my window. One may conjecture pretty well for whom that music was intended—ay, old gentleman, and for whom you suspected it to be intended."

In a very agreeable flutter I left my room, and descending the stairs, passed the Count's door very much at my leisure. There was just a chance that the beautiful songstress might emerge. I dropped my stick on the lobby, near their door, and you may be sure it took me some little time to pick it up! Fortune, nevertheless, did not favour me. I could not stay on the lobby all night picking up my stick, so I went down to the hall.

I consulted the clock, and found that there remained but a quarter of an hour to the moment of supper.

Every one was roughing it now, every inn in confusion; people might do at such a juncture what they never did before. Was it just possible that, for once, the Count and Countess would take their chairs at the table-d'hôte?

Chapter IV

Monsieur Droqville

FULL OF THIS exciting hope, I sauntered out, upon the steps of the Belle Etoile. It was now night, and a pleasant moonlight over everything. I had entered more into my romance since my arrival, and this poetic light heightened the sentiment. What a drama, if she turned out to be the Count's daughter, and in love with me! What a delightful—tragedy, if she turned out to be the Count's wife!

In this luxurious mood, I was accosted by a tall and very elegantly-made gentleman, who appeared to be about fifty. His air was courtly and graceful, and there was in his whole manner and appearance something so distinguished, that it was impossible not to suspect him of being a person of rank.

He had been standing upon the steps, looking out, like me, upon the moonlight effects that transformed, as it were, the objects and buildings in the little street. He accosted me, I say, with the politeness, at once easy and lofty, of a French nobleman of the old school. He asked me if I were not Mr. Beckett? I assented; and he immediately introduced himself as the Marquis d'Harmonville (this information he gave me in a low tone), and asked leave to present me with a letter from Lord R——, who knew my father slightly, and had once done me, also, a trifling kindness.

This English peer, I may mention, stood very high in the political world, and was named as the most probable successor to the distinguished post of English Minister at Paris.

I received it with a low bow, and read:

"MY DEAR BECKETT,

"I beg to introduce my very dear friend, the Marquis d'Harmonville, who will explain to you the nature of the services it may be in your power to render him and us."

He went on to speak of the Marquis as a man whose great wealth, whose intimate relations with the old families, and whose legitimate influence with the court rendered him the fittest possible person for those friendly offices which, at the desire of his own sovereign, and of our government, he has so obligingly undertaken.

It added a great deal to my perplexity, when I read further—

"By-the-bye, Walton was here yesterday, and told me that your seat was likely to be attacked; something, he says, is unquestionably going on at Domwell. You know there is an awkwardness in my meddling ever so cautiously. But I advise, if it is not very officious, your making Haxton look after it, and report immediately. I fear it is serious. I ought to have mentioned that, for reasons that you will see, when you have talked with him for five minutes, the Marquis—with the concurrence of all our friends—drops his title, for a few weeks, and is at present plain Monsieur Droqville.

"I am this moment going to town, and can say no more.

"Yours faithfully,

"R——."

I was utterly puzzled. I could scarcely boast of Lord ——'s acquaintance. I knew no one named Haxton, and, except my hatter, no one called Walton; and this peer wrote as if we were intimate friends! I looked at the back of the letter, and the mystery was solved. And now, to my consternation—for I was plain Richard Beckett—I read—

"*To George Stanhope Beckett, Esq., M.P.*"

I looked with consternation in the face of the Marquis.

"What apology can I offer to Monsieur the Mar—to Monsieur Droqville? It is true my name is Beckett—it is true I am known, though very slightly to Lord R——; but the letter was not intended for me. My name is Richard Beckett—this is to Mr. Stanhope Beckett, the member for Shillingsworth. What can I say, or do, in this unfortunate situation? I can only give you my honour as a gentleman, that, for me, the letter, which I now return, shall remain as unviolated a secret as before I opened it. I am so shocked and grieved that such a mistake should have occurred!"

I dare say my honest vexation and good faith were pretty legibly written in my countenance; for the look of gloomy embarrassment which had for a moment settled on the face of the Marquis, brightened; he smiled, kindly, and extended his hand.

"I have not the least doubt that Monsieur Beckett will respect my little secret. As a mistake was destined to occur, I have reason to thank my good stars that it should have been with a gentleman of honour. Monsieur Beckett will permit me, I hope, to place his name among those of my friends?"

I thanked the Marquis very much for his kind expression. He went on to say—

"If, Monsieur, I can persuade you to visit me at Claironville, in Normandy, where I hope to see, on the 15th of August, a great many friends, whose acquaintance it might interest you to make, I shall be too happy."

I thanked him, of course, very gratefully for his hospitality. He continued:

"I cannot, for the present, see my friends, for reasons which you may surmise, at my house in Paris. But Monsieur will be so good as to let me know the hotel he means to stay at in Paris; and he will find that although the Marquis d'Harmonville is not in town, that Monsieur Droqville will not lose sight of him."

With many acknowledgments I gave him the information he desired.

"And in the meantime," he continued, "if you think of any way in which Monsieur Droqville can be of use to you, our communication shall not be interrupted, and I shall so manage matters that you can easily let me know."

I was very much flattered. The Marquis had, as we say, taken a fancy to me. Such likings at first sight often ripen into lasting friendships. To be sure it was just possible that the Marquis might think it prudent to keep the involuntary depository of a political secret, even so vague a one, in good humour.

Very graciously the Marquis took his leave, going up the stairs of the Belle Etoile.

I remained upon the steps, for a minute lost in speculation upon this new theme of interest. But the wonderful eyes, the thrilling voice, the exquisite figure of the beautiful lady who had taken possession of my imagination, quickly reasserted their influence. I was again gazing at the sympathetic moon, and descending the steps, I loitered along the pavements among strange objects, and houses that were antique and picturesque, in a dreamy state, thinking.

In a little while, I turned into the inn-yard again. There had come a lull. Instead of the noisy place it was, an hour or two before, the yard was perfectly still and empty, except for the carriages that stood here and there. Perhaps there was a servants' table-d'hôte just then. I was rather pleased to find solitude; and undisturbed I found out my lady-love's carriage, in the moonlight. I mused, I walked round it; I was as utterly foolish and maudlin as very young men, in my situation, usually are. The blinds were down, the doors I suppose, locked. The brilliant moonlight revealed everything, and cast sharp, black shadows of wheel, and bar, and spring, on the pavement. I stood before the escutcheon painted on the door, which I had examined in the daylight. I wondered how often her eyes had rested on the same object. I pondered in a charming dream. A harsh, loud voice over my shoulder said suddenly.

"A red stork—good! The stork is a bird of prey; it is vigilant, greedy and catches gudgeons. Red, too!—blood red! Ha! ha! the symbol is appropriate."

I had turned about, and beheld the palest face I ever saw. It was broad, ugly, and malignant. The figure was that of a French officer, in undress, and was six feet high. Across the nose and eyebrow there was a deep scar, which made the repulsive face grimmer.

The officer elevated his chin and his eyebrows, with a scoffing chuckle, and said—"I have shot a stork, with a rifle bullet, when he thought himself safe in the clouds, for mere sport!" (He shrugged, and laughed malignantly). "See, Monsieur; when a man like me—

a man of energy, you understand, a man with all his wits about him, a man who has made the tour of Europe under canvas, and, *parbleu!* often without it—resolves to discover a secret, expose a crime, catch a thief, spit a robber on the point of his sword, it is odd if he does not succeed. Ha! ha! ha! Adieu, Monsieur!"

He turned with an angry whisk on his heel and swaggered with long strides out of the gate.

Chapter V

Supper at the Belle Etoile

THE FRENCH ARMY were in a rather savage temper, just then. The English, especially, had but scant courtesy to expect at their hands. It was plain, however, that the cadaverous gentleman who had just apostrophized the heraldry of the Count's carriage with such mysterious acrimony, had not intended any of his malevolence for me. He was stung by some old recollection, and had marched off, seething with fury.

I had received one of those unacknowledged shocks which startle us, when, fancying ourselves perfectly alone, we discover on a sudden, that our antics have been watched by a spectator, almost at our elbow. In this case, the effect was enhanced by the extreme repulsiveness of the face, and, I may add, its proximity, for, as I think, it almost touched mine. The enigmatical harangue of this person, so full of hatred and implied denunciation, was still in my ears. Here at all events was new matter for the industrious fancy of a lover to work upon.

It was time now to go to the table-d'hôte. Who could tell what lights the gossip of the supper-table might throw upon the subject that interested me so powerfully!

I stepped into the room, my eyes searching the little assembly, about thirty people, for the persons who specially interested me.

It was not easy to induce people, so hurried and overworked as those of the Belle Etoile just now, to send meals up to one's private apartments, in the midst of this unparalleled confusion; and, therefore many people who did not like it, might find themselves reduced to the alternative of supping at the table-d'hôte, or starving.

The Count was not there, nor his beautiful companion; but the Marquis d'Harmonville, whom I hardly expected to see in so public a place, signed, with a significant smile, to a vacant chair beside himself. I secured it, and he seemed pleased, and almost immediately entered into conversation with me.

"This is, probably, your first visit to France?" he said.

I told him it was, and he said:

"You must not think me very curious and impertinent; but Paris is about the most dangerous capital a high-spirited and generous young gentleman could visit without a Mentor. If you have not an experienced friend as a companion during your visit—" he paused.

I told him I was not so provided, but that I had my wits about me; that I had seen a good deal of life in England, and that, I fancied, human nature was pretty much the same in all parts of the world. The Marquis shook his head, smiling.

"You will find very marked differences, notwithstanding," he said. "Peculiarities of intellect and peculiarities of character, undoubtedly, do pervade different nations; and this results, among the criminal classes, in a style of villainy no less peculiar. In Paris, the class who live by their wits, is three or four times as great as in London; and they live much better; some of them even splendidly. They are more ingenious than the London rogues; they have more animation, and invention, and the dramatic faculty, in which your countrymen are deficient, is everywhere. These invaluable attributes place them upon a totally different level. They can affect the manners and enjoy the luxuries of people of distinction. They live, many of them, by play."

"So do many of our London rogues."

"Yes, but in a totally different way. They are the *habitués* of certain gaming-tables, billiard-rooms, and other places, including your races, where high play goes on; and by superior knowledge of chances, by masking their play, by means of confederates, by means of bribery, and other artifices, varying with the subject of their imposture, they rob the unwary. But here it is more elaborately done, and with a really exquisite *finesse*. There are people whose manners, style, conversation, are unexceptionable, living in handsome houses in the best situations, with everything about them in the most refined taste, and exquisitely luxurious, who impose even upon the Parisian bourgeois, who believe them to be, in good faith, people of rank and fashion, because their habits are expensive and refined, and their houses are frequented by foreigners of distinction, and, to a degree, by foolish young Frenchmen of rank. At all these houses play goes on. The ostensible host and hostess seldom join in it; they provide it simply to plunder their guests, by means of their accomplices, and thus wealthy strangers are inveigled and robbed."

"But I have heard of a young Englishman, a son of Lord Rooksbury, who broke two Parisian gaming-tables only last year."

"I see," he said laughing, "you are come here to do likewise. I, myself, at about your age, undertook the same spirited enterprise. I raised no less a sum than five hundred thousand francs to begin with; I expected to carry all before me by the simple expedient of going on doubling my stakes. I had heard of it, and I fancied that the sharpers, who kept the table knew nothing of the matter. I found, however, that they not only knew all about it, but had provided against the possibility of any such experiments; and I was pulled up before I had well begun, by a rule which forbids the doubling of an original stake more than four times, consecutively."

"And is that rule in force still?" I inquired, chap-fallen.

He laughed and shrugged, "Of course it is, my young friend. People who live by an art, always understand it better than an amateur. I see you had formed the same plan, and no doubt came provided."

I confessed I had prepared for conquest upon a still grander scale. I had arrived with a purse of thirty thousand pounds sterling.

"Any acquaintance of my very dear friend, Lord R——, interests me; and, besides my regard for him, I am charmed with you; so you will pardon all my, perhaps, too officious questions and advice."

I thanked him most earnestly for his valuable counsel, and begged that he would have the goodness to give me all the advice in his power.

"Then if you take my advice," said he, "you will leave your money in the bank where it lies. Never risk a Napoleon in a gaming-house. The night I went to break the bank, I lost between seven and eight thousand pounds sterling of your English money; and my next adventure, I had obtained an introduction to one of those elegant gaming-houses which affect to be the private mansions of persons of distinction, and was saved from ruin by a gentleman, whom, ever since, I have regarded with increasing respect and friendship. It oddly happens he is in this house at this moment. I recognized his servant, and made him a visit in his apartments here, and found him the same brave, kind, honourable man I always knew him. But that he is living so entirely out of the world, now, I should have made a point of introducing you. Fifteen years ago he would have been the man of all others to consult. The gentleman I speak of is the Comte de St. Alyre. He represents a very old family. He is the very soul of honour, and the most sensible man in the world, except in one particular."

"And that particular?" I hesitated. I was now deeply interested.

"Is that he has married a charming creature, at least five-and-forty years younger than himself, and is, of course, although I believe absolutely without cause, horribly jealous."

"And the lady?"

"The Countess is, I believe, in every way worthy of so good a man," he answered, a little drily.

"I think I heard her sing this evening."

"Yes, I daresay; she is very accomplished." After a few moments' silence he continued.

"I must not lose sight of you, for I should be sorry, when next you meet my friend Lord R——, that you had to tell him you had been pigeoned in Paris. A rich Englishman as you are, with so large a sum at his Paris bankers, young, gay, generous, a thousand ghouls and harpies will be contending who shall be first to seize and devour you."

At this moment I received something like a jerk from the elbow of the gentleman at my right. It was an accidental jog, as he turned in his seat.

"On the honour of a soldier, there is no man's flesh in this company heals so fast as mine."

The tone in which this was spoken was harsh and stentorian, and almost made me bounce. I looked round and recognised the officer, whose large white face had half scared me in the inn-yard, wiping his mouth furiously, and then with a gulp of Maçon, he went on——

"No one! It's not blood; it is ichor! it's miracle! Set aside stature, thew, bone, and muscle—set aside courage, and by all the angels of death, I'd fight a lion naked and dash his teeth down his jaws with my fist, and flog him to death with his own tail! Set aside, I say, all those attributes, which I am allowed to possess, and I am worth six men in any campaign, for that one quality of healing as I do—rip me up; punch me through, tear me to tatters with bomb-shells, and nature has me whole again, while your tailor would fine-draw an old-coat. *Parbleu!* gentlemen, if you saw me naked, you would laugh? Look at my hand, a sabre-cut across the palm, to the bone, to save my head, taken up with three stitches, and five days afterwards I was playing ball with an English general, a prisoner in Madrid, against the wall of the convent of the Santa Maria de la Castita! At Arcola, by the great devil himself! that was an action. Every man there, gentlemen, swallowed as much smoke in five minutes as would smother you all, in this room! I received, at the same moment, two musket balls in the thighs, a grape shot through the calf of my leg, a lance through my left shoulder, a piece of a shrapnel in the left deltoid, a bayonet through the cartilage of my right ribs, a sabre-cut that carried away a pound of flesh from my chest, and the better part of a congreve rocket on my forehead. Pretty well, ha, ha! and all while you'd say *bah!* and in eight days and a half I was making a forced march, without shoes, and only one gaiter, the life and soul of my company, and as sound as a roach!"

"Bravo! Bravissimo! Per Bacco! un galant uomo!" exclaimed, in a martial ecstasy, a fat little Italian, who manufactured toothpicks and wicker cradles on the island of Notre Dame; "your exploits shall resound through Europe! and the history of those wars should be written in your blood!"

"Never mind! a trifle!" exclaimed the soldier. "At Ligny, the other day, where we smashed the Prussians into ten hundred thousand milliards of atoms, a bit of a shell cut me across the leg and opened an artery. It was spouting as high as the chimney, and in half a minute I had lost enough to fill a pitcher. I must have expired in another minute, if I had not whipped off my sash like a flash of lightning, tied it round my leg above the wound, whipped a bayonet out of the back of a dead Prussian, and passing it under, made a tourniquet of it with a couple of twists, and so stayed the hemorrhage, and saved my life. But, *sacré bleu!* gentlemen, I lost so much blood, I have been as pale as the bottom of a plate ever since. No matter. A trifle. Blood well spent, gentlemen." He applied himself now to his bottle of *vin ordinaire.*

The Marquis had closed his eyes, and looked resigned and disgusted, while all this was going on.

"Garçon," said the officer, for the first time, speaking in a low tone over the back of his chair to the waiter; "who came in that travelling carriage, dark yellow and black, that stands in the middle of the yard, with arms and supporters emblazoned on the door, and a red stork, as red as my facings?"

The waiter could not say.

The eye of the eccentric officer, who had suddenly grown grim and serious, and seemed to have abandoned the general conversation to other people, lighted, as it were, accidentally, on me.

"Pardon me, Monsieur," he said. "Did I not see you examining the panel of that carriage at the same time that I did so, this evening? Can you tell me who arrived in it?"

"I rather think the Count and Countess de St. Alyre."

"And are they here, in the Belle Etoile?" he asked.

"They have got apartments upstairs," I answered.

He started up, and half pushed his chair from the table. He quickly sat down again, and I could hear him sacré-ing and muttering to himself, and grinning and scowling. I could not tell whether he was alarmed or furious.

I turned to say a word or two to the Marquis, but he was gone. Several other people had dropped out also, and the supper party soon broke up.

Two or three substantial pieces of wood smouldered on the hearth, for the night had turned out chilly. I sat down by the fire in a great arm-chair, of carved oak, with a marvellously high back, that looked as old as the days of Henry IV.

"Garçon," said I, "do you happen to know who that officer is?"

"That is Colonel Gaillarde, Monsieur."

"Has he been often here?"

"Once before, Monsieur, for a week; it is a year since."

"He is the palest man I ever saw."

"That is true, Monsieur; he has been often taken for a *revenant.*"

"Can you give me a bottle of really good Burgundy?"

"The best in France, Monsieur."

"Place it, and a glass by my side, on this table, if you please. I may sit here for half an hour?"

"Certainly, Monsieur."

I was very comfortable, the wine excellent, and my thoughts glowing and serene. "Beautiful Countess! Beautiful Countess! shall we ever be better acquainted."

Chapter VI

The Naked Sword

A MAN WHO HAS been posting all day long, and changing the air he breathes every half-hour, who is well pleased with himself, and has nothing on earth to trouble him, and who sits alone by a fire in a comfortable chair after having eaten a hearty supper, may be pardoned if he takes an accidental nap.

I had filled my fourth glass when I fell asleep. My head, I daresay, hung uncomfortably; and it is admitted, that a variety of French dishes is not the most favorable precursor to pleasant dreams.

I had a dream as I took mine ease in mine inn on this occasion. I fancied myself in a huge cathedral, without light except from four tapers that stood at the corners of a raised platform hung with black, on which lay, draped also in black, what seemed to me the dead body of the Countess de St. Alyre. The place seemed empty, it was cold, and I could see only (in the halo of the candles) a little way round.

The little I saw bore the character of Gothic gloom, and helped my fancy to shape and furnish the black void that yawned all round me. I heard a sound like the slow tread of two persons walking up the flagged aisle. A faint echo told of the vastness of the place. An awful sense of expectation was upon me, and I was horribly frightened when the body that lay on the catafalque said (without stirring), in a whisper that froze me, "They come to place me in the grave alive; save me."

I found that I could neither speak nor move. I was horribly frightened.

The two people who approached now emerged from the darkness. One, the Count de St. Alyre glided to the head of the figure and placed his long thin hands under it. The white-faced Colonel, with the scar across his face, and a look of infernal triumph, placed his hands under her feet, and they began to raise her.

With an indescribable effort I broke the spell that bound me, and started to my feet with a gasp.

I was wide awake, but the broad, wicked face of Colonel Gaillarde was staring, white as death, at me, from the other side of the hearth. "Where is she?" I shuddered.

"That depends on who she is, Monsieur," replied the Colonel curtly.

"Good heavens!" I gasped, looking about me.

The Colonel, who was eyeing me sarcastically, had had his *demitasse* of *café noir*, and now drank his *tasse*, diffusing a pleasant perfume of brandy.

"I fell asleep and was dreaming," I said, lest any strong language, founded on the *rôle* he played in my dream, should have escaped me. "I did not know for some moments where I was."

"You are the young gentleman who has the apartments over the Count and Countess de St. Alyre?" he said, winking one eye, close in meditation, and glaring at me with the other.

"I believe so—yes," I answered.

"Well, yonker, take care you have not worse dreams than that some night," he said enigmatically, and wagged his head with a chuckle. "Worse dreams," he repeated.

"What does Monsieur the Colonel mean?" I inquired.

"I am trying to find that out myself," said the Colonel; "and I think I shall. When *I* get the first inch of the thread fast between my finger and thumb, it goes hard but I follow it up, bit by bit, little by little, tracing it this way and that, and up and down, and round about, until the whole clue is wound up on my thumb, and the end, and its secret, fast in my fingers. Ingenious! Crafty as five foxes! wide awake as a weazel! *Parbleu!* if I had descended to that occupation I should have made my fortune as a spy. Good wine here?" he glanced interrogatively at my bottle.

"Very good," said I. "Will Monsieur the Colonel try a glass?"

He took the largest he could find, and filled it, raised it with a bow, and drank it slowly. "Ah! ah! Bah! That is not it," he exclaimed, with some disgust, filling it again. "You ought to have told me to order your Burgundy, and they would not have brought you that stuff."

I got away from this man as soon as I civilly could, and, putting on my hat, I walked out with no other company than my sturdy walking stick. I visited the inn-yard, and looked up to the windows of the Countess's apartments. They were closed, however, and I had not even the unsubstantial consolation of contemplating the light in which that beautiful lady was at that moment writing, or reading, or sitting and thinking of—any one you please.

I bore this serious privation as well as I could, and took a little saunter through the town. I shan't bore you with moonlight effects, nor with the maunderings of a man who has fallen in love at first sight with a beautiful face. My ramble, it is enough to say, occupied about half an hour, and, returning by a slight *détour*, I found myself in a little square, with about two high gabled houses on each side, and a rude stone statue, worn by centuries of rain, on a pedestal in the centre of the pavement. Looking at this statue was a slight and rather tall man, whom I instantly recognised as the Marquis d'Harmonville: he knew me almost as quickly. He walked a step towards me, shrugged and laughed:

"You are surprised to find Monsieur Droqville staring at that old stone figure by moonlight. Anything to pass the time. You, I see, suffer from *ennui*, as I do. These little provincial towns! Heavens! what an effort it is to live in them! If I could regret having formed in early life a friendship that does me honour, I think its condemning me to a sojourn in such a place would make me do so. You go on towards Paris, I suppose, in the morning?"

"I have ordered horses."

"As for me I await a letter, or an arrival, either would emancipate me; but I can't say how soon either event will happen."

"Can I be of any use in this matter?" I began.

"None, Monsieur, I thank you a thousand times. No, this is a piece in which every *rôle* is already cast. I am but an amateur, and induced, solely by friendship, to take a part."

So he talked on, for a time, as we walked slowly towards the Belle Etoile, and then came a silence, which I broke by asking him if he knew anything of Colonel Gaillarde.

"Oh! yes, to be sure. He is a little mad; he has had some bad injuries of the head. He used to plague the people in the War Office to death. He has always some delusion. They contrived some employment for him—not regimental, of course—but in this campaign Napoleon, who could spare nobody, placed him in command of a regiment. He was always a desperate fighter, and such men were more than ever needed."

There is, or was, a second inn, in this town, called l'Ecu de France. At its door the Marquis stopped, bade me a mysterious good night, and disappeared.

As I walked slowly towards my inn, I met, in the shadow of a row of poplars, the *garçon* who had brought me my Burgundy a little time ago. I was thinking of Colonel Gaillarde, and I stopped the little waiter as he passed me.

"You said, I think, that Colonel Gaillarde was at the Belle Etoile for a week at one time."

"Yes, Monsieur."

"Is he perfectly in his right mind?"

The waiter stared. "Perfectly, Monsieur."

"Has he been suspected at any time of being out of his mind?"

"Never, Monsieur; he is a little noisy, but a very shrewd man."

"What is a fellow to think?" I muttered, as I walked on.

I was soon within sight of the lights of the Belle Etoile. A carriage, with four horses, stood in the moonlight at the door, and a furious altercation was going on in the hall, in which the yell of Colonel Gaillarde out-topped all other sounds.

Most young men like, at least, to witness a row. But, intuitively, I felt that this would interest me in a very special manner. I had only fifty yards to run, when I found myself in the hall of the old inn. The principal actor in this strange drama was, indeed, the Colonel, who stood facing the old Count de St. Alyre, who, in his travelling costume, with his black silk scarf covering the lower part of his face, confronted him; he had evidently been intercepted in an endeavour to reach his carriage. A little in the rear of the Count stood the Countess, also in travelling costume, with her thick black veil down, and holding in her delicate fingers a white rose. You can't conceive a more diabolical effigy of hate and fury than the Colonel; the knotted veins stood out on his forehead, his eyes leaping from their sockets, he was grinding his teeth, and froth was on his lips. His sword was drawn, in his hand, and he accompanied his yelling denunciations with stamps upon the floor and flourishes of his weapon in the air.

The host of the Belle Etoile was talking to the Colonel in soothing terms utterly thrown away. Two waiters, pale with fear, stared uselessly from behind. The Colonel screamed, and thundered, and whirled his sword. "I was not sure of your red birds of prey; I could not believe you would have the audacity to travel on high roads, and to stop at honest inns, and lie under the same roof with honest men. You! you! *both*—vampires, wolves, ghouls. Summon the *gendarmes*, I say. By St. Peter and all the devils, if either of you try to get out of that door I'll take your heads off."

For a moment I had stood aghast. Here was a situation! I walked up to the lady; she laid her hand wildly upon my arm. "Oh! Monsieur," she whispered, in great agitation, "that dreadful madman! What are we to do? He won't let us pass; he will kill my husband."

"Fear nothing, Madame," I answered, with romantic devotion, and stepping between the Count and Gaillarde, as he shrieked his invective, "Hold your tongue, and clear the way, you ruffian, you bully, you coward!" I roared.

A faint cry escaped the lady, which more than repaid the risk I ran, as the sword of the frantic soldier, after a moment's astonished pause, flashed in the air to cut me down.

Chapter VII

The White Rose

I WAS TOO quick for Colonel Gaillarde. As he raised his sword, reckless of all consequences but my condign punishment, and quite resolved to cleave me to the teeth, I struck him across the side of his head, with my heavy stick; and while he staggered back, I struck him another blow, nearly in the same place, that felled him to the floor, where he lay as if dead.

I did not care one of his own regimental buttons, whether he was dead or not; I was, at that moment, carried away by such a tumult of delightful and diabolical emotions!

I broke his sword under my foot, and flung the pieces across the street. The old Count de St. Alyre skipped nimbly without looking to the right or left, or thanking anybody, over the floor, out of the door, down the steps, and into his carriage. Instantly I was at the side of the beautiful Countess, thus left to shift for herself; I offered her my arm, which she took, and I led her to her carriage. She entered, and I shut the door. All this without a word.

I was about to ask if there were any commands with which she would honour me—my hand was laid upon the lower edge of the window, which was open.

The lady's hand was laid upon mine timidly and excitedly. Her lips almost touched my cheek as she whispered hurriedly.

"I may never see you more, and, oh! that I could forget you. Go—farewell—for God's sake, go!"

I pressed her hand for a moment. She withdrew it, but tremblingly pressed into mine the rose which she had held in her fingers during the agitating scene she had just passed through.

All this took place while the Count was commanding, entreating, cursing his servants, tipsy, and out of the way during the crisis, my conscience afterwards insinuated, by my clever contrivance. They now mounted to their places with the agility of alarm. The postillions' whips cracked, the horses scrambled into a trot, and away rolled the carriage, with its precious freightage, along the quaint main street, in the moonlight, towards Paris.

I stood on the pavement, till it was quite lost to eye and ear in the distance.

With a deep sigh, I then turned, my white rose folded in my handkerchief—the little parting gage—the

"Favour secret, sweet, and precious;"

which no mortal eye but hers and mine had seen conveyed to me.

The care of the host of the Belle Etoile, and his assistants, had raised the wounded hero of a hundred fights partly against the wall, and propped him at each side with portmanteaus and pillows, and poured a glass of brandy, which was duly placed to his account, into his big mouth, where, for the first time, such a Godsend remained unswallowed.

A bald-headed little military surgeon of sixty, with spectacles, who had cut off eighty-seven legs and arms to his own share, after the battle of Eylau, having retired with his sword and his saw, his laurels and his sticking-plaster to this, his native town, was called in, and rather thought the gallant Colonel's skull was fractured, at all events there was concussion of the seat of thought, and quite enough work for his remarkable self-healing powers, to occupy him for a fortnight.

I began to grow a little uneasy. A disagreeable surprise, if my excursion, in which I was to break banks and hearts, and, as you see, heads, should end upon the gallows or the guillotine. I was not clear, in those times of political oscillation, which was the established apparatus.

The Colonel was conveyed, snorting apoplectically to his room.

I saw my host in the apartment in which we had supped. Wherever you employ a force of any sort, to carry a point of real importance, reject all nice calculations of economy. Better to be a thousand per cent over the mark, than the smallest fraction of a unit under it. I instinctively felt this.

I ordered a bottle of my landlord's very best wine; made him partake with me, in the proportion of two glasses to one; and then told him that he must not decline a trifling souvenir from a guest who had been so charmed with all he had seen of the renowned Belle Etoile. Thus saying, I placed five-and-thirty Napoleons in his hand. At touch of which his countenance, by no means encouraging before, grew sunny, his manners thawed, and it was plain, as he dropped the coins hastily into his pocket, that benevolent relations had been established between us.

I immediately placed the Colonel's broken head upon the tapis. We both agreed that if I had not given him that rather smart tap of my walking-cane, he would have beheaded half the inmates of the Belle Etoile. There was not a waiter in the house who would not verify that statement on oath.

The reader may suppose that I had other motives, beside the desire to escape the tedious inquisition of the law, for desiring to recommence my journey to Paris with the least possible delay. Judge what was my horror then to learn, that for love or money, horses were nowhere to be had that night. The last pair in the town had been obtained from the Ecu de France, by a gentleman who dined and supped at the Belle Etoile, and was obliged to proceed to Paris that night.

Who was the gentleman? Had he actually gone? Could he possibly be induced to wait till morning?

The gentleman was now upstairs getting his things together, and his name was Monsieur Droqville.

I ran upstairs. I found my servant St. Clair in my room. At sight of him, for a moment, my thoughts were turned into a different channel.

"Well, St. Clair, tell me this moment who the lady is?" I demanded.

"The lady is the daughter or wife, it matters not which, of the Count de St. Alyre;—the old gentleman who was so near being sliced like a cucumber to-night, I am informed, by the sword of the general whom Monsieur, by a turn of fortune, has put to bed of an apoplexy."

"Hold your tongue, fool! The man's beastly drunk—he's sulking —he could talk if he liked—who cares? Pack up my things. Which are Monsieur Droqville's apartments?"

He knew, of course; he always knew everything.

Half an hour later Monsieur Droqville and I were travelling towards Paris, in my carriage, and with his horses. I ventured to ask the Marquis d'Harmonville, in a little while, whether the lady, who accompanied the Count, was certainly the Countess. "Has he not a daughter?"

"Yes; I believe a very beautiful and charming young lady—I cannot say—it may have been she, his daughter by an earlier marriage. I saw only the Count himself to-day."

The Marquis was growing a little sleepy and, in a little while, he actually fell asleep in his corner. I dozed and nodded; but the Marquis slept like a top. He awoke only for a minute or two at the next postinghouse, where he had fortunately secured horses by sending on his man, he told me.

"You will excuse my being so dull a companion," he said, "but till to-night I have had but two hours' sleep, for more than sixty hours. I shall have a cup of coffee here; I have had my nap. Permit me to recommend you to do likewise. Their coffee is really excellent." He ordered two cups of *café noir*, and waited, with his head from the window. "We will keep the cups," he said, as he received them from the waiter, "and the tray. Thank you."

There was a little delay as he paid for these things; and then he took in the little tray, and handed me a cup of coffee.

I declined the tray; so he placed it on his own knees, to act as a miniature table.

"I can't endure being waited for and hurried," he said, "I like to sip my coffee at leisure."

I agreed. It really was the very perfection of coffee.

"I, like Monsieur le Marquis, have slept very little for the last two or three nights; and find it difficult to keep awake. This coffee will do wonders for me; it refreshes one so."

Before we had half done, the carriage was again in motion.

For a time our coffee made us chatty, and our conversation was animated.

The Marquis was extremely good-natured, as well as clever, and gave me a brilliant and amusing account of Parisian life, schemes, and dangers, all put so as to furnish me with practical warnings of the most valuable kind.

In spite of the amusing and curious stories which the Marquis related, with so much point and colour, I felt myself again becoming gradually drowsy and dreamy.

Perceiving this, no doubt, the Marquis good-naturedly suffered our conversation to subside into silence. The window next him was open. He threw his cup out of it; and did the same kind office for mine, and finally the little tray flew after, and I heard it clank on the road; a valuable waif, no doubt, for some early wayfarer in wooden shoes. I leaned back in my corner; I had my beloved *souvenir*—my white rose—close to my heart, folded, now, in white paper. It inspired all manner of romantic dreams. I began to grow more and more sleepy. But actual slumber did not come. I was still viewing, with my half-closed eyes, from my corner, diagonally, the interior of the carriage. I wished for sleep; but the barrier between waking and sleeping seemed absolutely insurmountable; and instead, I entered into a state of novel and indescribable indolence.

The Marquis lifted his despatch-box from the floor, placed it on his knees, unlocked it, and took out what proved to be a lamp, which he hung with two hooks, attached to it, to the window opposite to him. He lighted it with a match, put on his spectacles, and taking out a bundle of letters, began to read them carefully.

We were making way very slowly. My impatience had hitherto

employed four horses from stage to stage. We were in this emergency, only too happy to have secured two. But the difference in pace was depressing.

I grew tired of the monotony of seeing the spectacled Marquis reading, folding, and docketing, letter after letter. I wished to shut out the image which wearied me, but something prevented my being able to shut my eyes. I tried again and again; but, positively, I had lost the power of closing them.

I would have rubbed my eyes, but I could not stir my hand, my will no longer acted on my body—I found that I could not move one joint, or muscle, no more than I could, by an effort of my will, have turned the carriage about.

Up to this I had experienced no sense of horror. Whatever it was, simple nightmare was not the cause. I was awfully frightened! Was I in a fit?

It was horrible to see my good-natured companion pursue his occupation so serenely, when he might have dissipated my horrors by a single shake.

I made a stupendous exertion to call out but in vain; I repeated the effort again and again, with no result.

My companion now tied up his letters, and looked out of the window, humming an air from an opera. He drew back his head, and said, turning to me—

"Yes, I see the lights; we shall be there in two or three minutes."

He looked more closely at me, and with a kind smile, and a little shrug, he said, "Poor child! how fatigued he must have been —how profoundly he sleeps! when the carriage stops he will waken."

He then replaced his letters in the despatch-box, locked it, put his spectacles in his pocket, and again looked out of the window.

We had entered a little town. I suppose it was past two o'clock by this time. The carriage drew up, I saw an inn-door open, and a light issuing from it.

"Here we are!" said my companion, turning gaily to me. But I did not awake.

"Yes, how tired he must have been!" he exclaimed, after he had waited for an answer.

My servant was at the carriage door, and opened it.

"Your master sleeps soundly, he is so fatigued! It would be cruel to disturb him. You and I will go in, while they change the horses, and take some refreshment, and choose something that Monsieur Beckett will like to take in the carriage, for when he awakes by-and-by, he will, I am sure, be hungry."

He trimmed his lamp, poured in some oil; and taking care not to disturb me, with another kind smile, and another word of caution to my servant, he got out, and I heard him talking to St. Clair, as they entered the inn-door, and I was left in my corner, in the carriage, in the same state.

Chapter VIII

A Three Minutes' Visit

I HAVE SUFFERED extreme and protracted bodily pain, at different periods of my life, but anything like that misery, thank God, I never endured before or since. I earnestly hope it may not resemble any type of death, to which we are liable. I was, indeed, a spirit in prison; and unspeakable was my dumb and unmoving agony.

The power of thought remained clear and active. Dull terror filled my mind. How would this end? Was it actual death?

You will understand that my faculty of observing was unimpaired. I could hear and see anything as distinctly as ever I did in my life. It was simply that my will had, as it were, lost its hold of my body.

I told you that the Marquis d'Harmonville had not extinguished his carriage lamp on going into this village inn. I was listening intently, longing for his return, which might result, by some lucky accident, in awaking me from my catalepsy.

Without any sound of steps approaching, to announce an arrival, the carriage-door suddenly opened, and a total stranger got in silently and shut the door.

The lamp gave about as strong a light as a wax-candle, so I could see the intruder perfectly. He was a young man, with a dark grey, loose surtout, made with a sort of hood, which was pulled over his head. I thought, as he moved, that I saw the gold band of a military undress cap under it; and I certainly saw the lace and buttons of a uniform, on the cuffs of the coat that were visible under the wide sleeves of his outside wrapper.

This young man had thick moustaches, and an imperial, and I observed that he had a red scar running upward from his lip across his cheek.

He entered, shut the door softly, and sat down beside me. It was all done in a moment; leaning toward me, and shading his eyes with his gloved hand, he examined my face closely, for a few seconds.

This man had come as noiselessly as a ghost; and everything he did was accomplished with the rapidity and decision, that indicated a well defined and pre-arranged plan. His designs were evidently sinister. I thought he was going to rob, and, perhaps, murder me. I lay, nevertheless, like a corpse under his hands. He inserted his hand in my breast-pocket, from which he took my precious white rose and all the letters it contained, among which was a paper of some consequence to me.

My letters he glanced at. They were plainly not what he wanted. My precious rose, too, he laid aside with them. It was evidently about the paper I have mentioned, that he was concerned; for the moment he opened it, he began with a pencil, in a small pocket-book, to make rapid notes of its contents.

This man seemed to glide through his work with a noiseless and cool celerity which argued, I thought, the training of the police-department.

He re-arranged the papers, possibly in the very order in which he had found them, replaced them in my breast-pocket, and was gone.

His visit, I think, did not quite last three minutes. Very soon after his disappearance, I heard the voice of the Marquis once more. He got in, and I saw him look at me, and smile, half envying me, I fancied, my sound repose. If he had but known all!

He resumed his reading and docketing, by the light of the little lamp which had just subserved the purposes of a spy.

We were now out of the town, pursuing our journey at the same moderate pace. We had left the scene of my police visit, as I should have termed it, now two leagues behind us, when I suddenly felt a strange throbbing in one ear, and a sensation as if air passed through it into my throat. It seemed as if a bubble of air, formed deep in my ear, swelled, and burst there. The indescribable tension of my brain seemed all at once to give way; there was an odd humming in my head, and a sort of vibration through every nerve of my body, such as I have experienced in a limb that has been, in popular phraseology, asleep. I uttered a cry and half rose from my seat, and then fell back trembling, and with a sense of mortal faintness.

The Marquis stared at me, took my hand, and earnestly asked if I was ill. I could answer only with a deep groan.

Gradually the process of restoration was completed; and I was able, though very faintly, to tell him how very ill I had been; and then to describe the violation of my letters, during the time of his absence from the carriage.

"Good heaven!" he exclaimed, "the miscreant did not get at my despatch-box?"

I satisfied him, so far as I had observed, on that point. He placed the box on the seat beside him, and opened and examined its contents very minutely.

"Yes, undisturbed; all safe, thank heaven!" he murmured. "There are half a dozen letters here, that I would not have some people read, for a great deal."

He now asked with a very kind anxiety all about the illness I complained of. When he had heard me, he said—

"A friend of mine once had an attack as like yours as possible. It was on board ship, and followed a state of high excitement. He was a brave man like you; and was called on to exert both his strength and his courage suddenly. An hour or two after, fatigue overpowered him, and he appeared to fall into a sound sleep. He really sank into a state which he afterwards described so, that I think it must have been precisely the same affection as yours."

"I am happy to think that my attack was not unique. Did he ever experience a return of it?"

"I knew him for years after, and never heard of any such thing. What strikes me is a parallel in the predisposing causes of each attack. Your unexpected, and gallant hand-to-hand encounter, at such desperate odds, with an experienced swordsman, like that insane colonel of dragoons, your fatigue, and, finally, your composing yourself, as my other friend did, to sleep.

"I wish," he resumed, "one could make out who that *coquin* was, who examined your letters. It is not worth turning back, however, because we should learn nothing. Those people always manage so adroitly. I am satisfied, however, that he must have been an agent of the police. A rogue of any other kind would have robbed you."

I talked very little, being ill and exhausted, but the Marquis talked on agreeably.

"We grow so intimate," said he, at last, "that I must remind you that I am not, for the present, the Marquis d'Harmonville, but only Monsieur Droqville; nevertheless, when we get to Paris, although I cannot see you often, I may be of use. I shall ask you to name to me the hotel at which you mean to put up; because the Marquis being, as you are aware, on his travels, the Hotel d'Harmonville is, for the present, tenanted only by two or three old servants, who must not even see Monsieur Droqville. That gentleman will, nevertheless, contrive to get you access to the box of Monsieur le Marquis, at the Opera; as well, possibly, as to other places more difficult; and so soon as the diplomatic office of the Marquis d'Harmonville is ended, and he at liberty to declare himself, he will not excuse his friend, Monsieur Beckett, from fulfilling his promise to visit him this autumn at the Château d'Harmonville."

You may be sure I thanked the Marquis.

The nearer we got to Paris, the more I valued his protection. The countenance of a great man on the spot, just then, taking so kind an interest in the stranger whom he had, as it were, blundered upon, might make my visit ever so many degrees more delightful than I had anticipated.

Nothing could be more gracious than the manner and looks of the Marquis; and, as I still thanked him, the carriage suddenly stopped in front of the place where a relay of horses awaited us, and where, as it turned out, we were to part.

Chapter IX

Gossip and Counsel

MY EVENTFUL JOURNEY was over, at last. I sat in my hotel window looking out upon brilliant Paris, which had, in a moment, recovered all its gaiety, and more than its accustomed bustle. Every one has read of the kind of excitement that followed the catastrophe of Napoleon, and the second restoration of the Bourbons. I need not, therefore, even if, at this distance, I could, recall and describe my experiences and impressions of the peculiar aspect of Paris, in those strange times. It was, to be sure, my first visit. But, often as I have seen it since, I don't think I ever saw that delightful capital in a state, pleasurably, so excited and exciting.

I had been two days in Paris, and had seen all sorts of sights, and experienced none of that rudeness and insolence of which others complained, from the exasperated officers of the defeated French army.

I must say this, also. My romance had taken complete possession of me; and the chance of seeing the object of my dream, gave a secret and delightful interest to my rambles and drives in the streets and environs, and my visits to the galleries and other sights of the metropolis.

I had neither seen nor heard of Count or Countess, nor had the Marquis d'Harmonville made any sign. I had quite recovered from the strange indisposition under which I had suffered during my night journey.

It was now evening, and I was beginning to fear that my patrician acquaintance had quite forgotten me, when the waiter presented me the card of "Monsieur Droqville;" and, with no small elation and hurry, I desired him to show the gentleman up.

In came the Marquis d'Harmonville, kind and gracious as ever.

"I am a night-bird at present," said he, so soon as we had exchanged the little speeches which are usual. "I keep in the shade, during the daytime, and even now I hardly ventured to come in a close carriage. The friends for whom I have undertaken a rather critical service, have so ordained it. They think all is lost, if I am known to be in Paris. First let me present you with these orders for my box. I am so vexed that I cannot command it oftener during the next fortnight; during my absence, I had directed my secretary to give it for any night to the first of my friends who might apply, and the result is, that I find next to nothing left at my disposal."

I thanked him very much.

"And now, a word, in my office of Mentor. You have not come here, of course, without introductions?"

I produced half a dozen letters, the addresses of which he looked at.

"Don't mind these letters," he said. "I will introduce you. I will take you myself from house to house. One friend at your side is worth many letters. Make no intimacies, no acquaintances, until then. You young men like best to exhaust the public amusements of a great city, before embarrassing yourself with the engagements of society. Go to all these. It will occupy you, day and night, for at least three weeks. When this is over, I shall be at liberty, and will myself introduce you to the brilliant but comparatively quiet routine of society. Place yourself in my hands; and in Paris remember, when once in society, you are always there."

I thanked him very much, and promised to follow his counsels implicitly.

He seemed pleased, and said—

"I shall now tell you some of the places you ought to go to. Take your map, and write letters or numbers upon the points I will indicate, and we will make out a little list. All the places that I shall mention to you are worth seeing."

In this methodical way, and with a great deal of amusing and scandalous anecdote, he furnished me with a catalogue and a guide, which, to a seeker of novelty and pleasure, was invaluable.

"In a fortnight, perhaps in a week," he said, "I shall be at leisure to be of real use to you. In the meantime, be on your guard. You must not play; you will be robbed if you do. Remember, you are surrounded, here, by plausible swindlers and villains of all kinds, who subsist by devouring strangers. Trust no one but those you know."

I thanked him again, and promised to profit by his advice. But my heart was too full of the beautiful lady of the Belle Etoile, to allow our interview to close without an effort to learn something about her. I therefore asked for the Count and Countess de St. Alyre, whom I had had the good fortune to extricate from an extremely unpleasant row in the hall of the inn.

Alas! he had not seen them since. He did not know where they were staying. They had a fine old house only a few leagues from Paris; but he thought it probable that they would remain, for a few days at least, in the city, as preparations would, no doubt, be necessary, after so long an absence, for their reception at home.

"How long have they been away?"

"About eight months, I think."

"They are poor, I think you said?"

"What you would consider poor. But, Monsieur, the Count has an income which affords them the comforts, and even the elegancies of life, living as they do, in a very quiet and retired way, in this cheap country."

"Then they are very happy?"

"One would say they ought to be happy."

"And what prevents?"

"He is jealous."

"But his wife—she gives him no cause?"

"I am afraid she does."

"How, Monsieur?"

"I always thought she was a little too—a great deal too——"

"Too what, Monsieur?"

"Too handsome. But although she has remarkably fine eyes, exquisite features, and the most delicate complexion in the world, I believe that she is a woman of probity. You have never seen her?"

"There was a lady, muffled up in a cloak, with a very thick veil on, the other night, in the hall of the Belle Etoile, when I broke that fellow's head who was bullying the old Count. But her veil was so thick I could not see a feature through it." My answer was diplomatic, you observe. "She may have been the Count's daughter. Do they quarrel?"

"Who, he and his wife?"

"Yes."

"A little."

"Oh! and what do they quarrel about?"

"It is a long story; about the lady's diamonds. They are valuable—they are worth, La Perelleuse says, about a million of francs. The Count wishes them sold and turned into revenue, which he offers to settle as she pleases. The Countess, whose they are, resists, and for a reason which, I rather think, she can't disclose to him."

"And pray what is that?" I asked, my curiosity a good deal piqued.

"She is thinking, I conjecture, how well she will look in them when she marries her second husband."

"Oh?—yes, to be sure. But the Count de St. Alyre is a good man?"

"Admirable, and extremely intelligent."

"I should wish so much to be presented to the Count: you tell me he's so——"

"So agreeably married. But they are living quite out of the world. He takes her now and then to the Opera, or to a public entertainment; but that is all."

"And he must remember so much of the old *régime,* and so many of the scenes of the revolution!"

"Yes, the very man for a philosopher, like you! And he falls asleep after dinner; and his wife don't. But, seriously, he has re- tired from the gay and the great world, and has grown apathetic; and so has his wife; and nothing seems to interest her now, not even—her husband!"

The Marquis stood up to take his leave.

"Don't risk your money," said he. "You will soon have an op- portunity of laying out some of it to great advantage. Several collections of really good pictures, belonging to persons who have mixed themselves up in this Bonapartist restoration, must come within a few weeks to the hammer. You can do wonders when these sales commence. There will be startling bargains! Reserve yourself for them. I shall let you know all about it. By-the-bye," he said, stopping short as he approached the door, "I was so near forgetting. There is to be, next week, the very thing you would enjoy so much, because you see so little of it in England—I mean a *bal masqué,* conducted, it is said, with more than usual splen- dour. It takes place at Versailles—all the world will be there; there is such a rush for cards! But I think I may promise you one. Good night! Adieu!"

Chapter X

The Black Veil

SPEAKING THE LANGUAGE fluently and with unlimited money, there was nothing to prevent my enjoying all that was enjoyable in the French capital. You may easily suppose how two days were passed.

At the end of that time, and at about the same hour, Monsieur Droqville called again.

Courtly, good-natured, gay, as usual, he told me that the masquerade ball was fixed for the next Wednesday, and that he had applied for a card for me.

How awfully unlucky. I was so afraid I should not be able to go.

He stared at me for a moment with a suspicious and menacing look which I did not understand, in silence, and then inquired, rather sharply,

"And will Monsieur Beckett be good enough to say, why not?"

I was a little surprised, but answered the simple truth: I had made an engagement for that evening with two or three English friends, and did not see how I could.

"Just so! You English, wherever you are, always look out for your English boors, your beer and '*bifstek*'; and when you come here, instead of trying to learn something of the people you visit, and pretend to study, you are guzzling, and swearing, and smoking with one another, and no wiser or more polished at the end of your travels than if you had been all the time carousing in a booth at Greenwich."

He laughed sarcastically, and looked as if he could have poisoned me.

"There it is," said he, throwing the card on the table. "Take it or leave it, just as you please. I suppose I shall have my trouble for my pains; but it is not usual when a man such as I, takes trouble, asks a favour, and secures a privilege for an acquaintaince, to treat him so."

This was astonishingly impertinent!

I was shocked, offended, penitent. I had possibly committed unwittingly a breach of good-breeding, according to French ideas, which almost justified the brusque severity of the Marquis's undignified rebuke.

In a confusion, therefore, of many feelings, I hastened to make my apologies, and to propitiate the chance friend who had showed me so much disinterested kindness.

I told him that I would, at any cost, break through the engagement in which I had unluckily entangled myself; that I had spoken with too little reflection, and that I certainly had not thanked him at all in proportion to his kindness and to my real estimate of it.

"Pray say not a word more; my vexation was entirely on your account; and I expressed it, I am only too conscious, in terms a great deal too strong, which, I am sure, your good nature will pardon. Those who know me a little better are aware that I sometimes say a good deal more than I intend; and am always sorry when I do. Monsieur Beckett will forget that his old friend, Monsieur Droqville, has lost his temper in his cause, for a moment, and—we are as good friends as before."

He smiled like the Monsieur Droqville of the Belle Etoile, and extended his hand, which I took very respectfully and cordially.

Our momentary quarrel had left us only better friends.

The Marquis then told me I had better secure a bed in some hotel at Versailles, as a rush would be made to take them; and advised my going down next morning for the purpose.

I ordered horses accordingly for eleven o'clock; and, after a little more conversation, the Marquis d'Harmonville bid me good night, and ran down the stairs with his handkerchief to his mouth and nose, and, as I saw from my window, jumped into his close carriage again and drove away.

Next day I was at Versailles. As I approached the door of the Hotel de France, it was plain that I was not a moment too soon, if, indeed, I were not already too late.

A crowd of carriages were drawn up about the entrance, so that I had no chance of approaching except by dismounting and pushing my way among the horses. The hall was full of servants and gentlemen screaming to the proprietor, who, in a state of polite distraction, was assuring them, one and all, that there was not a room or a closet disengaged in his entire house.

I slipped out again, leaving the hall to those who were shouting, expostulating, wheeling, in the delusion that the host might, if he pleased, manage something for them. I jumped into my carriage and drove, at my horses' best pace, to the Hotel du Reservoir. The blockade about this door was as complete as the other. The result was the same. It was very provoking, but what was to be done? My postillion had, a little officiously, while I was in the hall talking with the hotel authorities, got his horses, bit by bit, as other carriages moved away, to the very steps of the inn door.

This arrangement was very convenient so far as getting in again was concerned. But, this accomplished, how were we to get on?

There were carriages in front, and carriages behind, and no less than four rows of carriages, of all sorts, outside.

I had at this time remarkably long and clear sight, and if I had been impatient before, guess what my feelings were when I saw an open carriage pass along the narrow strip of roadway left open at the other side, a barouche in which I was certain I recognised the veiled Countess and her husband. This carriage had been brought to a walk by a cart which occupied the whole breadth of the narrow way, and was moving with the customary tardiness of such vehicles.

I should have done more wisely if I had jumped down on the *trottoir*, and run round the block of carriages in front of the barouche. But, unfortunately, I was more of a Murat than a Moltke, and preferred a direct charge upon my object to relying on *tactique*. I dashed across the back seat of a carriage which was next mine, I don't know how; tumbled through a sort of gig, in which an old gentleman and a dog were dozing; stepped with an incoherent apology over the side of an open carriage, in which were four gentlemen engaged in a hot dispute; tipped at the far side in getting out, and fell flat across the backs of a pair of horses, who instantly began plunging and threw me head foremost in the dust.

To those who observed my reckless charge without being in the secret of my object I must have appeared demented. Fortunately, the interesting barouche had passed before the catastrophe, and covered as I was with dust, and my hat blocked, you may be sure I did not care to present myself before the object of my Quixotic devotion.

I stood for a while amid a storm of sacré-ing tempered disagreeably with laughter; and in the midst of these, while endeavouring to beat the dust from my clothes with my handkerchief, I heard a voice with which I was acquainted call, "Monsieur Beckett."

I looked and saw the Marquis peeping from a carriage-window. It was a welcome sight. In a moment I was at his carriage side.

"You may as well leave Versailles," he said; "you have learned, no doubt, that there is not a bed to hire in either of the hotels; and I can add that there is not a room to let in the whole town. But I have managed something for you that will answer just as well. Tell your servant to follow us, and get in here and sit beside me."

Fortunately an opening in the closely-packed carriages had just occurred, and mine was approaching.

I directed the servant to follow us; and the Marquis having said a word to his driver, we were immediately in motion.

"I will bring you to a comfortable place, the very existence of which is known to but few Parisians, where, knowing how things were here, I secured a room for you. It is only a mile away, and an old comfortable inn, called Le Dragon Volant. It was fortunate for you that my tiresome business called me to this place so early."

I think we had driven about a mile and a half to the farther side of the palace when we found ourselves upon a narrow old road, with the woods of Versailles on one side, and much older trees, of a size seldom seen in France, on the other.

We pulled up before an antique and solid inn, built of Caen stone, in a fashion richer and more florid than was ever usual in such houses, and which indicated that it was originally designed for the private mansion of some person of wealth, and probably, as the wall bore many carved shields and supporters, of distinction also. A kind of porch, less ancient than the rest, projected hospitably with a wide and florid arch, over which, cut in high relief in stone, and painted and gilded, was the sign of the inn. This was the Flying Dragon, with wings of brilliant red and gold, expanded, and its tail, pale green and gold, twisted and knotted into ever so many rings, and ending in a burnished point barbed like the dart of death.

"I shan't go in—but you will find it a comfortable place; at all events better than nothing. I would go in with you, but my incognito forbids. You will, I daresay, be all the better pleased to learn that the inn is haunted—I should have been, in my young days, I know. But don't allude to that awful fact in hearing of your host, for I believe it is a sore subject. Adieu. If you want to enjoy yourself at the ball take my advice, and go in a domino. I think I shall look in; and certainly, if I do, in the same costume. How shall we recognize one another? Let me see, something held in the fingers—a flower won't do, so many people will have flowers. Suppose you get a red cross a couple of inches long—you're an Englishman—stitched or pinned on the breast of your domino, and I a white one? Yes, that will do very well; and whatever room you go into keep near the door till we meet. I shall look for you at all the doors I pass; and you, in the same way, for me; and we must find each other soon. So that is understood. I can't enjoy a thing of that kind with any but a young person; a man of my age requires the contagion of young spirits and the companionship of someone who enjoys everything spontaneously. Farewell; we meet to-night."

By this time I was standing on the road; I shut the carriage-door; bid him good-bye; and away he drove.

Chapter XI

The Dragon Volant

I took one look about me.

The building was picturesque; the trees made it more so. The antique and sequestered character of the scene, contrasted strangely with the glare and bustle of the Parisian life, to which my eye and ear had become accustomed.

Then I examined the gorgeous old sign for a minute or two. Next I surveyed the exterior of the house more carefully. It was large and solid, and squared more with my ideas of an ancient English hostelry, such as the Canterbury pilgrims might have put up at, than a French house of entertainment. Except, indeed, for a round turret, that rose at the left flank of the house, and terminated in the extinguisher-shaped roof that suggests a French château.

I entered and announced myself as Monsieur Beckett, for whom a room had been taken. I was received with all the consideration due to an English milord, with, of course, an unfathomable purse.

My host conducted me to my apartment. It was a large room, a little sombre, panelled with dark wainscoting, and furnished in a stately and sombre style, long out of date. There was a wide hearth, and a heavy mantelpiece, carved with shields, in which I might, had I been curious enough, have discovered a correspondence with the heraldry on the outer walls. There was something interesting, melancholy, and even depressing in all this. I went to the stone-shafted window, and looked out upon a small park, with a thick wood, forming the background of a château, which presented a cluster of such conical-topped turrets as I have just now mentioned.

The wood and château were melancholy objects. They showed signs of neglect, and almost of decay; and the gloom of fallen grandeur, and a certain air of desertion hung oppressively over the scene.

I asked my host the name of the château.

"That, Monsieur, is the Château de la Carque," he answered.

"It is a pity it is so neglected," I observed. "I should say, perhaps, a pity that its proprietor is not more wealthy?"

"Perhaps so, Monsieur."

"Perhaps?"—I repeated, and looked at him. "Then I suppose he is not very popular."

"Neither one thing nor the other, Monsieur," he answered; "I meant only that we could not tell what use he might make of riches."

"And who is he?" I inquired.

"The Count de St. Alyre."

"Oh! The Count! You are quite sure?" I asked, very eagerly.

It was now the innkeeper's turn to look at me.

"Quite sure, Monsieur, the Count de St. Alyre."

"Do you see much of him in this part of the world?"

"Not a great deal, Monsieur; he is often absent for a considerable time."

"And is he poor?" I inquired.

"I pay rent to him for this house. It is not much; but I find he cannot wait long for it," he replied, smiling satirically.

"From what I have heard, however, I should think he cannot be very poor?" I continued.

"They say, Monsieur, he plays. I know not. He certainly is not rich. About seven months ago, a relation of his died in a distant place. His body was sent to the Count's house here, and by him buried in Père la Chaise, as the poor gentleman had desired. The Count was in profound affliction; although he got a handsome legacy, they say, by that death. But money never seems to do him good for any time."

"He is old, I believe?"

"Old? we call him the 'Wandering Jew,' except, indeed, that he has not always the five sous in his pocket. Yet, Monsieur, his courage does not fail him. He has taken a young and handsome wife."

"And, she?" I urged—

"Is the Countess de St. Alyre."

"Yes; but I fancy we may say something more? She has attributes?"

"Three, Monsieur, three, at least most amiable."

"Ah! And what are they?"

"Youth, beauty, and—diamonds."

I laughed. The sly old gentleman was foiling my curiosity.

"I see, my friend," said I, "you are reluctant——"

"To quarrel with the Count," he concluded. "True. You see, Monsieur, he could vex me in two or three ways; so could I him. But, on the whole, it is better each to mind his business, and to maintain peaceful relations; you understand."

It was, therefore, no use trying, at least for the present. Perhaps he had nothing to relate. Should I think differently, by-and-by, I could try the effect of a few Napoleons. Possibly he meant to extract them.

The host of the Dragon Volant was an elderly man, thin, bronzed, intelligent, and with an air of decision, perfectly military. I learned afterwards that he had served under Napoleon in his early Italian campaigns.

"One question, I think you may answer," I said, "without risking a quarrel. Is the Count at home?"

"He has many homes, I conjecture," said the host evasively. "But—but I think I may say, Monsieur, that he is, I believe, at present staying at the Château de la Carque."

I looked out of the window, more interested than ever, across the undulating grounds to the château, with its gloomy background of foliage.

"I saw him to-day, in his carriage at Versailles," I said.

"Very natural."

"Then his carriage and horses and servants are at the château?"

"The carriage he puts up here, Monsieur, and the servants are hired for the occasion. There is but one who sleeps at the château.

Such a life must be terrifying for Madame the Countess," he replied.

"The old screw!" I thought. "By this torture, he hopes to extract her diamonds. What a life! What fiends to contend with—jealousy and extortion!"

The knight having made this speech to himself, cast his eyes once more upon the enchanter's castle, and heaved a gentle sigh —a sigh of longing, of resolution, and of love.

What a fool I was! and yet, in the sight of angels, are we any wiser as we grow older? It seems to me, only, that our illusions change as we go on; but, still, we are madmen all the same.

"Well, St. Clair," said I, as my servant entered, and began to arrange my things. "You have got a bed?"

"In the cock-loft, Monsieur, among the spiders, and, *par ma foi!* the cats and the owls. But we agree very well. *Vive la bagatelle!*"

"I had no idea it was so full."

"Chiefly the servants, Monsieur, of those persons who were fortunate enough to get apartments at Versailles."

"And what do you think of the Dragon Volant?"

"The Dragon Volant! Monsieur; the old fiery dragon! The devil himself, if all is true! On the faith of a Christian, Monsieur, they say that diabolical miracles have taken place in this house."

"What do you mean? *Revenants?*"

"Not at all, sir; I wish it was no worse, *Revenants?* No! People who have *never* returned—who vanished, before the eyes of half a dozen men, all looking at them."

"What do you mean, St. Clair? Let us hear the story, or miracle, or whatever it is."

"It is only this, Monsieur, that an ex-master-of-the-horse of the late king, who lost his head—Monsieur will have the goodness to recollect, in the revolution—being permitted by the Emperor to return to France, lived here in this hotel, for a month, and at the end of that time vanished, visibly, as I told you, before the faces of half a dozen credible witnesses! The other was a Russian nobleman, six feet high and upwards, who, standing in the centre of the room, downstairs, describing to seven gentlemen of unquestionable veracity, the last moments of Peter the Great, and having a glass of *eau de vie* in his left hand, and his *tasse de café*, nearly finished, in his right, in like manner vanished. His boots were found on the floor where he had been standing; and the gentleman at his right, found, to his astonishment, his cup of coffee in his fingers, and the gentleman at his left, his glass of *eau de vie*——"

"Which he swallowed in his confusion," I suggested.

"Which was preserved for three years among the curious articles of this house, and was broken by the *curé* while conversing with Mademoiselle Fidone in the housekeeper's room; but of the Russian nobleman himself, nothing more was ever seen or heard! *Parbleu!* when we go out of the Dragon Volant, I hope it may be by the door. I heard all this, Monsieur, from the postillion who drove us."

"Then it *must* be true!" said I, jocularly: but I was beginning to feel the gloom of the view, and of the chamber in which I stood; there had stolen over me, I know not how, a presentiment of evil; and my joke was with an effort, and my spirit flagged.

Chapter XII

The Magician

No MORE BRILLIANT spectacle than this masked ball could be imagined. Among other *salons* and galleries, thrown open, was the enormous perspective of the "Grande Galerie des Glaces," lighted up on that occasion with no less than four thousand wax candles, reflected and repeated by all the mirrors, so that the effect was almost dazzling. The grand suite of *salons* was thronged with masques, in every conceivable costume. There was not a single room deserted. Every place was animated with music, voices, brilliant colours, flashing jewels, the hilarity of extemporised comedy, and all the spirited incidents of a cleverly sustained masquerade. I had never seen before anything, in the least, comparable to this magnificent *fête*. I moved along, indolently, in my domino and mask, loitering, now and then, to enjoy a clever dialogue, a farcical song, or an amusing monologue, but, at the same time, keeping my eyes about me, lest my friend in the black domino, with the little white cross on his breast, should pass me by.

I had delayed and looked about me, specially, at every door I passed, as the Marquis and I had agreed; but he had not yet appeared.

While I was thus employed, in the very luxury of lazy amusement, I saw a gilded sedan chair, or, rather, a Chinese palanquin, exhibiting the fantastic exuberance of "Celestial" decoration, borne forward on gilded poles by four richly-dressed Chinese; one with a wand in his hand marched in front, and another behind; and a slight and solemn man, with a long black beard, a tall fez, such as a dervish is represented as wearing, walked close to its side. A strangely-embroidered robe fell over his shoulders, covered with hieroglyphic symbols; the embroidery was in black and gold, upon a variegated ground of brilliant colours. The robe was bound about his waist with a broad belt of gold, with cabalistic devices traced on it, in dark red and black; red stockings, and shoes embroidered with gold, and pointed and curved upward at the toes, in Oriental fashion, appeared below the skirt of the robe. The man's face was dark, fixed, and solemn, and his eyebrows black, and enormously heavy—he carried a singular-looking book under his arm, a wand of polished black wood in his other hand, and walked with his chin sunk on his breast, and his eyes fixed upon the floor. The man in front waved his wand right and left to clear the way for the advancing palanquin, the curtains of which were closed; and there was something so singular, strange, and solemn about the whole thing, that I felt at once interested.

I was very well pleased when I saw the bearers set down their burthen within a few yards of the spot on which I stood.

The bearers and the men with the gilded wands forthwith clapped their hands, and in silence danced round the palanquin a curious and half frantic dance, which was yet, as to figures and postures, perfectly methodical. This was soon accomplished by a clapping of hands and a ha-ha-ing, rhythmically delivered.

While the dance was going on a hand was lightly laid on my arm, and, looking round, a black domino with a white cross stood beside me.

"I am so glad I have found you," said the Marquis; "and at this moment. This is the best group in the rooms. You must speak to the wizard. About an hour ago I lighted upon them, in another *salon*, and consulted the oracle, by putting questions. I never was more amazed. Although his answers were a little disguised it was soon perfectly plain that he knew every detail about the business, which no one on earth had heard of but himself, and two or three other men, about the most cautious persons in France. I shall never forget that shock. I saw other people who consulted him, evidently as much surprised, and more frightened than I. I came with the Count St. Alyre and the Countess."

He nodded towards a thin figure, also in a domino. It was the Count.

"Come," he said to me, "I'll introduce you."

I followed, you may suppose, readily enough.

The Marquis presented me, with a very prettily-turned allusion to my fortunate intervention in his favour at the Belle Etoile; and the Count overwhelmed me with polite speeches, and ended by saying what pleased me better still:

"The Countess is near us, in the next *salon* but one, chatting with her old friend the Duchesse d'Argensaque; I shall go for her in a few minutes; and when I bring her here, she shall make your acquaintance; and thank you, also, for your assistance, rendered with so much courage when we were so very disagreeably interrupted."

"You must, positively, speak with the magician," said the Marquis to the Count de St. Alyre, "you will be so much amused. I did so; and, I assure you, I could not have anticipated such answers! I don't know what to believe."

"Really! Then, by all means, let us try," he replied.

We three approached, together, the side of the palanquin, at which the black-bearded magician stood.

A young man, in a Spanish dress, who, with a friend at his side, had just conferred with the conjuror, was saying, as he passed us by:

"Ingenious mystification! Who is that in the palanquin. He seems to know everybody!"

The Count, in his mask and domino, moved along, stiffly, with us, towards the palanquin. A clear circle was maintained by the Chinese attendants, and the spectators crowded round in a ring.

One of these men—he who with a gilded wand had preceded the procession—advanced, extending his empty hand, palm upward.

"Money?" inquired the Count.

"Gold," replied the usher.

The Count placed a piece of money in his hand; and I and the Marquis were each called on in turn to do likewise as we entered the circle. We paid accordingly.

The conjuror stood beside the palanquin, its silk curtain in his hand; his chin sunk, with its long, jet-black beard, on his chest; the other hand grasping the black wand, on which he leaned; his eyes were lowered, as before, to the ground; his face looked absolutely lifeless. Indeed, I never saw face or figure so moveless, except in death.

The first question the Count put, was:

"Am I married, or unmarried?"

The conjuror drew back the curtain quickly, and placed his ear towards a richly-dressed Chinese, who sat in the litter; withdrew his head, and closed the curtain again; and then answered:

"Yes."

The same preliminary was observed each time, so that the man with the black wand presented himself, not as a prophet, but as a medium; and answered, as it seemed, in the words of a greater than himself.

Two or three questions followed, the answers to which seemed to amuse the Marquis very much; but the point of which I could not see, for I knew next to nothing of the Count's peculiarities and adventures.

"Does my wife love me?" asked he, playfully.

"As well as you deserve."

"Whom do I love best in the world?"

"Self."

"Oh! That I fancy is pretty much the case with every one. But, putting myself out of the question, do I love anything on earth better than my wife?"

"Her diamonds."

"Oh!" said the Count.

The Marquis, I could see, laughed.

"Is it true," said the Count, changing the conversation peremptorily, "that there has been a battle in Naples?"

"No; in France."

"Indeed," said the Count, satirically, with a glance round. "And may I inquire between what powers, and on what particular quarrel?"

"Between the Count and Countess de St. Alyre, and about a document they subscribed on the 25th July, 1811."

The Marquis afterwards told me that this was the date of their marriage settlement.

The Count stood stock-still for a minute or so; and one could fancy that they saw his face flushing through his mask.

Nobody, but we two, knew that the inquirer was the Count de St. Alyre.

I thought he was puzzled to find a subject for his next question; and, perhaps, repented having entangled himself in such a colloquy. If so, he was relieved; for the Marquis, touching his arm, whispered:

"Look to your right, and see who is coming."

I looked in the direction indicated by the Marquis, and I saw a gaunt figure stalking towards us. It was not a masque. The face was broad, scarred, and white. In a word, it was the ugly face of Colonel Gaillarde, in the costume of a corporal of the Imperial Guard, with his left arm so adjusted as to look like a stump, leaving the lower part of the coat-sleeve empty, and pinned up to the breast. There were strips of very real sticking-plaster across his eyebrows and temple, where my stick had left its mark, to score, hereafter, among the more honourable scars of war.

Chapter XIII

The Oracle Tells Me Wonders

I FORGOT FOR a moment how impervious my mask and domino were to the hard stare of the old campaigner, and was preparing for an animated scuffle. It was only for a moment, of course; but the Count cautiously drew a little back as the gasconading corporal, in blue uniform, white vest, and white gaiters—for my friend Gaillarde was as loud and swaggering in his assumed character as in his real one of a colonel of dragoons—drew near. He had already twice all but got himself turned out of doors for vaunting the exploits of Napoleon le Grand, in terrific mock-heroics, and had very nearly come to hand-grips with a Prussian hussar. In fact, he would have been involved in several sanguinary rows already, had not his discretion reminded him that the object of his coming there at all, namely, to arrange a meeting with an affluent widow, on whom he believed he had made a tender impression, would not have been promoted by his premature removal from the festive scene, of which he was an ornament, in charge of a couple of gendarmes.

"Money! Gold! Bah! What money can a wounded soldier like your humble servant have amassed, with but his sword-hand left, which, being necessarily occupied, places not a finger at his command with which to scrape together the spoils of a routed enemy?"

"No gold from him," said the magician. "His scars frank him."

"Bravo, Monsieur le prophète! Bravissimo! Here I am. Shall I begin, *mon sorcier*, without further loss of time, to question you?"

Without waiting for an answer, he commenced, in stentorian tones.

After half a dozen questions and answers, he asked:

"Whom do I pursue at present?"

"Two persons."

"Ha! Two? Well, who are they?"

"An Englishman, whom, if you catch, he will kill you; and a French widow, whom if you find, she will spit in your face."

"Monsieur le magicien calls a spade a spade, and knows that his cloth protects him. No matter! Why do I pursue them?"

"The widow has inflicted a wound on your heart, and the Englishman a wound on your head. They are each separately too strong for you; take care your pursuit does not unite them."

"Bah! How could that be?"

"The Englishman protects ladies. He has got that fact into your head. The widow, if she sees, will marry him. It takes some time, she will reflect, to become a colonel, and the Englishman is unquestionably young."

"I will cut his cock's-comb for him," he ejaculated with an oath and a grin; and in a softer tone he asked, "Where is she?"

"Near enough to be offended if you fail."

"So she ought, by my faith. You are right, Monsieur le prophète! A hundred thousand thanks! Farewell!" And staring about him, and stretching his lank neck as high as he could, he strode away with his scars, and white waistcoat and gaiters, and his bearskin shako.

I had been trying to see the person who sat in the palanquin. I had only once an opportunity of a tolerably steady peep. What I saw was singular. The oracle was dressed, as I have said, very richly, in the Chinese fashion. He was a figure altogether on a larger scale than the interpreter, who stood outside. The features seemed to me large and heavy, and the head was carried with a downward inclination! the eyes were closed, and the chin rested on the breast of his embroidered pelisse. The face seemed fixed, and the very image of apathy. Its character and pose seemed an exaggerated repetition of the immobility of the figure who communicated with the noisy outer world. This face looked blood-red; but that was caused, I concluded, by the light entering through the red silk curtains. All this struck me almost at a glance; I had not many seconds in which to make my observation. The ground was now clear, and the Marquis said, "Go forward, my friend."

I did so. When I reached the magician, as we called the man with the black wand, I glanced over my shoulder to see whether the Count was near.

No, he was some yards behind; and he and the Marquis, whose curiosity seemed to be, by this time, satisfied, were now conversing generally upon some subject of course quite different.

I was relieved, for the sage seemed to blurt out secrets in an unexpected way; and some of mine might not have amused the Count.

I thought for a moment. I wished to test the prophet. A Church-of-England man was a *rara avis* in Paris.

"What is my religion?" I asked.

"A beautiful heresy," answered the oracle instantly.

"A heresy?—and pray how is it named?"

"Love."

"Oh! Then I suppose I am a polytheist, and love a great many?"

"One."

"But, seriously," I asked, intending to turn the course of our colloquy a little out of an embarrassing channel, "have I ever learned any words of devotion by heart?"

"Yes."

"Can you repeat them?"

"Approach."

I did, and lowered my ear.

The man with the black wand closed the curtains, and whispered, slowly and distinctly, these words, which, I need scarcely tell you, I instantly recognised:

I may never see you more; and, oh! that I could forget you! go —farewell—for God's sake, go!

I started as I heard them. They were, you know, the last words whispered to me by the Countess.

Good Heaven! How miraculous! Words heard, most assuredly, by no ear on earth but my own and the lady's who uttered them, till now!

I looked at the impassive face of the spokesman with the wand. There was no trace of meaning, or even of a consciousness that the words he had uttered could possibly interest me.

"What do I most long for?" I asked, scarcely knowing what I said.

"Paradise."

"And what prevents my reaching it?"

"A black veil."

Stronger and stronger! The answers seemed to me to indicate the minutest acquaintance with every detail of my little romance, of which not even the Marquis knew anything! And I, the questioner, masked and robed so that my own brother could not have known me!

"You said I loved someone. Am I loved in return?" I asked.

"Try."

I was speaking lower than before, and stood near the dark man with the beard, to prevent the necessity of his speaking in a loud key.

"Does any one love me?" I repeated.

"Secretly," was the answer.

"Much or little?" I inquired.

"Too well."

"How long will that love last?"

"Till the rose casts its leaves."

The rose—another allusion!

"Then—darkness!" I sighed. "But till then I live in light."

223

"The light of violet eyes."

Love, if not a religion, as the oracle had just pronounced it, is, at least, a superstition. How it exalts the imagination! How it enervates the reason! How credulous it makes us!

All this which, in the case of another, I should have laughed at, most powerfully affected me in my own. It inflamed my ardour, and half crazed my brain, and even influenced my conduct.

The spokesman of this wonderful trick—if trick it were—now waved me backward with his wand, and as I withdrew, my eyes still fixed upon the group, by this time encircled with an aura of mystery in my fancy; backward toward the ring of spectators, I saw him raise his hand suddenly, with a gesture of command, as a signal to the usher who carried the golden wand in front.

The usher struck his wand on the ground, and, in a shrill voice, proclaimed: "The great Confu is silent for an hour."

Instantly the bearers pulled down a sort of blind of bamboo, which descended with a sharp clatter, and secured it at the bottom; and then the man in the tall fez, with the black beard and wand, began a sort of dervish dance. In this the men with the gold wands joined, and finally, in an outer ring, the bearers, the palanquin being the centre of the circles described by these solemn dancers, whose pace, little by little, quickened, whose gestures grew sudden, strange, frantic, as the motion became swifter and swifter, until at length the whirl became so rapid that the dancers seemed to fly by with the speed of a mill-wheel, and amid a general clapping of hands, and universal wonder, these strange performers mingled with the crowd, and the exhibition, for the time at least, ended.

The Marquis d'Harmonville was standing not far away, looking on the ground, as one could judge by his attitude and musing. I approached, and he said:

"The Count has just gone away to look for his wife. It is a pity she was not there to consult the prophet; it would have been amusing, I daresay, to see how the Count bore it. Suppose we follow him. I have asked him to introduce you."

With a beating heart, I accompanied the Marquis d'Harmonville.

Chapter XIV

Mademoiselle de la Vallière

WE WANDERED THROUGH the *salons*, the Marquis and I. It was no easy matter to find a friend in rooms so crowded.

"Stay here," said the Marquis, "I have thought of a way of finding him. Besides, his jealousy may have warned him that there is no particular advantage to be gained by presenting you to his wife, I had better go and reason with him; as you seem to wish an introduction so very much."

This occurred in the room that is now called the "Salon d'Apollon." The paintings remained in my memory, and my adventure of that evening was destined to occur there.

I sat down upon a sofa; and looked about me. Three or four persons beside myself were seated on this roomy piece of gilded furniture. They were chatting all very gaily; all—except the person who sat next to me, and she was a lady. Hardly two feet interposed between us. The lady sat apparently in a reverie. Nothing could be more graceful. She wore the costume perpetuated in Collignan's full-length portrait of Mademoiselle de la Vallière. It is, as you know, not only rich, but elegant. Her hair was powdered, but one could perceive that it was naturally a dark brown. One pretty little foot appeared, and could anything be more exquisite than her hand?

It was extremely provoking that this lady wore her mask, and did not, as many did, hold it for a time in her hand.

I was convinced that she was pretty. Availing myself of the privilege of a masquerade, a microcosm in which it is impossible, except by voice and allusion, to distinguish friend from foe, I spoke—

"It is not easy, Mademoiselle, to deceive me," I began.

"So much the better for Monsieur," answered the mask, quietly.

"I mean," I said, determined to tell my fib, "that beauty is a gift more difficult to conceal than Mademoiselle supposes."

"Yet Monsieur has succeeded very well," she said in the same sweet and careless tones.

"I see the costume of this, the beautiful Mademoiselle de la Vallière, upon a form that surpasses her own; I raise my eyes, and I behold a mask, and yet I recognise the lady; beauty is like that precious stone in the *Arabian Nights*, which emits, no matter how concealed, a light that betrays it."

"I know the story," said the young lady. "The light betrayed it, not in the sun, but in darkness. Is there so little light in these rooms, Monsieur, that a poor glow-worm can show so brightly. I thought we were in a luminous atmosphere, wherever a certain countess moved?"

Here was an awkward speech! How was I to answer? This lady might be, as they say some ladies are, a lover of mischief, or an intimate of the Countess de St. Alyre. Cautiously, therefore, I inquired,

"What countess?"

"If you know me, you must know that she is my dearest friend. Is she not beautiful?"

"How can I answer, there are so many countesses."

"Every one who knows me, knows who my best beloved friend is. You don't know me?"

"That is cruel. I can scarcely believe I am mistaken."

"With whom were you walking, just now?" she asked.

"A gentleman, a friend," I answered.

"I saw him, of course, a friend; but I think I know him, and should like to be certain. Is he not a certain marquis?"

Here was another question that was extremely awkward.

"There are so many people here, and one may walk, at one time, with one, and at another with a different one, that——"

"That an unscrupulous person has no difficulty in evading a simple question like mine. Know then, once for all, that nothing disgusts a person of spirit so much as suspicion. You, Monsieur, are a gentleman of discretion. I shall respect you accordingly."

"Mademoiselle would despise me, were I to violate a confidence."

"But you don't deceive me. You imitate your friend's diplomacy. I hate diplomacy. It means fraud and cowardice. Don't you think I know him. The gentleman with the cross of white ribbon on his breast. I know the Marquis d'Harmonville perfectly. You see to what good purpose your ingenuity has been expended."

"To that conjecture I can answer neither yes nor no."

"You need not. But what was your motive in mortifying a lady?"

"It is the last thing on earth I should do."

"You affected to know me, and you don't; through caprice or listlessness or curiosity you wished to converse, not with a lady, but with a costume. You admired, and you pretend to mistake me for another. But who is quite perfect? Is truth any longer to be found on earth?"

"Mademoiselle has formed a mistaken opinion of me."

"And you also of me; you find me less foolish than you supposed. I know perfectly whom you intend amusing with compliments and melancholy declamation, and whom, with that amiable purpose, you have been seeking."

"Tell me whom you mean," I entreated.

"Upon one condition."

"What is that?"

"That you will confess if I name the lady."

"You describe my object unfairly," I objected. "I can't admit that I proposed speaking to any lady in the tone you describe."

"Well, I shan't insist on that; only if I name the lady, you will promise to admit that I am right."

"*Must* I promise?"

"Certainly not, there is no compulsion; but your promise is the only condition on which I will speak to you again."

I hesitated for a moment; but how could she possibly tell? The Countess would scarcely have admitted this little romance to anyone; and the mask in the La Vallière costume could not possibly know who the masked domino beside her was.

"I consent," I said, "I promise."

"You must promise on the honour of a gentleman."

"Well, I do; on the honour of a gentleman."

"Then this lady is the Countess de St. Alyre." I was unspeakably surprised; I was disconcerted; but I remembered my promise, and said—

"The Countess de St. Alyre *is*, unquestionably, the lady to whom I hoped for an introduction to-night; but I beg to assure you also on the honour of a gentleman, that she has not the faintest imaginable suspicion that I was seeking such an honour, nor, in all probability, does she remember that such a person as I exists. I had the honour to render her and the Count a trifling service, too trifling, I fear, to have earned more than an hour's recollection."

"The world is not so ungrateful as you suppose; or if it be, there are, nevertheless, a few hearts that redeem it. I can answer for the Countess de St. Alyre, she never forgets a kindness. She does not show all she feels; for she is unhappy, and cannot."

"Unhappy! I feared, indeed, that might be. But for all the rest that you are good enough to suppose, it is but a flattering dream."

"I told you that I am the Countess's friend, and being so I must know something of her character; also, there are confidences between us, and I may know more than you think, of those trifling services of which you suppose the recollection is so transitory."

I was becoming more and more interested. I was as wicked as other young men, and the heinousness of such a pursuit was as nothing, now that self-love and all the passions that mingle in such a romance, were roused. The image of the beautiful Countess had now again quite superseded the pretty counterpart of La Vallière, who was before me. I would have given a great deal to hear, in solemn earnest, that she did remember the champion who, for her sake, had thrown himself before the sabre of an enraged dragoon, with only a cudgel in his hand, and conquered.

"You say the Countess is unhappy," said I. "What causes her unhappiness?"

"Many things. Her husband is old, jealous and tyrannical. Is not that enough? Even when relieved from his society, she is lonely."

"But you are her friend?" I suggested.

"And you think one friend enough?" she answered; "she has one alone, to whom she can open her heart."

"Is there room for another friend?"

"Try."

"How can I find a way?"

"She will aid you."

"How?"

She answered by question. "Have you secured rooms in either of the hotels of Versailles?"

"No, I could not. I am lodged in the Dragon Volant, which stands at the verge of the grounds of the Château de la Carque."

"That is better still. I need not ask if you have courage for an adventure. I need not ask if you are a man of honour. A lady may trust herself to you, and fear nothing. There are few men to whom the interview, such as I shall arrange, could be granted with safety. You shall meet her at two o'clock this morning in the Park of the Château de la Carque. What room do you occupy in the Dragon Volant?"

I was amazed at the audacity and decision of this girl. Was she, as we say in England, hoaxing me?

"I can describe that accurately," said I. "As I look from the rear of the house, in which my apartment is, I am at the extreme right, next the angle; and one pair of stairs up, from the hall."

"Very well; you must have observed, if you looked into the park, two or three clumps of chestnut and lime-trees, growing so close together as to form a small grove. You must return to your hotel, change your dress, and, preserving a scrupulous secrecy, as to why or where you go, leave the Dragon Volant, and climb the park-wall, unseen; you will easily recognise the grove I have mentioned; there you will meet the Countess, who will grant you an audience of a few minutes, who will expect the most scrupulous reserve on your part, and who will explain to you, in a few words, a great deal which I could not so well tell you here."

I cannot describe the feeling with which I heard these words. I was astounded. Doubt succeeded. I could not believe these agitating words.

"Mademoiselle will believe that if I only dared assure myself that so great a happiness and honour were really intended for me, my gratitude would be as lasting as my life. But how dare I believe that Mademoiselle does not speak, rather from her own sympathy or goodness, than from a certainty that the Countess de St. Alyre would concede so great an honour?"

"Monsieur believes either that I am not, as I pretend to be, in the secret which he hitherto supposed to be shared by no one but the Countess and himself, or else that I am cruelly mystifying him. That I am in her confidence, I swear by all that is dear in a whispered farewell. By the last companion of this flower!" and she took for a moment in her fingers the nodding head of a white rosebud that was nestled in her bouquet. "By my own good star, and hers—or shall I call it our '*belle étoile*'? Have I said enough?"

"Enough?" I repeated, "more than enough—a thousand thanks."

"And being thus in her confidence, I am clearly her friend; and being a friend would it be friendly to use her dear name so; and all for sake of practising a vulgar trick upon you—a stranger?"

"Mademoiselle will forgive me. Remember how very precious is the hope of seeing, and speaking to the Countess. Is it wonderful, then, that I should falter in my belief? You have convinced me, however, and will forgive my hesitation."

"You will be at the place I have described, then, at two o'clock?"

"Assuredly," I answered.

"And Monsieur, I know, will not fail, through fear. No, he need not assure me; his courage is already proved."

"No danger, in such a case, will be unwelcome to me."

"Had you not better go now, Monsieur, and rejoin your friend?"

"I promised to wait here for my friend's return. The Count de St. Alyre said that he intended to introduce me to the Countess."

"And Monsieur is so simple as to believe him?"

"Why should I not?"

"Because he is jealous and cunning. You will see. He will never introduce you to his wife. He will come here and say he cannot find her, and promise another time."

"I think I see him approaching, with my friend. No—there is no lady with him."

"I told you so. You will wait a long time for that happiness, if it is never to reach you except through his hands. In the meantime, you had better not let him see you so near me. He will suspect that we have been talking of his wife; and that will whet his jealousy and his vigilance."

I thanked my unknown friend in the mask, and withdrawing a few steps, came, by a little "circumbendibus," upon the flank of the Count.

I smiled under my mask, as he assured me that the Duchesse de la Roqueme had changed her place, and taken the Countess with her; but he hoped, at some very early time, to have an opportunity of enabling her to make my acquaintance.

I avoided the Marquis d'Harmonville, who was following the Count. I was afraid he might propose accompanying me home, and had no wish to be forced to make an explanation.

I lost myself quickly, therefore, in the crowd, and moved as rapidly as it would allow me, towards the Galerie des Glaces, which lay in the direction opposite to that in which I saw the Count and my friend the Marquis moving.

Chapter XV

Strange Story of the Dragon Volant

THESE FÊTES WERE earlier in those days, and in France, than our modern balls are in London. I consulted my watch. It was a little past twelve.

It was a still and sultry night; the magnificent suite of rooms, vast as some of them were, could not be kept at a temperature less than oppressive, especially to people with masks on. In some places the crowd was inconvenient, and the profusion of lights added to the heat. I removed my mask, therefore, as I saw some other people do, who were as careless of mystery as I. I had hardly done so, and began to breathe more comfortably, when I heard a friendly English voice call me by my name. It was Tom Whistlewick, of the —th Dragoons. He had unmasked, with a very flushed face, as I did. He was one of those Waterloo heroes, new from the mint of glory, whom, as a body, all the world, except France, revered; and the only thing I knew against him, was a habit of allaying his thirst, which was excessive, at balls, *fêtes*, musical parties, and all gatherings, where it was to be had, with champagne; and, as he introduced me to his friend, Monsieur Carmaignac, I observed that he spoke a little thick. Monsieur Carmaignac was little, lean, and as straight as a ramrod. He was bald, took snuff, and wore spectacles; and, as I soon learned, held an official position.

Tom was facetious, sly, and rather difficult to understand, in his present pleasant mood. He was elevating his eyebrows and screwing his lips oddly, and fanning himself vaguely with his mask.

After some agreeable conversation, I was glad to observe that he preferred silence, and was satisfied with the *rôle* of listener, as I and Monsieur Carmaignac chatted; and he seated himself, with extraordinary caution and indecision, upon a bench, beside us, and seemed very soon to find a difficulty in keeping his eyes open.

"I heard you mention," said the French gentleman, "that you had engaged an apartment in the Dragon Volant, about half a league from this. When I was in a different police department, about four years ago, two very strange cases were connected with that house. One was of a wealthy *émigré*, permitted to return to France, by the Em—by Napoleon. He vanished. The other—equally strange —was the case of a Russian of rank and wealth. He disappeared just as mysteriously."

"My servant," I said, "gave me a confused account of some occurrences, and, as well as I recollect he described the same persons—I mean a returned French nobleman, and a Russian gentleman. But he made the whole story so marvellous—I mean in the supernatural sense—that, I confess, I did not believe a word of it."

"No, there was nothing supernatural; but a great deal inexplicable," said the French gentleman. "Of course there may be theories; but the thing was never explained, nor, so far as I know, was a ray of light ever thrown upon it."

"Pray let me hear the story," I said. "I think I have a claim, as it affects my quarters. You don't suspect the people of the house?"

"Oh! it has changed hands since then. But there seemed to be a fatality about a particular room."

"Could you describe that room?"

"Certainly. It is a spacious, panelled bedroom, up one pair of stairs, in the back of the house, and at the extreme right, as you look from its windows."

"Ho! Really? Why, then, I have got the very room!" I said, beginning to be more interested—perhaps the least bit in the world, disagreeably. "Did the people die, or were they actually spirited away?"

"No, they did not die—they disappeared very oddly. I'll tell you the particulars—I happen to know them exactly, because I made an official visit, on the first occasion, to the house, to collect evidence; and although I did not go down there, upon the second, the papers came before me, and I dictated the official letter despatched to the relations of the people who had disappeared; they had applied to the government to investigate the affair. We had letters from the same relations more than two years later, from which we learned that the missing men had never turned up."

He took a pinch of snuff, and looked steadily at me.

"Never! I shall relate all that happened, so far as we could discover. The French noble, who was the Chevalier Chateau Blassemare, unlike most émigrés, had taken the matter in time, sold a large portion of his property before the revolution had proceeded so far as to render that next to impossible, and retired with a large sum. He brought with him about half a million of francs, the greater part of which he invested in the French funds; a much larger sum remained in Austrian land and securities. You will observe then that this gentleman was rich, and there was no allegation of his having lost money, or being, in any way, embarrassed. You see?"

I assented.

"This gentleman's habits were not expensive in proportion to his means. He had suitable lodgings in Paris; and for a time, society, the theatres, and other reasonable amusements, engrossed him. He did not play. He was a middle-aged man, affecting youth, with the vanities which are usual in such persons; but, for the rest, he was a gentle and polite person, who disturbed nobody—a person, you see, not likely to provoke an enmity."

"Certainly not," I agreed.

"Early in the summer of 1811, he got an order permitting him to copy a picture in one of these *salons*, and came down here, to Versailles, for the purpose. His work was getting on slowly. After a time he left his hotel, here, and went, by way of change, to the Dragon Volant: there he took, by special choice, the bedroom which has fallen to you by chance. From this time, it appeared, he painted little; and seldom visited his apartment in Paris. One night he saw the host of the Dragon Volant, and told him that he was going into Paris, to remain for a day or two, on very particular business; that his servant would accompany him, but that he would retain his apartments at the Dragon Volant, and return in a few days. He left some clothes there, but packed a portmanteau, took his dressing-case, and the rest, and, with his servant behind his carriage, drove into Paris. You observe all this, Monsieur?"

"Most attentively," I answered.

"Well, Monsieur, as soon as they were approaching his lodgings, he stopped the carriage on a sudden, told his servant that he had changed his mind; that he would sleep elsewhere that night, that he had very particular business in the north of France, not far from Rouen, that he would set out before daylight on his journey, and return in a fortnight. He called a fiacre, took in his hand a leather bag which, the servant said, was just large enough to hold a few shirts and a coat, but that it was enormously heavy, as he could testify, for he held it in his hand, while his master took out his purse to count thirty-six Napoleons, for which the servant was to account when he should return. He then sent him on, in the carriage; and he, with the bag I have mentioned, got into the fiacre. Up to that, you see, the narrative is quite clear."

"Perfectly," I agreed.

"Now comes the mystery," said Monsieur Carmaignac. "After that, the Count Chateau Blassemare was never more seen, so far as we can make out, by acquaintance or friend. We learned that the day before the Count's stockbroker had, by his direction, sold all his stock in the French funds, and handed him the cash it realised. The reason he gave him for this measure tallied with what he said to his servant. He told him that he was going to the north of France to settle some claims, and did not know exactly how much might be required. The bag, which had puzzled the servant by its weight, contained, no doubt, a large sum in gold. Will Monsieur try my snuff?"

He politely tendered his open snuff-box, of which I partook, experimentally.

"A reward was offered," he continued, "when the inquiry was instituted, for any information tending to throw a light upon the mystery, which might be afforded by the driver of the fiacre 'employed on the night of' (so-and-so), 'at about the hour of half-past ten, by a gentleman, with a black-leather travelling-bag in his hand, who descended from a private carriage, and gave his servant some money, which he counted twice over.' About a hundred and fifty drivers applied, but not one of them was the right man. We did, however, elicit a curious and unexpected piece of evidence in quite another quarter. What a racket that plaguey harlequin makes with his sword!"

"Intolerable!" I chimed in.

The harlequin was soon gone, and he resumed.

"The evidence I speak of, came from a boy, about twelve years old, who knew the appearance of the Count perfectly, having been often employed by him as a messenger. He stated that about half-past twelve o'clock, on the same night—upon which you are to observe, there was a brilliant moon—he was sent, his mother having been suddenly taken ill, for the *sage femme* who lived within a stone's throw of the Dragon Volant. His father's house, from which he started, was a mile away, or more, from that inn, in order to reach which he had to pass round the park of the Château de la Carque, at the site most remote from the point to which he was going. It passes the old churchyard of St. Aubin, which is separated from the road only by a very low fence, and two or three enormous old trees. The boy was a little nervous as he approached this ancient cemetery; and, under the bright moonlight, he saw a man whom he distinctly recognised as the Count, whom they designated by a soubriquet which means 'the man of smiles.' He was looking rueful enough now, and was seated on the side of a tombstone, on which he had laid a pistol, while he was ramming home the charge of another.

"The boy got cautiously by, on tiptoe, with his eyes all the time on the Count Chateau Blassemare, or the man he mistook for him; his dress was not what he usually wore, but the witness swore that he could not be mistaken as to his identity. He said his face looked grave and stern; but though he did not smile, it was the same face he knew so well. Nothing would make him swerve from that. If that were he, it was the last time he was seen. He has never been heard of since. Nothing could be heard of him in the neighbourhood of Rouen. There has been no evidence of his death; and there is no sign that he is living."

"That certainly is a most singular case," I replied; and was about to ask a question or two, when Tom Whistlewick who, without my observing it, had been taking a ramble, returned, a great deal more awake, and a great deal less tipsy.

"I say, Carmaignac, it is getting late, and I must go; I really must, for the reason I told you—and, Beckett, we must soon meet again."

"I regret very much, Monsieur, my not being able at present to relate to you the other case, that of another tenant of the very same room—a case more mysterious and sinister than the last—and which occurred in the autumn of the same year."

"Will you both do a very good-natured thing, and come and dine with me at the Dragon Volant to-morrow?"

So, as we pursued our way along the Galerie des Glaces, I extracted their promise.

"By Jove!" said Whistlewick, when this was done; "look at that pagoda, or sedan chair, or whatever it is, just where those fellows set it down, and not one of them near it! I can't imagine how they tell fortunes so devilish well. Jack Nuffles—I met him here to-night —says they are gipsies—where are they, I wonder? I'll go over and have a peep at the prophet."

I saw him plucking at the blinds, which were constructed something on the principle of Venetian blinds; the red curtains were inside; but they did not yield, and he could only peep under one that did not come quite down.

When he rejoined us, he related: "I could scarcely see the old fellow, it's so dark. He is covered with gold and red, and has an embroidered hat on like a mandarin's; he's fast asleep; and, by Jove, he smells like a pole-cat! It's worth going over only to have it to say. Fiew! pooh! oh! It *is* a perfume. Faugh!"

Not caring to accept this tempting invitation, we got along slowly towards the door. I bid them good night, reminding them of their promise. And so found my way at last to my carriage; and was soon rolling slowly towards the Dragon Volant, on the loneliest of roads, under old trees, and the soft moonlight.

What a number of things had happened within the last two hours! what a variety of strange and vivid pictures were crowded together in that brief space! What an adventure was before me!

The silent, moonlighted, solitary road, how it contrasted with the many-eddied whirl of pleasure from whose roar and music, lights, diamonds and colours, I had just extricated myself.

The sight of lonely Nature at such an hour, acts like a sudden sedative. The madness and guilt of my pursuit struck me with a momentary compunction and horror. I wished I had never entered the labyrinth which was leading me, I knew not whither. It was too late to think of that now; but the bitter was already stealing into my cup; and vague anticipations lay, for a few minutes, heavy on my heart. It would not have taken much to make me disclose my unmanly state of mind to my lively friend, Alfred Ogle, nor even to the milder ridicule of the agreeable Tom Whistlewick.

Chapter XVI

The Parc of the Château de la Carque

THERE WAS NO danger of the Dragon Volant's closing its doors on that occasion till three or four in the morning. There were quartered there many servants of great people, whose masters would not leave the ball till the last moment, and who could not return to their corners in the Dragon Volant, till their last services had been rendered.

I knew, therefore, I should have ample time for my mysterious excursion without exciting curiosity by being shut out.

And now we pulled up under the canopy of boughs, before the sign of the Dragon Volant, and the light that shone from its hall-door.

I dismissed my carriage, ran up the broad staircase, mask in hand, with my domino fluttering about me, and entered the large bed-room. The black wainscoting and stately furniture, with the dark curtains of the very tall bed, made the night there more sombre.

An oblique patch of moonlight was thrown upon the floor from the window to which I hastened. I looked out upon the landscape slumbering in those silvery beams. There stood the outline of the Château de la Carque, its chimneys, and many turrets with their extinguisher-shaped roofs black against the soft grey sky. There, also, more in the foreground, about midway between the window where I stood, and the château, but a little to the left, I traced the tufted masses of the grove which the lady in the mask had appointed as the trysting-place, where I and the beautiful Countess were to meet that night.

I took "the bearings" of this gloomy bit of wood, whose foliage glimmered softly at top in the light of the moon.

You may guess with what a strange interest and swelling of the heart I gazed on the unknown scene of my coming adventure.

But time was flying, and the hour already near. I threw my robe upon a sofa; I groped out a pair of boots, which I substituted for those thin heelless shoes, in those days called "pumps," without which a gentleman could not attend an evening party. I put on my hat, and lastly, I took a pair of loaded pistols which I had been advised were satisfactory companions in the then unsettled state of French society: swarms of disbanded soldiers, some of them alleged to be desperate characters, being everywhere to be met with. These preparations made, I confess I took a looking-glass to the window to see how I looked in the moonlight; and being satisfied, I replaced it, and ran downstairs.

In the hall I called for my servant.

"St. Clair," said I, "I mean to take a little moonlight ramble, only ten minutes or so. You must not go to bed until I return. If the night is very beautiful, I may possibly extend my ramble a little."

So down the steps I lounged, looking first over my right, and then over my left shoulder, like a man uncertain which direction to take, and I sauntered up the road, gazing now at the moon, and now at the thin white clouds in the opposite direction, whistling, all the time, an air which I had picked up at one of the theatres.

When I had got a couple of hundred yards away from the Dragon Volant, my minstrelsy totally ceased; and I turned about, and glanced sharply down the road that looked as white as hoar-frost under the moon, and saw the gable of the old inn, and a window, partly concealed by the foliage, with a dusky light shining from it.

No sound of footsteps was stirring; no sign of human figure in sight. I consulted my watch, which the light was sufficiently strong to enable me to do. It now wanted but eight minutes of the appointed hour. A thick mantle of ivy at this point covered the wall and rose in a clustering head at top.

It afforded me facilities for scaling the wall, and a partial screen for my operations, if any eye should chance to be looking that way. And now it was done. I was in the park of the Château de la Carque, as nefarious a poacher as ever trespassed on the grounds of unsuspicious lord!

Before me rose the appointed grove, which looked as black as a clump of gigantic hearse-plumes. It seemed to tower higher and higher at every step; and cast a broader and blacker shadow towards my feet. On I marched, and was glad when I plunged into the shadow which concealed me. Now I was among the grand old lime and chestnut trees—my heart beat fast with expectation.

This grove opened, a little, near the middle; and in the space thus cleared, there stood with a surrounding flight of steps, a small Greek temple or shrine, with a statue in the centre. It was built of white marble with fluted Corinthian columns, and the crevices were tufted with grass; moss had shown itself on pedestal and cornice, and signs of long neglect and decay were apparent in its discoloured and weather-worn marble. A few feet in front of the steps a fountain, fed from the great ponds at the other side of the château, was making a constant tinkle and plashing in a wide marble basin, and the jet of water glimmered like a shower of diamonds in the broken moonlight. The very neglect and half-ruinous state of all this made it only the prettier, as well as sadder. I was too intently watching for the arrival of the lady, in the direction of the château, to study these things; but the half-noted effect of them was romantic, and suggested somehow the grotto and the fountain, and the apparition of Egeria.

As I watched a voice spoke to me, a little behind my left shoulder. I turned, almost with a start, and the masque, in the costume of Mademoiselle de la Vallière stood there.

"The Countess will be here presently," she said. The lady stood upon the open space, and the moonlight fell unbroken upon her. Nothing could be more becoming; her figure looked more graceful and elegant than ever. "In the meantime I shall tell you some peculiarities of her situation. She is unhappy; miserable in an ill-assorted marriage, with a jealous tyrant who now would constrain her to sell her diamonds, which are——"

"Worth thirty thousand pounds sterling. I heard all that from a friend. Can I aid the Countess in her unequal struggle? Say but how, and the greater the danger or the sacrifice, the happier will it make me. Can I aid her?"

"If you despise a danger—which, yet, is not a danger; if you despise, as she does, the tyrannical canons of the world; and, if you are chivalrous enough to devote yourself to a lady's cause, with no reward but her poor gratitude; if you can do these things you can aid her, and earn a foremost place, not in her gratitude only, but in her friendship."

At those words the lady in the mask turned away, and seemed to weep. I vowed myself the willing slave of the Countess. "But," I added, "you told me she would soon be here."

"That is, if nothing unforeseen should happen; but with the eye of the Count de St. Alyre in the house, and open, it is seldom safe to stir."

"Does she wish to see me?" I asked, with a tender hesitation.

"First, say have you really thought of her, more than once, since the adventure of the Belle Etoile."

"She never leaves my thoughts; day and night her beautiful eyes haunt me; her sweet voice is always in my ear."

"Mine is said to resemble hers," said the mask.

"So it does," I answered. "But it is only a resemblance."

"Oh! then mine is better?"

"Pardon me, Madomoiselle, I did not say that. Yours is a sweet voice, but I fancy a little higher."

"A little shriller, you would say," answered the de la Vallière, I fancied a good deal vexed.

"No, not shriller: your voice is not shrill, it is beautifully sweet; but not so pathetically sweet as hers."

"That is prejudice, Monsieur; it is not true."

I bowed; I could not contradict a lady.

"I see, Monsieur, you laugh at me; you think me vain, because I claim in some points to be equal to the Countess de St. Alyre. I challenge you to say, my hand, at least, is less beautiful than hers." As she thus spoke, she drew her glove off, and extended her hand, back upward, in the moonlight.

The lady seemed really nettled. It was undignified and irritating; for in this uninteresting competition the precious moments were flying, and my interview leading apparently to nothing.

"You will admit, then, that my hand is as beautiful as hers?"

"I cannot admit it, Mademoiselle," said I, with the honesty of irritation. "I will not enter into comparisons, but the Countess de St. Alyre is, in all respects, the most beautiful lady I ever beheld."

The masque laughed coldly, and then, more and more softly, said, with a sigh, "I will prove all I say." And as she spoke she removed the mask: and the Countess de St. Alyre, smiling, confused, bashful, more beautiful than ever, stood before me!

"Good Heavens!" I exclaimed. "How monstrously stupid I have been. And it was to Madame la Comtesse that I spoke for so long in the salon!" I gazed on her in silence. And with a low sweet laugh of good-nature she extended her hand. I took it, and carried it to my lips.

"No, you must not do that," she said, quietly, "we are not old enough friends yet. I find, although you were mistaken, that you do remember the Countess of the Belle Etoile, and that you are a champion true and fearless. Had you yielded to the claims just now pressed upon you by the rivalry of Mademoiselle de la Vallière, in her mask, the Countess de St. Alyre should never have trusted or seen you more. I now am sure that you are true, as well as brave. You now know that I have not forgotten you; and, also that if you would risk your life for me, I, too, would brave some danger, rather than lose my friend for ever. I have but a few moments more. Will you come here again to-morrow night, at a quarter past eleven? I will be here at that moment; you must exercise the most scrupulous care to prevent suspicion that you have come here, Monsieur. You owe that to me."

She spoke these last words with the most solemn entreaty.

I vowed again and again, that I would die rather than permit the least rashness to endanger the secret which made all the interest and value of my life.

She was looking, I thought, more and more beautiful every moment. My enthusiasm expanded in proportion.

"You must come to-morrow night by a different route," she said; "and if you come again, we can change it once more. At the other side of the château there is a little churchyard, with a ruined chapel. The neighbours are afraid to pass it by night. The road is deserted there, and a stile opens a way into these grounds. Cross it and you can find a covert of thickets, to within fifty steps of this spot."

I promised, of course, to observe her instructions implicitly.

"I have lived for more than a year in an agony of irresolution. I have decided at last. I have lived a melancholy life; a lonelier life than is passed in the cloister. I have had no one to confide in; no one to advise me; no one to save me from the horrors of my existence. I have found a brave and prompt friend at last. Shall I ever forget the heroic tableau of the hall of the Belle Etoile? Have you —have you really kept the rose I gave you, as we parted? Yes— you swear it. You need not; I trust you. Richard, how often have I in solitude repeated your name, learned from my servant. Richard, my hero! Oh! Richard! Oh, my king! I love you."

I would have folded her to my heart—thrown myself at her feet. But this beautiful and—shall I say it—inconsistent woman repelled me.

"No, we must not waste our moments in extravagances. Understand my case. There is no such thing as indifference in the married state. Not to love one's husband," she continued, "is to hate him. The Count, ridiculous in all else, is formidable in his jealousy. In mercy, then, to me, observe caution. Affect to all you speak to, the most complete ignorance of all the people in the Château de la Carque; and, if any one in your presence mentions the Count or Countess de St. Alyre, be sure you say you never saw either. I shall have more to say to you to-morrow night. I have reasons that I cannot now explain, for all I do, and all I postpone. Farewell. Go! Leave me."

She waved me back, peremptorily. I echoed her "farewell," and obeyed.

This interview had not lasted, I think, more than ten minutes. I scaled the park-wall again, and reached the Dragon Volant before its doors were closed.

I lay awake in my bed, in a fever of elation. I saw, till the dawn broke, and chased the vision, the beautiful Countess de St. Alyre, always in the dark, before me.

Chapter XVII

The Tenant of the Palanquin

THE MARQUIS CALLED on me next day. My late breakfast was still upon the table.

He had come, he said, to ask a favour. An accident had happened to his carriage in the crowd on leaving the ball, and he begged, if I were going into Paris, a seat in mine—I was going in, and was extremely glad of his company. He came with me to my hotel; we went up to my rooms. I was surprised to see a man seated in an easy chair, with his back towards us, reading a newspaper. He rose. It was the Count de St. Alyre, his gold spectacles on his nose; his black wig, in oily curls, lying close to his narrow head, and showing, like carved ebony over a repulsive visage of boxwood. His black muffler had been pulled down. His right arm was in a sling. I don't know whether there was anything unusual in his countenance that day, or whether it was but the effect of prejudice arising from all I had heard in my mysterious interview in his park, but I thought his countenance was more strikingly forbidding than I had seen it before.

I was not callous enough in the ways of sin to meet this man, injured at least in intent, thus suddenly, without a momentary disturbance.

He smiled.

"I called, Monsieur Beckett, in the hope of finding you here," he croaked, "and I meditated, I fear, taking a great liberty, but my friend the Marquis d'Harmonville, on whom I have perhaps some claim, will perhaps give me the assistance I require so much."

"With great pleasure," said the Marquis, "but not till after six o'clock. I must go this moment to a meeting of three or four people, whom I cannot disappoint, and I know, perfectly, we cannot break up earlier."

"What am I to do?" exclaimed the Count. "An hour would have done it all. Was ever *contretemps* so unlucky!"

"I'll give you an hour, with pleasure," said I.

"How very good of you, Monsieur, I hardly dare to hope it. The business, for so gay and charming a man as Monsieur Beckett, is a little *funeste*. Pray read this note which reached me this morning."

It certainly was not cheerful. It was a note stating that the body of his, the Count's cousin, Monsieur de St. Amand, who had died at his house, the Château Clery, had been, in accordance with his written directions, sent for burial at Père la Chaise, and, with the permission of the Count de St. Alyre, would reach his house (the Château de la Carque), at about ten o'clock on the night following, to be conveyed thence in a hearse, with any member of the family who might wish to attend the obsequies.

"I did not see the poor gentleman twice in my life," said the Count, "but this office, as he has no other kinsman, disagreeable as it is, I could scarcely decline, and so I want to attend at the office to have the book signed, and the order entered. But here is another misery. By ill luck, I have sprained my thumb, and can't sign my name for a week to come. However, one name answers as well as another. Yours as well as mine. And as you are so good as to come with me, all will go right."

Away we drove. The Count gave me a memorandum of the christian and surnames of the deceased, his age, the complaint he died of, and the usual particulars; also a note of the exact position in which a grave, the dimensions of which were described, of the ordinary simple kind, was to be dug, between two vaults belonging to the family of St. Amand. The funeral, it was stated, would arrive at half-past one o'clock A.M. (the next night but one); and he handed me the money, with extra fees, for a burial by night. It was a good deal; and I asked him, as he entrusted the whole affair to me, in whose name I should take the receipt.

"Not in mine, my good friend. They wanted me to become an executor, which I, yesterday, wrote to decline; and I am informed that if the receipt were in my name it would constitute me an executor in the eye of the law, and fix me in that position. Take it, pray, if you have no objection, in your own name."

This, accordingly, I did.

"You will see, by-and-by, why I am obliged to mention all these particulars."

The Count, meanwhile, was leaning back in the carriage, with his black silk muffler up to his nose, and his hat shading his eyes, while he dozed in his corner; in which state I found him on my return.

Paris had lost its charm for me. I hurried through the little business I had to do, longed once more for my quiet room in the Dragon Volant, the melancholy woods of the Château de la Carque, and the tumultuous and thrilling influence of proximity to the object of my wild but wicked romance.

I was delayed some time by my stockbroker. I had a very large sum, as I told you, at my banker's, uninvested. I cared very little for a few days' interest—very little for the entire sum, compared with the image that occupied my thoughts, and beckoned me with a white arm, through the dark, towards the spreading lime-trees and chestnuts of the Château de la Carque. But I had fixed this day to meet him, and was relieved when he told me that I had better let it lie in my banker's hands for a few days longer, as the funds would certainly fall immediately. This accident, too, was not without its immediate bearing on my subsequent adventures.

The Room in the Dragon Volant

LE FANU

When I reached the Dragon Volant, I found, in my sitting-room, a good deal to my chagrin, my two guests, whom I had quite forgotten. I inwardly cursed my own stupidity for having embarrassed myself with their agreeable society. It could not be helped now, however, and a word to the waiters put all things in train for dinner.

Tom Whistlewick was in great force; and he commenced almost immediately with a very odd story.

He told me that not only Versailles, but all Paris, was in a ferment, in consequence of a revolting, and all but sacrilegious, practical joke, played off on the night before.

The pagoda, as he persisted in calling the palanquin, had been left standing on the spot where we last saw it. Neither conjuror, nor usher, nor bearers had ever returned. When the ball closed, and the company at length retired, the servants who attended to put out the lights, and secure the doors, found it still there.

It was determined, however, to let it stand where it was until next morning, by which time, it was conjectured, its owners would send messengers to remove it.

None arrived. The servants were then ordered to take it away; and its extraordinary weight, for the first time, reminded them of its forgotten human occupant. Its door was forced; and, judge what was their disgust, when they discovered, not a living man, but a corpse! Three or four days must have passed since the death of the burly man in the Chinese tunic and painted cap. Some people thought it was a trick designed to insult the Allies, in whose honour the ball was got up. Others were of opinion that it was nothing worse than a daring and cynical jocularity which, shocking as it was, might yet be forgiven to the high spirits and irrepressible buffoonery of youth. Others, again, fewer in number, and mystically given, insisted that the corpse was *bona fide* necessary to the exhibition, and that the disclosures and allusions which had astonished so many people were distinctly due to necromancy.

"The matter, however, is now in the hands of the police," observed Monsieur Carmaignac, "and they are not the body they were two or three months ago, if the offenders against propriety and public feeling are not traced, and convicted, unless, indeed, they have been a great deal more cunning than such fools generally are."

245

I was thinking within myself how utterly inexplicable was my colloquy with the conjuror, so cavalierly dismissed by Monsieur Carmaignac as a "fool"; and the more I thought, the more marvellous it seemed.

"It certainly was an original joke, though not a very clear one," said Whistlewick.

"Not even original," said Carmaignac. "Very nearly the same thing was done, a hundred years ago or more, at a state ball in Paris; and the rascals who played the trick were never found out."

In this Monsieur Carmaignac, as I afterwards discovered, spoke truly; for, among my books of French anecdote and memoirs, the very incident is marked, by my own hand.

While we were thus talking, the waiter told us that dinner was served; and we withdrew accordingly; my guests more than making amends for my comparative taciturnity.

Chapter XVIII

The Churchyard

Our DINNER WAS really good, so were the wines; better, perhaps, at this out-of-the-way inn, than at some of the more pretentious hotels in Paris. The moral effect of a really good dinner is immense—we all felt it. The serenity and goodnature that follow are more solid and comfortable than the tumultuous benevolences of Bacchus.

My friends were happy, therefore, and very chatty; which latter relieved me of the trouble of talking, and prompted them to entertain me and one another incessantly with agreeable stories and conversation, of which, until suddenly a subject emerged, which interested me powerfully, I confess, so much were my thoughts engaged elsewhere, I heard next to nothing.

"Yes," said Carmaignac, continuing a conversation which had escaped me, "there was another case, beside that Russian nobleman, odder still. I remembered it this morning, but cannot recall the name. He was a tenant of the very same room. By-the-by, Monsieur, might it not be as well," he added, turning to me, with a laugh, half joke whole earnest, as they say, "if you were to get into another apartment, now that the house is no longer crowded? that is, if you mean to make any stay here."

"A thousand thanks! no. I'm thinking of changing my hotel; and I can run into town so easily at night; and though I stay here, for this night, at least, I don't expect to vanish like those others. But you say there is another adventure, of the same kind, connected with the same room. Do let us hear it. But take some wine first." The story he told was curious.

"It happened," said Carmaignac, "as well as I recollect, before either of the other cases. A French gentleman—I wish I could remember his name—the son of a merchant, came to this inn (the Dragon Volant), and was put by the landlord into the same room of which we have been speaking. Your apartment, Monsieur. He was by no means young—past forty—and very far from good looking. The people here said that he was the ugliest man, and the most good-natured, that ever lived. He played on the fiddle, sang, and wrote poetry. His habits were odd and desultory. He would sometimes sit all day in his room writing, singing, and fiddling, and go out at night for a walk. An eccentric man! He was by no means a millionaire, but he had a *modicum bonum*, you understand—a trifle more than half a million francs. He consulted his stockbroker about investing this money in foreign stocks, and drew the entire sum from his banker. You now have the situation of affairs when the catastrophe occurred."

"Pray fill your glass," I said.

"Dutch courage, Monsieur, to face the catastrophe!" said Whistlewick, filling his own.

"Now, that was the last that ever was heard of his money," resumed Carmaignac. "You shall hear about himself. The night after this financial operation, he was seized with a poetic frenzy; he sent for the then landlord of this house, and told him that he long meditated an epic, and meant to commence that night, and that he was on no account to be disturbed until nine o'clock in the morning. He had two pairs of wax candles, a little cold supper on a side-table, his desk open, paper enough upon it to contain the entire Henriade, and a proportionate store of pens and ink.

"Seated at this desk he was seen by the waiter who brought him a cup of coffee at nine o'clock, at which time the intruder said he was writing fast enough to set fire to the paper—that was his phrase; he did not look up, he appeared too much engrossed. But, when the waiter came back, half an hour afterwards, the door was locked; and the poet, from within, answered, that he must not be disturbed.

"Away went the garçon; and next morning at nine o'clock knocked at his door, and receiving no answer, looked through the key-hole; the lights were still burning, the window-shutters were closed as he had left them; he renewed his knocking, knocked louder, no answer came. He reported this continued and alarming silence to the inn-keeper, who, finding that his guest had not left his key in the lock, succeeded in finding another that opened it. The candles were just giving up the ghost in their sockets, but there was light enough to ascertain that the tenant of the room was gone! The bed had not been disturbed; the window-shutter was barred. He must have let himself out, and, locking the door on the outside, put the key in his pocket, and so made his way out of the house. Here, however, was another difficulty, the Dragon Volant shut its doors and made all fast at twelve o'clock; after that hour no one could leave the house, except by obtaining the key and letting himself out, and of necessity leaving the door unsecured, or else by collusion and aid of some person in the house.

"Now it happened that, some time after the doors were secured, at half-past twelve, a servant who had not been apprized of his order to be left undisturbed, seeing a light shine through the key-hole, knocked at the door to inquire whether the poet wanted anything. He was very little obliged to his disturber, and dismissed him with a renewed charge that he was not to be interrupted again during the night. This incident established the fact that he was in the house after the doors had been locked and barred. The inn-keeper himself kept the keys, and swore that he found them hung on the wall above his head, in his bed, in their usual place, in the morning; and that nobody could have taken them away without awakening him. That was all we could discover. The Count de St. Alyre, to whom this house belongs, was very active and very much chagrined. But nothing was discovered."

"And nothing heard since of the epic poet?" I asked.

"Nothing—not the slightest clue—he never turned up again. I suppose he is dead; if he is not, he must have got into some devilish bad scrape, of which we have heard nothing, that compelled him to abscond with all the secrecy and expedition in his power. All that we know for certain is that, having occupied the room in which you sleep, he vanished, nobody ever knew how, and never was heard of since."

"You have now mentioned three cases," I said, "and all from the same room."

"Three. Yes, all equally unintelligible. When men are murdered, the great and immediate difficulty the assassins encounter is how to conceal the body. It is very hard to believe that three persons should have been consecutively murdered, in the same room, and their bodies so effectually disposed of that no trace of them was ever discovered."

From this we passed to other topics, and the grave Monsieur Carmaignac amused us with a perfectly prodigious collection of scandalous anecdote, which his opportunities in the police department had enabled him to accumulate.

My guests happily had engagements in Paris, and left me about ten.

I went up to my room, and looked out upon the grounds of the Château de la Carque. The moonlight was broken by clouds, and the view of the park in this desultory light, acquired a melancholy and fantastic character.

The strange anecdotes recounted of the room in which I stood, by Monsieur Carmaignac, returned vaguely upon my mind, drowning in sudden shadows the gaiety of the more frivolous stories with which he had followed them. I looked round me on the room that lay in ominous gloom, with an almost disagreeable sensation. I took my pistols now with an undefined apprehension that they might be really needed before my return to-night. This feeling, be it understood, in nowise chilled my ardour. Never had my enthusiasm mounted higher. My adventure absorbed and carried me away; but it added a strange and stern excitement to the expedition.

I loitered for a time in my room. I had ascertained the exact point at which the little churchyard lay. It was about a mile away; I did not wish to reach it earlier than necessary.

I stole quietly out, and sauntered along the road to my left, and thence entered a narrower track, still to my left, which, skirting the park-wall, and describing a circuitous route, all the way, under grand old trees, passes the ancient cemetery. That cemetery is embowered in trees, and occupies little more than half an acre of ground, to the left of the road, interposing between it and the park of the Château de la Carque.

Here, at this haunted spot, I paused and listened. The place was utterly silent. A thick cloud had darkened the moon, so that I could distinguish little more than the outlines of near objects, and that vaguely enough; and sometimes, as it were, floating in black fog, the white surface of a tombstone emerged.

Among the forms that met my eye against the iron-grey of the horizon, were some of those shrubs or trees that grow like our junipers, some six feet high, in form like a miniature poplar, with the darker foliage of the yew. I do not know the name of the plant, but I have often seen it in such funereal places.

Knowing that I was a little too early, I sat down upon the edge of a tombstone to wait, as, for aught I knew, the beautiful Countess might have wise reasons for not caring that I should enter the ground of the château earlier than she had appointed. In the listless state induced by waiting, I sat there, with my eyes on the object straight before me, which chanced to be that faint black outline I have described. It was right before me, about half a dozen steps away.

The moon now began to escape from under the skirt of the cloud that had hid her face for so long; and, as the light gradually improved, the tree on which I had been lazily staring began to take a new shape. It was no longer a tree, but a man standing motionless. Brighter and brighter grew the moonlight, clearer and clearer the image became, and at last stood out perfectly distinctly. It was Colonel Gaillarde.

Luckily, he was not looking towards me. I could only see him in profile; but there was no mistaking the white moustache, the farouche visage, and the gaunt six-foot stature. There he was, his shoulder towards me, listening and watching, plainly, for some signal or person expected, straight in front of him.

If he were, by chance, to turn his eyes in my direction, I knew that I must reckon upon an instantaneous renewal of the combat only commenced in the hall of the Belle Etoile. In any case, could malignant fortune have posted, at this place and hour, a more dangerous watcher? What ecstasy to him, by a single discovery, to hit me so hard, and blast the Countess de St. Alyre, whom he seemed to hate.

He raised his arm; he whistled softly; I heard an answering whistle as low; and, to my relief, the Colonel advanced in the direction of this sound, widening the distance between us at every step; and immediately I heard talking, but in a low and cautious key.

I recognised, I thought, even so, the peculiar voice of Gaillarde.

I stole softly forward in the direction in which those sounds were audible. In doing so, I had, of course, to use the extremest caution.

I thought I saw a hat above a jagged piece of ruined wall, and then a second—yes, I saw two hats conversing; the voices came from under them. They moved off, not in the direction of the park, but of the road, and I lay along the grass, peeping over a grave, as a skirmisher might, observing the enemy. One after the other, the figures emerged full into view as they mounted the stile at the road-side. The Colonel, who was last, stood on the wall for awhile, looking about him, and then jumped down on the road. I heard their steps and talk as they moved away together, with their backs towards me, in the direction which led them farther and farther from the Dragon Volant.

I waited until these sounds were quite lost in distance before I entered the park. I followed the instructions I had received from the Countess de St. Alyre, and made my way among brushwood and thickets to the point nearest the ruinous temple, and crossed the short intervening space of open ground rapidly.

I was now once more under the gigantic boughs of the old lime and chestnut trees; softly, and with a heart throbbing fast, I approached the little structure.

The moon was now shining steadily, pouring down its radiance on the soft foliage, and here and there mottling the verdure under my feet.

I reached the steps: I was among its worn marble shafts. She was not there, nor in the inner sanctuary, the arched windows of which were screened almost entirely by masses of ivy. The lady had not yet arrived.

Chapter XIX

The Key

I STOOD NOW upon the steps, watching and listening. In a minute or two I heard the crackle of withered sticks trod upon, and, looking in the direction, I saw a figure approaching among the trees, wrapped in a mantle.

I advanced eagerly. It was the Countess. She did not speak, but gave me her hand, and I led her to the scene of our last interview. She repressed the ardour of my impassioned greeting with a gentle but peremptory firmness. She removed her hood, shook back her beautiful hair, and, gazing on me with sad and glowing eyes, sighed deeply. Some awful thought seemed to weigh upon her.

"Richard, I must speak plainly. The crisis of my life has come. I am sure you would defend me. I think you pity me; perhaps you even love me."

At these words I became eloquent, as young madmen in my plight do. She silenced me, however, with the same melancholy firmness.

"Listen, dear friend, and then say whether you can aid me. How madly I am trusting you; and yet my heart tells me how wisely! To meet you here as I do—what insanity it seems! How poorly you must think of me! But when you know all, you will judge me fairly. Without your aid I cannot accomplish my purpose. That purpose unaccomplished, I must die. I am chained to a man whom I despise—whom I abhor. I have resolved to fly. I have jewels, principally diamonds, for which I am offered thirty thousand pounds of your English money. They are my separate property by my marriage settlement; I will take them with me. You are a judge, no doubt, of jewels. I was counting mine when the hour came, and brought this in my hand to show you. Look."

"It is magnificent!" I exclaimed, as a collar of diamonds twinkled and flashed in the moonlight, suspended from her pretty fingers. I thought, even at that tragic moment, that she prolonged the show, with a feminine delight in these brilliant toys.

"Yes," she said, "I shall part with them all. I will turn them into money, and break, for ever, the unnatural and wicked bonds that tied me, in the name of a sacrament, to a tyrant. A man young, handsome, generous, brave as you, can hardly be rich. Richard, you say you love me; you shall share all this with me. We will fly together to Switzerland; we will evade pursuit; my powerful friends will intervene and arrange a separation; and I shall, at length, be happy and reward my hero."

You may suppose the style, florid and vehement, in which I poured forth my gratitude, vowed the devotion of my life, and placed myself absolutely at her disposal.

"To-morrow night," she said, "my husband will attend the remains of his cousin, Monsieur de St. Amand, to Père la Chaise. The hearse, he says, will leave this at half-past nine. You must be here, where we stand, at nine o'clock."

I promised punctual obedience.

"I will not meet you here; but you see a red light in the window of the tower at that angle of the château?"

I assented.

"I placed it there, that, to-morrow night, when it comes, you may recognise it. So soon as that rose-coloured light appears at that window, it will be a signal to you that the funeral has left the château, and that you may approach safely. Come, then, to that window; I will open it, and admit you. Five minutes after a travelling-carriage, with four horses, shall stand ready in the *porte-cochère*. I will place my diamonds in your hands; and so soon as we enter the carriage, our flight commences. We shall have at least five hours' start; and with energy, stratagem, and resource, I fear nothing. Are you ready to undertake all this for my sake?"

Again I vowed myself her slave.

"My only difficulty," she said, "is how we shall quickly enough convert my diamonds into money; I dare not remove them while my husband is in the house."

Here was the opportunity I wished for. I now told her that I had in my banker's hands no less a sum than thirty thousand pounds, with which, in the shape of gold and notes, I should come furnished, and thus the risk and loss of disposing of her diamonds in too much haste would be avoided.

"Good heaven!" she exclaimed, with a kind of disappointment. "You are rich, then? and I have lost the felicity of making my generous friend more happy. Be it so! since so it must be. Let us contribute, each, in equal shares, to our common fund. Bring you, your money; I, my jewels. There is a happiness to me even in mingling my resources with yours."

On this there followed a romantic colloquy, all poetry and passion, such as I should, in vain, endeavour to reproduce.

Then came a very special instruction.

"I have come provided, too, with a key, the use of which I must explain."

It was a double key—a long, slender stem, with a key at each end —one about the size which opens an ordinary room door; the other, as small, almost, as the key of a dressing-case.

"You cannot employ too much caution to-morrow night. An interruption would murder all my hopes. I have learned that you occupy the haunted room in the Dragon Volant. It is the very room I would have wished you in. I will tell you why—there is a story of a man who, having shut himself up in that room one night, disappeared before morning. The truth is, he wanted, I believe, to escape from creditors; and the host of the Dragon Volant, at that time, being a rogue, aided him in absconding. My husband investigated the matter, and discovered how his escape was made. It was by means of this key. Here is a memorandum and a plan describing how they are to be applied. I have taken them from the Count's escritoire. And now, once more I must leave to your ingenuity how to mystify the people at the Dragon Volant. Be sure you try the keys first, to see that the locks turn freely. I will have my jewels ready. You, whatever we divide, had better bring your money, because it may be many months before you can revisit Paris, or disclose our place of residence to any one; and our passports—arrange all that; in what names, and whither, you please. And now, dear Richard" (she leaned her arm fondly on my shoulder, and looked with ineffable passion in my eyes, with her other hand clasped in mine), "my very life is in your hands; I have staked all on your fidelity."

As she spoke the last word, she, on a sudden, grew deadly pale, and gasped, "Good God! who is here?"

At the same moment she receded through the door in the marble screen, close to which she stood, and behind which was a small roofless chamber, as small as the shrine, the window of which was darkened by a clustering mass of ivy so dense that hardly a gleam of light came through the leaves.

I stood upon the threshold which she had just crossed, looking in the direction in which she had thrown that one terrified glance. No wonder she was frightened. Quite close upon us, not twenty yards away, and approaching at a quick step, very distinctly lighted by the moon, Colonel Gaillarde and his companion were coming. The shadow of the cornice and a piece of wall were upon me. Unconscious of this, I was expecting the moment when, with one of his frantic yells, he should spring forward to assail me.

I made a step backward, drew one of my pistols from my pocket, and cocked it. It was obvious he had not seen me.

I stood, with my finger on the trigger, determined to shoot him dead if he should attempt to enter the place where the Countess was. It would, no doubt, have been a murder; but, in my mind, I had no question or qualm about it. When once we engage in secret and guilty practices we are nearer other and greater crimes than we at all suspect.

"There's the statue," said the Colonel, in his brief discordant tones. "That's the figure."

"Alluded to in the stanzas?" inquired his companion.

"The very thing. We shall see more next time. Forward, Monsieur; let us march."

And, much to my relief, the gallant Colonel turned on his heel, and marched through the trees, with his back towards the château, striding over the grass, as I quickly saw, to the park-wall, which they crossed not far from the gables of the Dragon Volant.

I found the Countess trembling in no affected, but a very real terror. She would not hear of my accompanying her towards the château. But I told her that I would prevent the return of the mad Colonel; and upon that point, at least, that she need fear nothing. She quickly recovered, again bid me a fond and lingering good night, and left me, gazing after her, with the key in my hand, and such a phantasmagoria floating in my brain as amounted very nearly to madness.

There was I, ready to brave all dangers, all right and reason, plunge into murder itself, on the first summons, and entangle myself in consequences inextricable and horrible (what cared I?)

for a woman of whom I knew nothing, but that she was beautiful and reckless!

I have often thanked heaven for its mercy in conducting me through the labyrinths in which I had all but lost myself.

Chapter XX

A High-Cauld Cap

I WAS NOW upon the road, within two or three hundred yards of the Dragon Volant. I had undertaken an adventure with a vengeance! And by way of prelude, there not improbably awaited me, at my inn, another encounter, perhaps, this time, not so lucky, with the grotesque sabreur.

I was glad I had my pistols. I certainly was bound by no law to allow a ruffian to cut me down, unresisting.

Stooping boughs from the old park, gigantic poplars on the other side, and the moonlight over all, made the narrow road to the inn-door picturesque.

I could not think very clearly just now; events were succeeding one another so rapidly, and I, involved in the action of a drama so extravagant and guilty, hardly knew myself or believed my own story, as I slowly paced towards the still open door of the Flying Dragon.

No sign of the Colonel, visible or audible, was there. In the hall I inquired. No gentleman had arrived at the inn for the last half-hour. I looked into the public room. It was deserted. The clock struck twelve, and I heard the servant barring the great door. I took my candle. The lights in this rural hostelry were by this time out, and the house had the air of one that had settled to slumber for many hours. The cold moonlight streamed in at the window on the landing, as I ascended the broad staircase; and I paused for a moment to look over the wooded grounds to the turreted château, to me, so full of interest. I bethought me, however, that prying eyes might read a meaning in this midnight gazing, and possibly the Count himself might, in his jealous mood, surmise a signal in this unwonted light in the stair-window of the Dragon Volant.

On opening my room door, with a little start, I met an extremely old woman with the longest face I ever saw; she had what used to be termed a high-cauld cap on, the white border of which contrasted with her brown and yellow skin, and made her wrinkled face more ugly. She raised her curved shoulders, and looked up in my face, with eyes unnaturally black and bright.

"I have lighted a little wood, Monsieur, because the night is chill."

I thanked her, but she did not go. She stood with her candle in her tremulous fingers.

"Excuse an old woman, Monsieur," she said; "but what on earth can a young English *milord*, with all Paris at his feet, find to amuse him in the Dragon Volant?"

Had I been at the age of fairy tales, and in daily intercourse with the delightful Countess d'Aulnois, I should have seen in this withered apparition, the *genius loci*, the malignant fairy, at the stamp of whose foot, the ill-fated tenants of this very room had, from time to time, vanished. I was past that, however; but the old woman's dark eyes were fixed on mine, with a steady meaning that plainly told me that my secret was known. I was embarrassed and alarmed; I never thought of asking her what business that was of hers.

"These old eyes saw you in the park of the château to-night."

"*I!*" I began, with all the scornful surprise I could affect.

"It avails nothing, Monsieur; I know why you stay here; and I tell you to begone. Leave this house to-morrow morning and never come again."

She lifted her disengaged hand, as she looked at me with intense horror in her eyes.

"There is nothing on earth—I don't know what you mean," I answered; "and why should you care about me?"

"I don't care about you, Monsieur—I care about the honour of an ancient family, whom I served in their happier days, when to be noble, was to be honoured. But my words are thrown away, Monsieur; you are insolent. I will keep my secret, and you, yours; that is all. You will soon find it hard enough to divulge it."

The old woman went slowly from the room and shut the door, before I had made up my mind to say anything. I was standing where she had left me, nearly five minutes later. The jealousy of

257

Monsieur the Count, I assumed, appears to this old creature about the most terrible thing in creation. Whatever contempt I might entertain for the dangers which this old lady so darkly intimated, it was by no means pleasant, you may suppose, that a secret so dangerous should be so much as suspected by a stranger, and that stranger a partisan of the Count de St. Alyre.

Ought I not, at all risks, to apprize the Countess, who had trusted me so generously, or, as she said herself, so madly, of the fact that our secret was, at least, suspected by another? But was there not greater danger in attempting to communicate? What did the beldame mean by saying, "Keep your secret, and I'll keep mine"?

I had a thousand distracting questions before me. My progress seemed like a journey through the Spessart, where at every step some new goblin or monster starts from the ground or steps from behind a tree.

Peremptorily I dismissed these harassing and frightful doubts. I secured my door, sat myself down at my table, and with a candle at each side, placed before me the piece of vellum which contained the drawings and notes on which I was to rely for full instructions as to how to use the key.

When I had studied this for awhile, I made my investigation. The angle of the room at the right side of the window was cut off by an oblique turn in the wainscot. I examined this carefully, and, on pressure, a small bit of the frame of the woodwork slid aside, and disclosed a keyhole. On removing my finger, it shot back to its place again, with a spring. So far I had interpreted my instructions successfully. A similar search, next the door, and directly under this, was rewarded by a like discovery. The small end of the key fitted this, as it had the upper keyhole; and now, with two or three hard jerks at the key, a door in the panel opened, showing a strip of the bare wall, and a narrow, arched doorway, piercing the thickness of the wall; and within which I saw a screw-staircase of stone.

Candle in hand I stepped in. I do not know whether the quality of air, long undisturbed, is peculiar; to me it has always seemed so, and the damp smell of the old masonry hung in this atmosphere. My candle faintly lighted the bare stone wall that enclosed the stair, the foot of which I could not see. Down I went, and a few turns brought me to the stone floor. Here was another door, of the simple, old, oak kind, deep sunk in the thickness of the wall. The large end of the key fitted this. The lock was stiff; I set the candle down upon the stair, and applied both hands; it turned with difficulty, and as it revolved, uttered a shriek that alarmed me for my secret.

For some minutes I did not move. In a little time, however, I took courage, and opened the door. The night-air floating in, puffed out the candle. There was a thicket of holly and under-wood, as dense as a jungle, close about the door. I should have been in pitch-darkness, were it not that through the topmost leaves, there twinkled, here and there, a glimmer of moonshine.

Softly, lest anyone should have opened his window, at the sound of the rusty bolt, I struggled through this, till I gained a view of the open grounds. Here I found that the brushwood spread a good way up the park, uniting with the wood that approached the little temple I have described.

A general could not have chosen a more effectually-covered ap-proach from the Dragon Volant to the trysting-place where hitherto I had conferred with the idol of my lawless adoration.

Looking back upon the old inn, I discovered that the stair I had descended, was enclosed in one of those slender turrets that dec-orate such buildings. It was placed at that angle which corre-sponded with the part of the panelling of my room indicated in the plan I had been studying.

Thoroughly satisfied with my experiment, I made my way back to the door, with some little difficulty, re-mounted to my room, locked my secret door again; kissed the mysterious key that her hand had pressed that night, and placed it under my pillow, upon which, very soon after, my giddy head was laid, not, for some time, to sleep soundly.

Chapter XXI

I See Three Men in a Mirror

I AWOKE VERY early next morning, and was too excited to sleep again. As soon as I could, without exciting remark, I saw my host. I told him that I was going into town that night, and thence to ——, where I had to see some people on business, and requested him to mention my being there to any friend who might call. That I expected to be back in about a week, and that in the meantime my servant, St. Clair, would keep the key of my room, and look after my things.

Having prepared this mystification for my landlord, I drove into Paris, and there transacted the financial part of the affair. The problem was to reduce my balance, nearly thirty thousand pounds, to a shape in which it would be not only easily portable, but available, wherever I might go, without involving correspondence, or any other incident which would disclose my place of residence, for the time being. All these points were as nearly provided for as they could be. I need not trouble you about my arrangements for passports. It is enough to say that the point I selected for our flight was, in the spirit of romance, one of the most beautiful and sequestered nooks in Switzerland.

Luggage, I should start with none. The first considerable town we reached next morning, would supply an extemporised wardrobe. It was now two o'clock; only two! How on earth was I to dispose of the remainder of the day?

I had not yet seen the cathedral of Notre Dame; and thither I drove. I spent an hour or more there; and then to the Conciergerie, the Palais de Justice, and the beautiful Sainte Chapelle. Still there remained some time to get rid of, and I strolled into the narrow streets adjoining the cathedral. I recollect seeing, in one of them, an old house with a mural inscription stating that it had been the residence of Canon Fulbert, the uncle of Abelard's Eloise. I don't know whether these curious old streets, in which I observed fragments of ancient Gothic churches fitted up as warehouses, are still extant. I lighted, among other dingy and eccentric shops, upon one that seemed that of a broker of all sorts of old decorations, armour, china, furniture. I entered the shop; it was dark, dusty, and low. The proprietor was busy scouring a piece of inlaid armour, and allowed me to poke about his shop, and examine the curious things accumulated there, just as I pleased. Gradually I made my way to the farther end of it, where there was but one window with many panes, each with a bull's-eye in it, and in the dirtiest possible state. When I reached this window, I turned about, and in a recess, standing at right angles with the side wall of the shop, was a large mirror in an old-fashioned dingy frame. Reflected in this I saw, what in old houses I have heard termed an "alcove," in which, among lumber, and various dusty articles hanging on the wall, there stood a table, at which three persons were seated, as it seemed to me, in earnest conversation. Two of these persons I instantly recognized; one was Colonel Gaillarde, the other was the Marquis d'Harmonville. The third, who was fiddling with a pen, was a lean, pale man, pitted with the smallpox, with lank black hair, and about as mean-looking a person as I had ever seen in my life. The Marquis looked up, and his glance was instantaneously followed by his two companions. For a moment I hesitated what to do. But it was plain that I was not recognized, as indeed I could hardly have been, the light from the window being behind me, and the portion of the shop immediately before me, being very dark indeed.

Perceiving this, I had presence of mind to affect being entirely engrossed by the objects before me, and strolled slowly down the shop again. I paused for a moment to hear whether I was followed, and was relieved when I heard no step. You may be sure I did not waste more time in that shop, where I had just made a discovery so curious and so unexpected.

It was no business of mine to inquire what brought Colonel Gaillarde and the Marquis together, in so shabby, and even dirty a place, or who the mean person, biting the feather end of his pen, might be. Such employments as the Marquis had accepted sometimes make strange bed-fellows.

I was glad to get away, and just as the sun set, I had reached the steps of the Dragon Volant, and dismissed the vehicle in which I arrived, carrying in my hand a strong box, of marvellously small dimensions considering all it contained, strapped in a leather cover, which disguised its real character.

When I got to my room, I summoned St. Clair. I told him nearly the same story I had already told my host. I gave him fifty pounds, with orders to expend whatever was necessary on himself, and in payment for my rooms till my return. I then ate a slight and hasty dinner. My eyes were often upon the solemn old clock over the chimney-piece, which was my sole accomplice in keeping tryste in this inquitous venture. The sky favoured my design, and darkened all things with a sea of clouds.

The innkeeper met me in the hall, to ask whether I should

want a vehicle to Paris? I was prepared for this question, and instantly answered that I meant to walk to Versailles, and take a carriage there. I called St. Clair.

"Go," said I, "and drink a bottle of wine with your friends. I shall call you if I should want anything; in the meantime, here is the key of my room; I shall be writing some notes, so don't allow anyone to disturb me, for at least half an hour. At the end of that time you will probably find that I have left this for Versailles; and should you not find me in my room, you may take that for granted; and you may take charge of everything, and lock the door, you understand?"

St. Clair took his leave, wishing me all happiness and no doubt promising himself some little amusement with my money. With my candle in my hand, I hastened upstairs. It wanted now but five minutes to the appointed time. I do not think there is anything of the coward in my nature; but I confess, as the crisis approached, I felt something of the suspense and awe of a soldier going into action. Would I have receded? Not for all this earth could offer.

I bolted my door, put on my greatcoat, and placed my pistols, one in each pocket. I now applied my key to the secret locks; drew the wainscot-door a little open, took my strong box under my arm, extinguished my candle, unbolted my door, listened at it for a few moments to be sure that no one was approaching, and then crossed the floor of my room swiftly, entered the secret door, and closed the spring lock after me. I was upon the screw-stair in total darkness, the key in my fingers. Thus far the undertaking was successful.

Chapter XXII

Rapture

DOWN THE SCREW-STAIR I went in utter darkness; and having reached the stone floor, I discerned the door and groped out the keyhole. With more caution, and less noise than upon the night before, I opened the door, and stepped out into the thick brushwood. It was almost as dark in this jungle.

Having secured the door, I slowly pushed my way through the bushes, which soon became less dense. Then, with more ease, but still under thick cover, I pursued in the track of the wood, keeping near its edge.

At length, in the darkened air, about fifty yards away, the shafts of the marble temple rose like phantoms before me, seen through the trunks of the old trees. Everything favoured my enterprise. I had effectually mystified my servant and the people of the Dragon Volant, and so dark was the night, that even had I alarmed the suspicions of all the tenants of the inn, I might safely defy their united curiosity, though posted at every window of the house.

Through the trunks, over the roots of the old trees, I reached the appointed place of observation. I laid my treasure, in its leathern case, in the embrasure, and leaning my arms upon it, looked steadily in the direction of the château. The outline of the building was scarcely discernible, blending dimly, as it did, with the sky. No light in any window was visible. I was plainly to wait; but for how long?

Leaning on my box of treasure, gazing towards the massive shadow that represented the château, in the midst of my ardent and elated longings, there came upon me an odd thought, which you will think might well have struck me long before. It seemed on a sudden, as it came, that the darkness deepened, and a chill stole into the air around me.

Suppose I were to disappear finally, like those other men whose stories I had listened to! Had I not been at all the pains that mortal could, to obliterate every trace of my real proceedings, and to mislead every one to whom I spoke as to the direction in which I had gone?

This icy, snake-like thought stole through my mind, and was gone.

It was with me the full-blooded season of youth, conscious strength, rashness, passion, pursuit, the adventure! Here were a pair of double-barrelled pistols, four lives in my hands? What could possibly happen? The Count—except for the sake of my Dulcinea, what was it to me whether the old coward whom I had seen, in an ague of terror before the brawling Colonel, interposed or not? I was assuming the worst that could happen. But with an ally so clever and courageous as my beautiful Countess, could any such misadventure befall? Bah! I laughed at all such fancies.

As I thus communed with myself, the signal light sprang up. The rose-coloured light, *couleur de rose*, emblem of sanguine hope, and the dawn of a happy day.

Clear, soft, and steady, glowed the light from the window. The stone shafts showed black against it. Murmuring words of passionate love as I gazed upon the signal, I grasped my strong box under my arm, and with rapid strides approached the Château de la Carque. No sign of light or life, no human voice, no tread of foot, no bark of dog, indicated a chance of interruption. A blind was down; and as I came close to the tall window, I found that half a dozen steps led up to it and that a large lattice, answering for a door, lay open.

A shadow from within fell upon the blind; it was drawn aside, and as I ascended the steps, a soft voice murmured—"Richard, dearest Richard, come, oh! come! how I have longed for this moment!"

Never did she look so beautiful. My love rose to passionate enthusiasm. I only wished there were some real danger in the adventure worthy of such a creature. When the first tumultuous greeting was over, she made me sit beside her on a sofa. There we talked for a minute or two. She told me that the Count had gone, and was by that time more than a mile on his way, with the funeral, to Père la Chaise. Here were her diamonds. She exhibited, hastily, an open casket containing a profusion of the largest brilliants.

"What is this?" she asked.

"A box containing money to the amount of thirty thousand pounds," I answered.

"What! all that money?" she exclaimed.

"Every sou."

"Was it not unnecessary to bring so much, seeing all these," she said, touching the diamonds. "It would have been kind of you, to allow me to provide for both for a time, at least. It would have made me happier even than I am."

"Dearest, generous angel!" Such was my extravagant declamation. "You forget that it may be necessary, for a long time, to observe silence as to where we are, and impossible to communicate safely with any one."

264

"You have then here this great sum—are you certain; have you counted it?"

"Yes, certainly; I received it to-day," I answered, perhaps showing a little surprise in my face. "I counted it, of course, on drawing it from my bankers."

"It makes me feel a little nervous, travelling with so much money; but these jewels make as great a danger; *that* can add but little to it. Place them side by side; you shall take off your greatcoat when we are ready to go, and with it manage to conceal these boxes. I should not like the drivers to suspect that we were conveying such a treasure. I must ask you now to close the curtains of that window, and bar the shutters."

I had hardly done this when a knock was heard at the room-door.

"I know who this is," she said, in a whisper to me.

I saw that she was not alarmed. She went softly to the door, and a whispered conversation for a minute followed.

"My trusty maid, who is coming with us. She says we cannot safely go sooner than ten minutes. She is bringing some coffee to the next room."

She opened the door and looked in.

"I must tell her not to take too much luggage. She is so odd! Don't follow—stay where you are—it is better that she should not see you."

She left the room with a gesture of caution.

A change had come over the manner of this beautiful woman. For the last few minutes a shadow had been stealing over her, an air of abstraction, a look bordering on suspicion. Why was she pale? Why had there come that dark look in her eyes? Why had her very voice become changed? Had anything gone suddenly wrong? Did some danger threaten?

This doubt, however, speedily quieted itself. If there had been anything of the kind, she would, of course, have told me. It was only natural that, as the crisis approached, she should become more and more nervous. She did not return quite so soon as I had expected. To a man in my situation absolute quietude is next to impossible. I moved restlessly about the room. It was a small one. There was a door at the other end. I opened it, rashly enough. I listened, it was perfectly silent. I was in an excited, eager state, and every faculty engrossed about what was coming, and in so far detached, from the immediate present. I can't account, in any other way, for my having done so many foolish things that night, for I was, naturally, by no means deficient in cunning. About the most stupid of those was, that instead of immediately closing that door, which I never ought to have opened, I actually took a candle and walked into the room.

There I made, quite unexpectedly, a rather startling discovery.

Chapter XXIII

A Cup of Coffee

THE ROOM WAS carpetless. On the floor were a quantity of shavings and some score of bricks. Beyond these, on a narrow table, lay an object, which I could hardly believe I saw aright.

I approached and drew from it a sheet which had very slightly disguised its shape. There was no mistake about it. It was a coffin; and on the lid was a plate, with the inscription in French:

PIERRE DE LA ROCHE ST. AMAND.
GÉE DE XXIII ANS.

I drew back with a double shock. So, then, the funeral after all had not yet left! Here lay the body. I had been deceived. This, no doubt, accounted for the embarrassment so manifest in the Countess's manner. She would have done more wisely had she told me the true state of the case.

I drew back from this melancholy room, and closed the door. Her distrust of me was the worst rashness she could have committed. There is nothing more dangerous than misapplied caution. In entire ignorance of the fact I had entered the room, and there I might have lighted upon some of the very persons it was our special anxiety that I should avoid.

These reflections were interrupted, almost as soon as begun, by the return of the Countess de St. Alyre. I saw at a glance that she detected in my face some evidence of what had happened, for she threw a hasty look towards the door.

266

"Have you seen anything—anything to disturb you, dear Richard? Have you been out of this room?"

I answered promptly, "Yes," and told her frankly what had happened.

"Well, I did not like to make you more uneasy than necessary. Besides, it is disgusting and horrible. The body is there; but the Count had departed a quarter of an hour before I lighted the coloured lamp, and prepared to receive you. The body did not arrive till eight or ten minutes after he had set out. He was afraid lest the people at Père la Chaise should suppose that the funeral was postponed. He knew that the remains of poor Pierre would certainly reach this house to-night although an unexpected delay has occurred; and there are reasons why he wishes the funeral completed before to-morrow. The hearse with the body must leave this house in ten minutes. So soon as it is gone, we shall be free to set out upon our wild and happy journey. The horses are to the carriage in the *porte-cochère*. As for this *funeste* horror (she shuddered very prettily), let us think of it no more."

She bolted the door of communication, and when she turned, it was with such a pretty penitence in her face and attitude, that I was ready to throw myself at her feet.

"It is the last time," she said, in a sweet sad little pleading, "I shall ever practise a deception on my brave and beautiful Richard —my hero? Am I forgiven?"

Here was another scene of passionate effusion, and lovers' raptures and declamations, but only murmured, lest the ears of listeners should be busy.

At length, on a sudden, she raised her hand, as if to prevent my stirring, her eyes fixed on me, and her ear towards the door of the room in which the coffin was placed, and remained breathless in that attitude for a few moments. Then, with a little nod towards me, she moved on tip-toe to the door, and listened, extending her hand backward as if to warn me against advancing; and, after a little time, she returned still on tip-toe, and whispered to me, "They are removing the coffin—come with me."

I accompanied her into the room from which her maid, as she told me, had spoken to her. Coffee and some old china cups, which appeared to me quite beautiful, stood on a silver tray; and some liqueur glasses with a flask, which turned out to be noyeau, on a salver beside it.

"I shall attend you. I'm to be your servant here; I am to have my own way; I shall not think myself forgiven by my darling if he refuses to indulge me in anything."

She filled a cup with coffee, and handed it to me with her left hand, her right arm she fondly passed over my shoulder, and with her fingers through my curls caressingly, she whispered, "Take this, I shall take some just now."

It was excellent; and when I had done she handed me the liqueur which I also drank.

"Come back, dearest, to the next room," she said. "By this time those terrible people must have gone away, and we shall be safer there, for the present, than here."

"You shall direct, and I obey; you shall command me, not only now, but always, and in all things, my beautiful queen!" I murmured.

My heroics were unconsciously, I daresay, founded upon my ideal of the French school of lovemaking. I am, even now, ashamed as I recall the bombast to which I treated the Countess de St. Alyre.

"There, you shall have another miniature glass—a fairy glass— of noyeau," she said, gaily. In this volatile creature, the funereal gloom of the moment before, and the suspense of an adventure on which all her future was staked, disappeared in a moment. She ran and returned with another tiny glass, which, with an eloquent or tender little speech, I placed to my lips and sipped.

I kissed her hand, I kissed her lips, I gazed in her beautiful eyes, and kissed her again unresisting.

"You call me Richard, by what name am I to call my beautiful divinity?" I asked.

"You call me Eugenie, it is my name. Let us be quite real; that is, if you love as entirely as I do."

"Eugenie!" I exclaimed, and broke into a new rapture upon the name.

It ended by my telling her how impatient I was to set out upon our journey; and, as I spoke, suddenly an odd sensation overcame me. It was not in the slightest degree like faintness. I can find no phrase to describe it, but a sudden constraint of the brain; it was as if the membrane, in which it lies, if there be such a thing, contracted, and became inflexible.

"Dear Richard! what is the matter?" she exclaimed, with terror in her looks. "Good Heavens! are you ill? I conjure you, sit down; sit in this chair." She almost forced me into one; I was in no condition to offer the least resistance. I recognised but too truly the sensations that supervened. I was lying back in the chair in which I sat without the power, by this time, of uttering a syllable, of closing my eyelids, of moving my eyes, of stirring a muscle. I had in a few seconds glided into precisely the state in which I had passed so many appalling hours when approaching Paris, in my night-drive with the Marquis d'Harmonville.

Great and loud was the lady's agony. She seemed to have lost all sense of fear. She called me by my name, shook me by the shoulder, raised my arm and let it fall, all the time imploring of me, in distracting sentences, to make the slightest sign of life, and vowing that if I did not, she would make away with herself.

These ejaculations, after a minute or two, suddenly subsided. The lady was perfectly silent and cool. In a very business-like way she took a candle and stood before me, pale indeed, very pale, but with an expression only of intense scrutiny with a dash of horror in it. She moved the candle before my eyes slowly, evidently watching the effect. She then set it down, and rang a hand-bell two or three times sharply. She placed the two cases (I mean hers containing the jewels and my strong box) side by side on the table; and I saw her carefully lock the door that gave access to the room in which I had just now sipped my coffee.

Chapter XXIV

Hope

SHE HAD SCARCELY set down my heavy box, which she seemed to have considerable difficulty in raising on the table, when the door of the room in which I had seen the coffin, opened, and a sinister and unexpected apparition entered.

It was the Count de St. Alyre, who had been, as I have told you, reported to me to be, for some considerable time, on his way to Père la Chaise. He stood before me for a moment, with the frame of the doorway and a background of darkness enclosing him, like a portrait. His slight, mean figure was draped in the deepest mourning. He had a pair of black gloves in his hand, and his hat with crape round it.

When he was not speaking his face showed signs of agitation; his mouth was puckering and working. He looked damnably wicked and frightened.

"Well, my dear Eugenie? Well, child—eh? Well, it all goes admirably?"

"Yes," she answered, in a low, hard tone. "But you and Planard should not have left that door open."

This she said sternly. "He went in there and looked about wherever he liked; it was fortunate he did not move aside the lid of the coffin."

"Planard should have seen to that," said the Count, sharply. "*Ma foi!* I can't be everywhere!" He advanced half a dozen short quick steps into the room towards me, and placed his glasses to his eyes.

"Monsieur Beckett," he cried sharply, two or three times, "Hi! don't you know me?"

He approached and peered more closely in my face; raised my hand and shook it, calling me again, then let it drop, and said— "It has set in admirably, my pretty *mignonne*. When did it commence?"

The Countess came and stood beside him, and looked at me steadily for some seconds.

You can't conceive the effect of the silent gaze of those two pairs of evil eyes.

The lady glanced to where, I recollected, the mantelpiece stood, and upon it a clock, the regular click of which I sharply heard.

"Four—five—six minutes and a half," she said slowly, in a cold hard way.

"Brava! Bravissima! my beautiful queen! my little Venus! my Joan of Arc! my heroine! my paragon of women!"

He was gloating on me with an odious curiosity, smiling, as he groped backwards with his thin brown fingers to find the lady's hand; but she, not (I dare say) caring for his caresses, drew back a little.

"Come, *ma chère,* let us count these things. What is it? Pocket-book? Or—or—what?"

"It is *that!*" said the lady, pointing with a look of disgust to the box, which lay in its leather case on the table.

"Oh! Let us see—let us count—let us see," he said, as he was unbuckling the straps with his tremulous fingers. "We must count them—we must see to it. I have pencil and pocket-book—but—where's the key? See this cursed lock! My —— ! What is it? Where's the key?"

He was standing before the Countess, shuffling his feet, with his hands extended and all his fingers quivering.

"I have not got it; how could I? It is in his pocket, of course," said the lady.

In another instant the fingers of the old miscreant were in my pockets: he plucked out everything they contained, and some keys among the rest.

I lay in precisely the state in which I had been during my drive with the Marquis to Paris. This wretch I knew was about to rob me. The whole drama, and the Countess' *rôle* in it, I could not yet comprehend. I could not be sure—so much more presence of mind and histrionic resource have women than fall to the lot of our clumsy sex—whether the return of the Count was not, in truth, a surprise to her; and this scrutiny of the contents of my strong box, an extempore undertaking of the Count's. But it was clearing more and more every moment: and I was destined, very soon, to comprehend minutely my appalling situation.

I had not the power of turning my eyes this way or that, the smallest fraction of a hair's breadth. But let any one, placed as I was at the end of a room, ascertain for himself by experiment how wide is the field of sight, without the slightest alteration in the line of vision, he will find that it takes in the entire breadth of a large room, and that up to a very short distance before him; and imperfectly, by a refraction, I believe, in the eye itself, to a point very near indeed. Next to nothing that passed in the room, there-fore, was hidden from me.

The old man had, by this time, found the key. The leather case was open. The box cramped round with iron, was next unlocked. He turned out its contents upon the table.

"Rouleaux of a hundred Napoleons each. One, two, three. Yes, quick. Write down a thousand Napoleons. One, two; yes, right.

Another thousand, *write!*" And so, on and on till the gold was rapidly counted. Then came the notes.

"Ten thousand francs. *Write*. Ten thousand francs again: is it written? Another ten thousand francs: is it down? Smaller notes would have been better. They should have been smaller. These are horribly embarrassing. Bolt that door again; Planard would become unreasonable if he knew the amount. Why did you not tell him to get it in smaller notes? No matter now—go on—it can't be helped —write—another ten thousand francs—another—another." And so on, till my treasure was counted out, before my face, while I saw and heard all that passed with the sharpest distinctness, and my mental perceptions were horribly vivid. But in all other respects I was dead.

He had replaced in the box every note and rouleau as he counted it, and now having ascertained the sum total, he locked it, replaced it, very methodically, in its cover, opened a buffet in the wainscoting, and, having placed the Countess' jewel-case and my strong box in it, he locked it; and immediately on completing these arrangements he began to complain, with fresh acrimony and maledictions of Planard's delay.

He unbolted the door, looked in the dark room beyond, and listened. He closed the door again, and returned. The old man was in a fever of suspense.

"I have kept ten thousand francs for Planard," said the Count, touching his waistcoat pocket.

"Will that satisfy him?" asked the lady.

"Why—curse him!" screamed the Count. "Has he no conscience? I'll swear to him it's half the entire thing."

He and the lady again came and looked at me anxiously for a while, in silence; and then the old Count began to grumble again about Planard, and to compare his watch with the clock. The lady seemed less impatient; she sat no longer looking at me, but across the room, so that her profile was towards me—and strangely changed, dark and witch-like it looked. My last hope died as I beheld that jaded face from which the mask had dropped. I was certain that they intended to crown their robbery by murder. Why did they not despatch me at once? What object could there be in postponing the catastrophe which would expedite their own safety? I cannot recall, even to myself, adequately the horrors

272

unutterable that I underwent. You must suppose a real nightmare—I mean a nightmare in which the objects and the danger are real, and the spell of corporal death appears to be protractable at the pleasure of the persons who preside at your unearthly torments. I could have no doubt as to the cause of the state in which I was.

In this agony, to which I could not give the slighest expression, I saw the door of the room where the coffin had been, open slowly, and the Marquis d'Harmonville entered the room.

Chapter XXV

Despair

A MOMENT'S HOPE, hope violent and fluctuating, hope that was nearly torture, and then came a dialogue, and with it the terrors of despair.

"Thank heaven, Planard, you have come at last," said the Count, taking him, with both hands, by the arm and clinging to it, and drawing him towards me. "See, look at him. It has all gone sweetly, sweetly, sweetly up to this. Shall I hold the candle for you?"

My friend d'Harmonville, Planard, whatever he was, came to me, pulling off his gloves, which he popped into his pocket.

"The candle, a little this way," he said, and stooping over me he looked earnestly in my face. He touched my forehead, drew his hand across it, and then looked in my eyes for a time.

"Well, doctor, what do you think?" whispered the Count.

"How much did you give him?" said the Marquis, thus suddenly stunted down to a doctor.

"Seventy drops," said the lady.

"In the hot coffee?"

"Yes; sixty in a hot cup of coffee and ten in the liqueur."

Her voice, low and hard, seemed to me to tremble a little. It takes a long course of guilt to subjugate nature completely, and prevent those exterior signs of agitation that outlive all good.

The doctor, however, was treating me as coolly as he might a subject which he was about to place on the dissecting-table for a lecture.

He looked into my eyes again for a while, took my wrist, and applied his fingers to the pulse.

"That action suspended," he said to himself.

Then again he placed something that, for the moment I saw it, looked like a piece of gold-beater's leaf, to my lips, holding his head so far that his own breathing could not affect it.

"Yes," he said in soliloquy, very low.

Then he plucked my shirt-breast open and applied the stethoscope, shifted it from point to point, listened with his ear to its end, as if for a very far off sound, raised his head, and said, in like manner, softly to himself, "All appreciable action of the lungs has subsided."

Then turning from the sound, as I conjectured, he said:

"Seventy drops, allowing ten for waste, ought to hold him fast for six hours and a half—that is ample. The experiment I tried in the carriage was only thirty drops, and showed a highly sensitive brain. It would not do to kill him, you know. You are certain you did not exceed *seventy?*"

"Perfectly," said the lady.

"If he were to die the evaporation would be arrested, and foreign matter, some of it poisonous, would be found in the stomach, don't you see? If you are doubtful, it would be well to use the stomach-pump."

"Dearest Eugenie, be frank, be frank, do be frank," urged the Count.

"I am *not* doubtful, I am *certain*," she answered.

"How long ago, exactly? I told you to observe the time."

"I did; the minute-hand was exactly there, under the point of that Cupid's foot."

"It will last, then, probably for seven hours. He will recover then; the evaporation will be complete, and not one particle of the fluid will remain in the stomach."

It was reassuring, at all events, to hear that there was no intention to murder me. No one who has not tried it knows the terror of the approach of death, when the mind is clear, the instincts of life unimpaired, and no excitement to disturb the appreciation of that entirely new horror.

The nature and purpose of this tenderness was very, very peculiar, and as yet I had not a suspicion of it.

"You leave France, I suppose?" said the ex-Marquis.

"Yes, certainly, to-morrow," answered the Count.

"And where do you mean to go?"

"That I have not yet settled," he answered quickly.

"You won't tell a friend, eh?"

"I can't till I know. This has turned out an unprofitable affair."

"We shall settle that by-and-by."

"It is time we should get him lying down, eh?" said the Count, indicating me with one finger.

"Yes, we must proceed rapidly now. Are his night-shirt and night-cap—you understand—here?"

"All ready," said the Count.

"Now, Madame," said the doctor, turning to the lady, and making her, in spite of the emergency, a bow, "it is time you should retire."

The lady passed into the room, in which I had taken my cup of treacherous coffee, and I saw her no more.

The Count took a candle, and passed through the door at the farther end of the room, returning with a roll of linen in his hand. He bolted first one door, then the other.

They now, in silence, proceeded to undress me rapidly. They were not many minutes in accomplishing this.

What the doctor had termed my night-shirt, a long garment which reached below my feet, was now on, and a cap, that resembled a female nightcap more than anything I had ever seen upon a male head, was fitted upon mine, and tied under my chin.

And now, I thought, I shall be laid in a bed, to recover how I can, and, in the meantime, the conspirators will have escaped with their booty, and pursuit be in vain.

This was my best hope at the time; but it was soon clear that their plans were very different.

The Count and Planard now went, together, into the room that lay straight before me. I heard them talking low, and a sound of shuffling feet; then a long rumble; it suddenly stopped; it recommenced; it continued; side by side they came in at the door, their backs towards me. They were dragging something along the floor that made a continued boom and rumble, but they interposed between me and it, so that I could not see it until they had dragged it almost beside me; and then, merciful heaven! I saw it plainly enough. It was the coffin I had seen in the next room. It lay now flat on the floor, its edge against the chair in which I sat. Planard removed the lid. The coffin was empty.

Chapter XXVI

Catastrophe

"THOSE SEEM TO be good horses, and we change on the way," said Planard. "You give the men a Napoleon or two; we must do it within three hours and a quarter. Now, come; I'll lift him, upright, so as to place his feet in their proper berth, and you must keep them together, and draw the white shirt well down over them."

In another moment I was placed, as he described, sustained in Planard's arms, standing at the foot of the coffin, and so lowered backward, gradually, till I lay my length in it. Then the man, whom he called Planard, stretched my arms by my sides, and carefully arranged the frills at my breast, and the folds of the shroud, and after that, taking his stand at the foot of the coffin, made a survey which seemed to satisfy him.

The Count, who was very methodical, took my clothes, which had just been removed, folded them rapidly together and locked them up, as I afterwards heard, in one of the three presses which opened by doors in the panel.

I now understood their frightful plan. This coffin had been prepared for me; the funeral of St. Amand was a sham to mislead inquiry; I had myself given the order at Père la Chaise, signed it, and paid the fees for the interment of the fictitious Pierre de St. Amand, whose place I was to take, to lie in his coffin, with his name on the plate above my breast, and with a ton of clay packed down upon me; to waken from this catalepsy, after I had been for hours in the grave, there to perish by a death the most horrible that imagination can conceive.

If, hereafter, by any caprice of curiosity or suspicion, the coffin should be exhumed, and the body it enclosed examined, no chemistry could detect a trace of poison, nor the most cautious examination the slightest mark of violence.

276

I had myself been at the utmost pains to mystify inquiry, should my disappearance excite surmises, and had even written to my few correspondents in England to tell them that they were not to look for a letter from me for three weeks at least.

In the moment of my guilty elation death had caught me, and there was no escape. I tried to pray to God in my unearthly panic, but only thoughts of terror, judgment, and eternal anguish, crossed the distraction of my immediate doom.

I must not try to recall what is indeed indescribable—the multiform horrors of my own thoughts. I will relate, simply, what befell, every detail of which remains sharp in my memory as if cut in steel.

"The undertaker's men are in the hall," said the Count.

"They must not come till this is fixed," answered Planard. "Be good enough to take hold of the lower part while I take this end." I was not left long to conjecture what was coming, for in a few seconds more something slid across, a few inches above my face, and entirely excluded the light, and muffled sound, so that nothing that was not very distinct reached my ears henceforward; but very distinctly came the working of a turnscrew, and the crunching home of screws in succession. Than these vulgar sounds, no doom spoken in thunder could have been more tremendous.

The rest I must relate, not as it then reached my ears, which was too imperfectly and interruptedly to supply a connected narrative, but as it was afterwards told me by other people.

The coffin-lid being screwed down, the two gentlemen arranged the room, and adjusted the coffin so that it lay perfectly straight along the boards, the Count being specially anxious that there should be no appearance of hurry or disorder in the room, which might have suggested remark and conjecture.

When this was done, Doctor Planard said he would go to the hall to summon the men who were to carry the coffin out and place it in the hearse. The Count pulled on his black gloves, and held his white handkerchief in his hand, a very impressive chief-mourner. He stood a little behind the head of the coffin, awaiting the arrival of the persons who accompanied Planard, and whose fast steps he soon heard approaching.

Planard came first. He entered the room through the apartment in which the coffin had been originally placed. His manner was changed; there was something of a swagger in it.

"Monsieur le Comte," he said, as he strode through the door, followed by half a dozen persons. "I am sorry to have to announce to you a most unseasonable interruption. Here is Monsieur Carmaignac, a gentleman holding an office in the police department, who says that information to the effect that large quantities of smuggled English and other goods have been distributed in this neighbourhood, and that a portion of them is concealed in your house. I have ventured to assure him, of my own knowledge, that nothing can be more false than that information, and that you would be only too happy to throw open for his inspection, at a moment's notice, every room, closet, and cupboard in your house."

"Most assuredly," exclaimed the Count, with a stout voice, but a very white face. "Thank you, my good friend, for having anticipated me. I will place my house and keys at his disposal, for the purpose of his scrutiny, so soon as he is good enough to inform me, of what specific contraband goods he comes in search."

"The Count de St. Alyre will pardon me," answered Carmaignac, a little dryly. "I am forbidden by my instructions to make that disclosure; and that I am instructed to make a general search, this warrant will sufficiently apprise Monsieur le Comte."

"Monsieur Carmaignac, may I hope," interposed Planard, "that you will permit the Count de St. Alyre to attend the funeral of his kinsman, who lies here, as you see—" (he pointed to the plate upon the coffin)—"and to convey whom to Père la Chaise, a hearse waits at this moment at the door."

"That, I regret to say, I cannot permit. My instructions are precise; but the delay, I trust, will be but trifling. Monsieur le Comte will not suppose for a moment that I suspect him; but we have a duty to perform, and I must act as if I did. When I am ordered to search, I search; things are sometimes hid in such *bizarre* places. I can't say, for instance, what that coffin may contain."

"The body of my kinsman, Monsieur Pierre de St. Amand," answered the Count, loftily.

"Oh! then you've seen him?"

"Seen him? Often, too often!" The Count was evidently a good deal moved.

"I mean the body?"

The Count stole a quick glance at Planard.

"N—no, Monsieur—that is, I mean only for a moment." Another quick glance at Planard.

"But quite long enough, I fancy, to recognise him?" insinuated that gentleman.

"Of course—of course; instantly—perfectly. What! Pierre de St. Amand? Not know him at a glance? No, no, poor fellow, I know him too well for that."

"The things I am in search of," said Monsieur Carmaignac, "would fit in a narrow compass—servants are so ingenious sometimes. Let us raise the lid."

"Pardon me, Monsieur," said the Count, peremptorily, advancing to the side of the coffin, and extending his arm across it. "I cannot permit that indignity—that desecration."

"There shall be none, sir,—simply the raising of the lid; you shall remain in the room. If it should prove as we all hope, you shall have the pleasure of one other look, really the last, upon your beloved kinsman."

"But, sir, I can't."

"But, Monsieur, I must."

"But, besides, the thing, the turnscrew, broke when the last screw was turned; and I give you my sacred honour there is nothing but the body in this coffin."

"Of course Monsieur le Comte believes all that; but he does not know so well as I the legerdemain in use among servants, who are accustomed to smuggling. Here, Philippe, you must take off the lid of that coffin."

The Count protested; but Philippe—a man with a bald head, and a smirched face, looking like a working blacksmith—placed on the floor a leather bag of tools, from which, having looked at the coffin, and picked with his nail at the screw-heads, he selected a turn-screw, and, with a few deft twirls at each of the screws, they stood up like little rows of mushrooms, and the lid was raised. I saw the light, of which I thought I had seen my last, once more; but the axis of vision remained fixed. As I was reduced to the cataleptic state in a position nearly perpendicular, I continued looking straight before me, and thus my gaze was now fixed upon the ceiling. I saw the face of Carmaignac leaning over me with a curious frown. It seemed to me that there was no recognition in his eyes. Oh, heaven! that I could have uttered were it but one cry! I saw the dark, mean mask of the little Count staring down at me from the other side; the face of the pseudo-marquis also peering at me, but not so full in the line of vision; there were other faces also.

"I see, I see," said Carmaignac, withdrawing. "Nothing of the kind there."

"You will be good enough to direct your man to re-adjust the lid of the coffin, and to fix the screws," said the Count, taking courage; "and—and—really the funeral must proceed. It is not fair to the people who have but moderate fees for night-work, to keep them hour after hour beyond the time."

"Count de St. Alyre, you shall go in a very few minutes. I will direct, just now, all about the coffin."

The Count looked toward the door, and there saw a gendarme; and two or three more grave and stalwart specimens of the same force were also in the room. The Count was very uncomfortably excited; it was growing insupportable.

"As this gentleman makes a difficulty about my attending the obsequies of my kinsman, I will ask you, Planard, to accompany the funeral in my stead."

"In a few minutes," answered the incorrigible Carmaignac. "I must first trouble you for the key that opens that press."

He pointed direct at the press, in which the clothes had just been locked up.

"I—I have no objection," said the Count—"none, of course; only they have not been used for an age. I'll direct some one to look for the key."

"If you have not got it about you, it is quite unnecessary. Philippe, try your skeleton-keys with that press. I want it opened. Whose clothes are these?" inquired Carmaignac when, the press having been opened, he took out the suit that had been placed there scarcely two minutes since.

"I can't say," answered the Count. "I know nothing of the contents of that press. A roguish servant, named Lablais, whom I dismissed about a year ago, had the key. I have not seen it open for ten years or more. The clothes are probably his.

"Here are visiting cards, see, and here a marked pocket-handkerchief—'R.B.' upon it. He must have stolen them from a person named Beckett—R. Beckett. 'Mr. Beckett, Berkeley Square,' the card says; and, my faith! here's a watch and a bunch of seals; one of them with the initials 'R.B.' upon it. That servant, Lablais, must have been a consummate rogue!"

"So he was; you are right, sir.

"It strikes me that he possibly stole these clothes," continued Carmaignac, "from the man in the coffin, who, in that case, would be Monsieur Beckett, and not Monsieur de St. Amand. For, wonderful to relate, Monsieur, the watch is still going! That man in the coffin, I believe, is not dead, but simply drugged. And for having robbed and intended to murder him, I arrest you, Nicolas de la Marque, Count de St. Alyre."

In another moment the old villain was a prisoner. I heard his discordant voice break quaveringly into sudden vehemence and volubility; now croaking—now shrieking, as he oscillated between protests, threats, and impious appeals to the God who will "judge the secrets of men!" And thus lying and raving, he was removed from the room, and placed in the same coach with his beautiful and abandoned accomplice, already arrested; and, with two gendarmes sitting beside them, they were immediately driving at a rapid pace towards the Conciergerie.

There were now added to the general chorus two voices, very different in quality; one was that of the gasconading Colonel Gaillarde, who had with difficulty been kept in the background up to this; the other was that of my jolly friend Whistlewick, who had come to identify me.

I shall tell you, just now, how this project against my property and life, so ingenious and monstrous, was exploded. I must first say a word about myself. I was placed in a hot bath, under the direction of Planard, as consummate a villain as any of the gang, but now thoroughly in the interests of the prosecution. Thence I was laid in a warm bed, the window of the room being open. These simple measures restored me in about three hours; I should otherwise, probably, have continued under the spell for nearly seven.

The practices of these nefarious conspirators had been carried on with consummate skill and secrecy. Their dupes were led, as I was, to be themselves auxiliary to the mystery which made their own destruction both safe and certain.

A search was, of course, instituted. Graves were opened in Père la Chaise. The bodies exhumed had lain there too long, and were too much decomposed to be recognised. One only was identified. The notice for the burial, in this particular case, had been signed, the order given, and the fees paid, by Gabriel Gaillarde, who was known to the official clerk, who had to transact with him this little funereal business. The very trick, that had been arranged for me, had been successfully practised in his case. The person for whom the grave had been ordered, was purely fictitious; and Gabriel Gaillarde himself filled the coffin, on the cover of which that false name was inscribed as well as upon a tomb-stone over the grave. Possibly, the same honour, under my pseudonym, may have been intended for me.

The identification was curious. This Gabriel Gaillarde had had a bad fall from a run-away horse, about five years before his mysterious disappearance. He had lost an eye and some teeth, in this accident, besides sustaining a fracture of the right leg, immediately above the ankle. He had kept the injuries to his face as profound a secret as he could. The result was, that the glass eye which had done duty for the one he had lost, remained in the socket, slightly displaced, of course, but recognisable by the "artist" who had supplied it.

More pointedly recognisable were the teeth, peculiar in workmanship, which one of the ablest dentists in Paris had himself adapted to the chasms, the cast of which, owing to peculiarities in the accident, he happened to have preserved. This cast precisely fitted the gold plate found in the mouth of the skull. The mark, also, above the ankle, in the bone, where it had re-united, corresponded exactly with the place where the fracture had knit in the limb of Gabriel Gaillarde.

The Colonel, his younger brother, had been furious about the disappearance of Gabriel, and still more so about that of his money, which he had long regarded as his proper keepsake, whenever death should remove his brother from the vexations of living. He had suspected for a long time, for certain adroitly discovered reasons, that the Count de St. Alyre and the beautiful lady, his companion, countess, or whatever else she was, had pigeoned him. To this suspicion were added some others of a still darker kind; but in their first shape, rather the exaggerated reflections of his fury, ready to believe anything, than well-defined conjectures.

At length an accident had placed the Colonel very nearly upon the right scent; a chance, possibly lucky for himself, had apprised the scoundrel Planard that the conspirators—himself among the number—were in danger. The result was that he made terms for himself, became an informer, and concerted with the police this visit made to the Château de la Carque, at the critical moment when every measure had been completed that was necessary to construct a perfect case against his guilty accomplices.

I need not describe the minute industry or forethought with which the police collected all the details necessary to support the case. They had brought an able physician, who, even had Planard failed, would have supplied the necessary medical evidence.

My trip to Paris, you will believe, had not turned out quite so agreeably as I had anticipated. I was the principal witness for the prosecution in this *cause célèbre*, with all the *agréments* that attend that enviable position. Having had an escape, as my friend Whistlewick said, "with a squeak" for my life, I innocently fancied that I should have been an object of considerable interest to Parisian society; but, a good deal to my mortification, I discovered that I was the object for a good-natured but contemptuous merriment. I was a *balourd*, *abenêt*, *un âne*, and figured even in caricatures. I became a sort of public character, a dignity,

> "Unto which I was not born,"

and from which I fled as soon as I conveniently could, without even paying my friend the Marquis d'Harmonville a visit at his hospitable château.

The Marquis escaped scot-free. His accomplice, the Count, was executed. The fair Eugenie, under extenuating circumstances—consisting, so far as I could discover of her good looks—got off for six years' imprisonment.

Colonel Gaillarde recovered some of his brother's money, out of the not very affluent estate of the Count and *soi-disant* Countess. This, and the execution of the Count, put him in high good humour. So far from insisting on a hostile meeting, he shook me very graciously by the hand, told me that he looked upon the wound on his head, inflicted by the knob of my stick, as having been received in an honourable, though irregular duel, in which he had no disadvantage or unfairness to complain of.

I think I have only two additional details to mention. The bricks discovered in the room with the coffin, had been packed in it, in straw, to supply the weight of a dead body, and to prevent the suspicions and contradictions that might have been excited by the arrival of an empty coffin at the château.

Secondly, the Countess' magnificent brilliants were examined by a lapidary, and pronounced to be worth about five pounds to a tragedy-queen, who happened to be in want of a suite of paste.

The Countess had figured some years before as one of the cleverest actresses on the minor stage of Paris, where she had been picked up by the Count and used as his principal accomplice.

She it was who, admirably disguised, had rifled my papers in the carriage on my memorable night-journey to Paris. She also had figured as the interpreting magician of the palanquin at the ball at Versailles. So far as I was affected by that elaborate mystification it was intended to re-animate my interest, which, they feared, might flag in the beautiful Countess. It had its design and action upon other intended victims also; but of them there is, at present, no need to speak. The introduction of a real corpse—procured from a person who supplied the Parisian anatomists—involved no real danger, while it heightened the mystery and kept the prophet alive in the gossip of the town and in the thoughts of the noodles with whom he had conferred.

I divided the remainder of the summer and autumn between Switzerland and Italy.

As the well-worn phrase goes, I was a sadder if not a wiser man. A great deal of the horrible impression left upon my mind was due, of course, to the mere action of nerves and brain. But serious feelings of another and deeper kind remained. My after life was ultimately formed by the shock I had then received. Those impressions led me—but not till after many years—to happier though not less serious thoughts; and I have deep reason to be thankful to the all-merciful Ruler of events, for an early and terrible lesson in the ways of sin.

2. *The Expanding Psyche*

Cousin Phillis

1850

MRS. GASKELL

Mrs. Gaskell was born Elizabeth Cleghorn Stevenson, in 1810. Her father was a Unitarian minister and she married another. Most of her life was passed in Manchester or just outside it, at Knutsford, the original of Cranford. She is the most Victorian of Victorian novelists; gentle, good, reasonable, witty and self-effacing, and yet by an accident of place, rather than birth, she was brought into close contact with the Industrial Revolution and the bitter Nineteenth-Century class struggle. The comparison between rich and poor which was thrust upon her came to suggest a theme that she was not properly equipped to handle and her best work is either suburban pastoral like Cranford or a novel of county society like Wives and Daughters. There is an admirable essay on her by Lord David Cecil in his Early Victorian Novelists to which nothing can be added. He praises her taste, her feminine subtlety and command of detail and her freshness of outlook. "This freshness is Mrs. Gaskell's most significant quality for it gives a distinguishing twist to all her other qualities," he explains. "Other writers have been subtle and fastidious, other writers have been fresh. But no others have been both, exactly in the way she is. . . . Gladly forgetful of weakness and imperfection, we linger for hours in the lavender-scented atmosphere of her quiet, artless, narrow world. . . . Style, poetry, humor, pathos, sensibility to nature, knowledge of character; the recital of Mrs. Gaskell's virtues brings us to the same question as did those of the other Victorians. Why has she not got more reputation? With twenty times the talent of most novelists, why is she not read twenty times as much? Alas, the answer is the same. Like Dickens' and Charlotte Brontë's, Mrs. Gaskell's work is as faulty as it is inspired—and for the same reason. Like them she commits the novelist's fatal fault, she writes outside her range. For she too was the instinctive uncritical child of an instinctive uncritical age, ignorant alike of the laws governing her art and of her particular limitations."

It is all the more remarkable, then, that Cousin Phillis should be a minor work of art, worthy to be compared with certain novels of Hardy. We have four characters; the boy who tells the story, the Holmans, father and daughter, and the boy's exciting up-to-date friend, Mr. Holdsworth. The impact of the two young railwaymen on the Holman family is disastrous and everything is destroyed; the peace of the farm, the happy relationships between father and daughter, and between them and the boy who tells the story (who, by the end, is a young man). While appearing to conclude, as a good Victorian should, on a note of optimism, the artist in Mrs. Gaskell is not deceived—nor is the reader. We are present at a rural tragedy. The subtlety of Mrs. Gaskell is apparent in the complication of motive: she does not merely blame Holdsworth for being unstable or callous, she blames, more indirectly, the over-possessive Mr. Holman for having deliberately blinded himself to the age and appetites of his growing daughter. If he had not given her Dante, she would not have needed the travelled Holdsworth as her translator; if he had let her see more young men of her own age she would not have fallen so desperately 'in love' with him. All suffer, all are punished except the young railwayman who does the harm but never strays from his own code. And how beautifully Phillis herself misses being a prig! Here the author's celebrated freshness comes out in the many exquisite country scenes, none very remarkable for original writing or for the deep understanding of nature which Meredith and Hardy were soon to bring to the novel, but all strangely satisfying and true like the views of mellow aquatinted fields painted on old china.

Cousin Phillis

MRS. GASKELL

Part I

IT IS A great thing for a lad when he is first turned into the independence of lodgings. I do not think I ever was so satisfied and proud in my life as when, at seventeen, I sate down in a little three-cornered room above a pastry-cook's shop in the county town of Eltham. My father had left me that afternoon, after delivering himself of a few plain precepts, strongly expressed, for my guidance in the new course of life on which I was entering. I was to be a clerk under the engineer who had undertaken to make the little branch line from Eltham to Hornby. My father had got me this situation, which was in a position rather above his own in life; or perhaps I should say, above the station in which he was born and bred; for he was raising himself every year in men's consideration and respect. He was a mechanic by trade; but he had some inventive genius, and a great deal of perseverance, and had devised several valuable improvements in railway machinery. He did not do this for profit, though, as was reasonable, what came in the natural course of things was acceptable; he worked out his ideas, because, as he said, "until he could put them into shape, they plagued him by night and by day." But this is enough about my dear father; it is a good thing for a country where there are many like him. He was a sturdy Independent by descent and conviction; and this it was, I believe, which made him place me in the lodgings at the pastry-cook's. The shop was kept by the two sisters of our minister at home; and this was considered as a sort of safeguard to my morals, when I was turned loose upon the temptations of the county town, with a salary of thirty pounds a year.

My father had given up two precious days, and put on his Sunday clothes, in order to bring me to Eltham, and accompany me first to the office, to introduce me to my new master (who was under some obligations to my father for a suggestion), and next to take me to call on the Independent minister of the little congregation at Eltham. And then he left me; and, though sorry to part with him, I now began to taste with relish the pleasure of being my own master. I unpacked the hamper that my mother had provided me with, and smelt the pots of preserve with all the delight of a possessor who might break into their contents at any time he pleased. I handled and weighed in my fancy the home-cured ham, which seemed to promise me interminable feasts; and, above all, there was the fine savour of knowing that I might eat of these dainties when I liked, at my sole will, not dependent on the pleasure of any one else, however indulgent. I stowed my eatables away in the little corner cupboard—that room was all corners, and everything was placed in a corner, the fire-place, the window, the cupboard; I myself seemed to be the only thing in the middle, and there was hardly room for me. The table was made of a folding leaf under the window, and the window looked out upon the market-place; so the studies for the prosecution of which my father had brought himself to pay extra for a sitting-room for me, ran a considerable chance of being diverted from books to men and women. I was to have my meals with the two elderly Miss Browns in the little parlour behind the three-cornered shop downstairs; my breakfasts and dinners at least, for, as my hours in an evening were likely to be uncertain, my tea or supper was to be an independent meal.

Then, after this pride and satisfaction, came a sense of desolation. I had never been from home before, and I was an only child; and though my father's spoken maxim had been, "Spare the rod, and spoil the child," yet, unconsciously, his heart had yearned after me, and his ways towards me were more tender than he knew, or would have approved of in himself could he have known. My mother, who never professed sternness, was far more severe than my father: perhaps my boyish faults annoyed her more; for I remember, now that I have written the above words, how she pleaded for me once in my riper years, when I had really offended against my father's sense of right.

But I have nothing to do with that now. It is about cousin Phillis that I am going to write, and as yet I am far enough from even saying who cousin Phillis was.

For some months after I was settled in Eltham, the new employment in which I was engaged—the new independence of my life—occupied all my thoughts. I was at my desk by eight o'clock, home to dinner at one, back at the office by two. The afternoon work was more uncertain than the morning's; it might be the same, or it might be that I had to accompany Mr. Holdsworth, the managing engineer, to some point on the line between Eltham and Hornby. This I always enjoyed, because of the variety, and because of the country we traversed (which was very wild and pretty), and because I was thrown into companionship with Mr. Holdsworth, who held the position of hero in my boyish mind. He was a young man of five-and-twenty or so, and was in a station above mine, both by birth and education; and he had travelled on the Continent, and wore mustachios and whiskers of a somewhat foreign fashion. I was proud of being seen with him. He was really a fine fellow in a good number of ways, and I might have fallen into much worse hands.

Every Saturday I wrote home, telling of my weekly doings—my father had insisted upon this; but there was so little variety in my life that I often found it hard work to fill a letter. On Sundays I went twice to chapel, up a dark narrow entry, to hear droning hymns, and long prayers, and a still longer sermon, preached to a small congregation, of which I was, by nearly a score of years, the youngest member. Occasionally, Mr. Peters, the minister, would ask me home to tea after the second service. I dreaded the honour, for I usually sate on the edge of my chair all the evening, and answered solemn questions, put in a deep bass voice, until household prayer-time came, at eight o'clock, when Mrs. Peters came in, smoothing down her apron, and the maid-of-all-work followed, and first a sermon, and then a chapter was read, and a long impromptu prayer followed, till some instinct told Mr. Peters that supper-time had come, and we rose from our knees with hunger for our predominant feeling. Over supper the minister did unbend

293

a little into one or two ponderous jokes, as if to show me that ministers were men, after all. And then at ten o'clock I went home, and enjoyed my long-repressed yawns in the three-cornered room before going to bed.

Dinah and Hannah Dawson, so their names were put on the board above the shop-door—I always called them Miss Dawson and Miss Hannah—considered these visits of mine to Mr. Peters as the greatest honour a young man could have; and evidently thought that if, after such privileges, I did not work out my salvation, I was a sort of modern Judas Iscariot. On the contrary, they shook their heads over my intercourse with Mr. Holdsworth. He had been so kind to me in many ways, that when I cut into my ham, I hovered over the thought of asking him to tea in my room, more especially as the annual fair was being held in Eltham market-place, and the sight of the booths, the merry-go-rounds, the wild-beast shows, and such country pomps, was (as I thought at seventeen) very attractive. But when I ventured to allude to my wish in even distant terms, Miss Hannah caught me up, and spoke of the sinfulness of such sights, and something about wallowing in the mire, and then vaulted into France, and spoke evil of the nation, and all who had ever set foot therein, till, seeing that her anger was concentrating itself into a point, and that that point was Mr. Holdsworth, I thought it would be better to finish my breakfast, and make what haste I could out of the sound of her voice. I rather wondered afterwards to hear her and Miss Dawson counting up their weekly profits with glee, and saying that a pastry-cook's shop in the corner of the market-place, in Eltham fair week, was no such bad thing. However, I never ventured to ask Mr. Holdsworth to my lodgings.

There is not much to tell about this first year of mine at Eltham. But when I was nearly nineteen, and beginning to think of whiskers on my own account, I came to know cousin Phillis, whose very existence had been unknown to me till then. Mr. Holdsworth and I had been out to Heathbridge for a day, working hard. Heathbridge was near Hornby, for our line of railway was above half finished. Of course, a day's outing was a great thing to tell about in my weekly letters; and I fell to describing the country—a fault I was not often guilty of. I told my father of the bogs, all over wild myrtle and soft moss, and shaking ground over which we had to carry our line; and how Mr. Holdsworth and I had gone for our mid-day meals—for we had to stay here for two days and a night—to a pretty village hard by, Heathbridge proper; and how I hoped we should often have to go there, for the shaking, uncertain ground was puzzling our engineers—one end of the line going up as soon as the other was weighted down. (I had no thought for the share-holders' interests, as may be seen; we had to make a new line on firmer ground before the junction railway was completed.) I told all this at great length, thankful to fill up my paper. By return let-ter, I heard that a second-cousin of my mother's was married to the Independent minister of Hornby, Ebenezer Holman by name, and lived at Heathbridge proper; the very Heathbridge I had described, or so my mother believed, for she had never seen her cousin Phillis Green, who was something of an heiress (my father believed), being her father's only child, and old Thomas Green had owned an estate of near upon fifty acres, which must have come to his daughter. My mother's feeling of kinship seemed to have been strongly stirred by the mention of Heathbridge; for my father said she desired me, if ever I went thither again, to make inquiry for the Reverend Ebenezer Holman; and if indeed he lived there, I was further to ask if he had not married one Phillis Green; and if both these questions were answered in the affirma-tive, I was to go and introduce myself as the only child of Margaret Manning, born Moneypenny. I was enraged at myself for having named Heathbridge at all, when I found what it was drawing down upon me. One Independent minister, as I said to myself, was enough for any man; and here I knew (that is to say, I had been catechised on Sabbath mornings by) Mr. Hunter, our minis-ter at home; and I had had to be civil to old Peters at Eltham, and behave myself for five hours running whenever he asked me to tea at his house; and now, just as I felt the free air blowing about me up at Heathbridge, I was to ferret out another minister, and I should perhaps have to be catechised by him, or else asked to tea at his house. Besides, I did not like pushing myself upon strangers, who perhaps had never heard of my mother's name, and such an odd name as it was—Moneypenny; and if they had, had never cared more for her than she had for them, apparently, until this unlucky mention of Heathbridge.

Still, I would not disobey my parents in such a trifle, however irksome it might be. So the next time our business took me to Heathbridge, and we were dining in the little sanded inn-parlour, I took the opportunity of Mr. Holdsworth's being out of the room, and asked the questions which I was bidden to ask of the rosy-cheeked maid. I was either unintelligible or she was stupid; for she said she did not know, but would ask master; and of course the landlord came in to understand what it was I wanted to know; and I had to bring out all my stammering inquiries before Mr. Holdsworth, who would never have attended to them, I dare say, if I had not blushed and blundered, and made such a fool of myself.

"Yes," the landlord said, "the Hope Farm was in Heathbridge proper, and the owner's name was Holman, and he was an Independent minister, and, as far as the landlord could tell, his wife's Christian name was Phillis; anyhow, her maiden name was Green."

"Relations of yours?" asked Mr. Holdsworth.

"No, sir—only my mother's second-cousins. Yes, I suppose they are relations. But I never saw them in my life."

"The Hope Farm is not a stone's throw from here," said the officious landlord, going to the window. "If you carry your eye over yon bed of hollyhocks, over the damson-trees in the orchard yonder, you may see a stack of queer-like stone chimneys. Them is the Hope Farm chimneys; it's an old place, though Holman keeps it in good order."

Mr. Holdsworth had risen from the table with more promptitude than I had, and was standing by the window, looking. At the landlord's last words, he turned round, smiling,—"It is not often that parsons know how to keep land in order, is it?"

"Beg pardon, sir, but I must speak as I find; and minister Holman—we call the Church clergymen here 'parson,' sir; he would be a bit jealous if he heard a Dissenter called parson—minister Holman knows what he's about as well as e'er a farmer in the neighbourhood. He gives up five days a week to his own work, and two to the Lord's; and it is difficult to say which he works hardest at. He spends Saturday and Sunday a-writing sermons and a-visiting his flock at Hornby; and at five o'clock on Monday morning he'll be guiding his plough in the Hope Farm yonder just as well as if he could neither read nor write. But your dinner will be getting cold, gentlemen."

296

So we went back to table. After a while, Mr. Holdsworth broke the silence:—"If I were you, Manning, I'd look up these relations of yours. You can go and see what they're like while we're waiting for Dobson's estimates, and I'll smoke a cigar in the garden meanwhile."

"Thank you, sir. But I don't know them, and I don't think I want to know them."

"What did you ask all those questions for, then?" said he, looking quickly up at me. He had no notion of doing or saying things without a purpose. I did not answer, so he continued,—"Make up your mind, and go off and see what this farmer-minister is like, and come back and tell me—I should like to hear."

I was so in the habit of yielding to his authority, or influence, that I never thought of resisting, but went on my errand, though I remember feeling as if I would rather have had my head cut off. The landlord, who had evidently taken an interest in the event of our discussion in a way that country landlords have, accompanied me to the house-door, and gave me repeated directions, as if I was likely to miss my way in two hundred yards. But I listened to him, for I was glad of the delay, to screw up my courage for the effort of facing unknown people and introducing myself. I went along the lane, I recollect, switching at all the taller roadside weeds, till, after a turn or two, I found myself close in front of the Hope Farm. There was a garden between the house and the shady, grassy lane; I afterwards found that this garden was called the court; perhaps because there was a low wall round it, with an iron railing on the top of the wall, and two great gates between pillars crowned with stone balls for a state entrance to the flagged path leading up to the front door. It was not the habit of the place to go in either by these great gates or by the front door; the gates, indeed, were locked, as I found, though the door stood wide open. I had to go round by a side-path lightly worn on a broad, grassy way, which led past the court-wall, past a horse-mount, half covered with stonecrop and a little wild yellow fumitory, to another door—"the curate," as I found it was termed by the master of the house, while the front door, "handsome and all for show," was termed "the rector." I knocked with my hand upon the "curate" door; a tall girl, about my own age, as I thought, came and opened it, and stood there silent, waiting to know my errand. I see her now—

297

cousin Phillis. The westering sun shone full upon her, and made a slanting stream of light into the room within. She was dressed in dark blue cotton of some kind; up to her throat, down to her wrists, with a little frill of the same wherever it touched her white skin. And such a white skin as it was! I have never seen the like. She had light hair, nearer yellow than any other colour. She looked me steadily in the face with large, quiet eyes, wondering, but untroubled by the sight of a stranger. I thought it odd that so old, so full-grown as she was, she should wear a pinafore over her gown.

Before I had quite made up my mind what to say in reply to her mute inquiry of what I wanted there, a woman's voice called out, "Who is it, Phillis? If it is any one for butter-milk send them round to the back-door."

I thought I could rather speak to the owner of that voice than to the girl before me; so I passed her, and stood at the entrance of a room, hat in hand, for this side-door opened straight into the hall or house-place where the family sate when work was done. There was a brisk little woman of forty or so ironing some huge muslin cravats under the light of a long vine-shaded casement window. She looked at me distrustfully till I began to speak. "My name is Paul Manning," said I; but I saw she did not know the name. "My mother's name was Moneypenny," said I,—"Margaret Moneypenny."

"And she married one John Manning of Birmingham," said Mrs. Holman, eagerly. "And you'll be her son. Sit down! I am right glad to see you. To think of your being Margaret's son! Why, she was almost a child not so long ago. Well, to be sure, it is five-and-twenty years ago. And what brings you into these parts?"

She sate down herself, as if oppressed by her curiosity as to all the five-and-twenty years that had passed by since she had seen my mother. Her daughter Phillis took up her knitting—a long grey worsted man's stocking, I remember—and knitted away without looking at her work. I felt that the steady gaze of those deep grey eyes was upon me, though once, when I stealthily raised mine to hers, she was examining something on the wall above my head.

When I had answered all my cousin Holman's questions, she heaved a long breath, and said, "To think of Margaret Moneypenny's boy being in our house! I wish the minister was here. Phillis, in what field is thy father to-day?"

"In the five-acre; they are beginning to cut the corn."

"He'll not like being sent for, then, else I should have liked you to have seen the minister. But the five-acre is a good step off. You shall have a glass of wine and a bit of cake before you stir from this house, though. You're bound to go, you say, or else the minister comes in mostly when the men have their four o'clock."

"I must go—I ought to have been off before now."

"Here, then, Phillis, take the keys." She gave her daughter some whispered directions, and Phillis left the room.

"She is my cousin, is she not?" I asked. I knew she was, but somehow I wanted to talk of her, and did not know how to begin.

"Yes—Phillis Holman. She is our only child—now."

Either from that "now," or from a strange momentary wistfulness in her eyes, I knew that there had been more children, who were now dead.

"How old is cousin Phillis?" said I, scarcely venturing on the new name, it seemed too prettily familiar for me to call her by it; but cousin Holman took no notice of it, answering straight to the purpose.

"Seventeen last May-day; but the minister does not like to hear me calling it May-day," said she, checking herself with a little awe. "Phillis was seventeen on the first day of May last," she repeated in an emended edition.

"And I am nineteen in another month," thought I, to myself; I don't know why.

Then Phillis came in, carrying a tray with wine and cake upon it.

"We keep a house-servant," said cousin Holman, "but it is churning-day, and she is busy." It was meant as a little proud apology for her daughter's being the handmaiden.

"I like doing it, mother," said Phillis, in her grave, full voice.

I felt as if I were somebody in the Old Testament—who, I could not recollect—being served and waited upon by the daughter of the host. Was I like Abraham's steward, when Rebekah gave him to drink at the well? I thought Isaac had not gone the pleasantest way to work in winning him a wife. But Phillis never thought about such things. She was a stately, gracious young woman, in the dress and with the simplicity of a child.

As I had been taught, I drank to the health of my new-found

cousin and her husband; and then I ventured to name my cousin Phillis with a little bow of my head towards her; but I was too awkward to look and see how she took my compliment. "I must go, now," said I, rising.

Neither of the women had thought of sharing in the wine; cousin Holman had broken a bit of cake for form's sake.

"I wish the minister had been within," said his wife, rising too. Secretly I was very glad he was not. I did not take kindly to ministers in those days, and I thought he must be a particular kind of man, by his objecting to the term May-day. But before I went, cousin Holman made me promise that I would come back on the Saturday following and spend Sunday with them; when I should see something of "the minister."

"Come on Friday, if you can," were her last words as she stood at the curate-door, shading her eyes from the sinking sun with her hand.

Inside the house sate cousin Phillis, her golden hair, her dazzling complexion, lighting up the corner of the vine-shadowed room. She had not risen when I bade her good-bye; she had looked at me straight as she said her tranquil words of farewell.

I found Mr. Holdsworth down at the line, hard at work superintending. As soon as he had a pause, he said, "Well, Manning, what are the new cousins like? How do preaching and farming seem to get on together? If the minister turns out to be practical as well as reverend, I shall begin to respect him."

But he hardly attended to my answer, he was so much more occupied with directing his work-people. Indeed, my answer did not come very readily; and the most distinct part of it was the mention of the invitation that had been given me.

"Oh! of course you can go—and on Friday, too, if you like; there is no reason why not this week; and you've done a long spell of work this time, old fellow."

I thought that I did not want to go on Friday; but when the day came, I found that I should prefer going to staying away, so I availed myself of Mr. Holdsworth's permission, and went over to Hope Farm some time in the afternoon, a little later than my last visit. I found the "curate" open to admit the soft September air, so tempered by the warmth of the sun that it was warmer out of doors than in, although the wooden log lay smouldering in front of a heap of hot ashes on the hearth. The vine-leaves over the window had a tinge more yellow, their edges were here and there scorched and browned; there was no ironing about, and cousin Holman sate just outside the house, mending a shirt. Phillis was at her knitting indoors: it seemed as if she had been at it all the week. The many-speckled fowls were pecking about in the farmyard beyond, and the milk-cans glittered with brightness, hung out to sweeten. The court was so full of flowers that they crept out upon the low-covered wall and horse-mount, and were even to be found self-sown upon the turf that bordered the path to the back of the house. I fancied that my Sunday coat was scented for days afterwards by the bushes of sweetbriar and the fraxinella that perfumed the air. From time to time cousin Holman put her hand into a covered basket at her feet, and threw handsful of corn down for the pigeons that cooed and fluttered in the air around, in expectation of this treat.

I had a thorough welcome as soon as she saw me. "Now, this is kind—this is right down friendly," shaking my hand warmly. "Phillis, your cousin Manning is come!"

"Call me Paul, will you?" said I; "they call me so at home, and Manning in the office."

"Well; Paul, then. Your room is all ready for you, Paul, for, as I said to the minister, 'I'll have it ready whether he comes o' Friday or not.' And the minister said he must go up to the Ashfield whether you were to come or not; but he would come home betimes to see if you were here. I'll show you to your room, and you can wash the dust off a bit."

After I came down, I think she did not quite know what to do with me; or she might think that I was dull; or she might have work to do in which I hindered her; for she called Phillis, and bade her put on her bonnet, and go with me to the Ashfield, and find father. So we set off, I in a little flutter of a desire to make myself agreeable, but wishing that my companion were not quite so tall; for she was above me in height. While I was wondering how to begin our conversation, she took up the words.

"I suppose, cousin Paul, you have to be very busy at your work all day long in general?"

"Yes, we have to be in the office at half-past eight; and we have an hour for dinner, and then we go at it again till eight or nine."

"Then you have not much time for reading?"

"No," said I, with a sudden consciousness that I did not make the most of what leisure I had.

"No more have I. Father always gets an hour before going a-field in the mornings, but mother does not like me to get up so early."

"My mother is always wanting me to get up earlier when I am at home."

"What time do you get up?"

"Oh!—ah!—sometimes half-past six; not often though;" for I remembered only twice that I had done so during the past summer.

She turned her head, and looked at me.

"Father is up at three; and so was mother till she was ill. I should like to be up at four."

"Your father at three! Why, what has he to do at that hour?"

"What has he not to do? He has his private exercise in his own room; he always rings the great bell which calls the men to milking; he rouses up Betty, our maid; as often as not he gives the horses their feed before the man is up—for Jem, who takes care of the horses, is an old man; and father is always loth to disturb him; he looks at the calves, and the shoulders, heels, traces, chaff, and corn before the horses go a-field; he has often to whip-cord the plough-whips; he sees the hogs fed; he looks into the swill-tubs, and writes his orders for what is wanted for food for man and beast; yes, and for fuel, too. And then, if he has a bit of time to spare, he comes in and reads with me—but only English; we keep Latin for the evenings, that we may have time to enjoy it; and then he calls in the man to breakfast, and cuts the boys' bread and cheese, and sees their wooden bottles filled, and sends them off to their work; —and by this time it is half-past six, and we have our breakfast. There is father!" she exclaimed, pointing out to me a man in his shirt-sleeves, taller by the head than the other two with whom he was working. We only saw him through the leaves of the ash-trees growing in the hedge, and I thought I must be confusing the figures, or mistaken: that man still looked like a very powerful labourer, and had none of the precise demureness of appearance which I had always imagined was the characteristic of a minister. It was the Reverend Ebenezer Holman, however. He gave us a nod as we entered the stubble-field; and I think he would have

302

come to meet us but that he was in the middle of giving some directions to his men. I could see that Phillis was built more after his type than her mother's. He, like his daughter, was largely made, and of a fair, ruddy complexion, whereas hers was brilliant and delicate. His hair had been yellow or sandy, but now was grizzled. Yet his grey hairs betokened no failure in strength. I never saw a more powerful man—deep chest, lean flanks, well-planted head. By this time we were nearly up to him; and he interrupted himself and stepped forwards; holding out his hand to me, but addressing Phillis.

"Well, my lass, this is cousin Manning, I suppose. Wait a minute, young man, and I'll put on my coat, and give you a decorous and formal welcome. But—Ned Hall, there ought to be a water-furrow across this land: it's a nasty, stiff, clayey, dauby bit of ground, and thou and I must fall to, come next Monday— I beg your pardon, cousin Manning—and there's old Jem's cottage wants a bit of thatch; you can do that job tomorrow while I am busy." Then, suddenly changing the tone of his deep bass voice to an odd suggestion of chapels and preachers, he added, "Now, I will give out the psalm, 'Come all harmonious tongues,' to be sung to 'Mount Ephraim' tune."

He lifted his spade in his hand, and began to beat time with it; the two labourers seemed to know both words and music, though I did not; and so did Phillis: her rich voice followed her father's as he set the tune; and the men came in with more uncertainty, but still harmoniously. Phillis looked at me once or twice with a little surprise at my silence; but I did not know the words. There we five stood, bareheaded, excepting Phillis, in the tawny stubble-field, from which all the shocks of corn had not yet been carried— a dark wood on one side, where the woodpigeons were cooing; blue distance seen through the ash-trees on the other. Somehow, I think that if I had known the words, and could have sung, my throat would have been choked up by the feeling of the un-accustomed scene.

The hymn was ended, and the men had drawn off before I could stir. I saw the minister beginning to put on his coat, and looking at me with friendly inspection in his gaze, before I could rouse myself.

"I dare say you railway gentlemen don't wind up the day with singing a psalm together," said he; "but it is not a bad practice—not a bad practice. We have had it a bit earlier to-day for hospitality's sake—that's all."

I had nothing particular to say to this, though I was thinking a great deal. From time to time I stole a look at my companion. His coat was black, and so was his waistcoat; neckcloth he had none, his strong full throat being bare above the snow-white shirt. He wore drab-coloured knee-breeches, grey worsted stockings (I thought I knew the maker), and strong-nailed shoes. He carried his hat in his hand, as if he liked to feel the coming breeze lifting his hair. After a while, I saw that the father took hold of the daughter's hand, and so, they holding each other, went along towards home. We had to cross a lane. In it there were two little children—one lying prone on the grass in a passion of crying; the other standing stock still, with its finger in its mouth, the large tears slowly rolling down its cheeks for sympathy. The cause of their distress was evident; there was a broken brown pitcher, and a little pool of spilt milk on the road.

"Hollo! hollo! What's all this?" said the minister. "Why, what have you been about, Tommy?" lifting the little petticoated lad, who was lying sobbing, with one vigorous arm. Tommy looked at him with surprise in his round eyes, but no affright—they were evidently old acquaintances.

"Mammy's jug!" said he, at last, beginning to cry afresh.

"Well! and will crying piece mammy's jug, or pick up spilt milk? How did you manage it, Tommy?"

"He" (jerking his head at the other) "and me was running races."

"Tommy said he could beat me," put in the other.

"Now, I wonder what will make you two silly lads mind, and not run races again with a pitcher of milk between you," said the minister, as if musing. "I might flog you, and so save mammy the trouble; for I dare say she'll do it if I don't." The fresh burst of whimpering from both showed the probability of this. "Or I might take you to the Hope Farm, and give you some more milk; but then you'd be running races again, and my milk would follow that to the ground, and make another white pool. I think the flogging would be best—don't you?"

"We would never run races no more," said the elder of the two.

"Then you'd not be boys; you'd be angels."

"No, we shouldn't."

"Why not?"

They looked into each other's eyes for an answer to this puzzling question. At length, one said, "Angels is dead folk."

"Come; we'll not get too deep into theology. What do you think of my lending you a tin can with a lid to carry the milk home in? That would not break, at any rate; though I would not answer for the milk not spilling if you ran races. That's it!"

He had dropped his daughter's hand, and now held out each of his to the little fellows. Phillis and I followed, and listened to the prattle which the minister's companions now poured out to him, and which he was evidently enjoying. At a certain point, there was a sudden burst of the tawny, ruddy-evening landscape. The minister turned round and quoted a line or two of Latin.

"It's wonderful," said he, "how exactly Virgil has hit the enduring epithets, nearly two thousand years ago, and in Italy; and yet how it describes to a T what is now lying before us in the parish of Heathbridge, county ——, England."

"I dare say it does," said I, all aglow with shame, for I had forgotten the little Latin I ever knew.

The minister shifted his eyes to Phillis's face; it mutely gave him back the sympathetic appreciation that I, in my ignorance, could not bestow.

"Oh! this is worse than the catechism," thought I; "that was only remembering words."

"Phillis, lass, thou must go home with these lads, and tell their mother all about the race and the milk. Mammy must always know the truth," now speaking to the children. "And tell her, too, from me that I have got the best birch rod in the parish; and that if she ever thinks her children want a flogging she must bring them to me, and, if I think they deserve it, I'll give it them better than she can." So Phillis led the children towards the dairy, somewhere in the back yard, and I followed the minister in through the "curate" into the house-place.

"Their mother," said he, "is a bit of a vixen, and apt to punish her children without rhyme or reason. I try to keep the parish rod as well as the parish bull."

He sate down in the three-cornered chair by the fireside, and looked around the empty room.

"Where's the missus?" said he to himself. But she was there

in a minute; it was her regular plan to give him his welcome home —by a look, by a touch, nothing more—as soon as she could after his return, and he had missed her now. Regardless of my presence, he went over the day's doings to her; and then, getting up, he said he must go and make himself "reverend," and that then we would have a cup of tea in the parlour. The parlour was a large room with two casemented windows on the other side of the broad flagged passage leading from the rector-door to the wide staircase, with its shallow, polished oaken steps, on which no carpet was ever laid. The parlour-floor was covered in the middle by a home-made carpeting of needlework and list. One or two quaint family pictures of the Holman family hung round the walls; the fire-grate and irons were much ornamented with brass; and on a table against the wall between the windows, a great beau-pot of flowers was placed upon the folio volumes of Matthew Henry's Bible. It was a compliment to me to use this room, and I tried to be grateful for it; but we never had our meals there after that first day, and I was glad of it; for the large house-place, living-room, dining-room, whichever you might like to call it, was twice as comfortable and cheerful. There was a rug in front of the great large fire-place, and an oven by the grate, and a crook, with the kettle hanging from it, over the bright wood-fire; everything that ought to be black and polished in that room was black and polished; and the flags, and window-curtains, and such things as were to be white and clean, were just spotless in their purity. Opposite to the fire-place, extending the whole length of the room, was an oaken shovel-board, with the right incline for a skilful player to send the weights into the prescribed space. There were baskets of white work about, and a small shelf of books hung against the wall, books used for reading, and not for propping up a beau-pot of flowers. I took down one or two of those books once when I was left alone in the house-place on the first evening—Virgil, Cæsar, a Greek grammar—oh, dear! ah, me! and Phillis Holman's name in each of them! I shut them up, and put them back in their places, and walked as far away from the bookshelf as I could. Yes, and I gave my cousin Phillis a wide berth, although she was sitting at her work quietly enough, and her hair was looking more golden, her dark eyelashes longer, her round pillar of a throat whiter than ever. We had done tea, and we had returned into the house-place that the minister might smoke his pipe without fear of contaminating the drab damask window-curtains of the parlour. He had made himself "reverend" by putting on one of the voluminous white muslin neckcloths that I had seen cousin Holman ironing that first visit I had paid to the Hope Farm, and by making one or two other unimportant changes in his dress. He sate looking steadily at me, but whether he saw me or not I cannot tell. At the time I fancied that he did, and was gauging me in some unknown fashion in his secret mind. Every now and then he took his pipe out of his mouth, knocked out the ashes, and asked me some fresh question. As long as these related to my acquirements or my reading, I shuffled uneasily and did not know what to answer. By-and-by he got round to the more practical subject of railroads, and on this I was more at home. I really had taken an interest in my work; nor would Mr. Holdsworth, indeed, have kept me in his employment if I had not given my mind as well as my time to it; and I was, besides, full of the difficulties which beset us just then, owing to our not being able to find a steady bottom on the Heathbridge moss, over which we wished to carry our line. In the midst of all my eagerness in speaking about this, I could not help being struck with the extreme pertinence of his questions. I do not mean that he did not show ignorance of many of the details of engineering: that was to have been expected; but on the premises he had got hold of, he thought clearly and reasoned logically. Phillis—so like him as she was both in body and mind—kept stopping at her work and looking at me, trying to fully understand all that I said. I felt she did; and perhaps it made me take more pains in using clear expressions, and arranging my words, than I otherwise should.

"She shall see I know something worth knowing, though it mayn't be her dead-and-gone languages," thought I.

"I see," said the minister, at length. "I understand it all. You've a clear, good head of your own, my lad,—choose how you came by it."

"From my father," said I, proudly. "Have you not heard of his discovery of a new method of shunting? It was in the *Gazette*. It was patented. I thought every one had heard of Manning's patent winch."

"We don't know who invented the alphabet," said he, half smiling, and taking up his pipe.

"No, I dare say not, sir," replied I, half offended; "that's so long ago."

Puff—puff—puff.

"But your father must be a notable man. I heard of him once before; and it is not many a one fifty miles away whose fame reaches Heathbridge."

"My father is a notable man, sir. It is not me that says so; it is Mr. Holdsworth, and—and everybody."

"He is right to stand up for his father," said cousin Holman, as if she were pleading for me.

I chafed inwardly, thinking that my father needed no one to stand up for him. He was man sufficient for himself.

"Yes—he is right," said the minister, placidly. "Right, because it comes from his heart—right, too, as I believe in point of fact. Else there is many a young cockerel that will stand upon a dunghill and crow about his father, by way of making his own plumage to shine. I should like to know thy father," he went on, turning straight to me, with a kindly, frank look in his eyes.

But I was vexed, and would take no notice. Presently, having finished his pipe, he got up and left the room. Phillis put her work hastily down, and went after him. In a minute or two she returned, and sate down again. Not long after, and before I had quite recovered my good temper, he opened the door out of which he had passed, and called to me to come to him. I went across a narrow stone passage into a strange, many-cornered room, not ten feet in area, part study, part counting-house, looking into the farm-yard; with a desk to sit at, a desk to stand at, a spittoon, a set of shelves with old divinity books upon them; another, smaller, filled with books on farriery, farming, manures, and such subjects, with pieces of paper containing memoranda stuck against the whitewashed walls with wafers, nails, pins, anything that came readiest to hand; a box of carpenter's tools on the floor, and some manuscripts in short-hand on the desk.

He turned round half laughing. "That foolish girl of mine thinks I have vexed you"—putting his large, powerful hand on my shoulder. "'Nay,' says I; 'kindly meant is kindly taken'— is it not so?"

"It was not quite, sir," replied I, vanquished by his manner; "but it shall be in future."

"Come, that's right. You and I shall be friends. Indeed, it's not many a one I would bring in here. But I was reading a book this morning, and I could not make it out; it is a book that was left here by mistake one day; I had subscribed to Brother Robinson's sermons; and I was glad to see this instead of them, for sermons though they be, they're . . . well, never mind! I took 'em both, and made my old coat do a bit longer; but all's fish that comes to my net. I have fewer books than leisure to read them, and I have a prodigious big appetite. Here it is."

It was a volume of stiff mechanics, involving many technical terms, and some rather deep mathematics. These last, which would have puzzled me, seemed easy enough to him; all that he wanted was the explanations of the technical words, which I could easily give.

While he was looking through the book to find the places where he had been puzzled, my wandering eye caught on some of the papers on the wall, and I could not help reading one, which has stuck by me ever since. At first, it seemed a kind of weekly diary; but then I saw that the seven days were portioned out for special prayers and intercessions: Monday for his family, Tuesday for enemies, Wednesday for the Independent churches, Thursday for all other churches, Friday for persons afflicted, Saturday for his own soul, Sunday for all wanderers and sinners, that they might be brought home to the fold.

We were called back into the house-place to have supper. A door opening into the kitchen was opened; and all stood up in both rooms, while the minister, tall, large, one hand resting on the spread table, the other lifted up, said, in the deep voice that would have been loud had it not been so full and rich, but with the peculiar accent or twang that I believe is considered devout by some people, "Whether we eat or drink, or whatsoever we do, let us do all to the glory of God."

The supper was an immense meat-pie. We of the house-place were helped first; then the minister hit the handle of his buckhorn carving-knife on the table once, and said,—

"Now or never," which meant, did any of us want any more; and when we had all declined, either by silence or by words, he knocked twice with his knife on the table, and Betty came in through the open door, and carried off the great dish to the kitchen, where an old man and a young one, and a help-girl, were awaiting their meal.

"Shut the door, if you will," said the minister to Betty.

"That's in honour of you," said cousin Holman, in a tone of satisfaction, as the door was shut. "When we've no stranger with us, the minister is so fond of keeping the door open, and talking to the men and maids, just as much as to Phillis and me."

"It brings us all together like a household just before we meet as a household in prayer," said he, in explanation. "But to go back to what we were talking about—can you tell me of any simple book on dynamics that I could put in my pocket, and study a little at leisure times in the day?"

"Leisure times, father?" said Phillis, with a nearer approach to a smile than I had yet seen on her face.

"Yes; leisure times, daughter. There is many an odd minute lost in waiting for other folk; and now that railroads are coming so near us, it behooves us to know something about them."

I thought of his own description of his "prodigious big appetite" for learning. And he had a good appetite of his own for the more material victual before him. But I saw, or fancied I saw, that he had some rule for himself in the matter both of food and drink.

As soon as supper was done the household assembled for prayer. It was a long impromptu evening prayer; and it would have seemed desultory enough had I not had a glimpse of the kind of day that preceded it, and so been able to find a clue to the thoughts that preceded the disjointed utterances; for he kept there kneeling down in the centre of a circle, his eyes shut, his outstretched hands pressed palm to palm—sometimes with a long pause of silence, as if waiting to see if there was anything else he wished to "lay before the Lord" (to use his own expression)—before he concluded with the blessing. He prayed for the cattle and live creatures, rather to my surprise; for my attention had begun to wander, till it was recalled by the familiar words.

And here I must not forget to name an odd incident at the conclusion of the prayer, and before we had risen from our knees (indeed before Betty was well awake, for she made a nightly practice of having a sound nap, her weary head lying on her stalwart arms); the minister, still kneeling in our midst, but with his eyes wide open, and his arms dropped by his side, spoke to the elder man, who turned round on his knees to attend. "John, didst see that Daisy had her warm mash to-night; for we must not neglect the means, John—two quarts of gruel, a spoonful of ginger, and a gill of beer—the poor beast needs it, and I fear it slipped out of my mind to tell thee; and here was I asking a blessing and neglecting the means, which is a mockery," said he, dropping his voice.

Before we went to bed he told me he should see little or nothing more of me during my visit, which was to end on Sunday evening, as he always gave up both Saturday and Sabbath to his work in the ministry. I remembered that the landlord at the inn had told me this on the day when I first inquired about these new relations of mine; and I did not dislike the opportunity which I saw would be afforded me of becoming more acquainted with cousin Holman and Phillis, though I earnestly hoped that the latter would not attack me on the subject of the dead languages.

I went to bed, and dreamed that I was as tall as cousin Phillis, and had a sudden and miraculous growth of whisker, and a still more miraculous acquaintance with Latin and Greek. Alas! I wakened up still a short, beardless lad, with *"tempus fugit"* for my sole remembrance of the little Latin I had once learnt. While I was dressing, a bright thought came over me: I could question cousin Phillis, instead of her questioning me, and so manage to keep the choice of the subjects of conversation in my own power.

Early as it was, every one had breakfasted, and my basin of bread and milk was put on the oven-top to await my coming down. Every one was gone about their work. The first to come into the house-place was Phillis with a basket of eggs. Faithful to my resolution, I asked—

"What are those?"

She looked at me for a moment, and then said gravely—

"Potatoes!"

"No! they are not," said I. "They are eggs. What do you mean by saying they are potatoes?"

"What do you mean by asking me what they were, when they were plain to be seen?" retorted she.

We were both getting a little angry with each other.

"I don't know. I wanted to begin to talk to you; and I was afraid you would talk to me about books as you did yesterday. I have not read much; and you and the minister have read so much."

311

"I have not," said she. "But you are our guest; and mother says I must make it pleasant to you. We won't talk of books. What must we talk about?"

"I don't know. How old are you?"

"Seventeen last May. How old are you?"

"I am nineteen. Older than you by nearly two years," said I, drawing myself up to my full height.

"I should not have thought you were above sixteen," she replied, as quietly as if she were not saying the most provoking thing she possibly could. Then came a pause.

"What are you going to do now?" asked I.

"I should be dusting the bed-chambers; but mother said I had better stay and make it pleasant to you," said she, a little plaintively, as if dusting rooms was far the easiest task.

"Will you take me to see the live-stock? I like animals, though I don't know much about them."

"Oh, do you. I am so glad. I was afraid you would not like animals, as you did not like books."

I wondered why she said this. I think it was because she had begun to fancy all our tastes must be dissimilar. We went together all through the farm-yard; we fed the poultry, she kneeling down with her pinafore full of corn and meal, and tempting the little timid, downy chickens upon it, much to the anxiety of the fussy ruffled hen, their mother. She called to the pigeons, who fluttered down at the sound of her voice. She and I examined the great sleek cart-horses; sympathised in our dislike of pigs; fed the calves, coaxed the sick cow, Daisy; and admired the others out at pasture; and came back tired and hungry and dirty at dinner-time, having quite forgotten that there were such things as dead languages, and consequently capital friends.

Part II

COUSIN HOLMAN gave me the weekly county newspaper to read aloud to her, while she mended stockings out of a high piled-up basket, Phillis helping her mother. I read and read, unregardful of the words I was uttering, thinking of all manner of other things; of the bright colour of Phillis's hair, as the afternoon sun fell on

her bending head; of the silence of the house, which enabled me
to hear the double tick of the old clock which stood half-way up
the stairs; of the variety of inarticulate noises which cousin Holman made while I read, to show her sympathy, wonder, or horror at
the newspaper intelligence. The tranquil monotony of that hour
made me feel as if I had lived for ever, and should live for ever
droning out paragraphs in that warm sunny room, with my two
quiet hearers, and the curled-up pussy cat sleeping on the hearth-
rug, and the clock on the house-stairs perpetually clicking out the
passage of the moments. By-and-by Betty the servant came to the
door into the kitchen, and made a sign to Phillis, who put her
half-mended stocking down, and went away to the kitchen without
a word. Looking at cousin Holman a minute or two afterwards, I
saw that she had dropped her chin upon her breast, and had fallen
fast asleep. I put the newspaper down, and was nearly following
her example, when a waft of air from some unseen source slightly
opened the door of communication with the kitchen, that Phillis
must have left unfastened; and I saw part of her figure as she sate
by the dresser, peeling apples with quick dexterity of finger, but
with repeated turnings of her head towards some book lying on the
dresser by her. I softly rose, and as softly went into the kitchen,
and looked over her shoulder; before she was aware of my neighbourhood, I had seen that the book was in a language unknown to
me, and the running title was "L'Inferno." Just as I was making
out the relationship of this word to "infernal," she started and
turned round, and, as if continuing her thought as she spoke, she
sighed out,—

"Oh! it is so difficult! Can you help me?" putting her finger
below a line.

"Me! I! Not I! I don't even know what language it is in!"

"Don't you see it is Dante?" she replied, almost petulantly; she
did so want help.

"Italian, then?" said I dubiously; for I was not quite sure.

"Yes. And I do so want to make it out. Father can help me a
little, for he knows Latin; but then he has so little time."

"You have not much, I should think, if you have often to try
and do two things at once, as you are doing now."

"Oh! that's nothing! Father bought a heap of old books cheap.
And I knew something about Dante before; and I have always liked

Virgil so much. Paring apples is nothing, if I could only make out this old Italian. I wish you knew it."

"I wish I did," said I, moved by her impetuosity of tone. "If, now, only Mr. Holdsworth were here; he can speak Italian like anything, I believe."

"Who is Mr. Holdsworth?" said Phillis, looking up.

"Oh, he's our head engineer. He's a regular first-rate fellow! He can do anything;" my hero-worship and my pride in my chief all coming into play. Besides, if I was not clever and book-learned myself, it was something to belong to some one who was.

"How is it that he speaks Italian?" asked Phillis.

"He had to make a railway through Piedmont, which is in Italy, I believe; and he had to talk to all the workmen in Italian; and I have heard him say that for nearly two years he had only Italian books to read in the queer outlandish places he was in."

"Oh, dear!" said Phillis; "I wish——" and then she stopped. I was not quite sure whether to say the next thing that came into my mind; but I said it.

"Could I ask him anything about your book, or your difficulties?"

She was silent for a minute or so, and then she made reply—

"No! I think not. Thank you very much, though. I can generally puzzle a thing out in time. And then, perhaps, I remember it better than if some one had helped me. I'll put it away now, and you must move off, for I've got to make the paste for the pies; we always have a cold dinner on Sabbaths."

"But I may stay and help you, mayn't I?"

"Oh, yes; not that you can help at all, but I like to have you with me."

I was both flattered and annoyed at this straightforward avowal. I was pleased that she liked me; but I was young coxcomb enough to have wished to play the lover, and I was quite wise enough to perceive that if she had any idea of the kind in her head she would never have spoken out so frankly. I comforted myself immediately, however, by finding out that the grapes were sour. A great tall girl in a pinafore, half a head taller than I was, reading books that I had never heard of, and talking about them too, as of far more interest than any mere personal subjects; that was the last day on which I ever thought of my dear cousin Phillis as the possible

mistress of my heart and life. But we were all the greater friends
for this idea being utterly put away and buried out of sight.

Late in the evening the minister came home from Hornby. He
had been calling on the different members of his flock; and unsatisfactory work it had proved to him, it seemed from the fragments that dropped out of his thoughts into his talk.

"I don't see the men; they are all at their business, their shops,
or their warehouses; they ought to be there. I have no fault to
find with them; only if a pastor's teaching or words of admonition
are good for anything, they are needed by the men as much as by
the women."

"Cannot you go and see them in their places of business, and
remind them of their Christian privileges and duties, minister?"
asked cousin Holman, who evidently thought that her husband's
words could never be out of place.

"No!" said he, shaking his head. "I judge them by myself. If
there are clouds in the sky, and I am getting in the hay just ready
for loading, and rain sure to come in the night, I should look ill
upon Brother Robinson if he came into the field to speak about
serious things."

"But, at any rate, father, you do good to the women, and perhaps
they repeat what you have said to them to their husbands and
children?"

"It is to be hoped they do, for I cannot reach the men directly;
but the women are apt to tarry before coming to me, to put on
ribbons and gauds; as if they could hear the message I bear to them
best in their smart clothes. Mrs. Dobson to-day—Phillis, I am
thankful thou dost not care for the vanities of dress!"

Phillis reddened a little as she said, in a low humble voice,—

"But I do, father, I'm afraid. I often wish I could wear pretty-
coloured ribbons round my throat like the squire's daughters."

"It's but natural, minister!" said his wife; "I'm not above liking
a silk gown better than a cotton one myself!"

"The love of dress is a temptation and a snare," said he, gravely.
"The true adornment is a meek and quiet spirit. And, wife," said
he, as a sudden thought crossed his mind, "in that matter I, too,
have sinned. I wanted to ask you, could we not sleep in the grey
room, instead of our own?"

"Sleep in the grey room?—change our room at this time o' day?" cousin Holman asked, in dismay.

"Yes," said he. "It would save me from a daily temptation to anger. Look at my chin!" he continued; "I cut it this morning— I cut it on Wednesday when I was shaving; I do not know how many times I have cut it of late, and all from impatience at seeing Timothy Cooper at his work in the yard."

"He's a downright lazy tyke!" said cousin Holman. "He's not worth his wage. There's but little he can do, and what he can do, he does badly."

"True," said the minister. "But he is but, so to speak, a half-wit; and yet he has got a wife and children."

"More shame for him!"

"But that is past change. And if I turn him off, no one else will take him on. Yet I cannot help watching him of a morning as he goes sauntering about his work in the yard; and I watch, and I watch, till the old Adam rises strong within me at his lazy ways, and some day, I am afraid, I shall go down and send him about his business—let alone the way in which he makes me cut myself while I am shaving—and then his wife and children will starve. I wish we could move to the grey room."

I do not remember much more of my first visit to the Hope Farm. We went to chapel in Heathbridge, slowly and decorously walking along the lanes, ruddy and tawny with the colouring of the coming autumn. The minister walked a little before us, his hands behind his back, his head bent down, thinking about the discourse to be delivered to his people, cousin Holman said; and we spoke low and quietly, in order not to interrupt his thoughts. But I could not help noticing the respectful greetings which he received from both rich and poor as we went along; greetings which he acknowledged with a kindly wave of his hand, but with no words of reply. As we drew near the town, I could see some of the young fellows we met cast admiring looks on Phillis; and that made me look too. She had on a white gown, and a short black silk cloak, according to the fashion of the day. A straw bonnet, with brown ribbon strings; that was all. But what her dress wanted in colour, her sweet bonny face had. The walk made her cheeks bloom like the rose; the very whites of her eyes had a blue tinge in them, and her dark eyelashes brought out the depth of the blue eyes

themselves. Her yellow hair was put away as straight as its natural
curliness would allow. If she did not perceive the admiration she
excited, I am sure cousin Holman did; for she looked as fierce and
as proud as ever her quiet face could look, guarding her treasure,
and yet glad to perceive that others could see that it was a treasure.
That afternoon I had to return to Eltham to be ready for the next
day's work. I found out afterwards that the minister and his family
were all "exercised in spirit," as to whether they did well in asking
me to repeat my visits at the Hope Farm, seeing that of necessity
I must return to Eltham on the Sabbath-day. However, they did go
on asking me, and I went on visiting them, whenever my other engagements permitted me, Mr. Holdsworth being in this case, as in
all, a kind and indulgent friend. Nor did my new acquaintances oust
him from my strong regard and admiration. I had room in my heart
for all, I am happy to say, and as far as I can remember, I kept
praising each to the other in a manner which, if I had been an
older man, living more amongst people of the world, I should have
thought unwise, as well as a little ridiculous. It was unwise, certainly, as it was almost sure to cause disappointment if ever they
did become acquainted; and perhaps it was ridiculous, though I
do not think we any of us thought it so at the time. The minister
used to listen to my accounts of Mr. Holdsworth's many accomplishments and various adventures in travel with the truest interest,
and most kindly good faith; and Mr. Holdsworth in return liked to
hear about my visits to the farm, and description of my cousin's
life there—liked it, I mean, as much as he liked anything that was
merely narrative, without leading to action.

So I went to the farm certainly, on an average, once a month
during that autumn; the course of life there was so peaceful and
quiet, that I can only remember one small event, and that was one
that I think I took more notice of than any one else: Phillis left off
wearing the pinafores that had always been so obnoxious to me:
I do not know why they were banished, but on one of my visits I
found them replaced by pretty linen aprons in the morning, and a
black silk one in the afternoon. And the blue cotton gown became
a brown stuff one as winter drew on; this sounds like some book I
once read, in which a migration from the blue bed to the brown was
spoken of as a great family event.

Towards Christmas my dear father came to see me, and to consult Mr. Holdsworth about the improvement which has since been known as "Manning's driving wheel." Mr. Holdsworth, as I think I have before said, had a very great regard for my father, who had been employed in the same great machine-shop in which Mr. Holdsworth had served his apprenticeship; and he and my father had many mutual jokes about one of these gentlemen-apprentices who used to set about his smith's work in white wash-leather gloves, for fear of spoiling his hands. Mr. Holdsworth often spoke to me about my father as having the same kind of genius for mechanical invention as that of George Stephenson, and my father had come over now to consult him about several improvements, as well as an offer of partnership. It was a great pleasure to me to see the mutual regard of these two men. Mr. Holdsworth, young, handsome, keen, well-dressed, an object of admiration to all the youth of Eltham; my father, in his decent but unfashionable Sunday clothes, his plain, sensible face full of hard lines, the marks of toil and thought,—his hands, blackened beyond the power of soap and water by years of labour in the foundry; speaking a strong Northern dialect, while Mr. Holdsworth had a long soft drawl in his voice, as many of the Southerners have, and was reckoned in Eltham to give himself airs.

Although most of my father's leisure time was occupied with conversations about the business I have mentioned, he felt that he ought not to leave Eltham without going to pay his respects to the relations who had been so kind to his son. So he and I ran up on an engine along the incomplete line as far as Heathbridge, and went, by invitation, to spend a day at the farm.

It was odd and yet pleasant to me to perceive how these two men, each having led up to this point such totally dissimilar lives, seemed to come together by instinct, after one quiet straight look into each other's faces. My father was a thin, wiry man of five foot seven; the minister was a broad-shouldered, fresh-coloured man of six foot one; they were neither of them great talkers in general—perhaps the minister the most so—but they spoke much to each other. My father went into the fields with the minister; I think I see him now, with his hands behind his back, listening intently to all explanations of tillage, and the different processes of farming; occasionally taking up an implement, as if unconsciously, and examining it with a critical eye, and now and then asking a question, which I could

318

see was considered as pertinent by his companion. Then we re-turned to look at the cattle, housed and bedded in expectation of the snow-storm hanging black on the western horizon, and my father learned the points of a cow with as much attention as if he meant to turn farmer. He had his little book that he used for mechanical memoranda and measurements in his pocket, and he took it out to write down "straight back," "small muzzle," "deep barrel," and I know not what else, under the head "cow." He was very critical on a turnip-cutting machine, the clumsiness of which first incited him to talk; and when we went into the house he sat thinking and quiet for a bit, while Phillis and her mother made the last preparations for tea, with a little unheeded apology from cousin Holman, because we were not sitting in the best parlour, which she thought might be chilly on so cold a night. I wanted nothing better than the blazing, crackling fire that sent a glow over all the house-place, and warmed the snowy flags under our feet till they seemed to have more heat than the crimson rug right in front of the fire. After tea, as Phillis and I were talking together very happily, I heard an irrepressible exclamation from cousin Holman,—

"Whatever is the man about!"

And on looking round, I saw my father taking a straight burning stick out of the fire, and, after waiting for a minute, and examining the charred end to see if it was fitted for his purpose, he went to the hard-wood dresser, scoured to the last pitch of whiteness and cleanliness, and began drawing with the stick; the best substitute for chalk or charcoal within his reach, for his pocket-book pencil was not strong or bold enough for his purpose. When he had done, he began to explain his new model of a turnip-cutting machine to the minister, who had been watching him in silence all the time. Cousin Holman had, in the meantime, taken a duster out of a drawer, and, under pretence of being as much interested as her husband in the drawing, was secretly trying on an outside mark how easily it would come off, and whether it would leave her dresser as white as before. Then Phillis was sent for the book on dynamics, about which I had been consulted during my first visit, and my father had to explain many difficulties, which he did in language as clear as his mind, making drawings with his stick wherever they were needed as illustrations, the minister sitting with his massive head resting on his hands, his elbows on the table, almost unconscious of Phillis, leaning over and listening greedily, with her hand on his shoulder, sucking in information like her father's own daughter. I was rather sorry for cousin Holman; I had been so once or twice before; for do what she would, she was completely unable even to understand the pleasure her husband and daughter took in intellectual pursuits, much less to care in the least herself for the pursuits themselves, and was thus unavoidably thrown out of some of their interests. I had once or twice thought she was a little jealous of her own child, as a fitter companion for her husband than she was herself; and I fancied the minister himself was aware of this feeling, for I had noticed an occasional sudden change of subject, and a tenderness of appeal in his voice as he spoke to her, which always made her look contented and peaceful again. I do not think that Phillis ever perceived these little shadows; in the first place, she had such complete reverence for her parents that she listened to them both as if they had been St. Peter and St. Paul; and besides, she was always too much engrossed with any matter in hand to think about other people's manners and looks.

This night I could see, though she did not, how much she was winning on my father. She asked a few questions which showed that she had followed his explanations up to that point; possibly, too, her unusual beauty might have something to do with his favourable impression of her; but he made no scruple of expressing his admiration of her to her father and mother in her absence from the room; and from that evening I date a project of his which came out to me a day or two afterwards, as we sate in my little three-cornered room in Eltham.

"Paul," he began, "I never thought to be a rich man; but I think it's coming upon me. Some folk are making a deal of my new machine (calling it by its technical name), and Ellison, of the Borough Green Works, has gone so far as to ask me to be his partner."

"Mr. Ellison the Justice!—who lives in King Street? why, he drives his carriage!" said I, doubting, yet exultant.

"Ay, lad, John Ellison. But that's no sign that I shall drive my carriage. Though I should like to save thy mother walking, for she's not so young as she was. But that's a long way off, anyhow. I reckon I should start with a third profit. It might be seven hundred, or it might be more. I should like to have the power to work out some fancies o' mine. I care for that much more than for th' brass. And Ellison has no lads; and by nature the business would come to thee in course o' time. Ellison's lasses are but bits o' things, and are not like to come by husbands just yet; and when they do, maybe they'll not be in the mechanical line. It will be an opening for thee, lad, if thou art steady. Thou'rt not great shakes, I know, in th' inventing line; but many a one gets on better without having fancies for something he does not see and never has seen. I'm right down glad to see that mother's cousins are such uncommon folk for sense and goodness. I have taken the minister to my heart like a brother; and she is a womanly quiet sort of a body. And I'll tell you frank, Paul, it will be a happy day for me if ever you can come and tell me that Phillis Holman is like to be my daughter. I think if that lass had not a penny, she would be the making of a man; and she'll have yon house and lands, and you may be her match yet in fortune if all goes well."

I was growing as red as fire; I did not know what to say, and yet I wanted to say something; but the idea of having a wife of my own at some future day, though it had often floated about in my own head, sounded so strange when it was thus first spoken about by my father. He saw my confusion, and half smiling said,—

"Well, lad, what dost say to the old father's plans? Thou art but young, to be sure; but when I was thy age, I would ha' given my right hand if I might ha' thought of the chance of wedding the lass I cared for——"

"My mother?" asked I, a little struck by the change of his tone of voice.

"No! not thy mother. Thy mother is a very good woman—none better. No! the lass I cared for at nineteen ne'er knew how I loved her, and a year or two after and she was dead, and ne'er knew. I think she would ha' been glad to ha' known it, poor Molly; but I had to leave the place where we lived for to try to earn my bread —and I meant to come back—but before ever I did, she was dead and gone: I ha' never gone there since. But if you fancy Phillis Holman, and can get her to fancy you, my lad, it shall go different with you, Paul, to what it did with your father."

I took counsel with myself very rapidly, and I came to a clear conclusion.

"Father," said I, "if I fancied Phillis ever so much, she would never fancy me. I like her as much as I could like a sister; and she likes me as if I were her brother—her younger brother."

I could see my father's countenance fall a little.

"You see she's so clever—she's more like a man than a woman— she knows Latin and Greek."

"She'd forget 'em, if she'd a houseful of children," was my father's comment on this.

"But she knows many a thing besides, and is wise as well as learned: she has been so much with her father. She would never think much of me, and I should like my wife to think a deal of her husband."

"It is not just book-learning or the want of it as makes a wife think much or little of her husband," replied my father, evidently unwilling to give up a project which had taken deep root in his mind. "It's a something—I don't rightly know how to call it—if he's manly, and sensible, and straightforward; and I reckon you're that, my boy."

"I don't think I should like to have a wife taller than I am, father," said I, smiling; he smiled too, but not heartily.

"Well," said he, after a pause. "It's but a few days I've been thinking of it, but I'd got as fond of my notion as if it had been a new engine as I'd been planning out. Here's our Paul, thinks I to myself, a good sensible breed o' lad, as has never vexed or troubled his mother or me; with a good business opening out before him, age nineteen, not so bad-looking, though perhaps not to call handsome, and here's his cousin, not too near a cousin, but just nice, as one may say; aged seventeen, good and true, and well brought up to work with her hands as well as her head; a scholar—but that can't be helped, and is more her misfortune than her fault, seeing she is the only child of a scholar—and as I said afore, once she's a wife and a mother she'll forget it all, I'll be bound—with a good fortune in land and house when it shall please the Lord to take her parents to himself; with eyes like poor Molly's for beauty, a colour that comes and goes on a milk-white skin, and as pretty a mouth—"

"Why, Mr. Manning, what fair lady are you describing?" asked Mr. Holdsworth, who had come quickly and suddenly upon our tête-à-tête, and had caught my father's last words as he entered the room.

Both my father and I felt rather abashed; it was such an odd subject for us to be talking about; but my father, like a straight-forward simple man as he was, spoke out the truth.

"I've been telling Paul of Ellison's offer, and saying how good an opening it made for him—"

"I wish I'd as good," said Mr. Holdsworth. "But has the business a 'pretty mouth?'"

"You're always so full of your joking, Mr. Holdsworth," said my father. "I was going to say that if he and his cousin Phillis Holman liked to make it up between them, I would put no spoke in the wheel."

"Phillis Holman!" said Mr. Holdsworth. "Is she the daughter of the minister-farmer out at Heathbridge? Have I been helping on the course of true love by letting you go there so often? I knew nothing of it."

"There is nothing to know," said I, more annoyed than I chose to show. "There is no more true love in the case than may be between the first brother and sister you may choose to meet. I have been telling father she would never think of me; she's a great deal taller and cleverer; and I'd rather be taller and more learned than my wife when I have one."

"And it is she, then, that has the pretty mouth your father spoke about? I should think that would be an antidote to the cleverness and learning. But I ought to apologize for breaking in upon your last night; I came upon business to your father."

And then he and my father began to talk about many things that had no interest for me just then, and I began to go over again my conversation with my father. The more I thought about it, the more I felt that I had spoken truly about my feelings towards Phillis Holman. I loved her dearly as a sister, but I could never fancy her as my wife. Still less could I think of her ever—yes, *condescending*, that is the word—condescending to marry me. I was roused from a reverie on what I should like my possible wife to be, by hearing my father's warm praise of the minister, as a most unusual character; how they had got back from the diameter of driving-wheels to the subject of the Holmans I could never tell; but I saw that my father's weighty praises were exciting some curiosity in Mr. Holdsworth's mind; indeed, he said, almost in a voice of reproach,—

"Why, Paul, you never told me what kind of a fellow this minister-cousin of yours was!"

"I don't know that I found out, sir," said I. "But if I had, I don't think you'd have listened to me, as you have done to my father."

"No! most likely not, old fellow," replied Mr. Holdsworth, laughing. And again and afresh I saw what a handsome pleasant clear face his was; and though this evening I had been a bit put out with him—through his sudden coming, and his having heard my father's open-hearted confidence—my hero resumed all his empire over me by his bright merry laugh.

And if he had not resumed his old place that night, he would have done so the next day, when, after my father's departure, Mr. Holdsworth spoke about him with such just respect for his character, such ungrudging admiration of his great mechanical genius, that I was compelled to say, almost unawares,—

"Thank you, sir. I am very much obliged to you."

"Oh, you're not at all. I am only speaking the truth. Here's a Birmingham workman, self-educated, one may say—having never associated with stimulating minds, or had what advantages travel and contact with the world may be supposed to afford—working out his own thoughts into steel and iron, making a scientific name for himself—a fortune, if it pleases him to work for money —and keeping his singleness of heart, his perfect simplicity of manner; it puts me out of patience to think of my expensive schooling, my travels hither and thither, my heaps of scientific books, and I have done nothing to speak of. But it's evidently good blood; there's that Mr. Holman, that cousin of yours, made of the same stuff."

"But he's only cousin because he married my mother's second cousin," said I.

"That knocks a pretty theory on the head, and twice over, too. I should like to make Holman's acquaintance."

"I am sure they would be so glad to see you at Hope Farm," said I, eagerly. "In fact, they've asked me to bring you several times: only I thought you would find it dull."

"Not at all. I can't go yet though, even if you do get me an invitation; for the —— —— Company want me to go to the —— Valley, and look over the ground a bit for them, to see if it would do for a branch line; it's a job which may take me away for some time; but I shall be backwards and forwards, and you're quite up to doing what is needed in my absence; the only work that may be beyond you is keeping old Jevons from drinking."

He went on giving me directions about the management of the men employed on the line, and no more was said then, or for several months, about his going to Hope Farm. He went off into —— Valley, a dark overshadowed dale, where the sun seemed to set behind the hills before four o'clock on midsummer afternoon.

Perhaps it was this that brought on the attack of low fever which he had soon after the beginning of the new year; he was very ill for many weeks, almost many months; a married sister— his only relation, I think—came down from London to nurse him, and I went over to him when I could, to see him, and give him "masculine news," as he called it; reports of the progress of the line, which, I am glad to say, I was able to carry on in his absence, in the slow gradual way which suited the company best, while trade was in a languid state, and money dear in the market. Of course, with this occupation for my scanty leisure, I did not often go over to Hope Farm. Whenever I did go, I met with a thorough welcome; and many inquiries were made as to Holdsworth's illness, and the progress of his recovery.

At length, in June I think it was, he was sufficiently recovered to come back to his lodgings at Eltham, and resume part at least of his work. His sister, Mrs. Robinson, had been obliged to leave him some weeks before, owing to some epidemic amongst her own children. As long as I had seen Mr. Holdsworth in the rooms at the little inn at Hensleydale, where I had been accustomed to look upon him as an invalid, I had not been aware of the visible shake his fever had given to his health. But, once back in the old lodgings, where I had always seen him so buoyant, eloquent, decided, and vigorous in former days, my spirits sank at the change in one whom I had always regarded with a strong feeling of admiring affection. He sank into silence and despondency after the least exertion; he seemed as if he could not make up his mind to any action, or else that, when it was made up, he lacked strength to carry out his purpose. Of course, it was but the natural state of slow convalescence, after so sharp an illness; but, at the time, I did not know this, and perhaps I represented his state as more serious than it was to my kind relations at Hope Farm; who, in their grave, simple, eager way, immediately thought of the only help they could give.

"Bring him out here," said the minister. "Our air here is good to a proverb; the June days are fine; he may loiter away his time in the hay-field, and the sweet smells will be a balm in themselves— better than physic."

"And," said cousin Holman, scarcely waiting for her husband to finish his sentence, "tell him there is new milk and fresh eggs to be had for the asking; it's lucky Daisy has just calved, for her milk is always as good as other cow's cream; and there is the plaid room with the morning sun all streaming in."

Phillis said nothing, but looked as much interested in the project as any one. I took it up myself. I wanted them to see him; him to know them. I proposed it to him when I got home. He was too languid, after the day's fatigue, to be willing to make the little exertion of going amongst strangers; and disappointed me by almost declining to accept the invitation I brought. The next morning it was different; he apologized for his ungraciousness of the night before; and told me that he would get all things in train, so as to be ready to go out with me to Hope Farm on the following Saturday.

"For you must go with me, Manning," said he; "I used to be as impudent a fellow as need be, and rather liked going amongst strangers, and making my way; but since my illness I am almost like a girl, and turn hot and cold with shyness, as they do, I fancy."

So it was fixed. We were to go out to Hope Farm on Saturday afternoon; and it was also understood that if the air and the life suited Mr. Holdsworth, he was to remain there for a week or ten days, doing what work he could at that end of the line, while I took his place at Eltham to the best of my ability. I grew a little nervous, as the time drew near, and wondered how the brilliant Holdsworth would agree with the quiet quaint family of the minister; how they would like him and many of his half-foreign ways. I tried to prepare him, by telling him from time to time little things about the goings-on at Hope Farm.

"Manning," said he, "I see you don't think I am half good enough for your friends. Out with it, man."

"No," I replied boldly. "I think you are good; but I don't know if you are quite of their kind of goodness."

"And you've found out already that there is greater chance of disagreement between two 'kinds of goodness,' each having its own idea of right, than between a given goodness and a moderate degree of naughtiness—which last often arises from an indifference to right?"

"I don't know. I think you're talking metaphysics, and I am sure that is bad for you."

" 'When a man talks to you in a way that you don't understand about a thing which he does not understand, them's metaphysics.' You remember the clown's definition, don't you, Manning?"

"No, I don't," said I. "But what I do understand is, that you must go to bed; and tell me at what time we must start to-morrow, that I may go to Hepworth, and get those letters written we were talking about this morning."

"Wait till to-morrow, and let us see what the day is like," he answered, with such languid indecision as showed me he was over-fatigued. So I went my way.

The morrow was blue and sunny, and beautiful; the very perfection of an early summer's day. Mr. Holdsworth was all impatience to be off into the country; morning had brought back his freshness and strength, and consequent eagerness to be doing. I was afraid we were going to my cousin's farm rather too early, before they would expect us; but what could I do with such a restless vehement man as Holdsworth was that morning? We came down upon the Hope Farm before the dew was off the grass on the shady side of the lane; the great house-dog was loose, basking in the sun, near the closed side door. I was surprised at this door being shut, for all summer long it was open from morning to night; but it was only on latch. I opened it, Rover watching me with half-suspicious, half-trustful eyes. The room was empty.

"I don't know where they can be," said I. "But come in and sit down while I go and look for them. You must be tired."

"Not I. This sweet balmy air is like a thousand tonics. Besides, this room is hot, and smells of those pungent wood-ashes. What are we to do?"

"Go round to the kitchen. Betty will tell us where they are."

So we went round into the farmyard, Rover accompanying us

out of a grave sense of duty. Betty was washing out her milk-pans in the cold bubbling spring-water that constantly trickled in and out of a stone trough. In such weather as this most of her kitchen-work was done out of doors.

"Eh, dear!" said she, "the minister and missus is away at Hornby! They ne'er thought of your coming so betimes! The missus had some errands to do, and she thought as she'd walk with the minister and be back by dinner-time."

"Did not they expect us to dinner?" said I.

"Well, they did, and they did not, as I may say. Missus said to me the cold lamb would do well enough if you did not come; and if you did I was to put on a chicken and some bacon to boil; and I'll go do it now, for it is hard to boil bacon enough."

"And is Phillis gone, too?" Mr. Holdsworth was making friends with Rover.

"No! She's just somewhere about. I reckon you'll find her in the kitchen-garden, getting peas."

"Let us go there," said Holdsworth, suddenly leaving off his play with the dog.

So I led the way into the kitchen-garden. It was in the first promise of a summer profuse in vegetables and fruits. Perhaps it was not so much cared for as other parts of the property; but it was more attended to than most kitchen-gardens belonging to farm-houses. There were borders of flowers along each side of the gravel-walks; and there was an old sheltering wall on the north side covered with tolerably choice fruit-trees; there was a slope down to the fish-pond at the end, where there were great straw-berry-beds; and raspberry-bushes and rose-bushes grew wherever there was a space; it seemed a chance which had been planted. Long rows of peas stretched at right angles from the main walk, and I saw Phillis stooping down among them, before she saw us. As soon as she heard our crunching steps on the gravel, she stood up, and, shading her eyes from the sun, recognized us. She was quite still for a moment, and then came slowly towards us, blush-ing a little from evident shyness. I had never seen Phillis shy before.

"This is Mr. Holdsworth, Phillis," said I, as soon as I had shaken hands with her. She glanced up at him, and then looked down, more flushed than ever at his grand formality of taking his hat off and bowing; such manners had never been seen at Hope Farm before.

"Father and mother are out. They will be so sorry; you did not write, Paul, as you said you would."

"It was my fault," said Holdsworth, understanding what she meant as well as if she had put it more fully into words. "I have not yet given up all the privileges of an invalid; one of which is indecision. Last night, when your cousin asked me at what time we were to start, I really could not make up my mind."

Phillis seemed as if she could not make up her mind as to what to do with us. I tried to help her—

"Have you finished getting peas?" taking hold of the half-filled basket she was unconsciously holding in her hand; "or may we stay and help you?"

"If you would. But perhaps it will tire you, sir?" added she, speaking now to Holdsworth.

"Not a bit," said he. "It will carry me back twenty years in my life, when I used to gather peas in my grandfather's garden. I suppose I may eat a few as I go along?"

"Certainly, sir. But if you went to the strawberry-beds you would find some strawberries ripe, and Paul can show you where they are."

"I am afraid you distrust me. I can assure you I know the exact fulness at which peas should be gathered. I take great care not to pluck them when they are unripe. I will not be turned off, as unfit for my work."

This was a style of half-joking talk that Phillis was not accustomed to. She looked for a moment as if she would have liked to defend herself from the playful charge of distrust made against her, but she ended by not saying a word. We all plucked our peas in busy silence for the next five minutes. Then Holdsworth lifted himself up from between the rows, and said, a little wearily,—

"I am afraid I must strike work. I am not as strong as I fancied myself."

Phillis was full of penitence immediately. He did, indeed, look pale; and she blamed herself for having allowed him to help her.

"It was very thoughtless of me. I did not know—I thought, perhaps, you really liked it. I ought to have offered you something to eat, sir! Oh, Paul, we have gathered quite enough; how stupid I was to forget that Mr. Holdsworth had been ill!" And in a blushing hurry she led the way towards the house. We went in, and she moved a heavy cushioned chair forwards, into which Holdsworth was only too glad to sink. Then with deft and quiet speed she brought in a little tray, wine, water, cake, home-made bread, and newly-churned butter. She stood by in some anxiety till, after bite and sup, the colour returned to Mr. Holdsworth's face, and he would fain have made us some laughing apologies for the fright he had given us. But then Phillis drew back from her innocent show of care and interest, and relapsed into the cold shyness habitual to her when she was first thrown into the company of strangers. She brought out the last week's county paper (which Mr. Holdsworth had read five days ago), and then quietly withdrew; and then he subsided into languor, leaning back and shutting his eyes as if he would go to sleep. I stole into the kitchen after Phillis; but she had made the round of the corner of the house outside, and I found her sitting on the horse-mount, with her basket of peas, and a basin into which she was shelling them. Rover lay at her feet, snapping now and then at the flies. I went to her, and tried to help her; but somehow the sweet crisp young peas found their way more frequently into my mouth than into the basket, while we talked together in a low tone, fearful of being overheard through the open casements of the house-place in which Holdsworth was resting.

"Don't you think him handsome?" asked I.

"Perhaps—yes—I have hardly looked at him," she replied. "But is not he very like a foreigner?"

"Yes, he cuts his hair foreign fashion," said I.

"I like an Englishman to look like an Englishman."

"I don't think he thinks about it. He says he began that way when he was in Italy, because everybody wore it so, and it is natural to keep it on in England."

"Not if he began it in Italy because everybody there wore it so. Everybody here wears it differently."

I was a little offended with Phillis's logical fault-finding with my friend; and I determined to change the subject.

"When is your mother coming home?"

"I should think she might come any time now; but she had to go and see Mrs. Morton, who was ill, and she might be kept, and not be home till dinner. Don't you think you ought to go and see how Mr. Holdsworth is going on, Paul? He may be faint again."

I went at her bidding; but there was no need for it. Mr. Holdsworth was up, standing by the window, his hands in his pockets; he had evidently been watching us. He turned away as I entered.

"So that is the girl I found your good father planning for your wife, Paul, that evening when I interrupted you! Are you of the same coy mind still? It did not look like it a minute ago."

"Phillis and I understand each other," I replied, sturdily. "We are like brother and sister. She would not have me as a husband if there was not another man in the world; and it would take a deal to make me think of her—as my father wishes" (somehow I did not like to say "as a wife"), "but we love each other dearly."

"Well, I am rather surprised at it—not at your loving each other in a brother-and-sister kind of way—but at your finding it so impossible to fall in love with such a beautiful woman."

Woman! beautiful woman! I had thought of Phillis as a comely but awkward girl: and I could not banish the pinafore from my mind's eye when I tried to picture her to myself. Now I turned, as Mr. Holdsworth had done, to look at her again out of the window: she had just finished her task, and was standing up, her back to us, holding the basket, and the basin in it, high in air, out of Rover's reach, who was giving vent to his delight at the probability of a change of place by glad leaps and barks, and snatches at what he imagined to be a withheld prize. At length she grew tired of their mutual play, and with a feint of striking him, and a "Down, Rover! do hush!" she looked towards the window where we were standing, as if to reassure herself that no one had been disturbed by the noise, and seeing us, she coloured all over, and hurried away, with Rover still curving in sinuous lines about her as she walked.

"I should like to have sketched her," said Mr. Holdsworth, as he turned away. He went back to his chair, and rested in silence for a minute or two. Then he was up again.

"I would give a good deal for a book," said he. "It would keep me quiet." He began to look round; there were a few volumes at one end of the shovel-board.

"Fifth volume of Matthew Henry's *Commentary*," said he, reading their titles aloud. "*Housewife's complete Manual; Berridge on*

Prayer; L'Inferno—Dante!" in great surprise. "Why, who reads this?"

"I told you Phillis read it. Don't you remember? She knows Latin and Greek, too."

"To be sure! I remember! But somehow I never put two and two together. That quiet girl, full of household work, is the wonderful scholar, then, that put you to rout with her questions when you first began to come here. To be sure, 'Cousin Phillis!' What's here: a paper with the hard, obsolete words written out. I wonder what sort of a dictionary she has got. Baretti won't tell her all these words. Stay! I have got a pencil here. I'll write down the most accepted meanings, and save her a little trouble."

So he took her book and the paper back to the little round table, and employed himself in writing explanations and definitions of the words which had troubled her. I was not sure if he was not taking a liberty: it did not quite please me, and yet I did not know why. He had only just done, and replaced the paper in the book, and put the latter back in its place, when I heard the sound of wheels stopping in the lane, and looking out, I saw cousin Holman getting out of a neighbour's gig, making her little curtsey of acknowledgement, and then coming towards the house. I went out to meet her.

"Oh, Paul!" said she, "I am so sorry I was kept; and then Thomas Dobson said if I would wait a quarter of an hour he would—— But where's your friend Mr. Holdsworth? I hope he is come?"

Just then he came out, and with his pleasant cordial manner took her hand, and thanked her for asking him to come out here to get strong.

"I'm sure I am very glad to see you, sir. It was the minister's thought. I took it into my head you would be dull in our quiet house, for Paul says you've been such a great traveller; but the minister said that dulness would perhaps suit you while you were but ailing, and that I was to ask Paul to be here as much as he could. I hope you'll find yourself happy with us, I'm sure, sir. Has Phillis given you something to eat and drink, I wonder? there's a deal in eating a little often, if one has to get strong after an illness." And then she began to question him as to the details of his indisposition in her simple motherly way. He seemed at once to understand her, and to enter into friendly relations with her. It was not quite the same in the evening, when the minister came home. Men have always a little natural antipathy to get over when they first meet as strangers. But in this case each was disposed to make an effort to like the other; only each was to each a specimen of an unknown class. I had to leave the Hope Farm on Sunday afternoon, as I had Mr. Holdsworth's work as well as my own to look to in Eltham; and I was not at all sure how things would go on during the week that Holdsworth was to remain on his visit; I had been once or twice in hot water already at the near clash of opinions between the minister and my much-vaunted friend. On the Wednesday I received a short note from Holdsworth; he was going to stay on, and return with me on the following Sunday, and he wanted me to send him a certain list of books, his theodolite, and other surveying instruments, all of which could easily be conveyed down the line to Heathbridge. I went to his lodgings and picked out the books. Italian, Latin, trigonometry; a pretty considerable parcel they made, besides the implements. I began to be curious as to the general progress of affairs at Hope Farm, but I could not go over till the Saturday. At Heathbridge I found Holdsworth, come to meet me. He was looking quite a different man to what I had left him; embrowned, sparkles in his eyes, so languid before. I told him how much stronger he looked.

"Yes!" said he. "I am fidging fain to be at work again. Last week I dreaded the thoughts of my employment; now I am full of desire to begin. This week in the country has done wonders for me."

"You have enjoyed yourself, then?"

"Oh! it has been perfect in its way. Such a thorough country life! and yet removed from the dulness which I always used to fancy accompanied country life, by the extraordinary intelligence of the minister. I have fallen into calling him 'the minister,' like every one else."

"You get on with him, then?" said I. "I was a little afraid."

"I was on the verge of displeasing him once or twice, I fear, with random assertions and exaggerated expressions, such as one always uses with other people, and thinks nothing of; but I tried to check myself when I saw how it shocked the good man; and really it is very wholesome exercise, this trying to make one's words represent one's thoughts, instead of merely looking to their effect on others."

333

"Then you are quite friends now?" I asked.

"Yes, thoroughly; at any rate so far as I go. I never met a man with such a desire for knowledge. In information, as far as it can be gained from books, he far exceeds me on most subjects; but then I have travelled and seen—— Were not you surprised at the list of things I sent for?"

"Yes; I thought it did not promise much rest."

"Oh, some of the books were for the minister, and some for his daughter. (I call her Phillis to myself, but I use euphuisms in speaking about her to others. I don't like to seem familiar, and yet Miss Holman is a term I have never heard used)."

"I thought the Italian books were for her."

"Yes! Fancy her trying at Dante for her first book in Italian! I had a capital novel by Manzoni, *I Promessi Sposi*, just the thing for a beginner; and if she must still puzzle out Dante, my dictionary is far better than hers."

"Then she found out you had written those definitions on her list of words?"

"Oh! yes"—with a smile of amusement and pleasure. He was going to tell me what had taken place, but checked himself.

"But I don't think the minister will like your having given her a novel to read?"

"Pooh! What can be more harmless? Why make a bugbear of a word? It is as pretty and innocent a tale as can be met with. You don't suppose they take *Virgil* for gospel?"

By this time we were at the farm. I think Phillis gave me a warmer welcome than usual, and cousin Holman was kindness itself. Yet somehow I felt as if I had lost my place, and that Holdsworth had taken it. He knew all the ways of the house; he was full of little filial attentions to cousin Holman; he treated Phillis with the affectionate condescension of an elder brother; not a bit more; not in any way different. He questioned me about the progress of affairs in Eltham with eager interest.

"Ah!" said cousin Holman, "you'll be spending a different kind of time next week to what you have done this! I can see how busy you'll make yourself! But if you don't take care you'll be ill again, and have to come back to our quiet ways of going on."

"Do you suppose I shall need to be ill to wish to come back

here?" he answered warmly. "I am only afraid you have treated me so kindly that I shall always be turning up on your hands."

"That's right," she replied. "Only don't go and make yourself ill by over-work. I hope you'll go on with a cup of new milk every morning, for I am sure that is the best medicine; and put a teaspoonful of rum in it if you like; many a one speaks highly of that, only we had no rum in the house."

I brought with me an atmosphere of active life which I think he had begun to miss; and it was natural that he should seek my company, after his week of retirement. Once I saw Phillis looking at us as we talked together with a kind of wistful curiosity; but as soon as she caught my eye, she turned away, blushing deeply.

That evening I had a little talk with the minister. I strolled along the Hornby road to meet him; for Holdsworth was giving Phillis an Italian lesson, and cousin Holman had fallen asleep over her work.

Somehow, and not unwillingly on my part, our talk fell on the friend whom I had introduced to the Hope Farm.

"Yes! I like him!" said the minister, weighing his words a little as he spoke. "I like him. I hope I am justified in doing it, but he takes hold of me, as it were; and I have almost been afraid lest he carries me away, in spite of my judgment."

"He is a good fellow; indeed he is," said I. "My father thinks well of him; and I have seen a deal of him. I would not have had him come here if I did not know that you would approve of him."

"Yes" (once more hesitating), "I like him, and I think he is an upright man; there is a want of seriousness in his talk at times, but, at the same time, it is wonderful to listen to him! He makes Horace and Virgil living, instead of dead, by the stories he tells me of his sojourn in the very countries where they lived, and where to this day, he says—— But it is like dram-drinking. I listen to him till I forget my duties, and am carried off my feet. Last Sabbath evening he led us away into talk on profane subjects ill befitting the day."

By this time we were at the house, and our conversation stopped. But before the day was out, I saw the unconscious hold that my friend had got over all the family. And no wonder: he had seen so much and done so much as compared to them, and he told about it all so easily and naturally, and yet as I never heard any one else do; and his ready pencil was out in an instant to draw on scraps of paper all sorts of illustrations—modes of drawing up water in Northern Italy, wine-carts, buffaloes, stone-pines, I know not what. After we had all looked at these drawings, Phillis gathered them together, and took them.

It is many years since I have seen thee, Edward Holdsworth, but thou wast a delightful fellow! Ay, and a good one too; though much sorrow was caused by thee!

Part III

JUST AFTER THIS I went home for a week's holiday. Everything was prospering there; my father's new partnership gave evident satisfaction to both parties. There was no display of increased wealth in our modest household; but my mother had a few extra comforts provided for her by her husband. I made acquaintance with Mr. and Mrs. Ellison, and first saw pretty Margaret Ellison, who is now my wife. When I returned to Eltham, I found that a step was decided upon which had been in contemplation for some time; that Holdsworth and I should remove our quarters to Hornby; our daily presence, and as much of our time as possible, being required for the completion of the line at that end.

Of course this led to greater facility of intercourse with the Hope Farm people. We could easily walk out there after our day's work was done, and spend a balmy evening hour or two, and yet return before the summer's twilight had quite faded away. Many a time, indeed, we would fain have stayed longer—the open air, the fresh and pleasant country, made so agreeable a contrast to the close, hot town lodgings which I shared with Mr. Holdsworth; but early hours, both at eve and morn, were an imperative necessity with the minister, and he made no scruple at turning either or both of us out of the house directly after evening prayer, or "exercise," as he called it. The remembrance of many a happy day, and of several little scenes, comes back upon me as I think of that summer. They rise like pictures to my memory, and in this way I can date their succession; for I know that corn-harvest must have come after hay-making, apple-gathering after corn-harvest.

The removal to Hornby took up some time, during which we had neither of us any leisure to go out to the Hope Farm. Mr. Holdsworth had been out there once during my absence at home. One sultry evening, when work was done, he proposed our walking out and paying the Holmans a visit. It so happened that I had omitted to write my usual weekly letter home in our press of business, and I wished to finsh that before going out. Then he said that he would go, and that I could follow him if I liked. This I did in about an hour; the weather was so oppressive, I remember, that I took off my coat as I walked, and hung it over my arm. All the doors and windows at the farm were open when I arrived there, and every tiny leaf on the trees was still. The silence of the place was profound; at first I thought that it was entirely deserted; but just as I drew near the door I heard a weak sweet voice begin to sing; it was cousin Holman, all by herself in the house-place, piping up a hymn, as she knitted away in the clouded light. She gave me a kindly welcome, and poured out all the small domestic news of the fortnight past upon me, and, in return, I told her about my own people and my visit at home. "Where were the rest?" at length I asked.

Betty and the men were in the field helping with the last load of hay, for the minister said there would be rain before the morning. Yes, and the minister himself, and Phillis, and Mr. Holdsworth, were all there helping. She thought that she herself could have done something; but perhaps she was the least fit for hay-making of any one; and somebody must stay at home and take care of the house, there were so many tramps about; if I had not had something to do with the railroad she would have called them navvies. I asked her if she minded being left alone, as I should like to go and help; and having her full and glad permission to leave her alone, I went off, following her directions: through the farmyard, past the cattle-pond, into the ash-field, beyond into the higher field with two holly-bushes in the middle. I arrived there: there was Betty with all the farming men, and a cleared field, and a heavily laden cart; one man at the top of the great pile ready to catch the fragrant hay which the others threw up to him with their pitchforks; a little heap of cast-off clothes in a corner of the field (for the heat, even at seven o'clock, was insufferable), a few cans and baskets, and Rover lying by them panting, and keeping watch. Plenty of loud, hearty, cheerful talking; but no minister, no Phillis, no Mr. Holdsworth. Betty saw me first, and understanding who it was that I was in search of, she came towards me.

"They're out yonder—agait wi' them things o' Measter Holdsworth's."

So "out yonder" I went; out on to a broad upland common, full of red sand-banks, and sweeps and hollows; bordered by dark firs, purple in the coming shadows, but near at hand all ablaze with flowering gorse, or, as we call it in the south, furze-bushes, which, seen against the belt of distant trees, appeared brilliantly golden. On this heath, a little way from the field-gate, I saw the three. I counted their heads, joined together in an eager group over Holdsworth's theodolite. He was teaching the minister the practical art of surveying and taking a level. I was wanted to assist, and was quickly set to work to hold the chain. Phillis was as intent as her father; she had hardly time to greet me, so desirous was she to hear some answer to her father's question.

So we went on, the dark clouds still gathering, for perhaps five minutes after my arrival. Then came the blinding lightning and the rumble and quick-following rattling peal of thunder right over our heads. It came sooner than I expected, sooner than they had looked for: the rain delayed not; it came pouring down; and what were we to do for shelter? Phillis had nothing on but her indoor things—no bonnet, no shawl. Quick as the darting lightning around us, Holdsworth took off his coat and wrapped it round her neck and shoulders, and, almost without a word, hurried us all into such poor shelter as one of the over-hanging sand-banks could give. There we were, cowered down, close together, Phillis innermost, almost too tightly packed to free her arms enough to divest herself of the coat, which she, in her turn, tried to put lightly over Holdsworth's shoulders. In doing so she touched his shirt.

"Oh, how wet you are!" she cried, in pitying dismay; "and you've hardly got over your fever! Oh, Mr. Holdsworth, I am so sorry!" He turned his head a little, smiling at her.

"If I do catch cold, it is all my fault for having deluded you

338

into staying out here!" But she only murmured again "I am so sorry."

The minister spoke now. "It is a regular downpour. Please God that the hay is saved! But there is no likelihood of its ceasing, and I had better go home at once, and send you all some wraps; umbrellas will not be safe with yonder thunder and lightning."

Both Holdsworth and I offered to go instead of him; but he was resolved, although perhaps it would have been wiser if Holdsworth, wet as he already was, had kept himself in exercise. As he moved off, Phillis crept out, and could see on to the storm-swept heath. Part of Holdsworth's apparatus still remained exposed to all the rain. Before we could have any warning, she had rushed out of the shelter and collected the various things, and brought them back in triumph to where we crouched. Holdsworth had stood up, uncertain whether to go to her assistance or not. She came running back, her long lovely hair floating and dripping, her eyes glad and bright, and her colour freshened to a glow of health by the exercise and the rain.

"Now, Miss Holman, that's what I call wilful," said Holdsworth, as she gave them to him. "No, I won't thank you" (his looks were thanking her all the time). "My little bit of dampness annoyed you, because you thought I had got wet in your service; so you were determined to make me as uncomfortable as you were yourself. It was an unchristian piece of revenge!"

His tone of badinage (as the French call it) would have been palpable enough to any one accustomed to the world; but Phillis was not, and it distressed or rather bewildered her. "Unchristian" had to her a very serious meaning; it was not a word to be used lightly; and though she did not exactly understand what wrong it was that she was accused of doing, she was evidently desirous to throw off the imputation. At first her earnestness to disclaim unkind motives amused Holdsworth; while his light continuance of the joke perplexed her still more; but at last he said something gravely, and in too low a tone for me to hear, which made her all at once become silent, and called out her blushes. After a while, the minister came back, a moving mass of shawls, cloaks, and umbrellas. Phillis kept very close to her father's side on our return to the farm. She appeared to me to be shrinking away from Holdsworth, while he had not the slightest variation in his manner from what it usually was in his graver moods; kind, protecting, and thoughtful towards her. Of course, there was a great commotion about our wet clothes; but I name the little events of that evening now because I wondered at the time what he had said in that low voice to silence Phillis so effectually, and because, in thinking of their intercourse by the light of future events, that evening stands out with some prominence.

I have said that after our removal to Hornby our communications with the farm became almost of daily occurrence. Cousin Holman and I were the two who had least to do with this intimacy. After Mr. Holdsworth regained his health, he too often talked above her head in intellectual matters, and too often in his light bantering tone for her to feel quite at her ease with him. I really believe that he adopted this latter tone in speaking to her because he did not know what to talk about to a purely motherly woman, whose intellect had never been cultivated, and whose loving heart was entirely occupied with her husband, her child, her household affairs, and, perhaps, a little with the concerns of the members of her husband's congregation, because they, in a way, belonged to her husband. I had noticed before that she had fleeting shadows of jealousy even of Phillis, when her daughter and her husband appeared to have strong interests and sympathies in things which were quite beyond her comprehension. I had noticed it in my first acquaintance with them, I say, and had admired the delicate tact which made the minister, on such occasions, bring the conversation back to such subjects as those on which his wife, with her practical experience of every-day life, was an authority; while Phillis, devoted to her father, unconsciously followed his lead, totally unaware, in her filial reverence, of his motive for doing so.

To return to Holdsworth. The minister had at more than one time spoken of him to me with slight distrust, principally occasioned by the suspicion that his careless words were not always those of soberness and truth. But it was more as a protest against the fascination which the younger man evidently exercised over the elder one—more as it were to strengthen himself against yielding to this fascination—that the minister spoke out to me about this failing of Holdsworth's, as it appeared to him. In return

Holdsworth was subdued by the minister's uprightness and goodness, and delighted with his clear intellect—his strong healthy
craving after further knowledge. I never met two men who took
more thorough pleasure and relish in each other's society. To
Phillis his relation continued that of an elder brother: he directed
her studies into new paths, he patiently drew out the expression
of many of her thoughts, and perplexities, and unformed theories,
scarcely ever now falling into the vein of banter which she was
so slow to understand.

One day—harvest-time—he had been drawing on a loose piece
of paper—sketching ears of corn, sketching carts drawn by bul-
locks and laden with grapes—all the time talking with Phillis and
me, cousin Holman putting in her not pertinent remarks, when
suddenly he said to Phillis,—

"Keep your head still; I see a sketch! I have often tried to
draw your head from memory, and failed; but I think I can do it
now. If I succeed I will give it to your mother. You would like
a portrait of your daughter as Ceres, would you not, ma'am?"

"I should like a picture of her; yes, very much, thank you,
Mr. Holdsworth; but if you put that straw in her hair" (he was
holding some wheat ears above her passive head, looking at the
effect with an artistic eye), "you'll ruffle her hair. Phillis, my
dear, if you're to have your picture taken, go upstairs, and brush
your hair smooth."

"Not on any account. I beg your pardon, but I want hair
loosely flowing."

He began to draw, looking intently at Phillis; I could see this
stare of his discomposed her—her colour came and went, her
breath quickened with the consciousness of his regard; at last,
when he said, "Please look at me for a minute or two, I want to
get in the eyes," she looked up at him, quivered, and suddenly
got up and left the room. He did not say a word, but went on
with some other part of the drawing; his silence was unnatural,
and his dark cheek blanched a little. Cousin Holman looked up
from her work, and put her spectacles down.

"What's the matter? Where is she gone?"

Holdsworth never uttered a word, but went on drawing. I felt
obliged to say something; it was stupid enough, but stupidity was
better than silence just then.

"I'll go and call her," said I. So I went into the hall, and to the bottom of the stairs; but just as I was going to call Phillis, she came down swiftly with her bonnet on, and saying, "I'm going to father in the five-acre," passed out by the open "rector," right in front of the house-place windows, and out at the little white side-gate. She had been seen by her mother and Holdsworth as she passed; so there was no need for explanation, only cousin Holman and I had a long discussion as to whether she could have found the room too hot, or what had occasioned her sudden departure. Holdsworth was very quiet during all the rest of that day; nor did he resume the portrait-taking by his own desire, only at my cousin Holman's request the next time that he came; and then he said he should not require any more formal sittings for only such a slight sketch as he felt himself capable of making. Phillis was just the same as ever the next time I saw her after her abrupt passing me in the hall. She never gave any explanation of her rush out of the room.

So all things went on, at least as far as my observation reached at the time, or memory can recall now, till the great apple-gathering of the year. The nights were frosty, the mornings and evenings were misty, but at mid-day all was sunny and bright, and it was one mid-day that both of us being on the line near Heathbridge, and knowing that they were gathering apples at the farm, we resolved to spend the men's dinner-hour in going over there. We found the great clothes-baskets full of apples, scenting the house and stopping up the way; and an universal air of merry contentment with this the final produce of the year. The yellow leaves hung on the trees ready to flutter down at the slightest puff of air; the great bushes of Michaelmas daisies in the kitchen-garden were making their last show of flowers. We must needs taste the fruit off the different trees, and pass our judgment as to their flavour; and we went away with our pockets stuffed with those that we liked best. As we had passed to the orchard, Holdsworth had admired and spoken about some flower which he saw; it so happened he had never seen this old-fashioned kind since the days of his boyhood. I do not know whether he had thought anything more about this chance speech of his, but I know I had not—when Phillis, who had been missing just at the last moment of our hurried visit, re-appeared with a little nosegay of this same flower, which she was tying up with a blade of grass. She offered it to Holdsworth as he stood with her father on the point of departure. I saw their faces. I saw for the first time an unmistakable look of love in his black eyes; it was more than gratitude for the little attention; it was tender and beseeching—passionate. She shrank from it in confusion, her glance fell on me; and, partly to hide her emotion, partly out of real kindness at what might appear ungracious neglect of an older friend, she flew off to gather me a few late-blooming China roses. But it was the first time she had ever done anything of the kind for me.

We had to walk fast to be back on the line before the men's return, so we spoke but little to each other, and of course the afternoon was too much occupied for us to have any talk. In the evening we went back to our joint lodgings in Hornby. There, on the table, lay a letter for Holdsworth, which had been forwarded to him from Eltham. As our tea was ready, and I had had nothing to eat since morning, I fell to directly, without paying much attention to my companion as he opened and read his letter. He was very silent for a few minutes; at length he said,—

"Old fellow! I'm going to leave you!"

"Leave me!" said I. "How? When?"

"This letter ought to have come to hand sooner. It is from Greathed the engineer" (Greathed was well known in those days; he is dead now, and his name half-forgotten); "he wants to see me about some business; in fact, I may as well tell you, Paul, this letter contains a very advantageous proposal for me to go out to Canada, and superintend the making of a line there."

I was in utter dismay.

"But what will our company say to that?"

"Oh, Greathed has the superintendence of this line, you know; and he is going to be engineer in chief to this Canadian line; many of the shareholders in this company are going in for the other, so I fancy they will make no difficulty in following Greathed's lead. He says he has a young man ready to put in my place."

"I hate him," said I.

"Thank you," said Holdsworth, laughing.

"But you must not," he resumed; "for this is a very good thing for me; and, of course, if no one can be found to take my inferior work, I can't be spared to take the superior. I only wish

I had received this letter a day sooner. Every hour is of consequence, for Greathed says they are threatening a rival line. Do you know, Paul, I almost fancy I must go up to-night? I can take an engine back to Eltham, and catch the night train. I should not like Greathed to think me lukewarm."

"But you'll come back?" I asked, distressed at the thought of this sudden parting.

"Oh, yes! At least I hope so. They may want me to go out by the next steamer, that will be on Saturday." He began to eat and drink standing, but I think he was quite unconscious of the nature of either his food or his drink.

"I will go to-night. Activity and readiness go a long way in our profession. Remember that, my boy! I hope I shall come back, but if I don't, be sure and recollect all the words of wisdom that have fallen from my lips. Now, where's the portmanteau? If I can gain half an hour for a gathering up of my things in Eltham, so much the better. I'm clear of debt anyhow; and what I owe for my lodgings you can pay for me out of my quarter's salary, due November 4th."

"Then you don't think you will come back?" I said, despondingly.

"I will come back some time, never fear," said he kindly. "I may be back in a couple of days, having been found incompetent for the Canadian work; or I may not be wanted to go out so soon as I now anticipate. Anyhow, you don't suppose I am going to forget you, Paul—this work out there ought not to take me above two years, and, perhaps, after that, we may be employed together again."

Perhaps! I had very little hope. The same kind of happy days never returns. However, I did all I could in helping him: clothes, papers, books, instruments; how we pushed and struggled —how I stuffed. All was done in a much shorter time than we had calculated upon, when I had run down to the sheds to order the engine. I was going to drive him to Eltham. We sat ready for a summons. Holdsworth took up the little nosegay he had brought away from the Hope Farm, and had laid on the mantle-piece on first coming into the room. He smelt at it, and caressed it with his lips.

"What grieves me is that I did not know—that I have not said good-by to—to them."

He spoke in a grave tone, the shadow of the coming separation falling upon him at last.

"I will tell them," said I. "I am sure they will be very sorry." Then we were silent.

"I never liked any family so much."

"I knew you would like them."

"How one's thoughts change,—this morning I was full of a hope, Paul." He paused, and then he said,—

"You put that sketch in carefully?"

"That outline of a head?" asked I. But I knew he meant an abortive sketch of Phillis, which had not been successful enough for him to complete it with shading or colouring.

"Yes. What a sweet innocent face it is! and yet so—Oh, dear!"

He sighed and got up, his hands in his pockets, to walk up and down the room in evident disturbance of mind. He suddenly stopped opposite to me.

"You'll tell them how it all was. Be sure and tell the good minister that I was so sorry not to wish him good-by, and to thank him and his wife for all their kindness. As for Phillis,—please God in two years I'll be back and tell her myself all in my heart."

"You love Phillis, then?" said I.

"Love her!—Yes, that I do. Who could help it, seeing her as I have done? Her character as unusual and rare as her beauty! God bless her! God keep her in her high tranquillity, her pure innocence.—Two years! It is a long time. But she lives in such seclusion, almost like the sleeping beauty, Paul,"—(he was smiling now, though a minute before I had thought him on the verge of tears)—"but I shall come back like a prince from Canada, and waken her to my love. I can't help hoping that it won't be difficult, eh, Paul?"

This touch of coxcombry displeased me a little, and I made no answer. He went on, half apologetically,—

"You see, the salary they offer me is large; and besides that, this experience will give me a name which will entitle me to expect a still larger in any future undertaking."

"That won't influence Phillis."

"No! but it will make me more eligible in the eyes of her father and mother."

I made no answer.

"You give me your best wishes, Paul," said he, almost pleading. "You would like me for a cousin?"

I heard the scream and whistle of the engine ready down at the sheds.

"Ay, that I should," I replied, suddenly softened towards my friend now that he was going away. "I wish you were to be married to-morrow, and I were to be best man."

"Thank you, lad. Now for this cursed portmanteau (how the minister would be shocked); but it is heavy!" and off we sped into the darkness.

He only just caught the night train at Eltham, and I slept, desolately enough, at my old lodgings at Miss Dawson's, for that night. Of course the next few days I was busier than ever, doing both his work and my own. Then came a letter from him, very short and affectionate. He was going out in the Saturday steamer, as he had more than half expected; and by the following Monday the man who was to succeed him would be down at Eltham. There was a P.S., with only these words:—

"My nosegay goes with me to Canada, but I do not need it to remind me of Hope Farm."

Saturday came; but it was very late before I could go out to the farm. It was a frosty night, the stars shone clear above me, and the road was crisping beneath my feet. They must have heard my footsteps before I got up to the house. They were sitting at their usual employments in the house-place when I went in. Phillis's eyes went beyond me in their look of welcome, and then fell in quiet disappointment on her work.

"And where's Mr. Holdsworth?" asked cousin Holman, in a minute or two. "I hope his cold is not worse,—I did not like his short cough."

I laughed awkwardly; for I felt that I was the bearer of unpleasant news.

"His cold had need be better—for he's gone—gone away to Canada!"

I purposely looked away from Phillis, as I thus abruptly told my news.

"To Canada!" said the minister.

"Gone away!" said his wife.

But no word from Phillis.

"Yes!" said I. "He found a letter at Hornby when we got home the other night—when we got home from here; he ought to have got it sooner; he was ordered to go up to London directly, and to see some people about a new line in Canada, and he's gone to lay it down; he has sailed to-day. He was sadly grieved not to have time to come out and wish you all good-by; but he started for London within two hours after he got that letter. He bade me thank you most gratefully for all your kindnesses; he was very sorry not to come here once again."

Phillis got up and left the room with noiseless steps.

"I am very sorry," said the minister.

"I am sure so am I!" said cousin Holman. "I was real fond of that lad ever since I nursed him last June after that bad fever."

The minister went on asking me questions respecting Holdsworth's future plans; and brought out a large old-fashioned atlas, that he might find out the exact places between which the new railroad was to run. Then supper was ready; it was always on the table as soon as the clock on the stairs struck eight, and down came Phillis—her face white and set, her dry eyes looking defiance to me, for I am afraid I hurt her maidenly pride by my glance of sympathetic interest as she entered the room. Never a word did she say—never a question did she ask about the absent friend, yet she forced herself to talk.

And so it was all the next day. She was as pale as could be, like one who has received some shock; but she would not let me talk to her, and she tried hard to behave as usual. Two or three times I repeated, in public, the various affectionate messages to the family with which I was charged by Holdsworth; but she took no more notice of them than if my words had been empty air. And in this mood I left her on the Sabbath evening.

My new master was not half so indulgent as my old one. He kept up strict discipline as to hours, so that it was some time before I could again go out, even to pay a call at the Hope Farm.

It was a cold misty evening in November. The air, even indoors, seemed full of haze; yet there was a great log burning on the hearth, which ought to have made the room cheerful. Cousin Holman and Phillis were sitting at the little round table before the fire, working away in silence. The minister had his books out on the dresser, seemingly deep in study, by the light of his solitary candle; perhaps the fear of disturbing him made the unusual stillness of the room. But a welcome was ready for me from all; not noisy, not demonstrative—that it never was; my damp wrappers were taken off, the next meal was hastened, and a chair placed for me on one side the fire, so that I pretty much commanded a view of the room. My eye caught on Phillis, looking so pale and weary, and with a sort of aching tone (if I may call it so) in her voice. She was doing all the accustomed things —fulfilling small household duties, but somehow differently—I can't tell you how, for she was just as deft and quick in her movements, only the light spring was gone out of them. Cousin Holman began to question me; even the minister put aside his books, and came and stood on the opposite side of the fire-place, to hear what waft of intelligence I brought. I had first to tell them why I had not been to see them for so long—more than five weeks. The answer was simple enough; business and the necessity of attending strictly to the orders of a new superintendent, who had not yet learned trust, much less indulgence. The minister nodded his approval of my conduct, and said,—

"Right, Paul! 'Servants, obey in all things your masters according to the flesh.' I have had my fears lest you had too much license under Edward Holdsworth."

"Ah," said cousin Holman, "poor Mr. Holdsworth, he'll be on the salt seas by this time!"

"No, indeed," said I, "he's landed. I have had a letter from him from Halifax."

Immediately a shower of questions fell thick upon me. When? How? What was he doing? How did he like it? What sort of a voyage? &c.

"Many is the time we thought of him when the wind was blowing so hard; the old quince-tree is blown down, Paul, that on the right hand of the great pear-tree; it was blown down last Monday week, and it was that night that I asked the minister to pray in an especial manner for all them that went down in ships upon the great deep, and he said then, that Mr. Holdsworth might be already landed; but I said, even if the prayer did not fit him, it was sure to be fitting somebody out at sea, who would need the

Lord's care. Both Phillis and I thought he would be a month on the seas."

Phillis began to speak, but her voice did not come rightly at first. It was a little higher pitched than usual, when she said—

"We thought he would be a month if he went in a sailing-vessel, or perhaps longer. I suppose he went in a steamer?"

"Old Obadiah Grimshaw was more than six weeks in getting to America," observed cousin Holman.

"I presume he cannot as yet tell how he likes his new work?" asked the minister.

"No! he is but just landed; it is but one page long. I'll read it to you, shall I?—

"DEAR PAUL,—

"We are safe on shore, after a rough passage. Thought you would like to hear this, but homeward-bound steamer is making signals for letters. Will write again soon. It seems a year since I left Hornby. Longer since I was at the farm. I have got my nosegay safe. Remember me to the Holmans.

"Yours,

"E.H."

"That's not much, certainly," said the minister. "But it's a comfort to know he's on land these blowy nights."

Phillis said nothing. She kept her head bent down over her work; but I don't think she put a stitch in, while I was reading the letter. I wondered if she understood what nosegay was meant; but I could not tell. When next she lifted up her face, there were two spots of brilliant colour on the cheeks that had been so pale before. After I had spent an hour or two there, I was bound to return back to Hornby. I told them I did not know when I could come again, as we—by which I mean the company—had undertaken the Hensleydale line; that branch for which poor Holdsworth was surveying when he caught his fever.

"But you'll have a holiday at Christmas," said my cousin. "Surely they'll not be such heathens as to work you then?"

"Perhaps the lad will be going home," said the minister, as if to mitigate his wife's urgency; but for all that, I believe he wanted me to come. Phillis fixed her eyes on me with a wistful expression, hard to resist. But indeed, I had no thought of resisting. Under my new master I had no hope of a holiday long enough to enable me to go to Birmingham and see my parents with any comfort; and nothing could be pleasanter to me than to find myself at home at my cousin's for a day or two, then. So it was fixed that we were to meet in Hornby Chapel on Christmas Day, and that I was to accompany them home after service, and if possible to stay over the next day.

I was not able to get to chapel till late on the appointed day, and so I took a seat near the door in considerable shame, although it really was not my fault. When the service was ended I went and stood in the porch to await the coming out of my cousins. Some worthy people belonging to the congregation clustered into a group just where I stood, and exchanged the good wishes of the season. It had just begun to snow, and this occasioned a little delay, and they fell into further conversation. I was not attending to what was not meant for me to hear, till I caught the name of Phillis Holman. And then I listened; where was the harm?

"I never saw any one so changed!"

"I asked Mrs. Holman," quoth another, " 'Is Phillis well?' and she just said she had been having a cold which had pulled her down; she did not seem to think anything of it."

"They had best take care of her," said one of the oldest of the good ladies; "Phillis comes of a family as is not long-lived. Her mother's sister, Lydia Green, her own aunt as was, died of a decline just when she was about this lass's age."

This ill-omened talk was broken in upon by the coming out of the minister, his wife and daughter, and the consequent interchange of Christmas compliments. I had had a shock, and felt heavy-hearted and anxious, and hardly up to making the appropriate replies to the kind greetings of my relations. I looked askance at Phillis. She had certainly grown taller and slighter, and was thinner; but there was a flush of colour on her face which deceived me for a time, and made me think she was looking as well as ever. I only saw her paleness after we had returned to the farm, and she had subsided into silence and quiet. Her grey eyes looked hollow and sad; her complexion was of a dead white. But she went about just as usual; at least, just as she had done the last time I was there, and seemed to have no ailment; and I was inclined to think that my cousin was right when she had answered the inquiries of the good-natured gossips, and told them that Phillis was suffering from the consequences of a bad cold, nothing more.

I have said that I was to stay over the next day; a great deal of snow had come down, but not all, they said, though the ground was covered deep with the white fall. The minister was anxiously housing his cattle, and preparing all things for a long continuance of the same kind of weather. The men were chopping wood, sending wheat to the mill to be ground before the road should become impassable for a cart and horse. My cousin and Phillis had gone upstairs to the apple-room to cover up the fruit from the frost. I had been out the greater part of the morning, and came in about an hour before dinner. To my surprise, knowing how she had planned to be engaged, I found Phillis sitting at the dresser, resting her head on her two hands and reading, or seeming to read. She did not look up when I came in, but murmured something about her mother having sent her down out of the cold. It flashed across me that she was crying, but I put it down to some little spirit of temper; I might have known better than to suspect the gentle, serene Phillis of crossness, poor girl; I stooped down, and began to stir and build up the fire, which appeared to have been neglected. While my head was down I heard a noise which made me pause and listen—a sob, an unmistakable, irrepressible sob. I started up.

"Phillis!" I cried, going towards her, with my hand out, to take hers for sympathy with her sorrow, whatever it was. But she was too quick for me, she held her hand out of my grasp, for fear of my detaining her; as she quickly passed out of the house, she said,—

"Don't, Paul! I cannot bear it!" and passed me, still sobbing, and went out into the keen, open air.

I stood still and wondered. What could have come to Phillis? The most perfect harmony prevailed in the family, and Phillis especially, good and gentle as she was, was so beloved that if they had found out that her finger ached, it would have cast a shadow over their hearts. Had I done anything to vex her? No: she was crying before I came in. I went to look at her book—one of those unintelligible Italian books. I could make neither head nor tail of it. I saw some pencil-notes on the margin, in Holdsworth's handwriting.

Could that be it? Could that be the cause of her white looks, her weary eyes, her wasted figure, her struggling sobs? This idea came upon me like a flash of lightning on a dark night, making all things so clear we cannot forget them afterwards when the gloomy obscurity returns. I was still standing with the book in my hand when I heard cousin Holman's footsteps on the stairs, and as I did not wish to speak to her just then, I followed Phillis's example, and rushed out of the house. The snow was lying on the ground; I could track her feet by the marks they had made; I could see where Rover had joined her. I followed on till I came to a great stack of wood in the orchard—it was built up against the back wall of the outbuildings,—and I recollected then how Phillis had told me, that first day when we strolled about together, that underneath this stack had been her hermitage, her sanctuary, when she was a child; how she used to bring her book to study there, or her work, when she was not wanted in the house; and she had now evidently gone back to this quiet retreat of her childhood, forgetful of the clue given me by her footmarks on the new-fallen snow. The stack was built up very high; but through the interstices of the sticks I could see her figure, although I did not all at once perceive how I could get to her. She was sitting on a log of wood, Rover by her. She had laid her cheek on Rover's head, and had her arm around his neck, partly for a pillow, partly from an instinctive craving for warmth on that bitter cold day. She was making a low moan, like an animal in pain, or perhaps more like the sobbing of the wind. Rover, highly flattered by her caress, and also, perhaps, touched by sympathy, was flapping his heavy tail against the ground, but not otherwise moving a hair, until he heard my approach with his quick erect ears. Then, with a short, abrupt bark of distrust, he sprang up as if to leave his mistress. Both he and I were immovably still for a moment. I was not sure if what I longed to do was wise; and yet I could not bear to see the sweet serenity of my dear cousin's life so disturbed by a suffering which I thought I could assuage. But Rover's ears were sharper than my breathing was noiseless: he heard me, and sprang out from under Phillis's restraining hand.

"Oh, Rover, don't you leave me too," she plained out.

"Phillis!" said I, seeing by Rover's exit that the entrance to where she sat was to be found on the other side of the stack. "Phillis, come out! You have got a cold already; and it is not fit for you to sit there on such a day as this. You know how displeased and anxious it would make them all."

She sighed, but obeyed; stooping a little, she came out, and stood upright, opposite to me in the lonely, leafless orchard. Her face looked so meek and so sad that I felt as if I ought to beg her pardon for my necessarily authoritative words.

"Sometimes I feel the house so close," she said; "and I used to sit under the wood-stack when I was a child. It was very kind of you, but there was no need to come after me. I don't catch cold easily."

"Come with me into this cow-house, Phillis. I have got something to say to you; and I can't stand this cold, if you can."

I think she would have fain run away again; but her fit of energy was all spent. She followed me unwillingly enough—that I could see. The place to which I took her was of the fragrant breath of the cows, and was a little warmer than the outer air. I put her inside, and stood myself in the doorway, thinking how I could best begin. At last I plunged into it.

"I must see that you don't get cold for more reasons than one; if you are ill, Holdsworth will be so anxious and miserable out there" (by which I meant Canada)—

She shot one penetrating look at me, and then turned her face away with a slight impatient movement. If she could have run away then she would, but I held the means of exit in my own power. "In for a penny in for a pound," thought I, and I went on rapidly, anyhow.

"He talked so much about you, just before he left—that night after he had been here, you know—and you had given him those flowers." She put her hands up to hide her face, but she was listening now—listening with all her ears.

"He had never spoken much about you before, but the sudden going away unlocked his heart, and he told me how he loved you, and how he hoped on his return that you might be his wife."

"Don't," said she, almost gasping out the word, which she had tried once or twice before to speak; but her voice had been choked. Now she put her hand backwards; she had quite turned away from me, and felt for mine. She gave it a soft lingering pressure: and then she put her arms down on the wooden division, and laid her head on it, and cried quiet tears. I did not understand her at once, and feared lest I had mistaken the whole case, and only annoyed her. I went up to her. "Oh, Phillis; I am so sorry—I thought you would, perhaps, have cared to hear it; he did talk so feelingly, as if he did love you so much, and somehow I thought it would give you pleasure."

She lifted up her head and looked at me. Such a look! Her eyes, glittering with tears as they were, expressed an almost heavenly happiness; her tender mouth was curved with rapture— her colour vivid and blushing; but as if she was afraid her face expressed too much, more than the thankfulness to me she was essaying to speak, she hid it again almost immediately. So it was all right then, and my conjecture was well founded. I tried to remember something more to tell her of what he had said, but again she stopped me.

"Don't," she said. She still kept her face covered and hidden. In half a minute she added, in a very low voice, "Please, Paul, I think I would rather not hear any more—I don't mean but what I have—but what I am very much obliged—— Only—only, I think I would rather hear the rest from himself when he comes back."

And then she cried a little more, in quite a different way. I did not say any more, I waited for her. By-and-by she turned towards me—not meeting my eyes, however; and putting her hand in mine, just as if we were two children, she said,—

"We had best go back now—I don't look as if I had been crying, do I?"

"You look as if you had a bad cold," was all the answer I made.

"Oh! but I am—I am quite well, only cold; and a good run will warm me. Come along, Paul."

So we ran, hand in hand, till, just as we were on the threshold of the house, she stopped—

"Paul, please, we won't speak about that again."

Part IV

When I went over on Easter Day I heard the chapel-gossips complimenting cousin Holman on her daughter's blooming looks, quite forgetful of their sinister prophecies three months before.

354

And I looked at Phillis, and did not wonder at their words. I
had not seen her since the day after Christmas Day. I had left
the Hope Farm only a few hours after I had told her the news
which had quickened her heart into renewed life and vigour. The
remembrance of our conversation in the cow-house was vividly in
my mind as I looked at her when her bright healthy appearance
was remarked upon. As her eyes met mine our mutual recollections flashed intelligence from one to the other. She turned away,
her colour heightening as she did so. She seemed to be shy of
me for the first few hours after our meeting, and I felt rather
vexed with her for her conscious avoidance of me after my long
absence. I had stepped a little out of my usual line in telling her
what I did; not that I had received any charge of secrecy, or
given even the slightest promise to Holdsworth that I would not
repeat his words. But I had an uneasy feeling sometimes when I
thought of what I had done in the excitement of seeing Phillis so
ill and in so much trouble. I meant to have told Holdsworth
when I wrote next to him; but when I had my half-finished letter
before me I sate with my pen in my hand hesitating. I had more
scruple in revealing what I had found out or guessed at of Phillis's
secret than in repeating to her his spoken words. I did not think
I had any right to say out to him what I believed—namely, that
she loved him dearly, and had felt his absence even to the injury
of her health. Yet to explain what I had done in telling her how
he had spoken about her that last night, it would be necessary to
give my reasons, so I had settled within myself to leave it alone.
As she had told me she should like to hear all the details and
fuller particulars and more explicit declarations first from him, so
he should have the pleasure of extracting the delicious tender
secret from her maidenly lips. I would not betray my guesses,
my surmises, my all but certain knowledge of the state of her
heart. I had received two letters from him after he had settled
to his business; they were full of life and energy; but in each
there had been a message to the family at the Hope Farm of more
than common regard; and a slight but distinct mention of Phillis
herself, showing that she stood single and alone in his memory.
These letters I had sent on to the minister, for he was sure to care
for them, even supposing he had been unacquainted with their
writer, because they were so clever and so picturesquely worded.

355

that they brought, as it were, a whiff of foreign atmosphere into his circumscribed life. I used to wonder what was the trade or business in which the minister would not have thriven, mentally I mean, if it had so happened that he had been called into that state. He would have made a capital engineer, that I know; and he had a fancy for the sea, like many other land-locked men to whom the great deep is a mystery and a fascination. He read law-books with relish; and once happening to borrow *De Lolme on the British Constitution* (or some such title), he talked about jurisprudence till he was far beyond my depth. But to return to Holdsworth's letters. When the minister sent them back he also wrote out a list of questions suggested by their perusal, which I was to pass on in my answers to Holdsworth, until I thought of suggesting a direct correspondence between the two. That was the state of things as regarded the absent one when I went to the farm for my Easter visit, and when I found Phillis in that state of shy reserve towards me which I have named before. I thought she was ungrateful; for I was not quite sure if I had done wisely in having told her what I did. I had committed a fault, or a folly, perhaps, and all for her sake; and here was she, less friends with me than she had ever been before. This little estrangement only lasted a few hours. I think that as soon as she felt pretty sure of there being no recurrence, either by word, look, or allusion, to the one subject that was predominant in her mind, she came back to her old sisterly ways with me. She had much to tell me of her own familiar interests; how Rover had been ill, and how anxious they had all of them been, and how, after some little discussion between her father and her, both equally grieved by the sufferings of the old dog, he had been "remembered in the household prayers," and how he had begun to get better only the very next day, and then she would have led me into a conversation on the right ends of prayer, and on special providences, and I know not what; only I "jibbed" like their old cart-horse, and refused to stir a step in that direction. Then we talked about the different broods of chickens, and she showed me the hens that were good mothers, and told me the characters of all the poultry with the utmost good faith; and in all good faith I listened, for I believe there was a great deal of truth in all she said. And then we strolled on into the wood beyond the ash-meadow, and both of us

356

sought for early primroses, and the fresh green crinkled leaves. She was not afraid of being alone with me after the first day. I never saw her so lovely, or so happy. I think she hardly knew why she was so happy all the time. I can see her now, standing under the budding branches of the gray trees, over which a tinge of green seemed to be deepening day after day, her sun-bonnet fallen back on her neck, her hands full of delicate wood-flowers, quite unconscious of my gaze, but intent on sweet mockery of some bird in neighbouring bush or tree. She had the art of warbling, and replying to the notes of different birds, and knew their song, their habits and ways, more accurately than any one else I ever knew. She had often done it at my request the spring before; but this year she really gurgled, and whistled, and warbled just as they did, out of the very fulness and joy of her heart. She was more than ever the very apple of her father's eye; her mother gave her both her own share of love and that of the dead child who had died in infancy. I have heard cousin Holman murmur, after a long dreamy look at Phillis, and tell herself how like she was growing to Johnnie, and soothe herself with plaintive inarticulate sounds, and many gentle shakes of the head, for the aching sense of loss she would never get over in this world. The old servants about the place had the dumb loyal attachment to the child of the land, common to most agricultural labourers; not often stirred into activity or expression. My cousin Phillis was like a rose that had come to full bloom on the sunny side of a lonely house, sheltered from storms. I have read in some book of poetry—

> A maid whom there were none to praise,
> And very few to love.

And somehow those lines always reminded me of Phillis; yet they were not true of her either. I never heard her praised; and out of her own household there were very few to love her; but though no one spoke out their approbation, she always did right in her parents' eyes, out of her natural simple goodness and wisdom. Holdsworth's name was never mentioned between us when we were alone; but I had sent on his letters to the minister, as I have said; and more than once he began to talk about our absent friend, when he was smoking his pipe after the day's work was done. Then Phillis hung her head a little over her work, and listened in silence.

"I miss him more than I thought for; no offence to you, Paul. I said once his company was like dram-drinking; that was before I knew him; and perhaps I spoke in a spirit of judgment. To some men's minds everything presents itself strongly, and they speak accordingly; and so did he. And I thought in my vanity of censorship that his were not true and sober words; they would not have been if I had used them, but they were so to a man of his class of perceptions. I thought of the measure with which I had been meting to him when Brother Robinson was here last Thursday, and told me that a poor little quotation I was making from the *Georgics* savoured of vain babbling and profane heathenism. He went so far as to say that by learning other languages than our own, we were flying in the face of the Lord's purpose when He had said, at the building of the Tower of Babel, that he would confound their languages so that they should not understand each other's speech. As Brother Robinson was to me, so was I to the quick wits, bright senses, and ready words of Holdsworth."

The first little cloud upon my peace came in the shape of a letter from Canada, in which there were two or three sentences that troubled me more than they ought to have done, to judge merely from the words employed. It was this:—"I should feel dreary enough in this out-of-the-way place if it were not for a friendship I have formed with a French Canadian of the name of Ventadour. He and his family are a great resource to me in the long evenings. I never heard such delicious vocal music as the voices of these Ventadour boys and girls in their part songs; and the foreign element retained in their characters and manner of living reminds me of some of the happiest days of my life. Lucille, the second daughter, is curiously like Phillis Holman." In vain I said to myself that it was probably this likeness that made him take pleasure in the society of the Ventadour family. In vain I told my anxious fancy that nothing could be more natural than this intimacy, and that there was no sign of its leading to any consequence that ought to disturb me. I had a presentiment, and I was disturbed; and I could not reason it away. I dare say my presentiment was rendered more persistent and keen by the doubts which would force themselves into my mind, as to whether I had done well in repeating Holdsworth's words to Phillis. Her state of vivid happiness this summer was markedly different to the peaceful serenity of former days. If in my thoughtfulness at noticing this I caught her eye, she blushed and sparkled all over, guessing that I was remembering our joint secret. Her eyes fell before mine, as if she could hardly bear me to see the revelation of their bright glances. And yet I considered again, and comforted myself by the reflection that, if this change had been anything more than my silly fancy, her father or her mother would have perceived it. But they went on in tranquil unconsciousness and undisturbed peace.

A change in my own life was quickly approaching. In the July of this year my occupation on the —— railway and its branches came to an end. The lines were completed, and I was to leave ——shire, to return to Birmingham, where there was a niche already provided for me in my father's prosperous business. But before I left the north it was an understood thing amongst us all that I was to go and pay a visit of some weeks at the Hope Farm. My father was as much pleased at this plan as I was; and the dear family of cousins often spoke of things to be done, and sights to be shown me, during this visit. My want of wisdom in having told "that thing" (under such ambiguous words I concealed the injudicious confidence I had made to Phillis) was the only draw-back to my anticipations of pleasure.

The ways of life were too simple at the Hope Farm for my coming to them to make the slightest disturbance. I knew my room, like a son of the house. I knew the regular course of their days, and that I was expected to fall into it, like one of the family. Deep summer peace brooded over the place; the warm golden air was filled with the murmur of insects near at hand, the more distant sound of voices out in the fields, the clear far-away rumble of carts over the stone-paved lanes miles away. The heat was too great for the birds to be singing; only now and then one might hear the wood-pigeons in the trees beyond the ash-field. The cattle stood knee-deep in the pond, flicking their tails about to keep off the flies. The minister stood in the hay-field, without hat or cravat, coat or waist-coat, panting and smiling. Phillis had been leading the row of farm-servants, turning the swathes of

fragrant hay with measured movement. She went to the end—to
the hedge, and then, throwing down her rake, she came to me
with her free sisterly welcome. "Go, Paul!" said the minister.
"We need all hands to make use of the sunshine to-day. 'Whatsoever thine hand findeth to do, do it with all thy might.' It will
be a healthy change of work for thee, lad; and I find my best
rest in change of work." So off I went, a willing labourer, following Phillis's lead; it was the primitive distinction of rank;
the boy who frightened the sparrows off the fruit was the last in
our rear. We did not leave off till the red sun was gone down
behind the fir-trees bordering the common. Then we went home
to supper—prayers—to bed; some bird singing far into the night,
as I heard it through my open window, and the poultry beginning
their clatter and cackle in the earliest morning. I had carried
what luggage I immediately needed with me from my lodgings,
and the rest was to be sent by the carrier. He brought it to the
farm betimes that morning, and along with it he brought a letter
or two that had arrived since I had left. I was talking to cousin
Holman—about my mother's ways of making bread, I remember;
cousin Holman was questioning me, and had got me far beyond
my depth—in the house-place, when the letters were brought in
by one of the men, and I had to pay the carrier for his trouble
before I could look at them. A bill—a Canadian letter! What
instinct made me so thankful that I was alone with my dear unobservant cousin? What made me hurry them away into my
coat-pocket? I do not know. I felt strange and sick, and made
irrelevant answers, I am afraid. Then I went to my room, ostensibly to carry up my boxes. I sate on the side of my bed and
opened my letter from Holdsworth. It seemed to me as if I had
read its contents before, and knew exactly what he had got to say.
I knew he was going to be married to Lucille Ventadour; nay,
that he was married; for this was the 5th of July, and he wrote
word that his marriage was fixed to take place on the 29th of
June. I knew all the reasons he gave, all the raptures he went
into. I held the letter loosely in my hands, and looked into
vacancy, yet I saw a chaffinch's nest on the lichen-covered trunk
of an old apple-tree opposite my window, and saw the mother-
bird come fluttering in to feed her brood,—and yet I did not see it,
although it seemed to me afterwards as if I could have drawn

every fibre, every feather. I was stirred up to action by the merry sound of voices and the clamp of rustic feet coming home for the mid-day meal. I knew I must go down to dinner; I knew, too, I must tell Phillis; for in his happy egotism, his new-fangled foppery, Holdsworth had put in a P.S., saying that he should send wedding-cards to me and some other Hornby and Eltham acquaintances, and "to his kind friends at Hope Farm." Phillis had faded away to one among several "kind friends." I don't know how I got through dinner that day. I remember forcing myself to eat, and talking hard; but I also recollect the wondering look in the minister's eyes. He was not one to think evil without cause; but many a one would have taken me for drunk. As soon as I decently could I left the table, saying I would go out for a walk. At first I must have tried to stun reflection by rapid walking, for I had lost myself on the high moorlands far beyond the familiar gorse-covered common, before I was obliged for very weariness to slacken my pace. I kept wishing—oh! how fervently wishing I had never committed that blunder; that the one little half-hour's indiscretion could be blotted out. Alternating with this was anger against Holdsworth; unjust enough, I dare say. I suppose I stayed in that solitary place for a good hour or more, and then I turned homewards, resolving to get over the telling Phillis at the first opportunity, but shrinking from the fulfillment of my resolution so much that when I came into the house and saw Phillis (doors and windows open wide in the sultry weather) alone in the kitchen, I became quite sick with apprehension. She was standing by the dresser, cutting up a great household loaf into hunches of bread for the hungry labourers who might come in any minute, for the heavy thunder-clouds were overspreading the sky. She looked round as she heard my step.

"You should have been in the field, helping with the hay," said she, in her calm, pleasant voice. I had heard her as I came near the house softly chanting some hymn-tune, and the peacefulness of that seemed to be brooding over her now.

"Perhaps I should. It looks as if it was going to rain."

"Yes; there is thunder about. Mother has had to go to bed with one of her bad headaches. Now you are come in ——"

"Phillis," said I, rushing at my subject and interrupting her, "I went a long walk to think over a letter I had this morning—a letter from Canada. You don't know how it has grieved me." I held it out to her as I spoke. Her colour changed a little, but it was more the reflection of my face, I think, than because she formed any definite idea from my words. Still she did not take the letter. I had to bid her read it, before she quite understood what I wished. She sate down rather suddenly as she received it into her hands; and, spreading it on the dresser before her, she rested her forehead on the palms of her hands, her arms supported on the table, her figure a little averted, and her countenance thus shaded. I looked out of the open window; my heart was very heavy. How peaceful it all seemed in the farmyard! Peace and plenty. How still and deep was the silence of the house! Tick-tick went the unseen clock on the wide staircase. I had heard the rustle once, when she turned over the page of thin paper. She must have read to the end. Yet she did not move, or say a word, or even sigh. I kept on looking out of the window, my hands in my pockets. I wonder how long that time really was? It seemed to me interminable—unbearable. At length I looked round at her. She must have felt my look, for she changed her attitude with a quick sharp movement, and caught my eyes.

"Don't look so sorry, Paul," she said. "Don't, please. I can't bear it. There is nothing to be sorry for. I think not, at least. You have not done wrong, at any rate." I felt that I groaned, but I don't think she heard me. "And he,—there's no wrong in his marrying, is there? I'm sure I hope he'll be happy. Oh! how I hope it!" These last words were like a wail; but I believe she was afraid of breaking down, for she changed the key in which she spoke, and hurried on. "Lucille—that's our English Lucy, I suppose? Lucille Holdsworth! It's a pretty name; and I hope—I forget what I was going to say. Oh! it was this. Paul, I think we need never speak about this again; only remember you are not to be sorry. You have not done wrong; you have been very, very kind; and if I see you looking grieved I don't know what I might do;—I might break down, you know."

I think she was on the point of doing so then, but the dark storm came dashing down, and the thunder-cloud broke right above the house, as it seemed. Her mother, roused from sleep, called out for Phillis; the men and women from the hayfield came running into shelter, drenched through. The minister followed, smiling, and not unpleasantly excited by the war of elements; for, by dint of hard work through the long summer's day, the greater part of the hay was safely housed in the barn in the field. Once or twice in the succeeding bustle I came across Phillis, always busy, and, as it seemed to me, always doing the right thing. When I was alone in my own room at night I allowed myself to feel relieved: and to believe that the worst was over, and was not so very bad after all. But the succeeding days were very miserable. Sometimes I thought it must be my fancy that falsely represented Phillis to me as strangely changed, for surely, if this idea of mine was well-founded, her parents—her father and mother—her own flesh and blood—would have been the first to perceive it. Yet they went on in their household peace and content; if anything, a little more cheerfully than usual, for the "harvest of the first-fruits," as the minister called it, had been more bounteous than usual, and there was plenty all around, in which the humblest labourer was made to share. After the one thunderstorm, came one or two lovely serene summer days, during which the hay was all carried; and then succeeded long soft rains filling the ears of corn, and causing the mown grass to spring afresh. The minister allowed himself a few more hours of relaxation and home enjoyment than usual during this wet spell: hard earth-bound frost was his winter holiday; these wet days, after the hay harvest, his summer holiday. We sate with open windows, the fragrance and the freshness called out by the soft-falling rain filling the house-place; while the quiet ceaseless patter among the leaves outside ought to have had the same lulling effect as all other gentle perpetual sounds, such as mill-wheels and bubbling springs, have on the nerves of happy people. But two of us were not happy. I was sure enough of myself, for one. I was worse than sure,—I was wretchedly anxious about Phillis. Ever since that day of the thunderstorm there had been a new, sharp, discordant sound to me in her voice, a sort of jangle in her tone; and her restless eyes had no quietness in them; and her colour came and went without a cause that I could find out. The minister, happy in ignorance of what most concerned him, brought out his books; his learned volumes and classics. Whether he read and talked to Phillis, or to me, I do not know; but feeling by instinct that she was not, could not be, attending to the peaceful details, so strange and foreign to the turmoil in her heart, I forced myself to listen, and if possible to understand.

"Look here!" said the minister, tapping the old vellum-bound book he held; "in the first *Georgic* he speaks of rolling and irrigation; a little further on he insists on choice of the best seed, and advises us to keep the drains clear. Again, no Scotch farmer could give shrewder advice than to cut light meadows while the dew is on, even though it involve night-work. It is all living truth in these days." He began beating time with a ruler upon his knee, to some Latin lines he read aloud just then. I suppose the monotonous chant irritated Phillis to some irregular energy, for I remember the quick knotting and breaking of the thread with which she was sewing. I never hear that snap repeated now, without suspecting some sting or stab troubling the heart of the worker. Cousin Holman, at her peaceful knitting, noticed the reason why Phillis had so constantly to interrupt the progress of her seam.

"It is bad thread, I'm afraid," she said, in a gentle sympathetic voice. But it was too much for Phillis.

"The thread is bad—everything is bad—I am so tired of it all!" And she put down her work, and hastily left the room. I do not suppose that in all her life Phillis had ever shown so much temper before. In many a family the tone, the manner, would not have been noticed; but here it fell with a sharp surprise upon the sweet, calm atmosphere of home. The minister put down ruler and book, and pushed his spectacles up to his forehead. The mother looked distressed for a moment, and then smoothed her features and said in an explanatory tone,—"It's the weather, I think. Some people feel it different to others. It always brings on a headache with me." She got up to follow her daughter, but half-way to the door she thought better of it, and came back to her seat. Good mother! she hoped the better to conceal the unusual spirit of temper, by pretending not to take much notice of it. "Go on, minister," she said; "it is very interesting what you are reading about, and when I don't quite understand it, I like the sound of your voice." So he went on, but languidly and irregularly, and beat no more time with his ruler to any Latin lines. When the dusk came on, early that July night because of the cloudy sky, Phillis came softly back, making as though nothing had happened. She took up her work, but it was too dark to do many stitches; and she dropped it soon. Then I saw how her hand stole into her mother's, and how this latter fondled it with quiet little caresses, while the minister, as fully aware as I was of this tender pantomime, went on talking in a happier tone of voice about things as uninteresting to him, at the time, I verily believe, as they were to me; and that is saying a good deal, and shows how much more real what was passing before him was, even to a farmer, than the agricultural customs of the ancients.

I remember one thing more,—an attack which Betty the servant made upon me one day as I came in through the kitchen where she was churning, and stopped to ask her for a drink of buttermilk.

"I say, cousin Paul," (she had adopted the family habit of addressing me generally as cousin Paul, and always speaking of me in that form,) "something's amiss with our Phillis, and I reckon you've a good guess what it is. She's not one to take up wi' such as you" (not complimentary, but that Betty never was, even to those for whom she felt the highest respect), "but I'd as lief yon Holdsworth had never come near us. So there you've a bit o' my mind."

And a very unsatisfactory bit it was. I did not know what to answer to the glimpse at the real state of the case implied in the shrewd woman's speech; so I tried to put her off by assuming surprise at her first assertion.

"Amiss with Phillis! I should like to know why you think anything is wrong with her. She looks as blooming as any one can do."

"Poor lad! you're but a big child, after all; and you've likely never heared of a fever-flush. But you know better nor that, my fine fellow! so don't think for to put me off wi' blooms and blossoms and such-like talk. What makes her walk about for hours and hours o' nights when she used to be abed and asleep? I sleep next room to her, and hear her plain as can be. What makes her come in panting and ready to drop into that chair,"—nodding to one close to the door,—"and it's 'Oh! Betty, some water, please?' That's the way she comes in now, when she used to come back as fresh and bright as she went out. If yon friend o' yours has played her false, he's a deal for t' answer for: she's a lass who's as sweet and as sound as a nut, and the very apple of her father's eye, and of her mother's too, only wi' her she ranks second to th' minister. You'll have to look after yon chap, for I, for one, will stand no wrong to our Phillis."

What was I to do, or to say? I wanted to justify Holdsworth, to keep Phillis's secret, and to pacify the woman all in the same breath. I did not take the best course, I'm afraid.

"I don't believe Holdsworth ever spoke a word of—of love to her in all his life. I am sure he didn't."

"Ay, ay! but there's eyes, and there's hands, as well as tongues; and a man has two o' th' one and but one o' t'other."

"And she's so young; do you suppose her parents would not have seen it?"

"Well! if you axe me that, I'll say out boldly, 'No.' They've called her 'the child' so long—'the child' is always their name for her when they talk on her between themselves, as if never anybody else had a ewe-lamb before them—that she's grown up to be a woman under their very eyes, and they look on her still as if she were in her long clothes. And you ne'er heard on a man falling in love wi' a babby in long clothes!"

"No!" said I, half laughing. But she went on as grave as a judge.

"Ay! you see you'll laugh at the bare thought on it—and I'll be bound th' minister, though he's not a laughing man, would ha' sniggled at th' notion of falling in love wi' the child. Where's Holdsworth off to?"

"Canada," said I, shortly.

"Canada here, Canada there," she replied, testily. "Tell me how far he's off, instead of giving me your gibberish. Is he a two days' journey away? or a three? or a week?"

"He's ever so far off—three weeks at the least," cried I in despair. "And he's either married, or just going to be. So there!" I expected a fresh burst of anger. But no; the matter was too serious. Betty sate down, and kept silence for a minute or two. She looked so miserable and downcast, that I could not help going on, and taking her a little into my confidence.

"It is quite true what I said. I know he never spoke a word to her. I think he liked her, but it's all over now. The best thing we can do—the best and kindest for her—and I know you love her, Betty——"

"I nursed her in my arms; I gave her little brother his last taste o' earthly food," said Betty, putting her apron up to her eyes.

"Well! don't let us show her we guess that she is grieving; she'll get over it the sooner. Her father and mother don't even guess at it, and we must make as if we didn't. It's too late now to do anything else."

"I'll never let on; I know nought. I've known true love mysel', in my day. But I wish he'd been farred before he ever came near this house, with his 'Please Betty' this, and 'Please Betty' that, and drinking up our new milk as if he'd been a cat. I hate such beguiling ways."

I thought it was as well to let her exhaust herself in abusing the absent Holdsworth; if it was shabby and treacherous in me, I came in for my punishment directly.

"It's a caution to a man how he goes about beguiling. Some men do it as easy and innocent as cooing doves. Don't you be none of 'em, my lad. Not that you've got the gifts to do it, either; you're no great shakes to look at, neither for figure nor yet for face, and it would need be a deaf adder to be taken wi' your words, though there may be no great harm in 'em." A lad of nineteen or twenty is not flattered by such an outspoken opinion even from the oldest and ugliest of her sex; and I was only too glad to change the subject by my repeated injunctions to keep Phillis's secret. The end of our conversation was this speech of hers:—

"You great gaupus, for all you're called cousin o' th' minister —many a one is cursed wi' fools for cousins—d'ye think I can't see sense except through your spectacles? I give you leave to cut out my tongue, and nail it up on th' barn-door for a caution to magpies, if I let out on that poor wench, either to herself, or any one that is hers, as the Bible says. Now you've heard me speak Scripture language, perhaps you'll be content, and leave me my kitchen to myself."

During all these days, from the 5th of July to the 17th, I must have forgotten what Holdsworth had said about sending cards. And yet I think I could not have quite forgotten; but, once having told Phillis about his marriage, I must have looked upon the after consequence of cards as of no importance. At any rate, they came upon me as a surprise at last. The penny-post reform, as people call it, had come into operation a short time before; but the never-ending stream of notes and letters which seem now to flow in upon most households had not yet begun its course; at least in those remote parts. There was a post-office at Hornby; and an old fellow, who stowed away the few letters in any or all his pockets, as it best suited him, was the letter-carrier to Heathbridge and the neighbourhood. I have often met him in the lanes thereabouts, and asked him for letters. Sometimes I have come upon him, sitting on the hedge-bank resting; and he has begged me to read him an address, too illegible for his spectacled eyes to decipher. When I used to inquire if he had anything for me, or for Holdsworth (he was not particular to whom he gave up the letters, so that he got rid of them somehow, and could set off homewards), he would say he thought that he had, for such was his invariable safe form of answer; and would fumble in breast-pockets, waistcoat-pockets, breeches-pockets, and, as a last resource, in coat-tail pockets; and at length try to comfort me, if I looked disappointed, by telling me, "Hoo had missed this toime, but was sure to write to-morrow;" "Hoo" representing an imaginary sweetheart.

Sometimes I had seen the minister bring home a letter which he had found lying for him at the little shop that was the post-office at Heathbridge, or from the grander establishment at Hornby. Once or twice Josiah, the carter, remembered that the old letter-carrier had trusted him with an epistle to "Measter," as they had met in the lanes. I think it must have been about ten days after my arrival at the farm, and my talk to Phillis cutting bread-and-butter at the kitchen dresser, before the day on which the minister suddenly spoke at the dinner-table, and said—

"By-the-by, I've got a letter in my pocket. Reach me my coat here, Phillis." The weather was still sultry, and for coolness and ease the minister was sitting in his shirt-sleeves. "I went to Heathbridge about the paper they had sent me, which spoils all the pens—and I called at the post-office, and found a letter for me, unpaid,—and they did not like to trust it to old Zekiel. Ay! here it is! Now we shall hear news of Holdsworth, —I thought I'd keep it till we were all together." My heart seemed to stop beating, and I hung my head over my plate, not daring to look up. What would come of it now? What was Phillis doing? How was she looking? A moment of suspense, —and then he spoke again. "Why! what's this? Here are two visiting tickets with his name on, no writing at all. No! it's not his name on both. MRS. Holdsworth. The young man has gone and got married." I lifted my head at these words; I could not help looking just for one instant at Phillis. It seemed to me as if she had been keeping watch over my face and ways. Her face was brilliantly flushed; her eyes were dry and glittering; but she did not speak; her lips were set together almost as if she was pinching them tight to prevent words or sounds coming out. Cousin Holman's face expressed surprise and interest.

"Well!" said she, "who'd ha' thought it! He's made quick work of his wooing and wedding. I'm sure I wish him happy. Let me see"—counting on her fingers,—"October, November, December, January, February, March, April, May, June, July,— at least we're at the 28th,—it is nearly ten months after all, and reckon a month each way off——"

"Did you know of this news before?" said the minister, turning sharp round on me, surprised, I suppose, at my silence,— hardly suspicious, as yet.

"I knew—I had heard—something. It is to a French Canadian lady," I went on, forcing myself to talk. "Her name is Ventadour."

"Lucille Ventadour!" said Phillis, in a sharp voice, out of tune.

"Then you knew, too!" exclaimed the minister.

We both spoke at once. I said, "I heard of the probability of——, and told Phillis." She said, "He is married to Lucille Ventadour, of French descent; one of a large family near St. Meurice; am not I right?" I nodded. "Paul told me,—that is all we know, is not it? Did you see the Howsons, father, in Heathbridge?" and she forced herself to talk more than she had done for several days, asking many questions, trying, as I could see, to keep the conversation off the one raw surface, on which to touch was agony. I had less self-command; but I followed her lead. I was not so much absorbed in the conversation but what I could see that the minister was puzzled and uneasy; though he seconded Phillis's efforts to prevent her mother from recurring to the great piece of news, and uttering continual exclamations of wonder and surprise. But with that one exception we were all disturbed out of our natural equanimity, more or less. Every day, every hour, I was reproaching myself more and more for my blundering officiousness. If only I had held my foolish tongue for that one half-hour; if only I had not been in such impatient haste to do something to relieve pain! I could have knocked my stupid head against the wall in my remorse. Yet all I could do now was to second the brave girl in her efforts to conceal her disappointment and keep her maidenly secret. But I thought that dinner would never, never come to an end. I suffered for her, even more than for myself. Until now everything which I had heard spoken in that happy household were simple words of true meaning. If we had aught to say, we said it; and if any one preferred silence, nay if all did so, there would have been no spasmodic, forced efforts to talk for the sake of talking, or to keep off intrusive thoughts or suspicions.

At length we got up from our places, and prepared to disperse; but two or three of us had lost our zest and interest in the daily labour. The minister stood looking out of the window in silence, and when he roused himself to go out to the fields where his labourers were working, it was with a sigh; and he tried to avert his troubled face as he passed us on his way to the door. When he had left us, I caught sight of Phillis's face, as, thinking herself unobserved, her countenance relaxed for a moment or two into sad, woeful weariness. She started into briskness again when her mother spoke, and hurried away to do some little errand at her bidding. When we two were alone, cousin Holman recurred to Holdsworth's marriage. She was one of those people who like to view an event from every side of probability, or even possibility; and she had been cut short from indulging herself in this way during dinner.

"To think of Mr. Holdsworth's being married! I can't get over it, Paul. Not but what he was a very nice young man! I don't like her name, though; it sounds foreign. Say it again, my dear. I hope she'll know how to take care of him, English fashion. He is not strong, and if she does not see that his things are well aired, I should be afraid of the old cough."

"He always said he was stronger than he had ever been before, after that fever."

"He might think so, but I have my doubts. He was a very

pleasant young man, but he did not stand nursing very well. He got tired of being coddled, as he called it. I hope they'll soon come back to England, and then he'll have a chance for his health. I wonder now, if she speaks English; but, to be sure, he can speak foreign tongues like anything, as I've heard the minister say."

And so we went on for some time, till she became drowsy over her knitting, on the sultry summer afternoon; and I stole away for a walk, for I wanted some solitude in which to think over things, and, alas! to blame myself with poignant stabs of remorse.

I lounged lazily as soon as I got to the wood. Here and there the bubbling, brawling brook circled round a great stone, or a root of an old tree, and made a pool; otherwise it coursed brightly over the gravel and stones. I stood by one of these for more than half an hour, or, indeed, longer, throwing bits of wood or pebbles into the water, and wondering what I could do to remedy the present state of things. Of course all my meditation was of no use; and at length the distant sound of the horn employed to tell the men far afield to leave off work, warned me that it was six o'clock, and time for me to go home. Then I caught wafts of the loud-voiced singing of the evening psalm. As I was crossing the ash-field, I saw the minister at some distance talking to a man. I could not hear what they were saying, but I saw an impatient or dissentient (I could not tell which) gesture on the part of the former, who walked quickly away, and was apparently absorbed in his thoughts, for though he passed within twenty yards of me, as both our paths converged towards home, he took no notice of me. He passed the evening in a way which was even worse than dinner-time. The minister was silent, depressed, even irritable. Poor cousin Holman was utterly perplexed by this unusual frame of mind and temper in her husband; she was not well herself, and was suffering from the extreme and sultry heat, which made her less talkative than usual. Phillis, usually so reverently tender to her parents, so soft, so gentle, seemed now to take no notice of the unusual state of things, but talked to me—to any one, on indifferent subjects, regardless of her father's gravity, of her mother's piteous looks of bewilderment. But once my eyes fell upon her hands, concealed under the table, and I could see the passionate, convulsive manner in which she laced and interlaced her fingers perpetually, wringing them together from time to time, wringing till the compressed flesh became perfectly white. What could I do? I talked with her, as I saw she wished: her grey eyes had dark circles round them, and a strange kind of dark light in them; her cheeks were flushed, but her lips were white and wan. I wondered that others did not read these signs as clearly as I did. But perhaps they did; I think, from what came afterwards, the minister did.

Poor cousin Holman! she worshipped her husband; and the outward signs of his uneasiness were more patent to her simple heart than were her daughter's. After a while she could bear it no longer. She got up, and, softly laying her hand on his broad stooping shoulder, she said,—

"What is the matter, minister? Has anything gone wrong?"

He started as if from a dream. Phillis hung her head, and caught her breath in terror at the answer she feared. But he, looking round with a sweeping glance, turned his broad, wise face up to his anxious wife, and forced a smile, and took her hand in a reassuring manner.

"I am blaming myself, dear. I have been overcome with anger this afternoon. I scarcely knew what I was doing, but I turned away Timothy Cooper. He has killed the Ribstone pippin at the corner of the orchard; gone and piled the quicklime for the mortar for the new stable wall against the trunk of the tree—stupid fellow! killed the tree outright—and it loaded with apples!"

"And Ribstone pippins are so scarce," said sympathetic cousin Holman.

"Ay! But Timothy is but a half-wit; and he has a wife and children. He had often put me to it sore, with his slothful ways, but I had laid it before the Lord, and striven to bear with him. But I will not stand it any longer, it's past my patience. And he has notice to find another place. Wife, we won't talk more about it." He took her hand gently off his shoulder, touched it with his lips; but relapsed into a silence as profound, if not quite so morose in appearance, as before. I could not tell why, but this bit of talk between her father and mother seemed to take all the factitious spirits out of Phillis. She did not speak now, but looked out of the open casement at the calm large moon, slowly moving through the twilight sky. Once I thought her eyes were filling with tears; but, if so, she shook them off, and arose with

alacrity when her mother, tired and dispirited, proposed to go to
bed immediately after prayers. We all said good-night in our
separate ways to the minister, who still sat at the table with the
great Bible open before him, not much looking up at any of our
salutations, but returning them kindly. But when I, last of all, was
on the point of leaving the room, he said, still scarcely looking
up—

"Paul, you will oblige me by staying here a few minutes. I
would fain have some talk with you."

I knew what was coming, all in a moment. I carefully shut-to
the door, put out my candle, and sat down to my fate. He seemed
to find some difficulty in beginning, for, if I had not heard that he
wanted to speak to me, I should never have guessed it, he seemed
so much absorbed in reading a chapter to the end. Suddenly he
lifted his head up and said,—

"It is about that friend of yours, Holdsworth! Paul, have you
any reason for thinking he has played tricks upon Phillis?"

I saw that his eyes were blazing with such a fire of anger at the
bare idea, that I lost all my presence of mind, and only repeated,—

"Played tricks on Phillis!"

"Ay! you know what I mean: made love to her, courted her,
made her think that he loved her, and then gone away and left
her. Put it as you will, only give me an answer of some kind or
another—a true answer, I mean—and don't repeat my words,
Paul."

He was shaking all over as he said this. I did not delay a
moment in answering him,—

"I do not believe that Edward Holdsworth ever played tricks
on Phillis, ever made love to her; he never, to my knowledge,
made her believe that he loved her."

I stopped; I wanted to nerve up my courage for a confession,
yet I wished to save the secret of Phillis's love for Holdsworth as
much as I could; that secret which she had so striven to keep
sacred and safe; and I had need of some reflection before I went
on with what I had to say.

He began again before I had quite arranged my manner of
speech. It was almost as if to himself,—"She is my only child;
my little daughter! She is hardly out of childhood; I have
thought to gather her under my wings for years to come; her

373

mother and I would lay down our lives to keep her from harm and grief." Then, raising his voice, and looking at me, he said, "Something has gone wrong with the child; and it seems to me to date from the time she heard of that marriage. It is hard to think that you may know more of her secret cares and sorrows than I do,—but perhaps you do, Paul, perhaps you do,—only, if it be not a sin, tell me what I can do to make her happy again; tell me."

"It will not do much good, I am afraid," said I, "but I will own how wrong I did; I don't mean wrong in the way of sin, but in the way of judgment. Holdsworth told me just before he went that he loved Phillis, and hoped to make her his wife, and I told her."

There! it was out; all my part in it, at least; and I set my lips tight together, and waited for the words to come. I did not see his face; I looked straight at the wall opposite; but I heard him once begin to speak, and then turn over the leaves in the book before him. How awfully still that room was! The air outside, how still it was! The open window let in no rustle of leaves, no twitter or movement of birds—no sound whatever. The clock on the stairs—the minister's hard breathing—was it to go on for ever? Impatient beyond bearing at the deep quiet, I spoke again,—

"I did it for the best, as I thought."

The minister shut the book to hastily, and stood up. Then I saw how angry he was.

"For the best, do you say? It was best, was it, to go and tell a young girl what you never told a word of to her parents, who trusted you like a son of their own?"

He began walking about, up and down the room close under the open windows, churning up his bitter thoughts of me.

"To put such thoughts into the child's head," continued he; "to spoil her peaceful maidenhood with talk about another man's love; and such love, too," he spoke scornfully now—"a love that is ready for any young woman. Oh, the misery in my poor little daughter's face to-day at dinner—the misery, Paul! I thought you were one to be trusted—your father's son too, to go and put such thoughts into the child's mind; you two talking together about that man wishing to marry her."

I could not help remembering the pinafore, the childish garment which Phillis wore so long, as if her parents were unaware of her progress towards womanhood. Just in the same way the minister spoke and thought of her now, as a child, whose innocent peace I had spoiled by vain and foolish talk. I knew that the truth was different, though I could hardly have told it now; but, indeed, I never thought of trying to tell; it was far from my mind to add one iota to the sorrow which I had caused. The minister went on walking, occasionally stopping to move things on the table, or articles of furniture, in a sharp, impatient, meaningless way, then he began again,—

"So young, so pure from the world! how could you go and talk to such a child, raising hopes, exciting feelings—all to end thus; and best so, even though I saw her poor piteous face look as it did? I can't forgive you, Paul; it was more than wrong—it was wicked—to go and repeat that man's words."

His back was now to the door, and, in listening to his low angry tones, he did not hear it slowly open, nor did he see Phillis, standing just within the room, until he turned round; then he stood still. She must have been half undressed; but she had covered herself with a dark winter cloak, which fell in long folds to her white, naked, noiseless feet. Her face was strangely pale: her eyes heavy in the black circles round them. She came up to the table very slowly, and leant her hand upon it, saying mournfully,—

"Father, you must not blame Paul. I could not help hearing a great deal of what you were saying. He did tell me, and perhaps it would have been wiser not, dear Paul! But—oh, dear! oh, dear! I am so sick with shame! He told me out of his kind heart, because he saw—that I was so very unhappy at *his* going away."

She hung her head, and leant more heavily than before on her supporting hand.

"I don't understand," said her father; but he was beginning to understand. Phillis did not answer till he asked her again. I could have struck him now for his cruelty; but then I knew all.

"I loved him, father!" she said at length, raising her eyes to the minister's face.

"Had he ever spoken of love to you? Paul says not!"

"Never." She let fall her eyes, and drooped more than ever. I almost thought she would fall.

"I could not have believed it," said he, in a hard voice, yet sighing the moment he had spoken. A dead silence for a moment. "Paul! I was unjust to you. You deserved blame, but not all that I said." Then again a silence. I thought I saw Phillis's white lips moving, but it might be the flickering of the candlelight—a moth had flown in through the open casement, and was fluttering round the flame; I might have saved it, but I did not care to do so, my heart was too full of other things. At any rate, no sound was heard for long endless minutes. Then he said,—"Phillis! did we not make you happy here? Have we not loved you enough?"

She did not seem to understand the drift of this question; she looked up as if bewildered, and her beautiful eyes dilated with a painful, tortured expression. He went on without noticing the look on her face; he did not see it, I am sure.

"And yet you would have left us, left your home, left your father and your mother, and gone away with this stranger, wandering over the world."

He suffered, too; there were tones of pain in the voice in which he uttered this reproach. Probably the father and daughter were never so far apart in their lives, so unsympathetic. Yet some new terror came over her, and it was to him she turned for help. A shadow came over her face, and she tottered towards her father; falling down, her arms across his knees, and moaning out,—

"Father, my head! my head!" and then she slipped through his quick-enfolding arms, and lay on the ground at his feet.

I shall never forget his sudden look of agony while I live; never! We raised her up; her colour had strangely darkened; she was insensible. I ran through the back-kitchen to the yard pump, and brought back water. The minister had her on his knees, her head against his breast, almost as though she were a sleeping child. He was trying to rise up with his poor precious burden, but the momentary terror had robbed the strong man of his strength, and he sank back in his chair with sobbing breath.

"She is not dead, Paul! is she?" he whispered, hoarse, as I came near him.

I, too, could not speak, but I pointed to the quivering of the muscles round her mouth. Just then cousin Holman, attracted by some unwonted sound, came down. I remember I was surprised at the time at her presence of mind, she seemed to know so much better what to do than the minister, in the midst of the sick affright which blanched her countenance, and made her tremble all over. I think now that it was the recollection of what had gone before; the miserable thought that possibly his words had brought on this attack, whatever it might be, that so unmanned the minister. We carried her upstairs, and while the women were putting her to bed, still unconscious, still slightly convulsed, I slipped out, and saddled one of the horses, and rode as fast as the heavy-trotting beast could go, to Hornby, to find the doctor there, and bring him back. He was out, might be detained the whole night. I remember saying, "God help us all!" as I sate on my horse, under the window, through which the apprentice's head had appeared to answer my furious tugs at the night-bell. He was a good-natured fellow. He said,—

"He may be home in half an hour, there's no knowing; but I daresay he will. I'll send him out to the Hope Farm directly he comes in. It's that good-looking young woman, Holman's daughter, that's ill, isn't it?"

"Yes."

"It would be a pity if she was to go. She's an only child, isn't she? I'll get up, and smoke a pipe in the surgery, ready for the governor's coming home. I might go to sleep if I went to bed again."

"Thank you, you're a good fellow!" and I rode back almost as quickly as I came.

It was a brain fever. The doctor said so, when he came in the early summer morning. I believe we had come to know the nature of the illness in the night-watches that had gone before. As to hope of ultimate recovery, or even evil prophecy of the probable end, the cautious doctor would be entrapped into neither. He gave his directions, and promised to come again; so soon, that this one thing showed his opinion of the gravity of the case.

By God's mercy she recovered, but it was a long, weary time first. According to previously made plans, I was to have gone home at the beginning of August. But all such ideas were put aside now, without a word being spoken. I really think that I was necessary in the house, and especially necessary to the minister at this time; my father was the last man in the world, under such circumstances, to expect me home.

I say I think I was necessary in the house. Every person (I had almost said every creature, for all the dumb beasts seemed to know and love Phillis) about the place went grieving and sad, as though a cloud was over the sun. They did their work, each striving to steer clear of the temptation to eye-service, in fulfilment of the trust reposed in them by the minister. For the day after Phillis had been taken ill, he had called all the men employed on the farm into the empty barn; and there he had entreated their prayers for his only child; and then and there he had told them of his present incapacity for thought about any other thing in this world but his little daughter, lying nigh unto death, and he had asked them to go on with their daily labours as best they could, without his direction. So, as I say, these honest men did their work to the best of their ability, but they slouched along with sad and careful faces, coming one by one in the dim mornings to ask news of the sorrow that overshadowed the house; and receiving Betty's intelligence, always rather darkened by passing through her mind, with slow shakes of the head, and a dull wistfulness of sympathy. But, poor fellows, they were hardly fit to be trusted with hasty messages, and here my poor services came in. One time I was to ride hard to Sir William Bentinck's, and petition for ice out of his ice-house, to put on Phillis's head. Another it was to Eltham I must go, by train, horse, anyhow, and bid the doctor there come for a consultation, for fresh symptoms had appeared, which Mr. Brown, of Hornby, considered unfavourable. Many an hour have I sate on the window-seat, half-way up the stairs, close by the old clock, listening in the hot stillness of the house for the sounds in the sick-room. The minister and I met often, but spoke together seldom. He looked so old—so old! He shared the nursing with his wife; the strength that was needed seemed to be given to them both in that day. They required no one else about their child. Every office about her was sacred to them; even Betty only went into the room for the most necessary purposes. Once I saw Phillis through the open door; her pretty golden hair had been cut off long before; her head was covered with wet cloths, and she was moving it backwards and forwards on the pillow, with weary, never-ending motion, her poor eyes shut, trying in the old accustomed way to croon out a hymn tune, but perpetually breaking it up into moans of pain. Her mother sate by her, tearless, changing the cloths upon her head with patient solicitude. I did not see the minister at first, but there he was in a dark corner, down upon his knees, his hands clasped together in passionate prayer. Then the door shut, and I saw no more.

One day he was wanted; and I had to summon him. Brother Robinson and another minister, hearing of his "trial," had come to see him. I told him this upon the stair-landing in a whisper. He was strangely troubled.

"They will want me to lay bare my heart. I cannot do it. Paul, stay with me. They mean well; but as for spiritual help at such a time—it is God only, God only, who can give it."

So I went in with him. They were two ministers from the neighbourhood; both older than Ebenezer Holman; but evidently inferior to him in education and worldly position. I thought they looked at me as if I were an intruder, but remembering the minister's words I held my ground, and took up one of poor Phillis's books (of which I could not read a word) to have an ostensible occupation. Presently I was asked to "engage in prayer," and we all knelt down; Brother Robinson "leading," and quoting largely as I remember from the Book of Job. He seemed to take for his text, if texts are ever taken for prayers, "Behold thou hast instructed many; but now it is come upon thee, and thou faintest, it toucheth thee and thou art troubled." When we others rose up, the minister continued for some minutes on his knees. Then he too got up, and stood facing us, for a moment, before we all sate down in conclave. After a pause Robinson began—

"We grieve for you, Brother Holman, for your trouble is great. But we would fain have you remember you are as a light set on a hill; and the congregations are looking at you with watchful eyes. We have been talking as we came along on the two duties required of you in this strait; Brother Hodgson and me. And we have resolved to exhort you on these two points. First, God has given you the opportunity of showing forth an example of resignation." Poor Mr. Holman visibly winced at this word. I could fancy how he had tossed aside such brotherly preachings in his happier moments; but now his whole system was unstrung, and "resignation" seemed a term which presupposed that the dreaded misery of losing Phillis was inevitable. But good, stupid Mr. Robinson went on. "We hear on all sides that there are scarce any hopes of your child's recovery; and it may be well to bring you to mind of Abraham; and how he was willing to kill his only child when the Lord commanded. Take

379

example by him, Brother Holman. Let us hear you say, 'The Lord giveth and the Lord taketh away. Blessed be the name of the Lord!' "

There was a pause of expectancy. I verily believe the minister tried to feel it; but he could not. Heart of flesh was too strong. Heart of stone he had not.

"I will say it to my God, when he gives me strength—when the day comes," he spoke at last.

The other two looked at each other, and shook their heads. I think the reluctance to answer as they wished was not quite unexpected. The minister went on: "There are hopes yet," he said, as if to himself. "God has given me a great heart for hoping, and I will not look forward beyond the hour." Then turning more to them, and speaking louder, he added: "Brethren, God will strengthen me when the time comes, when such resignation as you speak of is needed. Till then I cannot feel it; and what I do not feel I will not express; using words as if they were a charm." He was getting chafed, I could see.

He had rather put them out by these speeches of his; but after a short time, and some more shakes of the head, Robinson began again,—

"Secondly, we would have you listen to the voice of the rod, and ask yourself for what sins this trial has been laid upon you; whether you may not have been too much given up to your farm and your cattle; whether this world's learning has not puffed you up to vain conceit and neglect of the things of God; whether you have not made an idol of your daughter?"

"I cannot answer—I will not answer!" exclaimed the minister. "My sins I confess to God. But if they were scarlet (and they are so in His sight," he added, humbly), "I hold with Christ that afflictions are not sent by God in wrath as penalties for sin."

"Is that orthodox, Brother Robinson?" asked the third minister, in a deferential tone of inquiry.

Despite the minister's injunction not to leave him, I thought matters were getting so serious that a little homely interruption would be more to the purpose than my continued presence, and I went round to the kitchen to ask for Betty's help.

" 'Od rot 'em!" said she; "they're always a-coming at illconvenient times; and they have such hearty appetites, they'll make nothing of

what would have served master and you since our poor lass has
been ill. I've but a bit of cold beef in th' house; but I'll do some
ham and eggs, and that'll rout 'em from worrying the minister.
They're a deal quieter after they've had their victual. Last time as
old Robinson came, he was very reprehensible upon master's learning, which he couldn't compass to save his life, so he needn't have
been afeard of that temptation, and used words long enough to
have knocked a body down; but after me and missus had given him
his fill of victual, and he'd had some good ale and a pipe, he spoke
just like any other man, and could crack a joke with me."

Their visit was the only break in the long weary days and
nights. I do not mean that no other inquiries were made. I believe
that all the neighbours hung about the place daily till they could
learn from some out-comer how Phillis Holman was. But they knew
better than to come up to the house, for the August weather was
so hot that every door and window was kept constantly open, and
the least sound outside penetrated all through. I am sure the cocks
and hens had a sad time of it; for Betty drove them all into an
empty barn, and kept them fastened up in the dark for several days,
with very little effect as regarded their crowing and clacking. At
length came a sleep which was the crisis, and from which she
wakened up with a new faint life. Her slumber had lasted many,
many hours. We scarcely dared to breathe or move during the
time; we had striven to hope so long, that we were sick at heart,
and durst not trust in the favourable signs: the even breathing, the
moistened skin, the slight return of delicate colour into the pale,
wan lips. I recollect stealing out that evening in the dusk, and
wandering down the grassy lane, under the shadow of the over-
arching elms to the little bridge at the foot of the hill, where the
lane to the Hope Farm joined another road to Hornby. On the
low parapet of that bridge I found Timothy Cooper, the stupid,
half-witted labourer, sitting, idly throwing bits of mortar into the
brook below. He just looked up at me as I came near, but gave me
no greeting, either by word or gesture. He had generally made
some sign of recognition to me, but this time I thought he was
sullen at being dismissed. Nevertheless I felt as if it would be a
relief to talk a little to some one, and I sate down by him. While
I was thinking how to begin, he yawned wearily.

"You are tired, Tim," said I.

"Ay," said he. "But I reckon I may go home now."

"Have you been sitting here long?"

"Welly all day long. Leastways sin' seven i' th' morning."

"Why, what in the world have you been doing?"

"Nought."

"Why have you been sitting here, then?"

"T' keep carts off." He was up now, stretching himself, and shaking his lubberly limbs.

"Carts! what carts?"

"Carts as might ha' wakened yon wench! It's Hornby marketday. I reckon yo're no better nor a half-wit yoursel'." He cocked his eye at me as if he were gauging my intellect.

"And have you been sitting here all day to keep the lane quiet?"

"Ay. I've nought else to do. Th' minister has turned me adrift. Have yo' heard how th' lass is faring to-night?"

"They hope she'll waken better for this long sleep. Goodnight to you, and God bless you, Timothy," said I.

He scarcely took any notice of my words, as he lumbered across a stile that led to his cottage. Presently I went home to the farm. Phillis had stirred, had spoken two or three faint words. Her mother was with her, dropping nourishment into her scarce conscious mouth. The rest of the household were summoned to evening prayer for the first time in many days. It was a return to the daily habits of happiness and health. But in these silent days our very lives had been an unspoken prayer. Now we met in the houseplace, and looked at each other with strange recognition of the thankfulness on all our faces. We knelt down; we waited for the minister's voice. He did not begin as usual. He could not; he was choking. Presently we heard the strong man's sob. Then old John turned round on his knees, and said—

"Minister, I reckon we have blessed the Lord wi' all our souls, though we've ne'er talked about it; and maybe He'll not need spoken words this night. God bless us all, and keep our Phillis safe from harm! Amen."

Old John's impromptu prayer was all we had that night.

"Our Phillis," as he had called her, grew better day by day from that time. Not quickly; I sometimes grew desponding, and feared that she would never be what she had been before; no more she has, in some ways.

I seized an early opportunity to tell the minister about Timothy Cooper's unsolicited watch on the bridge during the long summer's day.

"God forgive me!" said the minister. "I have been too proud in my own conceit. The first steps I take out of this house shall be to Cooper's cottage."

I need hardly say Timothy was reinstated in his place on the farm; and I have often since admired the patience with which his master tried to teach him how to do the easy work which was henceforward carefully adjusted to his capacity.

Phillis was carried downstairs, and lay for hour after hour quite silent on the great sofa, drawn up under the windows of the house-place. She seemed always the same, gentle, quiet, and sad. Her energy did not return with her bodily strength. It was sometimes pitiful to see her parents' vain endeavours to rouse her to interest. One day the minister brought her a set of blue ribbons, reminding her with a tender smile of a former conversation in which she had owned to a love of such feminine vanities. She spoke gratefully to him, but when he was gone she laid them on one side, and languidly shut her eyes. Another time I saw her mother bring her the Latin and Italian books that she had been so fond of before her illness—or, rather, before Holdsworth had gone away. That was worst of all. She turned her face to the wall, and cried as soon as her mother's back was turned. Betty was laying the cloth for the early dinner. Her sharp eyes saw the state of the case.

"Now, Phillis!" said she, coming up to the sofa; "we ha' done a' we can for you, and th' doctors has done a' they can for you, and I think the Lord has done a' He can for you, and more than you deserve, too, if you don't do something for yourself. If I were you, I'd rise up and snuff the moon, sooner than break your father's and your mother's hearts wi' watching and waiting till it pleases you to fight your own way back to cheerfulness. There, I never favoured long preachings, and I've said my say."

A day or two after Phillis asked me, when we were alone, if I thought my father and mother would allow her to go and stay with them for a couple of months. She blushed a little as she faltered out her wish for change of thought and scene.

"Only for a short time, Paul. Then—we will go back to the peace of the old days. I know we shall; I can, and I will!"

The Lifted Veil
1859

GEORGE ELIOT

GEORGE ELIOT was born in 1819, the same year as Whitman and Melville and two years before Flaubert and Dostoevsky. She belongs therefore to that crucial and marvellously gifted generation who shouldered the pale corpse of romanticism and marched forward into the modern world, creating the modern novel on their way. Even as one employs quite a different set of criteria to write about Madame Bovary to that one would apply to Balzac, even as there is nothing one could say about Flaubert to which he would not be qualified to reply, while there is a great deal one might say about Balzac or Stendhal which, despite their brilliance, they could never understand, so George Eliot is a not unworthy counterpart; an intellectual whom one could address in terms which would be meaningless to Trollope or Thackeray or Mrs. Gaskell. Alas, I am not the person to address her, for this story, The Lifted Veil, is the one work of hers that I have ever been able to read and only the demands of this anthology have led me to discover it! The very titles of her novels whisper to the sybarite, "Keep Out." Once again I must call Lord David Cecil to the rescue with his admirable evaluation of the only English lady to have won the friendship of Henry James and the admiration of Proust. "They are the first novels," he writes, "which set out to give a picture of life wholly unmodified by those formulas of a good plot which the novel had taken over from comedy and romance. Her story is conditioned solely by the logical demands of situation or character. It ends sadly or happily, it includes heroes or omits them, deals with the married or the unmarried, according as reason and observation lead her to think likely. In fact, the laws conditioning the form of George Eliot's novels are the same laws that condition those of Henry James and Wells and Conrad and Arnold Bennett. Hers are the first examples in English of the novel in its mature form;

in them it structurally comes of age. It comes of age in spirit too."

That she is not admired as much as Trollope or the Brontës, that she is not read or, if read, not enjoyed he ascribes to her puritanism, "nor does she, like some puritan writers, like Bunyan for instance, sweep away our antipathy to her moral system by the enthusiastic convictions with which she expounds it. It was impossible that she should; she did not feel enthusiastic about it herself. . . . Indeed—and here we come to the root cause of her failure to attain that supreme rank to which she aspired—there was something second-rate in the essential quality of George Eliot's inspiration. Her genius was built on the same grand scale as that of the greatest novelist; but it was not, as theirs was, compounded of the best material. She had more talents than most writers; they were none of them of the finest calibre. All the same, her achievement is a considerable one, more considerable than that of many more accomplished writers. Middlemarch may never give us the same feeling of unalloyed pleasure as Wives and Daughters does, but it rouses far deeper emotions, sets the mind far more seriously astir. For though she was not a supreme artist, George Eliot was not a minor one; laboriously but surely her insight, her integrity, her sad, mature wisdom, lifted her to the region of major art."

The Lifted Veil appeared in 1859. It is difficult to say anything about it without giving away the story, but I should like to draw attention both to the sustained intellectual sweep and the grace and skill of the construction of this lovely and moving tale. It is, one feels, all true—'sans style et sans epôque.' One sentence is outstanding: "The obtrusion on my mind of the mental process going forward in first one person and then another with whom I happened to be in contact; the vagrant frivolous ideas and emotions of some uninteresting acquaintance would force themselves on my consciousness like an importunate ill-played musical instrument, or the loud activity of an imprisoned insect." George Eliot seems to have possessed some such gift herself and it is that which makes this little known tale, by-product of a novelist who was a moralist by upbringing and a rationalist by environment, so haunting and poignant. There seems also a strange new quality about the writing—or is that a hallucination produced by the presence in the mid-Nineteenth Century of a genuine high-brow?

George Eliot's real name was Mary Ann Evans, she lived for many years in irreproachable sin with Henry Lewes, the biographer of Goethe. He died in 1878 and she married his old friend John Cross in 1880, dying herself in the same year, a few months after Flaubert. "She is magnificently ugly—deliciously hideous. She has a low forehead, a dull grey eye, a vast pendulous nose, a huge mouth full of uneven teeth and a chin and jaw bone qui n'en finissent pas . . . now in this vast ugliness resides a most powerful beauty which, in a very few minutes, steals forth and charms the mind, so that you end as I ended, in falling in love with her" (Henry James).

The Lifted Veil

GEORGE ELIOT

Chapter 1

THE TIME OF my end approaches. I have lately been subject to attacks of *angina pectoris*; and in the ordinary course of things, my physician tells me, I may fairly hope that my life will not be protracted many months. Unless, then, I am cursed with an exceptional physical constitution, as I am cursed with an exceptional mental character, I shall not much longer groan under the wearisome burden of this earthly existence. If it were to be otherwise—if I were to live on to the age most men desire and provide for—I should, for once, have known whether the miseries of delusive expectation can outweigh the miseries of true prevision. For I foresee when I shall die, and everything that will happen in my last moments.

Just a month from this day, on the twentieth of September, 1850, I shall be sitting in this chair, in this study, at ten o'clock at night, longing to die, weary of incessant insight and foresight, without delusions and without hope. Just as I am watching a tongue of blue flame rising in the fire, and my lamp is burning low, the horrible contraction will begin at my chest. I shall only have time to reach the bell and pull it violently, before the sense of suffocation will come. No one will answer my bell. I know why. My two servants are lovers, and will have quarreled. My housekeeper will have rushed out of the house, in a fury, two hours before, hoping that Perry will believe she has gone to drown herself. Perry is alarmed at last, and is gone out after her. The little scullery-maid is asleep on a bench: she never answers the bell; it does not wake her. The sense of suffocation increases: my lamp goes out with a horrible stench: I make a great effort and snatch at the bell again. I long for life, and there is no help. I thirsted for the unknown: the thirst is gone. O God, let me stay with the known, and be weary of it: I am content. Agony of pain and suffocation—and all the while the earth, the fields, the pebbly brook at the bottom of the rookery, the fresh scent after the rain, the light of the morning through my chamber window, the warmth of the hearth after the frosty air—will darkness close over them forever?

Darkness—darkness—no pain—nothing but darkness: but I am passing on and on through the darkness: my thought stays in the darkness, but always with a sense of moving onward—

Before that time comes, I wish to use my last hours of ease and strength in telling the strange story of my experience. I have never fully unbosomed myself to any human being; I have never been encouraged to trust much in the sympathy of my fellow-men. But we have all a chance of meeting with some pity, some tenderness, some charity when we are dead; it is the living only who cannot be forgiven—the living only from whom men's indulgence and reverence are held off, like the rain by the hard east wind. While the heart beats, bruise it—it is your only opportunity; while the eye can still turn toward you with moist, timid entreaty, freeze it with an icy, unanswering gaze; while the ear, that delicate messenger to the inmost sanctuary of the soul, can still take in the tones of kindness, put it off with hard civility, or sneering compliment, or envious affectation of indifference; while the creative brain can still throb with the sense of injustice, with the yearning for brotherly recognition—make haste—oppress it with your ill-considered judgments, your trivial comparisons, your careless misrepresentations. The heart will by-and-by be still—*ubi sœva indignatio ulterius cor lacerare nequit;*[1] the eye will cease to entreat; the ear will be deaf; the brain will have ceased from all wants as well as from all work. Then your charitable speeches may find vent; then you may remember and pity the toil and the struggle and the failure; then you may give due honor to the work achieved;

[1] Inscription on Swift's tombstone.

then you may find extenuation for errors, and may consent to bury them.

That is a trivial schoolboy text; why do I dwell on it? It has little reference to me, for I shall leave no works behind me for men to honor. I have no near relatives who will make up, by weeping over my grave, for the wounds they inflicted on me when I was among them. It is only the story of my life that will perhaps win a little more sympathy from strangers when I am dead, than I ever believed it would obtain from my friends while I was living.

My childhood perhaps seems happier to me than it really was, by contrast with all the after-years. For then the curtain of the future was as impenetrable to me as to other children: I had all their delight in the present hour, their sweet indefinite hopes for the morrow; and I had a tender mother: even now, after the dreary lapse of long years, a slight trace of sensation accompanies the remembrance of her caress as she held me on her knee—her arms round my little body, her cheek pressed against mine. I had a complaint of the eyes that made me blind for a little while, and she kept me on her knee from morning till night. That unequaled love soon vanished out of my life, and even to my childish consciousness it was as if that life had become more chill. I rode my little white pony with the groom by my side as before, but there were no loving eyes looking at me as I mounted, no glad arms open to me when I came back. Perhaps I missed my mother's love more than most children of seven or eight would have done, to whom the other pleasures of life remained as before; for I was certainly a very sensitive child. I remember still the mingled trepidation and delicious excitement with which I was affected by the tramping of the horses on the pavement in the echoing stables, by the loud resonance of the grooms' voices, by the booming bark of the dogs as my father's carriage thundered under the archway of the courtyard, by the din of the gong as it gave notice of luncheon and dinner. The measured tramp of soldiery which I sometimes heard—for my father's house lay near a county town where there were large barracks—made me sob and tremble; and yet when they were gone past, I longed for them to come back again.

I fancy my father thought me an odd child, and had little fondness for me; though he was very careful in fulfilling what he regarded as a parent's duties. But he was already past the middle of life, and I was not his only son. My mother had been his second wife, and he was five-and-forty when he married her. He was a firm, unbending, intensely orderly man, in root and stem a banker, but with a flourishing graft of the active landholder, aspiring to county influence: one of those people who are always like themselves from day to day, who are uninfluenced by the weather, and neither know melancholy nor high spirits. I held him in great awe, and appeared more timid and sensitive in his presence than at other times; a circumstance which, perhaps, helped to confirm him in the intention to educate me on a different plan from the prescriptive one with which he had complied in the case of my elder brother, already a tall youth at Eton. My brother was to be his representative and successor; he must go to Eton and Oxford, for the sake of making connections, of course: my father was not a man to underrate the bearing of Latin satirists or Greek dramatists on the attainment of an aristocratic position. But, intrinsically, he had slight esteem for "those dead but sceptred spirits"; having qualified himself for forming an independent opinion by reading Potter's "Æschylus," and dipping into Francis's "Horace." To this negative view he added a positive one, derived from a recent connection with mining speculations; namely, that a scientific education was the really useful training for a younger son. Moreover, it was clear that a shy, sensitive boy like me was not fit to encounter the rough experience of a public school. Mr. Letherall had said so very decidedly. Mr. Letherall was a large man in spectacles, who one day took my small head between his large hands, and pressed it here and there in an exploratory, suspicious manner—then placed each of his great thumbs on my temples, and pushed me a little way from him, and stared at me with glittering spectacles. The contemplation appeared to displease him, for he frowned sternly, and said to my father, drawing his thumbs across my eyebrows—

"The deficiency is there, sir—there; and here," he added, touching the upper sides of my head, "here is the excess. That must be brought out, sir, and this must be laid to sleep."

I was in a state of tremor, partly at the vague idea that I was the object of reprobation, partly in the agitation of my first hatred—hatred of this big, spectacled man, who pulled my head about as if he wanted to buy and cheapen it.

I am not aware how much Mr. Letherall had to do with the

system afterward adopted toward me, but it was presently clear that private tutors, natural history, science, and the modern languages, were the appliances by which the defects of my organization were to be remedied. I was very stupid about machines, so I was to be greatly occupied with them; I had no memory for classification, so it was particularly necessary that I should study systematic zoology and botany; I was hungry for human deeds and human emotions, so I was to be plentifully crammed with the mechanical powers, the elementary bodies, and the phenomena of electricity and magnetism. A better-constituted boy would certainly have profited under my intelligent tutors, with their scientific apparatus; and would, doubtless, have found the phenomena of electricity and magnetism as fascinating as I was, every Thursday, assured they were. As it was, I could have paired off, for ignorance of whatever was taught me, with the worst Latin scholar that was ever turned out of a classical academy. I read Plutarch, and Shakespeare, and Don Quixote by the sly, and supplied myself in that way with wandering thoughts, while my tutor was assuring me that "an improved man, as distinguished from an ignorant one, was a man who knew the reason why water ran down-hill." I had no desire to be this improved man; I was glad of the running water; I could watch it and listen to it gurgling among the pebbles, and bathing the bright green water-plants, by the hour together. I did not want to know why it ran; I had perfect confidence that there were good reasons for what was so very beautiful.

There is no need to dwell on this part of my life. I have said enough to indicate that my nature was of the sensitive, unpractical order, and that it grew up in an uncongenial medium, which could never foster it into happy, healthy development. When I was sixteen I was sent to Geneva to complete my course of education; and the change was a very happy one to me, for the first sight of the Alps, with the setting sun on them, as we descended the Jura, seemed to me like an entrance into heaven; and the three years of my life there were spent in a perpetual sense of exaltation, as if from a draught of delicious wine, at the presence of Nature in all her awful loveliness. You will think, perhaps, that I must have been a poet, from this early sensibility to Nature. But my lot was not so happy as that. A poet pours forth his song and *believes* in the listening ear and the answering soul, to which his song will be

floated sooner or later. But the poet's sensibility without his voice
—the poet's sensibility that finds no vent but in silent tears on the
sunny bank, when the noonday light sparkles on the water, or in
an inward shudder at the sound of harsh human tones, the sight
of a cold human eye—this dumb passion brings with it a fatal solitude of soul in the society of one's fellow-men. My least solitary
moments were those in which I pushed off in my boat, at evening,
toward the center of the lake; it seemed to me that the sky, and
the glowing mountain-tops, and the wide blue water, surrounded
me with a cherishing love such as no human face had shed on me
since my mother's love had vanished out of my life. I used to do
as Jean Jacques did—lie down in my boat and let it glide where it
would, while I looked up at the departing glow leaving one moun-
tain-top after the other, as if the prophet's chariot of fire were
passing over them on its way to the home of light. Then when the
white summits were all sad and corpse-like, I had to push homeward, for I was under careful surveillance, and was allowed no late
wanderings. This disposition of mine was not favorable to the
formation of intimate friendships among the numerous youths of
my own age who are always to be found studying at Geneva. Yet
I made one such friendship; and, singularly enough, it was with a
youth whose intellectual tendencies were the very reverse of my
own. I shall call him Charles Meunier; his real surname—an
English one, for he was of English extraction—having since become celebrated. He was an orphan, who lived on a miserable
pittance while he pursued the medical studies for which he had a
special genius. Strange! that with my vague mind, susceptible and
unobservant, hating inquiry and given up to contemplation, I
should have been drawn toward a youth whose strongest passion
was science. But the bond was not an intellectual one; it came
from a source that can happily blend the stupid with the brilliant,
the dreamy with the practical: it came from community of feeling.
Charles was poor and ugly, derided by Genevese *gamins*, and not
acceptable in drawing-rooms. I saw that he was isolated, as I was,
though from a different cause, and, stimulated by a sympathetic
resentment, I made timid advances toward him. It is enough to
say that there sprang up as much comradeship between us as our
different habits would allow; and in Charles's rare holidays we
went up the Salève together, or took the boat to Vevay, while

I listened dreamily to the monologues in which he unfolded his bold conceptions of future experiment and discovery. I mingled them confusedly in my thought with glimpses of blue water and delicate floating cloud, with the notes of birds and the distant glitter of the glacier. He knew quite well that my mind was half absent, yet he liked to talk to me in this way; for don't we talk of our hopes and our projects even to dogs and birds, when they love us? I have mentioned this one friendship because of its connection with a strange and terrible scene which I shall have to narrate in my subsequent life.

This happier life at Geneva was put an end to by a severe illness, which is partly a blank to me, partly a time of dimly-remembered suffering, with the presence of my father by my bed from time to time. Then came the languid monotony of convalescence, the days gradually breaking into variety and distinctness as my strength enabled me to take longer and longer drives. On one of these more vividly remembered days, my father said to me, as he sat beside my sofa—

"When you are quite well enough to travel, Latimer, I shall take you home with me. The journey will amuse you and do you good, for I shall go through the Tyrol and Austria, and you will see many new places. Our neighbors, the Filmores, are come; Alfred will join us at Basle, and we shall all go together to Vienna, and back by Prague——"

My father was called away before he had finished his sentence, and he left my mind resting on the word *Prague*, with a strange sense that a new and wondrous scene was breaking upon me: a city under the broad sunshine; that seemed to me as if it were the summer sunshine of a long-past century arrested in its course—unrefreshed for ages by the dews of night, or the rushing rain-cloud; scorching the dusty, weary, time-eaten grandeur of a people doomed to live on in the stale repetition of memories, like deposed and superannuated kings in their regal gold-inwoven tatters. The city looked so thirsty that the broad river seemed to me a sheet of metal; and the blackened statues, as I passed under their blank gaze, along the unending bridge, with their ancient garments and their saintly crowns, seemed to me the real inhabitants and owners of this place, while the busy, trivial men and women, hurrying to and fro, were a swarm of ephemeral visitants infesting it for a day.

397

It is such grim, stony beings as these, I thought, who are the fathers of ancient faded children, in those tanned time-fretted dwellings that crowd the steep before me; who pay their court in the worn and crumbling pomp of the palace which stretches its monotonous length on the height; who worship wearily in the stifling air of the churches, urged by no fear or hope, but compelled by their doom to be ever old and undying, to live on in the rigidity of habit, as they live on in perpetual midday, without the repose of night or the new birth of morning.

A stunning clang of metal suddenly thrilled through me, and I became conscious of the objects in my room again: one of the fire-irons had fallen as Pierre opened the door to bring me my draught. My heart was palpitating violently, and I begged Pierre to leave my draught beside me: I would take it presently.

As soon as I was alone again, I began to ask myself whether I had been sleeping. Was this a dream—this wonderfully distinct vision—minute in its distinctness down to a patch of rainbow light on the pavement, transmitted through a colored lamp in the shape of a star—of a strange city, quite unfamiliar to my imagination? I had seen no picture of Prague: it lay in my mind as a mere name, with vaguely-remembered historical associations—ill-defined memories of imperial grandeur and religious wars.

Nothing of this sort had ever occurred in my dreaming experience before, for I had often been humiliated because my dreams were only saved from being utterly disjointed and commonplace by the frequent terrors of nightmare. But I could not believe that I had been asleep, for I remembered distinctly the gradual breaking-in of the vision upon me, like the new images in a dissolving view, or the growing distinctness of the landscape as the sun lifts up the veil of the morning mist. And while I was conscious of this incipient vision, I was also conscious that Pierre came to tell my father Mr. Filmore was waiting for him, and that my father hurried out of the room. No, it was not a dream; was it—the thought was full of tremulous exultation—was it the poet's nature in me, hitherto only a troubled, yearning sensibility, now manifesting itself suddenly as spontaneous creation? Surely it was in this way that Homer saw the plain of Troy, that Dante saw the abodes of the departed, that Milton saw the earthward flight of the Tempter. Was it that my illness had wrought some happy change in my organization—given a firmer tension to my nerves —carried off some dull obstruction? I had often read of such effects—in works of fiction at least. Nay; in genuine biographies I had read of the subtilizing or exalting influence of some diseases on the mental powers. Did not Novalis feel his inspiration intensified under the progress of consumption?

When my mind had dwelt for some time on this blissful idea, it seemed to me that I might perhaps test it by an exertion of my will. The vision had begun when my father was speaking of our going to Prague. I did not for a moment believe it was really a representation of that city; I believed—I hoped it was a picture that my newly-liberated genius had painted in fiery haste, with the colors snatched from lazy memory. Suppose I were to fix my mind on some other place—Venice, for example, which was far more familiar to my imagination than Prague; perhaps the same sort of result would follow. I concentrated my thoughts on Venice; I stimulated my imagination with poetic memories, and strove to feel myself present in Venice, as I had felt myself present in Prague. But in vain. I was only coloring the Canaletto engravings that hung in my old bedroom at home; the picture was a shifting one, my mind wandering uncertainly in search of more vivid images; I could see no accident of form or shadow without conscious labor after the necessary conditions. It was all prosaic effort, not rapt passivity, such as I had experienced half an hour before. I was discouraged; but I remembered that inspiration was fitful.

For several days I was in a state of excited expectation, watching for a recurrence of my new gift. I sent my thoughts ranging over my world of knowledge, in the hope that they would find some object which would send a reawakening vibration through my slumbering genius. But no; my world remained as dim as ever, and that flash of strange light refused to come again, though I watched for it with palpitating eagerness.

My father accompanied me every day in a drive, and a gradually lengthening walk as my powers of walking increased; and one evening he had agreed to come and fetch me at twelve the next day, that we might go together to select a musical box, and other purchases rigorously demanded of a rich Englishman visiting Geneva. He was one of the most punctual of men and bankers, and I was always nervously anxious to be quite ready for him at the appointed time. But, to my surprise, at a quarter past twelve he had not appeared. I felt all the impatience of a convalescent who has nothing particular to do, and who has just taken a tonic in the prospect of immediate exercise that would carry off the stimulus.

Unable to sit still and reserve my strength, I walked up and down the room, looking out on the current of the Rhone, just where it leaves the dark-blue lake; but thinking all the while of the possible causes that could detain my father.

Suddenly I was conscious that my father was in the room, but not alone: there were two persons with him. Strange! I had heard no footstep, I had not seen the door open; but I saw my father, and at his right hand our neighbor Mrs. Filmore, whom I remembered very well, though I had not seen her for five years. She was a commonplace middle-aged woman, in silk and cashmere; but the lady on the left of my father was not more than twenty, a tall, slim, willowy figure, with luxuriant blonde hair, arranged in cunning braids and folds that looked almost too massive for the slight figure and the small-featured, thin-lipped face they crowned. But the face had not a girlish expression: the features were sharp, the pale gray eyes at once acute, restless, and sarcastic. They were fixed on me in half-smiling curiosity, and I felt a painful sensation as if a sharp wind were cutting me. The pale-green dress, and the green leaves that seemed to form a border about her pale blonde hair, made me think of a Water-Nixie—for my mind was full of German lyrics, and this pale, fatal-eyed woman, with the green weeds, looked like a birth from some cold sedgy stream, the daughter of an aged river.

"Well, Latimer, you thought me long," my father said——.

But while the last word was in my ears, the whole group vanished, and there was nothing between me and the Chinese painted folding-screen that stood before the door. I was cold and trembling; I could only totter forward and throw myself on the sofa. This strange new power had manifested itself again ——. But was it a power? Might it not rather be a disease—a sort of intermittent delirium, concentrating my energy of brain into moments of unhealthy activity, and leaving my saner hours all the more barren? I felt a dizzy sense of unreality in what my eye rested on; I grasped the bell convulsively, like one trying to free himself from nightmare, and rang it twice. Pierre came with a look of alarm in his face.

"Monsieur ne se trouve pas bien?" he said, anxiously.

"I'm tired of waiting, Pierre," I said, as distinctly and emphatically as I could, like a man determined to be sober in spite of wine; "I'm afraid something has happened to my father—he's usually so punctual. Run to the Hôtel des Bergues and see if he is there."

Pierre left the room at once, with a soothing "Bien, Monsieur"; and I felt the better for this scene of simple waking prose. Seeking to calm myself still further, I went into my bedroom, adjoining the *salon*, and opened a case of eau-de-Cologne; took out a bottle; went through the process of taking out the cork very neatly, and then rubbed the reviving spirit over my hands and forehead, and under my nostrils, drawing a new delight from the scent because I had procured it by slow details of labor, and by no strange sudden madness. Already I had begun to taste something of the horror that belongs to the lot of a human being whose nature is not adjusted to simple human conditions.

Still enjoying the scent, I returned to the *salon*, but it was not unoccupied, as it had been before I left it. In front of the Chinese folding-screen there was my father, with Mrs. Filmore on his right hand, and on his left——the slim blonde-haired girl, with the keen face and the keen eyes fixed on me in half-smiling curiosity.

"Well, Latimer, you thought me long," my father said——

I heard no more, felt no more, till I became conscious that I was lying with my head low on the sofa, Pierre and my father by my side. As soon as I was thoroughly revived, my father left the room, and presently returned, saying——

"I've been to tell the ladies how you are, Latimer. They were waiting in the next room. We shall put off our shopping expedition to-day."

Presently he said, "That young lady is Bertha Grant, Mrs. Filmore's orphan niece. Filmore has adopted her, and she lives with them, so you will have her for a neighbor when we go home— perhaps for a near relation; for there is a tenderness between her and Alfred, I suspect, and I should be gratified by the match, since Filmore means to provide for her in every way as if she were his daughter. It had not occurred to me that you knew nothing about her living with the Filmores."

He made no further allusion to the fact of my having fainted at the moment of seeing her, and I would not for the world have told him the reason: I shrank from the idea of disclosing to anyone what might be regarded as a pitiable peculiarity, most of all from betraying it to my father, who would have suspected my sanity ever after.

I do not mean to dwell with particularity on the details of my experience. I have described these two cases at length; because they had definite, clearly traceable results in my after-lot.

Shortly after this last occurrence—I think the very next day— I began to be aware of a phase in my abnormal sensibility, to which, from the languid and slight nature of my intercourse with others since my illness, I had not been alive before. This was the obtrusion on my mind of the mental process going forward in first one person, and then another, with whom I happened to be in contact: the vagrant, frivolous ideas and emotions of some uninteresting acquaintance—Mrs. Filmore, for example—would force themselves on my consciousness like an importunate, ill-played musical instrument, or the loud activity of an imprisoned insect. But this unpleasant sensibility was fitful, and left me moments of rest, when the souls of my companions were once more shut out from me, and I felt a relief such as silence brings to wearied nerves. I might have believed this importunate insight to be merely a diseased activity of the imagination, but that my prevision of incalculable words and actions proved it to have a fixed relation to the mental process in other minds. But this superadded consciousness, wearying and annoying enough when it urged on me the trivial experience of indifferent people became an intense pain and grief when it seemed to be opening to me the souls of those who were in a close relation to me—when the rational talk, the graceful attentions, the wittily-turned phrases, and the kindly deeds, which used to make the web of their characters, were seen as if thrust asunder by a microscopic vision, that showed all the intermediate frivolities, all the suppressed egoism, all the struggling chaos of puerilities, meanness, vague capricious memories, and indolent make-shift thoughts, from which human words and deeds emerge like leaflets covering a fermenting heap.

At Basle we were joined by my brother Alfred, now a handsome self-confident man of six-and-twenty—a thorough contrast to my fragile, nervous, ineffectual self. I believe I was held to have a sort of half-womanish, half-ghostly beauty; for the portrait-painters, who are thick as weeds at Geneva, had often asked me to sit to them, and I had been the model of a dying minstrel in a fancy picture. But I thoroughly disliked my own *physique*, and nothing but the belief that it was a condition of poetic genius would have reconciled me to it. That brief hope was quite fled, and I saw in my face now nothing but the stamp of a morbid organization, framed for passive suffering—too feeble for the sublime resistance of poetic production. Alfred, from whom I had been almost constantly separated, and who, in his present stage of character and appearance, came before me as a perfect stranger, was bent on being extremely friendly and brother-like to me. He had the superficial kindness of a good-humored, self-satisfied nature, that fears no rivalry, and has encountered no contrarieties. I am not sure that my disposition was good enough for me to have been quite free from envy toward him, even if our desires had not clashed, and if I had been in the healthy human condition which admits of generous confidence and charitable construction. There must always have been an antipathy between our natures. As it was, he became in a few weeks an object of intense hatred to me; and when he entered the room, still more when he spoke, it was as if a sensation of grating metal had set my teeth on edge. My diseased consciousness was more intensely and continually occupied with his thoughts and emotions than with those of any other person who came in my way. I was perpetually exasperated with the petty promptings of his conceit and his love of patronage, with his self-complacent belief in Bertha Grant's passion for him, with his half-pitying contempt for me—seen not in the ordinary indications of intonation and phrase and slight action, which an acute and suspicious mind is on the watch for, but in all their naked skinless complication.

For we were rivals, and our desires clashed, though he was not aware of it. I have said nothing yet of the effect Bertha Grant produced in me on a nearer acquaintance. That effect was chiefly determined by the fact that she made the only exception, among all the human beings about me, to my unhappy gift of insight.

About Bertha I was always in a state of uncertainty: I could watch the expression of her face, and speculate on its meaning; I could ask for her opinion with the real interest of ignorance; I could listen for her words and watch for her smile with hope and fear: she had for me the fascination of an unraveled destiny. I say it was this fact that chiefly determined the strong effect she produced on me: for, in the abstract, no womanly character could seem to have less affinity for that of a shrinking, romantic, passionate youth than Bertha's. She was keen, sarcastic, unimaginative, prematurely cynical, remaining critical and unmoved in the most impressive scenes, inclined to dissect all my favorite poems, and especially contemptuous toward the German lyrics which were my pet literature at that time. To this moment I am unable to define my feeling toward her: it was not ordinary boyish admiration, for she was the very opposite, even to the color of her hair, of the ideal woman who still remained to me the type of loveliness; and she was without that enthusiasm for the great and good, which, even at the moment of her strongest dominion over me, I should have declared to be the highest element of character. But there is no tyranny more complete than that which a self-centred negative nature exercises over a morbidly sensitive nature perpetually craving sympathy and support. The most independent people feel the effect of a man's silence in heightening their value for his opinion —feel an additional triumph in conquering the reverence of a critic habitually captious and satirical: no wonder, then, that an enthusiastic, self-distrusting youth should watch and wait before the closed secret of a sarcastic woman's face, as if it were the shrine of the doubtfully benignant deity who ruled his destiny. For a young enthusiast is unable to imagine the total negation in another mind of the emotions which are stirring his own: they may be feeble, latent, inactive, he thinks, but they are there—they may be called forth; sometimes, in moments of happy hallucination, he believes they may be there in all the greater strength because he sees no outward sign of them. And this effect, as I have intimated, was heightened to its utmost intensity in me, because Bertha was the only being who remained for me in the mysterious seclusion of soul that renders such youthful delusion possible. Doubtless there was another sort of fascination at work—that subtle physical attraction which delights in cheating our psychological predictions, and in compelling the men who paint sylphs to fall in love with some *bonne et brave femme*, heavy-heeled and freckled.

Bertha's behavior toward me was such as to encourage all my illusions, to heighten my boyish passion, and make me more and more dependent on her smiles. Looking back with my present wretched knowledge, I conclude that her vanity and love of power were intensely gratified by the belief that I had fainted on first seeing her purely from the strong impression her person had produced on me. The most prosaic woman likes to believe herself the object of a violent, a poetic passion; and without a grain of romance in her, Bertha had that spirit of intrigue which gave piquancy to the idea that the brother of the man she meant to marry was dying with love and jealousy for her sake. That she meant to marry my brother, was what at that time I did not believe; for though he was assiduous in his attentions to her, and I knew well enough that both he and my father had made up their minds to this result, there was not yet an understood engagement —there had been no explicit declaration; and Bertha habitually, while she flirted with my brother, and accepted his homage in a way that implied to him a thorough recognition of its intention, made me believe, by the subtlest looks and phrases—feminine nothings which could never be quoted against her—that he was really the object of her secret ridicule; that she thought him, as I did, a coxcomb, whom she would have pleasure in disappointing. Me she openly petted in my brother's presence, as if I were too young and sickly ever to be thought of as a lover; and that was the view he took of me. But I believe she must inwardly have delighted in the tremors into which she threw me by the coaxing way in which she patted my curls, while she laughed at my quotations. Such caresses were always given in the presence of our friends; for when we were alone together she affected a much greater distance toward me, and now and then took the opportunity, by words or slight actions, to stimulate my foolish timid hope that she really preferred me. And why should she not follow her inclination? I was not in so advantageous a position as my brother, but I had fortune, I was not a year younger than she was, and she was an heiress, who would soon be of age to decide for herself.

The fluctuations of hope and fear, confided to this one channel, made each day in her presence a delicious torment. There was one deliberate act of hers which especially helped to intoxicate me. When we were at Vienna her twentieth birthday occurred, and as she was very fond of ornaments, we all took the opportunity of the splendid jewelers' shops in that Teutonic Paris to purchase her a birthday present of jewelry. Mine, naturally, was the least expensive; it was an opal ring—the opal was my favorite stone, because it seemed to blush and turn pale as if it had a soul. I told Bertha so when I gave it her, and said that it was an emblem of the poetic nature, changing with the changing light of heaven and of woman's eyes. In the evening she appeared elegantly dressed, and wearing conspicuously all the birthday presents except mine. I looked eagerly at her fingers, but saw no opal. I had no opportunity of noticing this to her during the evening; but the next day, when I found her seated near the window alone, after breakfast, I said, "You scorn to wear my poor opal. I should have remembered that you despised poetic natures, and should have given you coral or turquoise, or some other opaque, unresponsive stone." "Do I despise it?" she answered, taking hold of a delicate gold chain which she always wore round her neck and drawing out the end from her bosom with my ring hanging to it; "it hurts me a little, I can tell you," she said, with her usual dubious smile, "to wear it in that secret place; and since your poetical nature is so stupid as to prefer a more public position, I shall not endure the pain any longer."

She took off the ring from the chain and put it on her finger, smiling still, while the blood rushed to my cheeks, and I could not trust myself to say a word of entreaty that she would keep the ring where it was before.

I was completely fooled by this, and for two days shut myself up in my room whenever Bertha was absent, that I might intoxicate myself afresh with the thought of this scene and all it implied.

I should mention that during these two months—which seemed a long life to me from the novelty and intensity of the pleasures and pains I underwent—my diseased participation in other people's consciousness continued to torment me; now it was my father, and now my brother, now Mrs. Filmore or her husband, and now our German courier, whose stream of thought rushed upon me like a ringing in the ears not to be got rid of, though it allowed my own impulses and ideas to continue their uninterrupted course. It was like a preternaturally heightened sense of hearing, making audible to one a roar of sound where others find perfect stillness. The weariness and disgust of this involuntary intrusion into other souls was counteracted only by my ignorance of Bertha, and my growing passion for her; a passion enormously stimulated, if not produced, by that ignorance. She was my oasis of mystery in the dreary desert of knowledge. I had never allowed my diseased condition to betray itself, or to drive me into any unusual speech or action, except once, when, in a moment of peculiar bitterness against my brother, I had forestalled some words which I knew he was going to utter—a clever observation, which he had prepared beforehand. He had occasionally a slightly-affected hesitation in his speech, and when he paused an instant after the second word, my impatience and jealousy impelled me to continue the speech for him, as if it were something we had both learned by rote. He colored and looked astonished, as well as annoyed; and the words had no sooner escaped my lips than I felt a shock of alarm lest such an anticipation of words—very far from being words of course, easy to divine—should have betrayed me as an exceptional being, a sort of quiet energumen, whom every one, Bertha, above all, would shudder at and avoid. But I magnified, as usual, the impression any word or deed of mine could produce on others; for no one gave any sign of having noticed my interruption as more than a rudeness, to be forgiven me on the score of my feeble nervous condition.

While this superadded consciousness of the actual was almost constant with me, I had never had a recurrence of that distinct prevision which I have described in relation to my first interview with Bertha; and I was waiting with eager curiosity to know whether or not my vision of Prague would prove to have been an instance of the same kind. A few days after the incident of the opal ring, we were paying one of our frequent visits to the Lichtenberg Palace. I could never look at many pictures in succession; for pictures, when they are at all powerful, affect me so strongly that one or two exhaust all my capability of contemplation. This morning I had been looking at Giorgione's picture of the cruel-eyed woman, said to be a likeness of Lucrezia Borgia. I had stood long alone before it, fascinated by the terrible reality of that cunning, relentless face, till I felt a strange poisoned sensation, as if I had long been inhaling a fatal odor, and was just beginning to be conscious of its effects. Perhaps even then I should not have moved away, if the rest of the party had not returned to this room, and announced that they were going to the Belvedere Gallery to settle a bet which had arisen between my brother and Mr. Filmore about a portrait. I followed them dreamily, and was hardly alive to what occurred till they had all gone up to the gallery, leaving me below; for I refused to come within sight of another picture that day. I made my way to the Grand Terrace, since it was agreed that we should saunter in the gardens when the dispute had been decided. I had been sitting here a short space, vaguely conscious of trim gardens, with a city and green hills in the distance, when, wishing to avoid the proximity of the sentinel, I rose and walked down the broad stone steps, intending to seat myself farther on in the gardens. Just as I reached the gravel walk, I felt an arm slipped within mine, and a light hand gently pressing my wrist. In the same instant a strange intoxicating numbness passed over me, like the continuance or climax of the sensation I was still feeling from the gaze of Lucrezia Borgia. The gardens, the summer sky, the consciousness of Bertha's arm being within mine, all vanished, and I seemed to be suddenly in darkness, out of which there gradually broke a dim firelight, and I felt myself sitting in my father's leather chair in the library at home. I knew the fireplace—the dogs for the wood-fire—the black marble chimney-piece with the white marble medallion of the dying Cleopatra in the centre. Intense and hopeless misery was pressing on my soul; the light became stronger, for Bertha was entering with a candle in her hand—Bertha, my wife—with cruel eyes, with green jewels and green leaves on her white ball-dress; every hateful thought within her present to me——"Madman, idiot! why don't you kill yourself, then?" It was a moment of hell. I saw into her pitiless soul—saw its barren worldliness, its scorching hate—and felt it clothe me round like an air I was obliged to breathe. She came with her candle and stood over me with a bitter smile of contempt; I saw the great emerald brooch on her bosom, a studded serpent with diamond eyes. I shuddered—I despised this woman with the barren soul and mean thoughts; but I felt helpless before her, as if she clutched my bleeding heart, and would clutch it till the last drop of life-blood ebbed away. She was my wife, and we hated each other. Gradually the hearth, the dim library, the candle-light disappeared—seemed to melt away into a background of light, the green serpent with the diamond eyes remaining a dark image on the retina. Then I had a sense of my eyelids quivering, and the living daylight broke in upon me; I saw gardens, and heard voices; I was seated on the steps of the Belvedere Terrace, and my friends were round me.

The tumult of mind into which I was thrown by this hideous vision made me ill for several days, and prolonged our stay at Vienna. I shuddered with horror as the scene recurred to me; and it recurred constantly, with all its minutiæ, as if they had been burned into my memory; and yet, such is the madness of the human heart under the influence of its immediate desires, I felt a wild hell-braving joy that Bertha was to be mine; for the fulfillment of my former prevision concerning her first appearance before me, left me little hope that this last hideous glimpse of the future was the mere diseased play of my own mind, and had no relation to external realities. One thing alone I looked toward as a possible means of casting doubt on my terrible conviction—the discovery that my vision of Prague had been false—and Prague was the next city on our route.

Meanwhile, I was no sooner in Bertha's society again, than I was as completely under her sway as before. What if I saw into the heart of Bertha, the matured woman—Bertha, my wife? Bertha, the *girl*, was a fascinating secret to me still: I trembled under her touch; I felt the witchery of her presence; I yearned to be assured of her love. The fear of poison is feeble against the sense of thirst. Nay, I was just as jealous of my brother as before—just as much irritated by his small patronizing ways; for my pride, my diseased sensibility, were there as they had always been, and winced as inevitably under every offense as my eye winced from an intruding mote. The future, even when brought within the compass of feeling by a vision that made me shudder, had still no more than the force of an idea, compared with the force of present emotion—of my love for Bertha, of my dislike and jealousy toward my brother.

It is an old story, that men sell themselves to the tempter, and sign a bond with their blood, because it is only to take effect at a distant day; then rush on to snatch the cup their souls thirst after with an impulse not the less savage because there is a dark shadow beside them forevermore. There is no short cut, no patent tram-road, to wisdom: after all the centuries of invention, the soul's path lies through the thorny wilderness which must be still trodden in solitude, with bleeding feet, with sobs for help, as it was trodden by them of old time.

My mind speculated eagerly on the means by which I should become my brother's successful rival, for I was still too timid, in my ignorance of Bertha's actual feeling, to venture on any step that would urge from her an avowal of it. I thought I should gain confidence even for this, if my vision of Prague proved to have been veracious; and yet, the horror of that certitude! Behind the slim girl Bertha, whose words and looks I watched for, whose touch was bliss, there stood continually that Bertha with the fuller form, the harder eyes, the more rigid mouth,—with the barren selfish soul laid bare; no longer a fascinating secret, but a measured fact, urging itself perpetually on my unwilling sight. Are you unable to give me your sympathy—you who read this? Are you unable to imagine this double consciousness at work within me, flowing on like two parallel streams which never mingle their waters and blend into a common hue? Yet you must have known something of the presentiments that spring from an insight at war with passion; and my visions were only like presentiments intensified to horror. You have known the powerlessness of ideas before the might of impulse; and my visions, when once they had passed into memory, were mere ideas—pale shadows that beckoned in vain, while my hand was grasped by the living and the loved.

In after-days I thought with bitter regret that if I had foreseen something more or something different—if instead of that hideous vision which poisoned the passion it could not destroy, or if even along with it I could have had a foreshadowing of that moment when I looked on my brother's face for the last time, some softening influence would have been shed over my feeling toward him: pride and hatred would surely have been subdued into pity, and the record of those hidden sins would have been shortened. But this is one of the vain thoughts with which we men flatter ourselves. We try to believe that the egoism within us would have easily been melted, and that it was only the narrowness of our knowledge which hemmed in our generosity, our awe, our human piety, and hindered them from submerging our hard indifference to the sensations and emotions of our fellow. Our tenderness and self-renunciation seem strong when our egoism has had its day—when, after our mean striving for a triumph that is to be another's loss, the triumph comes suddenly, and we shudder at it, because it is held out by the chill hand of death.

Our arrival in Prague happened at night, and I was glad of this, for it seemed like a deferring of a terribly decisive moment, to be in the city for hours without seeing it. As we were not to remain long in Prague, but to go on speedily to Dresden, it was proposed that we should drive out the next morning and take a general view of the place, as well as visit some of its specially interesting spots, before the heat became oppressive—for we were in August, and the season was hot and dry. But it happened that the ladies were rather late at their morning toilet, and to my father's politely-repressed but perceptible annoyance, we were not in the carriage till the morning was far advanced. I thought with a sense of relief, as we entered the Jews' quarter, where we were to visit the old synagogue, that we should be kept in this flat, shut-up part of the city, until we should all be too tired and too warm to go farther, and so we should return without seeing more than the streets through which we had already passed. That would give me another day's suspense—suspense, the only form in which a fearful spirit knows the solace of hope. But, as I stood under the blackened, groined arches of that old synagogue, made dimly visible by the seven thin candles in the sacred lamp, while our Jewish cicerone reached down the Book of the Law, and read to us in its ancient tongue,—I felt a shuddering impression that this strange building, with its shrunken lights, this surviving withered remnant of mediæval Judaism, was of a piece with my vision. Those darkened dusty Christian saints, with their loftier arches and their larger candles, needed the consolatory scorn with which they might point to a more shriveled death-in-life than their own.

As I expected, when we left the Jews' quarter the elders of our party wished to return to the hotel. But now, instead of rejoicing in this, as I had done beforehand, I felt a sudden overpowering impulse to go on at once to the bridge, and put an end to the suspense I had been wishing to protract. I declared, with unusual decision, that I would get out of the carriage and walk on alone; they might return without me. My father, thinking this merely a sample of my usual "poetic nonsense," objected that I should only do myself harm by walking in the heat; but when I persisted, he said angrily that I might follow my own absurd devices, but that Schmidt (our courier) must go with me. I assented to this, and set off with Schmidt toward the bridge. I had no sooner passed from under the archway of the grand old gate leading on to the bridge than a trembling seized me, and I turned cold under the midday sun; yet I went on; I was in search of something—a small detail which I remembered with special intensity as part of my vision. There is was, the patch of rainbow light on the pavement transmitted through a lamp in the shape of a star.

Chapter II

BEFORE THE AUTUMN was at an end, and while the brown leaves still stood thick on the beeches in our park, my brother and Bertha were engaged to each other, and it was understood that their marriage was to take place early in the next spring. In spite of the certainty I had felt from that moment on the bridge at Prague, that Bertha would one day be my wife, my constitutional timidity and distrust had continued to benumb me, and the words in which I had sometimes premeditated a confession of my love had died away unuttered. The same conflict had gone on within me as before—the longing for an assurance of love from Bertha's lips, the dread lest a word of contempt and denial should fall upon me like a corrosive acid. What was the conviction of a distant necessity to me? I trembled under a present glance, I hungered after a present joy, I was clogged and chilled by a present fear. And so the days passed on: I witnessed Bertha's engagement and heard her marriage discussed as if I were under a conscious nightmare— knowing it was a dream that would vanish, but feeling stifled under the grasp of hard-clutching fingers.

When I was not in Bertha's presence—and I was with her very often, for she continued to treat me with a playful patronage that wakened no jealousy in my brother—I spent my time chiefly in wandering, in strolling, or taking long rides while the daylight lasted, and then shutting myself up with my unread books; for

books had lost the power of chaining my attention. My self-consciousness was heightened to that pitch of intensity in which our
own emotions take the form of a drama which urges itself impera-
tively on our contemplation, and we begin to weep, less under the
sense of our suffering than at the thought of it. I felt a sort of
pitying anguish over the pathos of my own lot: the lot of a being
finely organized for pain, but with hardly any fibers that responded
to pleasure—to whom the idea of future evil robbed the present
of its joy, and for whom the idea of future good did not still the
uneasiness of a present yearning or a present dread. I went dumbly
through that stage of the poet's suffering, in which he feels the
delicious pang of utterance, and makes an image of his sorrows.

I was left entirely without remonstrance concerning this dreamy
wayward life: I knew my father's thought about me: "That lad
will never be good for anything in life: he may waste his years in
an insignificant way on the income that falls to him: I shall not
trouble myself about a career for him."

One mild morning in the beginning of November, it happened
that I was standing outside the portico patting lazy old Cæsar, a
Newfoundland almost blind with age, the only dog that ever took
any notice of me—for the very dogs shunned me, and fawned on
the happier people about me—when the groom brought up my
brother's horse which was to carry him to the hunt, and my
brother himself appeared at the door, florid, broad-chested, and
self-complacent, feeling what a good-natured fellow he was not to
behave insolently to us all on the strength of his great advantages.

"Latimer, old boy," he said to me in a tone of compassionate
cordiality, "what a pity it is you don't have a run with the hounds
now and then! The finest thing in the world for low spirits!"

"Low spirits!" I thought bitterly, as he rode away; "that is the
sort of phrase with which coarse, narrow natures like yours think
to describe experience of which you can know no more than your
horse knows. It is to such as you that the good of this world falls:
ready dullness, healthy selfishness, good-tempered conceit—these
are the keys to happiness."

The quick thought came that my selfishness was even stronger
than his—it was only a suffering selfishness instead of an enjoying
one. But then, again, my exasperating insight into Alfred's self-
complacent soul, his freedom from all the doubts and fears, the

unsatisfied yearnings, the exquisite tortures of sensitiveness, that had made the web of my life, seemed to absolve me from all bonds toward him. This man needed no pity, no love; those fine influences would have been as little felt by him as the delicate white mist is felt by the rock it caresses. There was no evil in store for him: if he was not to marry Bertha, it would be because he had found a lot pleasanter to himself.

Mr. Filmore's house lay not more than half a mile beyond our own gates, and whenever I knew my brother was gone in another direction, I went there for the chance of finding Bertha at home. Later on in the day I walked thither. By a rare accident she was alone, and we walked out in the grounds together, for she seldom went on foot beyond the trimly-swept gravel-walks. I remember what a beautiful sylph she looked to me as the low November sun shone on her blonde hair, and she tripped along teasing me with her usual light banter, to which I listened half fondly, half moodily; it was all the sign Bertha's mysterious inner self ever made to me. To-day perhaps the moodiness predominated, for I had not yet shaken off the access of jealous hate which my brother had raised in me by his parting patronage. Suddenly I interrupted and startled her by saying, almost fiercely, "Bertha, how can you love Alfred?"

She looked at me with surprise for a moment, but soon her light smile came again, and she answered sarcastically, "Why do you suppose I love him?"

"How can you ask that, Bertha?"

"What! your wisdom thinks I must love the man I'm going to marry? The most unpleasant thing in the world. I should quarrel with him; I should be jealous of him; our ménage would be conducted in a very ill-bred manner. A little quiet contempt contributes greatly to the elegance of life."

"Bertha, that is not your real feeling. Why do you delight in trying to deceive me by inventing such cynical speeches?"

"I need never take the trouble of invention in order to deceive you, my small Tasso"—(that was the mocking name she usually gave me). "The easiest way to deceive a poet is to tell him the truth."

She was testing the validity of her epigram in a daring way, and for a moment the shadow of my vision—the Bertha whose soul was no secret to me—passed between me and the radiant girl, the playful sylph whose feelings were a fascinating mystery. I suppose I must have shuddered, or betrayed in some other way my momentary chill of horror.

"Tasso!" she said, seizing my wrist, and peeping round into my face, "are you really beginning to discern what a heartless girl I am? Why, you are not half the poet I thought you were; you are actually capable of believing the truth about me."

The shadow passed from between us, and was no longer the object nearest to me. The girl whose light fingers grasped me, whose elfish, charming face looked into mine—who, I thought, was betraying an interest in my feelings that she would not have directly avowed,—this warm-breathing presence again possessed my senses and imagination like a returning siren melody which had been overpowered for an instant by the roar of threatening waves. It was a moment as delicious to me as the waking up to a consciousness of youth after a dream of middle age. I forgot everything but my passion, and said with swimming eyes—

"Bertha, shall you love me when we are first married? I wouldn't mind if you really loved me only for a little while."

Her look of astonishment, as she loosed my hand and started away from me recalled me to a sense of my strange, my criminal indiscretion.

"Forgive me," I said, hurriedly, as soon as I could speak again; "I did not know what I was saying."

"Ah, Tasso's mad fit has come on, I see," she answered, quietly, for she had recovered herself sooner than I had. "Let him go home and keep his head cool. I must go in, for the sun is setting."

I left her—full of indignation against myself. I had let slip words, which, if she reflected on them, might rouse in her a suspicion of my abnormal mental condition—a suspicion which of all things I dreaded. And besides that, I was ashamed of the apparent baseness I had committed in uttering them to my brother's betrothed wife. I wandered home slowly, entering our park through a private gate instead of by the lodges. As I approached the house, I saw a man dashing off at full speed from the stable-yard across the park. Had any accident happened at home? No; perhaps it was only one of my father's peremptory business errands that required this headlong haste. Nevertheless I quickened my pace without any distinct motive, and was soon at the house. I will not dwell on the scene I found there. My brother was dead—had been pitched from his horse, and killed on the spot by a concussion of the brain.

I went up to the room where he lay, and where my father was seated beside him with a look of rigid despair. I had shunned my father more than any one since our return home, for the radical antipathy between our natures made my insight into his inner self a constant affliction to me. But now, as I went up to him, and stood beside him in sad silence, I felt the presence of a new element that blended us as we had never been blent before. My father had been one of the most successful men in the money-getting world, he had had no sentimental sufferings, no illness. The heaviest trouble that had befallen him was the death of his first wife. But he married my mother soon after and I remember he seemed exactly the same, to my keen childish observation, the week after her death as before. But now, at last, a sorrow had come —the sorrow of old age, which suffers the more from the crushing of its pride and its hopes, in proportion as the pride and hope are narrow and prosaic. His son was to have been married soon— would probably have stood for the borough at the next election. That son's existence was the best motive that could be alleged for making new purchases of land every year to round off the estate. It is a dreary thing to live on doing the same things year after year, without knowing why we do them. Perhaps the tragedy of disappointed youth and passion is less piteous than the tragedy of disappointed age and worldliness.

As I saw into the desolation of my father's heart, I felt a movement of deep pity toward him, which was the beginning of a new affection—an affection that grew and strengthened in spite of the strange bitterness with which he regarded me in the first month or two after my brother's death. If it had not been for the softening influence of my compassion for him—the first deep compassion I had ever felt—I should have been stung by the perception that my father transferred the inheritance of an eldest son to me with a mortified sense that fate had compelled him to the unwelcome course of caring for me as an important being. It was only in spite of himself that he began to think of me with anxious regard. There is hardly any neglected child for whom death has made vacant a more favored place, who will not understand what I mean.

Gradually, however, my new deference to his wishes, the effect
of that patience which was born of my pity for him, won upon his
affection, and he began to please himself with the endeavor to
make me fill my brother's place as fully as my feebler personality
would admit. I saw that the prospect which by-and-by presented
itself of my becoming Bertha's husband was welcome to him, and
he even contemplated in my case what he had not intended in my
brother's—that his son and daughter-in-law should make one
household with him. My softened feeling toward my father made
this the happiest time I had known since childhood;—these last
months in which I retained the delicious illusion of loving Bertha,
of longing and doubting and hoping that she might love me. She
behaved with a certain new consciousness and distance toward me
after my brother's death; and I too was under a double constraint
—that of delicacy toward my brother's memory, and of anxiety as
to the impression my abrupt words had left on her mind. But the
additional screen this mutual reserve erected between us only
brought me more completely under her power: no matter how
empty the adytum, so that the veil be thick enough. So absolute
is our soul's need of something hidden and uncertain for the
maintenance of that doubt and hope and effort which are the
breath of its life, that if the whole future were laid bare to us
beyond to-day, the interest of all mankind would be bent on the
hours that lie between; we should pant after the uncertainties of
our one morning and our one afternoon; we should rush fiercely
to the Exchange for our last possibility of speculation, of success,
of disappointment; we should have a glut of political prophets fore-
telling a crisis or a no-crisis within the only twenty-four hours left
open to prophecy. Conceive the condition of the human mind if
all propositions whatsoever were self-evident except one, which
was to become self-evident at the close of a summer's day, but in
the meantime might be the subject of question, of hypothesis, of
debate. Art and philosophy, literature and science, would fasten
like bees on that one proposition which had the honey of probability in it, and be the more eager because their enjoyment would
end with sunset. Our impulses, our spiritual activities, no more
adjust themselves to the idea of their future nullity, than the beating of our heart, or the irritability of our muscles.

Bertha, the slim, fair-haired girl, whose present thoughts and
emotions were an enigma to me amidst the fatiguing obviousness

of the other minds around me, was as absorbing to me as a single unknown to-day—as a single hypothetic proposition to remain problematic till sunset; and all the cramped, hemmed-in belief and disbelief, trust and distrust, of my nature, welled out in this one narrow channel.

And she made me believe that she loved me. Without ever quitting her tone of *badinage* and playful superiority, she intoxicated me with the sense that I was necessary to her, that she was never at ease unless I was near her, submitting to her playful tyranny. It costs a woman so little effort to besot us in this way! A half-repressed word, a moment's unexpected silence, even an easy fit of petulance on our account, will serve us as *hashish* for a long while. Out of the subtlest web of scarcely perceptible signs, she set me weaving the fancy that she had always unconsciously loved me better than Alfred, but that, with the ignorant fluttered sensibility of a young girl, she had been imposed on by the charm that lay for her in the distinction of being admired and chosen by a man who made so brilliant a figure in the world as my brother. She satirized herself in a very graceful way for her vanity and ambition. What was it to me that I had the light of my wretched prevision on the fact that now it was I who possessed at least all but the personal part of my brother's adventures? Our sweet illusions are half of them conscious illusions, like effects of color that we know to be made up of tinsel, broken glass, and rags.

We were married eighteen months after Alfred's death, one cold, clear morning in April, when there came hail and sunshine both together; and Bertha, in her white silk and pale-green leaves, and the pale hues of her hair and face, looked like the spirit of the morning. My father was happier than he had thought of being again: my marriage, he felt sure, would complete the desirable modification of my character, and make me practical and worldly enough to take my place in society among sane men. For he delighted in Bertha's tact and acuteness, and felt sure she would be mistress of me, and make me what she chose: I was only twenty-one, and madly in love with her. Poor father! He kept that hope a little while after our first year of marriage, and it was not quite extinct when paralysis came and saved him from utter disappointment.

I shall hurry through the rest of my story, not dwelling so much as I have hitherto done on my inward experience. When people are well known to each other, they talk rather of what befalls them externally, leaving their feelings and sentiments to be inferred.

We lived in a round of visits for some time after our return home, giving splendid dinner-parties, and making a sensation in our neighborhood by the new luster of our equipage, for my father had reserved this display of his increased wealth for the period of his son's marriage; and we gave our acquaintances liberal opportunity for remarking that it was a pity I made so poor a figure as an heir and a bridegroom. The nervous fatigue of this existence, the insincerities and platitudes which I had to live through twice over—through my inner and outward sense—would have been maddening to me, if I had not had that sort of intoxicated callousness which came from the delights of a first passion. A bride and bridegroom surrounded by all the appliances of wealth, hurried through the day by the whirl of society, filling their solitary moments with hastily-snatched caresses, are prepared for their future life together as the novice is prepared for the cloister—by experiencing its utmost contrast.

Through all these crowded excited months, Bertha's inward self remained shrouded from me, and I still read her thoughts only through the language of her lips and demeanor: I had still the human interest of wondering whether what I did and said pleased her, of longing to hear a word of affection, of giving a delicious exaggeration of meaning to her smile. But I was conscious of a growing difference in her manner toward me; sometimes strong enough to be called haughty coldness, cutting and chilling me as the hail had done that came across the sunshine on our marriage morning; sometimes only perceptible in the dexterous avoidance of a tête-à-tête walk or dinner to which I had been looking forward. I had been deeply pained by this—had even felt a sort of crushing of the heart, from the sense that my brief day of happiness was near its setting; but still I remained dependent on Bertha, eager for the last rays of a bliss that would soon be gone forever, hoping and watching for some after-glow more beautiful from the impending night.

I remember—how should I not remember?—the time when that dependence and hope utterly left me, when the sadness I had felt in Bertha's growing estrangement became a joy that I looked back upon with longing, as a man might look back on the last pains in a paralyzed limb. It was just after the close of my father's last illness, which had necessarily withdrawn us from society and thrown us more upon each other. It was the evening of my father's death. On that evening the veil which had shrouded Bertha's soul from me—had made me find in her alone among my fellow-beings the blessed possibility of mystery, and doubt, and expectation— was first withdrawn. Perhaps it was the first day since the beginning of my passion for her, in which that passion was completely neutralized by the presence of an absorbing feeling of another kind. I had been watching by my father's deathbed: I had been witnessing the last fitful yearning glance his soul had cast back on the spent inheritance of life—the last faint consciousness of love he had gathered from the pressure of my hand. What are all our personal loves when we have been sharing in that supreme agony? In the first moments when we come away from the presence of death, every other relation to the living is merged, to our feeling, in the great relation of a common nature and a common destiny.

In that state of mind I joined Bertha in her private sitting-room. She was seated in a leaning posture on a settee, with her back toward the door; the great rich coils of her pale blonde hair surmounting her small neck, visible above the back of the settee. I remember, as I closed the door behind me, a cold tremulousness seizing me, and a vague sense of being hated and lonely—vague and strong, like a presentiment. I know how I looked at that moment, for I saw myself in Bertha's thought as she lifted her cutting gray eyes and looked at me: a miserable ghost-seer, surrounded by phantoms in the noonday, trembling under a breeze when the leaves were still, without appetite for the common objects of human desire, but pining after the moonbeams. We were front to front with each other, and judged each other. The terrible moment of complete illumination had come to me, and I saw that the darkness had hidden no landscape from me, but only a blank prosaic wall: from that evening forth, through the sickening years which followed, I saw all round the narrow room of this woman's soul— saw petty artifice and mere negation where I had delighted to believe in coy sensibilities and in wit at war with latent feeling— saw the light floating vanities of the girl defining themselves into the systematic coquetry, the scheming selfishness, of the woman—

saw repulsion and antipathy harden into cruel hatred, giving pain only for the sake of wreaking itself.

For Bertha, too, after her kind, felt the bitterness of disillusion. She had believed that my wild poet's passion for her would make me her slave; and that, being her slave, I should execute her will in all things. With the essential shallowness of a negative, unimaginative nature, she was unable to conceive the fact that sensibilities were anything else than weaknesses. She had thought my weaknesses would put me in her power, and she found them unmanageable forces. Our positions were reversed. Before marriage she had completely mastered my imagination, for she was a secret to me; and I created the unknown thought before which I trembled as if it were hers. But now that her soul was laid open to me, now that I was compelled to share the privacy of her motives, to follow all the petty devices that preceded her words and acts, she found herself powerless with me, except to produce in me the chill shudder of repulsion—powerless, because I could be acted on by no lever within her reach. I was dead to worldly ambitions, to social vanities, to all the incentives within the compass of her narrow imagination, and I lived under influences utterly invisible to her.

She was really pitiable to have such a husband, and so all the world thought. A graceful, brilliant woman, like Bertha, who smiled on morning callers, made a figure in ball-rooms, and was capable of that light repartee which, from such a woman, is accepted as wit, was secure of carrying off all sympathy from a husband who was sickly, abstracted, and, as some suspected, crack-brained. Even the servants in our house gave her the balance of their regard and pity. For there were no audible quarrels between us; our alienation, our repulsion from each other, lay within the silence of our own hearts; and if the mistress went out a great deal, and seemed to dislike the master's society, was it not natural, poor thing? The master was odd. I was kind and just to my dependents, but I excited in them a shrinking, half-contemptuous pity; for this class of men and women are but slightly determined in their estimate of others by general considerations, or even experience, of character. They judge of persons as they judge of coins, and value those who pass current at a high rate.

After a time I interfered so little with Bertha's habits, that it might seem wonderful how her hatred toward me could grow so intense and active as it did. But she had begun to suspect, by some involuntary betrayals of mine, that there was an abnormal power of penetration in me—that fitfully, at least, I was strangely cognizant of her thoughts and intentions, and she began to be haunted by a terror of me, which alternated every now and then with defiance. She meditated continually how the incubus could be shaken off her life—how she could be freed from this hateful bond to a being whom she at once despised as an imbecile, and dreaded as an inquisitor. For a long while she lived in the hope that my evident wretchedness would drive me to the commission of suicide; but suicide was not in my nature. I was too completely swayed by the sense that I was in the grasp of unknown forces, to believe in my power the self-release. Toward my own destiny I had become entirely passive; for my one ardent desire had spent itself, and impulse no longer predominated over knowledge. For this reason I never thought of taking any steps toward a complete separation, which would have made our alienation evident to the world. Why should I rush for help to a new course, when I was only suffering from the consequences of a deed which had been the act of my intensest will? That would have been the logic of one who had desires to gratify, and I had no desires. But Bertha and I lived more and more aloof from each other. The rich find it easy to live married and apart.

That course of our life which I have indicated in a few sentences filled the space of years. So much misery—so slow and hideous a growth of hatred and sin, may be compressed into a sentence! And men judge of each other's lives through this summary medium. They epitomize the experience of their fellow-mortal, and pronounce judgment on him in neat syntax, and feel themselves wise and virtuous—conquerors over the temptations they define in well-selected predicates. Seven years of wretchedness glide glibly over the lips of the man who has never counted them out in moments of chill disappointment, of head and heart throbbings, of dread and vain wrestling, of remorse and despair. We learn words by rote, but not their meaning; that must be paid for with our life-blood, and printed in the subtle fibres of our nerves.

But I will hasten to finish my story. Brevity is justified at once to those who readily understand, and to those who will never understand.

Some years after my father's death, I was sitting by the dim firelight in my library one January evening—sitting in the leather chair that used to be my father's—when Bertha appeared at the door, with a candle in her hand, and advanced toward me. I knew the ball-dress she had on—the white ball-dress, with the green jewels, shone upon by the light of the wax candle which lit up the medallion of the dying Cleopatra on the mantelpiece. Why did she come to me before going out? I had not seen her in the library, which was my habitual place, for months. Why did she stand before me with the candle in her hand, with her cruel contemptuous eyes fixed on me, and the glittering serpent, like a familiar demon, on her breast. For a moment I thought this fulfillment of my vision at Vienna marked some dreadful crisis in my fate, but I saw nothing in Bertha's mind, as she stood before me, except scorn for the look of overwhelming misery with which I sat before her.——"Fool, idiot, why don't you kill yourself, then?"—that was her thought. But at length her thoughts reverted to her errand, and she spoke aloud. The apparently indifferent nature of the errand seemed to make a ridiculous anticlimax to my prevision and my agitation.

"I have had to hire a new maid. Fletcher is going to be married, and she wants me to ask you to let her husband have the public-house and farm at Molton. I wish him to have it. You must give the promise now, because Fletcher is going to-morrow morning—and quickly, because I'm in a hurry."

"Very well; you may promise her," I said, indifferently, and Bertha swept out of the library again.

I always shrank from the sight of a new person, and all the more when it was a person whose mental life was likely to weary my reluctant insight with worldly ignorant trivialities. But I shrank especially from the sight of this new maid, because her advent had been announced to me at a moment to which I could not cease to attach some fatality: I had a vague dread that I should find her mixed up with the dreary drama of my life—that some new sickening vision would reveal her to me as an evil genius. When at last I did unavoidably meet her, the vague dread was changed into definite disgust. She was a tall, wiry, dark-eyed woman, this Mrs. Archer, with a face handsome enough to give her coarse hard nature the odious finish of bold, self-confident coquetry. That was enough to make me avoid her, quite apart from the contemptuous feeling with which she contemplated me. I seldom saw her; but I perceived that she rapidly became a favorite with her mistress, and, after the lapse of eight or nine months, I began to be aware that there had arisen in Bertha's mind toward this woman a mingled feeling of fear and dependence, and that this feeling was associated with ill-defined images of candle-light scenes in her dressing-room, and the locking-up of something in Bertha's cabinet. My interviews with my wife had become so brief and so rarely solitary, that I had no opportunity of perceiving these images in her mind with more definiteness. The recollections of the past become contracted in the rapidity of thought till they sometimes bear hardly a more distinct resemblance to the external reality than the forms of an oriental alphabet to the objects that suggested them.

Besides, for the last year or more a modification had been going forward in my mental condition, and was growing more and more marked. My insight into the minds of those around me was becoming dimmer and more fitful, and the ideas that crowded my double consciousness became less and less dependent on any personal contact. All that was personal in me seemed to be suffering a gradual death, so that I was losing the organ through which the personal agitations and projects of others could affect me. But along with this relief from wearisome insight, there was a new development of what I concluded—as I have since found rightly— to be a prevision of external scenes. It was as if the relation between me and my fellow-men was more and more deadened, and my relation to what we call the inanimate was quickened into new life. The more I lived apart from society, and in proportion as my wretchedness subsided from the violent throb of agonized passion into the dullness of habitual pain, the more frequent and vivid became such visions as that I had had of Prague—of strange cities, of sandy plains, of gigantic ruins, of midnight skies with strange bright constellations, of mountain passes, of grassy nooks flecked with the afternoon sunshine through the boughs: I was in the midst of such scenes, and in all of them one presence seemed to weigh on me in all these mighty shapes—the presence of something unknown and pitiless. For continual suffering had annihilated religious faith within me: to the utterly miserable—the unloving and the unloved—there is no religion possible, no worship but a worship of devils. And beyond all these, and continually recurring, was the vision of my death—the pangs, the suffocation, the last struggle, when life would be grasped at in vain.

Things were in this state near the end of the seventh year. I had become entirely free from insight, from my abnormal cognizance of any other consciousness than my own, and instead of intruding involuntarily into the world of other minds, was living continually in my own solitary future. Bertha was aware that I was greatly changed. To my surprise she had of late seemed to seek opportunities of remaining in my society, and had cultivated that kind of distant yet familiar talk which is customary between a husband and wife who live in polite and irrevocable alienation. I bore this with languid submission, and without feeling enough interest in her motives to be roused into keen observation; yet I could not help perceiving something triumphant and excited in her carriage and the expression of her face—something too subtle to express itself in words or tones, but giving one the idea that she lived in a state of expectation or hopeful suspense. My chief feeling was satisfaction that her inner self was once more shut out from me; and I almost revelled for the moment in the absent melancholy that made me answer her at cross purposes, and betray utter ignorance of what she had been saying. I remember well the look and the smile with which she one day said, after a mistake of this kind on my part: "I used to think you were a clairvoyant, and that was the reason why you were so bitter against other clairvoyants, wanting to keep your monopoly; but I see now you have become rather duller than the rest of the world."

I said nothing in reply. It occurred to me that her recent obtrusion of herself upon me might have been prompted by the wish to test my power of detecting some of her secrets; but I let the thought drop again at once; her motives and her deeds had no interest for me, and whatever pleasures she might be seeking, I had no wish to balk her. There was still pity in my soul for every living thing, and Bertha was living—was surrounded with possibilities of misery.

Just at this time there occurred an event which roused me somewhat from my inertia, and gave me an interest in the passing moment that I had thought impossible for me. It was a visit from

Charles Meunier, who had written me word that he was coming to England for relaxation from too strenuous labor, and would like to see me. Meunier had now a European reputation; but his letter to me expressed that keen remembrance of an early regard, an early debt of sympathy, which is inseparable from nobility of character; and I, too, felt as if his presence would be to me like a transient resurrection into a happier pre-existence.

He came, and as far as possible, I renewed our old pleasure of making *tête-à-tête* excursions, though, instead of mountains and glaciers and the wide blue lake, we had to content ourselves with mere slopes and ponds and artificial plantations. The years had changed us both, but with what different result! Meunier was now a brilliant figure in society, to whom elegant women pretended to listen, and whose acquaintance was boasted of by noblemen ambitious of brains. He repressed with the utmost delicacy all betrayal of the shock which I am sure he must have received from our meeting, or of a desire to penetrate into my condition and circumstances, and sought by the utmost exertion of his charming social powers to make our reunion agreeable. Bertha was much struck by the unexpected fascinations of a visitor who she had expected to find presentable only on the score of his celebrity, and put forth all her coquetries and accomplishments. Apparently she succeeded in attracting his admiration, for his manner toward her was attentive and flattering. The effect of his presence on me was so benignant, especially in those renewals of our old *tête-à-tête* wanderings, when he poured forth to me wonderful narratives of his professonal experience, that more than once, when his talk turned on the psychological relations of disease, the thought crossed my mind that, if his stay with me were long enough, I might possibly bring myself to tell this man the secrets of my lot. Might there not lie some remedy for me, too, in his science? Might there not at least lie some comprehension and sympathy ready for me in his large and susceptible mind? But the thought only flickered feebly now and then, and died out before it could become a wish. The horror I had of again breaking in on the privacy of another soul, made me, by an irrational instinct, draw the shroud of concealment more closely around my own, as we automatically perform the gesture we feel to be wanting in another.

When Meunier's visit was approaching its conclusion, there

happened an event which caused some excitement in our household, owing to the surprisingly strong effect it appeared to produce on Bertha—on Bertha, the self possessed, who usually seemed inaccessible to feminine agitations, and did even her hate in a self-restrained hygienic manner. This event was the sudden severe illness of her maid, Mrs. Archer. I have reserved to this moment the mention of a circumstance which had forced itself on my notice shortly before Meunier's arrival, namely, that there had been some quarrel between Bertha and this maid, apparently during a visit to a distant family, in which she had accompanied her mistress. I had overheard Archer speaking in a tone of bitter insolence, which I should have thought an adequate reason for immediate dismissal. No dismissal followed; on the contrary, Bertha seemed to be silently putting up with personal inconveniences from the exhibitions of this woman's temper. I was the more astonished to observe that her illness seemed a cause of strong solicitude to Bertha; that she was at the bedside night and day, and would allow no one else to officiate as head nurse. It happened that our family doctor was out on a holiday, an accident which made Meunier's presence in the house doubly welcome, and he apparently entered into the case with an interest which seemed so much stronger than the ordinary professional feeling, that one day when he had fallen into a long fit of silence after visiting her, I said to him—

"Is this a very peculiar case of disease, Meunier?"

"No," he answered, "it is an attack of peritonitis, which will be fatal, but which does not differ physically from many other cases that have come under my observation. But I'll tell you what I have on my mind. I want to make an experiment on this woman, if you will give me permission. It can do her no harm—will give her no pain—for I shall not make it until life is extinct to all purposes of sensation. I want to try the effect of transfusing blood into her arteries after the heart has ceased to beat for some minutes. I have tried the experiment again and again with animals that have died of this disease, with astounding results, and I want to try it on a human subject. I have the small tubes necessary, in a case I have with me, and the rest of the apparatus could be prepared readily. I should use my own blood—take it from my own arm. This woman won't live through the night, I'm convinced, and I want you to promise me your assistance in making the experiment.

I can't do without another hand, but it would perhaps not be well to call in a medical assistant from among your provincial doctors. A disagreeable foolish version of the thing might get abroad."

"Have you spoken to my wife on the subject?" I said, "because she appears to be peculiarly sensitive about this woman: she has been a favorite maid."

"To tell you the truth," said Meunier, "I don't want her to know about it. There are always insuperable difficulties with women in these matters, and the effect on the supposed dead body may be startling. You and I will sit up together, and be in readiness. When certain symptoms appear I shall take you in, and at the right moment we must manage to get every one else out of the room."

I need not give our farther conversation on the subject. He entered very fully into the details, and overcame my repulsion from them, by exciting in me a mingled awe and curiosity concerning the possible results of his experiment.

We prepared everything, and he instructed me in my part as assistant. He had not told Bertha of his absolute conviction that Archer would not survive through the night, and endeavored to persuade her to leave the patient and take a night's rest. But she was obstinate, suspecting the fact that death was at hand, and supposing that he wished merely to save her nerves. She refused to leave the sick-room. Meunier and I sat up together in the library, he making frequent visits to the sick-room, and returning with the information that the case was taking precisely the course he expected. Once he said to me, "Can you imagine any cause of ill feeling this woman has against her mistress, who is so devoted to her?"

"I think there was some misunderstanding between them before her illness. Why do you ask?"

"Because I have observed for the last five or six hours—since, I fancy, she has lost all hope of recovery—there seems a strange prompting in her to say something which pain and failing strength forbid her to utter; and there is a look of hideous meaning in her eyes, which she turns continually toward her mistress. In this disease the mind often remains singularly clear to the last."

"I am not surprised at an indication of malevolent feeling in her," I said. "She is a woman who has always inspired me with distrust and dislike, but she managed to insinuate herself into her mistress's favor." He was silent after this, looking at the fire with an air of absorption, till he went up-stairs again. He stayed away longer than usual, and on returning, said to me quietly, "Come now."

I followed him to the chamber where death was hovering. The dark hangings of the large bed made a background that gave a strong relief to Bertha's pale face as I entered. She started forward as she saw me enter, and then looked at Meunier with an expression of angry inquiry; but he lifted up his hand as if to impose silence, while he fixed his glance on the dying woman and felt her pulse. The face was pinched and ghastly, a cold perspiration was on the forehead, and the eyelids were lowered so as almost to conceal the large dark eyes. After a minute or two, Meunier walked round to the other side of the bed where Bertha stood, and with his usual air of gentle politeness toward her begged her to leave the patient under our care—everything should be done for her— she was no longer in a state to be conscious of an affectionate presence. Bertha was hesitating, apparently almost willing to believe his assurance and to comply. She looked round at the ghastly dying face, as if to read the confirmation of that assurance, when for a moment the lowered eyelids were raised again, and it seemed as if the eyes were looking toward Bertha, but blankly. A shudder passed through Bertha's frame, and she returned to her station near the pillow, tacitly implying that she would not leave the room.

The eyelids were lifted no more. Once I looked at Bertha as she watched the face of the dying one. She wore a rich *peignoir*, and her blonde hair was half covered by a lace cap: in her attire she was, as always, an elegant woman, fit to figure in a picture of modern aristocratic life: but I asked myself how that face of hers could ever have seemed to me the face of a woman born of woman, with memories of childhood, capable of pain, needing to be fondled? The features at that moment seemed so preternaturally sharp, the eyes were so hard and eager—she looked like a cruel immortal, finding her spiritual feast in the agonies of a dying race. For across those hard features there came something like a flash when the last hour had been breathed out, and we all felt that the dark veil had completely fallen. What secret was there between Bertha and this woman? I turned my eyes from her with a horrible dread lest my insight should return, and I should be obliged to see what had been breeding about two unloving women's hearts. I felt that Bertha had been watching for the moment of death as the sealing of her secret: I thanked Heaven it could remain sealed for me.

Meunier said quietly: "She is gone." He then gave his arm to Bertha, and she submitted to be led out of the room.

I suppose it was at her order that two female attendants came into the room, and dismissed the younger one who had been present before. When they entered, Meunier had already opened the artery in the long, thin neck that lay rigid on the pillow, and I dismissed them, ordering them to remain at a distance till we rang: the doctor, I said, had an operation to perform—he was not sure about the death. For the next twenty minutes I forgot everything but Meunier and the experiment in which he was so absorbed, that I think his senses would have been closed against all sounds or sights which had no relation to it. It was my task at first to keep up the artificial respiration in the body after the transfusion had been effected, but presently Meunier relieved me, and I could see the wondrous slow return of life; the breast began to heave, the inspirations became stronger, the eyelids quivered, and the soul seemed to have returned beneath them. The artificial respiration was withdrawn: still the breathing continued, and there was a movement of the lips.

Just then I heard the handle of the door moving: I suppose Bertha had heard from the women that they had been dismissed: probably a vague fear had arisen in her mind, for she entered with a look of alarm. She came to the foot of the bed and gave a stifled cry.

The dead woman's eyes were wide open, and met hers in full recognition—the recognition of hate. With a sudden strong effort, the hand that Bertha had thought for ever still was pointed toward her, and the haggard face moved. The gasping eager voice said—

"You mean to poison your husband——the poison is in the black cabinet——I got it for you——you laughed at me, and told lies about me behind my back, to make me disgusting——because you were jealous——are you sorry——now?"

The lips continued to murmur, but the sounds were no longer distinct. Soon there was no sound—only a slight movement: the flame had leaped out, and was being extinguished the faster. The wretched woman's heartstrings had been set to hatred and vengeance; the spirit of life had swept the chords for an instant, and was gone again for ever. Great God! Is this what it is to live again ——to wake up with our unstilled thirst upon us, with our unuttered curses rising to our lips, with our muscles ready to act out their half-committed sins?

Bertha stood pale at the foot of the bed, quivering and helpless, despairing of devices, like a cunning animal whose hiding-places are surrounded by swift-advancing flame. Even Meunier looked paralyzed; life for that moment ceased to be a scientific problem to him. As for me, this scene seemed of one texture with the rest of my existence: horror was my familiar, and this new revelation was only like an old pain recurring with new circumstances.

Since then Bertha and I have lived apart—she in her own neighborhood, the mistress of half our wealth, I as a wanderer in foreign countries, until I came to this Devonshire nest to die. Bertha lives pitied and admired; for what had I against that charming woman, whom every one but myself could have been happy with? There had been no witness of the scene in the dying room except Meunier, and while Meunier lived his lips were sealed by a promise to me.

Once or twice, weary of wandering, I rested in a favorite spot, and my heart went out toward the men and women and children whose faces were becoming familiar to me: but I was driven away again in terror at the approach of my old insight—driven away to live continually with the one Unknown Presence revealed and yet hidden by the moving curtain of the earth and sky. Till at last disease took hold of me and forced me to rest here—forced me to live in dependence on my servants. And then the curse of insight —of my double consciousness, came again, and has never left me. I know all their narrow thoughts, their feeble regard, their half-wearied pity.

It is the twentieth of September, 1850. I know these figures I have just written, as if they were a long familiar inscription. I have seen them on this page in my desk unnumbered times, when the scene of my dying struggle has opened upon me.

The Secret Sharer

1912

JOSEPH CONRAD

THE COLOSSUS of Henry James, who diminishes his predecessors, George Eliot and Meredith, also towered over those who came immediately after him. There is not room for more than one difficult author at a time. Conrad, besides learning late to write in English, also attempted to write English like Henry James, so that much of his prose has the artificiality of a translation. "Conrad haunts Winchelsea and Winchelsea (in discretion) haunts Rye" wrote James from his home in 1902. Yet prickly and self-conscious, involved and mannered though his style be, Conrad is the first of our authors to prefer the short novel to all others: his best work is given in this form, not just an occasional by-blow. Lord Jim, The Nigger of the Narcissus, Youth, Typhoon, Heart of Darkness, and a Set of Six, are among these. They are all well-known and are all marred in greater or less degree by the conventions of "yarn-spinning," the worst offender being his narrator Marlow. Whereas Hardy's short novels make one turn again to his longer ones, Conrad's are an end in themselves—such storms, such heroism, such chivalry and courtesy in a man's world—they are like stories by Hemingway or Malraux written by an upright christian gentleman, gallant, punctilious and ironical, yet preoccupied even as they are with the definition of courage. The Secret Sharer is taken from Twixt Land and Sea (1912). It is entirely devoid of yarn-spinning and seems to carry a symbolical meaning. Is Leggatt real or imaginary? If real how could he have hidden in the bath? if imaginary, why did the sailors seem to hear him? In either case, the author manages with marvellous skill the stress and tension of the testing time of the young Captain who, mad or sane, "was something of a stranger to himself."

Joseph Conrad's real name was Teodor Jozef Konrad Korzenowski. He was born in 1857 of Polish parents in the

Ukraine, who were afterwards exiled to Siberia. In 1874 he joined the crew of a French vessel, in 1878 an English one, in 1884 he got his master's certificate and became a British subject. In 1894 he abandoned the sea altogether for literature and died in 1924 at his cottage in Kent. England and the sea were his passions, Russia his bête noire, man's solitariness his theme. "My faculty to write in English," he wrote, "is as natural as any other aptitude with which I might have been born. I have a strange and overpowering feeling that it had always been an inherent part of myself . . . if I had not written in English I would not have written at all."

The Secret Sharer

JOSEPH CONRAD

Chapter I

ON MY RIGHT hand there were lines of fishing-stakes resembling a mysterious system of half-submerged bamboo fences, incomprehensible in its division of the domain of tropical fishes, and crazy of aspect as if abandoned for ever by some nomad tribe of fishermen now gone to the other end of the ocean; for there was no sign of human habitation as far as the eye could reach. To the left a group of barren islets, suggesting ruins of stone walls, towers, and blockhouses, had its foundations set in a blue sea that itself looked solid, so still and stable did it lie below my feet; even the track of light from the westering sun shone smoothly, without that animated glitter which tells of an imperceptible ripple. And when I turned my head to take a parting glance at the tug which had just left us anchored outside the bar, I saw the straight line of the flat shore joined to the stable sea, edge to edge, with a perfect and unmarked closeness, in one levelled floor half brown, half blue under the enormous dome of the sky. Corresponding in their insignificance to the islets of the sea, two small clumps of trees, one on each side of the only fault in the impeccable joint, marked the mouth of the river Meinam we had just left on the first preparatory stage of our homeward journey; and, far back on the inland level, a larger and loftier mass, the grove surrounding the great Paknam pagoda, was the only thing on which the eye could rest from the vain task of exploring the monotonous sweep of the horizon. Here and there gleams as of a few scattered pieces of silver marked the windings of the great river; and on the nearest of them, just within the bar, the tug steaming right into the land became lost to my sight, hull and funnel and masts, as though the impassive earth had swallowed her up without an effort, without a tremor. My eye followed the light cloud of her smoke, now here, now there, above the plain, according to the devious curves of the stream, but always fainter and farther away, till I lost it at last behind the mitre-shaped hill of the great pagoda. And then I was left alone with my ship, anchored at the head of the Gulf of Siam.

She floated at the starting-point of a long journey, very still in an immense stillness, the shadows of her spars flung far to the eastward by the setting sun. At that moment I was alone on her decks. There was not a sound in her—and around us nothing moved, nothing lived, not a canoe on the water, not a bird in the air, not a cloud in the sky. In this breathless pause at the threshold of a long passage we seemed to be measuring our fitness for a long and arduous enterprise, the appointed task of both our existences to be carried out, far from all human eyes, with only sky and sea for spectators and for judges.

There must have been some glare in the air to interfere with one's sight, because it was only just before the sun left us that my roaming eyes made out beyond the highest ridge of the principal islet of the group something which did away with the solemnity of perfect solitude. The tide of darkness flowed on swiftly; and with tropical suddenness a swarm of stars came out above the shadowy earth, while I lingered yet, my hand resting lightly on my ship's rail as if on the shoulder of a trusted friend. But, with all that multitude of celestial bodies staring down at one, the comfort of quiet communion with her was gone for good. And there were also disturbing sounds by this time—voices, footsteps forward; the steward flitted along the maindeck, a busily ministering spirit; a hand-bell tinkled urgently under the poop-deck. . . .

I found my two officers waiting for me near the supper table, in the lighted cuddy. We sat down at once, and as I helped the chief mate, I said:

"Are you aware that there is a ship anchored inside the islands? I saw her mastheads above the ridge as the sun went down."

He raised sharply his simple face, overcharged by a terrible growth of whisker, and emitted his usual ejaculations: "Bless my soul, sir! You don't say so!"

My second mate was a round-cheeked, silent young man, grave beyond his years, I thought; but as our eyes happened to meet I detected a slight quiver on his lips. I looked down at once. It was not my part to encourage sneering on board my ship. It must be said, too, that I knew very little of my officers. In consequence of certain events of no particular significance, except to myself, I had been appointed to the command only a fortnight before. Neither did I know much of the hands forward. All these people had been together for eighteen months or so, and my position was that of the only stranger on board. I mention this because it has some bearing on what is to follow. But what I felt most was my being a stranger to the ship; and if all the truth must be told, I was somewhat of a stranger to myself. The youngest man on board (barring the second mate), and untried as yet by a position of the fullest responsibility, I was willing to take the adequacy of the others for granted. They had simply to be equal to their tasks; but I wondered how far I should turn out faithful to that ideal conception of one's own personality every man sets up for himself secretly.

Meantime the chief mate, with an almost visible effect of collaboration on the part of his round eyes and frightful whiskers, was trying to evolve a theory of the anchored ship. His dominant trait was to take all things into earnest consideration. He was of a painstaking turn of mind. As he used to say, he "liked to account to himself" for practically everything that came in his way, down to a miserable scorpion he had found in his cabin a week before. The why and the wherefore of that scorpion—how it got on board and came to select his room rather than the pantry (which was a dark place and more what a scorpion would be partial to), and how on earth it managed to drown itself in the inkwell of his writing-desk—had exercised him infinitely. The ship within the islands was much more easily accounted for; and just as we were about to rise from table he made his pronouncement. She was, he doubted not, a ship from home lately arrived. Probably she drew too much water to cross the bar except at the top of spring tides.

Therefore she went into that natural harbour to wait for a few days in preference to remaining in an open roadstead.

"That's so," confirmed the second mate, suddenly, in his slightly hoarse voice. "She draws over twenty feet. She's the Liverpool ship *Sephora* with a cargo of coal. Hundred and twenty-three days from Cardiff."

We looked at him in surprise.

"The tugboat skipper told me when he came on board for your letters, sir," explained the young man. "He expects to take her up the river the day after tomorrow."

After thus overwhelming us with the extent of his information he slipped out of the cabin. The mate observed regretfully that he "could not account for that young fellow's whims." What prevented him telling us all about it at once, he wanted to know.

I detained him as he was making a move. For the last two days the crew had had plenty of hard work, and the night before they had very little sleep. I felt painfully that I—a stranger—was doing something unusual when I directed him to let all hands turn in without setting an anchor-watch. I proposed to keep on deck myself till one o'clock or thereabouts. I would get the second mate to relieve me at that hour.

"He will turn out the cook and the steward at four," I concluded, "and then give you a call. Of course at the slightest sign of any sort of wind we'll have the hands up and make a start at once."

He concealed his astonishment. "Very well, sir." Outside the cuddy he put his head in the second mate's door to inform him of my unheard-of caprice to take a five hours' anchor-watch on myself. I heard the other raise his voice incredulously—"What? The Captain himself?" Then a few more murmurs, a door closed, then another. A few moments later I went on deck.

My strangeness, which had made me sleepless, had prompted that unconventional arrangement, as if I had expected in those solitary hours of the night to get on terms with the ship of which I knew nothing, manned by men of whom I knew very little more. Fast alongside a wharf, littered like any ship in port with a tangle of unrelated things, invaded by unrelated shore people, I had hardly seen her yet properly. Now, as she lay cleared for sea, the stretch of her main-deck seemed to me very fine under the stars.

Very fine, very roomy for her size, and very inviting. I descended the poop and paced the waist, my mind picturing to myself the coming passage through the Malay Archipelago, down the Indian Ocean, and up the Atlantic. All its phases were familiar enough to me, every characteristic, all the alternatives which were likely to face me on the high seas—everything! . . . except the novel responsibility of command. But I took heart from the reasonable thought that the ship was like other ships, the men like other men, and that the sea was not likely to keep any special surprises expressly for my discomfiture.

Arrived at that comforting conclusion, I bethought myself of a cigar and went below to get it. All was still down there. Everybody at the after end of the ship was sleeping profoundly. I came out again on the quarter-deck, agreeably at ease in my sleeping-suit on that warm breathless night, barefooted, a glowing cigar in my teeth, and, going forward, I was met by the profound silence of the fore end of the ship. Only as I passed the door of the forecastle I heard a deep, quiet, trustful sigh of some sleeper inside. And suddenly I rejoiced in the great security of the sea as compared with the unrest of the land, in my choice of that untempted life presenting no disquieting problems, invested with an elementary moral beauty by the absolute straightforwardness of its appeal and by the singleness of its purpose.

The riding-light in the fore-rigging burned with a clear, untroubled, as if symbolic, flame, confident and bright in the mysterious shades of the night. Passing on my way aft along the other side of the ship, I observed that the rope side-ladder, put over, no doubt, for the master of the tug when he came to fetch away our letters, had not been hauled in as it should have been. I became annoyed at this, for exactitude in small matters is the very soul of discipline. Then I reflected that I had myself peremptorily dismissed my officers from duty, and by my own act had prevented the anchor-watch being formally set and things properly attended to. I asked myself whether it was wise ever to interfere with the established routine of duties even from the kindest of motives. My action might have made me appear eccentric. Goodness only knew how that absurdly whiskered mate would "account" for my conduct, and what the whole ship thought of that informality of their new captain. I was vexed with myself.

Not from compunction certainly, but, as it were mechanically, I proceeded to get the ladder in myself. Now a side-ladder of that sort is a light affair and comes in easily, yet my vigorous tug, which should have brought it flying on board, merely recoiled upon my body in a totally unexpected jerk. What the devil! . . . I was so astounded by the immovableness of that ladder that I remained stock-still, trying to account for it to myself like that imbecile mate of mine. In the end, of course, I put my head over the rail.

The side of the ship made an opaque belt of shadow on the darkling glassy shimmer of the sea. But I saw at once something elongated and pale floating very close to the ladder. Before I could form a guess a faint flash of phosphorescent light, which seemed to issue suddenly from the naked body of a man, flickered in the sleeping water with the elusive, silent play of summer lightning in a night sky. With a gasp I saw revealed to my stare a pair of feet, the long legs, a broad livid back immersed right up to the neck in a greenish cadaverous glow. One hand, awash, clutched the bottom rung of the ladder. He was complete but for the head. A headless corpse! The cigar dropped out of my gaping mouth with a tiny plop and a short hiss quite audible in the absolute stillness of all things under heaven. At that I suppose he raised up his face, a dimly pale oval in the shadow of the ship's side. But even then I could only barely make out down there the shape of his black-haired head. However, it was enough for the horrid, frost-bound sensation which had gripped me about the chest to pass off. The moment of vain exclamations was past, too. I only climbed on the spare spar and leaned over the rail as far as I could, to bring my eyes nearer to that mystery floating alongside.

As he hung by the ladder, like a resting swimmer, the sea-lightning played about his limbs at every stir; and he appeared in it ghastly, silvery, fish-like. He remained as mute as a fish, too. He made no motion to get out of the water, either. It was inconceivable that he should not attempt to come on board, and strangely troubling to suspect that perhaps he did not want to. And my first words were prompted by just that troubled incertitude.

"What's the matter?" I asked in my ordinary tone, speaking down to the face upturned exactly under mine.

"Cramp," it answered, no louder. Then slightly anxious, "I say, no need to call any one."

"I was not going to," I said.

"Are you alone on deck?"

"Yes."

I had somehow the impression that he was on the point of letting go the ladder to swim away beyond my ken—mysterious as he came. But, for the moment, this being appearing as if he had risen from the bottom of the sea (it was certainly the nearest land to the ship) wanted only to know the time. I told him. And he, down there, tentatively:

"I suppose your captain's turned in?"

"I am sure he isn't," I said.

He seemed to struggle with himself, for I heard something like the low, bitter murmur of doubt. "What's the good?" His next words came out with a hesitating effort.

"Look here, my man. Could you call him out quietly?"

I thought the time had come to declare myself.

"I am the captain."

I heard a "By Jove!" whispered at the level of the water. The phosphorescence flashed in the swirl of the water all about his limbs, his other hand seized the ladder.

"My name's Leggatt."

The voice was calm and resolute. A good voice. The self-possession of that man had somehow induced a corresponding state in myself. It was very quietly that I remarked:

"You must be a good swimmer."

"Yes. I've been in the water practically since nine o'clock. The question for me now is whether I am to let go this ladder and go on swimming till I sink from exhaustion, or—to come on board here."

I felt this was no mere formula of desperate speech, but a real alternative in the view of a strong soul. I should have gathered from this that he was young; indeed, it is only the young who are ever confronted by such clear issues. But at the time it was pure intuition on my part. A mysterious communication was established already between us two—in the face of that silent, darkened tropical sea. I was young, too; young enough to make no comment. The man in the water began suddenly to climb up the ladder, and I hastened away from the rail to fetch some clothes.

Before entering the cabin I stood still, listening in the lobby at the foot of the stairs. A faint snore came through the closed door of the chief mate's room. The second mate's door was on the hook, but the darkness in there was absolutely soundless. He, too, was young and could sleep like a stone. Remained the steward, but he was not likely to wake up before he was called. I got a sleeping-suit out of my room and, coming back on deck, saw the naked man from the sea sitting on the main-hatch, glimmering white in the darkness, his elbows on his knees and his head in his hands. In a moment he had concealed his damp body in a sleeping-suit of the same grey-stripe pattern as the one I was wearing and followed me like my double on the poop. Together we moved right aft, barefooted, silent.

"What is it?" I asked in a deadened voice, taking the lighted lamp out of the binnacle, and raising it to his face.

"An ugly business."

He had rather regular features; a good mouth; light eyes under somewhat heavy, dark eyebrows; a smooth, square forehead; no growth on his cheeks; a small, brown moustache, and a well-shaped, round chin. His expression was concentrated, meditative, under the inspecting light of the lamp I held up to his face; such as a man thinking hard in solitude might wear. My sleeping-suit was just right for his size. A well-knit young fellow of twenty-five at most. He caught his lower lip with the edge of white, even teeth.

"Yes," I said, replacing the lamp in the binnacle. The warm, heavy tropical night closed upon his head again.

"There's a ship over there," he murmured.

"Yes, I know. The *Sephora*. Did you know of us?"

"Hadn't the slightest idea. I am the mate of her——" He paused and corrected himself. "I should say I was."

"Aha! Something wrong?"

"Yes. Very wrong indeed. I've killed a man."

"What do you mean? Just now?"

"No, on the passage. Weeks ago. Thirty-nine south. When I say a man——"

"Fit of temper," I suggested, confidently.

The shadowy, dark head, like mine, seemed to nod imperceptibly above the ghostly grey of my sleeping-suit. It was, in the

444

night, as though I had been faced by my own reflection in the depths of a sombre and immense mirror.

"A pretty thing to have to own up to for a Conway boy," murmured my double, distinctly.

"You're a Conway boy?"

"I am," he said, as if startled. Then, slowly . . . "Perhaps you too——"

It was so; but being a couple of years older I had left before he joined. After a quick interchange of dates a silence fell; and I thought suddenly of my absurd mate with his terrific whiskers and the "Bless my soul—you don't say so" type of intellect. My double gave me an inkling of his thoughts by saying: "My father's a parson in Norfolk. Do you see me before a judge and jury on that charge? For myself I can't see the necessity. There are fellows that an angel from heaven—— And I am not that. He was one of those creatures that are just simmering all the time with a silly sort of wickedness. Miserable devils that have no business to live at all. He wouldn't do his duty and wouldn't let anybody else do theirs. But what's the good of talking! You know well enough the sort of ill-conditioned snarling cur——"

He appealed to me as if our experiences had been as identical as our clothes. And I knew well enough the pestiferous danger of such a character where there are no means of legal repression. And I knew well enough also that my double there was no homicidal ruffian. I did not think of asking him for details, and he told me the story roughly in brusque, disconnected sentences. I needed no more. I saw it all going on as though I were myself inside that other sleeping-suit.

"It happened while we were setting a reefed foresail, at dusk. Reefed foresail! You understand the sort of weather. The only sail we had left to keep the ship running; so you may guess what it had been like for days. Anxious sort of job, that. He gave me some of his cursed insolence at the sheet. I tell you I was overdone with this terrific weather that seemed to have no end to it. Terrific, I tell you—and a deep ship. I believe the fellow himself was half crazed with funk. It was no time for gentlemanly reproof, so I turned round and felled him like an ox. He up and at me. We closed just as an awful sea made for the ship. All hands saw it coming and took to the rigging, but I had him by the throat, and went on shaking him like a rat, the men above us yelling, 'Look out! look out!' " Then a crash as if the sky had fallen on my head. They say that for over ten minutes hardly anything was to be seen of the ship—just the three masts and a bit of the forecastle head and of the poop all awash driving along in a smother of foam. It was a miracle that they found us, jammed together behind the forebits. It's clear that I meant business, because I was holding him by the throat still when they picked us up. He was black in the face. It was too much for them. It seems they rushed us aft together, gripped as we were, screaming 'Murder!' like a lot of lunatics, and broke into the cuddy. And the ship running for her life, touch and go all the time, any minute her last in a sea fit to turn your hair grey only a-looking at it. I understand that the skipper, too, started raving like the rest of them. The man had been deprived of sleep for more than a week, and to have this sprung on him at the height of a furious gale nearly drove him out of his mind. I wonder they didn't fling me overboard after getting the carcass of their precious ship-mate out of my fingers. They had rather a job to separate us, I've been told. A sufficiently fierce story to make an old judge and a respectable jury sit up a bit. The first thing I heard when I came to myself was the maddening howling of that endless gale, and on that the voice of the old man. He was hanging on to my bunk, staring into my face out of his sou'wester.

" 'Mr. Leggatt, you have killed a man. You can act no longer as chief mate of this ship.' "

His care to subdue his voice made it sound monotonous. He rested a hand on the end of the skylight to steady himself with, and all that time did not stir a limb, so far as I could see. "Nice little tale for a quiet tea-party," he concluded in the same tone.

One of my hands, too, rested on the end of the sky-light; neither did I stir a limb, so far as I knew. We stood less than a foot from each other. It occurred to me that if old "Bless my soul —you don't say so" were to put his head up the companion and catch sight of us, he would think he was seeing double, or imagine himself come upon a scene of weird witchcraft; the strange captain having a quiet confabulation by the wheel with his own grey ghost. I became very much concerned to prevent anything of the sort. I heard the other's soothing undertone.

"My father's a parson in Norfolk," it said. Evidently he had forgotten he had told me this important fact before. Truly a nice little tale.

"You had better slip down into my stateroom now," I said, moving off stealthily. My double followed my movements; our bare feet made no sound; I let him in, closed the door with care, and, after giving a call to the second mate, returned on deck for my relief.

"Not much sign of any wind yet," I remarked when he approached.

"No, sir. Not much," he assented, sleepily, in his hoarse voice, with just enough deference, no more, and barely suppressing a yawn.

"Well, that's all you have to look out for. You have got your orders."

"Yes, sir."

I paced a turn or two on the poop and saw him take up his position face forward with his elbow in the ratlines of the mizzen-rigging before I went below. The mate's faint snoring was still going on peacefully. The cuddy lamp was burning over the table on which stood a vase with flowers, a polite attention from the ship's provision merchant—the last flowers we should see for the next three months at the very least. Two bunches of bananas hung from the beam symmetrically, one on each side of the rudder-casing. Everything was as before in the ship—except that two of her captain's sleeping-suits were simultaneously in use, one motionless in the cuddy, the other keeping very still in the captain's stateroom.

It must be explained here that my cabin had the form of the capital letter L the door being within the angle and opening into the short part of the letter. A couch was to the left, the bed-place to the right; my writing-desk and the chronometers' table faced the door. But any one opening it, unless he stepped right inside, had no view of what I call the long (or vertical) part of the letter. It contained some lockers surmounted by a bookcase; and a few clothes, a thick jacket or two, caps, oilskin coat, and such like, hung on hooks. There was at the bottom of that part a door opening into my bath-room, which could be entered also directly from the saloon. But that way was never used.

The mysterious arrival had discovered the advantage of this particular shape. Entering my room, lighted strongly by a big bulkhead lamp swung on gimbals above my writing-desk, I did not see him anywhere till he stepped out quietly from behind the coats hung in the recessed part.

"I heard somebody moving about, and went in there at once," he whispered.

I, too, spoke under my breath.

"Nobody is likely to come in here without knocking and getting permission."

He nodded. His face was thin and the sunburn faded, as though he had been ill. And no wonder. He had been, I heard presently, kept under arrest in his cabin for nearly seven weeks. But there was nothing sickly in his eyes or in his expression. He was not a bit like me, really; yet, as we stood leaning over my bed-place, whispering side by side, with our dark heads together and our backs to the door, anybody bold enough to open it stealthily would have been treated to the uncanny sight of a double captain busy talking in whispers with his other self.

"But all this doesn't tell me how you came to hang on to our side-ladder," I inquired, in the hardly audible murmurs we used, after he had told me something more of the proceedings on board the *Sephora* once the bad weather was over.

"When we sighted Java Head I had had time to think all those matters out several times over. I had six weeks of doing nothing else, and with only an hour or so every evening for a tramp on the quarter-deck."

He whispered, his arms folded on the side of my bed-place, staring through the open port. And I could imagine perfectly the manner of this thinking out—a stubborn if not a steadfast operation; something of which I should have been perfectly incapable.

"I reckoned it would be dark before we closed with the land," he continued, so low that I had to strain my hearing, near as we were to each other, shoulder touching shoulder almost. "So I asked to speak to the old man. He always seemed very sick when he came to see me—as if he could not look me in the face. You know, that foresail saved the ship. She was too deep to have run long under bare poles. And it was I that managed to set it for him. Anyway, he came. When I had him in my cabin—he stood by the door looking at me as if I had the halter round my neck already—I asked him right away to leave my cabin door unlocked at night while the ship was going through Sunda Straits. There would be the Java coast within two or three miles, off Angier Point. I wanted nothing more. I've had a prize for swimming my second year in the Conway."

"I can believe it," I breathed out.

"God only knows why they locked me in every night. To see some of their faces you'd have thought they were afraid I'd go about at night strangling people. Am I a murdering brute? Do I look it? By Jove! if I had been he wouldn't have trusted himself like that into my room. You'll say I might have chucked him aside and bolted out, there and then—it was dark already. Well, no. And for the same reason I wouldn't think of trying to smash the door. There would have been a rush to stop me at the noise, and I did not mean to get into a confounded scrimmage. Somebody else might have got killed—for I would not have broken out only to get chucked back, and I did not want any more of that work. He refused, looking more sick than ever. He was afraid of the men, and also of that old second mate of his who had been sailing with him for years—a grey-headed old humbug; and his steward, too, had been with him devil knows how long— seventeen years or more—a dogmatic sort of loafer who hated me like poison, just because I was the chief mate. No chief mate ever made more than one voyage in the *Sephora*, you know. Those two old chaps ran the ship. Devil only knows what the skipper wasn't afraid of (all his nerve went to pieces altogether in that hellish spell of bad weather we had)—of what the law would do to him—of his wife, perhaps. Oh, yes! she's on board. Though I don't think she would have meddled. She would have been only too glad to have me out of the ship in any way. The 'brand of Cain' business, don't you see. That's all right. I was ready enough to go off wandering on the face of the earth—and that was price enough to pay for an Abel of that sort. Anyhow, he wouldn't listen to me. 'This thing must take its course. I represent the law here.' He was shaking like a leaf. 'So you won't?' 'No!' 'Then I hope you will be able to sleep on that,' I said, and turned my back on him. 'I wonder that you can,' cries he, and locks the door.

"Well, after that, I couldn't. Not very well. That was three weeks ago. We have had a slow passage through the Java Sea; drifted about Carimata for ten days. When we anchored here they thought, I suppose, it was all right. The nearest land (and that's five miles) is the ship's destination; the consul would soon set about catching me; and there would have been no object in bolting to these islets there. I don't suppose there's a drop of water on them. I don't know how it was, but to-night that steward, after bringing me my supper, went out to let me eat it, and left the door unlocked. And I ate it—all there was, too. After I had finished I strolled out on the quarter-deck. I don't know that I meant to do anything. A breath of fresh air was all I wanted, I believe. Then a sudden temptation came over me. I kicked off my slippers and was in the water before I had made up my mind fairly. Somebody heard the splash and they raised an awful hullabaloo. 'He's gone! Lower the boats! He's committed suicide! No, he's swimming.' Certainly I was swimming. It's not so easy for a swimmer like me to commit suicide by drowning. I landed on the nearest islet before the boat left the ship's side. I heard them pulling about in the dark, hailing, and so on, but after a bit they gave up. Everything quieted down and the anchorage became as still as death. I sat down on a stone and began to think. I felt certain they would start searching for me at daylight. There was no place to hide on those stony things—and if there had been, what would have been the good? But now I was clear of that ship, I was not going back. So after a while I took off all my clothes, tied them up in a bundle with a stone inside, and dropped them in the deep water on the outer side of that islet. That was suicide enough for me. Let them think what they liked, but I didn't mean to drown myself. I meant to swim till I sank—but that's not the same thing. I struck out for another of these little islands, and it was from that one that I first saw your riding-light. Something to swim for. I went on easily, and on the way I came upon a flat rock a foot or two above water. In the daytime, I dare say, you might make it out with a glass from your poop. I scrambled up on it and rested myself for a bit. Then I made another start. That last spell must have been over a mile."

His whisper was getting fainter and fainter, and all the time he stared straight out through the port-hole, in which there was not even a star to be seen. I had not interrupted him. There was something that made comment impossible in his narrative, or perhaps in himself; a sort of feeling, a quality, which I can't find a name for. And when he ceased, all I found was a futile whisper: "So you swam for our light?"

"Yes—straight for it. It was something to swim for. I couldn't see any stars low down because the coast was in the way, and I couldn't see the land, either. The water was like glass. One might have been swimming in a confounded thousand-feet deep cistern with no place for scrambling out anywhere; but what I didn't like was the notion of swimming round and round like a crazed bullock before I gave out; and as I didn't mean to go back . . . No. Do you see me being hauled back, stark naked, off one of these little islands by the scruff of the neck and fighting like a wild beast? Somebody would have got killed for certain, and I did not want any of that. So I went on. Then your ladder——"

"Why didn't you hail the ship?" I asked, a little louder.

He touched my shoulder lightly. Lazy footsteps came right over our heads and stopped. The second mate had crossed from the other side of the poop and might have been hanging over the rail, for all we knew.

"He couldn't hear us talking—could he?" My double breathed into my very ear, anxiously.

His anxiety was an answer, a sufficient answer, to the question I had put to him. An answer containing all the difficulty of that situation. I closed the port hole quietly, to make sure. A louder word might have been overheard.

"Who's that?" he whispered then.

"My second mate. But I don't know much more of the fellow than you do."

And I told him a little about myself. I had been appointed to take charge while I least expected anything of the sort, not quite a fortnight ago. I didn't know either the ship or the people. Hadn't had the time in port to look about me or size anybody up. And as to the crew, all they knew was that I was appointed to take the ship home. For the rest, I was almost as much of a stranger on board as himself, I said. And at the moment I felt it most acutely. I felt that it would take very little to make me a suspect person in the eyes of the ship's company.

He had turned about meantime; and we, the two strangers in the ship, faced each other in identical attitudes.

"Your ladder——" he murmured, after a silence. "Who'd have thought of finding a ladder hanging over at night in a ship anchored out here! I felt just then a very unpleasant faintness. After the life I've been leading for nine weeks, anybody would have got out of condition. I wasn't capable of swimming round as far as your rudder-chains. And, lo and behold! there was a ladder to get hold of. After I gripped it I said to myself, 'What's the good?' When I saw a man's head looking over I thought I would swim away presently and leave him shouting—in whatever language it was. I didn't mind being looked at. I—I liked it. And then you speaking to me so quietly—as if you had expected me—made me hold on a little longer. It had been a confounded lonely time— I don't mean while swimming. I was glad to talk a little to somebody that didn't belong to the *Sephora*. As to asking for the captain, that was a mere impulse. It could have been no use, with all the ship knowing about me and the other people pretty certain to be round here in the morning. I don't know—I wanted to be seen, to talk with somebody, before I went on. I don't know what I would have said. . . . 'Fine night, isn't it?' or something of the sort."

"Do you think they will be round here presently?" I asked with some incredulity.

"Quite likely," he said, faintly.

He looked extremely haggard all of a sudden. His head rolled on his shoulders.

"H'm. We shall see then. Meantime get into that bed," I whispered. "Want help? There."

It was a rather high bed-place with a set of drawers underneath. This amazing swimmer really needed the lift I gave him by seizing his leg. He tumbled in, rolled over on his back, and flung one arm across his eyes. And then, with his face nearly hidden, he must have looked exactly as I used to look in that bed. I gazed upon my other self for a while before drawing across carefully the two green serge curtains which ran on a brass rod. I thought for a moment of pinning them together for greater safety, but I sat down on the couch, and once there I felt unwilling to rise and hunt for a pin. I would do it in a moment. I was extremely tired, in a peculiarly intimate way, by the strain of stealthiness, by the effort of whispering and the general secrecy of this excitement. It was three o'clock by now and I had been on my feet since nine, but I was not sleepy; I could not have gone to sleep. I sat there, fagged out, looking at the curtains, trying to clear my mind of the confused sensation of being in two places at once, and greatly bothered by an exasperating knocking in my head. It was a relief to discover suddenly that it was not in my head at all, but on the outside of the door. Before I could collect myself the words "Come in" were out of my mouth, and the steward entered with a tray, bringing in my morning coffee. I had slept, after all, and I was so frightened that I shouted, "This way! I am here, steward," as though he had been miles away. He put down the tray on the table next the couch and only then said, very quietly, "I can see you are here, sir." I felt him give me a keen look, but I dared not meet his eyes just then. He must have wondered why I had drawn the curtains of my bed before going to sleep on the couch. He went out, hooking the door open as usual.

I heard the crew washing decks above me. I knew I would have been told at once if there had been any wind. Calm, I thought, and I was doubly vexed. Indeed, I felt dual more than ever. The steward reappeared suddenly in the doorway. I jumped up from the couch so quickly that he gave a start.

"What do you want here?"

"Close your port, sir—they are washing decks."

"It is closed," I said, reddening.

"Very well, sir." But he did not move from the doorway and returned my stare in an extraordinary, equivocal manner for a time. Then his eyes wavered, all his expression changed, and in a voice unusually gentle, almost coaxingly:

"May I come in to take the empty cup away, sir?"

"Of course!" I turned my back on him while he popped in and out. Then I unhooked and closed the door and even pushed the bolt. This sort of thing could not go on very long. The cabin was as hot as an oven, too. I took a peep at my double, and discovered that he had not moved, his arm was still over his eyes; but his chest heaved; his hair was wet; his chin glistened with perspiration. I reached over him and opened the port.

"I must show myself on deck," I reflected.

Of course, theoretically, I could do what I liked, with no one to say nay to me within the whole circle of the horizon; but to lock my cabin door and take the key away I did not dare. Directly I put my head out of the companion I saw the group of my two officers, the second mate barefooted, the chief mate in long india-rubber boots, near the break of the poop, and the steward half-way down the poop-ladder talking to them eagerly. He happened to catch sight of me and dived, the second ran down on the main-deck shouting some order or other, and the chief mate came to meet me, touching his cap.

There was a sort of curiosity in his eye that I did not like. I don't know whether the steward had told them that I was "queer" only, or downright drunk, but I know the man meant to have a good look at me. I watched him coming with a smile which, as he got into point-blank range, took effect and froze his very whiskers. I did not give him time to open his lips.

"Square the yards by lifts and braces before the hands go to breakfast."

It was the first particular order I had given on board that ship; and I stayed on deck to see it executed, too. I had felt the need of asserting myself without loss of time. That sneering young cub got taken down a peg or two on that occasion, and I also seized the opportunity of having a good look at the face of every foremast man as they filed past me to go to the after braces. At breakfast time, eating nothing myself, I presided with such frigid dignity that the two mates were only too glad to escape from the cabin as soon as decency permitted; and all the time the dual working of my mind distracted me almost to the point of insanity. I was constantly watching myself, my secret self, as dependent on my actions as my own personality, sleeping in that bed, behind that door which faced me as I sat at the head of the table. It was very much like being mad, only it was worse because one was aware of it.

I had to shake him for a solid minute, but when at last he opened his eyes it was in the full possession of his senses, with an inquiring look.

"All's well so far," I whispered. "Now you must vanish into the bath-room."

He did so, as noiseless as a ghost, and then I rang for the

steward, and facing him boldly, directed him to tidy up my state-room while I was having my bath—"and be quick about it." As my tone admitted of no excuses, he said, "Yes, sir," and ran off to fetch his dust-pan and brushes. I took a bath and did most of my dressing, splashing, and whistling softly for the steward's edification, while the secret sharer of my life stood drawn up bolt upright in that little space, his face looking very sunken in daylight, his eyelids lowered under the stern, dark line of his eyebrows drawn together by a slight frown.

When I left him there to go back to my room the steward was finishing dusting. I sent for the mate and engaged him in some insignificant conversation. It was, as it were, trifling with the terrific character of his whiskers; but my object was to give him an opportunity for a good look at my cabin. And then I could at last shut, with a clear conscience, the door of my stateroom and get my double back into the recessed part. There was nothing else for it. He had to sit still on a small folding stool, half smothered by the heavy coats hanging there. We listened to the steward going into the bath-room out of the saloon, filling the water-bottles there, scrubbing the bath, setting things to rights, whisk, bang, clatter—out again into the saloon—turn the key—click. Such was my scheme for keeping my second self invisible. Nothing better could be contrived under the circumstances. And there we sat; I at my writing-desk ready to appear busy with some papers, he behind me out of sight of the door. It would not have been prudent to talk in daytime; and I could not have stood the excite-ment of that queer sense of whispering to myself. Now and then, glancing over my shoulder, I saw him far back there, sitting rigidly on the low stool, his bare feet close together, his arms folded, his head hanging on his breast—and perfectly still. Anybody would have taken him for me.

I was fascinated by it myself. Every moment I had to glance over my shoulder. I was looking at him when a voice outside the door said:

"Beg pardon, sir."

"Well!" . . . I kept my eyes on him, and so when the voice outside the door announced, "There's a ship's boat coming our way, sir," I saw him give a start—the first movement he had made for hours. But he did not raise his bowed head.

"All right. Get the ladder over."

I hesitated. Should I whisper something to him? But what? His immobility seemed to have been never disturbed. What could I tell him he did not know already? . . . Finally I went on deck.

Chapter II

THE SKIPPER OF the *Sephora* had a thin red whisker all round his face, and the sort of complexion that goes with hair of that colour; also the particular, rather smeary shade of blue in the eyes. He was not exactly a showy figure; his shoulders were high, his stature but middling—one leg slightly more bandy than the other. He shook hands, looking vaguely around. A spiritless tenacity was his main characteristic, I judged. I behaved with a politeness which seemed to disconcert him. Perhaps he was shy. He mumbled to me as if he were ashamed of what he was saying; gave his name (it was something like Archbold—but at this distance of years I hardly am sure), his ship's name, and a few other particulars of that sort, in the manner of a criminal making a reluctant and doleful confession. He had had terrible weather on the passage out—terrible—terrible—wife aboard, too.

By this time we were seated in the cabin and the steward brought in a tray with a bottle and glasses. "Thanks! No." Never took liquor. Would have some water, though. He drank two tumblerfuls. Terrible thirsty work. Ever since daylight had been exploring the islands round his ship.

"What was that for—fun?" I asked, with an appearance of polite interest.

"No!" He sighed. "Painful duty."

As he persisted in his mumbling and I wanted my double to hear every word, I hit upon the notion of informing him that I regretted to say I was hard of hearing.

"Such a young man, too!" he nodded, keeping his smeary blue, unintelligent eyes fastened upon me. "What was the cause of it—some disease?" he inquired, without the least sympathy and as if he thought that, if so, I'd got no more than I deserved.

"Yes; disease," I admitted in a cheerful tone which seemed to shock him. But my point was gained, because he had to raise his voice to give me his tale. It is not worth while to record that version. It was just over two months since all this had happened, and he had thought so much about it that he seemed completely muddled as to its bearings, but still immensely impressed.

"What would you think of such a thing happening on board your own ship? I've had the *Sephora* for these fifteen years. I am a well-known shipmaster."

He was densely distressed—and perhaps I should have sympathised with him if I had been able to detach my mental vision from the unsuspected sharer of my cabin as though he were my second self. There he was on the other side of the bulkhead, four or five feet from us, no more, as we sat in the saloon. I looked politely at Captain Archbold (if that was his name), but it was the other I saw, in a grey sleeping-suit, seated on a low stool, his bare feet close together, his arms folded, and every word said between us falling into the ears of his dark head bowed on his chest.

"I have been at sea now, man and boy, for seven-and-thirty years, and I've never heard of such a thing happening in an English ship. And that it should be my ship. Wife on board, too."

I was hardly listening to him.

"Don't you think," I said, "that the heavy sea which, you told me, came aboard just then might have killed the man? I have seen the sheer weight of a sea kill a man very neatly, by simply breaking his neck."

"Good God!" he uttered, impressively, fixing his smeary blue eyes on me. "The sea! No man killed by the sea ever looked like that." He seemed positively scandalised at my suggestion. And as I gazed at him, certainly not prepared for anything original on his part, he advanced his head close to mine and thrust his tongue out at me so suddenly that I couldn't help starting back.

After scoring over my calmness in this graphic way he nodded wisely. If I had seen the sight, he assured me, I would never forget it as long as I lived. The weather was too bad to give the corpse a proper sea burial. So next day at dawn they took it up on the poop, covering its face with a bit of bunting; he read a short prayer, and then, just as it was, in its oilskins and long boots, they

457

launched it amongst those mountainous seas that seemed ready every moment to swallow up the ship herself and the terrified lives on board of her.

"That reefed foresail saved you," I threw in.

"Under God—it did," he exclaimed fervently. "It was by a special mercy, I firmly believe, that it stood some of those hurricane squalls."

"It was the setting of that sail which——" I began.

"God's own hand in it," he interrupted me. "Nothing less could have done it. I don't mind telling you that I hardly dared give the order. It seemed impossible that we could touch anything without losing it, and then our last hope would have been gone."

The terror of that gale was on him yet. I let him go on for a bit, then said, casually—as if returning to a minor subject:

"You were very anxious to give up your mate to the shore people, I believe?"

He was. To the law. His obscure tenacity on that point had in it something incomprehensible and a little awful; something, as it were, mystical, quite apart from his anxiety that he should not be suspected of "countenancing any doings of that sort." Seven-and-thirty virtuous years at sea, of which over twenty of immaculate command, and the last fifteen in the *Sephora*, seemed to have laid him under some pitiless obligation.

"And you know," he went on, groping shamefacedly amongst his feelings, "I did not engage that young fellow. His people had some interest with my owners. I was in a way forced to take him on. He looked very smart, very gentlemanly, and all that. But do you know—I never liked him, somehow. I am a plain man. You see, he wasn't exactly the sort for the chief mate of a ship like the *Sephora*."

I had become so connected in thought and impressions with the secret sharer of my cabin that I felt as if I, personally, were being given to understand that I, too, was not the sort that would have done for the chief mate of a ship like the *Sephora*. I had no doubt of it in my mind.

"Not at all the style of man. You understand," he insisted, superfluously, looking hard at me.

I smiled urbanely. He seemed at a loss for a while.

"I suppose I must report a suicide."

"Beg pardon?"

"Sui-cide! That's what I'll have to write to my owners directly I get in."

"Unless you manage to recover him before to-morrow," I assented, dispassionately. . . . "I mean, alive."

He mumbled something which I really did not catch, and I turned my ear to him in a puzzled manner. He fairly bawled:

"The land—I say, the mainland is at least seven miles off my anchorage."

"About that."

My lack of excitement, of curiosity, of surprise, of any sort of pronounced interest, began to arouse his distrust. But except for the felicitous pretence of deafness I had not tried to pretend anything. I had felt utterly incapable of playing the part of ignorance properly, and therefore was afraid to try. It is also certain that he had brought some ready-made suspicions with him, and that he viewed my politeness as a strange and unnatural phenomenon. And yet how else could I have received him? Not heartily! That was impossible for psychological reasons, which I need not state here. My only object was to keep off his inquiries. Surlily? Yes, but surliness might have provoked a point-blank question. From its novelty to him and from its nature, punctilious courtesy was the manner best calculated to restrain the man. But there was the danger of his breaking through my defence bluntly. I could not, I think, have met him by a direct lie, also for psychological (not moral) reasons. If he had only known how afraid I was of his putting my feeling of identity with the other to the test! But, strangely enough—(I thought of it only afterwards)—I believe that he was not a little disconcerted by the reverse side of that weird situation, by something in me that reminded him of the man he was seeking—suggested a mysterious similitude to the young fellow he had distrusted and disliked from the first.

However that might have been, the silence was not very prolonged. He took another oblique step.

"I reckon I had no more than a two-mile pull to your ship. Not a bit more."

"And quite enough, too, in this awful heat," I said.

Another pause full of mistrust followed. Necessity, they say, is mother of invention, but fear, too, is not barren of ingenious suggestions. And I was afraid he would ask me point-blank for news of my other self.

"Nice little saloon, isn't it?" I remarked, as if noticing for the first time the way his eyes roamed from one closed door to the other. "And very well fitted out, too. Here, for instance," I continued, reaching over the back of my seat negligently and flinging the door open, "is my bath-room."

He made an eager movement, but hardly gave it a glance. I got up, shut the door of the bath-room, and invited him to have a look round, as if I were very proud of my accommodation. He had to rise and be shown round, but he went through the business without any raptures whatever.

"And now we'll have a look at my stateroom," I declared, in a voice as loud as I dared to make it, crossing the cabin to the starboard side with purposely heavy steps.

He followed me in and gazed around. My intelligent double had vanished. I played my part.

"Very convenient—isn't it?"

"Very nice. Very comf . . ." He didn't finish and went out brusquely as if to escape from some unrighteous wiles of mine. But it was not to be. I had been too frightened not to feel vengeful; I felt I had him on the run, and I meant to keep him on the run. My polite insistence must have had something menacing in it, because he gave in suddenly. And I did not let him off a single item; mate's room, pantry, storerooms, the very sail-locker which was also under the poop—he had to look into them all. When at last I showed him out on the quarter-deck he drew a long, spiritless sigh, and mumbled dismally that he must really be going back to his ship now. I desired my mate, who had joined us, to see to the captain's boat.

The man of whiskers gave a blast on the whistle which he used to wear hanging round his neck, and yelled, "Sephora's away!" My double down there in my cabin must have heard, and certainly could not feel more relieved than I. Four fellows came running out from somewhere forward and went over the side, while my own men, appearing on deck too, lined the rail. I escorted my visitor to the gangway ceremoniously, and nearly overdid it. He was a tenacious beast. On the very ladder he lingered, and in that unique, guiltily conscientious manner of sticking to the point:

"I say . . . you . . . you don't think that——"

I covered his voice loudly:

"Certainly not. . . . I am delighted. Goodbye."

I had an idea of what he meant to say, and just saved myself by the privilege of defective hearing. He was too shaken generally to insist, but my mate, close witness of that parting, looked mystified and his face took on a thoughtful cast. As I did not want to appear as if I wished to avoid all communication with my officers, he had the opportunity to address me.

"Seems a very nice man. His boat's crew told our chaps a very extraordinary story, if what I am told by the steward is true. I suppose you had it from the captain, sir?"

"Yes. I had a story from the captain."

"A very horrible affair—isn't it, sir?"

"It is."

"Beats all these tales we hear about murders in Yankee ships."

"I don't think it beats them. I don't think it resembles them in the least."

"Bless my soul—you don't say so! But of course I've no acquaintance whatever with American ships, not I, so I couldn't go against your knowledge. It's horrible enough for me. . . . But the queerest part is that those fellows seemed to have some idea the man was hidden aboard here. They had really. Did you ever hear of such a thing?"

"Preposterous—isn't it?"

We were walking to and fro athwart the quarterdeck. No one of the crew forward could be seen (the day was Sunday), and the mate pursued:

"There was some little dispute about it. Our chaps took offence. 'As if we would harbour a thing like that,' they said. 'Wouldn't you like to look for him in our coal-hole?' Quite a tiff. But they made it up in the end. I suppose he did drown himself. Don't you, sir?"

"I don't suppose anything."

"You have no doubt in the matter, sir?"

"None whatever."

I left him suddenly. I felt I was producing a bad impression, but with my double down there it was most trying to be on deck. And it was almost as trying to be below. Altogether a nerve-trying situation. But on the whole I felt less torn in two when I was with him. There was no one in the whole ship whom I dared take into my confidence. Since the hands had got to know his story, it would have been impossible to pass him off for any one else, and an accidental discovery was to be dreaded now more than ever. . . .

The steward being engaged in laying the table for dinner, we could talk only with our eyes when I first went down. Later in the afternoon we had a cautious try at whispering. The Sunday quietness of the ship was against us; the stillness of air and water around her was against us; the elements, the men were against us—everything was against us in our secret partnership; time itself—for this could not go on forever. The very trust in Providence was, I suppose, denied to his guilt. Shall I confess that this thought cast me down very much? And as to the chapter of accidents which counts for so much in the book of success, I could only hope that it was closed. For what favourable accident could be expected?

"Did you hear everything?" were my first words as soon as we took up our position side by side, leaning over my bed-place.

He had. And the proof of it was his earnest whisper, "The man told you he hardly dared to give the order."

I understood the reference to be to that saving foresail.

"Yes. He was afraid of it being lost in the setting."

"I assure you he never gave the order. He may think he did, but he never gave it. He stood there with me on the break of the poop after the maintopsail blew away, and whimpered about our last hope—positively whimpered about it and nothing else—and the night coming on! To hear one's skipper go on like that in such weather was enough to drive any fellow out of his mind. It worked me up into a sort of desperation. I just took it into my own hands and went away from him, boiling, and—— But what's the use telling you? You know! . . . Do you think that if I had not been pretty fierce with them I should have got the men to do anything? Not it! The bo's'n perhaps? Perhaps! It wasn't a heavy sea—it was a sea gone mad! I suppose the end of the world will be something like that; and a man may have the heart to see it coming once and be done with it—but to have to face it day after day—— I don't blame anybody. I was precious little better than the rest. Only—I was an officer of that old coal-wagon, anyhow——"

"I quite understand," I conveyed that sincere assurance into his ear. He was out of breath with whispering; I could hear him pant slightly. It was all very simple. The same strung-up force which had given twenty-four men a chance, at least, for their lives, had, in a sort of recoil, crushed an unworthy mutinous existence.

But I had no leisure to weigh the merits of the matter—footsteps in the saloon, a heavy knock. "There's enough wind to get under way with, sir." Here was the call of a new claim upon my thoughts and even upon my feelings.

"Turn the hands up," I cried through the door. "I'll be on deck directly."

I was going out to make the acquaintance of my ship. Before I left the cabin our eyes met—the eyes of the only two strangers on board. I pointed to the recessed part where the little camp-stool awaited him and laid my finger on my lips. He made a gesture—somewhat vague—a little mysterious, accompanied by a faint smile, as if of regret.

This is not the place to enlarge upon the sensations of a man who feels for the first time a ship move under his feet to his own independent word. In my case they were not unalloyed. I was not wholly alone with my command; for there was that stranger in my cabin. Or rather, I was not completely and wholly with her. Part of me was absent. That mental feeling of being in two places at once affected me physically as if the mood of secrecy had penetrated my very soul. Before an hour had elapsed since the ship had begun to move, having occasion to ask the mate (he stood by my side) to take a compass bearing of the Pagoda, I caught myself reaching up to his ear in whispers. I say I caught myself, but enough had escaped to startle the man. I can't describe it otherwise than by saying that he shied. A grave, preoccupied manner, as though he were in possession of some perplexing intelligence, did not leave him henceforth. A little later I moved away from the rail to look at the compass with such a stealthy gait that the helmsman noticed it—and I could not help noticing the unusual roundness of his eyes. These are trifling instances, though it's to no commander's advantage to be suspected of ludicrous eccentricities. But I was also more seriously affected. There are to a seaman certain words, gestures, that should in given conditions come as naturally, as instinctively as the winking of a menaced eye. A certain order should spring on to his lips without thinking; a certain sign should get itself made, so to speak, without reflection. But all unconscious alertness had abandoned me. I had to make an effort of will to recall myself back (from the cabin) to the conditions of the moment. I felt that I was appearing an irresolute commander to those people who were watching me more or less critically.

And, besides, there were the scares. On the second day out, for instance, coming off the deck in the afternoon (I had straw slippers on my bare feet) I stopped at the open pantry door and spoke to the steward. He was doing something there with his back to me. At the sound of my voice he nearly jumped out of his skin, as the saying is, and incidentally broke a cup.

"What on earth's the matter with you?" I asked, astonished.

He was extremely confused. "Beg your pardon, sir. I made sure you were in your cabin."

"You see I wasn't."

"No, sir. I could have sworn I had heard you moving in there not a moment ago. It's most extraordinary . . . very sorry, sir."

I passed on with an inward shudder. I was so identified with my secret double that I did not even mention the fact in those scanty, fearful whispers we exchanged. I suppose he had made some slight noise of some kind or other. It would have been miraculous if he hadn't at one time or another. And yet, haggard as he appeared, he looked always perfectly self-controlled, more than calm—almost invulnerable. On my suggestion he remained almost entirely in the bathroom, which, upon the whole, was the safest place. There could be really no shadow of an excuse for any one ever wanting to go in there, once the steward had done with it. It was a very tiny place. Sometimes he reclined on the floor, his legs bent, his head sustained on one elbow. At others I would find him on the campstool, sitting in his grey sleeping-suit and with his cropped dark hair like a patient, unmoved convict. At night I would smuggle him into my bed-place, and we would whisper together, with the regular footfalls of the officer of the watch passing and repassing over our heads. It was an infinitely miserable time. It was lucky that some tins of fine preserves were stowed in a locker in my stateroom; hard bread I could always get hold of; and so he lived on stewed chicken, paté de foie gras, asparagus, cooked oysters, sardines—on all sorts of abominable sham delicacies out of tins. My early morning coffee he always drank; and it was all I dared do for him in that respect.

Every day there was the horrible manœuvring to go through so that my room and then the bath-room should be done in the usual way. I came to hate the sight of the steward, to abhor the voice of that harmless man. I felt that it was he who would bring on the disaster of discovery. It hung like a sword over our heads.

The fourth day out, I think (we were then working down the east side of the Gulf of Siam, tack for tack, in light winds and smooth water)—the fourth day, I say, of this miserable juggling with the unavoidable, as we sat at our evening meal, that man, whose slightest movement I dreaded, after putting down the dishes ran up on deck busily. This could not be dangerous. Presently he came down again; and then it appeared that he had remembered a coat of mine which I had thrown over a rail to dry after having been wetted in a shower which had passed over the ship in the afternoon. Sitting stolidly at the head of the table I became terrified at the sight of the garment on his arm. Of course he made for my door. There was no time to lose.

"Steward," I thundered. My nerves were so shaken that I could not govern my voice and conceal my agitation. This was the sort of thing that made my terrifically whiskered mate tap his forehead with his forefinger. I had detected him using that gesture while talking on deck with a confidential air to the carpenter. It was too far to hear a word, but I had no doubt that this pantomime could only refer to the strange new captain.

"Yes, sir," the pale-faced steward turned resignedly to me. It was this maddening course of being shouted at, checked without rhyme or reason, arbitrarily chased out of my cabin, suddenly called into it, sent flying out of his pantry on incomprehensible errands, that accounted for the growing wretchedness of his expression.

"Where are you going with that coat?"

"To your room, sir."

"Is there another shower coming?"

"I'm sure I don't know, sir. Shall I go up again and see, sir?"

"No! never mind."

My object was attained, as of course my other self in there would have heard everything that passed. During this interlude my two officers never raised their eyes off their respective plates; but the lip of that confounded cub, the second mate, quivered visibly.

I expected the steward to hook my coat on and come out at once. He was very slow about it; but I dominated my nervousness sufficiently not to shout after him. Suddenly I became aware (it could be heard plainly enough) that the fellow for some reason or other was opening the door of the bath-room. It was the end. The place was literally not big enough to swing a cat in. My voice died in my throat and I went stony all over. I expected to hear a yell of surprise and terror, and made a movement, but had not the strength to get on my legs. Everything remained still. Had my second self taken the poor wretch by the throat? I don't know what I could have done next moment if I had not seen the steward come out of my room, close the door, and then stand quietly by the sideboard.

"Saved," I thought. "But, no! Lost! Gone! He was gone!"

I laid my knife and fork down and leaned back in my chair. My head swam. After a while, when sufficiently recovered to speak in a steady voice, I instructed my mate to put the ship round at eight o'clock himself.

"I won't come on deck," I went on. "I think I'll turn in, and unless the wind shifts I don't want to be disturbed before midnight. I feel a bit seedy."

"You did look middling bad a little while ago," the chief mate remarked without showing any great concern.

They both went out, and I stared at the steward clearing the table. There was nothing to be read on that wretched man's face. But why did he avoid my eyes I asked myself. Then I thought I should like to hear the sound of his voice.

"Steward!"

"Sir!" Startled as usual.

"Where did you hang up that coat?"

"In the bath-room, sir." The usual anxious tone. "It's not quite dry yet, sir."

For some time longer I sat in the cuddy. Had my double vanished as he had come? But of his coming there was an explanation, whereas his disappearance would be inexplicable. . . . I went slowly into my dark room, shut the door, lighted the lamp, and for a time dared not turn round. When at last I did I saw him standing bolt-upright in the narrow recessed part. It would not be true to say I had a shock, but an irresistible doubt of his bodily existence flitted through my mind. Can it be, I asked myself, that he is not visible to other eyes than mine? It was like being haunted. Motionless, with a grave face, he raised his hands slightly at me in a gesture which meant clearly, "Heavens! what a narrow escape!" Narrow indeed. I think I had come creeping quietly as near insanity as any man who has not actually gone over the border. That gesture restrained me, so to speak.

The mate with the terrific whiskers was now putting the ship on the other tack. In the moment of profound silence which follows upon the hands going to their stations I heard on the poop his raised voice: "Hard alee!" and the distant shout of the order repeated on the maindeck. The sails, in that light breeze, made but a faint fluttering noise. It ceased. The ship was coming round slowly; I held my breath in the renewed stillness of expectation; one wouldn't have thought that there was a single living soul on her decks. A sudden brisk shout, "Mainsail haul!" broke the spell, and in the noisy cries and rush overhead of the men running away with the main-brace we two, down in my cabin, came together in our usual position by the bed-place.

He did not wait for my question. "I heard him fumbling here and just managed to squat myself down in the bath," he whispered to me. "The fellow only opened the door and put his arm in to hang the coat up. All the same——"

"I never thought of that," I whispered back, even more appalled than before at the closeness of the shave, and marvelling at that something unyielding in his character which was carrying him through so finely. There was no agitation in his whisper. Whoever was being driven distracted, it was not he. He was sane. And the proof of his sanity was continued when he took up the whispering again.

"It would never do for me to come to life again."

It was something that a ghost might have said. But what he was alluding to was his old captain's reluctant admission of the theory of suicide. It would obviously serve his turn—if I had understood at all the view which seemed to govern the unalterable purpose of his action.

"You must maroon me as soon as ever you can get amongst these islands off the Cambodge shore," he went on.

467

"Maroon you! We are not living in a boy's adventure tale," I protested. His scornful whispering took me up.

"We aren't indeed! There's nothing of a boy's tale in this. But there's nothing else for it. I want no more. You don't suppose I am afraid of what can be done to me? Prison or gallows or whatever they may please. But you don't see me coming back to explain such things to an old fellow in a wig and twelve respectable tradesmen, do you? What can they know whether I am guilty or not— or of what I am guilty, either? That's my affair. What does the Bible say? 'Driven off the face of the earth.' Very well. I am off the face of the earth now. As I came at night so I shall go."

"Impossible!" I murmured. "You can't."

"Can't? . . . Not naked like a soul on the Day of Judgment. I shall freeze on to this sleeping-suit. The Last Day is not yet— and . . . you have understood thoroughly. Didn't you?"

I felt suddenly ashamed of myself. I may say truly that I understood—and my hesitation in letting that man swim away from my ship's side had been a mere sham sentiment, a sort of cowardice.

"It can't be done now till next night," I breathed out. "The ship is on the off-shore tack and the wind may fail us."

"As long as I know that you understand," he whispered. "But of course you do. It's a great satisfaction to have got somebody to understand. You seem to have been there on purpose." And in the same whisper, as if we two whenever we talked had to say things to each other which were not fit for the world to hear, he added, "It's very wonderful."

We remained side by side talking in our secret way—but sometimes silent or just exchanging a whispered word or two at long intervals. And as usual he stared through the port. A breath of wind came now and again into our faces. The ship might have been moored in dock, so gently and on an even keel she slipped through the water, that did not murmur even at our passage, shadowy and silent like a phantom sea.

At midnight I went on deck, and to my mate's great surprise put the ship round on the other tack. His terrible whiskers flitted round me in silent criticism. I certainly should not have done it if it had been only a question of getting out of that sleepy gulf as quickly as possible. I believe he told the second mate, who relieved him, that it was a great want of judgment. The other only yawned. That intolerable cub shuffled about so sleepily and lolled against the rails in such a slack, improper fashion that I came down on him sharply.

"Aren't you properly awake yet?"

"Yes, sir! I am awake."

"Well, then, be good enough to hold yourself as if you were. And keep a look-out. If there's any current we'll be closing with some islands before daylight."

The east side of the gulf is fringed with islands, some solitary, others in groups. On the blue background of the high coast they seem to float on silvery patches of calm water, arid and grey, or dark green and rounded like clumps of evergreen bushes, with the larger ones, a mile or two long, showing the outlines of ridges, ribs of grey rock under the dank mantle of matted leafage. Unknown to trade, to travel, almost to geography, the manner of life they harbour is an unsolved secret. There must be villages—settlements of fishermen at least—on the largest of them, and some communication with the world is probably kept up by native craft. But all that forenoon, as we headed for them, fanned along by the faintest of breezes, I saw no sign of man or canoe in the field of the telescope I kept on pointing at the scattered group.

At noon I gave no orders for a change of course, and the mate's whiskers became much concerned and seemed to be offering themselves unduly to my notice. At last I said:

"I am going to stand right in. Quite in—as far as I can take her."

The stare of extreme surprise imparted an air of ferocity also to his eyes, and he looked truly terrific for a moment.

"We're not doing well in the middle of the gulf," I continued, casually. "I am going to look for the land breezes to-night."

"Bless my soul! Do you mean, sir, in the dark amongst the lot of all them islands and reefs and shoals?"

"Well—if there are any regular land breezes at all on this coast one must get close inshore to find them, mustn't one?"

"Bless my soul!" he exclaimed again under his breath. All that afternoon he wore a dreamy, contemplative appearance which in him was a mark of perplexity. After dinner I went into my stateroom as if I meant to take some rest. There we two bent our dark heads over a half-unrolled chart lying on my bed.

"There," I said. "It's got to be Koh-ring. I've been looking at

469

it ever since sunrise. It has got two hills and a low point. It must be inhabited. And on the coast opposite there is what looks like the mouth of a biggish river—with some town, no doubt, not far up. It's the best chance for you that I can see."

"Anything. Koh-ring let it be."

He looked thoughtfully at the chart as if surveying chances and distances from a lofty height—and following with his eyes his own figure wandering on the blank land of Cochin-China, and then passing off that piece of paper clean out of sight into uncharted regions. And it was as if the ship had two captains to plan her course for her. I had been so worried and restless running up and down that I had not had the patience to dress that day. I had remained in my sleeping-suit, with straw slippers and a soft floppy hat. The closeness of the heat in the gulf had been most oppressive, and the crew were used to see me wandering in that airy attire.

"She will clear the south point as she heads now," I whispered into his ear. "Goodness only knows when, though, but certainly after dark. I'll edge her in to half a mile, as far as I may be able to judge in the dark——"

"Be careful," he murmured, warningly—and I realised suddenly that all my future, the only future for which I was fit, would perhaps go irretrievably to pieces in any mishap to my first command.

I could not stop a moment longer in the room. I motioned him to get out of sight and made my way on the poop. That unplayful cub had the watch. I walked up and down for a while thinking things out, then beckoned him over.

"Send a couple of hands to open the two quarterdeck ports," I said, mildly.

He actually had the impudence, or else so forgot himself in his wonder at such an incomprehensible order, as to repeat:

"Open the quarter-deck ports! What for, sir?"

"The only reason you need concern yourself about is because I tell you to do so. Have them opened wide and fastened properly."

He reddened and went off, but I believe made some jeering remark to the carpenter as to the sensible practice of ventilating a ship's quarter-deck. I know he popped into the mate's cabin to impart the fact to him because the whiskers came on deck, as it were by chance, and stole glances at me from below—for signs of lunacy or drunkenness, I suppose.

A little before supper, feeling more restless than ever, I rejoined, for a moment, my second self. And to find him sitting so quietly was surprising, like something against nature, inhuman.

I developed my plan in a hurried whisper.

"I shall stand in as close as I dare and then put her round. I will presently find means to smuggle you out of here into the sail-locker, which communicates with the lobby. But there is an opening, a sort of square for hauling the sails out, which gives straight on the quarter-deck and which is never closed in fine weather, so as to give air to the sails. When the ship's way is deadened in stays and all the hands are aft at the main-braces you will have a clear road to slip out and get overboard through the open quarter-deck port. I've had them both fastened up. Use a rope's end to lower yourself into the water so as to avoid a splash— you know. It could be heard and cause some beastly complication."

He kept silent for a while, then whispered, "I understand."

"I won't be there to see you go," I began with an effort. "The rest . . . I only hope I have understood, too."

"You have. From first to last"—and for the first time there seemed to be a faltering, something strained in his whisper. He caught hold of my arm, but the ringing of the supper bell made me start. He didn't, though; he only released his grip.

After supper I didn't come below again till well past eight o'clock. The faint, steady breeze was loaded with dew; and the wet, darkened sails held all there was of propelling power in it. The night, clear and starry, sparkled darkly, and the opaque, light-less patches shifting slowly against the low stars were the drifting islets. On the port bow there was a big one more distant and shadowily imposing by the great space of sky it eclipsed.

On opening the door I had a back view of my very own self looking at a chart. He had come out of the recess and was standing near the table.

"Quite dark enough," I whispered.

He stepped back and leaned against my bed with a level, quiet glance. I sat on the couch. We had nothing to say to each other. Over our heads the officer of the watch moved here and there. Then I heard him move quickly. I knew what that meant. He was

471

making for the companion; and presently his voice was outside my door.

"We are drawing in pretty fast, sir. Land looks rather close."

"Very well," I answered. "I am coming on deck directly."

I waited till he was gone out of the cuddy, then rose. My double moved too. The time had come to exchange our last whispers, for neither of us was ever to hear each other's natural voice.

"Look here!" I opened a drawer and took out three sovereigns. "Take this anyhow. I've got six and I'd give you the lot, only I must keep a little money to buy some fruit and vegetables for the crew from native boats as we go through Sunda Straits."

He shook his head.

"Take it," I urged him, whispering desperately. "No one can tell what——"

He smiled and slapped meaningly the only pocket of the sleeping-jacket. It was not safe, certainly. But I produced a large old silk handkerchief of mine, and tying the three pieces of gold in a corner, pressed it on him. He was touched, I suppose, because he took it at last and tied it quickly round his waist under the jacket, on his bare skin.

Our eyes met; several seconds elapsed, till, our glances still mingled, I extended my hand and turned the lamp out. Then I passed through the cuddy, leaving the door of my room wide open. . . . "Steward!"

He was still lingering in the pantry in the greatness of his zeal, giving a rub-up to a plated cruet stand the last thing before going to bed. Being careful not to wake up the mate, whose room was opposite, I spoke in an undertone.

He looked round anxiously. "Sir!"

"Can you get me a little hot water from the galley?"

"I am afraid, sir, the galley fire's been out for some time now."

"Go and see."

He flew up the stairs.

"Now," I whispered, loudly, into the saloon—too loudly, perhaps, but I was afraid I couldn't make a sound. He was by my side in an instant—the double captain slipped past the stairs—through a tiny dark passage . . . a sliding door. We were in the sail-locker, scrambling on our knees over the sails. A sudden thought struck me. I saw myself wandering barefooted, bareheaded, the sun beating on my dark poll. I snatched off my floppy hat and tried hurriedly in the dark to ram it on my other self. He dodged and fended off silently. I wonder what he thought had come to me before he understood and suddenly desisted. Our hands met gropingly, lingered united in a steady, motionless clasp for a second. . . . No word was breathed by either of us when they separated.

I was standing quietly by the pantry door when the steward returned.

"Sorry, sir. Kettle barely warm. Shall I light the spirit-lamp?"

"Never mind."

I came out on deck slowly. It was now a matter of conscience to shave the land as close as possible—for now he must go overboard whenever the ship was put in stays. Must! There could be no going back for him. After a moment I walked over to leeward and my heart flew into my mouth at the nearness of the land on the bow. Under any other circumstances I would not have held on a minute longer. The second mate had followed me anxiously.

I looked on till I felt I could command my voice.

"She will weather," I said in a quiet tone.

"Are you going to try that, sir?" he stammered out incredulously.

I took no notice of him and raised my tone just enough to be heard by the helmsman.

"Keep her good full."

"Good full, sir."

The wind fanned my cheek, the sails slept, the world was silent. The strain of watching the dark loom of the land grow bigger and denser was too much for me. I had shut my eyes—because the ship must go closer. She must! The stillness was intolerable. Were we standing still?

When I opened my eyes the second view started my heart with a thump. The black southern hill of Koh-ring seemed to hang right over the ship like a towering fragment of the everlasting night. On that enormous mass of blackness there was not a gleam to be seen, not a sound to be heard. It was gliding irresistibly towards us and yet seemed already within reach of the hand. I saw the vague figures of the watch grouped in the waist, gazing in awed silence.

473

"Are you going on, sir?" inquired an unsteady voice at my elbow.

I ignored it. I had to go on.

"Keep her full. Don't check her way. That won't do now," I said, warningly.

"I can't see the sails very well," the helmsman answered me, in strange, quavering tones.

Was she close enough? Already she was, I won't say in the shadow of the land, but in the very blackness of it, already swallowed up as it were, gone too close to be recalled, gone from me altogether.

"Give the mate a call," I said to the young man who stood at my elbow as still as death. "And turn all hands up."

My tone had a borrowed loudness reverberated from the height of the land. Several voices cried out together: "We are all on deck, sir."

Then stillness again, with the great shadow gliding closer, towering higher, without a light, without a sound. Such a hush had fallen on the ship that she might have been a bark of the dead floating in slowly under the very gate of Erebus.

"My God! Where are we?"

It was the mate moaning at my elbow. He was thunderstruck, and as it were deprived of the moral support of his whiskers. He clapped his hands and absolutely cried out, "Lost!"

"Be quiet," I said, sternly.

He lowered his tone, but I saw the shadowy gesture of his despair. "What are we doing here?"

"Looking for the land wind."

He made as if to tear his hair, and addressed me recklessly.

"She will never get out. You have done it, sir. I knew it'd end in something like this. She will never weather, and you are too close now to stay. She'll drift ashore before she's round. O my God!"

I caught his arm as he was raising it to batter his poor devoted head, and shook it violently.

"She's ashore already," he wailed, trying to tear himself away.

"Is she? . . . Keep good full there!"

"Good full, sir," cried the helmsman in a frightened, thin, child-like voice.

I hadn't let go the mate's arm and went on shaking it. "Ready about, do you hear? You go forward"—shake—"and stop there"— shake—"and hold your noise"—shake—"and see these head-sheets properly overhauled"—shake, shake—shake.

And all the time I dared not look towards the land lest my heart should fail me. I released my grip at last and he ran forward as if fleeing for dear life.

I wondered what my double there in the sail-locker thought of this commotion. He was able to hear everything—and perhaps he was able to understand why, on my conscience, it had to be thus close—no less. My first order "Hard alee!" re-echoed ominously under the towering shadow of Koh-ring as if I had shouted in a mountain gorge. And then I watched the land intently. In that smooth water and light wind it was impossible to feel the ship coming-to. No! I could not feel her. And my second self was making now ready to slip out and lower himself overboard. Perhaps he was gone already . . . ?

The great black mass brooding over our very mastheads began to pivot away from the ship's side silently. And now I forgot the secret stranger ready to depart, and remembered only that I was a total stranger to the ship. I did not know her. Would she do it? How was she to be handled?

I swung the mainyard and waited helplessly. She was perhaps stopped, and her very fate hung in the balance, with the black mass of Koh-ring like the gate of the everlasting night towering over her taffrail. What would she do now? Had she way on her yet? I stepped to the side swiftly, and on the shadowy water I could see nothing except a faint phosphorescent flash revealing the glassy smoothness of the sleeping surface. It was impossible to tell—and I had not learned yet the feel of my ship. Was she moving? What I needed was something easily seen, a piece of paper, which I could throw overboard and watch. I had nothing on me. To run down for it I didn't dare. There was no time. All at once my strained, yearning stare distinguished a white object floating within a yard of the ship's side. White on the black water. A phosphorescent flash passed under it. What was that thing? . . . I recognised my own floppy hat. It must have fallen off his head . . . and he didn't bother. Now I had what I wanted—the saving mark for my eyes. But I hardly thought of my other self, now gone from the ship, to be hidden for ever from all friendly faces, to be a fugitive and a vagabond on the earth, with no brand of the curse on his sane forehead to stay a slaying hand . . . too proud to explain.

And I watched the hat—the expression of my sudden pity for his mere flesh. It had been meant to save his homeless head from the dangers of the sun. And now—behold—it was saving the ship, by serving me for a mark to help out the ignorance of my strangeness. Ha! It was drifting forward, warning me just in time that the ship had gathered sternway.

"Shift the helm," I said in a low voice to the seaman standing still like a statue.

The man's eyes glistened wildly in the binnacle light as he jumped round to the other side and spun round the wheel.

I walked to the break of the poop. On the over-shadowed deck all hands stood by the forebraces waiting for my order. The stars ahead seemed to be gliding from right to left. And all was so still in the world that I heard the quiet remark, "She's round," passed in a tone of intense relief between two seamen.

"Let go and haul."

The foreyards ran round with a great noise, amidst cheery cries. And now the frightful whiskers made themselves heard giving various orders. Already the ship was drawing ahead. And I was alone with her. Nothing! no one in the world should stand now between us, throwing a shadow on the way of silent knowledge and mute affection, the perfect communion of a seaman with his first command.

Walking to the taffrail, I was in time to make out, on the very edge of a darkness thrown by a towering black mass like the very gateway of Erebus—yes, I was in time to catch an evanescent glimpse of my white hat left behind to mark the spot where the secret sharer of my cabin and of my thoughts, as though he were my second self, had lowered himself into the water to take his punishment: a free man, a proud swimmer striking out for a new destiny.

The Farcical History of
Richard Greenow
1920

ALDOUS HUXLEY

ALDOUS HUXLEY is so well-known that there is almost nothing one need say about him. He was born in 1894, a writer with every gift but one. Immensely intelligent, deeply imaginative, with an outlook both scientific and aesthetic, with both a comic and a tragic sense, with moral feeling and a seeing eye, the general and the particular all compounded, he should have been the Michelangelo of modern prose rather than one of the most fragmentated old masters in an age of self-dispersion. What is the gift he lacks? It is certainly one which would have unified all the others and which we might call the love of artistic perfection, the unhappy tormenting love which was experienced by Mallarmé and Valéry, and by Proust's 'Swann' who on his death-bed felt he would have given his whole life and fortune to have created something like the Petit pan de mur jaune, the little yellow slab of wall in the corner of his Vermeer. Huxley's perfectionism has gone into his search for the Absolute, he is a better man than most other writers but his books have never been ends in themselves; they began as expressions of his personality, experiments in a contemporary manner, they ended as tracts and vehicles for conversion. Point Counterpoint, although it set out to be a great novel, over-strained its author's mechanism which did not recover until Time Must Have a Stop. This does not of course imply that all his other gifts were not employed in his work and they have certainly made his contribution outstanding. D. H. Lawrence had genius and Huxley all the talents, yet D. H. Lawrence abused his genius, turning it to didactic purposes and sealing its fate with his jesting catchphrase 'Art For My Sake' while Huxley did try to harness his gifts to the Flaubertian conception "L'homme c'est rien, l'oeuvre c'est tout" but failed. In all his mature work there is a constant buzzing of adjectives and adverbs, a mannered obviousness, a reverberation which is the noise made by the very absence of perfectionism, the human engine in need of holy oil. Despite their limitations as novelists E. M. Forster and Virginia Woolf belong on one side of an invisible frontier, D. H. Lawrence and Aldous Huxley, with all their gifts, on the other.

I have always found the early works of Huxley fascinating; they are slight and modest in conception and parade his natural powers, his wit and erudition, his crisp and lively charm, and also his favorite phobias—before his style hardens and they become obsessions. He is like a precocious child trying on fancy dresses out of an old chest. Apart from two slim volumes of poetry, they are Limbo (1920), Crome Yellow (1921), Mortal Coils (1922), and Antic Hay (1923), his first full-length novel. The Farcical History of Richard Greenow is the first story in Limbo, which also contains a revealing account of a frustrated love affair Happily Ever After in which the philosopher Santayana is said to play a central part.

Like most of Huxley's early work Richard Greenow is largely autobiographical, 'Aesop College' is Eton, 'Canteloup' is Balliol, where Huxley took a first in English literature and the Weekly International is probably Middleton Murray's Athenaeum which Huxley joined in 1919. Mrs. Cravister is certainly Mrs. Warre-Cornish, wife of the Vice-Provost of Eton and famous for her gnomic sayings. Ten years later I followed Huxley to Eton and Balliol and as a schoolboy I vividly remember the excitement of reading Richard Greenow, even of identifying Mr. Copthorne-Slazenger before the book was seized by the authorities. I felt like the child of Victorian parents who learns of a divine Order when the pinks in his garden come up and spell his name. It has always seemed to me a fresh and delightful story, a tour-de-force in the Jekyll and Hyde tradition and one which eliminates the clumsy pill swallowing of the original. Besides giving a picture of the brilliant young men of the 1914 generation, The Farcical History must be the first story about psychoanalysis and one which attacks what has proved to be the weak point of Freudian psychology—its complete inability to treat psychotic schizoids of which 'Richard Greenow' is so formidable an example!

The Farcical History of Richard Greenow

Chapter I

THE MOST SUMPTUOUS present that Millicent received on her seventh birthday was a doll's house. "With love to darling little Mill from Aunty Loo." Aunt Loo was immensely rich, and the doll's house was almost as grandiose and massive as herself.

It was divided into four rooms, each papered in a different colour and each furnished as was fitting: beds and washstands and wardrobes in the upstair rooms, arm-chairs and artificial plants below. "Replete with every modern convenience; sumptuous appointments." There was even a cold collation ready spread on the dining-room table—two scarlet lobsters on a dish, and a ham that had been sliced into just enough to reveal an internal complexion of the loveliest pink and white. One might go on talking about the doll's house for ever, it was so beautiful. Such, at any rate, was the opinion of Millicent's brother Dick. He would spend hours opening and shutting the front door, peeping through the windows, arranging and rearranging the furniture. As for Millicent, the gorgeous present left her cold. She had been hoping—and, what is more, praying, fervently, every night for a month—that Aunty Loo would give her a toy sewing-machine (one of the kind that works, though) for her birthday.

She was bitterly disappointed when the doll's house came instead. But she bore it all stoically and managed to be wonderfully polite to Aunty Loo about the whole affair. She never looked at the doll's house: it simply didn't interest her.

481

Dick had already been at a preparatory school for a couple of terms. Mr. Killigrew, the headmaster, thought him a promising boy. "Has quite a remarkable aptitude for mathematics," he wrote in his report. "He has started Algebra this term and shows a"— "quite remarkable" scratched out (the language of reports is apt to be somewhat limited)—"a very unusual grasp of the subject." Mr. Killigrew didn't know that his pupil also took an interest in dolls: if he had, he would have gibed at Dick as unmercifully and in nearly the same terms as Dick's fellow-schoolboys—for shepherds grow to resemble their sheep and pedagogues their childish charges. But of course Dick would never have dreamt of telling anyone at school about it. He was chary of letting even the people at home divine his weakness, and when anyone came into the room where the doll's house was, he would put his hands in his pockets and stroll out, whistling the tune of, "There is a Happy Land far, far away, where they have Ham and Eggs seven times a day," as though he had merely stepped in to have a look at the beastly thing—just to give it a kick.

When he wasn't playing with the doll's house, Dick spent his holiday time in reading, largely, devouringly. No length or incomprehensibility could put him off; he had swallowed down *Robert Elsmere* in the three-volume edition at the age of eight. When he wasn't reading he used to sit and think about Things in General and Nothing in Particular; in fact, as Millicent reproachfully put it, he just mooned about. Millicent, on the other hand, was always busily doing something: weeding in the garden, or hoeing, or fruit-picking (she could be trusted not to eat more than the recognized tariff—one in twenty raspberries or one in forty plums); helping Kate in the kitchen; knitting mufflers for those beings known vaguely as The Cripples, while her mother read aloud in the evenings before bedtime. She disapproved of Dick's mooning, but Dick mooned all the same.

When Dick was twelve and a half he knew enough about mathematics and history and the dead languages to realize that his dear parents were profoundly ignorant and uncultured. But, what was more pleasing to the dear parents, he knew enough to win a scholarship at Æsop College, which is one of our Greatest Public Schools.

If this were a Public School story, I should record the fact that, while at Æsop, Dick swore, lied, blasphemed, repeated dirty stories, read the articles in John Bull about brothels disguised as nursing-homes and satyrs disguised as curates; that he regarded his masters, with very few exceptions, as fools, not even always well-meaning. And so on. All which would be quite true, but beside the point. For this is not one of the conventional studies of those clever young men who discover Atheism and Art at School, Socialism at the University, and, passing through the inevitable stage of Sex and Syphilis after taking their B.A., turn into maturely brilliant novelists at the age of twenty-five. I prefer, therefore, to pass over the minor incidents of a difficult pubescence, touching only on those points which seem to throw a light on the future career of our hero.

It is possible for those who desire it—incredible as the thing may appear—to learn something at Æsop College. Dick even learnt a great deal. From the beginning he was the young Benjamin of his mathematical tutor, Mr. Skewbauld, a man of great abilities in his own art, and who, though wholly incapable of keeping a form in order, could make his private tuition a source of much profit to a mathematically minded boy. Mr. Skewbauld's house was the worst in Æsop: Dick described it as a mixture between a ghetto and a home for the mentally deficient, and when he read in Sir Thomas Browne that it was a Vulgar Error to suppose that Jews stink, he wrote a letter to the School Magazine exploding that famous doctor as a quack and a charlatan, whose statements ran counter to the manifest facts of everyday life in Mr. Skewbauld's house. It may seem surprising that Dick should have read Sir Thomas Browne at all. But he was more than a mere mathematician. He filled the ample leisure, which is Æsop's most precious gift to those of its Alumni who know how to use it, with much and varied reading in history, in literature, in physical science, and in more than one foreign language. Dick was something of a prodigy.

"Greenow's an intellectual," was Mr. Copthorne-Slazenger's contemptuous verdict. "I have the misfortune to have two or three intellectuals in my house. They're all of them friends of his. I think he's a Bad Influence in the School." Copthorne-Slazenger regarded himself as the perfect example of *mens sana in corpore sano*, the soul of an English gentleman in the body of a Greek god.

Unfortunately his legs were rather too short and his lower lip was underhung like a salmon's.

Dick had, indeed, collected about him a band of kindred spirits. There was Partington, who specialized in history; Gay, who had read all the classical writings of the golden age and was engaged in the study of mediæval Latin; Fletton, who was fantastically clever and had brought the art of being idle to a pitch never previously reached in the annals of Æsop. These were his chief friends, and a queer-looking group they made—Dick, small and dark and nervous; Partington, all roundness, and whose spectacles were two moons in a moonface; Gay, with the stiff walk of a little old man; and Fletton, who looked like nobody so much as Mr. Jingle, tall and thin with a twisted, comical face.

"An ugly skulking crew," Copthorne-Slazenger, conscious of his own Olympian splendour, would say as he saw them pass.

With these faithful friends Dick should have been—and indeed for the most part was—very happy. Between them they mustered up a great stock of knowledge; they could discuss every subject under the sun. They were a liberal education and an amusement to one another. There were times, however, when Dick was filled with a vague, but acute, discontent. He wanted something which his friends could not give him; but what, but what? The discontent rankled under the surface, like a suppressed measles. It was Lord Francis Quarles who brought it out and made the symptoms manifest.

Francis Quarles was a superb creature, with the curly forehead of a bull and the face and limbs of a Græco-Roman statue. It was a sight worth seeing when he looked down through half-shut eyelids, in his usual attitude of sleepy arrogance, on the world about him. He was in effect what Mr. Copthorne-Slazenger imagined himself to be, and he shared that gentleman's dislike for Dick and his friends. "Yellow little atheists," he called them. He always stood up for God and the Church of England; they were essential adjuncts to the aristocracy. God, indeed, was almost a member of the Family; lack of belief in Him amounted to a personal insult to the name of Quarles.

It was half-way through the summer term, when Dick was sixteen, on one of those days of brilliant sunshine and cloudless blue, when the sight of beautiful and ancient buildings is peculiarly poignant. Their age and quiet stand out in melancholy contrast against the radiant life of the summer; and at Æsop the boys go laughing under their antique shadow; "Little victims"—you feel how right Gray was. Dick was idly strolling across the quadrangle, engaged in merely observing the beauty about him—the golden-grey chapel, with its deep geometrical shadows between the buttresses, the comely rose-coloured shapes of the brick-built Tudor buildings, the weathercocks glittering in the sun, the wheeling flurries of pigeons. His old discontent had seized on him again, and to-day in the presence of all this beauty it had become almost unbearable. All at once, out of the mouth of one of the dark little tunnelled doors pierced in the flanks of the sleeping building, a figure emerged into the light. It was Francis Quarles, clad in white flannels and the radiance of the sunshine. He appeared like a revelation, bright, beautiful, and sudden, before Dick's eyes. A violent emotion seized him; his heart leapt, his bowels were moved within him; he felt a little sick and faint—he had fallen in love.

Francis passed by without deigning to notice him. His head was high, his eyes drowsy under their drooping lids. He was gone, and for Dick all the light was out, the beloved quadrangle was a prison-yard, the pigeons a loathsome flock of carrion eaters. Gay and Partington came up behind him with shouts of invitation. Dick walked rudely away. God! how he hated them and their wretched, silly talk and their yellow, ugly faces.

The weeks that followed were full of strangeness. For the first time in his life Dick took to writing poetry. There was one sonnet which began:

> Is it a vision or a waking dream?
> Or is it truly Apollo that I see,
> Come from his sylvan haunts in Arcady
> To $\left\{ \begin{array}{l} \text{laugh and loiter} \\ \text{sing and saunter} \end{array} \right.$ by an English stream. . . .

He kept on repeating the words to himself, "Sylvan haunts in Arcady," "laugh and loiter" (after much thought he had adopted that as more liquidly mélodious than "sing and saunter"). How beautiful they sounded!—as beautiful as Keats—more beautiful, for they were his own.

He avoided the company of Gay and Fletton and Partington;

they had become odious to him, and their conversation, when he could bring himself to listen to it, was, somehow, almost incomprehensible. He would sit for hours alone in his study; not working —for he could not understand the mathematical problems on which he had been engaged before the fateful day in the quadrangle—but reading novels and the poetry of Mrs. Browning, and at intervals writing something rather ecstatic of his own. After a long preparatory screwing up of his courage, he dared at last to send a fag with a note to Francis, asking him to tea; and when Francis rather frigidly refused, he actually burst into tears. He had not cried like that since he was a child.

He became suddenly very religious. He would spend an hour on his knees every night, praying, praying with frenzy. He mortified the flesh with fasting and watching. He even went so far as to flagellate himself—or at least tried to; for it is very difficult to flagellate yourself adequately with a cane in a room so small that any violent gesture imperils the bric-à-brac. He would pass half the night stark naked, in absurd postures, trying to hurt himself. And then, after the dolorously pleasant process of self-maceration was over, he used to lean out of the window and listen to the murmurs of the night and fill his spirit with the warm velvet darkness of midsummer. Copthorne-Slazenger, coming back by the late train from town one night, happened to see his moon-pale face hanging out of window and was delighted to be able to give him two hundred Greek lines to remind him that even a member of the Sixth Form requires sleep sometimes.

The fit lasted three weeks. "I can't think what's the matter with you, Greenow," complained Mr. Skewbauld snufflingly. "You seem incapable or unwilling to do anything at all. I suspect the cause is constipation. If only everyone would take a little paraffin every night before going to bed! . . ." Mr. Skewbauld's self-imposed mission in life was the propagation of the paraffin habit. It was the universal panacea—the cure for every ill.

His friends of before the crisis shook their heads and could only suppose him mad. And then the fit ended as suddenly as it had begun.

It happened at a dinner-party given by the Cravisters. Dr. Cravister was the Headmaster of Æsop—a good, gentle, learned old man, with snow-white hair and a saintly face which the spirit of comic irony had embellished with a nose that might, so red and bulbous it was, have been borrowed from the properties of a music-hall funny man. And then there was Mrs. Cravister, large and stately as a galleon with all sails set. Those who met her for the first time might be awed by the dignity of what an Elizabethan would have called her "swelling port." But those who knew her well went in terror of the fantastic spirit which lurked behind the outward majesty. They were afraid of what that richly modulated voice of hers might utter. It was not merely that she was malicious —and she had a gift of ever-ready irony; no, what was alarming in all her conversation was the element of the unexpected. With most people one feels comfortably secure that they will always say the obvious and ordinary things; with Mrs. Cravister, never. The best one could do was to be on guard and to try and look, when she made a more than usually characteristic remark, less of a be-wildered fool than one felt.

Mrs. Cravister received her guests—they were all of them boys —with stately courtesy. They found it pleasant to be taken so seriously, to be treated as perfectly grown men; but at the same time, they always had with Mrs. Cravister a faint uncomfortable suspicion that all her politeness was an irony so exquisite as to be practically undistinguishable from ingenuousness.

"Good evening, Mr. Gay," she said, holding out her hand and shutting her eyes; it was one of her disconcerting habits, this shut-ting of the eyes. "What a pleasure it will be to hear you talking to us again about eschatology."

Gay, who had never talked about eschatology and did not know the meaning of the word, smiled a little dimly and made a pro-testing noise.

"Eschatology? What a charming subject!" The fluty voice be-longed to Henry Cravister, the Headmaster's son, a man of about forty who worked in the British Museum. He was almost too cul-tured, too erudite.

"But I don't know anything about it," said Gay desperately.

"Spare us your modesty," Henry Cravister protested.

His mother shook hands with the other guests, putting some at their ease with a charming phrase and embarrassing others by saying something baffling and unexpected that would have dis-mayed even the hardiest diner-out, much more a schoolboy tremblingly on his good behaviour. At the tail end of the group of boys stood Dick and Francis Quarles. Mrs. Cravister slowly raised her heavy waxen eyelids and regarded them a moment in silence.

"The Græco-Roman and the Gothic side by side!" she exclaimed. "Lord Francis is something in the Vatican, a rather late piece of work; and Mr. Greenow is a little gargoyle from the roof of Notre Dame de Paris. Two epochs of art—how clearly one sees the difference. And my husband, I always think, is purely Malayan in design—purely Malayan," she repeated as she shook hands with the two boys.

Dick blushed to the roots of his hair, but Francis' impassive arrogance remained unmoved. Dick stole a glance in his direction, and at the sight of his calm face he felt a new wave of adoring admiration sweeping through him.

The company was assembled and complete. Mrs. Cravister looked round the room and remarking, "We won't wait for Mr. Copthorne-Slazenger," sailed majestically in the direction of the door. She particularly disliked this member of her husband's staff, and lost no opportunity of being rude to him. Thus, where an ordinary hostess might have said, "Shall we come in to dinner?" Mrs. Cravister employed the formula, "We won't wait for Mr. Copthorne-Slazenger"; and a guest unacquainted with Mrs. Cravister's habits would be surprised on entering the dining-room to find that all the seats at the table were filled, and that the meal proceeded smoothly without a single further reference to the missing Copthorne, who never turned up at all, for the good reason that he had never been invited.

Dinner began a little nervously and uncomfortably. At one end of the table the Headmaster was telling anecdotes of Æsop in the sixties, at which the boys in his neighbourhood laughed with a violent nervous insincerity. Henry Cravister, still talking about eschatology, was quoting from Sidonius Apollinarius and Commodianus of Gaza. Mrs. Cravister, who had been engaged in a long colloquy with the butler, suddenly turned on Dick with the remark, "And so you have a deep, passionate fondness for cats," as though they had been intimately discussing the subject for the last hour. Dick had enough presence of mind to say that, yes, he did like cats—all except those Manx ones that had no tails.

"No tails," Mrs. Cravister repeated—"no tails. Like men. How symbolical everything is!"

Francis Quarles was sitting opposite him, so that Dick had ample opportunity to look at his idol. How perfectly he did everything, down to eating his soup! The first lines of a new poem began to buzz in Dick's head:

"All, all I lay at thy proud marble feet—
My heart, my love and all my future days.
Upon thy brow for ever let me gaze,
For ever touch thy hair: oh (something) sweet . . ."

Would he be able to find enough rhymes to make it into a sonnet? Mrs. Cravister, who had been leaning back in her chair for the last few minutes in a state of exhausted abstraction, opened her eyes and said to nobody in particular:

"Ah, how I envy the calm of those Chinese dynasties!"

"Which Chinese dynasties?" a well-meaning youth inquired.

"Any Chinese dynasty, the more remote the better. Henry, tell us the names of some Chinese dynasties."

In obedience to his mother, Henry delivered a brief disquisition on the history of politics, art, and letters in the Far East.

The Headmaster continued his reminiscences.

An angel of silence passed. The boys, whose shyness had begun to wear off, became suddenly and painfully conscious of hearing themselves eating. Mrs. Cravister saved the situation.

"Lord Francis knows all about birds," she said in her most thrilling voice. "Perhaps he can tell us why it is the unhappy fate of the carrion crow to mate for life."

Conversation again became general. Dick was still thinking about his sonnet. Oh, these rhymes!—praise, bays, roundelays, amaze: greet, bleat, defeat, beat, paraclete. . . .

" . . . to sing the praise
In anthems high and solemn roundelays
Of Holy Father, Son and Paraclete."

That was good—damned good; but it hardly seemed to fit in with the first quatrain. It would do for one of his religious poems, though. He had written a lot of sacred verse lately.

Then suddenly, cutting across his ecstatic thoughts, came the sound of Henry Cravister's reedy voice.

"But I always find Pater's style so coarse," it said.

Something explosive took place in Dick's head. It often happens

489

when one blows one's nose that some passage in the labyrinth connecting ears and nose and throat is momentarily blocked, and one
becomes deaf and strangely dizzy. Then, suddenly, the mucous
bubble bursts, sound rushes back to the brain, the head feels clear
and stable once more. It was something like this, but transposed
into terms of the spirit, that seemed now to have happened to
Dick.

It was as though some mysterious obstruction in his brain, which
had dammed up and diverted his faculties from their normal course
during the past three weeks, had been on a sudden overthrown.
His life seemed to be flowing once more along familiar channels.

He was himself again.

"But I always find Pater's style so coarse."

These few words of solemn foolery were the spell which had
somehow performed the miracle. It was just the sort of remark he
might have made three weeks ago, before the crisis. For a moment,
indeed, he almost thought it was he himself who had spoken; his
own authentic voice, carried across the separating gulf of days, had
woken him again to life!

He looked at Francis Quarles. Why, the fellow was nothing but
a great prize ox, a monstrous animal. "There was a Lady loved a
Swine. Honey, said she . . ." It was ignoble, it was ridiculous. He
could have hidden his face in his hands for pure shame; shame
tingled through his body. Goodness, how grotesquely he had
behaved!

He leaned across and began talking to Henry Cravister about
Pater and style and books in general. Cravister was amazed at the
maturity of the boy's mind; for he possessed to a remarkable degree that critical faculty which in the vast majority of boys is—
and from their lack of experience must be—wholly lacking.

"You must come and see me some time when you're in London," Henry Cravister said to him when the time came for the
boys to get back to their houses. Dick was flattered; he had not
said that to any of the others. He walked home with Gay, laughing
and talking quite in his old fashion. Gay marvelled at the change
in his companion; strange, inexplicable fellow! but it was pleasant
to have him back again, to repossess the lost friend. Arrived in his
room, Dick sat down to attack the last set of mathematical problems that had been set him. Three hours ago they had appeared

490

utterly incomprehensible; now he understood them perfectly. His mind was like a giant refreshed, delighting in its strength.

Next day Mr. Skewbauld congratulated him on his answers.

"You seem quite to have recovered your old form, Greenow," he said. "Did you take my advice? Paraffin regularly . . ."

Looking back on the events of the last weeks, Dick was disquieted. Mr. Skewbauld might be wrong in recommending paraffin, but he was surely right in supposing that something was the matter and required a remedy. What could it be? He felt so well; but that, of course, proved nothing. He began doing Müller's exercises, and he bought a jar of malt extract and a bottle of hypophosphites. After much consultation of medical handbooks and the encyclopædia, he came to the conclusion that he was suffering from anæmia of the brain; and for some time one fixed idea haunted him: Suppose the blood completely ceased to flow to his brain, suppose he were to fall down suddenly dead or, worse, become utterly and hopelessly paralysed. . . . Happily the distractions of Æsop in the summer term were sufficiently numerous and delightful to divert his mind from this gloomy brooding, and he felt so well and in such high spirits that it was impossible to go on seriously believing that he was at death's door. Still, whenever he thought of the events of those strange weeks he was troubled. He did not like being confronted by problems which he could not solve. During the rest of his stay at school he was troubled by no more than the merest velleities of a relapse. A fit of moon-gazing and incapacity to understand the higher mathematics had threatened him one time when he was working rather too strenuously for a scholarship. But a couple of days' complete rest had staved off the peril. There had been rather a painful scene, too, at Dick's last School Concert. Oh, those Æsop concerts! Musically speaking, of course, they are deplorable; but how rich from all other points of view than the merely æsthetic! The supreme moment arrives at the very end when three of the most eminent and popular of those about to leave mount the platform together and sing the famous "Æsop, Farewell." Greatest of school songs! The words are not much, but the tune, which goes swooning along in three-four time, is perhaps the masterpiece of the late organist, Dr. Pilch.

Dick was leaving, but he was not a sufficiently heroic figure to have been asked to sing, "Æsop, Farewell." He was simply a member of the audience, and one, moreover, who had come to the concert in a critical and mocking spirit. For, as he had an ear for music, it was impossible for him to take the concert very seriously. The choir had clamorously re-crucified the Messiah; the soloists had all done their worst; and now it was time for "Æsop, Farewell." The heroes climbed on to the stage. They were three demigods, but Francis Quarles was the most splendid of the group as he stood there with head thrown back, eyes almost closed, calm and apparently unconscious of the crowd that seethed, actually and metaphorically, beneath him. He was wearing an enormous pink orchid in the buttonhole of his evening coat; his shirt-front twinkled with diamond studs; the buttons of his waistcoat were of fine gold. At the sight of him, Dick felt his heart beating violently; he was not, he painfully realized, master of himself.

The music struck up—Dum, dum, dumdidi, dumdidi; dum, dum, dum, and so on. So like the Merry Widow. In two days' time he would have left Æsop for ever. The prospect had never affected him very intensely. He had enjoyed himself at school, but he had never, like so many Æsopians, fallen in love with the place. It remained for him an institution; for others it was almost an adored person. But to-night his spirit, rocked on a treacly ocean of dominant sevenths, succumbed utterly to the sweet sorrow of parting. And there on the platform stood Francis. Oh, how radiantly beautiful! And when he began, in his rich tenor, the first verse of the Valedictory:

> "Farewell, Mother Æsop,
> Our childhood's home!
> Our spirit is with thee,
> Though far we roam . . ."

he found himself hysterically sobbing.

Chapter II

CANTELOUP COLLEGE IS perhaps the most frightful building in Oxford—and to those who know their Oxford well this will mean not a little. Up till the middle of last century Canteloup possessed

two quadrangles of fifteenth-century buildings, unimpressive and
petty, like so much of College architecture, but at least quiet,
unassuming, decent. After the accession of Victoria the College
began to grow in numbers, wealth, and pride. The old buildings
were too small and unpretentious for what had now become a
Great College. In the summer of 1867 a great madness fell upon
the Master and Fellows. They hired a most distinguished architect,
bred up in the school of Ruskin, who incontinently razed all the
existing buildings to the ground and erected in their stead a vast
pile in the approved Mauro-Venetian Gothic of the period. The
New Buildings contained a great number of rooms, each served by
a separate and almost perpendicular staircase; and if nearly half
of them were so dark as to make it necessary to light them artificially for all but three hours out of the twenty-four, this slight
defect was wholly outweighed by the striking beauty, from outside, of the Neo-Byzantine loopholes by which they were, euphe-
mistically, "lighted."

Prospects in Canteloup may not please; but man, on the other
hand, tends to be less vile there than in many other places. There
is an equal profusion at Canteloup of Firsts and Blues; there are
Union orators of every shade of opinion and young men so languidly well bred as to take no interest in politics of any kind; there
are drinkers of cocoa and drinkers of champagne. Canteloup is a
microcosm, a whole world in miniature; and whatever your temperament and habits may be, whether you wish to drink, or row,
or work, or hunt, Canteloup will provide you with congenial companions and a spiritual home.

Lack of athletic distinction had prevented Dick from being, at
Æsop, a hero or anything like one. At Canteloup, in a less
barbarically ordered state of society, things were different. His
rooms in the Venetian gazebo over the North Gate became the
meeting-place of all that was most intellectually distinguished in
Canteloup and the University at large. He had had his sitting-
room austerely upholstered and papered in grey. A large white
Chinese figure of the best period stood pedestalled in one corner,
and on the walls there hung a few uncompromisingly good drawings and lithographs by modern artists. Fletton, who had accompanied Dick from Æsop to Canteloup, called it the "cerebral
chamber"; and with its prevailing tone of brain-coloured grey and

493

the rather dry intellectual taste of its decorations it deserved the name.

To-night the cerebral chamber had been crammed. The Canteloup branch of the Fabian Society, under Dick's presidency, had been holding a meeting. "Art in the Socialist State" was what they had been discussing. And now the meeting had broken up, leaving nothing but three empty jugs that had once contained mulled claret and a general air of untidiness to testify to its having taken place at all. Dick stood leaning an elbow on the mantelpiece and absent-mindedly kicking, to the great detriment of his pumps, at the expiring red embers in the grate. From the depths of a huge and cavernous arm-chair, Fletton, pipe in mouth, fumed like a sleepy volcano.

"I liked the way, Dick," he said, with a laugh—"the way you went for the Arty-Crafties. You utterly destroyed them."

"I merely pointed out, what is sufficiently obvious, that crafts are not art, nor anything like it, that's all." Dick snapped out the words. He was nervous and excited, and his body felt as though it were full of compressed springs ready to jump at the most imponderable touch. He was always like that after making a speech.

"You did it very effectively," said Fletton. There was a silence between the two young men.

A noise like the throaty yelling of savages in rut came wafting up from the quadrangle on which the windows of the cerebral chamber opened. Dick started; all the springs within him had gone off at once—a thousand simultaneous Jack-in-the-boxes.

"It's only Francis Quarles' dinner-party becoming vocal," Fletton explained. "Blind mouths, as Milton would call them."

Dick began restlessly pacing up and down the room. When Fletton spoke to him, he did not reply or, at best, gave utterance to a monosyllable or a grunt.

"My dear Dick," said the other at last, "you're not very good company to-night," and heaving himself up from the arm-chair, Fletton went shuffling in his loose, heelless slippers towards the door. "I'm going to bed."

Dick paused in his lion-like prowling to listen to the receding sound of feet on the stairs. All was silent now: Gott sei dank. He went into his bedroom. It was there that he kept his piano, for it was a piece of furniture too smugly black and polished to have a place in the cerebral chamber. He had been thirsting after his piano all the time Fletton was sitting there, damn him! He drew up a chair and began to play over and over a certain series of chords. With his left hand he struck an octave G in the bass, while his right dwelt lovingly on F, B, and E. A luscious chord, beloved by Mendelssohn—a chord in which the native richness of the dominant seventh is made more rich, more piercing sweet by the addition of a divine discord. G, F, B, and E—he let the notes hang tremulously on the silence, savoured to the full their angelic overtones; then, when the sound of the chord had almost died away, he let it droop reluctantly through D to the simple, triumphal beauty of C natural—the diapason closing full in what was for Dick a wholly ineffable emotion.

He repeated that dying fall again and again, perhaps twenty times. Then, when he was satiated with its deliciousness, he rose from the piano and opening the lowest drawer of the wardrobe pulled out from under his evening clothes a large portfolio. He undid the strings; it was full of photogravure reproductions from various Old Masters. There was an almost complete set of Greuze's works, several of the most striking Ary Scheffers, some Alma Tadema, some Leighton, photographs of sculpture by Torwaldsen and Canova, Boecklin's "Island of the Dead," religious pieces by Holman Hunt, and a large packet of miscellaneous pictures from the Paris Salons of the last forty years. He took them into the cerebral chamber where the light was better, and began to study them, lovingly, one by one. The Cézanne lithograph, the three admirable etchings by Van Gogh, the little Picasso looked on, unmoved, from the walls.

It was three o'clock before Dick got to bed. He was stiff and cold, but full of the satisfaction of having accomplished something. And, indeed, he had cause to be satisfied; for he had written the first four thousand words of a novel, a chapter and a half of *Heartsease Fitzroy: the Story of a Young Girl*.

Next morning Dick looked at what he had written overnight, and was alarmed. He had never produced anything quite like this since the days of the Quarles incident at Æsop. A relapse? He wondered. Not a serious one in any case; for this morning he felt himself in full possession of all his ordinary faculties. He must have got overtired speaking to the Fabians in the evening. He looked at his manuscript again, and read: " 'Daddy, do the little girl angels in heaven have toys and kittens and teddy-bears?'

" 'I don't know,' said Sir Christopher gently. 'Why does my little one ask?'

" 'Because, daddy,' said the child—'because I think that soon I too may be a little angel, and I should so like to have my teddy-bear with me in heaven.'

"Sir Christopher clasped her to his breast. How frail she was, how ethereal, how nearly an angel already! Would she have her teddy-bear in heaven? The childish question rang in his ears. Great, strong man though he was, he was weeping. His tears fell in a rain upon her auburn curls.

" 'Tell me, daddy,' she insisted, "will dearest God allow me my teddy-bear?'

" 'My child,' he sobbed, 'my child . . .' "

The blushes mounted hot to his cheeks; he turned away his head in horror. He would really have to look after himself for a bit, go to bed early, take exercise, not do much work. This sort of thing couldn't be allowed to go on.

He went to bed at half-past nine that night, and woke up the following morning to find that he had added a dozen or more closely written pages to his original manuscript during the night. He supposed he must have written them in his sleep. It was all very disquieting. The days passed by; every morning a fresh instalment was added to the rapidly growing bulk of *Heartsease Fitzroy*. It was as though some goblin, some Lob-lie-by-the-Fire, came each night to perform the appointed task, vanishing before the morning. In a little while Dick's alarm wore off; during the day he was perfectly well; his mind functioned with marvellous efficiency. It really didn't seem to matter what he did in his sleep provided he was all right in his waking hours. He almost forgot about *Heartsease*, and was only reminded of her existence when by chance he opened the drawer in which the steadily growing pile of manuscript reposed.

In five weeks *Heartsease Fitzroy* was finished. Dick made a parcel of the manuscript and sent it to a literary agent. He had no hopes of any publisher taking the thing; but he was in sore straits for money at the moment, and it seemed worth trying, on the off-chance. A fortnight later Dick received a letter beginning: "DEAR MADAM,—Permit me to hail in you a new authoress of real talent.

Heartsease Fitzroy is GREAT,"—and signed "EBOR W. SIMS, Editor, *Hildebrand's Home Weekly.*"

Details of the circulation of *Hildebrand's Home Weekly* were printed at the head of the paper; its average net sale was said to exceed three and a quarter millions. The terms offered by Mr. Sims seemed to Dick positively fabulous. And there would be the royalties on the thing in book form after the serial had run its course.

The letter arrived at breakfast; Dick cancelled all engagements for the day and set out immediately for a long and solitary walk. It was necessary to be alone, to think. He made his way along the Seven Bridges Road, up Cumnor Hill, through the village, and down the footpath to Bablock Hithe, thence to pursue the course of the "stripling Thames"—haunted at every step by the Scholar Gipsy, damn him! He drank beer and ate some bread and cheese in a little inn by a bridge, farther up the river; and it was there, in the inn parlour, surrounded by engravings of the late Queen, and breathing the slightly mouldy preserved air bottled some three centuries ago into that hermetically sealed chamber—it was there that he solved the problem, perceived the strange truth about himself.

He was a hermaphrodite.

A hermaphrodite, not in the gross obvious sense, of course, but spiritually. Two persons in one, male and female. Dr. Jekyll and Mr. Hyde: or rather a new William Sharp and Fiona MacLeod—a more intelligent William, a vulgarer Fiona. Everything was explained; the deplorable Quarles incident was simple and obvious now. A sentimental young lady of literary tastes writing sonnets to her Ouida guardsman. And what an unerring flair Mr. Sims had shown by addressing him so roundly and unhesitatingly as "madam"!

Dick was elated at this discovery. He had an orderly mind that disliked mysteries. He had been a puzzle to himself for a long time; now he was solved. He was not in the least distressed to discover this abnormality in his character. As long as the two parts of him kept well apart, as long as his male self could understand mathematics, and as long as his lady novelist's self kept up her regular habit of writing at night and retiring from business during the day, the arrangement would be admirable. The more he thought about it, the more it seemed an ideal state of affairs. His life would arrange itself so easily and well. He would devote the day to the disinterested pursuit of knowledge, to philosophy and mathematics, with perhaps an occasional excursion into politics. After midnight he would write novels with a feminine pen, earning the money that would make his unproductive male labours possible. A kind of spiritual *souteneur*. But the fear of poverty need haunt him no more; no need to become a wage-slave, to sacrifice his intelligence to the needs of his belly. Like a gentleman of the East, he would sit still and smoke his philosophic pipe while the womenfolk did the dirty work. Could anything be more satisfactory?

He paid for his bread and beer, and walked home, whistling as he went.

Chapter III

Two months later the first instalment of *Heartsease Fitzroy: the Story of a Young Girl,* by Pearl Bellairs, appeared in the pages of *Hildebrand's Home Weekly.* Three and a quarter millions read and approved. When the story appeared in book form, two hundred thousand copies were sold in six weeks; and in the course of the next two years no less than sixteen thousand female infants in London alone were christened Heartsease. With her fourth novel and her two hundred and fiftieth Sunday paper article, Pearl Bellairs was well on her way to becoming a household word.

Meanwhile Dick was in receipt of an income far beyond the wildest dreams of his avarice. He was able to realize the two great ambitions of his life—to wear silk underclothing and to smoke good (but really good) cigars.

Chapter IV

Dick went down from Canteloup in a blaze of glory. The most brilliant man of his generation, exceptional mind, prospects, career. But his head was not turned. When people congratulated him on his academic successes, he thanked them politely and then invited them to come and see his Memento Mori. His Memento Mori was called Mr. Glottenham and could be found at any hour of the day in the premises of the Union, or if it was evening, in the Senior Common Room at Canteloup. He was an old member of the College, and the dons in pity for his age and loneliness had made him, some years before, a member of their Common Room. This act of charity was as bitterly regretted as any generous impulse in the history of the world. Mr. Glottenham made the life of the Canteloup fellows a burden to them; he dined in Hall with fiendish regularity, never missing a night, and he was always the last to leave the Common Room. Mr. Glottenham did not prepossess at a first glance; the furrows of his face were covered with a short grey sordid stubble; his clothes were disgusting with the spilth of many years of dirty feeding; he had the shoulders and long hanging arms of an ape—an ape with a horribly human look about it. When he spoke, it was like the sound of a man breaking coke; he spoke incessantly and on every subject. His knowledge was enormous; but he possessed the secret of a strange inverted alchemy—he knew how to turn the richest gold to lead, could make the most interesting topic so intolerably tedious that it was impossible, when he talked, not to loathe it.

This was the death's-head to which Dick, like an ancient philosopher at a banquet, would direct the attention of his heartiest congratulators. Mr. Glottenham had had the most dazzling academic career of his generation. His tutors had prophesied for him a future far more brilliant than that of any of his contemporaries. They were now Ministers of State, poets, philosophers, judges, millionaires. Mr. Glottenham frequented the Union and the Canteloup Senior Common Room, and was—well, he was just Mr. Glottenham. Which was why Dick did not think too highly of his own laurels.

Chapter V

"What shall I do? What ought I to do?" Dick walked up and down the room smoking, furiously and without at all savouring its richness, one of his opulent cigars.

499

"My dear," said Cravister—for it was in Cravister's high-ceilinged Bloomsbury room that Dick was thus unveiling his distress of spirit—"my dear, this isn't a revival meeting. You speak as though there were an urgent need for your soul to be saved from hell fire. It's not as bad as that, you know."

"But it *is* a revival meeting," Dick shouted in exasperation—"it is. I'm a revivalist. You don't know what it's like to have a feeling about your soul. I'm terrifyingly earnest; you don't seem to understand that. I have all the feelings of Bunyan without his religion. I regard the salvation of my soul as important. How simple everything would be if one could go out with those creatures in bonnets and sing hymns like, 'Hip, hip for the blood of the Lamb, hurrah!' or that exquisite one:

> " 'The bells of Hell ring tingalingaling
> For you, but not for me.
> For me the angels singalingaling;
> They've got the goods for me.'

Unhappily it's impossible."

"Your ideas," said Cravister in his flutiest voice, "are somewhat Gothic. I think I can understand them, though of course I don't sympathize or approve. My advice to people in doubt about what course of action they ought to pursue is always the same: do what you want to."

"Cravister, you're hopeless," said Dick, laughing. "I suppose I am rather Gothic, but I do feel sometimes that the question of ought as well as of want does arise."

Dick had come to his old friend for advice about Life. What ought he to do? The indefatigable pen of Pearl Bellairs solved for him the financial problem. There remained only the moral problem: how could he best expend his energies and his time? Should he devote himself to knowing or doing, philosophy or politics? He felt in himself the desire to search for truth and the ability— who knows?—to find it. On the other hand, the horrors of the world about him seemed to call on him to put forth all his strength in an effort to ameliorate what was so patently and repulsively bad. Actually, what had to be decided was this: Should he devote himself to the researches necessary to carry out the plan, long ripening in his brain, of a new system of scientific philosophy; or should he devote his powers and Pearl Bellairs' money in propaganda that should put life into the English revolutionary movement? Great moral principles were in the balance. And Cravister's advice was, do what you want to!

After a month of painful indecision, Dick, who was a real Englishman, arrived at a satisfactory compromise. He started work on his new Synthetic Philosophy, and at the same time joined the staff of the *Weekly International*, to which he contributed both money and articles. The weeks slipped pleasantly and profitably along. The secret of happiness lies in congenial work, and no one could have worked harder than Dick, unless it was the indefatigable Pearl Bellairs, whose nightly output of five thousand words sufficed to support not only Dick but the *Weekly International* as well. These months were perhaps the happiest period of Dick's life. He had friends, money, liberty; he knew himself to be working well; and it was an extra, a supererogatory happiness that he began at this time to get on much better with his sister Millicent than he had ever done before. Millicent had come up to Oxford as a student at St. Mungo Hall in Dick's third year. She had grown into a very efficient and very intelligent young woman. A particularly handsome young woman as well. She was boyishly slender, and a natural grace kept on breaking through the somewhat rigid deportment, which she always tried to impose upon herself, in little beautiful gestures and movements that made the onlooker catch his breath with astonished pleasure.

> "Wincing she was as is a jolly colt,
>   Straight as a mast and upright as a bolt:"

Chaucer had as good an eye for youthful grace as for mormals and bristly nostrils and thick red jovial villainousness.

Millicent lost no time in making her presence at St. Mungo's felt. Second- and third-year heroines might snort at the forwardness of a mere fresh-girl, might resent the complete absence of veneration for their glory exhibited by this youthful bejauna; Millicent pursued her course unmoved. She founded new societies and put fresh life into the institutions which already existed at St. Mungo's to take cocoa and discuss the problems of the universe. She played hockey like a tornado, and she worked alarmingly hard. Decidedly, Millicent was a Force, very soon the biggest Force in the St. Mungo world. In her fifth term she organized the famous St. Mungo general strike, which compelled the authorities to relax a few of the more intolerably tyrannical and anachronistic rules restricting the liberty of the students. It was she who went, on behalf of the strikers, to interview the redoubtable Miss Prosser, Principal of St. Mungo's. The redoubtable Miss Prosser looked grim and invited her to sit down. Millicent sat down and, without quailing, delivered a short but pointed speech attacking the fundamental principles of the St. Mungo system of discipline.

"Your whole point of view," she assured Miss Prosser, "is radically wrong. It's an insult to the female sex; it's positively obscene. Your root assumption is simply this: that we're all in a chronic state of sexual excitement; leave us alone for a moment and we'll immediately put our desires into practice. It's disgusting. It makes me blush. After all, Miss Prosser, we are a college of intelligent women, not an asylum of nymphomaniacs."

For the first time in her career, Miss Prosser had to admit herself beaten. The authorities gave in—reluctantly and on only a few points; but the principle had been shaken, and that, as Millicent pointed out, was what really mattered.

Dick used to see a good deal of his sister while he was still in residence at Canteloup, and after he had gone down he used to come regularly once a fortnight during term to visit her. That horrible mutual reserve, which poisons the social life of most families and which had effectively made of their brotherly and sisterly relation a prolonged discomfort in the past, began to disappear. They became the best of friends.

"I like you, Dick, a great deal better than I did," said Millicent one day as they were parting at the gate of St. Mungo's after a long walk together.

Dick took off his hat and bowed. "My dear, I reciprocate the sentiment. And, what's more, I esteem and admire you. So there."

Millicent curtsied, and they laughed. They both felt very happy.

Chapter VI

"What a life!" said Dick, with a sigh of weariness as the train moved out of Euston.

Not a bad life, Millicent thought.

"But horribly fatiguing. I am quite outreined by it."

"Outreined" was Dick's translation of *éreinté*. He liked using words of his own manufacture; one had to learn his idiom before one could properly appreciate his intimate conversation.

Dick had every justification for being outreined. The spring and summer had passed for him in a whirl of incessant activity. He had written three long chapters of the *New Synthetic Philosophy*, and had the material for two more ready in the form of notes. He had helped to organize and bring to its successful conclusion the great carpenters' strike of May and June. He had written four pamphlets and a small army of political articles. And this comprised only half his labour; for nightly, from twelve till two, Pearl Bellairs emerged to compose the masterpieces which supplied Dick with his bread and butter. *Apes in Purple* had been published in May. Since then she had finished *La Belle Dame sans Morality*, and had embarked on the first chapters of *Daisy's Voyage to Cythera*. Her weekly articles, "For the Girls of Britain," had become, during this period, a regular and favourite feature in the pages of *Hildebrand's Sabbath*, that prince of Sunday papers. At the beginning of July, Dick considered that he had earned a holiday, and now they were off, he and Millicent, for the North.

Dick had taken a cottage on the shore of one of those long salt-water lochs that give to the west coast of Scotland such a dissipated appearance on the map. For miles around there was not a living soul who did not bear the name of Campbell—two families only excepted, one of whom was called Murray-Drummond and the other Drummond-Murray. However, it was not for the people that Dick and Millicent had come, so much as for the landscape, which made up in variety for anything that the inhabitants might lack. Behind the cottage, in the midst of a narrow strip of bog lying between the loch and the foot of the mountains, stood one of the numerous tombs of Ossian, a great barrow of ancient stones. And a couple of miles away the remains of Deirdre's Scottish refuge bore witness to the Celtic past. The countryside was dotted with the black skeletons of mediæval castles. Astonishing country, convulsed into fantastic mountain shapes, cut and indented by winding fiords. On summer days the whole of this improbable landscape became blue and remote and aerially transparent. Its beauty lacked all verisimilitude. It was for that reason that Dick chose the neighbourhood for his holidays. After the insistent actuality of London this frankly unreal coast was particularly refreshing to a jaded spirit.

"Nous sommes ici en plein romantisme," said Dick on the day of their arrival, making a comprehensive gesture towards the dream-like scenery, and for the rest of his holiday he acted the part of a young romantic of the palmy period. He sat at the foot of Ossian's tomb and read Lamartine; he declaimed Byron from the summit of the mountains and Shelley as he rode along the loch. In the evening he read George Sand's *Indiana*; he agonized with the pure, but passionate, heroine, while his admiration for Sir Brown, her English lover, the impassive giant who never speaks and is always clothed in faultless hunting costume, knew no bounds. He saturated himself in the verses of Victor Hugo, and at last almost came to persuade himself that the words, *Dieu, infinité, eternité*, with which the works of that deplorable genius are so profusely sprinkled, actually possessed some meaning, though what that meaning was he could not, even in his most romantic transports, discover. Pearl Bellairs, of course, understood quite clearly their significance, and though she was a very poor French scholar she used sometimes to be moved almost to tears by the books she found lying about when she came into existence after midnight. She even copied out extracts into her notebooks with a view to using them in her next novel.

> "Les plus désespérés sont les chants les plus beaux,
> Et j'en sais d'immortels qui sont de purs sanglots,"

was a couplet which struck her as sublime.

Millicent, meanwhile, did the housekeeping with extraordinary efficiency, took a great deal of exercise, and read long, serious books; she humoured her brother in his holiday romanticism, but refused to take part in the game.

The declaration of war took them completely by surprise. It is true that a *Scotsman* found its way into the cottage by about lunch-time every day, but it was never read, and served only to light fires and wrap up fish and things of that sort. No letters were being forwarded, for they had left no address; they were isolated from the world. On the fatal morning Dick had, indeed, glanced at the paper, without however noticing anything out of the ordinary. It was only later when, alarmed by the rumours floating round the village shop, he came to examine his *Scotsman* more closely, that he found about half-way down the third column of one of the middle pages an admirable account of all that had been so tragically happening in the last twenty-four hours; he learnt with horror that Europe was at war and that his country too had entered the arena. Even in the midst of his anguish of spirit he could not help admiring the *Scotsman's* splendid impassivity—no headlines, no ruffling of the traditional aristocratic dignity. Like Sir Rodolphe Brown in *Indiana*, he thought, with a sickly smile.

Dick determined to start for London at once. He felt that he must act, or at least create the illusion of action; he could not stay quietly where he was. It was arranged that he should set out that afternoon, while Millicent should follow a day or two later with the bulk of the luggage. The train which took him to Glasgow was slower than he thought it possible for any train to be. He tried to read, he tried to sleep; it was no good. His nervous agitation was pitiable; he made little involuntary movements with his limbs, and every now and then the muscles of his face began twitching in a spasmodic and uncontrollable tic. There were three hours to wait in Glasgow; he spent them in wandering about the streets. In the interminable summer twilight the inhabitants of Glasgow came forth into the open to amuse themselves; the sight almost made him sick. Was it possible that there should be human beings so numerous and so uniformly hideous? Small, deformed, sallow, they seemed malignantly ugly, as if on purpose. The words they spoke were incomprehensible. He shuddered; it was an alien place —it was hell.

The London train was crammed. Three gross Italians got into Dick's carriage, and after they had drunk and eaten with loud, unpleasant gusto, they prepared themselves for sleep by taking off their boots. Their feet smelt strongly ammoniac, like a cage of mice long uncleaned. Acutely awake, while the other occupants of the compartment enjoyed a happy unconsciousness, he looked at the huddled carcasses that surrounded him. The warmth and the smell of them was suffocating, and there came to his mind, with the nightmarish insistence of a fixed idea, the thought that every breath they exhaled was saturated with disease. To be condemned to sit in a hot bath of consumption and syphilis—it was too horrible! The moment came at last when he could bear it no longer; he got up and went into the corridor. Standing there, or sitting sometimes for a few dreary minutes in the lavatory, he passed the rest of the night. The train roared along without a stop. The roaring became articulate: in the days of his childhood trains used to run to the tune of "Lancashire, to Lancashire, to fetch a pocket-handkercher; to Lancashire, to Lancashire . . ." But to-night the wheels were shouting insistently, a million times over, two words only—"the War, the War; the War, the War." He tried desperately to make them say something else, but they refused to recite Milton; they refused to go to Lancashire; they went on with their endless Tibetan litany—the War, the War, the War.

By the time he reached London, Dick was in a wretched state. His nerves were twittering and jumping within him; he felt like a walking aviary. The tic in his face had become more violent and persistent. As he stood in the station, waiting for a cab, he overheard a small child saying to its mother, "What's the matter with that man's face, mother?"

"Sh—sh, darling," was the reply. "It's rude."

Dick turned and saw the child's big round eyes fixed with fascinated curiosity upon him, as though he were a kind of monster. He put his hand to his forehead and tried to stop the twitching of the muscles beneath the skin. It pained him to think that he had become a scarecrow for children.

Arrived at his flat, Dick drank a glass of brandy and lay down for a rest. He felt exhausted—ill. At half-past one he got up, drank some more brandy, and crept down into the street. It was intensely hot; the pavements reverberated the sunlight in a glare which hurt his eyes; they seemed to be in a state of grey incandescence. A nauseating smell of wetted dust rose from the roadway, along which a water-cart was slowly piddling its way. He realized suddenly that he ought not to have drunk all that brandy on an empty stomach; he was definitely rather tipsy. He had arrived at that state of drunkenness when the senses perceive things clearly, but do not transmit their knowledge to the understanding. He was painfully conscious of this division, and it needed all the power of his will to establish contact between his parted faculties. It was as though he were, by a great and prolonged effort, keeping his brain pressed against the back of his eyes; as soon as he relaxed the pressure, the understanding part slipped back, the contact was broken, and he relapsed into a state bordering on imbecility. The actions which ordinarily one does by habit and without thinking, he had to perform consciously and voluntarily. He had to reason out the problem of walking—first the left foot forward, then the right. How ingeniously he worked his ankles and knees and hips! How delicately the thighs slid past one another!

He found a restaurant and sat there drinking coffee and trying to eat an omelette until he felt quite sober. Then he drove to the offices of the *Weekly International* to have a talk with Hyman, the editor. Hyman was sitting in his shirt-sleeves, writing.

He lifted his head as Dick came in. "Greenow," he shouted delightedly, "we were all wondering what had become of you. We thought you'd joined the Army."

Dick shook his head, but did not speak; the hot stuffy smell of printer's ink and machinery combined with the atrocious reek of Hyman's Virginian cigarettes to make him feel rather faint. He sat down on the window-ledge, so as to be able to breathe an uncontaminated air.

"Well," he said at last, "what about it?"

"It's going to be hell."

"Did you suppose I thought it was going to be paradise?" Dick replied irritably. "Internationalism looks rather funny now, doesn't it?"

"I believe in it more than ever I did," cried Hyman. His face lit up with the fervour of his enthusiasm. It was a fine face, gaunt, furrowed, and angular, for all that he was barely thirty, looking as though it had been boldly chiselled from some hard stone. "The rest of the world may go mad; we'll try and keep our sanity. The time will come when they'll see we were right."

Hyman talked on. His passionate sincerity and singleness of purpose were an inspiration to Dick. He had always admired Hyman—with the reservations, of course, that the man was rather a fanatic and not so well-educated as he might have been—but to-day he admired him more than ever. He was even moved by that perhaps too facile eloquence which of old had been used to leave him cold. After promising to do a series of articles on international relations for the paper, Dick went home, feeling better than he had done all day.

He decided that he would begin writing his articles at once. He collected pens, paper, and ink and sat down in a businesslike way at his bureau. He remembered distinctly biting the tip of his penholder; it tasted rather bitter.

And then he realized he was standing in Regent Street, looking in at one of the windows of Liberty's.

For a long time he stood there quite still, absorbed to all appearance in the contemplation of a piece of peacock-blue fabric. But all his attention was concentrated within himself, not on anything outside. He was wondering—wondering how it came about that he was sitting at his writing-table at one moment, and standing, at the next, in Regent Street. He hadn't—the thought flashed upon him—he hadn't been drinking any more of that brandy, had he? No, he felt himself to be perfectly sober. He moved slowly away and continued to speculate as he walked.

At Oxford Circus he bought an evening paper. He almost screamed aloud when he saw that the date printed at the head of the page was August 12th. It was on August 7th that he had sat down at his writing-table to compose those articles. Five days ago, and he had not the faintest recollection of what had happened in those five days.

He made all haste back to the flat. Everything was in perfect order. He had evidently had a picnic lunch that morning—sardines, bread and jam, and raisins; the remains of it still covered the table. He opened the sideboard and took out the brandy bottle. Better make quite sure. He held it up to the light; it was more than three-quarters full. Not a drop had gone since the day of his return. If brandy wasn't the cause, then what was?

As he sat there thinking, he began in an absent-minded way to look at his evening paper. He read the news on the front page, then turned to the inner sheets. His eye fell on these words printed at the head of the column next the leading article:

"To the Women of the Empire. Thoughts in War-Time. By Pearl Bellairs." Underneath in brackets: "The first of a series of inspiring patriotic articles by Miss Bellairs, the well-known novelist."

Dick groaned in agony. He saw in a flash what had happened to his five missing days. Pearl had got hold of them somehow, had trespassed upon his life out of her own reserved nocturnal existence. She had taken advantage of his agitated mental state to have a little fun in her own horrible way.

He picked up the paper once more and began to read Pearl's article. "Inspiring and patriotic": those were feeble words in which to describe Pearl's shrilly raucous chauvinism. And the style! Christ! to think that he was responsible, at least in part, for this. Responsible, for had not the words been written by his own hand and composed in some horrible bluebeard's chamber of his own brain? They had, there was no denying it. Pearl's literary atrocities had never much distressed him; he had long given up reading a word she wrote. Her bank balance was the only thing about her that interested him. But now she was invading the sanctities of his private life. She was trampling on his dearest convictions, denying his faith. She was a public danger. It was all too frightful.

He passed the afternoon in misery. Suicide or brandy seemed the only cures. Not very satisfactory ones, though. Towards evening an illuminating idea occurred to him. He would go and see Rogers. Rogers knew all about psychology—from books, at any rate: Freud, Jung, Morton Prince, and people like that. He used to try hypnotic experiments on his friends and even dabbled in amateur psychotherapy. Rogers might help him to lay the ghost of Pearl. He ate a hasty dinner and went to see Rogers in his Kensington rooms.

Rogers was sitting at a table with a great book open in front of him. The reading-lamp, which was the only light in the room, brightly illuminated one side of the pallid, puffy, spectacled face, leaving the other in complete darkness, save for a little cedilla of golden light caught on the fold of flesh at the corner of his mouth. His huge shadow crossed the floor, began to climb the wall, and from the shoulders upwards mingled itself with the general darkness of the room.

"Good evening, Rogers," said Dick wearily. "I wish you wouldn't try and look like Rembrandt's 'Christ at Emmaus' with these spectacular chiaroscuro effects."

Rogers gave vent to his usual nervous giggling laugh. "This is very nice of you to come and see me, Greenow."

"How's the Board of Trade?" Rogers was a Civil Servant by profession.

"Oh, business as usual, as the *Daily Mail* would say." Rogers laughed again as though he had made a joke.

After a little talk of things indifferent, Dick brought the conversation round to himself.

"I believe I'm getting a bit neurasthenic," he said. "Fits of depression, nervous pains, lassitude, anæmia of the will. I've come to you for professional advice. I want you to nose out my suppressed complexes, analyse me, dissect me. Will you do that for me?"

Rogers was evidently delighted. "I'll do my best," he said, with assumed modesty. "But I'm no good at the thing, so you mustn't expect much."

"I'm at your disposal," said Dick.

Rogers placed his guest in a large armchair. "Relax your muscles and think of nothing at all." Dick sat there flabby and abstracted while Rogers made his preparations. His apparatus consisted chiefly in a notebook and a stop-watch. He seated himself at the table.

"Now," he said solemnly, "I want you to listen to me. I propose to read out a list of words; after each of the words you must say the first word that comes into your head. The very first, mind, however foolish it may seem. And say it as soon as it crosses your mind; don't wait to think. I shall write down your answers and take the time between each question and reply."

Rogers cleared his throat and started.

"Mother," he said in a loud, clear voice. He always began his analyses with the family. For since the majority of kinks and complexes date from childhood, it is instructive to investigate the relations between the patient and those who surrounded him at an early age. "Mother."

"Dead," replied Dick immediately. He had scarcely known his mother.

"Father."

"Dull." One and a fifth seconds' interval.

"Sister." Rogers pricked his ears for the reply: his favourite incest-theory depended on it.

"Fabian Society," said Dick, after two seconds' interval. Rogers was a little disappointed. He was agreeably thrilled and excited by the answer he received to his next word: "Aunt."

The seconds passed, bringing nothing with them; and then at last there floated into Dick's mind the image of himself as a child, dressed in a green velvet and lace, a perfect Bubbles boy, kneeling on Auntie Loo's lap and arranging a troop of lead soldiers on the horizontal projection of her corsage.

"Bosom," he said.

Rogers wrote down the word and underlined it. Six and three-fifths seconds: very significant. He turned now to the chapter of possible accidents productive of nervous shocks.

"Fire."

"Coal.

"Sea."

"Sick."

"Train."

"Smell."

And so on. Dull answers all the time. Evidently, nothing very catastrophic had ever happened to him. Now for a frontal attack on the fortress of sex itself.

"Women." There was rather a long pause, four seconds, and then Dick replied, "Novelist." Rogers was puzzled.

"Breast."

"Chicken." That was disappointing. Rogers could find no trace of those sinister moral censors, expurgators of impulse, suppressors of happiness. Perhaps the trouble lay in religion.

"Christ," he said.

Dick replied, "Amen," with the promptitude of a parish clerk.

"God."

Dick's mind remained a perfect blank. The word seemed to convey to him nothing at all. God, God. After a long time there appeared before his inward eye the face of a boy he had known at school and at Oxford, one Godfrey Wilkinson, called God for short.

"Wilkinson." Ten seconds and a fifth.

A few more miscellaneous questions, and the list was exhausted. Almost suddenly, Dick fell into a kind of hypnotic sleep. Rogers sat pensive in front of his notes; sometimes he consulted a text-book. At the end of half an hour he awakened Dick to tell him that he had had, as a child, consciously or unconsciously, a great Freudian passion for his aunt; that later on he had had another

511

passion, almost religious in its fervour and intensity, for somebody called Wilkinson; and that the cause of all his present troubles lay in one or other of these episodes. If he liked, he (Rogers) would investigate the matter further with a view to establishing a cure.

Dick thanked him very much, thought it wasn't worth taking any more trouble, and went home.

Chapter VII

MILLICENT WAS ORGANIZING a hospital supply dépôt, organizing indefatigably, from morning till night. It was October; Dick had not seen his sister since those first hours of the war in Scotland; he had had too much to think about these last months to pay attention to anyone but himself. To-day, at last, he decided that he would go and pay her a visit. Millicent had commandeered a large house in Kensington from a family of Jews, who were anxious to live down a deplorable name by a display of patriotism. Dick found her sitting there in her office—young, formidable, beautiful, severe—at a big desk covered with papers.

"Well," said Dick, "you're winning the war, I see."

"You, I gather, are not," Millicent replied.

"I believe in the things I always believed in."

"So do I."

"But in a different way, my dear—in a different way," said Dick sadly. There was a silence.

"Had we better quarrel?" Millicent asked meditatively.

"I think we can manage with nothing worse than a coolness— for the duration."

"Very well, a coolness."

"A smouldering coolness."

"Good," said Millicent briskly. "Let it start smouldering at once. I must get on with my work. Good-bye, Dick. God bless you. Let me know sometimes how you get on."

"No need to ask how you get on," said Dick with a smile, as he shook her hand. "I know by experience that you always get on, only too well, ruthlessly well."

He went out. Millicent returned to her letters with concentrated ardour; a frown puckered the skin between her eyebrows.

Probably, Dick reflected as he made his way down the stairs, he wouldn't see her again for a year or so. He couldn't honestly say that it affected him much. Other people became daily more and more like ghosts, unreal, thin, vaporous; while every hour the consciousness of himself grew more intense and all-absorbing. The only person who was more than a shadow to him now was Hyman of the *Weekly International*. In those first horrible months of the war, when he was wrestling with Pearl Bellairs and failing to cast her out, it was Hyman who kept him from melancholy and suicide. Hyman made him write a long article every week, dragged him into the office to do sub-editorial work, kept him so busy that there were long hours when he had no time to brood over his own insoluble problems. And his enthusiasm was so passionate and sincere that sometimes even Dick was infected by it; he could believe that life was worth living and the cause worth fighting for. But not for long; for the devil would return, insistent and untiring. Pearl Bellairs was greedy for life; she was not content with her short midnight hours; she wanted the freedom of whole days. And whenever Dick was overtired, or ill or nervous, she leapt upon him and stamped him out of existence, till enough strength came back for him to reassert his personality. And the articles she wrote! The short stories! The recruiting songs! Dick dared not read them; they were terrible, terrible.

Chapter VIII

THE MONTHS PASSED by. The longer the war lasted, the longer it seemed likely to last. Dick supported life somehow. Then came the menace of conscription. The *Weekly International* organized a great anti-conscription campaign, in which Hyman and Dick were the leading spirits. Dick was almost happy. This kind of active work was new to him and he enjoyed it, finding it exciting and at the same time sedative. For a self-absorbed and brooding mind, pain itself is an anodyne. He enjoyed his incessant journeys, his speechmaking to queer audiences in obscure halls and chapels;

he liked talking with earnest members of impossible Christian sects, pacifists who took not the faintest interest in the welfare of humanity at large, but were wholly absorbed in the salvation of their own souls and in keeping their consciences clear from the faintest trace of blood-guiltiness. He enjoyed the sense of power which came to him, when he roused the passion of the crowd to enthusiastic assent, or breasted the storm of antagonism. He enjoyed everything—even getting a bloody nose from a patriot hired and intoxicated by a great evening paper to break up one of his meetings. It all seemed tremendously exciting and important at the time. And yet when, in quiet moments, he came to look back on his days of activity, they seemed utterly empty and futile. What was left of them? Nothing, nothing at all. The momentary intoxication had died away, the stirred ant's-nest had gone back to normal life. Futility of action! There was nothing permanent, or decent, or worth while, except thought. And of that he was almost incapable now. His mind, when it was not occupied by the immediate and actual, turned inward morbidly upon itself. He looked at the manuscript of his book and wondered whether he would ever be able to go on with it. It seemed doubtful. Was he, then, condemned to pass the rest of his existence enslaved to the beastliness and futility of mere quotidian action? And even in action his powers were limited; if he exerted himself too much—and the limits of fatigue were soon reached—Pearl Bellairs, watching perpetually like a hungry tigress for her opportunity, leapt upon him and took possession of his conscious faculties. And then, it might be for a matter of hours or of days, he was lost, blotted off the register of living souls, while she performed, with intense and hideous industry, her self-appointed task. More than once his anti-conscription campaigns had been cut short and he himself had suddenly disappeared from public life, to return with the vaguest stories of illness or private affairs—stories that made his friends shake their heads and wonder which it was among the noble army of vices that Poor Dick Greenow was so mysteriously addicted to. Some said drink, some said women, some said opium, and some hinted at things infinitely darker and more horrid. Hyman asked him point-blank what it was, one morning when he had returned to the office after three days' unaccountable absence.

Dick blushed painfully. "It isn't anything you think," he said.

"What is it, then?" Hyman insisted.

"I can't tell you," Dick replied desperately and in torture, "but I swear it's nothing discreditable. I beg you won't ask me any more."

Hyman had to pretend to be satisfied with that.

Chapter IX

A TACTICAL MOVE in the anti-conscription campaign was the foundation of a club, a place where people with pacific or generally advanced ideas could congregate.

"A club like this would soon be the intellectual centre of London," said Hyman, ever sanguine.

Dick shrugged his shoulders. He had a wide experience of pacifists.

"If you bring people together," Hyman went on, "they encourage one another to be bold—strengthen one another's faith."

"Yes," said Dick dyspeptically. "When they're in a herd, they can believe that they're much more numerous and important than they really are."

"But, man, they are numerous, they are important!" Hyman shouted and gesticulated.

Dick allowed himself to be persuaded into an optimism which he knew to be ill-founded. The consolations of religion do not console the less efficaciously for being illusory.

It was a long time before they could think of a suitable name for their club. Dick suggested that it should be called the Sclopis Club. "Such a lovely name," he explained. "Sclopis—Sclopis; it tastes precious in the mouth." But the rest of the committee would not hear of it; they wanted a name that meant something. One lady suggested that it should be called the Everyman Club; Dick objected with passion. "It makes one shudder," he said. The lady thought it was a beautiful and uplifting name, but as Mr. Greenow was so strongly opposed, she wouldn't press the claims of Everyman. Hyman wanted to call it the Pacifist Club, but that was judged too provocative. Finally, they agreed to call it the

Novembrist Club, because it was November and they could think of no better title.

The inaugural dinner of the Novembrist Club was held at Piccolomini's Restaurant. Piccolomini is in, but not exactly of, Soho, for it is a cross between a Soho restaurant and a Corner House, a hybrid which combines the worst qualities of both parents— the dirt and inefficiency of Soho, the size and vulgarity of Lyons. There is a large upper chamber reserved for agapes. Here, one wet and dismal winter's evening, the Novembrists assembled.

Dick arrived early, and from his place near the door he watched his fellow-members come in. He didn't much like the look of them. "Middle class" was what he found himself thinking; and he had to admit, when his conscience reproached him for it, that he did not like the middle classes, the lower middle classes, the lower classes. He was, there was no denying it, a bloodsucker at heart—cultured and intelligent, perhaps, but a bloodsucker none the less.

The meal began. Everything about it was profoundly suspect. The spoons were made of some pale pinchbeck metal, very light and flimsy; one expected them to melt in the soup, or one would have done, if the soup had been even tepid. The food was thick and greasy. Dick wondered what it really looked like under the concealing sauces. The wine left an indescribable taste that lingered on the palate, like the savour of brass or of charcoal fumes.

From childhood upwards Dick had suffered from the intensity of his visceral reactions to emotion. Fear and shyness were apt to make him feel very sick, and disgust produced in him a sensation of intolerable queasiness. Disgust had seized upon his mind tonight. He grew paler with the arrival of every dish, and the wine, instead of cheering him, made him feel much worse. His neighbours to right and left ate with revolting heartiness. On one side sat Miss Gibbs, garishly dressed in ill-assorted colours that might be called futuristic; on the other was Mr. Something in pince-nez, rather ambrosial about the hair. Mr. Something was a poet, or so the man who introduced them had said. Miss Gibbs was just an ordinary member of the Intelligentsia, like the rest of us.

The Lower Classes, the Lower Classes . . .

"Are you interested in the Modern Theatre?" asked Mr. Something in his mellow voice. Too mellow—oh, much too mellow!

"Passably," said Dick.

"So am I," said Mr. Thingummy. "I am a vice-president of the Craftsmen's League of Joy, which perhaps you may have heard of."

Dick shook his head; this was going to be terrible.

"The objects of the Craftsmen's League of Joy," Mr. Thingummy continued, "or rather, one of the objects—for it has many —is to establish Little Theatres in every town and village in England, where simple, uplifting, beautiful plays might be acted. The people have no joy."

"They have the cinema and the music hall," said Dick. He was filled with a sudden senseless irritation. "They get all the joy they want out of the jokes of the comics and the legs of the women."

"Ah, but that is an impure joy," Mr. What's-his-name protested.

"Impure purple, Herbert Spenser's favourite colour," flashed irrelevantly through Dick's brain.

"Well, speaking for myself," he said aloud, "I know I get more joy out of a good pair of legs than out of any number of uplifting plays of the kind they'd be sure to act in your little theatres. The people ask for sex and you give them a stone."

How was it, he wondered, that the right opinions in the mouths of these people sounded so horribly cheap and wrong? They degraded what was noble; beauty became fly-blown at their touch. Their intellectual tradition was all wrong. Lower classes, it always came back to that. When they talked about war and the International, Dick felt a hot geyser of chauvinism bubbling up in his breast. In order to say nothing stupid, he refrained from speaking at all. Miss Gibbs switched the conversation on to art. She admired all the right people. Dick told her that he thought Sir Luke Fildes to be the best modern artist. But his irritation knew no bounds when he found out a little later that Mr. Something had read the poems of Fulke Greville, Lord Brooke. He felt inclined to say, "You may have read them, but of course you can't understand or appreciate them."

Lower Classes . . .

How clear and splendid were the ideas of right and justice! If only one could filter away the contaminating human element. . . . Reason compelled him to believe in democracy, in internationalism, in revolution; morality demanded justice for the oppressed.

But neither morality nor reason would ever bring him to take pleasure in the company of democrats or revolutionaries, or make him find the oppressed, individually, any less antipathetic.

At the end of this nauseating meal, Dick was called on to make a speech. Rising to his feet, he began stammering and hesitating; he felt like an imbecile. Then suddenly inspiration came. The great religious ideas of Justice and Democracy swept like a rushing wind through his mind, purging it of all insignificant human and personal preferences or dislikes. He was filled with pentecostal fire. He spoke in a white heat of intellectual passion, dominating his hearers, infecting them with his own high enthusiasm. He sat down amid cheers. Miss Gibbs and Mr. Thingummy leaned towards him with flushed, shining faces.

"That was wonderful, Mr. Greenow. I've never heard anything like it," exclaimed Miss Gibbs, with genuine, unflattering enthusiasm.

Mr. Thing said something poetical about a trumpet-call. Dick looked from one to the other with blank and fishy eyes. So it was for these creatures he had been speaking!

Good God! . . .

Chapter X

DICK'S LIFE WAS now a monotonous nightmare. The same impossible situation was repeated again and again. If it were not for the fact that he knew Pearl Bellairs to be entirely devoid of humour, Dick might have suspected that she was having a little quiet fun with him, so grotesque were the anomalies of his double life. Grotesque, but dreary, intolerably dreary. Situations which seem, in contemplation, romantic and adventurous have a habit of proving, when actually experienced, as dull and daily as a bank clerk's routine. When you read about it, a Jekyll and Hyde existence sounds delightfully amusing; but when you live through it, as Dick found to his cost, it is merely a boring horror.

In due course Dick was called up by the Military Authorities. He pleaded conscientious objection. The date of his appearance before the Tribunal was fixed. Dick did not much relish the prospect of being a Christian martyr; it seemed an anachronism. However, it would have to be done. He would be an absolutist; there would be a little buffeting, spitting, and scourging, followed by an indefinite term of hard labour. It was all very unpleasant. But nothing could be much more unpleasant than life as he was now living it. He didn't even mind very much if they killed him. Being or not being—the alternatives left him equally cold.

The days that preceded his appearance before the Tribunal were busy days, spent in consulting solicitors, preparing speeches, collecting witnesses.

"We'll give you a good run for your money," said Hyman. "I hope they'll be feeling a little uncomfortable by the time they have done with you, Greenow."

"Not nearly so uncomfortable as I shall be feeling," Dick replied, with a slightly melancholy smile.

The South Marylebone Tribunal sat in a gloomy and fetid chamber in a police station. Dick, who was extremely sensitive to his surroundings, felt his fatigue and nervousness perceptibly increase as he entered the room. Five or six pitiable creatures with paralytic mothers or one-man businesses were briskly disposed of, and then it was Dick's turn to present himself before his judges. He looked round the court, nodded to Hyman, smiled at Millicent, who had so far thawed their wartime coolness as to come and see him condemned, caught other friendly eyes. It was as though he were about to be electrocuted. The preliminaries passed off; he found himself answering questions in a loud, clear voice. Then the Military Representative began to loom horribly large. The Military Representative was a solicitor's clerk disguised as a lieutenant in the Army Service Corps. He spoke in an accent that was more than genteel; it was rich, noble, aristocratic. Dick tried to remember where he had heard a man speaking like that before. He had it now. Once when he had been at Oxford after term was over. He had gone to see the Varieties, which come twice nightly and with cheap seats to the theatre after the undergraduates have departed. One of the turns had been a Nut, a descendant of the bloods and Champagne Charlies of earlier days. A young man in an alpaca evening suit and a monocle. He had danced, sung a song, spoken some patter. Sitting in the front row of the stalls, Dick had been able to see the large, swollen, tuberculous glands in his neck. They wobbled when he danced or sang. Fascinatingly horrible, those glands; and the young man, how terribly, painfully pathetic. . . . When the Military Representative spoke, he could hear again that wretched Nut's rendering of the Eton and Oxford voice. It unnerved him.

"What is your religion, Mr. Greenow?" the Military Representative asked.

Fascinated, Dick looked to see whether he too had tuberculous glands. The Lieutenant had to repeat his question sharply. When he was irritated, his voice went back to its more natural nasal twang. Dick recovered his presence of mind.

"I have no religion," he answered.

"But, surely, sir, you must have some kind of religion."

"Well, if I must, if it's in the Army Regulations, you had better put me down as an Albigensian, or a Bogomile, or, better still, as a Manichean. One can't find oneself in this court without possessing a profound sense of the reality and active existence of a power of evil equal to, if not greater than, the power of good."

"This is rather irrelevant, Mr. Greenow," said the Chairman.

"I apologize." Dick bowed to the court.

"But if," the Military Representative continued—"if your objection is not religious, may I ask what it is?"

"It is based on a belief that all war is wrong, and that the solidarity of the human race can only be achieved in practice by protesting against war, wherever it appears and in whatever form."

"Do you disbelieve in force, Mr. Greenow?"

"You might as well ask me if I disbelieve in gravitation. Of course, I believe in force: it is a fact."

"What would you do if you saw a German violating your sister?" said the Military Representative, putting his deadliest question.

"Perhaps I had better ask my sister first," Dick replied. "She is sitting just behind you in the court."

The Military Representative was covered with confusion. He coughed and blew his nose. The case dragged on. Dick made a speech; the Military Representative made a speech; the Chairman made a speech. The atmosphere of the court-room grew fouler and fouler. Dick sickened and suffocated in the second-hand air. An immense lassitude took possession of him; he did not care about anything—about the cause, about himself, about Hyman or Millicent or Pearl Bellairs. He was just tired. Voices buzzed and drawled in his ears—sometimes his own voice, sometimes other people's. He did not listen to what they said. He was tired—tired of all this idiotic talk, tired of the heat and smell. . . .

Tired of picking up very thistly wheat sheaves and propping them up in stooks on the yellow stubble. For that was what, suddenly, he found himself doing. Overhead the sky expanded in endless steppes of blue-hot cobalt. The pungent prickly dust of the dried sheaves plucked at his nose with imminent sneezes, made his eyes smart and water. In the distance a reaping-machine whirred and hummed. Dick looked blankly about him, wondering where he was. He was thankful, at any rate, not to be in that sweltering courtroom; and it was a mercy, too, to have escaped from the odious gentility of the Military Representative's accent. And, after all, there were worse occupations than harvesting.

Gradually, and bit by bit, Dick pieced together his history. He had, it seemed, done a cowardly and treacherous thing: deserted in the face of the enemy, betrayed his cause. He had a bitter letter from Hyman. "Why couldn't you have stuck it out? I thought it was in you. You've urged others to go to prison for their beliefs, but you get out of it yourself by sneaking off to a soft alternative service job on a friend's estate. You've brought discredit on the whole movement." It was very painful, but what could he answer? The truth was so ridiculous that nobody could be expected to swallow it. And yet the fact was that he had been as much startled to find himself working at Crome as anyone. It was all Pearl's doing.

He had found in his room a piece of paper covered with the large, flamboyant feminine writing which he knew to be Pearl's. It was evidently the rough copy of an article on the delights of being a land-girl: dewy dawns, rosy children's faces, quaint cottages, mossy thatch, milkmaids, healthy exercise. Pearl was being a land-girl; but he could hardly explain the fact to Hyman. Better not attempt to answer him.

Dick hated the manual labour of the farm. It was hard, monotonous, dirty, and depressing. It inhibited almost completely the functions of his brain. He was unable to think about anything at all; there was no opportunity to do anything but feel uncomfortable. God had not made him a Caliban to scatter ordure over fields, to pick up ordure from cattle-yards. His rôle was Prospero.

"Ban, Ban, Caliban"—it was to that derisive measure that he pumped water, sawed wood, mowed grass; it was a march for his slow, clotted feet as he followed the dung-carts up the winding lanes. "Ban, Ban, Caliban—Ban, Ban, Ban . . ."

"Oh, that bloody old fool Tolstoy," was his profoundest reflection on a general subject in three months of manual labour and communion with mother earth.

He hated the work, and his fellow-workers hated him. They mistrusted him because they could not understand him, taking the silence of his overpowering shyness for arrogance and the contempt of one class for another. Dick longed to become friendly with them. His chief trouble was that he did not know what to say. At meal-times he would spend long minutes in cudgelling his brains for some suitable remark to make. And even if he thought of something good, like—"It looks as though it were going to be a good year for roots," he somehow hesitated to speak, feeling that such a remark, uttered in his exquisitely modulated tones, would be, somehow, a little ridiculous. It was the sort of thing that ought to be said rustically, with plenty of Z's and long vowels, in the manner of William Barnes. In the end, for lack of courage to act the yokel's part, he generally remained silent. While the others were eating their bread and cheese with laughter and talk, he sat like the skeleton at the feast—a skeleton that longed to join in the revelry, but had not the power to move its stony jaws. On the rare occasions that he actually succeeded in uttering something, the labourers looked at one another in surprise and alarm, as though it were indeed a skeleton that had spoken.

He was not much more popular with the other inhabitants of the village. Often, in the evenings, as he was returning from work, the children would pursue him, yelling. With the unerringly cruel instinct of the young they had recognized in him a fit object for abuse and lapidation. An outcast member of another class, from whom that class in casting him out had withdrawn its protection, an alien in speech and habit, a criminal, as their zealous schoolmaster lost no opportunity of reminding them, guilty of the

blackest treason against God and man—he was the obviously pre-
destined victim of childish persecution. When stones began to
fly, and dung and precocious obscenity, he bowed his head and
pretended not to notice that anything unusual was happening.
It was difficult, however, to look quite dignified.

There were occasional short alleviations to the dreariness of his
existence. One day, when he was engaged in his usual occupation
of manuring, a familiar figure suddenly appeared along the footpath
through the field. It was Mrs. Cravister. She was evidently staying at the big house; one of the Manorial dachshunds preceded
her. He took off his cap.

"Mr. Greenow!" she exclaimed, coming to a halt. "Ah, what
a pleasure to see you again! Working on the land: so Tolstoyan.
But I trust it doesn't affect your æsthetic ideas in the same way
as it did his. Fifty peasants singing together is music; but Bach's
chromatic fantasia is mere gibbering incomprehensibility."

"I don't do this for pleasure," Dick explained. "It's hard labour,
meted out to the Conscientious Objector."

"Of course, of course," said Mrs. Cravister, raising her hand to
arrest any further explanation. "I had forgotten. A conscientious
objector, a Bible student. I remember how passionately devoted
you were, even at school, to the Bible."

She closed her eyes and nodded her head several times.

"On the contrary——" Dick began; but it was no good. Mrs.
Cravister had determined that he should be a Bible student and it
was no use gainsaying her. She cut him short.

"Dear me, the Bible. . . . What a style! That alone would prove
it to have been directly inspired. You remember how Mahomet
appealed to the beauty of his style as a sign of his divine mission.
Why has nobody done the same for the Bible? It remains for
you, Mr. Greenow, to do so. You will write a book about it. How
I envy you!"

"The style is very fine," Dick ventured, "but don't you think
the matter occasionally leaves something to be desired?"

"The matter is nothing," cried Mrs. Cravister, making a gesture
that seemed to send all meaning flying like a pinch of salt along
the wind—"nothing at all. It's the style that counts. Think of
Madame Bovary."

"I certainly will," said Dick.

Mrs. Cravister held out her hand. "Good-bye. Yes, I certainly envy you. I envy you your innocent labour and your incessant study of that most wonderful of books. If I were asked, Mr. Greenow, what book I should take with me to a desert island, what single solitary book, I should certainly say the Bible, though, indeed, there are moments when I think I should choose *Tristram Shandy*. Good-bye."

Mrs. Cravister sailed slowly away. The little brown basset trotted ahead, straining his leash. One had the impression of a great ship being towed into harbour by a diminutive tug.

Dick was cheered by this glimpse of civilization and humanity. The unexpected arrival, one Saturday afternoon, of Millicent was not quite such an unmixed pleasure. "I've come to see how you're getting on," she announced, "and to put your cottage straight and make you comfortable."

"Very kind of you," said Dick. He didn't want his cottage put straight.

Millicent was in the Ministry of Munitions now, controlling three thousand female clerks with unsurpassed efficiency. Dick looked at her curiously, as she talked that evening of her doings. "To think I should have a sister like that," he said to himself. She was terrifying.

"You do enjoy bullying other people!" he exclaimed at last. "You've found your true vocation. One sees now how the new world will be arranged after the war. The women will continue to do all the bureaucratic jobs, all that entails routine and neatness and interfering with other people's affairs. And man, it is to be hoped, will be left free for the important statesman's business, free for creation and thought. He will stay at home and give proper education to the children, too. He is fit to do these things, because his mind is disinterested and detached. It's an arrangement which will liberate all man's best energies for their proper uses. The only flaw I can see in the system is that you women will be so fiendishly and ruthlessly tyrannical in your administration."

"You can't seriously expect me to argue with you," said Millicent.

"No, please don't. I am not strong enough. My dung-carrying has taken the edge off all my reasoning powers."

Millicent spent the next morning in completely rearranging

Dick's furniture. By lunch-time every article in the cottage was occupying a new position.

"That's much nicer," said Millicent, surveying her work and seeing that it was good.

There was a knock at the door. Dick opened it and was astonished to find Hyman.

"I just ran down to see how you were getting on," he explained.

"I'm getting on very well since my sister rearranged my furniture," said Dick. He found it pleasing to have an opportunity of exercising his long unused powers of malicious irony. This was very mild, but with practice he would soon come on to something more spiteful and amusing.

Hyman shook hands with Millicent, scowling as he did so. He was irritated that she was there; he wanted to talk with Dick alone. He turned his back on her and began addressing Dick.

"Well," he said, "I haven't seen you since the fatal day. How is the turnip-hoeing?"

"Pretty beastly," said Dick.

"Better than doing hard labour in a gaol, I suppose?"

Dick nodded his head wearily, foreseeing what must inevitably come.

"You've escaped that all right," Hyman went on.

"Yes; you ought to be thankful," Millicent chimed in.

"I still can't understand why you did it, Greenow. It was a blow to me. I didn't expect it of you." Hyman spoke with feeling. "It was desertion; it was treason."

"I agree," said Millicent judicially. "He ought to have stuck to his principles."

"He ought to have stuck to what was right, oughtn't he, Miss Greenow?" Hyman turned towards Millicent, pleased at finding someone who shared his views.

"Of course," she replied—"of course. I totally disagree with you about what is right. But if he believed it right not to fight, he certainly ought to have gone to prison for his belief."

Dick lit a pipe with an air of nonchalance. He tried to disguise the fact that he was feeling extremely uncomfortable under these two pairs of merciless, accusing eyes.

"To my mind, at any rate," said Millicent, "your position seems quite illogical and untenable, Dick."

It was a relief to be talked to and not about.

"I'm sorry about that," said Dick rather huskily—not a very intelligent remark, but what was there to say?

"Of course, it's illogical and untenable. Your sister is quite right." Hyman banged the table.

"I can't understand what induced you to take it up——"

"After you'd said you were going to be one of the absolutes," cried Hyman, interrupting and continuing Millicent's words.

"Why?" said Millicent.

"Why, why, why?" Hyman echoed.

Dick, who had been blowing out smoke at a great rate, put down his pipe. The taste of the tobacco was making him feel rather sick. "I wish you would stop," he said wearily. "If I gave you the real reason, you wouldn't believe me. And I can't invent any others that would be in the least convincing."

"I believe the real reason is that you were afraid of prison."

Dick leaned back in his chair and shut his eyes. He did not mind being insulted now; it made no difference. Hyman and Millicent were still talking about him, but what they said did not interest him; he scarcely listened.

They went back to London together in the evening.

"Very intelligent woman, your sister," said Hyman just before they were starting. "Pity she's not on the right side about the war and so forth."

Four weeks later Dick received a letter in which Hyman announced that he and Millicent had decided to get married.

"I am happy to think," Dick wrote in his congratulatory reply, "that it was I who brought you together."

He smiled as he read through the sentence; that was what the Christian martyr might say to the two lions who had scraped acquaintance over his bones in the amphitheatre.

One warm afternoon in the summer of 1918, Mr. Hobart, Clerk to the Wibley Town Council, was disturbed in the midst of his duties by the sudden entry into his office of a small dark man, dressed in corduroys and gaiters, but not having the air of a genuine agricultural labourer.

"What may I do for you?" inquired Mr. Hobart.

"I have come to inquire about my vote," said the stranger.

"Aren't you already registered?"

"Not yet. You see, it isn't long since the Act was passed giving us the vote."

Mr. Hobart stared.

"I don't quite follow," he said.

"I may not look it," said the stranger, putting his head on one side and looking arch—"I may not look it, but I will confess to you, Mr.—er—Mr.—er——"

"Hobart."

"Mr. Hobart, that I am a woman of over thirty."

Mr. Hobart grew visibly paler. Then, assuming a forced smile and speaking as one speaks to a child or a spoiled animal, he said:

"I see—I see. Over thirty, dear me."

He looked at the bell, which was over by the fireplace at the other side of the room, and wondered how he should ring it without rousing the maniac's suspicions.

"Over thirty," the stranger went on. "You know my woman's secret. I am Miss Pearl Bellairs, the novelist. Perhaps you have read some of my books. Or are you too busy?"

"Oh no, I've read several," Mr. Hobart replied, smiling more and more brightly and speaking in even more coaxing and indulgent tones.

"Then we're friends already, Mr. Hobart. Anyone who knows my books, knows me. My whole heart is in them. Now, you must tell me all about my poor little vote. I shall be very patriotic with it when the time comes to use it."

Mr. Hobart saw his opportunity.

"Certainly, Miss Bellairs," he said. "I will ring for my clerk and we'll—er—we'll take down the details."

He got up, crossed the room, and rang the bell with violence.

"I'll just go and see that he brings the right books," he added, and darted to the door. Once outside in the passage, he mopped his face and heaved a sigh of relief. That had been a narrow shave, by Jove. A loony in the office—dangerous-looking brute, too.

On the following day Dick woke up and found himself in a bare whitewashed room, sparsely furnished with a little iron bed, a washstand, a chair, and table. He looked round him in surprise.

Where had he got to this time? He went to the door and tried to open it; it was locked. An idea entered his mind: he was in barracks somewhere; the Military Authorities must have got hold of him somehow in spite of his exemption certificate. Or perhaps Pearl had gone and enlisted. . . . He turned next to the window, which was barred. Outside, he could see a courtyard, filled, not with soldiers, as he had expected, but a curious motley crew of individuals, some men and some women, wandering hither and thither with an air of complete aimlessness. Very odd, he thought —very odd. Beyond the courtyard, on the farther side of a phenomenally high wall, ran a railway line and beyond it a village, roofed with tile and thatch, and a tall church spire in the midst. Dick looked carefully at the spire. Didn't he know it? Surely— yes, those imbricated copper plates with which it was covered, that gilded ship that served as wind vane, the little gargoyles at the corner of the tower—there could be no doubt; it was Belbury church. Belbury—that was where the . . . No, no; he wouldn't believe it. But looking down again into that high-walled courtyard, full of those queer, aimless folk, he was forced to admit it. The County Asylum stands at Belbury. He had often noticed it from the train, a huge, gaunt building of sausage-coloured brick, standing close to the railway, on the opposite side of the line to Belbury village and church. He remembered how, the last time he had passed in the train, he had wondered what they did in the asylum. He had regarded it then as one of those mysterious, unapproachable places, like Lhassa or a Ladies' Lavatory, into which he would never penetrate. And now, here he was, looking out through the bars, like any other madman. It was all Pearl's doing, as usual. If there had been no bars, he would have thrown himself out of the window.

He sat down on his bed and began to think about what he should do. He would have to be very sane and show them by his behaviour and speech that he was no more mad than the commonalty of mankind. He would be extremely dignified about it all. If a warder or a doctor or somebody came in to see him, he would rise to his feet and say in the calmest and severest tones: "May I ask, pray, why I am detained here and upon whose authority?" That ought to stagger them. He practised that sentence, and the noble attitude with which he would accompany it, for the best part of an hour. Then, suddenly, there was the sound of a key in the lock. He hastily sat down again on the bed. A brisk little man of about forty, clean-shaven and with pince-nez, stepped into the room, followed by a nurse and a warder in uniform. The doctor! Dick's heart was beating with absurd violence; he felt like an amateur actor at the first performance of an imperfectly rehearsed play. He rose, rather unsteadily, to his feet, and in a voice that quavered a little with an emotion he could not suppress, began:

"Pray I ask, may . . ."

Then, realizing that something had gone wrong, he hesitated, stammered, and came to a pause.

The doctor turned to the nurse.

"Did you hear that?" he asked. "He called me May. He seems to think everybody's a woman, not only himself."

Turning to Dick with a cheerful smile, he went on:

"Sit down, Miss Bellairs, please sit down."

It was too much. Dick burst into tears, flung himself upon the bed, and buried his face in the pillow. The doctor looked at him as he lay there sobbing, his whole body shaken and convulsed.

"A bad case, I fear."

And the nurse nodded.

For the next three days Dick refused to eat. It was certainly unreasonable, but it seemed the only way of making a protest. On the fourth day the doctor signed a certificate to the effect that forcible feeding had become necessary. Accompanied by two warders and a nurse, he entered Dick's room.

"Now, Miss Bellairs," he said, making a last persuasive appeal, "do have a little of this nice soup. We have come to have lunch with you."

"I refused to eat," said Dick icily, "as a protest against my unlawful detention in this place. I am as sane as any of you here."

"Yes, yes." The doctor's voice was soothing. He made a sign to the warders. One was very large and stout, the other wiry, thin, sinister, like the second murderer in a play. They closed in on Dick.

"I won't eat and I won't be made to eat!" Dick cried. "Let me go!" he shouted at the fat warder, who had laid a hand on his shoulder. His temper was beginning to rise.

"Now, do behave yourself," said the fat warder. "It ain't a bit of use kicking up a row. Now, do take a little of this lovely soup," he added wheedlingly.

"Let me go!" Dick screamed again, all his self-control gone. "I will not let myself be bullied."

He began to struggle violently. The fat warder put an arm round his shoulders, as though he were an immense mother comforting an irritable child. Dick felt himself helpless; the struggle had quite exhausted him; he was weaker than he had any idea of. He began kicking the fat man's shins; it was the only way he could still show fight.

"Temper, temper," remonstrated the warder, more motherly than ever. The thin warden stooped down, slipped a strap round the kicking legs, and drew it tight. Dick could move no more. His fury found vent in words—vain, abusive, filthy words, such as he had not used since he was a schoolboy.

"Le me go," he screamed—"let me go, you devils! You beasts, you swine! beasts and swine!" he howled again and again.

They soon had him securely strapped in a chair, his head held back ready for the doctor and his horrible-looking tubes. They were pushing the horrors up his nostrils. He coughed and choked, spat, shouted inarticulately, retched. It was like having a spoon put on your tongue and being told to say A-a-h, but worse; it was like jumping into the river and getting water up your nose— how he had always hated that!—only much worse. It was like almost everything unpleasant, only much, much worse than all. He exhausted himself struggling against his utterly immovable bonds. They had to carry him to his bed, he was so weak.

He lay there, unmoving—for he was unable to move—staring at the ceiling. He felt as though he were floating on air, unsupported, solid no longer; the sensation was not unpleasant. For that reason he refused to let his mind dwell upon it; he would think of nothing that was not painful, odious, horrible. He thought about the torture which had just been inflicted on him and of the monstrous injustice of which he was a victim. He thought of the millions who had been and were still being slaughtered in the war; he thought of their pain, all the countless separate pains of them; pain incommunicable, individual, beyond the reach of sympathy; infinities of pain pent within frail finite bodies; pain without sense or object, bringing with it no hope and no redemption, futile, unnecessary, stupid. In one supreme apocalyptic moment he saw, he felt the universe in all its horror.

They forcibly fed him again the following morning and again on the day after. On the fourth day pneumonia, the result of shock, complicated by acute inflammation of the throat and pleura, set in. The fever and pain gained ground. Dick had not the strength to resist their ravages, and his condition grew hourly worse. His mind, however, continued to work clearly—too clearly. It occurred to him that he might very likely die. He asked for pencil and paper to be brought him, and putting forth all the little strength he had left, he began to make his testament.

"I am perfectly sane," he wrote at the top of the page, and underlined the words three times. "I am confined here by the most intol. injust." As soon as he began, he realized how little time and strength were left him; it was a waste to finish the long words. "They are killing me for my opins. I regard this war and all wars as utter bad. Capitalists' war. The devils will be smashed sooner later. Wish I could help. But it won't make any difference," he added on a new line and as though by an afterthought. "World will always be hell. Cap. or Lab., Engl. or Germ.—all beasts. One in a mill. is GOOD. I wasn't. Selfish intellect. Perhaps Pearl Bellairs better. If die, send corp. to hosp. for anatomy. Useful for once in my life!"

Quite suddenly, he lapsed into delirium. The clear lucidity of his mind became troubled. The real world disappeared from before his eyes, and in its place he saw a succession of bright, unsteady visions created by his sick fantasy. Scenes from his childhood, long forgotten, bubbled up and disappeared. Unknown, hideous faces crowded in upon him; old friends revisited him. He was living in a bewildering mixture of the familiar and the strange. And all the while, across this changing unsubstantial world, there hurried a continual, interminable procession of dromedaries—countless high-domed beasts, with gargoyle faces and stiff legs and necks that bobbed as though on springs. Do what he could, he was unable to drive them away. He lost his temper with the brutes at last, struck at them, shouted; but in vain. The room rang with his cries of, "Get away, you beasts. Bloody humps. None of your nonconformist faces here." And while he was yelling and gesticulating (with his left hand only), his right hand was still busily engaged in writing. The words were clear and legible; the sentences consecutive and eminently sane. Dick might rave, but Pearl Bellairs remained calm and in full possession of her deplorable faculties. And what was Pearl doing with her busy pencil, while Dick, like a frenzied Betsy Trotwood, shouted at the trespassing camels? The first thing she did was to scratch out all that poor Dick had said about the war. Underneath it she wrote:

"We shall not sheathe the sword, which we have not lightly . . ."
And then, evidently finding that memorable sentence too long, particularly so since the addition of Poland and Czecho-Slovakia to the list of Allies, she began again.

"We are fighting for honour and the defense of Small Nationalities. Plucky little Belgium! We went into the war with clean hands."

A little of Pearl's thought seemed at this moment to have slopped over into Dick's mind; for he suddenly stopped abusing his dromedaries and began to cry out in the most pitiable fashion, "Clean hands, clean hands! I can't get mine clean. I can't, I can't, I can't. I contaminate everything." And he kept rubbing his left hand against the bedclothes and putting his fingers to his nose, only to exclaim, "Ugh, they still stink of goat!" and then to start rubbing again.

The right hand wrote on unperturbed. "No peace with the Hun until he is crushed and humiliated. Self-respecting Britons will refuse to shake a Hunnish hand for many a long year after the war. No more German waiters. Intern the Forty-Seven Thousand Hidden Hands in High Places!"

At this point, Pearl seemed to have been struck by a new idea. She took a clean page and began:

"To the Girls of England. I am a woman and proud of the fact. But, girls, I blushed for my sex to-day when I read in the papers that there had been cases of English girls talking to Hun prisoners, and not only talking to them, but allowing themselves to be kissed by them. Imagine! Clean, healthy British girls allowing themselves to be kissed by the swinish and bloodstained lips of the unspeakable Hun! Do you wonder that I blush for my sex? Stands England where she did? No, emphatically no, if these stories are true, and true—sadly and with a heavy bleeding heart do I admit it—true they are."

"Clean hands, clean hands," Dick was still muttering, and applying his fingers to his nose once more, "Christ," he cried, "how they stink! Goats, dung . . ."

"Is there any excuse for such conduct?" the pencil continued. "The most that can be said in palliation of the offense is that girls are thoughtless, that they do not consider the full significance of their actions. But listen to me, girls of all ages, classes and creeds, from the blue-eyed, light-hearted flapper of sixteen to the stern-faced, hard-headed business woman—listen to me. There is a girlish charm about thoughtlessness, but there is a point beyond which thoughtlessness becomes criminal. A flapper may kiss a Hun without thinking what she is doing, merely for the fun of the thing; perhaps, even, out of misguided pity. Will she repeat the offense if she realizes, as she must realize if she will only think, that this thoughtless fun, this mawkish and hysterical pity, is nothing less than Treason? Treason—it is a sinister word, but . . ."

The pencil stopped writing; even Pearl was beginning to grow tired. Dick's shouting had died away to a hoarse, faint whisper. Suddenly her attention was caught by the last words that Dick had written—the injunction to send his body if he died, to a hospital for an anatomy. She put forth a great effort.

"NO. NO," she wrote in huge capitals. "Bury me in a little country churchyard, with lovely marble angels like the ones in St. George's at Windsor, over Princess Charlotte's tomb. Not anatomy. Too horrible, too disgus . . ."

The coma which had blotted out Dick's mind fell now upon hers as well. Two hours later Dick Greenow was dead; the fingers of his right hand still grasped a pencil. The scribbled papers were thrown away as being merely the written ravings of a madman; they were accustomed to that sort of thing at the asylum.

3. *The Limits of the Form*

The Case of General Ople
and Lady Camper
1890

GEORGE MEREDITH

tempt to feel at home there. His wonderful sonnet sequence
Modern Love published in 1862 might have been written fifty
years later and The Egoist is a novel which affords a standing

IN THE INTRODUCTION to this anthology I said we would have
to go out into the byways of English literature to find short
novels; I did not know then that the byways were going to run
into one another, that the preoccupation with the long short
story, the conte or nouvelle is something that is handed on
like an hereditary trait or a professional secret. I suppose the
master of the long short story in England to-day is David
Garnett. And it is no accident that he has recently produced an
edition of Peacock to whom Aldous Huxley's early novels owed
so much. Meredith married Peacock's daughter, and in The
Egoist (1879) he presents two minor characters, Doctor Middleton, an epicurean port-loving professor who was drawn
from Peacock, and Vernon Whitford ("Phoebus Apollo
turned fasting friar") who was taken from Leslie Stephen, the
father of Virginia Woolf. And one of the finest of Henry
James' long short stories, The Death of the Lion, is reputed
to be about Meredith.

George Meredith, grandson of a prosperous Portsmouth
tailor, was born in 1828 and died in 1909, the same year as his
friend Swinburne. He is thus of a generation seven years later
than George Eliot, Flaubert, Turgeniev and Dostoevsky who
were born around 1820 while he was exactly of an age with
Tolstoi who died a year later. He is a central figure in the
development of the English novel standing mid-way between
the great Victorians and the 1840 generation of Hardy and
Henry James. Meredith was an intellectual and a man of
genius. His books are worked out with great originality and
deal with real people, they would be more read were his style
less feverish and exacting. As a poet Meredith was somewhat
extravagant in the pre-Raphaelite manner and his poetry spills
over into his fiction. He seems at times like a man of the twentieth century with outstanding gifts who finds himself transported to mid-Victorian England and makes a desperate at-

tempt to feel at home there. His wonderful sonnet sequence
Modern Love published in 1862 might have been written fifty
years later, and The Egoist is a novel which affords a rewarding
pleasure to-day. Marriage provided the main theme of his
work and in particular, the ravages of family pride in relation
to the deeper significance of marriage and the rights of women.
Although he takes his themes from aristocratic and not very
Victorian society, poverty dogged Meredith all his life and
Diana of the Crossways (1885) was his first popular success.
For more than thirty years he read for a publisher and for the
last forty years of his life he lived in a cottage on Box Hill.

"He is the master of us all," wrote Stevenson, and the master is now beginning to turn in the sleep of his collected
editions. Certainly he is one of the last English novelists whom
we can call 'great,' great in imagination, in courage, sanity,
comic spirit and passion for nature and in that mysterious
dignity of calling which also characterises Hardy and which is
somehow lacking in the next generation of able craftsmen.

The Case of General Ople qualifies 'for the limits of the
form' not by its construction for, although there are four
characters, Lady Camper's nephew and the General's daughter
are very slightly drawn. No, it is the texture of the writing,
the verbal brilliance and radiant golden comedy of the story
that is so remarkable. It is of course a very sophisticated love
story, a far far cry from Cousin Phillis, but it is more than
that, a soap bubble blown by some god in the mischief of his
charity. Compared to it, Henry James' stories of London social
life in the nineties seem rather cold and laboured, there is a
warmth of genius, a compassion about The Case of General
Ople like a landscape of Watteau beside a landscape of
Boucher, or a conversation piece of Renoir or Monet in a cold
municipal gallery. It is very compressed, no word is wasted,
and when the narrator suddenly appears with a disquisition on
love and nature it is at exactly the right moment. After this
brief Mozartian melody, the farce proceeds to its conclusion of
unexpected yet foregone felicity.

The Case of General Ople and Lady Camper

GEORGE MEREDITH

Chapter I

AN EXCURSION BEYOND the immediate suburbs of London, projected long before his pony-carriage was hired to conduct him, in fact, ever since his retirement from active service, led General Ople across a famous common, with which he fell in love at once, to a lofty highway along the borders of a park, for which he promptly exchanged his heart, and so gradually within a stone's-throw or so of the river-side, where he determined not solely to bestow his affections but to settle for life. It may be seen that he was of an impulsive temperament, though he had thought fit to loosen his sword-belt. The pony-carriage, however, had been hired for the very special purpose of helping him to pass in review the lines of what he called country houses, cottages, or even sites for building, not too remote from sweet London; and as when Coelebs goes forth intending to pursue and obtain, there is no doubt of his bringing home a wife, the circumstances that there stood a house to let, in an airy situation, at a certain distance in hail of the metropolis he worshiped, was enough to kindle the general's enthusiasm. He would have taken the first he saw had it not been for his daughter, who accompanied, and at the age of eighteen was about to undertake the management of his house. Fortune, under Elizabeth Ople's guiding restraint, directed him to an epitome of the comforts. The place he fell upon is only to be described in the tongue of auctioneers, and for the first week after taking it he

541

modestly followed them by terming it *bijou*. In time, when his own imagination, instigated by a state of something more than mere contentment, had been at work on it, he chose the happy phrase "a gentlemanly residence." For it was, he declared, a small estate. There was a lodge to it, resembling two sentry-boxes forced into union, where in one half an old couple sat bent, in the other half lay compressed; there was a back-drive to discoverable stables; there was a bit of grass that would have appeared a meadow if magnified; and there was a wall round the kitchen garden and a strip of wood round the flower garden. The prying of the outside world was impossible. Comfort, fortification, and gentlemanliness made the place, as the general said, an ideal English home.

The compass of the estate was half an acre, and perhaps a perch or two, just the size for the hugging love General Ople was happiest in giving. He wisely decided to retain the old couple at the lodge, whose members were used to restriction, and also not to purchase a cow, that would have wanted pasture. With the old man, while the old woman attended to the bell at the handsome front entrance with its gilt spiked gates, he undertook to do the gardening—a business he delighted in, so long as he could perform it in a gentlemanly manner; that is to say, so long as he was not overlooked. He was perfectly concealed from the road. Only one house, and curiously indeed, only one window of the house, and further to show the protection extended to Douro Lodge, that window an attic, overlooked him. And the house was empty.

The house (for who can hope, and who should desire a commodious house with conservatories, aviaries, pond, and boat-shed, and other joys of wealth, to remain unoccupied) was taken two seasons later by a lady of whom Fame, rolling like a dust-cloud from the place she had left, reported that she was eccentric. The word is uninstructive; it does not frighten. In a lady of a certain age it is rather a characteristic of aristocracy in retirement. And at least it implies wealth.

General Ople was very anxious to see her. He had the sentiment of humble respectfulness toward aristocracy, and there was that in riches which roused his admiration. London, for instance, he was not afraid to say he thought the wonder of the world. He remarked, in addition, that the sacking of London would suffice to make every common soldier of the foreign army of occupation an independent gentleman for the term of his natural days. But this is a nightmare! said he, startling himself with an abhorrent dream of envy of those enriched invading officers: for Booty is the one lovely thing which the military mind can contemplate in the abstract. His habit was to go off in an explosion of heavy sighs when he had delivered himself so far, like a man at war with himself.

The lady arrived in time: she received the cards of the neighborhood, and signalized her eccentricity by paying no attention to them, excepting the card of a Mrs. Baerens, who had audience of her at once. By express arrangement, the card of General Wilson Ople, as her nearest neighbor, followed the card of the rector, the social head of the district; and the rector was granted an interview, but Lady Camper was not at home to General Ople. "She is of superior station to me, and may not wish to associate with me," the general modestly said.

Nevertheless, he was wounded; for in spite of himself, and without the slightest wish to obtrude his own person, as he explained the meaning that he had in him, his rank in the British army forced him to be the representative of it in the absence of any one of a superior rank. So that he was professionally hurt, and his heart being in his profession, it may be honestly stated that he was wounded in his feelings, though he said no, and insisted on the distinction. Once a day his walk for constitutional exercise compelled him to pass before Lady Camper's windows, which were not bashfully withdrawn, as he said humorously of Douro Lodge, in the seclusion of half-pay, but bowed out imperiously, militarily, like a generalissimo on horseback, and had full command of the road and levels up to the swelling park foliage. He went by at a smart stride, with a delicate depression of his upright bearing, as though hastening to greet a friend in view, whose hand was getting ready for the shake. This much would have been observed by a house-maid; and considering his fine figure and the peculiar shining silveriness of his hair, the acceleration of his gait was noticeable. When he drove by, the pony's right ear was flicked to the extreme indignation of the mettlesome little animal. It ensued in consequence that the general was borne flying under the eyes of Lady Camper, and such pace displeasing him, he reduced it invariably at a step or two beyond the corner of her grounds.

But neither he nor his daughter Elizabeth attached importance to so trivial a circumstance. The general punctiliously avoided glancing at the windows during the passage past them, whether in his wild career or on foot. Elizabeth took a side-shot as one looks at a way-side tree. Their speech concerning Lady Camper was an exchange of commonplaces over her loneliness; and this condition of hers was the more perplexing to General Ople on his hearing from his daughter that the lady was very fine-looking, and not so very old, as he had fancied eccentric ladies must be.

The rector's account of her, too, excited the mind. She had informed him bluntly that she now and then went to church to save appearances, but was not a church-goer, finding it impossible to support the length of the service; might, however, be reckoned in subscriptions for all the charities, and left her pew open to poor people, and none but the poor. She had traveled over Europe, and knew the East.

Sketches in water-colors of the scenes she had visited adorned her walls, and a pair of pistols, that she had found useful, she affirmed, lay on the writing-desk in her drawing-room. General Ople gathered from the rector that she had a great contempt for men; yet it was curiously varied with lamentations over the weakness of women. "Really she can not possibly be an example of that," said the general, thinking of the pistols.

Now we learn from those who have studied women on the chess-board, and know what ebony or ivory will do along particular lines, or hopping, that men much talked about will take possession of their thoughts; and certainly the fact may be accepted for one of their moves. But the whole fabric of our knowledge of them, which we are taught to build on this originally acute perception, is shattered when we hear that it is exactly the same, in the same degree, in proportion to the amount of work they have to do, exactly the same with men and their thoughts in the case of women much talked about. So it was with General Ople, and nothing is left for me to say except that there is broader ground than the chess-board. I am earnest in protesting the similarity of the singular couples on common earth, because otherwise the general is in peril of the accusation that he is a feminine character; and not simply was he a gallant officer and a veteran in gunpowder strife, he was also (and it is an extraordinary thing that a genuine humility did not prevent it, and did survive it) a lord and conqueror of the sex. He had done his pretty bit of mischief, all in the way of honor, of course, but hearts had knocked. And now, with his bright white hair, his close-brushed white whiskers on a face burned brown, his clear-cut features, and a winning droop of his eyelids, there was powder in him still—if not shot.

There was a lamentable susceptibility to ladies' charms. On the other hand, for the protection of the sex, a remainder of shyness kept him from active enterprise, and in the state of suffering so long as indications of encouragement were wanting. He had killed the soft ones who came to him, attracted by the softness in him, to be killed; but clever women alarmed and paralyzed him. Their aptitude to question and require immediate, sparkling answers; their demand for fresh wit of a kind that is not furnished by publications which strike it into heads with a hammer, and supply it wholesale; their various reading; their power of ridicule too, made them awful in his contemplation.

Supposing—for the inflammable officer was now thinking, and deeply thinking, of a clever woman—supposing that Lady Camper's pistols were needed in her defense one night! at the first report proclaiming her extremity, valor might gain an introduction to her upon easy terms, and would not be expected to be witty. She would, perhaps, after the excitement, admit his masculine superiority in the beautiful old fashion by fainting in his arms. Such was the reverie he passingly indulged, and only so could he venture to hope for an acquaintance with the formidable lady who was his next neighbor. But the proud society of the burglarious denied him opportunity.

Meanwhile he learned that Lady Camper had a nephew, and the young gentleman was in a cavalry regiment. General Ople met him outside his gates, received and returned a polite salute, liked his appearance and manners, and talked of him to Elizabeth, asking her if by chance she had seen him. She replied that she believed that she had, and praised his horsemanship. The general discovered that he was an excellent sculler. His daughter was rowing him up the river when the young gentleman shot by with a splendid stroke, in an outrigger, backed, and floating alongside presumed to enter into conversation, during which he managed to express regrets at his aunt's turn for solitariness. As they belonged to sister branches of the same service, the general and Mr. Reginald Rolles had a theme in common, and a passion.

Elizabeth told her father that nothing afforded her so much pleasure as to hear him talk with Mr. Rolles on military matters. General Ople assured her that it pleased him likewise. He began to spy about for Mr. Rolles, and it sometimes occurred that they conversed across the wall—it could hardly be avoided. A hint or two, an undefinable flying allusion, gave the general to understand that Lady Camper had not been happy in her marriage. He was pained to think of her misfortune; but as she was not over forty, the disaster was, perhaps, not irremediable; that is to say, if she could be taught to extend her forgiveness to men and abandon her solitude. "If," he said to his daughter, "Lady Camper should by any chance be induced to contract a second alliance, she would, one might expect, be humanized, and we should have highly agreeable neighbors."

Elizabeth artlessly hoped for such an event to take place.

She rarely differed with her father, up to whom, taking example from the world around him, she looked as the pattern of a man of wise conduct.

And he was one; and though modest, he was in good humor with himself, approved himself, and could say that, without boasting of success, he was a satisfied man until he met his touchstone in Lady Camper.

Chapter II

THIS IS THE pathetic matter of my story, and it requires pointing out, because he never could explain what it was that seemed to him so cruel in it, for he was no brilliant son of fortune; he was no great pretender; none of those who are logically displaced from the heights they have been raised to, manifestly created to show the moral in Providence. He was modest, retiring, humbly contented; a gentlemanly residence appeased his ambition. Popular he could own that he was, but not meteorically; rather by reason of his willingness to receive light than to shed it. Why, then, was the terrible test brought to bear upon him of all men? He was one of us; no worse, and not strikingly or perilously better; and he could not but feel, in the bitterness of his reflections upon an inexplicable destiny, that the punishment befalling him, unmerited as it was, looked like absence of design in the scheme of things above. It looked as if the blow had been dealt him by reckless chance. And to believe that was for the mind of General Ople the having to return to his alphabet and recommence the ascent of the laborious mountain of understanding.

To proceed, the general's introduction to Lady Camper was owing to a message she sent him by her gardener with a request that he would cut down a branch of a wych-elm obscuring her view across his grounds toward the river. The general consulted with his daughter, and came to the conclusion that, as he could hardly dispatch a written reply to a verbal message, yet greatly wished to subscribe to the wishes of Lady Camper, the best thing for him to do was to apply for an interview.

He sent word that he would wait on Lady Camper immediately, and betook himself forthwith to his toilet.

She was the niece of an earl!

Elizabeth commended his appearance, "passed him," as he would have said; and well she might, for his hat, surtout, trousers and boots were worthy of an introduction to royalty. A touch of scarlet silk round the neck gave him bloom, and better than that, the blooming consciousness of it.

"You are not to be nervous, papa," Elizabeth said.

"Not at all," replied the general. "I say, not at all, my dear," he repeated, and so betrayed that he had fallen into the nervous mood. "I was saying, I have known worse mornings than this."

He turned to her and smiled brightly, nodded, and set his face to meet the future.

He was absent an hour and a half.

He came back with his radiance a little subdued, by no means eclipsed; as, when experience has afforded us matter for thought, we cease to shine dazzlingly, yet are not clouded; the rays have merely grown serener. The sum of his impressions was conveyed in the reflective utterance, "It only shows, my dear, how different the reality is from our anticipation of it."

Lady Camper had been charming; full of condescension, neighborly, friendly, willing to be satisfied with the sacrifice of the smallest branch of the wych-elm, and only requiring that much for complimentary reasons.

Elizabeth wished to hear what they were, and she thought the request rather singular; but the general begged her to bear in mind that they were dealing with a very extraordinary woman. "Highly accomplished, really exceeding handsome," he said to himself, aloud.

The reasons were, her liking for air and view, and desire to see into her neighbor's grounds without having to mount to the attic.

Elizabeth gave a slight exclamation, and blushed.

"So, my dear, we are objects of interest to her ladyship," said the general.

He assured her that Lady Camper's manners were delightful. Stranger to tell, she knew a great deal of his antecedent history, things he had not supposed were known. "Little matters," he remarked, by which his daughter faintly conceived a reference to the conquests of his dashing days. Lady Camper had deigned to impart some of her own, incidentally: that she was of Welsh blood, and born among the mountains. "She has a romantic look," was the general's comment; and that her husband had been an insatiable traveler before he became an invalid, and had never cared for art. "Quite an extraordinary circumstance, with such a wife!" the general said.

He fell upon the wych-elm with his own hands under cover of the leafage, and the next day he paid his respects to Lady Camper, to inquire if her ladyship saw any further obstruction to the view.

"None," she replied. "And now we shall see what the two birds will do."

Apparently, then, she entertained an animosity to a pair of birds in the tree.

"Yes, yes; I say they chirp early in the morning," said General Ople.

"At all hours."

"The song of birds—" he pleaded softly for nature.

"If the nest is provided for them; but I don't like vagabond chirping."

The general perfectly acquiesced. This, in an engagement with a clever woman, is what you should do, or else you are likely to find yourself planted unawares in a high wind, your hat blown off, and your coat-tails anywhere; in other words, you will stand ridiculous in your bewilderment; and General Ople ever footed with the utmost caution to avoid that quagmire of the ridiculous. The extremer quags he had hitherto escaped; the smaller, into which he fell in his agile evasions of the big, he had hitherto been blessed in finding none to notice.

He requested her ladyship's permission to present his daughter. Lady Camper sent in her card.

Elizabeth Ople beheld a tall, handsomely mannered lady, with good features and penetrating dark eyes, an easy carriage of her person and an agreeable voice; but (the vision of her age flashed out under the compelling eyes of youth) fifty if a day. The rich coloring confessed to it. But she was very pleasing; and Elizabeth's perception dwelt on it only because her father's manly chivalry had defended the lady against one year more than forty.

The richness of the coloring, Elizabeth feared, was artificial, and it caused her ingenuous young blood a shudder. For we are so devoted to nature when the dame is flattering us with her gifts, that we loathe the substitute, omitting to think how much less it is an imposition than a form of practical adoration of the genuine.

Our young detective, however, concealed her emotion of childish horror.

Lady Camper remarked of her: "She seems honest, and that is the most we can hope of girls."

"She is a jewel for an honest man," the general sighed, "some day!"

"Let us hope it will be a distant day."

"Yet," said the general, "girls expect to marry."

Lady Camper fixed her black eyes on him, but did not speak.

He told Elizabeth that her ladyship's eyes were exceedingly searching. "Only," said he, "as I have nothing to hide, I am able to submit to inspection," and he laughed slightly up to arresting cough, and made the mantel-piece ornaments pass muster.

General Ople was the hero to champion a lady whose airs of haughtiness caused her to be somewhat backbitten. He assured everybody that Lady Camper was much misunderstood; she was a most remarkable woman; she was a most affable and highly intelligent lady. Building up her attributes to a splendid climax, he declared that she was pious, charitable, witty, and really an extraordinary artist. He laid particular stress on her artistic qualities, describing her power with the brush, her water-color sketches, and also some immensely clever caricatures. As he talked of no one else, his friends heard enough of Lady Camper, who was anything but a favorite. The Pollingtons, the Wilders, the Wardens, the Baerens, the Goslings, and others of his acquaintance, talked of Lady Camper and General Ople rather maliciously. They were all City people, and they admired the general, but mourned that he should so abjectly have fallen at the feet of a lady as red with rouge as a railway bill. His not seeing it showed the state he was in. The sister of Mrs. Pollington, an amiable widow, relict of a large City warehouseman, named Barcop, was chilled by a falling off in his attentions. His apology for not appearing at garden-parties was that he was engaged to wait on Lady Camper.

And at one time, her not condescending to exchange visits with the obsequious general was a topic fertile in irony. But she did condescend.

Lady Camper came to his gate unexpectedly, rang the bell, and was let in like an ordinary visitor. It happened that the general was gardening—not the pretty occupation of pruning, he was digging—and of necessity his coat was off, and he was hot, dusty, unpresentable.

From adoring earth as the mother of roses, you may pass into a lady's presence without purification; you can not—or so the general thought—when you are caught in the act of adoring the mother of cabbages. And though he himself loved the cabbage equally with the rose, in his heart respected the vegetable yet more than he esteemed the flower, for he gloried in his kitchen garden, this was not a secret for the world to know, and he almost heeled over on his beam ends when word was brought of the extreme honor Lady Camper had done him. He worked his arms hurriedly into his fatigue jacket, trusting to get away to the house and spend a couple of minutes on his adornment; and with any other visitor it might have been accomplished, but Lady Camper disliked sitting alone in a room. She was on the square of lawn as the general stole along the walk. Had she kept her back to him he might have rounded her, like the shadow of a dial, undetected. She was frightfully acute of hearing. She turned while he was in the agony of hesitation, in a queer attitude, one leg on the march, projected by a frenzied tiptoe of the hinder leg, the very fatalest moment she could possibly have selected for unveiling him.

Of course there was no choice but to surrender on the spot.

He began to squander his dizzy wits in profuse apologies. Lady Camper simply spoke of the nice little nest of a garden, smelled the flowers, accepted a Niel rose and a Rohan, a Celine, a Falcot, and La France.

"A beautiful rose indeed," she said of the latter, "only it smells of macassar oil."

"Really, it never struck me. I say it never struck me before," rejoined the general, smelling it as at a pinch of snuff. "I was saying, I always—" and he tacitly, with the absurdest of smiles, begged permission to leave unterminated a sentence not in itself particularly difficult.

"I have a nose," observed Lady Camper.

Like the nobly bred person she was, according to General Ople's version of the interview on his estate, when he stood before her in his gardening costume, she put him at his ease, or she exerted herself to do so; and if he underwent considerable anguish, it was the fault of his excessive scrupulousness regarding dress, propriety, appearance.

He conducted her at her request to the kitchen garden and the handful of paddock, the stables and coach-house, then back to the lawn.

"It is the home for a young couple," she said.

"I am no longer young," the general bowed, with the sigh peculiar to this confession. "I say I am no longer young, but I call the place a gentlemanly residence. I was saying I—"

"Yes, yes!" Lady Camper tossed her head, half closing her eyes with a contraction of the brows as if in pain.

He perceived a similar expression whenever he spoke of his residence.

Perhaps it recalled happier days to enter such a nest. Perhaps it had been such a home for a young couple that she had entered on her marriage with Sir Scrope Camper, before he inherited his title and estates.

The general was at a loss to conceive what it was.

It recurred at another mention of his idea of the nature of the residence. It was almost a paroxysm. He determined not to vex her reminiscences again; and as this resolution directed his mind to his residence, thinking it pre-eminently gentlemanly, his tongue committed the error of repeating it, with "gentleman-like" for a variation.

Elizabeth was out—he knew not where. The house-maid informed him that Miss Elizabeth was out rowing on the water.

"Is she alone?" Lady Camper inquired of him.

"I fancy so," the general replied.

"The poor child has no mother."

"It has been a sad loss to us both, Lady Camper."

"No doubt. She is too pretty to go out alone."

"I can trust her."

"Girls!"

"She has the spirit of a man."

"That is well. She has a spirit; it will be tried."

The general modestly furnished an instance or two of her spiritedness.

Lady Camper seemed to like this theme; she looked graciously interested.

"Still, you should not suffer her to go out alone," she said.

"I place implicit confidence in her," said the general; and Lady Camper gave it up.

She proposed to walk down the lanes to the river-side to meet Elizabeth returning.

The general manifested alacrity checked by reluctance. Lady Camper had told him she objected to sit in a strange room by herself; after that, he could hardly leave her to dash upstairs to change his clothes; yet how, attired as he was, in a fatigue jacket, that warned him not to imagine his back view, and held him constantly a little to the rear of Lady Camper lest she should be troubled by it; and he knew the habit of the second rank to criticise the front—how consent to face the outer world in such style side by side with the lady he admired?

"Come," said she; and he shot forward a step, looking as if he had missed fire.

"Are you not coming, general?"

He advanced mechanically.

Not a soul met them down the lanes, except a little one, to

whom Lady Camper gave a small silver piece, because she was a picture.

The act of charity sunk into the general's heart, as any pretty performance will do upon a warm waxen bed.

Lady Camper surprised him by answering his thoughts. "No; it's for my own pleasure."

Presently she said: "Here they are."

General Ople beheld his daughter by the river-side at the end of the lane, under escort of Mr. Reginald Rolles.

It was another picture, and a pleasing one. The young lady and the young gentleman wore boating hats, and were both dressed in white, and standing by or just turning from the outrigger and light skiff they were about to leave in charge of a waterman. Elizabeth stretched a finger at arm's-length, issuing directions, which Mr. Rolles took up and worded further to the man for the sake of emphasis; and he, rather than Elizabeth, was guilty of the half start at sight of the persons who were approaching.

"My nephew, you should know, is intended for a working soldier," said Lady Camper; "I like that sort of soldier best."

General Ople drooped his shoulders at the personal compliment.

She resumed. "His pay is a matter of importance to him. You are aware of the smallness of a subaltern's pay."

"I," said the general, "I say I feel my poor half-pay, having always been a working soldier myself, very important, I was saying, very important to me."

"Why did you retire?"

Her interest in him seemed promising. He replied conscientiously: "Beyond the duties of general of brigade, I could not, I say I could not, dare to aspire; I can accept and execute orders; I shrink from responsibility."

"It is a pity," said she, "that you were not, like my nephew Reginald, entirely dependent on your profession."

She laid such stress on her remark that the general, who had just expressed a very modest estimate of his abilities, was unable to reject the flattery of her assuming him to be a man of some fortune. He coughed and said, "Very little." The thought came to him that he might have to make a statement to her in time, and he emphasized: "Very little indeed. Sufficient," he assured her, "for a gentlemanly appearance."

"I have given you your warning," was her inscrutable rejoinder, uttered within earshot of the young people, to whom, especially to Elizabeth, she was gracious. The damsel's boating uniform was praised, and her sunny flush of exercise and exposure.

Lady Camper regretted that she could not abandon her parasol. "I freckle so easily."

The general, puzzling over her strange words about a warning, gazed at the red rose of art on her cheek with an air of profound abstraction.

"I freckle so easily," she repeated, dropping her parasol to defend her face from the calculating scrutiny.

"I burn brown," said Elizabeth.

Lady Camper laid the bud of a Falcot rose against the young girl's cheek, but fetched streams of color that overwhelmed the momentary comparison of the sun-swathed skin with the rich dusky yellow of the rose in its deepening inward to soft brown.

Reginald stretched his hand for the privileged flower, and she let him take it; then she looked at the general; but the general was looking, with his usual air of satisfaction, nowhere.

Chapter III

"LADY CAMPER IS no common enigma," General Ople observed to his daughter.

Elizabeth inclined to be pleased with her, for at her suggestion the general had bought a couple of horses, that she might ride in the park accompanied by her father or the little groom. Still, the great lady was hard to read.

She tested the resources of his income by all sorts of instigation to expenditure, which his gallantry could not withstand; she encouraged him to talk of his deeds in arms; she was friendly, almost affectionate, and most bountiful in the presents of fruit, peaches, nectarines, grapes, and hot-house wonders, that she showered on his table; but she was an enigma in her evident dissatisfaction with him for something he seemed to have left unsaid. And what could that be?

At their last interview she had asked him: "Are you sure, general, you have nothing more to tell me?"

And as he remarked, when relating it to Elizabeth: "One might really be tempted to misapprehend her ladyship's— I say one might commit one's self beyond recovery. Now, my dear, what do you think she intended?"

Elizabeth was "burning brown," or darkly blushing, as her manner was.

She answered: "I am certain you know of nothing that would interest her; nothing, unless—"

"Well?" the general urged her.

"How can I speak it, papa?"

"You really can't mean—"

"Papa, what could I mean?"

"If I were fool enough!" he murmured. "No, no, I am an old man. I was saying, I am past the age of folly."

One day Elizabeth came home from her ride in a thoughtful mood. She had not, further than has been mentioned, incited her father to think of the age of folly; but voluntarily or not, Lady Camper had, by an excess of graciousness amounting to downright invitation; as thus: "Will you persist in withholding your confidence from me, general?" She added: "I am not so difficult a person."

These prompting speeches occurred on the morning of the day when Elizabeth sat at his table, after a long ride into the country, profoundly meditative.

A note was handed to General Ople, with the request that he would step in to speak with Lady Camper in the course of the evening or next morning. Elizabeth waited till his hat was on, then said: "Papa, on my ride to-day, I met Mr. Rolles."

"I am glad you had an agreeable escort, my dear."

"I could not refuse his company."

"Certainly not. And where did you ride?"

"To a beautiful valley; and there we met—"

"Her ladyship?"

"Yes."

"She always admires you on horseback."

"So you know it, papa, if she should speak of it."

"And I am bound to tell you, my child," said the general, "that this morning Lady Camper's manner to me was—if I were a fool— I say, this morning—I beat a retreat, but apparently she—I see no way out of it—supposing she—"

"I am sure she esteems you, dear papa," said Elizabeth.

"You take to her, my dear?" the general inquired, anxiously, "a little? A little afraid of her?"

"A little," Elizabeth replied, "only a little."

"Don't be agitated about me."

"No, papa; you are sure to do right."

"But you are trembling."

"Oh, no! I wish you success."

General Ople was overjoyed to be re-enforced by his daughter's good wishes. He kissed her to thank her. He turned back to her to kiss her again. She had greatly lightened the difficulty at least of a delicate position.

It was just like the imperious nature of Lady Camper to summon him in the evening to terminate the conversation of the morning, from the visible pitfall of which he had beaten a rather precipitate retreat. But if his daughter cordially wished him success, and Lady Camper offered him the crown of it, why then he had only to pluck up spirit, like a good commander who has to pass a fordable river in the enemy's presence; a dash, a splash, a rattling volley or two, and you are over, established on the opposite bank. But you must be positive of victory, otherwise, with the river behind you, your new position is likely to be ticklish. So the general entered Lady Camper's drawing-room warily, watching the fair enemy. He knew he was captivating, his old conquests whispered in his ears, and her reception of him all but pointed to a footstool at her feet. He might have fallen there at once, had he not remembered a hint that Mr. Reginald Rolles had dropped concerning Lady Camper's amazing variability.

Lady Camper began:

"General, you ran away from me this morning. Let me speak. And, by the way, I must reproach you; you should not have left it to me. Things have now gone so far that I can not pretend to be blind. I know your feelings as a father. Your daughter's happiness—"

"My lady," the general interposed, "I have her distinct assurance that it is, I say it is wrapped up in mine."

"Let me speak. Young people will say anything. Well, they have a certain excuse for selfishness; we have not. I am in some degree bound to my nephew; he is my sister's son."

"Assuredly, my lady. I would not stand in his light, be quite as-

556

sured. If I am, I was saying if I am not mistaken, I— And he is, or has the making of an excellent soldier in him, and is likely to be a distinguished cavalry officer."

"He has to carve his own way in the world, general."

"All good soldiers have, my lady. And if my position is not, after a considerable term of service, I say if—"

"To continue," said Lady Camper, "I never have liked early marriages. I was married in my teens before I knew men. Now I do know them, and now—"

The general plunged forward. "The honor you do us now—a mature experience is worth—my dear Lady Camper, I have admired you; and your objection to early marriages can not apply to —indeed, madame, vigor, they say—though youth, of course—yet young people, as you observe—and I have, though perhaps my reputation is against it, I was saying I have a natural timidity with your sex, and I am gray-headed, white-headed, but happily without a single malady."

Lady Camper's brows showed a trifling bewilderment. "I am speaking of these young people. General Ople."

"I consent to everything beforehand, my dear lady. He should be, I say Mr. Rolles should be provided for."

"So should she, general, so should Elizabeth."

"She shall be, she will, dear madame. What I have, with your permission, if—good Heaven! Lady Camper, I scarcely know where I am. She would—I shall not like to lose her; you would not wish it. In time she will—she has every quality of a good wife."

"There, stay there, and be intelligible," said Lady Camper. "She has every quality. Money should be one of them. Has she money?"

"Oh! my lady," the general exclaimed, "we shall not come upon your purse when her time comes."

"Has she ten thousand pounds?"

"Elizabeth? She will have, at her father's death—but as for my income, it is moderate, and only sufficient to maintain a gentlemanly appearance in proper self-respect. I make no show. I say I make no show. A wealthy marriage is the last thing on earth I should have aimed at. I prefer quiet and retirement. Personally, I mean. That is my personal taste. But if the lady: I say if it should happen that the lady—and indeed I am not one to press a suit;

but if she who distinguishes and honors me should chance to be wealthy, all I can do is to leave her wealth at her disposal, and that I do: I do that unreservedly. I feel I am very confused, alarmingly confused. Your ladyship merits a superior—I trust I have not—I am entirely at your ladyship's mercy."

"Are you prepared, if your daughter is asked in marriage, to settle ten thousand pounds on her, General Ople?"

The general collected himself. In his heart he thoroughly appreciated the moral beauty of Lady Camper's extreme solicitude on behalf of his daughter's provision; but he would have desired a postponement of that and other material questions belonging to a distant future until his own fate was decided.

So he said: "Your ladyship's generosity is very marked. I say it is very marked."

"Now, my good General Ople! how is it marked in any degree?" cried Lady Camper. "I am not generous. I don't pretend to be; and certainly I don't want the young people to think me so. I want to be just. I have assumed that you intend to be the same. Then will you do me the favor to reply to me?"

The general smiled winningly and intently, to show her that he prized her, and would not let her escape his eulogies.

"Marked, in this way, dear madame, that you think of my daughter's future more than I. I say more than her father himself does. I know I ought to speak more warmly, I feel warmly. I was never an eloquent man, and if you take me as a soldier, I am, as I have ever been in the service—I was saying I am Wilson Ople, of the grade of general, to be relied on for executing orders; and, madame, you are Lady Camper, and you command me. I can not be more precise. In fact, it is the feeling of the necessity for keeping close to the business that destroys what I would say. I am in fact lamentably incompetent to conduct my own case."

Lady Camper left her chair.

"Dear me, this is very strange, unless I am singularly in error," she said.

The general now faintly guessed that he might be in error, for his part.

But she had burned his ships, blown up his bridges; retreat could not be thought of.

He stood up, his head bent and appealing to her side-face like one pleadingly in pursuit, and very deferentially, with a courteous vehemence, he entreated first her ladyship's pardon for his presumption, and then the gift of her ladyship's hand.

As for his language, it was the tongue of General Ople. But his bearing was fine. If his clipped white silken hair spoke of age, his figure breathed manliness. He was a picture, and she loved pictures.

For his own sake, she begged him to cease. She dreaded to hear of something "gentlemanly."

"This is a new idea to me, my dear general," she said. "You must give me time. People at our age have to think of the fitness. Of course, in a sense, we are both free to do as we like. Perhaps I may be of some aid to you. My preference is for absolute independence. And I wished to talk of a different affair. Come to me tomorrow. Do not be hurt if I decide that we had better remain as we are."

The general bowed. His efforts, and the wavering of the fair enemy's flag, had inspired him with a positive reawakening of masculine passion to gain this fortress. He said well: "I have, then, the happiness, madame, of being allowed to hope until to-morrow?"

She replied: "I would not deprive you of a moment of happiness. Bring good sense with you when you do come."

The general asked, eagerly: "I have your ladyship's permission to come early?"

"Consult your happiness," she answered; and if to his mind she seemed returning to the state of enigma, it was on the whole deliciously. She restored him his youth. He told Elizabeth that night he really must begin to think of marrying her to some worthy young fellow. "Though," said he, with an air of frank intoxication, "my opinion is, the young ones are not so lively as the old in these days, or I should have been besieged before now."

The exact substance of the interview he forbore to relate to his inquisitive daughter, with a very honorable discretion.

Chapter IV

ELIZABETH CAME RIDING home to breakfast from a gallop round the park, and passing Lady Camper's gates, received the salutation of her parasol. Lady Camper talked with her through the bars. There was not a sign to tell of a change or twist in her neighborly affability. She remarked simply enough that it was her nephew's habit to take early gallops, and possibly Elizabeth might have seen him, for his quarters were proximate; but she did not demand an answer. She had passed a rather restless night, she said. "How is the general?"

"Papa must have slept soundly, for he usually calls to me through his door when he hears I am up," said Elizabeth.

Lady Camper nodded kindly and walked on.

At seven in the morning General Ople was ready for battle. His forces were, the anticipation of victory, a carefully arranged toilet, and an unaccustomed spirit of enterprise in the realms of speech; for he was no longer in such awe of Lady Camper.

"You have slept well?" she inquired.

"Excellently, my lady."

"Yes, your daughter tells me she heard you, as she went by your door in the morning for a ride to meet my nephew. You are, I shall assume, prepared for business?"

"Elizabeth—to meet—!" General Ople's impression of anything extraneous to his emotion was feeble and passed instantly. "Prepared! Oh, certainly!" and he struck in a compliment on her ladyship's fresh morning bloom.

"It can hardly be visible," she responded. "I have not painted yet."

"Does your ladyship proceed to your painting in the very early morning?"

"Rouge. I rouge."

"Dear me! I should not have supposed it."

"You have speculated on it very openly, general. I remember your trying to see a freckle through the rouge; but the truth is, I am of a supernatural paleness if I do not rouge, so I do. You understand, therefore, I have a false complexion. Now to business."

"If your ladyship insists on calling it business. I have little to offer—myself!"

"You have a gentlemanly residence."

"It is, my lady, it is. It is a *bijou*."

"Ah!" Lady Camper sighed dejectedly.

"It is a perfect *bijou*!"

"Oblige me, general, by not pronouncing the French word as if you were swearing by something in English, like a trooper."

General Ople started, admitted that the word was French, and apologized for his pronunciation. Her variability was now visible over a corner of the battlefield like a thundercloud.

"The business we have to discuss concerns the young people, general."

"Yes," brightened by this, he assented. "Yes, dear Lady Camper, it is a part of the business; it is a secondary part; it has to be discussed; I say I subscribe beforehand. I may say that honoring, esteeming you as I do, and hoping ardently for your consent—"

"They must have a home and an income, general."

"I presume, dearest lady, Elizabeth will be welcome in your home. I certainly shall never chase Reginald out of mine."

Lady Camper threw back her head. "Then you are not yet awake, or you practice the art of sleeping with open eyes! Now listen to me. I rouge, I have told you. I like colors, and I do not like to see wrinkles or have them seen. Therefore I rouge. I do not expect to deceive the world so flagrantly as to my age, and you I would not deceive for a moment. I am seventy."

The effect of this noble frankness on the general was to raise him from his chair in a sitting posture as if he had been blown up.

Her countenance was inexorably imperturbable under his alternate blinking and gazing that drew her close and shot her distant, like a mysterious toy.

"But," said she, "I am an artist; I dislike the look of extreme age, so I conceal it as well as I can. You are very kind to fall in with the deception; an innocent, and, I think, a proper one, before the world, though not to the gentleman who does me the honor to propose to me for my hand. You desire to settle our business first. You esteem me; I suppose you mean as much as young people mean when they say they love. Do you? Let us come to an understanding."

"I can," the melancholy general gasped, "I say I can—I can not—I can not credit your ladyship's—"

"You are at liberty to call me Angela."

"Ange—" he tried it, and in shame relapsed. "Madame. Yes. Thanks."

"Ah," cried Lady Camper, "do not use these vulgar contractions of decent speech in my presence. I abhor the word 'thanks.' It is fit for fribbles."

"Dear me, I have used it all my life," groaned the general.

"Then for the remainder, be it understood that you renounce it. To continue, my age is—"

"Oh, impossible, impossible," the general almost wailed; there was really a crack in his voice.

"Advancing to seventy. But, like you, I am happy to say I have not a malady. I bring no invalid frame to a union that necessitates the leaving of the front door open day and night to the doctor. My belief is, I could follow my husband still on a campaign, if he were a warrior instead of a pensioner."

General Ople winced.

He was about to say humbly, "As general of brigade—"

"Yes, yes, you want a commanding officer, and that I have seen, and that has caused me to meditate on your proposal," she interrupted him; while he, studying her countenance hard, with the painful aspect of a youth who lashes a donkey memory in an examination by word of mouth, attempted to marshal her signs of younger years against her awful confession of the extremely ancient, the witheringly ancient. But for the manifest rouge, manifest in spite of her declaration that she had not yet that morning proceeded to her paint-brush, he would have thrown down his glove to challenge her on the subject of her age. She actually had charms. Her mouth had a charm; her eyes were lively; her figure, mature if you like, was at least full and good; she stood upright, she had a queenly seat. His mental ejaculation was: "What a wonderful constitution!"

By a lapse of politeness he repeated it to himself half aloud; he was shockingly nervous.

"Yes, I have finer health than many a younger woman," she said. "An ordinary calculation would give me twenty good years to come. I am a widow, as you know. And, by the way, you have a leaning for widows. Have you not? I thought I had heard of a Widow Barcop in this parish. Do not protest. I assure you I am a stranger to jealousy. My income—"

The general raised his hands.

"Well, then," said the cool and self-contained lady, "before I go further, I may ask you, knowing what you have forced me to confess, are you still of the same mind as to marriage? And one moment, general. I promise you most sincerely that your withdrawing a step shall not, as far as it touches me, affect my neighborly and friendly sentiments, not in any degree. Shall we be as we were?"

Lady Camper extended her delicate hand to him.

He took it respectfully, inspected the aristocratic and unshrunken fingers, and kissing them, said: "I never withdraw from a position unless I am beaten back. Lady Camper, I—"

"My name is Angela."

The general tried again; he could not utter the name.

To call a lady of seventy Angela is difficult in itself. It is, it seems, thrice difficult in the way of courtship.

"Angela!" said she.

"Yes. I say, there is not a more beautiful female name, dear Lady Camper."

"Spare me that word 'female' as long as you live. Address me by that name, if you please."

The general smiled. The smile was meant for propitiation and sweetness. It became a brazen smile.

"Unless you wish to step back," said she.

"Indeed, no. I am happy, Lady Camper. My life is yours. I say my life is devoted to you, dear madame."

"Angela!"

General Ople was blushingly delivered of the name.

"That will do," said she. "And as I think it possible one may be admired too much as an artist, I must request you to keep my number of years a secret."

"To the death, madame!" said the general.

"And now we will take a turn in the garden, Wilson Ople. And beware of one thing, for a commencement, for you are full of weeds, and I mean to pluck out a few: never call any place a gentlemanly residence in my hearing, nor let it come to my ears that you have been using the phrase elsewhere. Don't express astonishment. At present it is enough that I dislike it. But this only," Lady Camper added, "this only if it is not your intention to withdraw from your position."

"Madame, my lady, I was saying—hem!—Angela, I could not wish to withdraw!"

Lady Camper leaned with some pressure on his arm, observing: "You have a curious attachment to antiquities."

"My dear lady, it is your mind; I say it is your mind; I was saying I am in love with your mind," the general endeavored to assure her, and himself too.

"Or is it my powers as an artist?"

"Your mind, your extraordinary powers of mind."

"Well," said Lady Camper, "a veteran general of brigade is as good a crutch as a childless old grannam can have."

And such, as a crutch, General Ople, parading her grounds with the aged woman, found himself used and treated.

The accuracy of his perceptions might be questioned. He was like a man stunned by some great tropical fruit, which responds to the longing of his eyes by falling on his head; but it appeared to him that she increased in bitterness at every step they took, as if determined to make him realize her wrinkles.

He was even so inconsequent, or so little recognized his position as to object in his heart to hear himself called Wilson.

It is true that she uttered Wilson Ople as if the names formed one word. And on a second occasion (when he inclined to feel hurt) she remarked, "I fear, Wilsonople, if we are to speak plainly, thou art but a fool."

He, perhaps, naturally objected to that. He was, however, giddy, and barely knew.

Yet once more the magical woman changed. All semblance of harshness and harridan-like spike-tonguedness vanished when she said adieu.

The astronomer, looking at the crusty jag and scoria of the magnified moon through his telescope, and again with naked eyes at the soft-beaming moon, when the crater-ridges are faint as eyebrow pencilings, has a similar sharp alternation of prospect to that which mystified General Ople.

But between watching an orb that is only variable at our caprice, and contemplating a woman who shifts and quivers ever at her own, how vast the difference!

And consider that this woman is about to be one's wife!

He could have believed (if he had not known full surely that such things are not) he was in the hands of a witch.

Lady Camper's "adieu" was perfectly beautiful—a kind, cordial, intimate, above all, to satisfy his present craving, it was a ladylike adieu—the adieu of a delicate and elegant woman, who had hardly left her anchorage by forty to sail into the fifties.

Alas! he had her word for it that she was not less than seventy. And worse, she had betrayed most melancholy signs of sourness and agedness as soon as he had sworn himself to her fast and fixed.

"The road is open to you to retreat," were her last words.

"My road," he answered, gallantly, "is forward."

He was drawing backward as he said it, and something provoked her to smile.

Chapter V

IT IS A noble thing to say that your road is forward, and it befits a man of battles. General Ople was too loyal a gentleman to think of any other road. Still, albeit not gifted with imagination, he could not avoid the feeling that he had set his face to winter. He found himself suddenly walking straight into the heart of winter, and a nipping winter. For her ladyship had proved acutely nipping. His little customary phrases, to which Lady Camper objected, he could see no harm in whatever. Conversing with her in the privacy of domestic life would never be the flowing business that it is for other men. It would demand perpetual vigilance, hop, skip, jump, floundering, and apologies.

This was not a pleasing prospect.

On the other hand, she was the niece of an earl. She was wealthy. She might be an excellent friend to Elizabeth; and she could be, when she liked, both commandingly and bewitchingly lady-like.

Good! But he was a general officer of not more than fifty-five, in his full vigor, and she a woman of seventy!

The prospect was bleak. It resembled an outlook on the steppes. In point of the discipline he was to expect, he might be compared to a raw recruit, and in his own home!

However, she was a woman of mind. One would be proud of her.

But did he know the worst of her? A dreadful presentiment that he did not know the worst of her rolled an ocean of gloom upon General Ople, striking out one solitary thought in the obscurity—namely, that he was about to receive punishment for retiring from active service to a life of ease at a comparatively early age, when still in marching trim. And the shadow of the thought was that he deserved the punishment!

He was in his garden with the dawn. Hard exercise is the best of opiates for dismal reflections. The general discomposed his daughter by offering to accompany her on her morning ride before breakfast. She considered that it would fatigue him. "I am not a man of eighty!" he cried. He could have wished that he had been.

He led the way to the park, where they soon had sight of young Rolles, who checked his horse and spied them like a vedette, but, perceiving that he had been seen, came cantering and hailing the general with hearty wonderment.

"And what's this the world says, general?" said he. "But we all applaud your taste. My aunt Angela was the handsomest woman of her time."

The general murmured in confusion: "Dear me!" and looked at the young man, thinking that he could not have known the time. "Is all arranged, my dear general?"

"Nothing is arranged; and I beg—I say I beg—I came out for fresh air and pace."

The general rode frantically.

In spite of the fresh air he was unable to eat at breakfast. He was bound, of course, to present himself to Lady Camper, in common civility, immediately after it.

And first, what were the phrases he had to avoid uttering in her presence? He could remember only the "gentlemanly residence." And it was a gentlemanly residence, he thought, as he took leave of it. It was one, neatly named to fit the place. Lady Camper is indeed a most eccentric person! he decided from his experience of her.

He was rather astonished that young Rolles should have spoken so coolly of his aunt's leaning to matrimony; but perhaps her exact age was unknown to the younger members of her family.

This idea refreshed him by suggesting the extremely honorable nature of Lady Camper's uncomfortable confession.

He himself had an uncomfortable confession to make. He would have to speak of his income. He was living up to the edges of it.

566

"She is an upright woman, and I must be the same!" he said, fortunately not in her hearing.

The subject was disagreeable to a man sensitive on the topic of money, and feeling that his prudence had recently been misled to keep up appearances.

Lady Camper was in her garden, reclining under her parasol. A chair was beside her, to which, acknowledging the salutation of her suitor, she waved him.

"You have met my nephew Reginald this morning, general?"

"Curiously, in the park, this morning, before breakfast, I did— yes. Hem! I—I say I did meet him. Has your ladyship seen him?"

"No. The park is very pretty in the early morning."

"Sweetly pretty."

Lady Camper raised her head, and with the mildness of assured dictatorship, pronounced:

"Never say that before me."

"I submit, my lady," said the poor scourged man.

"Why, naturally you do. Vulgar phrases have to be endured, except when our intimates are guilty, and then we are not merely offended—we are compromised by them. You are still of the mind in which you left me yesterday? You are one day older. But, I warn you, so am I."

"Yes, my lady, we can not—I say we can not check—time. Decidedly of the same mind. Quite so."

"Oblige me by never saying 'Quite so.' My lawyer says it. It reeks of the city of London. And do not look so miserable."

"I, madame?—my dear lady!" the general flashed out in a radiance that dulled instantly.

"Well," said she, cheerfully, "and you're for the old woman?"

"For Lady Camper."

"You are seductive in your flatteries, general. Well, then, we have to speak of business."

"My affairs—"

General Ople was beginning, with perturbed forehead, but Lady Camper held up her finger.

"We will touch on your affairs incidentally. Now, listen to me, and do not exclaim until I have finished. You know that these two young ones have been whispering over the wall for some months. They have been meeting on the river and in the park habitually, apparently with your consent."

"My lady!"

"I did not say with your connivance."

"You mean my daughter Elizabeth?"

"And my nephew Reginald. We have named them, if that advances us. Now, the end of such meetings is marriage, and the sooner the better, if they are to continue. I would rather they should not; I do not hold it good for young soldiers to marry. But if they do, it is very certain that their pay will not support a family; and in a marriage of two healthy young people, we have to assume the existence of the family. You have allowed matters to go so far that the boy is hot in love; I suppose the girl is, too. She is a nice girl. I do not object to her personally. But I insist that a settlement be made on her before I give my nephew one penny. Hear me out, for I am not fond of business, and shall be glad to have done with these explanations. Reginald has nothing of his own. He is my sister's son, and I loved her, and rather like the boy. He has at present four hundred a year from me. I will double it, on the condition that you at once make over ten thousand pounds—not less; and let it be yes or no—to be settled on your daughter and go to her children, independent of the husband—*cela va sans dire*. Now you may speak, general."

The general spoke, with breath fetched from the deeps:

"Ten thousand pounds! Hem! Ten! frankly, ten, my lady! One's income—I am quite taken by surprise. I say Elizabeth's conduct—though, poor child, it is natural to her to seek a mate—I mean, to accept a mate and an establishment; and Reginald is a very hopeful fellow—I was saying they jump on me out of an ambush, and I wish them every happiness. And she is an ardent soldier, and a soldier she must marry. But ten thousand!"

"It is to secure the happiness of your daughter, general!"

"Pounds! my lady. It would rather cripple me."

"You would have my house, general; you would have the moiety, as the lawyers say, of my purse; you would have horses, carriages, servants; I do not divine what more you would wish to have."

"But, madame—a pensioner on the government! I can look back on past services—I say old services—and I accept my position. But, madame, a pensioner on my wife, bringing next to nothing to the common estate! I fear my self-respect would, I say would—"

"Well, and what would it do, General Ople?"

"I was saying my self-respect as my wife's pensioner, my lady. I could not come to her empty-handed."

"Do you expect that I should be the person to settle money on your daughter, to save her from mischances? A rakish husband, for example, for Reginald is young, and no one can guess what will be made of him."

"Undoubtedly your ladyship is correct. We might try absence for the poor girl. I have no female relation, but I could send her to the sea-side to a lady friend."

"General Ople, I forbid you, as you value my esteem, ever—and I repeat, I forbid you ever—to afflict my ears with that phrase 'lady friend!' "

The general blinked in a state of insurgent humility.

These incessant whippings could not but sting the humblest of men; and "lady friend," he was sure, was a very common term, used, he was sure, in the very best society. He had never heard her majesty speak at levees of a lady friend, but he was quite sure that she had one; and if so, what could be the objection to her subjects mentioning it as a term to suit their own circumstances?

He was harassed and perplexed by old Lady Camper's treatment of him, and he resolved not to call her Angela, even upon supplication—not that day, at least.

She said: "You will not need to bring property of any kind to the common estate; I neither look for it nor desire it. The generous thing for you to do would be to give your daughter all you have, and come to me."

"But, Lady Camper, if I denude myself or curtail my income— a man at his wife's discretion, I was saying a man at his wife's mercy—"

General Ople was really forced, by his manly dignity, to make this protest on its behalf. He did not see how he could have escaped doing so; he was more an agent than a principal. "My wife's mercy," he said again, but simply as a herald proclaiming superior orders.

Lady Camper's brows were wrathful. A deep blood-crimson overcame the rouge, and gave her a terrible stormy look.

"The congress now ceases to sit, and the treaty is not concluded," was all she said.

She rose, bowed to him, "Good-morning, general," and turned her back.

He sighed. He was a free man. But this could not be denied—whatever the lady's age, she was a grand woman in her carriage, and when looking angry she had a queen-like aspect that raised her out of the reckoning of time.

So now he knew there was a worse behind what he had previously known. He was precipitate in calling it the worst.

"Now," said he to himself, "I know the worst!"

No man should ever say it. Least of all, one who has entered into relations with an eccentric lady.

Chapter VI

POLITENESS REQUIRED THAT General Ople should not appear to rejoice in his dismissal as a suitor, and should at least make some show of holding himself at the beck of a reconsidering mind. He was guilty of running up to London early next day, and remaining absent until nightfall; and he did the same on the two following days. When he presented himself at Lady Camper's lodge gates, the astonishing intelligence that her ladyship had departed for the Continent and Egypt gave him qualms of remorse, which assumed a more definite shape in something like awe of her triumphant constitution. He forbore to mention her age, for he was the most honorable of men, but a habit of tea-table talkativeness impelled him to say and repeat an idea that had visited him, to the effect that Lady Camper was one of those wonderful women who are comparable to brilliant generals, and defend themselves from the siege of Time by various aggressive movements. Fearful of not being understood, owing to the rarity of the occasions when the squat, plain squad of honest Saxon regulars at his command were called upon to explain an idea, he recast the sentence. But, as it happened that the regulars of his vocabulary were not numerous, and not accustomed to work upon thoughts and images, his repetitions rather succeeded in exposing the piece of knowledge he had recently acquired than in making his meaning plainer. So we need not marvel that his acquaintances should suppose him to be secretly aware of an extreme degree in which Lady Camper was a veteran.

General Ople entered into the gayeties of the neighborhood

once more, and passed through the winter cheerfully. In justice to
him, however, it should be said that to the intent dwelling of his
mind upon Lady Camper, and not to the festive life he led, was
due his entire ignorance of his daughter's unhappiness. She lived
with him, and yet it was in other houses he learned that she was
unhappy. After his last interview with Lady Camper, he had informed Elizabeth of the ruinous and preposterous amount of money
demanded of him for a settlement upon her; and Elizabeth, like the
girl of good sense that she was, had replied immediately, "It could
not be thought of, papa."

He had spoken to Reginald likewise. The young man fell into
a dramatic tearing-of-hair and long-stride fury not ill-becoming an
enamored dragoon. But he maintained that his aunt, though an
eccentric, was a cordially kind woman. He seemed to feel, if he did
not partly hint, that the general might have accepted Lady Camper's
terms. The young officer could not longer be welcome at Douro
Lodge, so the general paid him a morning call at his quarters, and
was distressed to find him breakfasting very late, tapping eggs that
he forgot to open—one of the surest signs of a young man downright and deeply in love, as the general knew from experience—
and surrounded by uncut sporting journals of past weeks, which
dated from the day when his blow had struck him, as accurately
as the watch of the drowned man marks his minute.

Lady Camper had gone to Italy, and was in communication with
her nephew. Reginald was not further explicit. His legs were very
prominent in his despair, and his fingers frequently performed the
part of blunt combs, consequently the general was impressed by his
passion for Elizabeth. The girl who, if she was often meditative,
always met his eyes with a smile, and quietly said: "Yes, papa," and
"No, papa," gave him little concern as to the state of her feelings.
Yet everybody said now that she was unhappy.

Mrs. Barcop, the widow, raised her voice above the rest. So
attentive was she to Elizabeth that the general had it kindly suggested to him that some one was courting him through his daughter.
He gazed at the widow.

Now she was not much past thirty; and it was really singular—he
could have laughed—the thinking of Mrs. Barcop set him per-
sistently thinking of Lady Camper. That is to say, his mad fancy
reverted from the lady of perhaps thirty-five to the lady of seventy.

Such, thought he, is genius in a woman. Of his neighbors generally, Mrs. Baerens, the wife of a German merchant, an exquisite player on the pianoforte, was the most inclined to lead him to speak of Lady Camper. She was a kind, prattling woman, and was known to have been a governess before her charms withdrew the gastronomic Gottfried Baerens from his devotion to the well-served City club, where, as he exclaimed (ever turning fondly to his wife as he vocalized the compliment), he had found every necessity, every luxury, in life "as you can not have dem out of London—all save de female!" Mrs. Baerens, a lady of Teutonic extraction, was distinguishable as one of that sex; at least she was not masculine. She spoke with great respect of Lady Camper and her family, and seemed to agree in the general's eulogies of Lady Camper's constitution. Still he thought she eyed him strangely.

One April morning the general received a letter with the Italian postmark. Opening it with his usual calm and happy curiosity, he perceived that it was composed of pen-and-ink drawings. And suddenly his heart sunk like a scuttled ship. He saw himself the victim of a caricature.

The first sketch had merely seemed picturesque, and he supposed it a clever play of fancy by some traveling friend, or perhaps an actual scene slightly exaggerated.

Even on reading "A distant View of the City of Wilsonople," he was only slightly enlightened. His heart beat still with befitting regularity. But the second and the third sketches betrayed the terrible hand. The distant view of the city of Wilsonople was fair with glittering domes, which, in the succeeding near view, proved to have been soap-bubbles, for a place of extreme flatness, begirt with crazy old-fashioned fortifications, was shown; and in the third view, representing the interior, stood for sole place of habitation, a sentry-box.

Most minutely drawn, and, alas, with fearful accuracy, a military gentleman in undress occupied the box. Not a doubt could exist as to the person it was meant to be.

The general tried hard to remain incredulous. He remembered too well who had called him Wilsonople.

But here was the extraordinary thing that sent him over the neighborhood canvassing for exclamations: on the fourth page was the outline of a lovely feminine hand holding a pen, as in the act of shading, and under it was written these words: "What I say is, I say I think it exceedingly unlady-like."

Now consider the general's feelings when, turning to this fourth page, having these very words in his mouth, as the accurate expression of his thoughts, he discovered them written.

An enemy who anticipates the actions of our mind has a quality of the malignant divine that may well inspire terror. The senses of General Ople were struck by the aspect of a black goddess who penetrated him, read him through, and had both power and will to expose and make him ridiculous forever.

The loveliness of the hand, too, in a perplexing manner contested his denunciation of her conduct. It was lady-like eminently, and it involved him in a confused mixture of the moral and material, as great as young people are known to feel when they make the attempt to separate them, in one of their frenzies.

With a petty, bitter laugh he folded the letter, put it in his breast-pocket, and sallied forth for a walk, chiefly to talk to himself about it. But as it absorbed him entirely, he showed it to the rector, whom he met, and what the rector said is of no consequence, for General Ople listened to no remarks, calling in succession on the Pollingtons, the Goslings, the Baerens, and others, early though it was, and the lords of those houses absent amassing hoards; and to the ladies everywhere he displayed the sketches he had received, observing that Wilsonople meant himself; and there he was, he said, pointing at the capped fellow in the sentry box, done unmistakably. The likeness indeed was remarkable. "She is a woman of genius," he ejaculated, with utter melancholy.

Mrs. Baerens, by the aid of a magnifying-glass, assisted him to read a line under the sentry box, that he had taken for a mere trembling dash; it ran: "A gentlemanly residence."

"What eyes she has!" the general exclaimed. "I say it is miraculous what eyes she has at her time of— I was saying, I should never have known it was writing."

He sighed heavily. His shuddering sensitiveness to caricature was increased by a certain evident dread of the hand which struck; the knowing that he was absolutely bare to this woman, defenseless, open to exposure in his little whims, foibles, tricks, incompetencies, in what lay in his heart, and the words that would come to his tongue. He felt like a man haunted.

So deeply did he feel the blow that people asked how it was that he could be so foolish as to dance about assisting Lady Camper in her efforts to make him ridiculous; he acted the parts of publisher and agent for the fearful caricaturist. In truth there was a strangely double reason for his conduct, he danced about for sympathy, he had the intensest craving for sympathy, but more than this, or quite as much, he desired to have the powers of his enemy widely appreciated; in the first place, that he might be excused to himself for wincing under them, and secondly, because an awful admiration of her that should be deepened by a corresponding sentiment around him, helped him to enjoy luxurious recollections of an hour when he was near making her his own—his own, in the holy abstract contemplation of marriage, without realizing their probable relative conditions after the ceremony.

"I say that is the very image of her ladyship's hand," he was especially fond of remarking, "I say it is a beautiful hand."

He carried the letter in his pocket-book; and beginning to fancy that she had done her worst, for he could not imagine an inventive malignity capable of pursuing the theme, he spoke of her treatment of him with compassionate regret, not badly assumed from being partly sincere.

Two letters dated in France, the one Dijon, the other Fontainebleau, arrived together; and as the general knew Lady Camper to be returning to England, he expected that she was anxious to excuse herself to him. His fingers were not so confident, for he tore one of the letters to open it.

The city of Wilsonople was recognizable immediately. So likewise was the sole inhabitant.

General Ople's petty, bitter laugh returned, like a weak-chested patient's cough in the shifting of our winds eastward.

A faceless woman's shadow kneels on the ground near the sentry box, weeping. A faceless shadow of a young man on horseback is beheld galloping toward a gulf. The sole inhabitant contemplates his largely substantial full-fleshed face and figure in a glass.

Next, we see the standard of Great Britain furled; next, unfurled and borne by a troop of shadows to the sentry-box. The officer within says: "I say I should be very happy to carry it, but I can not quit this gentlemanly residence."

Next, the standard is shown assailed by popguns. Several of the shadows are prostrate. "I was saying, I assure you that nothing but this gentlemanly residence prevents me from heading you," says the gallant officer.

General Ople trembled with protestant indignation when he saw himself reclining in a magnified sentry box, while the detachments of shadows hurry to him to show him the standard of his country trailing in the dust; and he is maliciously made to say: "I dislike responsibility. I say I am a fervent patriot, and very fond of my comforts, but I shun responsibility."

The second letter contained scenes between Wilsonople and the Moon.

He addresses her as his neighbor, and tells her of his triumphs over the sex.

He requests her to inform him whether she is a "female," that she may be triumphed over.

He hastens past her window on foot, with his head bent, just as the general had been in the habit of walking.

He drives a mouse-pony furiously by.

He cuts down a tree that she may peep through.

Then, from the Moon's point of view, Wilsonople, a Silenus, is discerned in an armchair winking at a couple too plainly pouting their lips for a doubt of their intentions to be entertained.

A fourth letter arrived, bearing date of Paris. This one illustrated Wilsonople's courtship of the Moon, and ended with his "saying," in his peculiar manner: "In spite of her paint I could not have conceived her age to be so enormous."

How break off his engagement with the Lady Moon? Consent to none of her terms!

Little used as he was to read behind a veil, acuteness of suffering sharpened the general's intelligence to a degree that sustained him in animated dialogue with each succeeding sketch or poisoned arrow whirring at him, from the moment his eyes rested on it; and here are a few samples:

"Wilsonople informs the Moon that she is 'sweetly pretty.'"

"He thanks her with 'Thanks!' for a handsome piece of lunar green cheese."

"He points to her, apparently saying to some one 'My lady friend.'"

"He sneezes '*Bijou! bijou! bijou!*'"

They were trifles, but they attacked his habits of speech; and he began to grow more and more alarmingly absurd in each fresh caricature of his person.

He looked at himself as the malicious woman's hand had shaped him. It was unjust; it was no resemblance—and yet it was! There was a corner of likeness left that leavened the lump; henceforth he must walk abroad with this distressing image of himself before his eyes, instead of the satisfactory reflex of the man who had, and was happy in thinking that he had done mischief in his time. Such an end for a conquering man was too pathetic.

The general surprised himself talking to himself in something louder than a hum at neighbors' dinner-tables. He looked about and noticed that people were silently watching him.

Chapter VII

LADY CAMPER'S RETURN was the subject of speculation in the neighborhood, for most people thought she would cease to persecute the general with her preposterous and unwarrantable pen-and-ink sketches when living so closely proximate; and how he would behave was the question. Those who made a hero of him were sure he would treat her with disdain. Others were uncertain. He had been so severely hit that it seemed possible he would not show much spirit.

He, for his part, had come to entertain such dread of the post, that Lady Camper's return relieved him of his morning apprehensions; and he would have forgiven her, though he feared to see her, if only she had promised to leave him in peace for the future. He feared to see her, because of the too probable furnishing of fresh matter for her ladyship's hand. Of course he could not avoid being seen by her, and that was a particular misery. A gentlemanly humility or demureness of aspect when seen, would, he hoped, disarm his enemy. It should, he thought. He had borne unheard-of things. No one of his friends and acquaintances knew, they could not know, what he had endured. It had caused him fits of stammering. It had destroyed the composure of his gait. Elizabeth had informed him that he talked to himself incessantly, and aloud. She, poor child, looked pale, too. She was evidently anxious about him.

Young Rolles, whom he had met now and then, persisted in praising his aunt's good heart. So, perhaps, having satiated her revenge, she might now be inclined for peace, on the terms of distant civility.

"Yes. Poor Elizabeth!" sighed the general, in pity of the poor girl's disappointment; "poor Elizabeth! she little guesses what her father has gone through. Poor child! I say, she hasn't any idea of my sufferings." He commended himself for keeping them from her.

General Ople delivered his card at Lady Camper's lodge gates, and escaped to his residence in a state of prickly heat that required the brushing of his hair with hard brushes for ten minutes to comfort and re-establish him.

He fell to working in his garden, when Lady Camper's card was brought to him an hour after the delivery of his own, a pleasing promptitude, showing signs of repentance, and suggesting to the general instantly some sharp sarcasms upon women, which he had come upon in quotation in the papers and the pulpit, his two main sources of information.

Instead of handing back the card to the maid, he stuck it in his hat and went on digging.

The first of a series of letters containing shameless realistic caricatures was handed to him the afternoon following. They came fast and thick. Not a day's interval of grace was allowed. Niobe under the shafts of Diana was hardly less violently and morally assailed. The deadliness of the attack lay in the ridicule of the daily habits of one of the most sensitive of men, as to his personal appearance, and the opinion of the world. He might have concealed the sketches, but he could not have concealed the bruises, and people were perpetually asking the unhappy general what he was saying, for he spoke to himself as if he were repeating something to them for the tenth time.

"I say," said he, "I say, that for a lady, really an educated lady, to sit, as she must—I was saying, she must have sat in an attic to have the right view of me. And there, you see, this is what she has done. This is the last; this is the afternoon's delivery. Her ladyship has me correctly as to costume, but I could not exhibit such a sketch to ladies."

577

A back view of the general was displayed in his act of digging. "I say I could not allow ladies to see it," he informed the gentlemen, who were suffered to inspect it freely.

"But you see I have no means of escape; I am at her mercy from morning to night," the general said, with a quivering tongue, "unless I stay at home inside the house; and that is death to me, or unless I abandon the place, and my lease; and I shall—I say, I shall find nowhere in England for anything like the money or conveniences such a gent—a residence you would call fit for a gentleman. I call it a bi—it is, in short, a gem. But I shall have to go."

Young Rolles offered to expostulate with his aunt Angela.

The general said: "Tha—I thank you very much. I would not have her ladyship suppose I am so susceptible. I hardly know," he confessed pitiably, "what it is right to say, and what not—what not. I—I—I never know that I am not looking a fool. I hurry from tree to tree to shun the light. I am seriously affected in my appetite. I say I shall have to go."

Reginald gave him to understand that if he flew the shafts would follow him, for Lady Camper would never forgive his running away, and was quite equal to publishing a book of the adventures of Wilsonople.

Sunday afternoon, walking in the park with his daughter on his arm, General Ople met Mr. Rolles. He saw that the young man and Elizabeth were mortally pale, and as the very idea of wretchedness directed his attention to himself, he adressed them conjointly on the subject of his persecution, giving neither of them a chance of speaking until they were constrained to part.

A sketch was the consequence, in which a withered Cupid and a fading Psyche were seen divided by Wilsonople, who keeps them forcibly asunder with policeman's fists, while courteously and elegantly entreating them to hear him. "Meet," he tells them, "as often as you like, in my company, so long as you listen to me"; and the pathos of his aspect makes hungry demand for a sympathetic audience.

Now this, and not the series representing the martyrdom of the old couple at Douro Lodge gates, whose rigid frames bore witness to the close packing of a gentlemanly residence, this was the sketch General Ople, in his madness from the pursuing bite of the gadfly, handed about at Mrs. Pollington's lawn-party. Some have said that he would not have betrayed his daughter; but it is reasonable to suppose he had no idea of his daughter's being the Psyche. Or if he had, it was indistinct, owing to the violence of his personal emotion. Assuming this to have been the very sketch, he handed it to two or three ladies in turn, and was heard to deliver himself at intervals in the following snatches: "As you like, my lady, as you like; strike, I say, strike; I bear it; I say I bear it. If her ladyship is unforgiving, I say I am enduring—I may go— I was saying I may go mad, but while I have my reason I walk upright—I walk upright."

Mr. Pollington and certain City gentlemen hearing the poor general's renewed soliloquies, were seized with disgust of Lady Camper's conduct, and stoutly advised an application to the law courts.

He gave ear to them abstractedly, but after pulling out the whole chapter of the caricatures (which it seemed that he kept in a case of morocco leather in his breast-pocket), showing them, with comments on them, and observing, "There will be more—there must be more—I say I am sure there are things I do that her lady-ship will discover and expose," he declined to seek redress or simple protection; and the miserable spectacle was exhibited soon after of this courtly man listening to Mrs. Barcop on the weather, and replying in acquiescence: "It is hot— If your ladyship will only abstain from colors. Very hot, as you say, madame—I do not complain of pen and ink, but I would rather escape colors. And I dare say you find it hot, too?"

Mrs. Barcop shut her eyes and sighed over the wreck of a hand-some military officer.

She asked him: "What is your objection to colors?"

His hand was at his breast-pocket immediately, as he said: "Have you not seen?"—though but a few minutes back he had shown her the contents of the packet, including a hurried glance of the famous digging scene.

By this time the entire district was in fervid sympathy with General Ople. The ladies did not, as their lords did, proclaim as-tonishment that a man should suffer a woman to goad him to a state of semi-lunacy; but one or two confessed to their husbands that it required a great admiration of General Ople not to despise him, both for his susceptibility and his patience. As for the men, they knew him to have faced the balls in bellowing battle-strife; they knew him to have endured privation, not only cold, but downright want of food and drink—an almost unimaginable horror to these brave daily feasters; so they could not quite look on him in contempt; but his want of sense was offensive, and still more so his submission to a scourging by a woman. Not one of them would have deigned to feel it. Would they have allowed her to see that she could sting them? They would have laughed at her. Or they would have dragged her before a magistrate.

It was a Sunday in early summer when General Ople walked to morning service, unaccompanied by Elizabeth, who was unwell. The church was of the considerate, old-fashioned order, with square pews, permitting the mind to abstract itself from the sermon, or wrestle at leisure with the difficulties presented by the preacher, as General Ople often did, feeling not a little in love with his sincere attentiveness for grappling with the knotty point, and partially allowing the struggle to be seen. The church was, besides, a sanctuary for him. Hither his enemy did not come. He had this one place of refuge, and he almost looked a happy man again.

He had passed into his hat and out of it, which he habitually did standing, when who should walk up to within a couple of yards of him but Lady Camper. Her pew was full of poor people, who made signs of retiring. She signified to them that they were to sit, then quietly took her seat among them, fronting the general across the aisle.

During the sermon a low voice, sharp in contradistinction to the monotone of the preacher's, was heard to repeat these words: "I say I am not sure I shall survive it." Considerable muttering in the same quarter was heard besides.

After the customary ceremonious game, when all were free to move, of nobody liking to move first, Lady Camper and a charity boy were the persons who took the lead. But Lady Camper could not quit her pew, owing to the sticking of the door. She smiled, as with her pretty hand she twice or thrice essayed to shake it open. General Ople strode to her aid. He pulled the door, gave the shadow of a respectful bow, and no doubt he would have withdrawn, had not Lady Camper, while acknowledging the civility, placed her prayerbook in his hands to carry at her heels. There was no choice for him. He made a sort of slipping dance back for his hat, and followed her ladyship. All present being eager to witness the spectacle, the passage of Lady Camper dragging the victim general behind her was observed without a stir of the well-dressed members of the congregation, until a desire overcame them to see how Lady Camper would behave to her fish when she had him outside the sacred edifice.

None could have imagined such a scene. Lady Camper was in her carriage; General Ople was, hat in hand, at the carriage-step, and he looked as if he were toasting before the bars of a furnace, for while he stood there, Lady Camper was rapidly penciling outlines in a small pocket sketch-book. There are dogs whose shyness is put to it to endure human observation and a direct address to them, even on the part of their masters; and these dear simple dogs wag tail and turn their heads aside waveringly, as though to entreat you not to eye them and talk to them so. General Ople, in the presence of the sketch-book, was much like the nervous animal. He would fain have run away. He glanced at it, and round about, and again at it, and at the heavens. Her ladyship's cruelty, and his inexplicable submission to it, were witnessed of the multitude.

The general's friends walked very slowly. Lady Camper's carriage whirled by, and the general came up with them, accosting them and himself alternately. They asked him where Elizabeth was, and he replied, "Poor child, yes! I am told she is pale, but I can not believe I am so perfectly—I say so perfectly—ridiculous when I join in the responses." He drew forth half a dozen sheets, and showed them sketches that Lady Camper had taken in church, caricaturing him in the sitting down and the standing up. She had torn them out of the book, and presented them to him when driving off. "I was saying, worship in the ordinary sense will be interdicted to me if her ladyship—" said the general, woefully, shuffling the sketch-paper sheets in which he figured.

He made the following odd confession to Mr. and Mrs. Gosling on the road—that he had gone to his chest, and taken out his sword-belt to measure his girth, and found himself thinner than when he left the service, which had not been the case before his attendance at the last levee of the foregoing season. So the deduction was obvious—that Lady Camper had reduced him. She had reduced him as effectually as a harassing siege.

"But why do you pay attention to her! Why—" exclaimed Mr. Gosling, a gentleman of the City, whose roundness would have turned a rifle-shot.

"To allow her to wound you so seriously!" exclaimed Mrs. Gosling.

"Madame, if she were my wife," the general explained, "I should feel it. I say it is the fact of it; I feel it, if I appear so extremely ridiculous to a human eye, to any one eye."

"To Lady Camper's eye!"

He admitted it might be that. He had not thought of ascribing the acuteness of his pain to the miserable image he presented to this particular lady's eye. No; it really was true, curiously true; another lady's eye might have transformed him to a pumpkin shape, exaggerated all his foibles fifty-fold, and he, though not liking it, of course not, would yet have preserved a certain manly equanimity. How was it Lady Camper had such power over him —a lady concealing seventy years with a rouge-box or paint-pot? It was witchcraft in its worst character. He had for six months at her bidding been actually living the life of a beast, degraded in his own esteem; scorched by every laugh he heard; running, pursued, overtaken, and, as it were, scored or branded, and then let go for the process to be repeated.

Chapter VIII

OUR YOUNG BARBARIANS have it all their own way with us when they fall into love-liking; they lead us whither they please, and interest us in their wishings, their weepings, and that fine performance, their kissings. But when we see our veterans tottering to their fall, we scarcely consent to their having a wish; as for a kiss, we halloo at them if we discover them on a by-way to the sacred grove where such things are supposed to be done by the venerable. And this piece of rank injustice, not to say impoliteness, is entirely because of an unsound opinion that Nature is not in it, as though it were our esteem for Nature which caused us to disrespect them.

They, in truth, show her to us discreet, civilized, in a decent moral aspect; vistas of real life, views of the mind's eye, are opened by their touching little emotions; whereas those bully youngsters who came bellowing at us and catch us by the senses plainly prove either that we are no better than they or that we give our attention of Nature only when she makes us afraid of her. If we cared for her, we should be up and after her reverentially in her sedater steps, deeply studying her in her slower paces. Whirling, she teaches nothing. Our closest instructors, the true philosophers —the story-tellers, in short—will learn in time that Nature is not of necessity always roaring, and as soon as they do, the world may be said to be enlightened. Meantime, in the contemplation of a pair of white whiskers fluttering round a pair of manifestly painted cheeks, be assured that Nature is in it, very Nature, domesticated Nature, the Nature of gradations, Nature with a perspective. Art in days to come will dote on the theme. It is Nature calling to Nature, Nature amazed with brains, and pursuing the direction of their index; not that hectoring old wanton—but let the young have their fun. Let the superior interest of the passions of the aged be conceded, and not a word shall be said against the young. They are young, and happily they can not clothe themselves.

If, then, Nature is in it, with a couple properly attired, how has she been made active? The reason of her launch upon this last adventure is, that she has perceived the person who can supply the virtue known to her by experience to be wanting. Thus, in the broader instance, many who have journeyed far down the road, turn back to the worship of youth, which they have lost. Some are for the graceful worldliness of wit, of which they have just share enough to admire it. Some are captivated by hands that can wield the rod, which in earlier days they escaped to their cost. In the case of General Ople it was partly her whippings of him, partly her penetration, her ability, that sat so finely on a wealthy woman; her indifference to conventional manners, that so well beseemed a nobly born one, and more than all, her correction of his little weaknesses and incompetencies, in spite of his dislike of it, won him. He began to feel a sort of nibbling pleasure in her grotesque sketches of his person; a tendency to recur to the old ones, while dreading the arrival of new. You hear old gentlemen speak fondly of the switch; and they are not attached to pain, but the instrument revives their feeling of youth; and General Ople half enjoyed, while shrinking, Lady Camper's foregone outlines of him. For in the distance, the whip's end may look like a clinging caress instead of a stinging flick. But this craven melting in his heart was rebuked by a very worthy pride, that flew for support to the injury she had done to his devotions and the offense to the sacred edifice. After thinking over it he decided that he must quit his residence; and as it appeared to him in the light of a duty, with an unspoken anguish, commissioned the house-agent of his town to sell his lease or let the house furnished, without further parley.

From the house-agent's shop he turned into the chemist's for a tonic—a foolish proceeding—for he had received bracing enough in the blow he had just dealt himself, but he had been cogitating on tonics recently, imagining certain valiant effects of them, with visions of a former careless happiness that they were likely to restore. So he requested to have the tonic strong, and he took one glass of it over the counter.

Fifteen minutes after the draught he came in sight of his house, and beholding it, he could have called it a gentlemanly residence aloud under Lady Camper's windows, his insurgency was of such violence. He talked of it incessantly, but forbore to tell Elizabeth, as she was looking pale, the reason why its modest merits touched him so. He longed for the hour of his next dose, and for a caricature to follow, that he might drink and defy it. A caricature was really due to him, he thought; otherwise why had he abandoned his *bijou* dwelling. Lady Camper, however, sent none. He had to wait a fortnight before one came, and that was rather a likeness, and a handsome likeness, except as regarded a certain disorderliness in his dress, which he knew to be very unlike him. Still it dispatched him to the looking-glass, to bring that verifier of fact in evidence against the sketch. While sitting there he heard the house-maid's knock at the door, and the strange intelligence that his daughter was with Lady Camper, and had left word that she hoped he would not forget his engagement to go to Mrs. Baerens' lawn-party.

The general jumped away from the glass, censuring the absent Elizabeth in a fit of wrath so foreign to him that he returned hurriedly to have another look at himself, and exclaimed at the pitch of his voice: "I say, I attribute it to an indigestion of that tonic. Do you hear?" The house-maid faintly answered outside the door that she did, alarming him, for there seemed to be confusion somewhere. His hope was that no one would mention Lady Camper's name, for the mere thought of her caused a rush to his head. "I believe I am in for a touch of apoplexy," he said to the rector, who greeted him, in advance of the ladies, on Mrs. Baerens' lawn. He said it smilingly, but wanting some show of sympathy, instead of the whisper and meaningless hand at his clerical band, with which the rector responded, he cried, "Apoplexy," and his friend seemed then to understand, and disappeared among the ladies.

Several of them surrounded the general, and one inquired whether the series was being continued. He drew forth his pocket-book, handed her the latest, and remarked on the gross injustice of it; for, as he requested them to take the note, her ladyship now sketched him as a person inattentive to his dress, and he begged them to observe that she had drawn him with his necktie hanging loose. "And that—I say that has never been known of me since I first entered society."

The ladies exchanged looks of profound concern, for the fact was, the general had come without any necktie and any collar, and he appeared to be unaware of the circumstance. The rector had told them that, in answer to a hint he had dropped on the subject of neckties, General Ople expressed a slight apprehension of apoplexy; but his careless or merely partial observance of the laws of buttonment could have nothing to do with such fears. They signified rather a disorder of the intelligence. Elizabeth was condemned for leaving him to go about alone. The situation was really most painful, for a word to so sensitive a man would drive him away in shame and for good; and still, to let him parade the ground in the state, compared with his natural self, of scarecrow, and with the dreadful habit of talking to himself quite raging, was a horrible alternative. Mrs. Baerens at last directed her husband upon the general, trembling as though she watched for the operations of a fish torpedo; and other ladies shared her excessive anxiousness, for Mr. Baerens had the manner and look of artillery, and on this occasion carried a surcharge of powder.

The general bent his ear to Mr. Baerens, whose German-English and repeated remark, "I am to do it wid delicassy," did not assist his comprehension, and when he might have been enlightened, he was petrified by seeing Lady Camper walk on the lawn with Elizabeth. The great lady stood a moment beside Mrs. Baerens; she came straight over to him, contemplating him in silence.

Then she said, "Your arm, General Ople," and she made one circuit of the lawn with him, barely speaking.

At her request he conducted her to her carriage. He took a seat beside her, obediently. He felt that he was being sketched, and comported himself like a child's flat man, that jumps at the pulling of a string.

"Where have you left your girl, general?" Before he could rally his wits to answer the question, he was asked:

"And what have you done with your necktie and collar?"

He touched his throat.

"I am rather nervous to-day; I forgot, Elizabeth," he said, sending his fingers in a dotting run of wonderment round his neck.

Lady Camper smiled with a triumphing humor on her close-drawn lips.

The verified absence of necktie and collar seemed to be choking him.

"Never mind, you have been abroad without them," said Lady Camper, "and that is a victory for me. And you thought of Elizabeth first when I drew your attention to it, and that is a victory for you. It is a very great victory. Pray do not be dismayed, general. You have a handsome campaigning air. And no apologies, if you please; I like you well enough as you are. There is my hand."

General Ople understood her last remark. He pressed the lady's hand in silence very nervously.

"But do not shrug your head into your shoulders as if there were any possibility of concealing the thunderingly evident," said Lady Camper, electrifying him what with her cordial squeeze, her kind eyes, and her singular language. "You have omitted the collar. Well? The collar is the fatal finishing touch in men's dress; it would make Apollo look *bourgeois*."

Her hand was in his; and watching the play of her features, a spark entered General Ople's brain, causing him, in forgetfulness of collar and caricatures, to ejaculate:

"Seventy? Did your ladyship say seventy? Utterly impossible! You trifled with me."

"We will talk when we are free of this accompaniment of carriage-wheels, general," said Lady Camper.

"I will beg permission to go and fetch Elizabeth, madame."

"Rightly thought of. Fetch her in my carriage. And, by the way, Mrs. Baerens was my old music-mistress, and is, I think, one year older than I. She can tell you on which side of seventy I am."

"I shall not require to ask, my lady," he said, sighing.

"Then we will send the carriage for Elizabeth, and have it out together at once. I am impatient; yes, general, impatient—for what? forgiveness."

"Of me, my lady?" The general breathed profoundly.

"Of whom else? Do you know what it is? I don't think you do. You English have the smallest experience of humanity. I mean this: to strike so hard that, in the end, you soften your heart to the victim. Well, that is my weakness. And we of our blood put no restraint on the blows we strike, so we are always overdoing it."

General Ople assisted Lady Camper to alight from the carriage, which was forthwith dispatched for Elizabeth.

He prepared to listen to her with a disconnected smile of acute attentiveness.

She had changed. She spoke of money. Ten thousand pounds must be settled on his daughter. "And now," said she, "you will remember that you are wanting a collar."

He acquiesced. He craved permission to retire for ten minutes.

"Simplest of men! What will cover you?" she exclaimed, and peremptorily bidding him sit down in the drawing-room she took one of the famous pair of pistols in her hand, and said: "If I put myself in a similar position, and make myself décolletée, too, will that satisfy you? You see these murderous weapons? Well, I am a coward. I dread fire-arms. They are hid there to impose on the world, and I believe they do. They have imposed on you. Now you would never think of pretending to a moral quality you do not possess. But, silly, simple man that you are! you can give yourself the airs of wealth, buy horses to conceal your nakedness, and when you are taken upon the standard of your apparent income, you would rather seem to be beating a miserly retreat than behave frankly and honestly. I have a little overstated it, but I am near the mark."

"Your ladyship wanting courage!" cried the general.

"Refresh yourself by meditating on it," said she. "And to prove it to you, I was glad to take this house when I knew I was to have a gallant gentleman for a neighbor. No visitors will be admitted, General Ople, so you are bare-throated only to me—sit quietly. One day you speculated on the paint on my cheeks for the space of a minute and a half—I had said that I freckled easily. Your look signified that you really could not detect a single freckle for the paint. I forgave you, or I did not. But when I found you, on closer acquaintance, as indifferent to your daughter's happiness as you had been to her reputation—"

"My daughter! her reputation! her happiness!"

General Ople raised his eyes under a wave, half uttering the outcries.

"So indifferent to her reputation that you allowed a young man to talk with her over the wall, and meet her by appointment: so reckless of the girl's happiness that when I tried to bring you to a treaty on her behalf, you could not be dragged from thinking of yourself and your own affairs. When I found that, perhaps I was predisposed to give you some of what my sisters used to call my spice. You would not honestly state the proportions of your income, and you affected to be faithful to the woman of seventy. Most preposterous! Could any caricature of mine exceed in grotesqueness your sketch of yourself? You are a brave and a generous man all the same; and I suspect it is more hoodwinking than egotism—or extreme egotism—that blinds you. A certain amount you must have to be a man. You did not like my paint, still less did you like my sincerity; you were annoyed by my corrections of your habits of speech; you were horrified by the age of seventy, and you were credulous. General Ople, listen to me, and remember that you have no collar on! you were credulous of my statement of my great age, or you chose to be so, or chose to seem so because I had brushed your cat's coat against the fur. And then, full of yourself, not thinking of Elizabeth, but to withdraw in the chivalrous attitude of the man true to his word to the old woman, only stickling to bring a certain independence to the common stock, because—I quote you, and you have no collar on, mind—

'you could not be at your wife's mercy,' you broke from your proposal on the money question. Where was your consideration for Elizabeth then? Well, general, you were fond of thinking of yourself, and I thought I would assist you. I gave you plenty of subject matter. I will not say I meant to work a homeopathic cure. But if I drive you to forget your collar is it or is it not a triumph? No," added Lady Camper, "it is no triumph for me; but it is one for you, if you like to make the most of it. Your fault has been to quit active service, general, and love your ease too well. It is the fault of your countrymen. You must get a militia regiment, or inspectorship of militia. You are ten times the man in exercise. Why, do you mean to tell me that you would have cared for those drawings of mine when marching?"

"I think so—I say I think so," remarked the general, seriously.

"I doubt it," said she. "But to the point: here comes Elizabeth. If you have not much money to spare for her, according to your prudent calculation, reflect how this money has enfeebled you and reduced you to the level of the people round about us here—who are what? Inhabitants of gentlemanly residences—yes! But what kind of creatures? They have no mental standard, no moral aim, no native chivalry. You were rapidly becoming one of them, only, fortunately for you, you were sensitive to ridicule."

"Elizabeth shall have half my money settled on her," said the general; "though I fear it is not much. And if I can find occupation, my lady—"

"Something worthier than that," said Lady Camper, penciling outlines rapidly on the margin of a book, and he saw himself lashing a pony; "or that," and he was plucking at a cabbage; "or that," and he was bowing to three petticoated posts.

"The likeness is exact," General Ople groaned.

"So you may suppose I have studied you," said she. "But there is no real likeness. Slight exaggerations do more harm to truth than reckless violations of it. You would not have cared one bit for a caricature if you had not nursed the absurd idea of being one of our conquerors. It is the very tragedy of modesty for a man like you to have such notions, my poor dear good friend. The modest are the most easily intoxicated when they sip at vanity. And reflect whether you have not been intoxicated; for these young people have been wretched, and you have not observed it, though one of them was living with you, and is the child you love. There, I have done. Pray show a good face to Elizabeth."

The general obeyed as well as he could. He felt very like a sheep that has come from a shearing, and when released he wished to run away. But hardly had he escaped before he had a desire for the renewal of the operation. "She sees me through, she sees me through," he was heard saying to himself; and in the end he taught himself to say it with a secret exultation, for as it was on her part an extraordinary piece of insight to see him through, it struck him that in acknowledging the truth of it he made a discovery of new powers in human nature.

General Ople studied Lady Camper diligently for fresh proofs of her penetration of the mysteries in his bosom, by which means, as it happened that she was diligently observing the two betrothed young ones, he began to watch them likewise, and took pleasure in the sight. Their meetings, their partings, their rides out and home, furnished him themes of converse. He soon had enough to talk of, and previously, as he remembered, he had never sustained a conversation of any length with composure and the beneficent sense of fullness. Five thousand pounds, to which sum Lady Camper reduced her stipulation for Elizabeth's dowry, he signed over to his dear girl gladly, and came out with the confession to her ladyship that a well-invested twelve thousand comprised his fortune. She shrugged; she had left off pulling him this way and that, so his chains were enjoyable; and he said to himself: "If ever she should in the dead of night want a man to defend her!" He mentioned it to Reginald, who had been the repository of Elizabeth's lamentations about her father being left alone, forsaken, and the young man conceived a scheme for causing his aunt's great bell to be rung at midnight, which would certainly have led to a dramatic issue and the happy re-establishment of our masculine ascendency at the close of this history. But he forgot it, in his bridegroom's delight, until he was making his miserable official speech at the wedding-breakfast, and set Elizabeth winking over a tear. As she stood in the hall ready to depart, a great van was observed in the road at the gates of Douro Lodge; and this the men in custody declared to contain the goods and knickknacks of the people who had taken the house furnished for a year, and were coming in that very afternoon.

"I remember—I say now I remember—I had a notice," the general said, cheerily, to his troubled daughter.

"But where are you to go, papa?" the poor girl cried, close on sobbing.

"I shall get employment of some sort," said he. "I was saying I want it, I need it, I require it."

"You are saying three times what once would have sufficed for," said Lady Camper, and she asked him a few questions, frowned with a smile, and offered him a lodgment in his neighbor's house.

"Really, dearest Aunt Angela?" said Elizabeth.

"What else can I do, child? I have, it seems, driven him out of a gentlemanly residence, and I must give him a lady-like one. True, I would rather have had him at call, but as I have always wished for a policeman in the house, I may as well be satisfied with a soldier."

"But if you lose your character, my lady?" said Reginald.

"Then I must look to the general to restore it."

General Ople immediately bowed his head over Lady Camper's fingers.

"An odd thing to happen to a woman of forty-one!" she said to her great people; and they submitted with the best grace in the world, while the general's ears tingled till he felt younger than Reginald. This—his reflections ran, or it would be more correct to say waltzed—this is the result of painting! that you can believe a woman to be any age when her cheeks are tinted!

As for Lady Camper, she had been floated accidentally over the ridicule of the bruit of a marriage at a time of life as terrible to her as her fiction of seventy had been to General Ople; she resigned herself to let things go with the tide. She had not been blissful in her first marriage, she had abandoned the chase of an ideal man, and she had found one who was tunable so as not to offend her ears—likely ever to be a fund of amusement for her humor—good, impressible, and, above all, very picturesque. There is the secret of her and of how it came to pass that a simple man and a complex woman fell to union after the strangest division.

Nightmare Abbey

1818

THOMAS LOVE PEACOCK

PEACOCK's whole literary output consists of short novels. One would expect him therefore to have explored the form to the full. This is not the case, for being a civil servant, he remained an amateur, faithful to the same simple formula, an arrangement of extreme viewpoints which give their name to the characters and are whipped up into a philosophical omelette with some fines herbes of romance and gallantry. There are Welsh omelettes, Thames valley omelettes, New Forest omelettes but the ingredients and the process remain the same, Peacock's satirical mind is the whisk and a country house the copper frying pan. Nightmare Abbey is a Lincolnshire omelette flavoured with Gothic and marsh gas but the lightest and crispest of them all, if a shade soggy in the middle. Much has been written about Peacock; his admirers, though few, are vocal. But his fame has been faintly tarnished by the uncritical enthusiasm of some rather deadly old people; garrulous lawyers, crusted tories, dons and high bureaucrats, for he was very much one of them himself, in his old age.

But he is more than that. With Landor, Lamb and the youthful De Quincey of the Opium Eater he is one of the custodians of good prose; prose of a dry and sparkling freshness which, although it never achieves the heights of the other three, never falters, and seems to spring from an innate sense of proportion operating on a benign and incessantly rejuvenated imagination. Although he was born in 1785 it is a mistake to regard Peacock as exemplifying a delayed reaction of Eighteenth-Century common sense to the evils and humbug of romanticism. Romanticism formed him, but he soon removed his small capital of genius from the splendid ill-starred undertaking and reinvested it in long life and talent. In his novels there is always one resolute opponent of romanticism (generally in holy orders) but he is no more than the bassoon in the orchestra. By remaining a romantic Peacock would have accomplished nothing, while by withdrawing he was able to harness his romantic energy to a small but useful engine; a happy childhood and a classical education appear to triumph over the romantic rebellion against the father and all his works but, without the romantic impulse to revolt, he would have accomplished nothing. Diffused romanticism, epicurean common sense, metallic wit combine in Peacock's novels to depict the good life—a warm and happy place where we would all like to be. That is his permanent attraction.

Son of a glass merchant, Thomas Love Peacock was brought up by his mother and her father, a retired sea captain. He lived with his mother all his life; she remained in his home after his marriage and he read her every manuscript. She was a reader of history and an admirer of Gibbon and from her he acquired the permanent internal serenity of the well-loved only child. "I passed many of my best years with my mother, taking more pleasure in reading than society." Aged twenty-two, he fell in love with his neighbour Fanny Falkner and became engaged to her. The engagement was broken off owing to a misunderstanding; she married another and died the following year. In 1812, at the age of twenty-seven, he met Shelley who was seven years his junior. The friendship lasted for the remainder of the poet's life, during which he allowed Peacock a hundred pounds a year, and made him his executor with a legacy of two thousand pounds. Peacock taught Shelley to read the classics while Shelley kept alive the romantic spark and prevented his fossilising into bureaucracy before he had produced anything. The first two novels, Headlong Hall and Melincourt were written in 1815 and 1817, the latter containing a somewhat idealised portrait of Shelley. In 1818 Shelley went to Italy and Peacock consoled himself by writing Nightmare Abbey, making friendly fun of Shelley as Scythrop, Coleridge as Flosky and Byron as Cypress. Byron enjoyed the tale and sent him a rosebud which is still preserved, while Shelley wrote, "I think Scythrop a character admirably conceived and executed; and I know not how to praise sufficiently the lightness and chastity of the language." Peacock had noticed how the fashionable melancholy of the romantics was seldom allowed to interfere with the various enjoyments dependent on a private income and he rammed home the point. But he well knew that, even so, Nightmare Abbey would be insupportable without them and so would sensible Mr. Hilary and the agreeable Reverend Larynx, the platitudinous chorus to this drama of bright affected young people. His characters seldom develop; they blow the same phrase on their flutes at the right moment as the jolly conductor waves his baton and then are silent, awaiting the time to repeat it in a slightly different setting. Only Scythrop has a certain faint reality and then only in his relationship with his father. Anything more might perhaps upset this whirling farce (a trifle slow when the girls are away for too long), but redeemed by much exquisite satire where the prose rhythm alone conveys the hint of parody.

"Mr. Cypress: 'I have no hope for myself or for others. Our life is a false nature; it is not in the harmony of things; it is an all-blasting upas, whose root is earth, and whose leaves are the skies which rain their poison dews upon mankind. We wither from our youth; we gasp with unslaked thirst for unattainable goods; lured from the first to the last by phantoms—love, fame, ambition, avarice—all idle, and all ill—one meteor of many names, that vanishes in the smoke of death.' Mr. Flosky: 'A most delightful speech, Mr. Cypress, a most amiable and instructive philosophy.' "

Nightmare Abbey

THOMAS LOVE PEACOCK

Chapter I

NIGHTMARE ABBEY, a venerable family-mansion, in a highly picturesque state of semi-dilapidation, pleasantly situated on a strip of dry land between the sea and the fens at the verge of the county of Lincoln, had the honour to be the seat of Christopher Glowry, Esquire. This gentleman was naturally of an atrabilarious temperament, and much troubled with those phantoms of indigestion which are commonly called *blue devils*. He had been deceived in an early friendship: he had been crossed in love; and had offered his hand, from pique, to a lady, who accepted it from interest, and who, in so doing, violently tore asunder the bonds of a tried and youthful attachment. Her vanity was gratified by being the mistress of a very extensive, if not very lively establishment; but all the springs of her sympathies were frozen. Riches she possessed, but that which enriches them, the participation of affection, was wanting. All that they could purchase for her became indifferent to her, because that which they could not purchase, and which was more valuable than themselves, she had, for their sake, thrown away. She discovered, when it was too late, that she had mistaken the means for the end—that riches, rightly used, are instruments of happiness, but are not in themselves happiness. In this wilful blight of her affections, she found them valueless as means: they had been the end to which she had immolated all her affections, and were now the only end that remained to her.

599

She did not confess this to herself as a principle of action, but it operated through the medium of unconscious self-deception, and terminated in inveterate avarice. She laid on external things the blame of her mind's internal disorder, and thus became by degrees an accomplished scold. She often went her daily rounds through a series of deserted apartments, every creature in the house vanishing at the creak of her shoe, much more at the sound of her voice, to which the nature of things affords no simile; for, as far as the voice of woman, when attuned by gentleness and love, transcends all other sounds in harmony, so far does it surpass all others in discord when stretched into unnatural shrillness by anger and impatience.

Mr. Glowry used to say that his house was no better than a spacious kennel, for every one in it led the life of a dog. Disappointed both in love and in friendship, and looking upon human learning as vanity, he had come to a conclusion that there was but one good thing in the world, *videlicet*, a good dinner; and this his parsimonious lady seldom suffered him to enjoy: but one morning, like Sir Leoline, in *Christabel*, "he woke and found his lady dead," and remained a very consolate widower, with one small child.

This only son and heir Mr. Glowry had christened Scythrop, from the name of a maternal ancestor, who had hanged himself one rainy day in a fit of *tædium vitæ*, and had been eulogized by a coroner's jury in the comprehensive phrase of *felo de se*; on which account Mr. Glowry held his memory in high honour, and made a punch-bowl of his skull.

When Scythrop grew up, he was sent, as usual, to a public school, where a little learning was painfully beaten into him, and thence to the University, where it was carefully taken out of him; and he was sent home, like a well-threshed ear of corn, with nothing in his head: having finished his education to the high satisfaction of the master and fellows of his college, who had, in testimony of their approbation, presented him with a silver fish-slice, on which his name figured at the head of a laudatory inscription in some semi-barbarous dialect of Anglo-Saxonized Latin.

His fellow-students, however, who drove tandem and random in great perfection, and were connoisseurs in good inns, had taught him to drink deep ere he departed. He had passed much of his time with these choice spirits, and had seen the rays of the midnight lamp tremble on many a lengthening file of empty bottles. He passed his vacations sometimes at Nightmare Abbey, sometimes in London, at the house of his uncle, Mr. Hilary, a very cheerful and elastic gentleman, who had married the sister of the melancholy Mr. Glowry. The company that frequented his house was the gayest of the gay. Scythrop danced with the ladies and drank with the gentlemen, and was pronounced by both a very accomplished, charming fellow and an honour to the University.

At the house of Mr. Hilary, Scythrop first saw the beautiful Miss Emily Girouette. He fell in love; which is nothing new. He was favourably received; which is nothing strange. Mr. Glowry and Mr. Girouette had a meeting on the occasion, and quarrelled about the terms of the bargain; which is neither new nor strange. The lovers were torn asunder, weeping and vowing everlasting constancy; and, in three weeks after this tragical event, the lady was led a smiling bride to the altar, by the Honourable Mr. Lackwit; which is neither strange nor new.

Scythrop received this intelligence at Nightmare Abbey, and was half distracted on the occasion. It was his first disappointment, and preyed deeply on his sensitive spirit. His father, to comfort him, read him a Commentary on Ecclesiastes, which he had himself composed, and which demonstrated incontrovertibly that all is vanity. He insisted particularly on the text, "One man among a thousand have I found, but a woman amongst all those have I not found."

"How would he expect it," said Scythrop, "when the whole thousand were locked up in his seraglio? His experience is no precedent for a free state of society like that in which we live."

"Locked up or at large," said Mr. Glowry, "the result is the same: their minds are always locked up, and vanity and interest keep the key. I speak feelingly, Scythrop."

"I am sorry for it, sir," said Scythrop. "But how is it that their minds are locked up? The fault is in their artificial education, which studiously models them into mere musical dolls, to be set out for sale in the great toy-shop of society."

"To be sure," said Mr. Glowry, "their education is not so well finished as yours has been; and your idea of a musical doll is good. I bought one myself, but it was confoundedly out of tune; but, whatever be the cause, Scythrop, the effect is certainly this, that one is pretty nearly as good as another, as far as any judgment can be formed of them before marriage. It is only after marriage that they show their true qualities, as I know by bitter experience. Marriage is, therefore, a lottery, and the less choice and selection a man bestows on his ticket the better; for if he has incurred considerable pains and expense to obtain a lucky number, and his lucky number proves a blank, he experiences not a simple, but a complicated disappointment; the loss of labour and money being superadded to the disappointment of drawing a blank, which, constituting simply and entirely the grievance of him who has chosen his ticket at random, is, from its simplicity, the more endurable." This very excellent reasoning was thrown away upon Scythrop, who retired to his tower as dismal and disconsolate as before.

The tower which Scythrop inhabited stood at the south-eastern angle of the Abbey; and, on the southern side, the foot of the tower opened on a terrace, which was called the garden, though nothing grew on it but ivy, and a few amphibious weeds. The south-western tower, which was ruinous and full of owls, might, with equal propriety, have been called the aviary. This terrace or garden, or terrace-garden, or garden-terrace (the reader may name it ad libitum), took in an oblique view of the open sea, and fronted a long tract of level sea-coast, and a fine monotony of fens and windmills.

The reader will judge, from what we have said, that this building was a sort of castellated abbey; and it will, probably, occur to him to inquire if it had been one of the strongholds of the ancient church militant. Whether this was the case, or how far it had been indebted to the taste of Mr. Glowry's ancestors for any transmutations from its original taste, are, unfortunately, circumstances not within the pale of our knowledge.

The north-western tower contained the apartments of Mr. Glowry. The moat at its base, and the fens beyond, comprised the whole of his prospect. The moat surrounded the Abbey, and was in immediate contact with the walls on every side but the south.

The north-eastern tower was appropriated to the domestics, whom Mr. Glowry always chose by one of two criterions,—a long face or a dismal name. His butler was Raven; his steward was Crow; his valet was Skellet. Mr. Glowry maintained that the valet was of French extraction, and that his name was Squelette. His grooms were Mattocks and Graves. On one occasion, being in want of a footman, he received a letter from a person signing himself Diggory Deathshead, and lost no time in securing this acquisition; but on Diggory's arrival, Mr. Glowry was horror-struck by the sight of a round ruddy face, and a pair of laughing eyes. Deathshead was always grinning,—not a ghastly smile, but the grin of a comic mask; and disturbed the echoes of the hall with so much unhallowed laughter, that Mr. Glowry gave him his discharge. Diggory, however, had stayed long enough to make conquests of all the old gentleman's maids, and left him a flourishing colony of young Deathsheads to join chorus with the owls, that had before been the exclusive choristers of Nightmare Abbey.

The main body of the building was divided into rooms of state, spacious apartments for feasting, and numerous bedrooms for visitors, who, however, were few and far between.

Family interests compelled Mr. Glowry to receive occasional visits from Mr. and Mrs. Hilary, who paid them from the same motive; and, as the lively gentleman on these occasions found few conductors for his exuberant gaiety, he became like a double-charged electric jar, which often exploded in some burst of outrageous merriment to the signal discomposure of Mr. Glowry's nerves.

Another occasional visitor, much more to Mr. Glowry's taste, was Mr. Flosky,[1] a very lachrymose and morbid gentleman, of some note in the literary world, but in his own estimation of much more merit than name. The part of his character which recommended him to Mr. Glowry, was his very fine sense of the grim and the tearful. No one could relate a dismal story with so many minutiæ of supererogatory wretchedness. No one could call up a *rawhead and bloody bones* with so many adjuncts and circumstances of ghastliness. Mystery was his mental element. He lived in the midst of that visionary world in which nothing is but what is not. He dreamed with his eyes open, and saw ghosts dancing round him at noontide. He had been in his youth an enthusiast for liberty, and had hailed the dawn of the French Revolution as the promise of a day that was to banish war and slavery, and every form of vice and misery, from the face of the earth. Because all this was not done, he deduced that nothing was done; and from this deduction,

[1] A *corruption* of Filosky, quasi φιλοσκιος, a lover, or sector, of shadows.

according to his system of logic, he drew a conclusion that worse than nothing was done; that the overthrow of the feudal fortresses of tyranny and superstition was the greatest calamity that had ever befallen mankind; and that their only hope now was to rake the rubbish together, and rebuild it without any of those loopholes by which the light had originally crept in. To qualify himself for a coadjustor in this laudable task, he plunged into the central opacity of Kantian metaphysics, and lay *perdu* several years in transcendental darkness, till the common daylight of common sense became intolerable to his eyes. He called the sun an *ignis fatuus*; and exhorted all who would listen to his friendly voice, which were about as many as called "God save King Richard," to shelter themselves, from its delusive radiance in the obscure haunt of Old Philosophy. This word Old had great charms for him. The good old times were always on his lips; meaning the days when polemic theology was in its prime, and rival prelates beat the drum ecclesiastic with Herculean vigour, till the one wound up his series of syllogisms with the very orthodox conclusion of roasting the other.

But the dearest friend of Mr. Glowry, and his most welcome guest, was Mr. Toobad, the Manichæan Millenarian. The twelfth verse of the twelfth chapter of Revelations was always in his mouth: "Woe to the inhabiters of the earth and of the sea! for the devil is come among you, having great wrath, because he knoweth that he hath but a short time." He maintained that the supreme dominion of the world was, for wise purposes, given over for a while to the Evil Principle; and that this precise period of time, commonly called the enlightened age, was the point of his plenitude of power. He used to add that by-and-by he would be cast down, and a high and happy order of things succeed; but he never omitted the saving clause, "Not in our time": which last words were always echoed in doleful response by the sympathetic Mr. Glowry.

Another and very frequent visitor, was the Reverend Mr. Larynx, the vicar of Cladyke, a village about ten miles distant;—a good-natured accommodating divine, who was always most obligingly ready to take a dinner and a bed at the house of any country gentleman in distress for a companion. Nothing came amiss to him,— a game at billiards, at chess, at draughts, at backgammon, at piquet, or at all-fours in a *tête-à-tête*,—or any game on the cards, round, square, or triangular, in a party of any number exceeding two. He would even dance among friends, rather than that a lady, even if she were on the wrong side of thirty, should sit still for want of a partner. For a ride, a walk, or a sail, in the morning,—a song after dinner, a ghost story after supper,—a bottle of port with the squire, or a cup of green tea with his lady,—for all or any of these, or for anything else that was agreeable to any one else, consistently with the dye of his coat, the Reverend Mr. Larynx was at all times equally ready. When at Nightmare Abbey, he would condole with Mr. Glowry,—drink Madeira with Scythrop,—crack jokes with Mr. Hilary,—hand Mrs. Hilary to the piano, take charge of her fan and gloves, and turn over her music with surprising dexterity,— quote Revelations with Mr. Toobad,—and lament the good old times of feudal darkness with the transcendental Mr. Flosky.

Chapter II

SHORTLY AFTER THE disastrous termination of Scythrop's passion for Miss Emily Girouette, Mr. Glowry found himself, much against his will, involved in a lawsuit, which compelled him to dance attendance on the High Court of Chancery. Scythrop was left alone at Nightmare Abbey. He was a burnt child, and dreaded the fire of female eyes. He wandered about the ample pile, or along the garden terrace, with "his cogitative faculties immersed in cogi-bundity of cogitation." The terrace terminated at the south-western tower, which, as we have said, was ruinous and full of owls. Here would Scythrop take his evening seat, on a fallen fragment of mossy stone, with his back resting against the ruined wall,—a thick canopy of ivy, with an owl in it, over his head,—and the *Sorrows of Werter* in his hand. He had some taste for romance reading before he went to the University, where, we must confess, in justice to his college, he was cured of the love of reading in all its shapes; and the cure would have been radical, if disappointment in love, and total solitude, had not conspired to bring on a relapse. He began to devour romances and German tragedies, and, by the recommendation of Mr. Flosky, to pore over ponderous tomes of transcendental philosophy, which reconciled him to the labour of studying them by their mystical jargon and necromantic imagery.

In the congenial solitude of Nightmare Abbey, the distempered ideas of metaphysical romance and romantic metaphysics had ample time and space to germinate into a fertile crop of chimeras, which rapidly shot up into vigorous and abundant vegetation.

He now became troubled with the *passion for reforming the world*. He built many castles in the air, and peopled them with secret tribunals, and bands of illuminati, who were always the imaginary instruments of his projected regeneration of the human species. As he intended to institute a perfect republic, he invested himself with absolute sovereignty over these mystical dispensers of liberty. He slept with Horrid Mysteries under his pillow, and dreamed of venerable eleutherarchs and ghastly confederates holding midnight conventions in subterranean caves. He passed whole mornings in his study, immersed in gloomy reverie, stalking about the room in his night-cap, which he pulled over his eyes like a cowl, and folding his striped calico dressing-gown about him like the mantle of a conspirator.

"Action," thus he soliloquized, "is the result of opinion, and to new-model opinion would be to new-model society. Knowledge is power; it is in the hands of a few, who employ it to mislead the many, for their own selfish purposes of aggrandisement and appropriation. What if it were in the hands of a few who should employ it to lead the many? What if it were universal, and the multitude were enlightened? No. The many must be always in leading-strings; but let them have wise and honest conductors. A few to think, and many to act; that is the only basis of perfect society. So thought the ancient philosophers: they had their esoterical and exoterical doctrines. So thinks the sublime Kant, who delivers his oracles in language which none but the initiated can comprehend. Such were the views of those secret associations of illuminati, which were the terror of superstition and tyranny, and which, carefully selecting wisdom and genius from the great wilderness of society, as the bee selects honey from the flowers of the thorn and the nettle, bound all human excellence in a chain, which, if it had not been prematurely broken, would have commanded opinion, and regenerated the world."

Scythrop proceeded to meditate on the practicability of reviving a confederation of regenerators. To get a clear view of his own ideas, and to feel the pulse of the wisdom and genius of the age, he wrote and published a treatise, in which his meanings were carefully wrapt up in the monk's hood of transcendental technology, but filled with hints of matter deep and dangerous, which he thought would set the whole nation in a ferment; and he awaited the result in awful expectation, as a miner who has fired a train awaits the explosion of a rock. However, he listened and heard nothing; for the explosion, if any ensued, was not sufficiently loud to shake a single leaf of the ivy on the towers of Nightmare Abbey; and some months afterwards he received a letter from his bookseller, informing him that only seven copies had been sold, and concluding with a polite request for the balance.

Scythrop did not despair. "Seven copies," he thought, "have been sold. Seven is a mystical number, and the omen is good. Let me find the seven purchasers of my seven copies, and they shall be the seven golden candlesticks with which I will illuminate the world."

Scythrop had a certain portion of mechanical genius, which his romantic projects tended to develop. He constructed models of cells and recesses, sliding panels and secret passages, that would have baffled the skill of the Parisian police. He took the opportunity of his father's absence to smuggle a dumb carpenter into the Abbey, and between them they gave reality to one of these models in Scythrop's tower. Scythrop foresaw that a great leader of human regeneration would be involved in fearful dilemmas, and determined, for the benefit of mankind in general, to adopt all possible precautions for the preservation of himself.

The servants, even the women, had been tutored into silence. Profound stillness reigned throughout and around the Abbey, except when the occasional shutting of a door would peal in long reverberations through the galleries, or the heavy tread of the pensive butler would wake the hollow echoes of the hall. Scythrop stalked about like the grand inquisitor, and the servants flitted past him like familiars. In his evening meditations on the terrace, under the ivy of the ruined tower, the only sounds that came to his ear were the rustling of the wind in the ivy, the plaintive voices of the feathered choristers, the owls, the occasional striking of the Abbey clock, and the monotonous dash of the sea on its low and level shore. In the meantime, he drank Madeira, and laid deep schemes for a thorough repair of the crazy fabric of human nature.

Chapter III

MR. GLOWRY RETURNED from London with the loss of his lawsuit. Justice was with him, but the law was against him. He found Scythrop in a mood most sympathetically tragic; and they vied with each other in enlivening their cups by lamenting the depravity of this degenerate age, and occasionally interspersing divers grim jokes about graves, worms, and epitaphs. Mr. Glowry's friends, whom we have mentioned in the first chapter, availed themselves of his return to pay him a simultaneous visit. At the same time arrived Scythrop's friend and fellow-collegian, the Honourable Mr. Listless. Mr. Glowry had discovered this fashionable young gentleman in London, "stretched on the rack of a too easy chair," and devoured with a gloomy and misanthropical *nil curo*, and had pressed him so earnestly to take the benefit of the pure country air at Nightmare Abbey, that Mr. Listless, finding it would give him more trouble to refuse than to comply, summoned his French valet, Fatout, and told him he was going to Lincolnshire. On this simple hint, Fatout went to work, and the imperials were packed, and the post-chariot was at the door, without the Honourable Mr. Listless having said or thought another syllable on the subject.

Mr. and Mrs. Hilary brought with them an orphan niece, a daughter of Mr. Glowry's youngest sister, who had made a runaway love-match with an Irish officer. The lady's fortune disappeared in the first year: love, by a natural consequence, disappeared in the second: the Irishman himself, by a still more natural consequence, disappeared in the third. Mr. Glowry had allowed his sister an annuity, and she had lived in retirement with her only daughter, whom, at her death, which had recently happened, she commended to the care of Mrs. Hilary.

Miss Marionetta Celestina O'Carroll was a very blooming and accomplished young lady. Being a compound of the *Allegro Vivace* of the O'Carrolls, and of the *Andante Doloroso* of the Glowries, she exhibited in her own character all the diversities of an April sky. Her hair was light-brown; her eyes hazel, and sparkling with a mild but fluctuating light; her features regular; her lips full, and of equal size; and her person surpassingly graceful. She was a proficient in music. Her conversation was sprightly, but always on subjects light in their nature and limited in their interest: for moral sympathies, in any general sense, had no place in her mind. She had some coquetry, and more caprice, liking and disliking almost in the same moment; pursuing an object with earnestness while it seemed unattainable, and rejecting it when in her power as not worth the trouble of possession.

Whether she was touched with a *penchant* for her cousin Scythrop, or was merely curious to see what effect the tender passion would have on so *outré* a person, she had not been three days in the Abbey before she threw out all the lures of her beauty and accomplishments to make a prize of his heart. Scythrop proved an easy conquest. The image of Miss Emily Girouette was already sufficiently dimmed by the power of philosophy and the exercise of reason: for to these influences, or to any influence but the true one, are usually ascribed the mental cures performed by the great physician Time. Scythrop's romantic dreams had indeed given him many *pure anticipated cognitions* of combinations of beauty and intelligence, which, he had some misgivings, were not exactly realized in his cousin Marionetta; but, in spite of these misgivings, he soon became distractedly in love; which, when the young lady clearly perceived, she altered her tactics, and assumed as much coldness and reserve as she had before shown ardent and ingenuous attachment. Scythrop was confounded at the sudden change; but, instead of falling at her feet and requesting an explanation, he retreated to his tower, muffled himself in his night-cap, seated himself in the president's chair of his imaginary secret tribunal, summoned Marionetta with all terrible formalities, frightened her out of her wits, disclosed himself, and clasped the beautiful penitent to his bosom.

While he was acting this reverie—in the moment in which the awful president of the secret tribunal was throwing back his cowl and his mantle, and discovering himself to the lovely culprit, as her adoring and magnanimous lover, the door of the study opened, and the real Marionetta appeared.

The motives which had led her to the tower were, a little penitence, a little concern, a little affection, and a little fear as to what the sudden secession of Scythrop, occasioned by her sudden change of manner, might portend. She had tapped several times unheard, and of course unanswered; and at length, timidly and cautiously opening the door, she discovered him standing before a black velvet chair, which was mounted on an old oak table, in the act of throwing open his striped calico dressing gown, and flinging away his night-cap, which is what the French call an imposing attitude.

Each stood a few moments fixed in their respective places—the lady in astonishment, and the gentleman in confusion. Marionetta was the first to break silence. "For heaven's sake," said she, "my dear Scythrop, what is the matter?"

"For heaven's sake, indeed!" said Scythrop, springing from the table; "for your sake, Marionetta, and you are my heaven,—distraction is the matter. I adore you, Marionetta, and your cruelty drives me mad." He threw himself at her knees, devoured her hand with kisses, and breathed a thousand vows in the most passionate language of romance.

Marionetta listened a long time in silence, till her lover had exhausted his eloquence and paused for a reply. She then said, with a very arch look, "I prithee deliver thyself like a man of this world." The levity of this quotation, and of the manner in which it was delivered, jarred so discordantly on the high-wrought enthusiasm of the romantic inamorato, that he sprang upon his feet, and beat his forehead with his clenched fists. The young lady was terrified; and deeming it expedient to soothe him, took one of his hands in hers, placed the other hand on his shoulder, looked up in his face with a winning seriousness, and said, in the tenderest possible tone, "What would you have, Scythrop?"

Scythrop was in heaven again. "What would I have? What but you, Marionetta? You, for the companion of my studies, the partner of my thoughts, the auxiliary of my great designs for the emancipation of mankind."

"I am afraid I should be but a poor auxiliary, Scythrop, what would you have me do?"

"Do as Rosalie does with Carlos, divine Marionetta. Let us each open a vein in the other's arm, mix our blood in a bowl, and drink it as a sacrament of love. Then we shall see visions of transcendental illumination, and soar on the wings of ideas into the space of pure intelligence."

Marionetta could not reply; she had not so strong a stomach as Rosalie, and turned sick at the proposition. She disengaged herself suddenly from Scythrop, sprang through the door of the tower, and fled with precipitation along the corridors. Scythrop pursued her, crying, "Stop, stop, Marionetta—my life, my love!" and was gaining rapidly on her flight, when, at an ill-omened corner, where two corridors ended in an angle, at the head of a staircase, he came into sudden and violent contact with Mr. Toobad, and they both plunged together to the foot of the stairs, like two billiard-balls into one pocket. This gave the young lady time to escape, and enclose herself in her chamber; while Mr. Toobad, rising slowly, and rubbing his knees and shoulders, said, "You see, my dear Scythrop, in this little incident, one of the innumerable proofs of the temporary supremacy of the devil; for what but a systematic design and concurrent contrivance of evil could have made the angles of time and place coincide in our unfortunate persons at the head of this accursed staircase?"

"Nothing else, certainly," said Scythrop: "you are perfectly in the right, Mr. Toobad. Evil, and mischief, and misery, and confusion, and vanity, and vexation of spirit, and death, and disease, and assassination, and war, and poverty, and pestilence, and famine, and avarice, and selfishness, and rancour, and jealousy, and spleen, and malevolence, and the disappointments of philanthropy, and the faithlessness of friendship, and the crosses of love—all prove the accuracy of your views, and the truth of your system; and it is not impossible that the infernal interruption of this fall down stairs may throw a colour of evil on the whole of my future existence."

"My dear boy," said Mr. Toobad, "you have a fine eye for consequences."

So saying, he embraced Scythrop, who retired with a disconsolate step, to dress for dinner; while Mr. Toobad stalked across the hall, repeating, "Woe to the inhabiters of the earth, and of the sea, for the devil is come among you, having great wrath."

Chapter IV

THE FLIGHT OF Marionetta, and the pursuit of Scythrop, had been witnessed by Mr. Glowry, who, in consequence, narrowly observed his son and his niece in the evening; and, concluding from their manner, that there was a better understanding between them than he wished to see, he determined on obtaining the next morning from Scythrop a full and satisfactory explanation. He, therefore, shortly after breakfast, entered Scythrop's tower, with a very grave face, and said, without ceremony or preface, "So, sir, you are in love with your cousin."

Scythrop, with a little hesitation, answered, "Yes, sir."

"That is candid, at least; and she is in love with you?"

"I wish she were, sir."

"You know she is, sir."

"Indeed, sir, I do not."

"But you hope she is."

"I do, from my soul."

"Now that is very provoking, Scythrop, and very disappointing: I could not have supposed that you, Scythrop Glowry, of Nightmare Abbey, would have been infatuated with such a dancing, laughing, singing, thoughtless, careless, merry-hearted thing as Marionetta, in all respects the reverse of you and me. It is very disappointing, Scythrop. And do you know, sir, that Marionetta has no fortune?"

"It is the more reason, sir, that her husband should have one."

"The more reason for her; but not for you. My wife had no fortune, and I had no consolation in my calamity. And do you reflect, sir, what an enormous slice this lawsuit has cut out of our family estate? we who used to be the greatest landed proprietors in Lincolnshire."

"To be sure, sir, we had more acres of fen than any man on this coast: but what are fens to love? What are dykes and windmills to Marionetta?"

"And what, sir, is love to a windmill? Not grist, I am certain: besides, sir, I have made a choice for you. I have made a choice for you, Scythrop. Beauty, genius, accomplishments, and a great fortune into the bargain. Such a lovely, serious creature, in a fine state of high dissatisfaction with the world, and everything in it. Such a delightful surprise I had prepared for you. Sir, I have pledged my honour to the contract—the honor of the Glowrys of Nightmare Abbey: and now, sir, what is to be done?"

"Indeed, sir, I cannot say. I claim, on this occasion, that liberty of action which is the co-natal prerogative of every rational being."

"Liberty of action, sir? There is no such thing as liberty of action. We are all slaves and puppets of a blind and unpathetic necessity."

"Very true, sir; but liberty of action, between individuals, consists in their being differently influenced, or modified, by the same universal necessity; so that the results are unconsentaneous, and their respective necessitated volitions clash and fly off in a tangent."

"Your logic is good sir: but you are aware, too, that one individual may be a medium of adhibiting to another a mode or form of necessity, which may have more or less influence in the production of consentaneity; and therefore, sir, if you do not comply with my wishes in this instance (you have had your own way in everything else), I shall be under the necessity of disinheriting you, though I shall do it with tears in my eyes." Having said these words, he vanished suddenly, in the dread of Scythrop's logic.

Mr. Glowry immediately sought Mrs. Hilary, and communicated to her his views of the case in point. Mrs. Hilary, as the phrase is, was as fond of Marionetta as if she had been her own child: but—there is always a *but* on these occasions—she could do nothing for her in the way of fortune, as she had two hopeful sons, who were finishing their education at Brazen-nose, and who would not like to encounter any diminution of their prospects, when they should be brought out of the house of mental bondage —*i.e.*, the University—to the land flowing with milk and honey— *i.e.*, the west end of London.

Mrs. Hilary hinted to Marionetta that propriety, and delicacy, and decorum, and dignity, etc., etc., etc., would require them to leave the Abbey immediately. Marionetta listened in silent submission, for she knew that her inheritance was passive obedience; but when Scythrop, who had watched the opportunity of Mrs. Hilary's departure, entered, and, without speaking a word, threw himself at her feet in a paroxysm of grief, the young lady, in equal silence and sorrow, threw her arms round his neck and burst into tears. A very tender scene ensued, which the sympathetic susceptibilities of the soft-hearted reader can more accurately imagine than we can delineate. But when Marionetta hinted that she was to leave the Abbey immediately, Scythrop snatched from its repository his ancestor's skull, filled it with Madeira, and presenting himself before Mr. Glowry, threatened to drink off the contents, if Mr. Glowry did not immediately promise that Marionetta should not be taken from the Abbey without her own consent. Mr. Glowry, who took the Madeira to be some deadly brewage, gave the required promise in dismal panic. Scythrop returned to Marionetta with a joyful heart, and drank the Madeira by the way.

Mr. Glowry, during his residence in London, had come to an agreement with his friend, Mr. Toobad, that a match between Scythrop and Mr. Toobad's daughter would be a very desirable occurrence. She was finishing her education in a German convent, but Mr. Toobad described her as being fully impressed with the truth of his Ahrimanic philosophy, and being altogether as gloomy and anti-Thalian a young lady as Mr. Glowry himself could desire for the future mistress of Nightmare Abbey. She had a great fortune in her own right, which was not, as we have seen, without its weight in inducing Mr. Glowry to set his heart upon her as his daughter-in-law that was to be; he was therefore very much disturbed by Scythrop's untoward attachment to Marionetta. He condoled on the occasion with Mr. Toobad; who said that he had been too long accustomed to the intermeddling of the devil in all his affairs to be astonished at this new trace of his cloven claw; but that he hoped to outwit him yet, for he was sure there could be no comparison between his daughter and Marionetta, in the mind of any one who had a proper perception of the fact that, the world being a great theatre of evil, seriousness and solemnity are the characteristics of wisdom, and laughter and merriment make a human being no better than a baboon. Mr. Glowry comforted himself with this view of the subject, and urged Mr. Toobad to expedite his daughter's return from Germany. Mr. Toobad said he was in daily expectation of her arrival in London, and would set off immediately to meet her, that he might lose no time in bringing her to Nightmare Abbey. "Then," he added, "we shall see whether Thalia or Melpomene—whether the Allegra or the Penserosa—will carry off the symbol of victory."

"There can be no doubt," said Mr. Glowry, "which way the scale will incline, or Scythrop is no true scion of the venerable stem of the Glowrys."

Chapter V

MARIONETTA FELT SECURE of Scythrop's heart; and, notwithstanding the difficulties that surrounded her, she could not debar herself
from the pleasure of tormenting her lover, whom she kept in a
perpetual fever. Sometimes she would meet him with the most
unqualified affection: sometimes with the most chilling indifference; rousing him to anger by artificial coldness—softening him
to love by eloquent tenderness—or inflaming him to jealousy by
coquetting with the Honourable Mr. Listless, who seemed, under
her magical influence, to burst into sudden life, like the bud of
the evening primrose. Sometimes she would sit by the piano, and
listen with becoming attention to Scythrop's pathetic remonstrances; but, in the most impassioned part of his oratory, she
would convert all his ideas into a chaos, by striking up some
Rondo Allegro, and saying, "Is it not pretty?" Scythrop would
begin to storm, and she would answer him with,

> "Zitti, zitti, piano, piano,
> Non facciamo confusione."[1]

or some similar facezia, till he would start away from her, and
enclose himself in his tower, in an agony of agitation, vowing to
renounce her, and her whole sex, for ever; and returning to her
presence at the summons of the billet, which she never failed to
send with many expressions of penitence, and promises of amend-
ment. Scythrop's schemes for regenerating the world, and detecting his seven golden candlesticks, went on very slowly in this fever
of his spirit.

Things proceeded in this train for several days; and Mr. Glowry
began to be uneasy at receiving no intelligence from Mr. Toobad;
when one evening the latter rushed into the library, where the
family and the visitors were assembled, vociferating, "The devil is
come among you, having great wrath!" He then drew Mr. Glowry
aside into another apartment, and after remaining some time together, they re-entered the library with faces of great dismay, but

[1] Quiet, quiet, softly, softly; let us have no confusion.

did not condescend to explain to any one the cause of their discomfiture.

The next morning, early, Mr. Toobad departed. Mr. Glowry sighed and groaned all day, and said not a word to any one. Scythrop had quarrelled, as usual, with Marionetta, and was enclosed in his tower, in a fit of morbid sensibility. Marionetta was comforting herself at the piano, with singing the airs of *Nina pazza per amore*; and the Honourable Mr. Listless was listening to the harmony, as he lay supine on the sofa, with a book in his hand, into which he peeped at intervals. The Reverend Mr. Larynx approached the sofa, and proposed a game at billiards.

The Honourable Mr. Listless.—Billiards! Really I should be very happy; but, in my present exhausted state, the exertion is too much for me. I do not know when I have been equal to such an effort. (*He rang the bell for his valet. Fatout entered.*) Fatout, when did I play at billiards last?

Fatout.—De fourteen December de last year, Monsieur. (*Fatout bowed and retired.*)

The Honourable Mr. Listless.—So it was. Seven months ago. You see, Mr. Larynx; you see, sir. My nerves, Miss O'Carroll, my nerves are shattered. I have been advised to try Bath. Some of the faculty recommend Cheltenham. I think of trying both, as the seasons don't clash. The season, you know, Mr. Larynx—the season, Miss O'Carroll—the season is everything.

Marionetta.—And health is something. *N'est-ce pas*, Mr. Larynx?

The Reverend Mr. Larynx.—Most assuredly, Miss O'Carroll. For, however reasoners may dispute about the *summum bonum*, none of them will deny that a very good dinner is a very good thing: and what is a good dinner without a good appetite? and whence is a good appetite but from good health? Now, Cheltenham, Mr. Listless, is famous for good appetites.

The Honourable Mr. Listless.—The best piece of logic I ever heard, Mr. Larynx; the very best I assure you. I have thought very seriously of Cheltenham: very seriously and profoundly. I thought of it—let me see—when did I think of it? (*He rang again, and Fatout re-appeared.*) Fatout, when did I think of going to Cheltenham, and did not go?

Fatout.—De Juillet twenty-von, de last summer, Monsieur. (*Fatout retired.*)

The Honourable Mr. Listless.—So it was. An invaluable fellow that, Mr. Larynx—invaluable, Miss O'Carroll.

Marionetta.—So I should judge, indeed. He seems to serve you as a walking memory, and to be a living chronicle, not of your actions only, but of your thoughts.

The Honourable Mr. Listless.—An excellent definition of the fellow, Miss O'Carroll,—excellent, upon my honour. Ha! ha! he! Heigho! Laughter is pleasant, but the exertion is too much for me.

A parcel was brought in for Mr. Listless; it had been sent express. Fatout was summoned to unpack it; and it proved to contain a new novel, and a new poem, both of which had long been anxiously expected by a whole host of fashionable readers; and the last number of a popular Review, of which the editor and his coadjutors were in high favour at court, and enjoyed ample pensions for their services to church and state. As Fatout left the room, Mr. Flosky entered, and curiously inspected the literary arrivals.

Mr. Flosky.—(*Turning over the leaves.*) "Devilman, a novel." Hm. Hatred—revenge—misanthropy—and quotations from the Bible. Hm. This is the morbid anatomy of black bile.—"Paul Jones, a poem." Hm. I see how it is. Paul Jones, an amiable enthusiast—disappointed in his affections—turns pirate from ennui and magnanimity—cuts various masculine throats, wins various feminine hearts—is hanged at the yard-arm! The catastrophe is very awkward, and very unpoetical.—"The Downing Street Review." Hm. First article—An Ode to the Red Book, by Roderick Sackbut, Esquire. Hm. His own poem reviewed by himself. Hm-m-m.

(*Mr. Flosky proceeded in silence to look over the other articles of the Review; Marionetta inspected the novel, and Mr. Listless the poem.*)

The Reverend Mr. Larynx.—For a young man of fashion and family, Mr. Listless, you seem to be of a very studious turn.

The Honourable Mr. Listless.—Studious! You are pleased to be facetious, Mr. Larynx. I hope you do not suspect me of being studious. I have finished my education. But there are some fashionable books that one must read, because they are ingredients of the talk of the day: otherwise I am no fonder of books than I dare say you yourself are, Mr. Larynx.

The Reverend Mr. Larynx.—Why, sir, I cannot say that I am indeed particularly fond of books; yet neither can I say that I never do read. A tale or a poem, now and then, to a circle of ladies over their work, is no very heterodox employment of the vocal energy. And I must say, for myself, that few men have a more Job-like endurance of the eternally recurring questions and answers that interweave themselves, on these occasions, with the crisis of an adventure, and heighten the distress of a tragedy.

The Honourable Mr. Listless.—And very often make the distress when the author has omitted it.

Marionetta.—I shall try your patience some rainy morning, Mr. Larynx; and Mr. Listless shall recommend us the very newest book, that everybody reads.

The Honourable Mr. Listless.—You shall receive it, Miss O'Carroll, with all the gloss of novelty; fresh as a ripe green-gage in all the downiness of its bloom. A mail-coach copy from Edinburgh, forwarded express from London.

Mr. Flosky.—This rage for novelty is the bane of literature. Except my works and those of my particular friends, nothing is good that is not as old as Jeremy Taylor: and *entre nous*, the best parts of my friends' books were either written or suggested by myself.

The Honourable Mr. Listless.—Sir, I reverence you. But I must say, modern books are very consolatory and congenial to my feelings. There is, as it were, a delightful north-east wind, an intellectual blight breathing through them; a delicious misanthropy and discontent, that demonstrates the nullity of virtue and energy, and puts me in good humour with myself and my sofa.

Mr. Flosky.—Very true, sir. Modern literature is a north-east wind—a blight of the human soul. I take credit to myself for having helped to make it so. The way to produce fine fruit is to blight the flower. You call this a paradox. Marry, so be it. Ponder thereon.

The conversation was interrupted by the re-appearance of Mr. Toobad, covered with mud. He just showed himself at the door, muttered "The devil is come among you!" and vanished. The road which connected Nightmare Abby with the civilized world was artificially raised above the level of the fens, and ran through them in a straight line as far as the eye could reach, with a ditch on each side, of which the water was rendered invisible by the aquatic vegetation that covered the surface. Into one of these ditches the sudden action of a shy horse which took fright at a windmill, had precipitated the travelling chariot of Mr. Toobad, who had been reduced to the necessity of scrambling in dismal plight through

618

the window. One of the wheels was found to be broken; and Mr.
Toobad, leaving the postilion to get the chariot as well as he could
to Claydyke for the purpose of cleaning and repairing, had walked
back to Nightmare Abbey, followed by his servant with the imperial, and repeating all the way his favourite quotation from the
Revelations.

Chapter VI

Mr. Toobad had found his daughter Celinda in London, and
after the first joy of meeting was over, told her he had a husband
ready for her. The young lady replied, very gravely, that she should
take the liberty to choose for herself. Mr. Toobad said he saw the
devil was determined to interfere with all his projects, but he was
resolved on his own part, not to have on his conscience the crime
of passive obedience and non-resistance to Lucifer, and therefore
she should marry the person he had chosen for her. Miss Toobad
replied, *très posément,* she assuredly would not. "Celinda, Celinda,"
said Mr. Toobad, "you most assuredly shall."—"Have I not a fortune in my own right, sir?" said Celinda. "The more is the pity,"
said Mr. Toobad: "but I can find means, miss; I can find means.
There are more ways than one of breaking in obstinate girls." They
parted for the night with the expression of opposite resolutions,
and in the morning the young lady's chamber was found empty,
and what was become of her Mr. Toobad had no clue to conjecture. He continued to investigate town and country in search of
her; visiting and revisiting Nightmare Abby at intervals, to consult
with his friend, Mr. Glowry. Mr. Glowry agreed with Mr. Toobad
that this was a very flagrant instance of filial disobedience and rebellion; and Mr. Toobad declared, that when he discovered the
fugitive, she should find that "the devil was come unto her, having
great wrath."

In the evening, the whole party met, as usual, in the library.
Marionetta sat at the harp; the Honourable Mr. Listless sat by her
and turned over her music, though the exertion was almost too
much for him. The Reverend Mr. Larynx relieved him occasionally in this delightful labour. Scythrop, tormented by the demon

619

Jealousy, sat in the corner biting his lips and fingers. Marionetta looked at him every now and then with a smile of most provoking good humor, which he pretended not to see, and which only the more exasperated his troubled spirit. He took down a volume of Dante, and pretended to be deeply interested in the Purgatorio, though he knew not a word he was reading, as Marionetta was well aware; who, tripping across the room, peeped into his book, and said to him, "I see you are in the middle of Purgatory."—"I am in the middle of hell," said Scythrop furiously. "Are you?" said she; "then come across the room, and I will sing you the finale of *Don Giovanni*."

"Let me alone," said Scythrop. Marionetta looked at him with a deprecating smile, and said, "You unjust, cross creature, you."—"Let me alone," said Scythrop, but much less emphatically than at first, and by no means wishing to be taken at his word. Marionetta left him immediately, and returning to the harp, said, just loud enough for Scythrop to hear—"Did you ever read Dante, Mr. Listless? Scythrop is reading Dante, and is just now in Purgatory."—"And I," said the Honourable Mr. Listless, "am not reading Dante, and am just now in Paradise," bowing to Marionetta.

Marionetta.—You are very gallant, Mr. Listless; and I dare say you are very fond of reading Dante.

The Honourable Mr. Listless.—I don't know how it is, but Dante never came in my way till lately. I never had him in my collection, and if I had had him I should not have read him. But I find he is growing fashionable, and I am afraid I must read him some wet morning.

Marionetta.—No, read him some evening, by all means. Were you ever in love, Mr. Listless?

The Honourable Mr. Listless.—I assure you, Miss O'Carroll, never—till I came to Nightmare Abbey. I dare say it is very pleasant; but it seems to give so much trouble that I fear the exertion would be too much for me.

Marionetta.—Shall I teach you a compendious method of courtship, that will give you no trouble whatever?

The Honourable Mr. Listless.—You will confer on me an inexpressible obligation. I am all impatience to learn it.

Marionetta.—Sit with your back to the lady and read Dante; only be sure to begin in the middle, and turn over three or four pages at once—backwards as well as forwards, and she will immediately perceive that you are desperately in love with her—desperately.

(The Honourable Mr. Listless, sitting between Scythrop and Marionetta, and fixing all his attention on the beautiful speaker, did not observe Scythrop, who was doing as she described).

The Honourable Mr. Listless.—You are pleased to be facetious, Miss O'Carroll. The lady would infallibly conclude that I was the greatest brute in town.

Marionetta.—Far from it. She would say, perhaps, some people have odd methods of showing their affection.

The Honourable Mr. Listless.—But I should think, with submission—

Mr. Flosky.—*(Joining them from another part of the room.)* Did I not hear Mr. Listless observe that Dante is becoming fashionable?

The Honourable Mr. Listless.—I did hazard a remark to that effect, Mr. Flosky, though I speak on such subjects with a consciousness of my own nothingness, in the presence of so great a man as Mr. Flosky. I know not what is the colour of Dante's devils, but as he is certainly becoming fashionable I conclude they are blue; for the blue devils, as it seems to me, Mr. Flosky, constitute the fundamental feature of fashionable literature.

Mr. Flosky.—The blue are, indeed, the staple commodity; but as they will not always be commanded, the black, red, and gray may be admitted as substitutes. Tea, late dinners, and the French Revolution have played the devil, Mr. Listless, and brought the devil into play.

Mr. Toobad (starting up).—Having great wrath.

Mr. Flosky.—This is no play upon words, but the sober sadness of veritable fact.

The Honourable Mr. Listless.—Tea, late dinners, and the French Revolution. I cannot exactly see the connection of ideas.

Mr. Flosky.—I should be sorry if you could; I pity the man who can see the connection of his own ideas. Still more do I pity him, the connection of whose ideas any other person can see. Sir, the great evil is, that there is too much commonplace light in our moral and political literature; and light is a great enemy to mystery, and mystery is a great friend to enthusiasm. Now the enthusiasm for abstract truth is an exceedingly fine thing, as long as the truth, which is the object of the enthusiasm, is so completely abstract as to be altogether out of the reach of the human faculties; and, in that sense, I have myself an enthusiasm for truth, but in no other, for the pleasure of metaphysical investigation lies in the means, not in the end; and if the end could be found, the pleasure of the means would cease. The mind, to be kept in health, must be kept in exercise. The proper exercise of the mind is elaborate reasoning. Analytical reasoning is a base and mechanical process, which takes to pieces and examines, bit by bit, the rude material of knowledge, and extracts therefrom a few hard and obstinate things called facts, everything in the shape of which I cordially hate. By synthetical reasoning, setting up as its goal some unattainable abstraction, like an imaginary quantity in algebra, and commencing its course with taking for granted some two assertions which cannot be proved, from the union of these two assumed truths produces a third assumption, and so on in infinite series, to the unspeakable benefit of the human intellect. The beauty of this process is, that at every step it strikes out into two branches, in a compound ratio of ramification; so that you are perfectly sure of losing your way, and keeping your mind in perfect health, by the perpetual exercise of an interminable quest; and for these reasons I have christened my eldest son Emmanuel Kant Flosky.

The Reverend Mr. Larynx.—Nothing can be more luminous.

The Honourable Mr. Listless.—And what has all that to do with Dante, and the blue devils?

Mr. Hilary.—Not much, I should think, with Dante, but a great deal with the blue devils.

Mr. Flosky.—It is very certain, and much to be rejoiced at, that our literature is hag-ridden. Tea has shattered our nerves; late dinners make us slaves of indigestion; the French Revolution has made us shrink from the name of philosophy, and has destroyed, in the more refined part of the community (of which number I am one), all enthusiasm for political liberty. That part of the reading public which shuns the solid food of reason for the light diet of fiction, requires a perpetual adhibition of sauce piquante to the palate of its depraved imagination. It lived upon ghosts, goblins, and skeletons (I and my friend Mr. Sackbut served up a few of the best), till even the devil himself, though magnified to the size of Mount

622

Athos, became too base, common, and popular for its surfeited appetite. The ghosts have therefore been laid, and the devil has been cast into outer darkness, and now the delight of our spirts is to dwell on all the vices and blackest passions of our nature, tricked out in a masquerade dress of heroism and disappointed benevolence; the whole secret of which lies in forming combinations that contradict all our experience, and affixing the purple shed of some particular virtue to that precise character, in which we should be most certain not to find it in the living world; and making this single virtue not only redeem all the real and manifest vices of the character, but make them actually pass for necessary adjuncts, and indispensable accompaniments and characteristics of the said virtue.

Mr. Toobad.—That is, because the devil is come among us, and finds it for his interest to destroy all our perceptions of the distinctions of right and wrong.

Marionetta.—I do not precisely enter into your meaning, Mr. Flosky, and should be glad if you would make it a little more plain to me.

Mr. Flosky.—One or two examples will do it, Miss O'Carroll. If I were to take all the mean and sordid qualities of a money-dealing Jew, and tack on to them, as with a nail, the quality of extreme benevolence, I should have a very decent hero for a modern novel; and should contribute my quota to the fashionable method of administering a mass of vice, under a thin and unnatural covering of virtue, like a spider wrapt in a bit of gold leaf, and administered as a wholesome pill. On the same principle, if a man knocks me down, and takes my purse and watch by main force, I turn him to account, and set him forth in a tragedy as a dashing young fellow, disinherited for his romantic generosity, and full of a most amiable hatred of the world in general, and his own country in particular, and of a most enlightened and chivalrous affection for himself: then, with the addition of a wild girl to fall in love with him, and a series of adventures in which they break all the Ten Commandments in succession (always, you will observe, for some sublime motive, which must be carefully analyzed in its progress), I have as amiable a pair of tragic characters as ever issued from that new region of the belles lettres, which I have called the Morbid Anatomy of Black Bile, and which is greatly to be admired and rejoiced at, as affording a fine scope for the exhibition of mental power.

Mr. Hilary.—Which is about as well employed as the power of a hothouse would be in forcing up a nettle to the size of an elm. If we go on in this way, we shall have a new art of poetry, of which one of the first rules will be: To remember to forget that there are any such things as sunshine and music in the world.

The Honourable Mr. Listless.—It seems to be the case with us at present, or we should not have interrupted Miss O'Carroll's music with this exceedingly dry conversation.

Mr. Flosky.—I should be most happy if Miss O'Carroll would remind us that there are yet both music and sunshine——

The Honourable Mr. Listless.—In the voice and the smile of beauty. May I entreat the favour of—(*turning over the pages of music.*)

All were silent, and Marionetta sung:—

> Why are thy looks so blank, gray friar?
> Why are thy looks so blue?
> Thou seem'st more pale and lank, gray friar,
> Than thou wast used to do:—
> Say, what has made thee rue?
>
> Thy form was plump, and a light did shine
> In thy round and ruby face,
> Which showed an outward visible sign
> Of an inward spiritual grace:—
> Say, what has changed thy case?
>
> Yet will I tell thee true, gray friar?
> I very well can see,
> That, if thy looks are blue, gray friar,
> 'Tis all for love of me,—
> 'Tis all for love of me.
>
> But breathe not thy vows to me, gray friar,
> Oh! breathe them not, I pray;
> For ill beseems in a reverend friar,
> The love of a mortal may;
> And I needs must say thee nay.

> But, could'st thou think my heart to move
> With that pale and silent scowl?
> Know, he who would win a maiden's love,
> Whether clad in cap or cowl,
> Must be more of a lark than an owl.

Scythrop immediately replaced Dante on the shelf, and joined the circle round the beautiful singer. Marionetta gave him a smile of approbation that fully restored his complacency, and they continued on the best possible terms during the remainder of the evening. The Honourable Mr. Listless turned over the leaves with double alacrity, saying, "You are severe upon invalids, Miss O'Carroll: to escape your satire, I must try to be sprightly, though the exertion is too much for me."

Chapter VII

A NEW VISITOR arrived at the Abbey, in the person of Mr. Asterias, the ichthyologist. This gentleman had passed his life in seeking the living wonders of the deep through the four quarters of the world; he had a cabinet of stuffed and dried fishes, of shells, sea-weeds, corals, and madrepores, that was the admiration and envy of the Royal Society. He had penetrated into the watery den of the Sepia Octopus, disturbed the conjugal happiness of that turtle-dove of the ocean, and come off victorious in a sanguinary conflict. He had been becalmed in the tropical seas, and had watched, in eager expectation, though unhappily always in vain, to see the colossal polypus rise from the water, and entwine its enormous arms round the masts and the rigging. He maintained the original of all things from water, and insisted that the polypodes were the first of animated things, and that, from their round bodies and many-shooting arms, the Hindoos had taken their gods, the most ancient of deities. But the chief object of his ambition, the end and aim of his researches, was to discover a triton and a mermaid, the existence of which he most potently and implicitly believed, and was prepared to demonstrate, à priori, à posteriori, à fortiori, synthetically and analytically, syllogistically and inductively, by arguments deduced both from acknowledged facts and plausible hypotheses. A report that a mermaid had been seen "sleeking her soft alluring locks" on the sea-coast of Lincolnshire, had brought him in great haste from London, to pay a long-promised and often-postponed visit to his old acquaintance, Mr. Glowry.

Mr. Asterias was accompanied by his son, to whom he had given the name of Aquarius—flattering himself that he would, in the process of time, become a constellation among the stars of ich-thyological science. What charitable female had lent him the mould in which this son was cast, no one pretended to know; and, as he never dropped the most distant allusion to Aquarius's mother, some of the wags of London maintained that he had re-ceived the favours of a mermaid, and that the scientific perquisi-tions which kept him always prowling about the sea-shore, were directed by the less philosophical motive of regaining his lost love.

Mr. Asterias perlustrated the sea-coast for several days, and reaped disappointment, but not despair. One night, shortly after his arrival, he was sitting in one of the windows of the library, looking towards the sea, when his attention was attracted by a figure which was moving near the edge of the surf, and which was dimly visible through the moonless summer night. Its motions were irregular, like those of a person in a state of indecision. It had extremely long hair, which floated in the wind. Whatever else it might be, it certainly was not a fisherman. It might be a lady; but it was neither Mrs. Hilary nor Miss O'Carroll, for they were both in the library. It might be one of the female servants; but it had too much grace, and too striking an air of habitual liberty to render it probable. Besides, what should one of the female servants be doing there at this hour, moving to and fro, as it seemed, without any visible purpose? It could scarcely be a stranger, for Claydyke, the nearest village was ten miles distant; and what female would come ten miles across the fens, for no purpose but to hover over the surf, under the walls of Nightmare Abbey? Might it not be a mermaid? It was possibly a mermaid. It was probably a mermaid. It was very probably a mermaid. Nay, what else could it be but a mermaid? It certainly was a mermaid. Mr. Asterias stole out of the library on tip-toe, with his finger on his lips, having beckoned Aquarius to follow him.

The rest of the party was in great surprise at Mr. Asterias's move-ment, and some of them approached the window to see if the locality would tend to elucidate the mystery. Presently they saw him and Aquarius cautiously stealing along on the other side of the moat, but they saw nothing more; and Mr. Asterias, returning, told them, with accents of great disappointment, that he had had a glimpse of a mermaid, but she had eluded him in the darkness, and was gone, he presumed, to sup with some enamoured triton, in a submarine grotto.

"But, seriously, Mr. Asterias," said the Honourable Mr. Listless, "do you positively believe there are such things as mermaids?"

Mr. Asterias.—Most assuredly; and tritons too.

The Honourable Mr. Listless.—What! things that are half human and half fish?

Mr. Asterias.—Precisely. They are the oran outangs of the sea. But I am persuaded that there are also complete sea men, differing in no respect from us, but that they are stupid and covered with scales; for, though our organization seems to exclude us essentially from the class of amphibious animals, yet anatomists well know that the foramen ovale may remain open in an adult, and that respiration is, in that case, not necessary to life: and how can it be otherwise explained that the Indian divers, employed in the pearl fishery, pass whole hours under the water; and that the famous Swedish gardener of Troningholm lived a day and a half under the ice without being drowned? A Nereid, or mermaid, was taken in the year 1403 in a Dutch lake, and was in every respect like a Frenchwoman except that she did not speak. Towards the end of the seventeenth century, an English ship a hunded and fifty leagues from land, in the Greenland seas, discovered a flotilla of sixty or seventy little skiffs, in each of which was a triton, or sea man: at the approach of the English vessel, the whole of them, seized with simultaneous fear, disappeared, skiffs and all, under the water, as if they had been a human variety of the nautilus. The illustrious Don Feijoo has preserved an authentic and well-attested story of a young Spaniard, named Francis de la Vega, who, bathing with some of his friends in June, 1674, suddenly dived under the sea and rose no more. His friends thought him drowned: they were plebeians and pious Catholics; but a philosopher might very legitimately have drawn the same conclusion.

The Reverend Mr. Larynx.—Nothing could be more logical.

Mr. Asterias.—Five years afterwards, some fishermen near Cadiz found in their nets a triton, or sea man; they spoke to him in several languages——

The Reverend Mr. Larynx.—They were very learned fishermen.

Mr. Hilary.—They had the gift of tongues by especial favour of their brother fisherman, St. Peter.

The Honourable Mr. Listless.—Is Saint Peter the tutelar saint of Cadiz? (*None of the company could answer this question, and Mr. Asterias proceeded.*)

They spoke to him in several languages, but he was as mute as a fish. They handed him over to some holy friars, who exorcised him; but the devil was mute too. After some days he pronounced the name Lierganes. A monk took him to that village. His mother and brothers recognized and embraced him; but he was as insensible to their caresses as any other fish would have been. He had some scales on his body, which dropped off by degrees; but his skin was as hard and rough as shagreen. He stayed at home nine years, without recovering his speech or his reason: he then disappeared again; and one of his old acquaintance, some years after, saw him pop his head out of the water, near the coast of the Asturias. These facts were certified by his brothers, and by Don Gaspardo de la Riba Aguero, Knight of Saint James, who lived near Lierganes, and often had the pleasure of our triton's company to dinner. Pliny mentions an embassy of the Olyssiponians to Tiberius, to give him intelligence of a triton which had been heard playing on its shell in a certain cave; with several other authenticated facts on the subject of Tritons and Nereids.

The Honourable Mr. Listless.—You astonish me. I have been much on the sea-shore, in the season, but I do not think I ever saw a mermaid. (*He rang, and summoned Fatout, who made his appearance half-seas-over.*) Fatout, did I ever see a mermaid?

Fatout.—Mermaid! mer-r-m-m-maid! Ah! merry maid! Oui, monsieur. Yes, sir, very many. I vish dere was one or two here in de kitchen—ma foi! Dey be all as melancholic as so many tombstone!

The Honourable Mr. Listless.—I mean, Fatout, an odd kind of human fish.

Fatout.—De odd fish! Ah, oui! I understand the phrase: ve have seen nothing else since ve left town—ma foi!

The Honourable Mr. Listless.—You seem to have a cup too much, sir.

Fatout.—Non, monsieur: de cup too little. De fen be very unwholesome, and I drink-a-de ponch vid Raven de butler, to keep out de bad air.

The Honourable Mr. Listless.—Fatout! I insist on your being sober.

Fatout.—Oui, monsieur; I vil be as sober as de révérendissime père Jean. I should be ver glad of de merry maid; but de butler be de odd fish, and he swim in de bowl de ponch. Ah! ah! I do recollect de little-a song:—"About fair maids, and about fair maids, and about my merry maids all." (*Fatout reeled out, singing.*)

The Honourable Mr. Listless.—I am overwhelmed: I never saw the rascal in such a condition before. But will you allow me, Mr. Asterias, to inquire into the *cui bono* of all the pains and expense you have incurred to discover a mermaid? The *cui bono*, sir, is the question I always take the liberty to ask when I see any one taking much trouble for any object. I am myself a sort of Signor Pococurante, and should like to know if there be anything better or pleasanter, than the state of existing and doing nothing?

Mr. Asterias.—I have made many voyages, Mr. Listless, to remote and barren shores: I have travelled over desert and inhospitable lands: I have defied danger—I have endured fatigue—I have submitted to privation. In the midst of these I have experienced pleasures which I would not at any time have exchanged for that of existing and doing nothing. I have known many evils, but I have never know the worst of all, which, as it seems to me, are those which are comprehended in the inexhaustible varieties of *ennui*: spleen, chagrin, vapours, blue devils, time-killing, discontent, misanthropy, and all their interminable train of fretfulness, querulousness, suspicions, jealousies, and fears, which have alike infected society, and the literature of society; and which would make an arctic ocean of the human mind, if the more humane pursuits of philosophy and science did not keep alive the better feelings and more valuable energies of our nature.

The Honourable Mr. Listless.—You are pleased to be severe upon our fashionable belles lettres.

Mr. Asterias.—Surely not without reason, when pirates, highwaymen, and other varieties of the extensive genus Marauder, are the only *beau idéal* of the active, as splenetic and railing misanthropy is of the speculative energy. A gloomy brow and a tragical voice seem to have been of late the characteristics of fashionable manners: and a morbid, withering, deadly, antisocial sirocco, loaded with moral and political despair, breathes through all the groves and valleys of the modern Parnassus; while science moves on in the calm dignity of its course, affording to youth delights equally pure and vivid—to maturity, calm and grateful occupation—to old age, the most pleasing recollections and inexhaustible materials of agreeable and salutary reflection; and, while its votary enjoys the disinterested pleasure of enlarging the intellect and increasing the comforts of society, he is himself independent of the caprices of human intercourse and the accidents of human fortune. Nature is his great and inexhaustible treasure. His days are always too short for his enjoyment: *ennui* is a stranger to his door. At peace with the world and with his own mind, he suffices to himself, makes all around him happy, and the close of his pleasing and beneficial existence is the evening of a beautiful day.

The Honourable Mr. Listless.—Really I should like very well to lead such a life myself, but the exertion would be too much for me. Besides, I have been at college. I contrive to get through my day by sinking my morning in bed, and killing the evening in company; dressing and dining in the intermediate space, and stopping the chinks and crevices of the few vacant moments that remain with a little easy reading. And that amiable discontent and antisociality which you reprobate in our present drawing-room table literature, I find, I do assure you, a very fine mental tonic, which reconciles me to my favourite pursuit of doing nothing, by showing me that nobody is worth doing anything for.

Marionetta.—But is there not in such compositions a kind of unconscious self-detection, which seems to carry their own antidote with them? For surely no one who cordially and truly either hates or despises the world will publish a volume every three months to say so.

Mr. Flosky.—There is a secret in all this, which I will elucidate with a dusky remark. According to Berkeley, the *esse* of things is *percipi*. They exist as they are perceived. But, leaving for the present, as far as relates to the material world, the materialists, hyloists, and antihyloists, to settle this point among them, which is indeed

A subtle question, raised among
Those out o' their wits, and those i' the wrong,

for only we transcendentalists are in the right: we may very safely
assert that the *esse* of happiness is *percipi*. It exists as it is perceived. "It is the mind that maketh well or ill." The elements of
pleasure and pain are everywhere. The degree of happiness that
any circumstances or objects can confer on us depends on the
mental disposition with which we approach them. If you consider
what is meant by the common phrases, a happy disposition and
a discontented temper, you will perceive that the truth for which
I am contending is universally admitted. (*Mr. Flosky suddenly
stopped; he found himself unintentionally trespassing within the
limits of common sense.*)

Mr. Hilary.—It is very true; a happy disposition finds materials
of enjoyment everywhere. In the city, or the country—in society,
or in solitude—in the theatre, or the forest—in the hum of the
multitude, or in the silence of the mountains, are alike materials
of reflection and elements of pleasure. It is one mode of pleasure
to listen to the music of *Don Giovanni*, in a theatre glittering
with light, and crowded with elegance and beauty: it is another to
glide at sunset over the bosom of a lonely lake, where no sound
disturbs the silence but the motion of the boat through the waters.
A happy disposition derives pleasure from both, a discontented
temper from neither, but is always busy in detecting deficiencies,
and feeding dissatisfaction with comparisons. The one gathers all
the flowers, the other all the nettles, in its path. The one has the
faculty of enjoying everything, the other of enjoying nothing. The
one realizes all the pleasure of the present good; the other con-
verts it into pain, by pining after something better, which is
only better because it is not present, and which, if it were present,
would not be enjoyed. These morbid spirits are in life what professed critics are in literature; they see nothing but faults, because
they are predetermined to shut their eyes to beauties. The critic
does his utmost to blight genius in its infancy; that which rises
in spite of him he will not see; and then he complains of the
decline of literature. In like manner, these cankers of society complain of human nature and society, when they have wilfully de-
barred themselves from all the good they contain, and done their
utmost to blight their own happiness and that of all around them.

Misanthropy is sometimes the product of disappointed benevolence; but it is more frequently the offspring of overweening and mortified vanity, quarrelling with the world for not being better treated than it deserves.

Scythrop (to Marionetta).—These remarks are rather uncharitable. There is great good in human nature, but it is at present ill-conditioned. Ardent spirits cannot but be dissatisfied with things as they are; and, according to their views of the probabilities of amelioration, they will rush into the extremes of either hope or despair—of which the first is enthusiasm, and the second misanthropy; but their sources in this case are the same, as the Severn and the Wye run in different directions, and both rise in Plinlimmon.

Marionetta.—"And there is salmon in both"; for the resemblance is about as close as that between Macedon and Monmouth.

Chapter VIII

MARIONETTA OBSERVED THE next day a remarkable perturbation in Scythrop, for which she could not imagine any probable cause. She was willing to believe at first that it had some transient and trifling source, and would pass off in a day or two; but, contrary to this expectation, it daily increased. She was well aware that Scythrop had a strong tendency to the love of mystery, for its own sake; that is to say, he would employ mystery to serve a purpose, but would first choose his purpose by its capability of mystery. He seemed now to have more mystery on his hands than the laws of the system allowed, and to wear his coat of darkness with an air of great discomfort. All her little playful arts lost by degrees much of their power, either to irritate or to soothe; and the first perception of her diminished influence produced in her an immediate depression of spirits, and a consequent sadness of demeanour, that rendered her very interesting to Mr. Glowry; who, duly considering the improbability of accomplishing his wishes with respect to Miss Toobad (which improbability naturally increased in the diurnal ratio of that young lady's absence), began to reconcile himself by degrees to the idea of Marionetta being his daughter.

Marionetta made many ineffectual attempts to extract from Scythrop the secret of his mystery; and, in despair of drawing it from himself, began to form hopes that she might find a clue to it from Mr. Flosky, who was Scythrop's dearest friend, and was more frequently than any other person admitted to his solitary tower. Mr. Flosky, however, had ceased to be visible in a morning. He was engaged in the composition of a dismal ballad; and Marionetta's uneasiness overcoming her scruples of decorum, she determined to seek him in the apartment which he had chosen for his study. She tapped at the door, and at the sound "Come in," entered the apartment. It was noon, and the sun was shining in full splendour, much to the annoyance of Mr. Flosky, who had obviated the inconvenience by closing the shutters, and drawing the window-curtains. He was sitting at his table by the light of a solitary candle, with a pen in one hand, and a muffiner in the other, with which he occasionally sprinkled salt on the wick to make it burn blue. He sate with "his eye in a fine frenzy rolling," and turned his inspired gaze on Marionetta as if she had been the ghastly ladie of a magical vision; then placed his hand before his eyes, with an appearance of manifest pain—shook his head—withdrew his hand—rubbed his eyes, like a waking man—and said, in a tone of ruefulness most jeremitalorically pathetic, "To what am I to attribute this very unexpected pleasure, my dear Miss O'Carroll?"

Marionetta.—I must apologise for intruding on you, Mr. Flosky; but the interest which I—you—take in my cousin Scythrop——

Mr. Flosky.—Pardon me, Miss O'Carroll; I do not take any interest in any person or thing on the face of the earth; which sentiment, if you analyse it, you will find to be the quintessence of the most refined philanthropy.

Marionetta.—I will take it for granted that it is so, Mr. Flosky; I am not conversant with metaphysical subtleties, but——

Mr. Flosky.—Subtleties! my dear Miss O'Carroll. I am sorry to find you participating in the vulgar error of the *reading public*, to whom an unusual collocation of words, involving a juxtaposition of antiperistatical ideas, immediately suggests the notion of hyperoxysophistical paradoxology.

Marionetta.—Indeed, Mr. Flosky, it suggests no such notion to me. I have sought you for the purpose of obtaining information.

633

Mr. Flosky (shaking his head).—No one ever sought me for such a purpose before.

Marionetta.—I think, Mr. Flosky—that is, I believe—that is, I fancy—that is, I imagine——

Mr. Flosky.—The τουτεστι, the *id est*, the *cioè*, the *c'est à dire*, the that is, my dear Miss O'Carroll, is not applicable in this case —if you will permit me to take the liberty of saying so. Think is not synonymous with believe—for belief, in many most important particulars, results from the total absence, the absolute negation of thought, and is thereby the sane and orthodox condition of mind; and thought and belief are both essentially different from fancy, and fancy, again, is distinct from imagination. This distinction between fancy and imagination is one of the most abstruse and important points of metaphysics. I have written seven hundred pages of promise to elucidate it, which promise I shall keep as faithfully as the bank will its promise to pay.

Marionetta.—I assure you, Mr. Flosky, I care no more about metaphysics than I do about the bank; and, if you will condescend to talk to a simple girl in intelligible terms——

Mr. Flosky.—Say not condescend! Know you not that you talk to the most humble of men, to one who has buckled on the armour of sanctity, and clothed himself with humility as with a garment?

Marionetta.—My cousin Scythrop has of late had an air of mystery about him, which gives me great uneasiness.

Mr. Flosky.—That is strange: nothing is so becoming to a man as an air of mystery. Mystery is the very key-stone of all that is beautiful in poetry, all that is sacred in faith, and all that is recondite in transcendental psychology. I am writing a ballad which is all mystery; it is "such stuff as dreams are made of," and is, indeed, stuff made of a dream; for, last night I fell asleep as usual over my book, and had a vision of pure reason. I composed five hundred lines in my sleep; so that, having had a dream of a ballad, I am now officiating as my own Peter Quince, and making a ballad of my dream, and it shall be called Bottom's Dream, because it has no bottom.

Marionetta.—I see, Mr. Flosky, you think my intrusion unseasonable, and are inclined to punish it, by talking nonsense to me. *(Mr. Flosky gave a start at the word nonsense, which almost overturned the table.)* I assure you, I would not have intruded if I had not been very much interested in the question I wish to ask you.—(*Mr. Flosky listened in sullen dignity.*)—My cousin Scythrop seems to have some secret preying on his mind.—(*Mr. Flosky was silent.*)—He seems very unhappy—Mr. Flosky.—Perhaps you are acquainted with the cause.—(*Mr. Flosky was still silent.*)—I only wish to know—Mr. Flosky—if it is anything—that could be remedied by anything—that any one—of whom I know anything—could do.

Mr. Flosky (after a pause).—There are various ways of getting at secrets. The most approved methods, as recommended both theoretically and practically in philosophical novels, are eavesdropping at key-holes, picking the locks of chests and desks, peeping into letters, steaming wafers, and insinuating hot wire under sealing-wax; none of which methods I hold it lawful to practise.

Marionetta.—Surely, Mr. Flosky, you cannot suspect me of wishing to adopt or encourage such base and contemptible arts.

Mr. Flosky.—Yet are they recommended, and with well-strung reasons, by writers of gravity and note, as simple and easy methods of studying character, and gratifying that laudable curiosity which aims at the knowledge of man.

Marionetta.—I am as ignorant of this morality which you do not approve, as of the metaphysics which you do: I should be glad to know by your means, what is the matter with my cousin; I do not like to see him unhappy, and I suppose there is some reason for it.

Mr. Flosky.—Now I should rather suppose there is no reason for it: it is the fashion to be unhappy. To have a reason for being so would be exceedingly commonplace: to be so without any is the province of genius: the art of being miserable for misery's sake, has been brought to great perfection in our days; and the ancient *Odyssey*, which held forth a shining example of the endurance of real misfortune, will give place to a modern one, setting out a more instructive picture of querulous impatience under imaginary evils.

Marionetta.—Will you oblige me, Mr. Flosky, by giving me a plain answer to a plain question?

Mr. Flosky.—It is impossible, my dear Miss O'Carroll. I never gave a plain answer to a question in my life.

Marionetta.—Do you, or do you not, know what is the matter with my cousin?

Mr. Flosky.—To say that I do not know, would be to say that I am ignorant of something; and God forbid that a transcendental metaphysician, who has pure anticipated cognitions of everything, and carries the whole science of geometry in his head without ever having looked into Euclid, should fall into so empirical an error as to declare himself ignorant of anything: to say that I do know, would be to pretend to positive and circumstantial knowledge touching present matter of fact, which, when you consider the nature of evidence, and the various lights in which the same thing may be seen——

Marionetta.—I see, Mr. Flosky, that either you have no information, or are determined not to impart it; and I beg your pardon for having given you this unnecessary trouble.

Mr. Flosky.—My dear Miss O'Carroll, it would have given me great pleasure to have said anything that would have given you pleasure; but if any person living could make report of having obtained any information on any subject from Ferdinando Flosky, my transcendental reputation would be ruined for ever.

Chapter IX

SCYTHROP GREW EVERY day more reserved, mysterious, and *distrait*; and gradually lengthened the duration of his diurnal seclusions in his tower. Marionetta thought she perceived in all this very manifest symptoms of a warm love cooling.

It was seldom that she found herself alone with him in the morning, and, on these occasions, if she was silent in the hope of his speaking first, not a syllable would he utter; if she spoke to him indirectly, he assented monosyllabically; if she questioned him, his answers were brief, constrained, and evasive. Still, though her spirits were depressed, her playfulness had not so totally forsaken her, but that it illuminated at intervals the gloom of Nightmare Abbey; and if, on any occasion, she observed in Scythrop tokens of unextinguished or returning passion, her love of tormenting her lover immediately got the better both of her grief and her sympathy, though not of her curiosity, which Scythrop seemed determined not to satisfy. This playfulness, however, was in a great measure artificial, and usually vanished with the irritable Strephon, to whose annoyance it had been exerted. The Genius Loci, the *tutela* of Nightmare Abbey, the spirit of black melancholy, began to set his seal on her pallescent countenance. Scythrop perceived the change, found his tender sympathies awakened, and did his utmost to comfort the afflicted damsel, assuring her that his seeming inattention had only proceeded from his being involved in a profound meditation on a very hopeful scheme for the regeneration of human society. Marionetta called him ungrateful, cruel, cold-hearted, and accompanied her reproaches with many sobs and tears: poor Scythrop growing every moment more soft and submissive—till, at length, he threw himself at her feet, and declared that no competition of beauty, however dazzling, genius, however transcendent, talents, however cultivated, or philosophy, however enlightened, should ever make him renounce his divine Marionetta.

"Competition!" thought Marionetta, and suddenly, with an air of the most freezing indifference, she said, "You are perfectly at liberty, sir, to do as you please; I beg you will follow your own plans, without any reference to me."

Scythrop was confounded. What was become of all her passion and her tears? Still kneeling, he kissed her hand with rueful timidity, and said, in most pathetic accents, "Do you not love me, Marionetta?"

"No," said Marionetta, with a look of cold composure: "No." Scythrop still looked up incredulously. "No I tell you."

"Oh! very well, madam," said Scythrop, rising, "if that is the case, there are those in the world——"

"To be sure there are, sir;—and do you suppose that I do not see through your designs, you ungenerous monster?"

"My designs, Marionetta!"

"Yes, your designs, Scythrop. You have come here to cast me off, and artfully contrive that it should appear to be my doing, and not yours, thinking to quiet your tender conscience with this pitiful stratagem. But do not suppose that you are of so much consequence to me; do not suppose it: you are of no consequence to me at all—not at all, therefore, leave me: I renounce you: leave me: why do you not leave me?"

Scythrop endeavoured to remonstrate, but without success. She

637

reiterated her injunctions to him to leave her, till, in the simplicity of his spirit, he was preparing to comply. When he had nearly reached the door, Marionetta said, "Farewell." Scythrop looked back. "Farewell, Scythrop," she repeated, "you will never see me again."

"Never see you again, Marionetta?"

"I shall go from hence to-morrow, perhaps to-day; and before we meet again, one of us will be married, and we might as well be dead, you know, Scythrop."

The sudden change of her voice in the last few words, and the burst of tears that accompanied them, acted like electricity on the tender-hearted youth; and, in another instant, a complete reconciliation was accomplished without the intervention of words.

There are, indeed, some learned casuists, who maintain that love has no language, and that all the misunderstandings and dissensions of lovers arise from the fatal habit of employing words on a subject to which words are inapplicable; that love, beginning with looks, that is to say, with the physiognomical expression of congenial mental dispositions, tends through a regular gradation of signs and symbols of affection, to that consummation which is most devoutly to be wished; and that it neither is necessary that there should be, nor probable that there would be, a single word spoken from first to last between two sympathetic spirits, were it not that the arbitrary institutions of society have raised, at every step of this very simple process, so many complicated impediments and barriers in the shape of settlements and ceremonies, parents and guardians, lawyers, Jew-brokers, and parsons, that many an adventurous knight (who, in order to obtain the conquest of a Hesperian fruit, is obliged to fight his way through all these monsters) is either repulsed at the onset, or vanquished before the achievement of his enterprise: and such a quantity of unnatural talking is rendered inevitably necessary through all the stages of the progression, that the tender and volatile spirit of love often takes flight on the pinions of some of the $\epsilon\pi\epsilon\alpha$ $\pi\tau\epsilon\rho o\epsilon\nu\tau\alpha$, or *winged* words, which are pressed into his service in despite of himself.

At this conjunction, Mr. Glowry entered, and sitting down near them, said, "I see how it is: and as we are all sure to be miserable do what we may, there is no need of taking pains to make one another more so; therefore with God's blessing and mine, there"—joining their hands as he spoke.

Scythrop was not exactly prepared for this decisive step; but he could only stammer out, "Really, sir, you are too good"; and Mr. Glowry departed to bring Mr. Hilary to ratify the act.

Now, whatever truth there may be in the theory of love and language, of which we have so recently spoken, certain it is, that during Mr. Glowry's absence, which lasted half an hour, not a single word was said by either Scythrop or Marionetta.

Mr. Glowry returned with Mr. Hilary, who was delighted at the prospect of so advantageous an establishment for his orphan niece, of whom he considered himself in some manner the guardian, and nothing remained, as Mr. Glowry observed, but to fix the day.

Marionetta blushed, and was silent. Scythrop was also silent for a time, and at length hesitatingly said, "My dear sir, your goodness overpowers me; but really you are so precipitate."

Now, this remark, if the young lady had made it, would, whether she thought it or not—for sincerity is a thing of no account on these occasions, nor indeed on any other, according to Mr. Flosky—this remark, if the young lady had made it, would have been perfectly *comme il faut*; but being made by the young gentleman, it was *toute autre chose*, and was, indeed, in the eyes of his mistress, a most heinous and irremissible offense. Marionetta was angry, very angry, but she concealed her anger, and said, calmly and coldly, "Certainly, you are much too precipitate, Mr. Glowry. I assure you, sir, I have by no means made up my mind; and, indeed, as far as I know it, it inclines the other way; but it will be quite time enough to think of these matters seven years hence." Before surprise permitted reply, the young lady had locked herself up in her own apartment.

"Why, Scythrop," said Mr. Glowry, elongating his face exceedingly, "the devil is come among us sure enough, as Mr. Toobad observes: I thought you and Marionetta were both of a mind."

"So we are, I believe, sir," said Scythrop, gloomily, and stalked away to his tower.

"Mr. Glowry," said Mr. Hilary, "I do not very well understand all this."

"Whims, brother Hilary," said Mr. Glowry; "some little foolish love quarrel, nothing more. Whims, freaks, April showers. They will be blown over by to-morrow."

"If not," said Mr. Hilary, "these April showers have made us April fools."

"Ah!" said Mr. Glowry, "you are a happy man, and in all your afflictions you can console yourself with a joke, let it be ever so bad, provided you crack it yourself. I should be very happy to laugh with you, if it would give you any satisfaction; but, really at present, my heart is so sad, that I find it impossible to levy a contribution on my muscles."

Chapter X

ON THE EVENING on which Mr. Asterias had caught a glimpse of a female figure on the sea-shore, which he had translated into the visual sign of his interior cognition of a mermaid, Scythrop, retiring to his tower, found his study pre-occupied. A stranger, muffled in a cloak, was sitting at his table. Scythrop paused in surprise. The stranger rose at his entrance, and looked at him intently a few moments, in silence. The eyes of the stranger alone were visible. All the rest of his figure was muffled and mantled in the folds of a black cloak, which was raised, by the right hand, to the level of the eyes. This scrutiny being completed, the stranger, dropping the cloak, said, "I see, by your physiognomy, that you may be trusted"; and revealed to the astonished Scythrop a female form and countenance of dazzling grace and beauty, with long flowing hair of raven blackness, and large black eyes of almost oppressive brilliancy, which strikingly contrasted with a complexion of snowy whiteness. Her dress was extremely elegant, but had an appearance of foreign fashion, as if both the lady and the mantuamaker were of "far countree."

> "I guess 't was frightful there to see
> A lady so richly clad as she,
> Beautiful exceedingly."

For, if it be terrible for one young lady to find another under a tree at midnight, it must, à fortiori, be much more terrible to a young gentleman to find a young lady in his study at that hour. If the logical consecutiveness of this conclusion be not manifest to my readers, I am sorry for their dulness, and must refer them, for more ample elucidation, to a treatise which Mr. Flosky intends to write, on the Categories of Relation, which comprehend Substance and Accident, Cause and Effect, Action and Re-action.

Scythrop, therefore, either was or ought to have been, frightened; at all events, he was astonished; and astonishment, though not in itself fear, is nevertheless a good stage towards it, and is, indeed, as it were the half-way house between respect and terror, according to Mr. Burke's graduated scale of the sublime.

"You are surprised," said the lady; "yet why should you be surprised? If you had met me in a drawing-room, and I had been introduced to you by an old woman, it would have been a matter of course: can the division of two or three walls, and the absence of an unimportant personage, make the same object essentially different in the perception of a philosopher?"

"Certainly not," said Scythrop; "but when any class of objects has habitually presented itself to our perceptions in invariable conjunction with particular relations, then, on the sudden appearance of one object of the class divested of those accompaniments, the essential difference of the relation is, by an involuntary process transferred to the object itself, which thus offers itself to our perceptions with all the strangeness of novelty."

"You are a philosopher," said the lady, "and a lover of liberty. You are the author of a treatise, called 'Philosophical Gas; or, a Project for a General Illumination of the Human Mind.'"

"I am," said Scythrop, delighted at this first blossom of his renown.

"I am a stranger in this country," said the lady; "I have been but a few days in it, yet I find myself immediately under the necessity of seeking refuge from an atrocious persecution. I had no friend to whom I could apply; and, in the midst of my difficulties, accident threw your pamphlet in my way. I saw that I had, at least, one kindred mind in this nation, and determined to apply to you."

"And what would you have me do?" said Scythrop, more and more amazed, and not a little perplexed.

"I would have you," said the young lady, "assist me in finding some place of retreat, where I can remain concealed from the indefatigable search that is being made for me. I have been so nearly caught once or twice already, that I cannot confide any longer in my own ingenuity."

Doubtless, thought Scythrop, this is one of my golden candlesticks. "I have constructed," said he, "in this tower, an entrance to a small suite of unknown apartments in the main building, which I defy any creature living to detect. If you would like to remain there a day or two, till I can find you a more suitable concealment, you may rely on the honour of a transcendental eleutherarch."

"I rely on myself," said the lady. "I act as I please, go where I please, and let the world say what it will. I am rich enough to set it at defiance. It is the tyrant of the poor and the feeble, but the slave of those who are above the reach of its injury."

Scythrop ventured to inquire the name of his fair *protégée*. "What is a name?" said the lady: "any name will serve the purpose of distinction. Call me Stella. I see by your looks," she added, "that you think all this very strange. When you know me better, your surprise will cease. I submit not to be an accomplice in my sex's slavery. I am, like yourself, a lover of freedom, and I carry my theory into practice. *They alone are subject to blind authority who have no reliance on their own strength.*"

Stella took possession of the recondite apartments. Scythrop intended to find her another asylum; but from day to day he postponed his intention, and by degrees forgot it. The young lady reminded him of it from day to day, till she also forgot it. Scythrop was anxious to learn her history; but she would add nothing to what she had already communicated, that she was shunning an atrocious persecution. Scythrop thought of Lord C. and the Alien Act, and said, "As you will not tell your name, I suppose it is in the green bag." Stella, not understanding what he meant, was silent; and Scythrop, translating silence into acquiescence, concluded that he was sheltering an *illuminée* whom Lord S. suspected of an intention to take the Tower, and set fire to the Bank: exploits, at least, as likely to be accomplished by the hands and eyes of a young beauty, as by a drunken cobbler and doctor, armed with a pamphlet and an old stocking.

Stella, in her conversations with Scythrop displayed a highly cultivated and energetic mind, full of impassioned schemes of liberty, and impatience of masculine usurpation. She had a lively sense of all the oppressions that are done under the sun; and the vivid pictures which her imagination presented to her of the numberless scenes of injustice and misery which are being acted at every moment in every part of the inhabited world, gave an habitual seriousness to her physiognomy, that made it seem as if a smile had never once hovered on her lips. She was intimately conversant with the German language and literature; and Scythrop listened with delight to her repetitions of her favourite passages from Schiller and Göthe, and to her encomiums on the sublime Spartacus Weishaupt, the immortal founder of the sect of the Illuminati. Scythrop found that his soul had a greater capacity of love than the image of Marionetta had filled. The form of Stella took possession of every vacant corner of the cavity, and by degrees displaced that of Marionetta from many of the outworks of the citadel; though the latter still held possession of the *keep*. He judged, from his new friend calling herself Stella, that, if it were not her real name, she was an admirer of the principles of the German play from which she had taken it, and took an opportunity of leading the conversation to that subject; but to his great surprise, the lady spoke very ardently of the singleness and exclusiveness of love, and declared that the reign of affection was one and indivisible; that it might be transferred, but could not be participated. "If I ever love," said she, "I shall do so without limit or restriction. I shall hold all difficulties light, all sacrifices cheap, all obstacles gossamer. But for love so total, I shall claim a return as absolute. I will have no rival: whether more or less favoured will be of little moment. I will be neither first nor second—I will be alone. The heart which I shall possess I will possess entirely, or entirely renounce."

Scythrop did not dare to mention the name of Marionetta; he trembled lest some unlucky accident should reveal it to Stella, though he scarcely knew what result to wish or anticipate, and lived in the double fever of a perpetual dilemma. He could not dissemble to himself that he was not in love, at the same time, with two damsels of minds and habits as remote as the antipodes. The scale of predilection always inclined to the fair one who happened to be present; but the absent was never effectually outweighed, though the degrees of exaltation and depression varied according to accidental variations in the outward and visible signs of the inward and spiritual graces of his respective charmers. Passing and repassing several times a day from the company of the one to that of the other, he was like a shuttlecock between two battledores, changing its direction as rapidly as the oscillations of a pendulum, receiving many a hard knock on the cork of a sensitive heart, and flying from point to point on the feathers of a super-sublimated head. This was an awful state of things. He had now as much mystery about him as any romantic transcendentalist or transcendental romancer could desire. He had his esoterical and his exoterical love. He could not endure the thought of losing either of them, but he trembled when he imagined the possibility that some fatal discovery might deprive him of both. The old proverb concerning two strings in a bow gave him some gleams of comfort; but that concerning two stools occurred to him more frequently, and covered his forehead with a cold perspiration. With Stella, he would indulge freely in all his romantic and philosophical visions. He could build castles in the air, and she would pile towers and turrets on the imaginary edifices. With Marionetta it was otherwise: she knew nothing of the world and society beyond the sphere of her own experience. Her life was all music and sunshine, and she wondered what any one could see to complain of in such a pleasant state of things. She loved Scythrop, she hardly knew why; indeed, she was not always sure that she loved him at all: she felt her fondness increase or diminish in an inverse ratio to his. When she had manœuvered him into a fever of passionate love, she often felt and always assumed indifference: if she found that her coldness was contagious, and that Scythrop either was, or pretended to be, as indifferent as herself, she would become doubly kind, and raise him again to that elevation from which she had previously thrown him down. Thus, when his love was flowing, hers was ebbing: when his was ebbing hers was flowing. Now and then there were moments of level tide, when reciprocal affection seemed to promise imperturbable harmony; but Scythrop could scarcely resign his spirit to the pleasing illusion, before the pinnace of the lover's affections was caught in some eddy of the lady's caprice, and he was whirled away from the shore of his hopes, without rudder or compass, into an ocean of mists and storms. It resulted, from this system of conduct, that all that passed between Scythrop and Marionetta consisted in making and unmaking love.

644

He had no opportunity to take measure of her understanding by conversations on general subjects, and on his favourite designs; and being left in this respect to the exercise of indefinite conjecture, he took it for granted, as most lovers would do in similar circumstances, that she had great natural talents, which she wasted at present on trifles: but coquetry would end with marriage, and leave room for philosophy to exert its influence on her mind. Stella had no coquetry, no disguise: she was an enthusiast in subjects of general interest; and her conduct to Scythrop was always uniform, or rather showed a regular progression of partiality which seemed fast ripening into love.

Chapter XI

SCYTHROP, ATTENDING ONE day the summons to dinner, found in the drawing-room his friend Mr. Cypress, the poet, whom he had known at college, and who was a great favourite of Mr. Glowry. Mr. Cypress said, he was on the point of leaving England, but could not think of doing so without a farewell-look at Nightmare Abbey and his respected friends, the moody Mr. Glowry and the mysterious Mr. Scythrop, the sublime Mr. Flosky and the pathetic Mr. Listless; to all of whom, and the morbid hospitality of the melancholy dwelling in which they were then assembled, he assured them he should always look back with as much affection as his lacerated spirit could feel for anything. The sympathetic condolence of their respective replies were cut short by Raven's announcement of "dinner on table."

The conversation that took place when the wine was in circulation, and the ladies were withdrawn, we shall report with our usual scrupulous fidelity.

Mr. Glowry.—You are leaving England, Mr. Cypress. There is a delightful melancholy in saying farewell to an old acquaintance, when the chances are twenty to one against ever meeting again. A smiling bumper to sad parting, and let us all be unhappy together.

Mr. Cypress (filling a bumper).—This is the only social habit that the disappointed spirit never unlearns.

The Reverend Mr. Larynx (filling).—It is the only piece of academical learning that the finished educatee retains.

Mr. Flosky (filling.)—It is the only objective fact which the sceptic can realize.

Scythrop (filling).—It is the only styptic for a bleeding heart.

The Honorable Mr. Listless (filling).—It is the only trouble that is very well worth taking.

Mr. Asterias (filling).—It is the only key of conversational truth.

Mr. Toobad (filling).—It is the only antidote to the great wrath of the devil.

Mr. Hilary (filling.)—It is the only symbol of perfect life. The inscription "HIC NON BIBITUR"[1] will suit nothing but a tombstone.

Mr. Glowry.—You will see many fine old ruins, Mr. Cypress; crumbling pillars and mossy walls—many a one-legged Venus and headless Minerva—many a Neptune buried in sand—many a Jupiter turned topsy-turvy—many a perforated Bacchus doing duty as a waterpipe—many reminiscences of the ancient world, which I hope was better worth living in than the modern; though, for myself, I care not a straw more for one than the other, and would not go twenty miles to see anything that either could show.

Mr. Cypress.—It is something to seek, Mr. Glowry. The mind is restless, and must persist in seeking, though to find is to be disappointed. Do you feel no aspirations towards the countries of Socrates and Cicero? No wish to wander among the venerable remains of the greatness that has passed for ever?

Mr. Glowry.—Not a grain.

Scythrop.—It is, indeed, much the same as if a lover should dig up the buried form of his mistress, and gaze upon relics which are anything but herself, to wander among a few mouldy ruins, that are only imperfect indexes to lost volumes of glory, and meet at every step the more melancholy ruins of human nature—a degenerate race of stupid and shrivelled slaves, grovelling in the lowest depths of servility and superstition.

The Honorable Mr. Listless.—It is the fashion to go abroad. I have thought of it myself, but am hardly equal to the exertion. To be sure, a little eccentricity and originality are allowable in some cases; and the most eccentric and original of all characters is an Englishman who stays at home.

[1] No drinking here.

Scythrop.—I should have no pleasure in visiting countries that are past all hope of regeneration. There is great hope of our own; and it seems to me that an Englishman, who, either by his station in society, or by his genius, or (as in your instance, Mr. Cypress) by both, has the power of essentially serving his country in its arduous struggle with its domestic enemies, yet forsakes his country, which is still so rich in hope, to dwell in others which are only fertile in the ruins of memory, does what none of those ancients, whose fragmentary memorials you venerate, would have done in similar circumstances.

Mr. Cypress.—Sir, I have quarrelled with my wife; and a man who has quarrelled with his wife is absolved from all duty to his country. I have written an ode to tell the people as much, and they may take it as they list.

Scythrop.—Do you suppose, if Brutus had quarrelled with his wife, he would have given it as a reason to Cassius for having nothing to do with his enterprise? Or would Cassius have been satisfied with such an excuse?

Mr. Flosky.—Brutus was a senator: so is our dear friend: but the cases are different. Brutus had some hope of political good: Mr. Cypress has none. How should he, after what we have seen in France?

Scythrop.—A Frenchman is born in harness, ready saddled, bitted, and bridled, for any tyrant to ride. He will fawn under his rider one moment, and throw him and kick him to death the next, but another adventurer springs on his back, and by dint of whip and spur, on he goes as before. We may, without much vanity, hope better of ourselves.

Mr. Cypress.—I have no hope for myself or for others. Our life is a false nature; it is not in the harmony of things; it is an all-blasting upas, whose root is earth, and whose leaves are the skies which rain their poison-dews upon mankind. We wither from our youth; we gasp with unslaked thirst for unattainable good; lured from the first to the last by phantoms—love, fame, ambition, avarice—all idle, and all ill—one meteor of many names, that vanishes in the smoke of death.

Mr. Flosky.—A most delightful speech, Mr. Cypress. A most amiable and instructive philosophy. You have only to impress its truth on the minds of all living men, and life will then, indeed,

647

be the desert and the solitude; and I must do you, myself, and our mutual friends the justice to observe that let society only give fair play, at one and the same time, as I flatter myself it is inclined to do, to your system of morals, and my system of metaphysics, and Scythrop's system of politics, and Mr. Listless's system of manners, and Mr. Toobad's system of religion, and the result will be as fine a mental chaos as ever the immortal Kant himself could ever have hoped to see; in the prospect of which I rejoice.

Mr. Hilary.—"Certainly, ancient, it is not a thing to rejoice at:" I am one of those who cannot see the good that is to result from all this mystifying and blue-devilling of society. The contrast it presents to the cheerful and solid wisdom of antiquity is too forcible not to strike any one who has the least knowledge of classical literature. To represent vice and misery as the necessary accompaniments of genius, is as mischievous as it is false, and the feeling is as unclassical as the language in which it is usually expressed.

Mr. Toobad.—It is our calamity. The devil has come among us, and has begun by taking possession of all the cleverest fellows. Yet, forsooth, this is the enlightened age. Marry, how? Did our ancestors go peeping about with dark lanterns, and do we walk at our ease in broad sunshine? Where is the manifestation of our light? By what symptoms do you recognize it? What are its signs, its tokens, its symptoms, its symbols, its categories, its conditions? What is it, and why? How, where, when is it to be seen, felt, and understood? What do we see by it which our ancestors saw not, and which at the same time is worth seeing? We see a hundred men hanged, where they saw one. We see five hundred transported, where they saw one. We see five thousand in the workhouse, where they saw one. We see scores of Bible societies, where they saw none. We see paper, where they saw gold. We see men in stays, where they saw men in armour. We see painted faces, where they saw healthy ones. We see children perishing in manufactories, where they saw them flourishing in the fields. We see prisons, where they saw castles. We see masters, where they saw representatives. In short, they saw true men, where we see false knaves. They saw Milton, and we see Mr. Sackbut.

Mr. Flosky.—The false knave, sir, is my honest friend; therefore, I beseech you, let him be countenanced. God forbid but a knave should have some countenance at his friend's request.

Mr. Toobad.—"Good men and true" was their common term, like the καλος κάγανος[1] of the Athenians. It is so long since men have been either good or true, that it is to be questioned which is most obsolete, the fact or the phraseology.

Mr. Cypress.—There is no worth nor beauty but in the mind's idea. Love sows the wind and reaps the whirlwind. Confusion, thrice confounded, is the portion of him who rests even for an instant on that most brittle of reeds—the affection of a human being. The sum of our social destiny is to inflict or to endure.

Mr. Hilary.—Rather to bear and forbear, Mr. Cypress—a maxim which you perhaps despise. Ideal beauty is not the mind's creation: it is real beauty, refined and purified in the mind's alembic, from the alloy which always more or less accompanies it in our mixed and imperfect nature. But still the gold exists in a very ample degree. To expect too much is a disease in the expectant, for which human nature is not responsible; and, in the common name of humanity, I protest against these false and mischievous ravings. To rail against humanity for not being abstract perfection, and against human love for not realizing all the splendid visions of the poets of chivalry, is to rail at the summer for not being all sunshine, and at the rose for not being always in bloom.

Mr. Cypress.—Human love! Love is not an inhabitant of the earth. We worship him as the Athenians did their unknown God: but broken hearts are the martyrs of his faith, and the eye shall never see the form which phantasy paints, and which passion pursues through paths of delusive beauty, among flowers whose odours are agonies, and trees whose gums are poison.

Mr. Hilary.—You talk like a Rosicrusian, who will love nothing but a sylph, who does not believe in the existence of a sylph, and who yet quarrels with the whole universe for not containing a sylph.

Mr. Cypress.—The mind is diseased of its own beauty, and fevers into false creation. The forms which the sculptor's soul has seized exist only in himself.

Mr. Flosky.—Permit me to discept. They are the mediums of common forms combined and arranged into a common standard. The ideal beauty of the Helen of Zeuxis was the combined medium of the real beauty of the virgins of Crotona.

[1] the beautiful and the good.

Mr. Hilary.—But to make ideal beauty the shadow in the water, and like the dog in the fable, to throw away the substance in catching at the shadow, is scarcely the characteristic of wisdom, whatever it may be of genius. To reconcile man as he is to the world as it is, to preserve and improve all that is good, and destroy or alleviate all that is evil, in physical and moral nature—have been the hope and aim of the greatest teachers and ornaments of our species. I will say, too, that the highest wisdom and the highest genius have been invariably accompanied with cheerfulness. We have sufficient proofs on record that Shakespeare and Socrates were the most festive companions. But now the little wisdom and genius we have seem to be entering into a conspiracy against cheerfulness.

Mr. Toobad.—How can we be cheerful with the devil among us?

The Honourable Mr. Listless.—How can we be cheerful when our nerves are shattered?

Mr. Flosky.—How can we be cheerful when we are surrounded by a *reading public*, that is growing too wise for its betters?

Scythrop.—How can we be cheerful when our great general designs are crossed every moment by our little particular passions?

Mr. Cypress.—How can we be cheerful in the midst of disappointment and despair?

Mr. Glowry.—Let us all be unhappy together.

Mr. Hilary.—Let us sing a catch.

Mr. Glowry.—No: a nice tragical ballad. The Norfolk Tragedy to the tune of the Hundredth Psalm.

Mr. Hilary.—I say a catch.

Mr. Glowry.—I say no. A song from Mr. Cypress.

All.—A song from Mr. Cypress.

Mr. Cypress sung—

> There is a fever of the spirit,
>   The brand of Cain's unresting doom,
> Which in the lone dark souls that bear it
>   Glows like the lamp in Tullia's tomb:
> Unlike that lamp, its subtle fire
>   Burns, blasts, consumes its cell, the heart.
> Till, one by one hope, joy, desire,
>   Like dreams of shadowy smoke depart.

When hope, love, life itself, are only
    Dust—spectral memories—dead and cold—
The unfed fire burns bright and lonely,
    Like that undying lamp of old:
And by that dreary illumination,
    Till time its clay-built home has rent,
Thought broods on feeling's desolation—
    The soul is its own monument.

Mr. Glowry.—Admirable. Let us all be unhappy together.

Mr. Hilary.—Now, I say again, a catch.

The Reverend Mr. Larynx.—I am for you.

Mr. Hilary.—"Seamen three."

The Reverend Mr. Larynx.—Agreed. I'll be Harry Gill, with the voice of three. Begin.

Mr. Hilary and the Reverend Mr. Larynx—

Seamen three! What men be ye?
Gotham's three wise men we be.
Whither in your bowl so free?
To rake the moon from out the sea.
The bowl goes trim. The moon doth shine.
And our ballast is old wine;
And your ballast is old wine.

Who art thou, so fast adrift?
I am he they call Old Care.
Here on board we will thee lift.
No: I may not enter there.
Wherefore so? 'Tis Jove's degree,
In a bowl Care may not be;
In a bowl Care may not be.

Fear ye not the waves that roll?
No: in charmed bowl we swim.
What the charm that floats the bowl?
Water may not pass the brim.
The bowl goes trim. The moon doth shine.
And our ballast is old wine;
And your ballast is old wine.

This catch was so well executed by the spirit and science of Mr. Hilary, and the deep tri-une voice of the reverend gentleman, that the whole party, in spite of themselves, caught the contagion, and joined in chorus at the conclusion, each raising a bumper to his lips:

> The bowl goes trim: the moon doth shine.
> And our ballast is old wine.

Mr. Cypress, having his ballast on board, stepped, the same evening, into his bowl, or travelling chariot, and departed to rake seas and rivers, lakes and canals, for the moon of ideal beauty.

Chapter XII

IT WAS THE custom of the Honourable Mr. Listless, on adjourning from the bottle to the ladies, to retire for a few moments to make a second toilette, that he might present himself in becoming taste. Fatout, attending as usual, appeared with a countenance of great dismay, and informed his master that he had just ascertained that the abbey was haunted. Mrs. Hilary's *gentlewoman*, for whom Fatout had lately conceived a *tendresse*, had been, as she expressed it, "fritted out of her seventeen senses" the preceding night as she was retiring to her bedchamber, by a ghostly figure she had met stalking along one of the galleries, wrapped in a white shroud, with a bloody turban on its head. She had fainted away with fear; and, when she recovered, she found herself in the dark, and the figure was gone. "*Sacré—cochon—bleu!*" exclaimed Fatout, giving very deliberate emphasis to every portion of his terrible oath—"I vould not meet de *revenant*, de ghost—*non*—not for all de *bowl-de-ponch* in de vorld."

"Fatout," said the Honourable Mr. Listless, "did I ever see a ghost?"

"*Jamais*, monsieur, never."

"Then I hope I never shall, for, in the present shattered state of my nerves, I am afraid it would be too much for me. There— loosen the lace of my stays a little, for really this plebeian practice

652

of eating—Not too loose—consider my shape. That will do. And
I desire that you bring me no more stories of ghosts; for, though I
do not believe in such things, yet, when one is awake in the night,
one is apt, if one thinks of them, to have fancies that give one a
kind of a chill, particularly if one opens one's eyes suddenly on
one's dressing gown hanging in the moonlight, between the bed
and the window."

The Honourable Mr. Listless, though he had prohibited Fatout
from bringing him any more stories of ghosts, could not help thinking of that which Fatout had already brought; and, as it was upper-
most in his mind, when he descended to the tea and coffee cups,
and the rest of the company in the library, he almost involuntarily
asked Mr. Flosky, whom he looked up to as a most oraculous personage, whether any story of any ghost that had ever appeared to
any one, was entitled to any degree of belief?

Mr. Flosky.—By far the greater number to a very great degree.

The Honourable Mr. Listless.—Really, that is very alarming!

Mr. Flosky.—Sunt geminæ somni portæ.[1] There are two gates
through which ghosts find their way to the upper air: fraud and
self-delusion. In the latter case a ghost is a *deceptio visûs*, an ocular
spectrum, an idea with the force of a sensation. I have seen many
ghosts myself. I dare say there are few in this company who have
not seen a ghost.

The Honourable Mr. Listless.—I am happy to say, I never have,
for one.

The Reverend Mr. Larynx.—We have such high authority for
ghosts, that it is rank scepticism to disbelieve them. Job saw a
ghost, which came for the express purpose of asking a question, but
did not wait for an answer.

The Honourable Mr. Listless.—Because Job was too frightened
to give one.

The Reverend Mr. Larynx.—Spectres appeared to the Egyptians
during the darkness with which Moses covered Egypt. The witch
of Endor raised the ghost of Samuel. Moses and Elias appeared on
Mount Tabor. An evil spirit was sent into the army of Sennacherib,
and exterminated it in a single night.

Mr. Toobad.—Saying, The devil has come among you, having
great wrath.

[1] There are two gates of sleep.

653

Mr. Flosky.—Saint Macarius interrogated a skull, which was found in the desert, and made it relate, in presence of several witnesses, what was going forward in hell. Saint Martin of Tours, being jealous of a pretended martyr, who was the rival saint of his neighbourhood, called up his ghost, and made him confess that he was damned. Saint Germain, being on his travels, turned out of an inn a large party of ghosts, who had every night taken possessions of the *table d'hôte*, and consumed a copious supper.

Mr. Hilary.—Jolly ghosts, and no doubt all friars. A similar party took possession of the cellar of M. Swebach, the painter, in Paris, drank his wine, and threw the empty bottles at his head.

The Reverend Mr. Larynx.—An atrocious act.

Mr. Flosky.—Pausanias relates, that the neighing of horses and the tumult of combatants were heard every night on the field of Marathon: but those who went purposely to hear these sounds suffered severely for their curiosity; but those who heard them by accident passed with impunity.

The Reverend Mr. Larynx.—I once saw a ghost myself in my study, which is the last place where any one but a ghost would look for me. I had not been into it for three months, and was going to consult Tillotson, when on opening the door, I saw a venerable figure in a flannel dressing gown, sitting in my arm-chair, and reading my Jeremy Taylor. It vanished in a moment, and so did I; and what it was or what it wanted I have never been able to ascertain.

Mr. Flosky.—It was an idea with the force of a sensation. It is seldom that ghosts appeal to two senses at once; but, when I was in Devonshire, the following story was well attested to me. A young woman, whose lover was at sea, returning one evening over some solitary fields, saw her lover sitting on a stile over which she was to pass. Her first emotions were surprise and joy, but there was a paleness and seriousness in his face that made them give place to alarm. She advanced towards him, and he said to her, in a solemn voice, "The eye that hath seen me shall see me no more. Thine eye is upon me, but I am not." And with these words he vanished; and on that very day and hour, as it afterwards appeared, he had perished by shipwreck.

The whole party now drew round in a circle, and each related some ghostly anecdote, heedless of the flight of time, till, in a pause of the conversation, they heard the hollow tongue of midnight sounding twelve.

Mr. Hilary.—All these anecdotes admit of solution on psychological principles. It is more easy for a soldier, a philosopher, or even a saint, to be frightened at his own shadow, than for a dead man to come out of his grave. Medical writers cite a thousand singular examples of the force of imagination. Persons of feeble, nervous, melancholy temperament, exhausted by fever, by labour, or by spare diet, will readily conjure up, in the magic ring of their old phantasy, spectres, gorgons, chimæras, and all the objects of their hatred and their love. We are most of us like Don Quixote, to whom a windmill was a giant, and Dulcinea was a magnificent princess: all more or less the dupes of our own imagination, though we do not all go so far as to see ghosts, or to fancy ourselves pipkins and teapots.

Mr. Flosky.—I can safely say, I have seen too many ghosts myself to believe in their external existence. I have seen all kinds of ghosts: black spirits and white, red spirits and gray. Some in the shape of venerable old men, who have met me in my rambles at noon; some of beautiful young women, who have peeped through my curtains at midnight.

The Honourable Mr. Listless.—And have proved, I doubt not, "palpable to feeling as to sight."

Mr. Flosky.—By no means, sir. You reflect upon my purity. Myself and my friends, particularly my friend Mr. Sackbut, are famous for our purity. No, sir, genuine untangible ghosts. I live in a world of ghosts. I see a ghost at this moment.

Mr. Flosky fixed his eyes on the door at the further end of the library. The company looked in the same direction. The door silently opened, and a ghastly figure, shrouded in white drapery, with the semblance of a bloody turban on its head, entered and stalked slowly up the apartment. Mr. Flosky, familiar as he was with ghosts, was not prepared for this apparition, and made the best of his way out at the opposite door. Mrs. Hilary and Marionetta followed, screaming. The Honourable Mr. Listless, by two turns of his body, rolled first off the sofa and then under it. The Reverend Mr. Larynx leaped up and fled with so much precipitation, that he overturned the table on the foot of Mr. Glowry. Mr. Glowry roared with pain in the ear of Mr. Toobad. Mr. Toobad's alarm so bewildered his senses, that, missing the door, he threw up one of the windows, jumped out in his panic, and plunged over head and ears in the moat. Mr. Asterias and his son, who were on the watch for their mermaid, were attracted by the splashing, threw a net over him, and dragged him to land.

Scythrop and Mr. Hilary meanwhile had hastened to his assistance, and, on arriving at the edge of the moat, followed by several servants with ropes and torches, found Mr. Asterias and Aquarius busy in endeavouring to extricate Mr. Toobad from the net, who was entangled in the meshes, and floundering with rage. Scythrop was lost in amazement; but Mr. Hilary saw, at one view, all the circumstances of the adventure, and burst into an immoderate fit of laughter; on recovering from which, he said to Mr. Asterias, "You have caught an odd fish, indeed." Mr. Toobad was highly exasperated at this unseasonable pleasantry; but Mr. Hilary softened his anger, by producing a knife, and cutting the Gordian knot of his reticular envelopment. "You see," said Mr. Toobad— "you see, gentlemen, in my unfortunate person proof upon proof of the present dominion of the devil in the affairs of this world; and I have no doubt but that the apparition of this night was Apollyon himself in disguise, sent for the express purpose of terrifying me into this complication of misadventures. The devil is come among you, having great wrath, because he knoweth that he hath but a short time."

Chapter XIII

MR. GLOWRY WAS much surprised, on occasionally visiting Scythrop's tower, to find the door always locked, and to be kept sometimes waiting many minutes for admission: during which he invariably heard a heavy rolling sound like that of a ponderous mangle, or of a waggon on a weighing-bridge, or of theatrical thunder.

He took little notice of this for some time: at length his curiosity was excited, and, one day, instead of knocking at the door, as usual, the instant he reached it, he applied his ear to the key-hole, and like Bottom, in the *Midsummer Night's Dream*, "spied a voice," which he guessed to be of the feminine gender, and knew to be not Scythrop's, whose deeper tones he distinguished at intervals. Having attempted in vain to catch a syllable of the discourse, he knocked violently at the door, and roared for immediate admission. The voices ceased, and Scythrop was discovered alone. Mr. Glowry looked round to every corner of the apartment, and then said, "Where is the lady?"

"The lady, sir?" said Scythrop.

"Yes, sir, the lady."

"Sir, I do not understand you."

"You don't, sir?"

"No, indeed, sir. There is no lady here."

"But, sir, this is not the only apartment in the tower, and I make no doubt there is a lady upstairs."

"You are welcome to search, sir."

"Yes, and while I am searching, she will slip out from some lurking-place, and make her escape."

"You may lock this door, sir, and take the key with you."

"But there is the terrace door: she has escaped by the terrace."

"The terrace, sir, has no other outlet, and the walls are too high for a lady to jump down."

"Well, sir, give me the key."

Mr. Glowry took the key, searched every nook of the tower, and returned.

"You are a fox, Scythrop; you are an exceedingly cunning fox, with that demure visage of yours. What was that lumbering sound I heard before you opened the door?"

"Sound, sir?"

"Yes, sir, sound."

"My dear sir, I am not aware of any sound, except my great table, which I moved on rising to let you in."

"The table!—let me see that. No, sir; not a tenth part heavy enough, not a tenth part."

"But, sir, you do not consider the laws of acoustics: a whisper becomes a peal of thunder in the focus of reverberation. Allow me to explain this: sounds striking on concave surfaces are reflected from them, and, after reflection, converge to points which are the foci of these surfaces. It follows, therefore, that the ear may be so placed in one, as that it shall hear a sound better than when situated nearer to the point of the first impulse: again, in the case of two concave surfaces placed opposite to each other——"

"Nonsense, sir. Don't tell me of foci. Pray, sir, will concave surfaces produce two voices when nobody speaks? I heard two voices, and one was feminine; feminine, sir: what say you to that?"

"Oh, sir, I perceive your mistake: I am writing a tragedy, and was acting over a scene to myself. To convince you, I will give you a specimen; but you must first understand the plot. It is a tragedy on the German model. The Great Mogul is in exile, and has taken lodgings at Kensington, with his only daughter, the Princess Rantrorina, who takes in needlework, and keeps a day-school. *The Princess is discovered hemming a set of shirts for the parson of the parish: they are to be marked with a large R. Enter to her the Great Mogul. A pause, during which they look at each other expressively. The princess changes colour several times. The Mogul takes snuff in great agitation. Several grains are heard to fall on the stage. His heart is seen to beat through his upper benjamin.*—THE MOGUL (*with a mournful look at his left shoe*). "My shoestring is broken." THE PRINCESS (*after an interval of melancholy reflection*). "I know it."—THE MOGUL. "My second shoe-string! The first broke when I lost my empire: the second has broken to-day. When will my poor heart break!"—THE PRINCESS. "Shoe-strings, hearts, and empires! Mysterious sympathy!"

"Nonsense, sir," interrupted Mr. Glowry. "That is not at all like the voice I heard."

"But, sir," said Scythrop, "a key-hole may be so constructed as to act like an acoustic tube, and an acoustic tube, sir, will modify sound in a very remarkable manner. Consider the construction of the ear, and the nature and causes of sound. The external part of the ear is a cartilaginous funnel."

"It won't do, Scythrop. There is a girl concealed in this tower, and find her I will. There are such things as sliding panels and secret closets."—He sounded round the room with his cane, but detected no hollowness.—"I have heard, sir," he continued, "that during my absence, two years ago, you had a dumb carpenter closeted with you, day after day. I did not dream that you were laying contrivances for carrying on secret intrigues. Young men will have their way: I had my way when I was a young man: but, sir, when your cousin Marionetta——"

Scythrop now saw that the affair was growing serious. To have clapped his hand upon his father's mouth, to have entreated him to be silent, would, in the first place, not have made him so; and, in the second, would have shown a dread of being overheard by somebody. His only resource, therefore, was to try and drown Mr. Glowry's voice; and, having no other subject, he continued his description of the ear, raising his voice continually as Mr. Glowry raised his.

"When your cousin Marionetta," said Mr. Glowry, "whom you profess to love—whom you profess to love, sir——"

"The internal canal of the ear," said Scythrop, "is partly bony and partly cartilaginous. This internal canal is—"

"Is actually in the house, sir; and, when you are so shortly to be —as I expect——"

"Closed at the further end by the *membrana tympani*—"

"Joined together in holy matrimony—"

"Under which is carried a branch of the fifth pair of nerves—"

"I say, sir, when you are so shortly to be married to your cousin Marionetta—"

"The *cavitas tympani*—"

A loud noise was heard behind the bookcase, which, to the astonishment of Mr. Glowry, opened in the middle, and the massy compartments, with all their weight of books, receding from each other in the manner of a theatrical scene, with a heavy rolling sound (which Mr. Glowry immediately recognized to be the same which had excited his curiosity) disclosed an interior apartment, in the entrance of which stood the beautiful Stella, who, stepping forward, exclaimed, "Married! Is he going to be married? The profligate!"

"Really, madam," said Mr. Glowry, "I do not know what he is going to do, or what I am going to do, or what any one is going to do; for all this is incomprehensible."

"I can explain it all," said Scythrop, "in a most satisfactory manner, if you will but have the goodness to leave us alone."

"Pray, sir, to which act of the tragedy of the Great Mogul does this incident belong?"

"I entreat you, my dear sir, leave us alone."

Stella threw herself into a chair, and burst into a tempest of tears. Scythrop sat down by her, and took her hand. She snatched her hand away, and turned her back upon him. He rose, sat down on the other side, and took her other hand. She snatched it away, and turned from him again. Scythrop continued entreating Mr.

Glowry to leave them alone; but the old gentleman was obstinate, and would not go.

"I suppose, after all," said Mr. Glowry maliciously, "it is only a phænomenon in acoustics, and this young lady is a reflection of sound from concave surfaces."

Some one tapped at the door: Mr. Glowry opened it, and Mr. Hilary entered. He had been seeking Mr. Glowry, and had traced him to Scythrop's tower. He stood a few moments in silent surprise, and then addressed himself to Mr. Glowry for an explanation.

"The explanation," said Mr. Glowry, "is very satisfactory. The Great Mogul has taken lodgings at Kensington, and the external part of the ear is a cartilaginous funnel."

"Mr. Glowry, that is no explanation."

"Mr. Hilary, it is all I know about the matter."

"Sir, this pleasantry is very unseasonable. I perceive that my niece is sported with in a most unjustifiable manner, and I shall see if she will be more successful in obtaining an intelligible answer." And he departed in search of Marionetta.

Scythrop was now in a hopeful predicament. Mr. Hilary made a hue and cry in the abbey, and summoned his wife and Marionetta to Scythrop's apartment. The ladies, not knowing what was the matter, hastened in great consternation. Mr. Toobad saw them sweeping along the corridor, and judging from their manner that the devil had manifested his wrath in some new shape, followed from pure curiosity.

Scythrop, meanwhile, vainly endeavoured to get rid of Mr. Glowry and to pacify Stella. The latter attempted to escape from the tower, declaring she would leave the abbey immediately, and he should never see or hear of her more. Scythrop held her hand, and detained her by force, till Mr. Hilary reappeared with Mrs. Hilary and Marionetta. Marionetta, seeing Scythrop grasping the hand of a strange beauty, fainted away in the arms of her aunt. Scythrop flew to her assistance; and Stella, with redoubled anger, sprang towards the door, but was intercepted in her intended flight by being caught in the arms of Mr. Toobad, who exclaimed —"Celinda!"

"Papa!" said the young lady disconsolately.

"The devil is come among you," said Mr. Toobad, "how came my daughter here?"

"Your daughter!" exclaimed Mr. Glowry.

"Your daughter!" exclaimed Scythrop, and Mr. and Mrs. Hilary.

"Yes," said Mr. Toobad, "my daughter Celinda."

Marionetta opened her eyes and fixed them on Celinda; Celinda, in return, fixed hers on Marionetta. They were at remote points of the apartment. Scythrop was equidistant from both of them, central and motionless, like Mahomet's coffin.

"Mr. Glowry," said Mr. Toobad, "can you tell by what means my daughter came here?"

"I know no more," said Mr. Glowry, "than the Great Mogul."

"Mr. Scythrop," said Mr. Toobad, "how came my daughter here?"

"I did not know, sir, that the lady was your daughter."

"But how came she here?"

"By spontaneous locomotion," said Scythrop, sullenly.

"Celinda," said Toobad, "what does all this mean?"

"I really do not know, sir."

"This is most unaccountable. When I told you in London that I had chosen a husband for you, you thought proper to run away from him; and now, to all appearance, you have run away to him."

"How, sir! was that your choice?"

"Precisely; and if he is yours too we shall be both of a mind, for the first time in our lives."

"He is not my choice, sir. This lady has a prior claim: I renounce him."

"And I renounce him," said Marionetta.

Scythrop knew not what to do. He could not attempt to conciliate the one without irreparably offending the other; and he was so fond of both, that the idea of depriving himself for ever of the society of either was intolerable to him: he therefore retreated into his stronghold, mystery; maintained an impenetrable silence; and contented himself with stealing occasionally a deprecating glance at each of the objects of his idolatry. Mr. Toobad and Mr. Hilary, in the meantime, were each insisting on an explanation from Mr. Glowry, who they thought had been playing a double game on this occasion. Mr. Glowry was vainly endeavouring to persuade them of his innocence in the whole transaction. Mrs. Hilary was endeavour-

ing to mediate between her husband and brother. The Honourable
Mr. Listless, the Reverend Mr. Larynx, Mr. Flosky, Mr. Asterias,
and Aquarius, were attracted by the tumult to the scene of action,
and were appealed to severally and conjointly by the respective
disputants. Multitudinous questions, and answers *en masse*, composed a charivari, to which the genius of Rossini alone could have
given a suitable accompaniment, and which was only terminated
by Mrs. Hilary and Mr. Toobad retreating with the captive damsels. The whole party followed, with the exception of Scythrop,
who threw himself into his armchair, crossed his left foot over his
right knee, placed the hollow of his left hand on the interior ankle
of his left leg, rested his right elbow on the elbow of the chair,
placed the ball of his right thumb against his right temple, curved
the fore-finger along the upper part of his forehead, rested the
point of the middle finger on the bridge of his nose, and the points
of the two others on the lower part of the palm, fixed his eyes intently on the veins in the back of his left hand, and sat in this
position like the immovable Theseus, who, as is well known to
many who have not been at college, and to some few who have,
sedet, æternumque sedebit.[1] We hope the admirers of the *minutiæ*
in poetry and romance will appreciate this accurate description of
a pensive attitude.

Chapter XIV

SCYTHROP WAS STILL in this position when Raven entered to announce that dinner was on table.

"I cannot come," said Scythrop.

Raven sighed. "Something is the matter," said Raven: "but man
is born to trouble."

"Leave me," said Scythrop; "go, and croak elsewhere."

"Thus it is," said Raven. "Five-and-twenty years have I lived in
Nightmare Abbey, and now all the reward of my affection is—Go,
and croak elsewhere. I have danced you on my knee, and fed you
with marrow."

"Good Raven," said Scythrop, "I entreat you to leave me."

[1] Sits, and will sit for ever.

"Shall I bring your dinner here?" said Raven. "A boiled fowl and a glass of Madeira are prescribed by the faculty in cases of low spirits. But you had better join the party: it is very much reduced already."

"Reduced! How?"

"The Honourable Mr. Listless is gone. He declared that, what with family quarrels in the morning, and ghosts at night, he could get neither sleep nor peace; and that the agitation was too much for his nerves: though Mr. Glowry assured him that the ghost was only poor Crow walking in his sleep, and that the shroud and bloody turban were a sheet and a red night-cap."

"Well, sir?"

"The Reverend Mr. Larynx has been called off on duty, to marry or bury (I don't know which) some unfortunate person or persons, at Claydyke: but man is born to trouble!"

"Is that all?"

"No. Mr. Toobad is gone too, and a strange lady with him."

"Gone!"

"Gone. And Mr. and Mrs. Hilary, and Miss O'Carroll: they are all gone. There is nobody left but Mr. Asterias and his son, and they are going to-night."

"Then I have lost them both!"

"Won't you come to dinner?"

"No."

"Shall I bring your dinner here?"

"Yes."

"What will you have?"

"A pint of port and a pistol."

"A pistol!"

"And a pint of port. I will make my exit like Werter. Go. Stay. Did Miss O'Carroll say anything?"

"No."

"Did Miss Toobad say anything?"

"The strange lady? No."

"Did either of them cry?"

"No."

"What did they do?"

"Nothing."

"What did Mr. Toobad say?"

"He said, fifty times over, the devil was come among us."

"And they are gone?"

"Yes; and the dinner is getting cold. There is a time for everything under the sun. You may as well dine first, and be miserable afterwards."

"True, Raven. There is something in that. I will take your advice: therefore bring me——"

"The port and the pistol?"

"No; the boiled fowl and Madeira."

Scythrop had dined, and was sipping his Madeira alone, immersed in melancholy musing, when Mr. Glowry entered, followed by Raven, who, having placed an additional glass, and set a chair for Mr. Glowry, withdrew. Mr. Glowry sat down opposite Scythrop. After a pause, during which each filled and drank in silence, Mr. Glowry said, "So, sir, you have played your cards well. I proposed Miss Toobad to you: you refused her. Mr. Toobad proposed you to her: she refused you. You fell in love with Marionetta, and were going to poison yourself, because, from pure fatherly regard to your temporal interests, I withheld my consent. When, at length, I offered you my consent, you told me I was too precipitate. And, after all, I find you and Miss Toobad living together in the same tower, and behaving in every respect like two plighted lovers. Now, sir, if there be any rational solution of all this absurdity, I shall be very much obliged to you for a small glimmering of information."

"The solution, sir, is of little moment; but I will leave it in writing for your satisfaction. The crisis of my fate is come: the world is a stage, and my direction is exit."

"Do not talk so, sir;—do not talk so, Scythrop. What would you have?"

"I would have my love."

"And pray, sir, who is your love?"

"Celinda—Marionetta—either—both."

"Both! That may do very well in a German tragedy; and the Great Mogul might have found it very feasible in his lodgings at Kensington; but it will not do in Lincolnshire. Will you have Miss Toobad?"

"Yes."

"And renounce Marionetta?"

"No."

"But you must renounce one."

"I cannot."

"And you cannot have both. What is to be done?"

"I must shoot myself."

"Don't talk so, Scythrop. Be rational, my dear Scythrop. Consider, and make a cool, calm choice, and I will exert myself in your behalf."

"Why should I choose, sir? Both have renounced *me*: I have no hope of either."

"Tell me which you would have, and I will plead your cause irresistibly."

"Well, sir,—I will have—no, sir, I cannot renounce either. I cannot choose either. I am doomed to be the victim of eternal disappointments; and I have no resource but a pistol."

"Scythrop—Scythrop;—if one of them should come to you— what then?"

"That, sir, might alter the case: but that cannot be."

"It can be, Scythrop; it will be: I promise you it will be. Have but a little patience—but a week's patience; and it shall be."

"A week, sir, is an age: but, to oblige you, as a last act of filial duty, I will live another week. It is now Thursday evening, twenty-five minutes past seven. At this hour and minute, on Thursday next, love and fate shall smile on me, or I will drink my last pint of port in this world."

Mr. Glowry ordered his travelling-chariot, and departed from the abbey.

Chapter XV

The day after Mr. Glowry's departure was one of incessant rain, and Scythrop repented of the promise he had given. The next day was one of bright sunshine: he sat on the terrace, read a tragedy of Sophocles, and was not sorry, when Raven announced dinner, to find himself alive. On the third evening, the wind blew, and the rain beat, and the owl flapped against his windows; and he put a new flint in his pistol. On the fourth day, the sun shone again; and he locked the pistol up in a drawer, where he left it undisturbed till the morning of the eventful Thursday, when he ascended the turret with a telescope, and spied anxiously along the road that crossed the fens from Claydyke: but nothing appeared on it. He watched in this manner from ten A.M. till Raven summoned him to dinner at five; when he stationed Crow at the telescope, and descended to his own funeral-feast. He left open the communications between the tower and the turret, and called aloud at intervals to Crow,—"Crow, Crow, is anything coming?" Crow answered, "The wind blows, and the windmills turn, but I see nothing coming"; and, at every answer, Scythrop found the necessity of raising his spirits with a bumper. After dinner, he gave Raven his watch to set by the abbey clock. Raven brought it, Scythrop placed it on the table, and Raven departed. Scythrop called again to Crow; and Crow, who had fallen asleep, answered mechanically, "I see nothing coming." Scythrop laid his pistol between his watch and his bottle. The hour-hand passed the VII.—the minute-hand moved on;—it was within three minutes of the appointed time. Scythrop called again to Crow. Crow answered as before. Scythrop rang the bell: Raven appeared.

"Raven," said Scythrop, "the clock is too fast."

"No, indeed," said Raven, who knew nothing of Scythrop's intentions; "if anything, it is too slow."

"Villain!" said Scythrop, pointing the pistol at him; "it is too fast!"

"Yes—yes—too fast, I meant," said Raven, in manifest fear.

"How much too fast?" said Scythrop.

"As much as you please," said Raven.

"How much, I say?" said Scythrop, pointing the pistol again.

"An hour, a full hour, sir," said the terrified butler.

"Put back my watch," said Scythrop.

Raven, with trembling hand, was putting back the watch, when the rattle of wheels was heard in the court; and Scythrop, springing downstairs by three steps together, was at the door in sufficient time to have handed either of the young ladies from the carriage, if she had happened to be in it; but Mr. Glowry was alone.

"I rejoice to see you," said Mr. Glowry; "I was fearful of being too late, for I waited till the last moment, in the hope of accomplishing my promise; but all my endeavours have been vain, as these letters will show."

Scythrop impatiently broke the seals. The contents were these:—

"Almost a stranger in England, I fled from parental tyranny, and the dread of an arbitrary marriage, to the protection of a stranger and a philosopher, whom I expected to find something better than, or at least something different from the rest of his worthless species. Could I, after what has occurred, have expected nothing more from you than the commonplace impertinence of sending your father to treat with me, and with mine, for me? I should be a little moved in your favour, if I could believe you capable of carrying into effect the resolutions which your father says you have taken, in the event of my proving inflexible; though I doubt not you will execute them as far as relates to the pint of wine, twice over, at least. I wish you much happiness with Miss O'Carroll. I shall always cherish a grateful recollection of Nightmare Abbey, for having been the means of introducing me to a true transcendentalist; and, though he is a little older than myself, which is all one in Germany, I shall very soon have the pleasure of subscribing myself

CELINDA FLOSKY."

"I hope, my dear cousin, that you will not be angry with me, but that you will always think of me as a sincere friend, who will always feel interested in your welfare; I am sure you love Miss Toobad much better than me, and I wish you much happiness with her. Mr. Listless assures me that people do not kill themselves for love nowadays, though it is still the fashion to talk about it. I shall, in a very short time, change my name and situation, and shall always be happy to see you in Berkeley Square, when, to the unalterable designation of your affectionate cousin, I shall subjoin the signature of

MARIONETTA LISTLESS."

Scythrop tore both the letters to atoms, and railed in good set terms against the fickleness of women.

"Calm yourself, my dear Scythrop," said Mr. Glowry; "there are yet maidens in England."

"Very true, sir," said Scythrop.

"And the next time," said Mr. Glowry, "have but one string to your bow."

"Very good advice," said Scythrop.

"And, besides," said Mr. Glowry, "the fatal time is past, for it is now almost eight."

"Then that villain Raven," said Scythrop, "deceived me, when he said that the clock was too fast; but, as you observe very justly, the time has gone by, and I have just reflected that these repeated crosses in love qualify me to take a very advanced degree in misanthropy; and there is, therefore, good hope that I may make a figure in the world. But I shall ring for the rascal Raven, and admonish him."

Raven appeared. Scythrop looked at him very fiercely two or three minues; and Raven, still remembering the pistol, stood quaking in mute apprehension, till Scythrop, pointing significantly towards the dining-room, said, "Bring some Madeira."

Liber Amoris

1823

WILLIAM HAZLITT

THE LIBER AMORIS is a record of the most unfortunate love story in literature from Propertius' meeting with Cynthia to Baudelaire's with Jeanne Duval. It is something between a work of art and a case history, containing some of the loveliest pages in English and some of the silliest, aiming at the perfection of art but held back by proximity to the raw and painful experiences of life. There is nothing else like it in the language. It remains a pièce unique, a romantic catastrophe.

Let us first observe the episode as the world saw it. Benjamin Robert Haydon is writing to Miss Mitford (1822):

"Hazlitt at present gives me great pain by the folly with which he is conducting himself. He has fallen in love with a lodging-house hussy, who will be his death, he has been to Scotland to divorce his wife although he has a fine little boy by her; and after doing this to marry this girl, he comes back to find she has been making a fool of him in order to get presents and in reality has been admitting a lover more favoured. Hazlitt's torture is beyond expression; you may imagine it. The girl really incited in him a devoted and intense love . . . he talks of nothing else day and night. He has written down all the conversations without colour, literally as they happen; he has preserved all the love letters, many of which are equal to anything of the sort, and really affecting; and I believe, in order to ease his soul of this burden, means, with certain arrangements, to publish it as a tale of character. He will sink into idiocy if he does not get rid of it."

In 1822, Hazlitt was 44 years old. He had been married in 1808 and had lived apart from his wife since 1819. For two years he had been in lodgings off Chancery Lane kept by a tailor named Walker, who had three daughters. Though his marriage had been a sensible one, for his wife had intellectual tastes and a little property, it was not founded on mutual attraction and their temperaments were utterly dissimilar. Sarah Hazlitt was prosaic, secretive, conventional and thrifty, her husband brilliant, reckless, moody and improvident. He had never been loved nor had a happy love affair; young girls, he said, drove him mad, and he had a sentiment of physical inferiority kept alive by personal attacks on him in right-wing papers. 'Pimpled Hazlitt' was a favorite epithet and Blackwood's magazine described him as a 'small fetid blear-eyed pug.' In fact, like many political journalists, he was attractive when animated and insignificant when silent and brooding. "His figure was indeed indifferent," wrote Barry Cornwall, "and his movements shy and awkward, but there was something in his earnest irritable face, his restless eyes, his black hair, combed backwards and curling (not too resolutely) about a well-shaped head, that was very striking."

For the last year at his lodgings he had been titivated by the morning visits of his landlady's daughter, Sally Walker, who brought him his breakfast, sat on his lap and kissed him. "Her face was round and small" (I quote Barry Cornwall again) "and her eyes emotionless, glassy and without any speculation (apparently) in them. Her movements in walking were very remarkable. For I never observed her to make a step. She went onwards in a sort of wavy sinuous manner, like the movements of a snake. She was silent, or uttered monosyllables only, and was very demure. Her steady unmoving gaze upon the person whom she was addressing was exceedingly unpleasant. To this girl he gave all his valuable time, all his wealth of thought, and all the loving frenzy of his heart. For a time I think that on this point he was substantially insane—certainly beyond self control." There must have been a manic depressive streak in Hazlitt and I believe that the transition from depression to mania (cf. Goethe) is generally accompanied by falling in love which is, perhaps, provoked by glandular disturbance. Sally Walker was like a cancer of the soul to Hazlitt, an obsessional growth on the spirit set in motion through sexual repression, and a last middle aged clutching at innocence and

672

youth. She attacked him in his weak spot as an insect paralyzes a grub, and from that moment genius was of no avail; "glued to a bitch," he was in the grip of a disease that had seized on a centre of retarded adolescence. He developed the manic's loquacity and on the same day told five people, two of them strangers, of his passion, down to the minutest detail. Some of his original letters are hysterical, obscene and illegible and he develops the typical exhibitionism, reading aloud his most abject letters, boasting of imaginary success, behaving to his wife and friends with meanness, aggression and blatant want of tact. He is clearly possessed and, at moments, consciously so, though perhaps not aware that his rising tide of mania will also protect him, will enable him to write a whole volume of essays in less than a month and at the last float his hopeless passion into rage, rather than self destruction.

Sally Walker is attractive in the way of so many artful modest maidens of the early nineteenth century, Juliets of the back parlour, paintable by Etty or Fuseli. A servant girl's conventionality appeared modesty, her sententiousness high principles, her ignorance simplicity, her lumpish heaviness deep understanding. A quiet flirtatiousness, the prevarication of indifference and the gleam of cupidity wove round her victims a mysterious texture of unfathomable charm. She would make the perfect whore, he thought, or the perfect wife. Seizing with the desperate naivety of middle age on the latter alternative, he persuaded Mrs. Hazlitt, in return for a settlement, to go to Scotland to divorce him and they set out in the spring of 1822 for the sombre Reno of the North.

Mrs. Hazlitt kept a diary of her trip to Scotland. It is an extraordinary document. She and Hazlitt constantly met to arrange the details of the divorce and she was always asking him for small sums of money which he owed her. As he was famous and seldom paid, she soon acquired a reputation for thinking of nothing else. Those who have examined this journal have pronounced her phlegmatic and callous. I think she was a proud and undemonstrative woman who loved her husband and tried to deaden her mortification by compulsive walking. Although each painful scene laid her low with stomach trouble, she covered one hundred and seventy miles in a week. "Mrs. Bell said that he seemed quite enamoured of a letter he had been writing to Patmore; that in their walk the day before, he pulled it out of his pocket twenty times, and wanted to read it to her; that he talked so loud and acted so extravagantly that the people stood and stared at them as they passed, they seemed to take him for a madman. . . . walked to the Glasgow canal; seemed so restless; as if I should go mad; and could not swallow, I was so choked."

Like many abandoned wives of men of genius Sarah Hazlitt continued to observe paintings and landscape with the eyes her husband had opened for her and one day, as she was leaving the picture gallery at Dalkeith Palace, she met Hazlitt and a friend coming in. In a letter to Patmore about Sally he writes afterwards, "Do you know I saw a picture, the pattern of her, the other day at Dalkeith Palace (Hope finding Fortune in the Sea) and the resemblance almost drove me out of my senses." When they met a week later, Mrs. Hazlitt asked him if he thought it a good collection. "No," he said, "very poor; there were but two tolerable, one a female figure floating on the water in an historical picture, which he thought a copy of some good picture. I told him I had remarked it and thought that figure exceedingly good. The other was a Claude but in a very dirty condition." Three days later they had a long and final discussion when he tried to explain the nature of his infatuation, how Sally had made a dead set at him from the first . . . 'she was not at all pretty; her eyes were the worst and had the worst expression he had ever seen of hypocrisy and design, and had a poor slimy watery look, yet she was well made and had handsome arms.' I said it did not appear to me at all the beauty he used to admire, which was plump, and she was as thin and bony as the scrag end of a neck of mutton; that I thought the female figure in the picture at Dalkeith House much more to his taste; he fancied it was like her. I said it was much nearer my form in the thighs, the fall of the back, and the contour of the whole figure; he said, I was very well made. He said he had two opposite opinions of Sarah Walker at different times. . . . He asked me where I should be in town and I told him at Christies; he enquired what sort of people they were. I told him a very respectable quiet young couple lately married; he desired me to take care of myself, and keep up a respectable appearance, as I had money enough to do so. He wished he could marry some woman with a good fortune, that he might not be under the necessity of writing another line."

The Liber Amoris is in three parts—the Overture, a series of dialogues which present the characters in their period of felicity, then the letters to Patmore from Scotland, and finally the denouement, a long letter to Sheridan Knowles from London. There are also some fragments of diary. We see three Hazlitts, the gallant lover as with Sally, the doggy or despairing one with Patmore, and the solitary artist in the Journal. Hazlitt made a considerable effort to produce a work of art and rewrote many of the letters, toning down his ravings and accusations until he very nearly succeeded. It is instructive to compare the rough and finished states, and I give two versions of the passage recounting the visit to Rosslyn.

I

"I was at Roslin Castle yesterday, and the exquisite beauty of the scene, with the thought of what I should feel, should I ever be restored to her, and have to lead her through such places as my adored, my angel-wife, almost drove me beside myself. For this picture, this ecstatic vision, what have I instead as the image of the reality? Demoniacal possessions. I see the young witch seated in another's lap, twining her serpent arms round him, her eyes glancing, and her cheeks on fire. Damn the unnatural hag. Oh! Oh! Why does not the hideous thought choke me? It is so, and she can make no more confidences. The gentleman who lodges in the old room is a red-faced, pot-bellied, powdered gentleman of sixty—a pleasant successor! . . . The bitch likes the nasty, the wilful, the antipathetic . . . Get someone to try her or I am destroyed for ever. It would be sweet and full revenge. You may try her if you like—a pot-belly and a slender waist match by contrast. Do they not? I shall soon be in town and see. Pity me, Pity [a word indistinct]

"Looking in the glass to see why I am so hated, I think I see FREEDOM written on my brow."

II

"I was at Rosslyn Castle yesterday. It lies low in a rude but sheltered valley, hid from the vulgar gaze, and powerfully reminds one of the old song. The straggling fragments of the russet ruins, suspended smiling and graceful in the air as if they would linger out another century to please the curious beholder, the green larch trees trembling in between, with the blue sky and white silver clouds, the wild mountain plants starting out here and there, the date of the year on an old low doorway, but still more, the beds of flowers in orderly decay, that seem to have no hand to tend them, but keep up a sort of traditional remembrance of civilisation in former ages, present altogether an amiable subject for contemplation." But the reader can compare the rest for himself.

Perhaps because Hazlitt was hard up (a general consequence of infatuation) and had even been arrested for debt—or perhaps through neurotic insensitiveness, the Liber Amoris appeared too soon and after inadequate gestation. The effect was disastrous and the book was attacked on all sides. Crabb Robinson wrote in his diary: "Finished early Hazlitt's disgusting 'New Pygmalion', such a story as this is nauseous and revolting. It ought to exclude the author from all decent society." Half a century later it deterred Stevenson from writing the life of the most imaginative essayist since Bacon.

Hazlitt had hoped to be cured by the knowledge of Sally's infidelity but four months after the publication of his book he was still passing most of the night watching her door. "If we have drunk poison, finding it out does not prevent its being in our veins." What repels so many people about the *Liber Amoris* is indeed the helplessness of a brilliant mind in the grip of adolescent lust. Hazlitt is unmanned by it, he is no longer master of himself and this morbidity is something that, like jealousy, we cannot forgive in other people because we so dread it for ourselves. Fortunately a trip abroad and the rewarding company of Landor and of Stendhal (who gave him *De l'Amour*) worked wonders. He married again, a widow with a little money, and again unhappily—and died in 1830. His last words were, "Well, I have had a happy life."

Mrs. Hazlitt did not re-marry and on her son announcing his engagement she wrote advising him, "to pay ready money for everything, to lay by a little every year in case of a family or illness, and to let neither of you have any secret or separate schemes unconfided to the other." Of the "slimy marble varnished fiend," "the little damned incubus," the "sweet apparition" whose lingering glance, as she turned in the doorway that August morning, had set in motion such a coil, we can only conjecture.

Liber Amoris

WILLIAM HAZLITT

Advertisement

The circumstances, an outline of which is given in these pages, happened a very short time ago to a native of North Britain, who left his own country early in life, in consequence of political animosities and an ill-advised connection in marriage. It was some years after that he formed the fatal attachment which is the subject of the following narrative. The whole was transcribed very carefully with his own hand, a little before he set out for the Continent in hopes of benefiting by a change of scene, but he died soon after in the Netherlands—it is supposed, of disappointment preying on a sickly frame and morbid state of mind. It was his wish that what had been his strongest feeling while living, should be preserved in this shape when he was no more.—It has been suggested to the friend, into whose hands the manuscript was entrusted, that many things (particularly in the Conversations in the first Part) either childish or redundant, might have been omitted; but a promise was given that not a word should be altered, and the pledge was held sacred. The names and circumstances are so far disguised, it is presumed, as to prevent any consequences resulting from the publication, farther than the amusement or sympathy of the reader.

Part I

The Picture

H. OH! IS IT you? I had something to show you—I have got a picture here. Do you know any one it's like?

S. No, Sir.

H. Don't you think it like yourself?

S. No: it's much handsomer than I can pretend to be.

H. That's because you don't see yourself with the same eyes that others do. *I* don't think it handsomer, and the expression is hardly so fine as yours sometimes is.

S. Now you flatter me. Besides, the complexion is fair, and mine is dark.

H. Thine is pale and beautiful, my love, not dark! But if your colour were a little heightened, and you wore the same dress, and your hair were let down over your shoulders, as it is here, it might be taken for a picture of you. Look here, only see how like it is. The forehead is like, with that little obstinate protrusion in the middle; the eyebrows are like, and the eyes are just like yours, when you look up and say—"No—never!"

S. What then, do I always say "No—never!" when I look up?

H. I don't know about that—I never heard you say so but once: but that was once too often for my peace. It was when you told me, "you could never be mine." Ah! if you are never to be mine, I shall not long be myself. I cannot go on as I am. My faculties leave me: I think of nothing, I have no feeling about any thing but thee: thy sweet image has taken possession of me, haunts me, and will drive me to distraction. Yet I could almost wish to go mad for thy sake: for then I might fancy that I had thy love in return, which I cannot live without!

S. Do not, I beg, talk in that manner, but tell me what this is a picture of.

H. I hardly know; but it is a very small and delicate copy (painted in oil on a gold ground) of some fine old Italian picture, Guido's or Raphael's, but I think Raphael's. Some say it is a Madonna; others call it a Magdalen, and say you may distinguish the tear upon the cheek, though no tear is there. But it seems to me more like Raphael's St. Cecilia, "with looks commercing with the skies," than any thing else.—See, Sarah, how beautiful it is! Ah! dear girl, these are the ideas I have cherished in my heart, and in my brain; and I never found anything to realize them on earth till I met with thee, my love! While thou didst seem sensible of my kindness, I was but too happy: but now thou hast cruelly cast me off.

S. You have no reason to say so: you are the same to me as ever.

H. That is nothing. You are to me everything, and I am nothing to you. Is it not too true?

S. No.

H. Then kiss me, my sweetest. Oh! could you see your face now—your mouth full of suppressed sensibility, your down-cast eyes, the soft blush upon that cheek, you would not say the picture is not like because it is too handsome, or because you want complexion. Thou art heavenly-fair, my love—like her from whom the picture was taken—the idol of the painter's heart, as thou art of mine! Shall I make a drawing of it, altering the dress a little, to show you how like it is?

S. As you please.—

The Invitation

H. BUT I AM afraid I tire you with this prosing description of the French character and abuse of the English? You know there is but one subject on which I should ever wish to talk, if you would let me.

S. I must say, you don't seem to have a very high opinion of this country.

H. Yes, it is the place that gave you birth.

S. Do you like the French women better than the English?

H. No: though they have finer eyes, talk better, and are better

681

made. But they none of them look like you. I like the Italian women I have seen, much better than the French: they have darker eyes, darker hair, and the accents of their native tongue are much richer and more melodious. But I will give you a better account of them when I come back from Italy, if you would like to hear it.

S. I should much. It is for that I have sometimes had a wish for travelling abroad, to understand something of the manners and characters of different people.

H. My sweet girl! I will give you the best account I can—unless you would rather go and judge for yourself.

S. I cannot.

H. Yes, you shall go with me, and you shall go *with honour*—you know what I mean.

S. You know it is not in your power to take me so.

H. But it soon may: and if you would consent to bear me company, I would swear never to think of an Italian woman while I am abroad, nor of an English one after I return home. Thou art to me more than thy whole sex.

S. I require no such sacrifices.

H. Is that what you thought I meant by *sacrifices* last night? But sacrifices are no sacrifices when they are repaid a thousand fold.

S. I have no way of doing it.

H. You have not the will.—

S. I must go now.

H. Stay, and hear me a little. I shall soon be where I can no more hear thy voice, far distant from her I love, to see what change of climate and bright skies will do for a sad heart. I shall perhaps see thee no more, but I shall still think of thee the same as ever—I shall say to myself, "Where is she now?—what is she doing?" But I shall hardly wish you to think of me, unless you could do so more favourably than I am afraid you will. Ah! dearest creature, I shall be "far distant from you," as you once said of another, but you will not think of me as of him, "with the sincerest affection." The smallest share of thy tenderness would make me blest; but couldst thou ever love me as thou didst him, I should feel like a God! My face would change to a different expression: my whole form would undergo alteration. I was getting well, I was growing

young in the sweet proofs of your friendship: you see how I droop
and wither under your displeasure! Thou art divine, my love, and
canst make me either more or less than mortal. Indeed I am thy
creature, thy slave—I only wish to live for your sake—I would
gladly die for you—

S. That would give me no pleasure. But indeed you greatly
over-rate my power.

H. Your power over me is that of sovereign grace and beauty.
When I am near thee, nothing can harm me. Thou art an angel
of light, shadowing me with thy softness. But when I let go thy
hand, I stagger on a precipice: out of thy sight the world is dark
to me and comfortless. There is no breathing out of this house:
the air of Italy will stifle me. Go with me and lighten it. I can
know no pleasure away from thee—

> "But I will come again, my love,
> "An it were ten thousand mile!"

The Message

S. MRS. E—— has called for the book, Sir.

H. Oh! it is there. Let her wait a minute or two. I see this is a
busy-day with you. How beautiful your arms look in those short
sleeves!

S. I do not like to wear them.

H. Then that is because you are merciful, and would spare frail
mortals who might die with gazing.

S. I have no power to kill.

H. You have, you have—Your charms are irresistible as your
will is inexorable. I wish I could see you always thus. But I would
have no one else see you so. I am jealous of all eyes but my own.
I should almost like you to wear a veil, and to be muffled up
from head to foot; but even if you were, and not a glimpse of
you could be seen, it would be to no purpose—you would only
have to move, and you would be admired as the most graceful
creature in the world. You smile—Well, if you were to be won
by fine speeches—

S. You could supply them!

H. It is however no laughing matter with me; thy beauty kills me daily, and I shall think of nothing but thy charms, till the last word trembles on my tongue, and that will be thy name, my love—the name of my Infelice! You will live by that name, you rogue, fifty years after you are dead. Don't you thank me for that?

S. I have no such ambition, Sir. But Mrs. E—— is waiting.

H. She is not in love, like me. You look so handsome to-day, I cannot let you go. You have got a colour.

S. But you say I look best when I am pale.

H. When you are pale, I think so; but when you have a colour, I then think you still more beautiful. It is you that I admire; and whatever you are, I like best. I like you as Miss L——, I should like you still more as Mrs. ——. I once thought you were half-inclined to be a prude, and I admired you as a "pensive nun, devout and pure." I now think you are more than half a coquet, and I like you for your roguery. The truth is, I am in love with you, my angel; and whatever you are, is to me the perfection of thy sex. I care not what thou art, while thou art still thyself. Smile but so, and turn my heart to what shape you please!

S. I am afraid, Sir, Mrs. E—— will think you have forgotten her.

H. I had, my charmer. But go, and make her a sweet apology, all graceful as thou art. One kiss! Ah! ought I not to think myself the happiest of men?

The Flageolet

H. WHERE HAVE you been, my love!

S. I have been down to see my aunt, Sir.

H. And I hope she has been giving you good advice.

S. I did not go to ask her opinion about anything.

H. And yet you seem anxious and agitated. You appear pale and dejected, as if your refusal of me had touched your own breast with pity. Cruel girl! you look at this moment heavenly-soft, saint-like, or resemble some graceful marble statue, in the moon's pale ray! Sadness only heightens the elegance of your features. How can I escape from you, when every new occasion, even your cruelty and scorn, brings out some new charm. Nay, your rejection of me, by the way in which you do it, is only a new link added to my chain. Raise those down-cast eyes, bend as if an angel stooped, and kiss me. . . . Ah! enchanting little trembler! if such is thy sweetness where thou dost not love, what must thy love have been? I cannot think how any man, having the heart of one, could go and leave it.

S. No one did, that I know of.

H. Yes, you told me yourself he left you (though he liked you, and though he knew—Oh! gracious God!—that you loved him) he left you because "the pride of birth would not permit a union." —For myself, I would leave a throne to ascend to the heaven of thy charms. I live but for thee, here—I only wish to live again to pass all eternity with thee. But even in another world, I suppose you would turn from me to seek him out, who scorned you here.

S. If the proud scorn us here, in that place we shall all be equal.

H. Do not look so—do not talk so—unless you would drive me mad. I could worship you at this moment. Can I witness such perfection, and bear to think I have lost you for ever? Oh! let me hope! You see you can mould me as you like. You can lead me by the hand, like a little child; and with you my way would be like a little child's:—you could strew flowers in my path, and pour new life and hope into me. I should then indeed hail the return of spring with joy, could I indulge the faintest hope—would you but let me try to please you!

S. Nothing can alter my resolution, Sir.

H. Will you go and leave me so?

S. It is late, and my father will be getting impatient at my stopping so long.

H. You know he has nothing to fear for you—it is poor I that am alone in danger. But I wanted to ask about buying you a flageolet. Could I see that which you have? If it is a pretty one, it would hardly be worth while; but if it isn't, I thought of be-speaking an ivory one for you. Can't you bring up your own to show me?

S. Not to-night, Sir.

H. I wish you could.

S. I cannot—but I will in the morning.

H. Whatever you determine, I must submit to. Good night, and bless thee!

[*The next morning, S. brought up the tea-kettle as usual; and looking towards the tea-tray, she said, "Oh! I see my sister has forgot the tea-pot." It was not there, sure enough; and tripping down stairs, she came up in a minute, with the tea-pot in one hand, and the flageolet in the other, balanced so sweetly and gracefully. It would have been awkward to have brought up the flageolet in the tea-tray, and she could not well have gone down again on purpose to fetch it. Something therefore was to be omitted as an excuse. Exquisite witch! But do I love her the less dearly for it? I cannot.*]

The Confession

H. YOU SAY you cannot love. Is there not a prior attachment in the case? Was there any one else that you *did* like?

S. Yes, there was another.

H. Ah! I thought as much. Is it long ago then?

S. It is two years, Sir.

H. And has time made no alteration? Or do you still see him sometimes?

S. No, Sir! But he is one to whom I feel the sincerest affection, and ever shall, though he is far distant.

H. And did he return your regard?

S. I had every reason to think so.

H. What then broke off your intimacy?

S. It was the pride of birth, Sir, that would not permit him to think of an union.

H. Was he a young man of rank, then?

S. His connections were high.

H. And did he never attempt to persuade you to any other step?

S. No—he had too great a regard for me.

H. Tell me, my angel, how was it? Was he so very handsome? Or was it the fineness of his manners?

S. It was more his manner: but I can't tell how it was. It was chiefly my own fault. I was foolish to suppose he could ever think seriously of me. But he used to make me read with him—and I used to be with him a good deal, though not much neither—and I found my affections entangled before I was aware of it.

H. And did your mother and family know of it?

S. No—I have never told any one but you; nor I should not have mentioned it now, but I thought it might give you some satisfaction.

H. Why did he go at last?

S. We thought it better to part.

H. And do you correspond?

S. No, Sir. But perhaps I may see him again some time or other, though it will be only in the way of friendship.

H. My God! what a heart is thine, to live for years upon that bare hope!

S. I did not wish to live always, Sir—I wished to die for a long time after, till I thought it not right; and since then I have endeavoured to be as resigned as I can.

H. And do you think the impression will never wear out?

S. Not if I can judge from my feelings hitherto. It is now some time since,—and I find no difference.

H. May God for ever bless you! How can I thank you for your condescension in letting me know your sweet sentiments? You have changed my esteem into adoration.—Never can I harbour a thought of ill in thee again.

S. Indeed, Sir, I wish for your good opinion and your friendship.

H. And can you return them?

S. Yes.

H. And nothing more?

S. No, Sir.

H. You are an angel, and I will spend my life, if you will let me, in paying you the homage that my heart feels towards you.

The Quarrel

H. YOU ARE angry with me?

S. Have I not reason?

H. I hope you have; for I would give the world to believe my suspicions unjust. But, oh! my God! after what I have thought of

you and felt towards you, as little less than an angel, to have but
a doubt cross my mind for an instant that you were what I dare
not name—a common lodging-house decoy, a kissing convenience,
that your lips were as common as the stairs—

S. Let me go, Sir!

H. Nay—prove to me that you are not so, and I will fall down
and worship you. You were the only creature that ever seemed to
love me; and to have my hopes, and all my fondness for you, thus
turned to a mockery—it is too much! Tell me why you have deceived me, and singled me out as your victim?

S. I never have, Sir. I always said I could not love.

H. There is a difference between love and making me a laughing-stock. Yet what else could be the meaning of your little sister's
running out to you, and saying "He thought I did not see him!"
when I had followed you into the other room? Is it a joke upon
me that I make free with you? Or is not the joke rather against
her sister, unless you make my courtship of you a jest to the whole
house? Indeed I do not well see how you can come and stay with
me as you do, by the hour together, and day after day, as openly
as you do, unless you give it some such turn with your family. Or
do you deceive them as well as me?

S. I deceive no one, Sir. But my sister Betsey was always watching and listening when Mr. M—— was courting my eldest sister,
till he was obliged to complain of it.

H. That I can understand, but not the other. You may remember, when your servant Maria looked in and found you sitting
in my lap one day, and I was afraid she might tell your mother, you
said "You did not care, for you had no secrets from your mother."
This seemed to me odd at the time, but I thought no more of it,
till other things brought it to my mind. Am I to suppose, then, that
you are acting a part, a vile part, all this time, and that you come
up here, and stay as long as I like, that you sit on my knee and
put your arms round my neck, and feed me with kisses, and let me
take other liberties with you, and that for a year together; and
that you do all this not out of love, or liking, or regard, but go
through your regular task, like some young witch, without one
natural feeling, to show your cleverness, and get a few presents
out of me, and go down into the kitchen to make a fine laugh

of it? There is something monstrous in it, that I cannot believe of you.

S. Sir, you have no right to harass my feelings in the manner you do. I have never made a jest of you to any one, but always felt and expressed the greatest esteem for you. You have no ground for complaint in my conduct; and I cannot help what Betsey or others do. I have always been consistent from the first. I told you my regard could amount to no more than friendship.

H. Nay, Sarah, it was more than half a year before I knew that there was an insurmountable obstacle in the way. You say your regard is merely friendship, and that you are sorry I have ever felt any thing more for you. Yet the first time I ever asked you, you let me kiss you: the first time I ever saw you, as you went out of the room, you turned full round at the door, with that inimitable grace with which you do everything, and fixed your eyes full upon me, as much as to say, "Is he caught?"—that very week you sat upon my knee, twined your arms round me, caressed me with every mark of tenderness consistent with modesty; and I have not got much farther since. Now if you did all this with me, a perfect stranger to you, and without any particular liking to me, must I not conclude you do so as a matter of course with every one?—Or if you do not do so with others, it was because you took a liking to me for some reason or other.

S. It was gratitude, Sir, for different obligations.

H. If you mean by obligations the presents I made you, I had given you none the first day I came. You do not consider yourself *obliged* to every one who asks you for a kiss?

S. No, Sir.

H. I should not have thought any thing of it in any one but you. But you seemed so reserved and modest, so soft, so timid, you spoke so low, you looked so innocent—I thought it impossible you could deceive me. Whatever favors you granted must proceed from pure regard. No betrothed virgin ever gave the object of her choice kisses, caresses more modest or more bewitching than those you have given me a thousand and a thousand times. Could I have thought I should ever live to believe them an inhuman mockery of one who had the sincerest regard for you? Do you think they will not now turn to rank poison in my veins, and kill me, soul and body? You say it is friendship—but if this is friendship, I'll forswear love. Ah! Sarah! it must be something more or less than friendship. If your caresses are sincere, they show fondness—if they are not, I must be more than indifferent to you. Indeed you once let some words drop, as if I were out of the question in such matters, and you could trifle with me with impunity. Yet you complain at other times that no one ever took such liberties with you as I have done. I remember once in particular your saying, as you went out at the door in anger—"I had an attachment before, but that person never attempted any thing of the kind." Good God! How did I dwell on that word *before*, thinking it implied an attachment to me also; but you have since disclaimed any such meaning. You say you have never professed more than esteem. Yet once, when you were sitting in your old place, on my knee, embracing and fondly embraced, and I asked you if you could not love, you made answer, "I could easily say so, whether I did or not—YOU SHOULD JUDGE BY MY ACTIONS!" And another time, when you were in the same posture, and I reproached you with indifference, you replied in these words, "Do I SEEM INDIFFERENT?" Was I to blame after this to indulge my passion for the loveliest of her sex? Or what can I think?

S. I am no prude, Sir.

H. Yet you might be taken for one. So your mother said, "It was hard if you might not indulge in a little levity." She has strange notions of levity. But levity, my dear, is quite out of character in you. Your ordinary walk is as if you were performing some religious ceremony: you come up to my table of a morning, when you merely bring in the tea-things, as if you were advancing to the altar. You move in minuet-time: you measure every step, as if you were afraid of offending in the smallest things. I never hear your approach on the stairs, but by a sort of hushed silence. When you enter the room, the Graces wait on you, and Love waves round your person in gentle undulations, breathing balm into the soul! By Heaven, you are an angel! You look like one at this instant! Do I not adore you—and have I merited this return?

S. I have repeatedly answered that question. You sit and fancy things out of your own head, and then lay them to my charge. There is not a word of truth in your suspicions.

H. Did I not overhear the conversation down-stairs last night, to which you were a party? Shall I repeat it?

S. I had rather not hear it!

H. Or what am I to think of this story of the footman?

S. It is false, Sir, I never did any thing of the sort.

H. Nay, when I told your mother I wished she wouldn't * (as I heard she did) she said "Oh, there's nothing in that, for Sarah very often * * * * * * * * * * *" and your doing so before company, is only a trifling addition to the sport.

S. I'll call my mother, Sir, and she shall contradict you.

H. Then she'll contradict herself. But did not you boast you were "very persevering in your resistance to gay young men," and had been "several times obliged to ring the bell?" Did you always ring it? Or did you get into these dilemmas that made it necessary, merely by the demureness of your looks and ways? Or had nothing else passed? Or have you two characters, one that you palm off upon me, and another, your natural one, that you resume when you get out of the room, like an actress who throws aside her artificial part behind the scenes? Did you not, when I was courting you on the staircase the first night Mr. C—— came, beg me to desist, for if the new lodger heard us, he'd take you for a light character? Was that all? Were you only afraid of being *taken* for a light character? Oh! Sarah!

S. I'll stay and hear this no longer.

H. Yes, one word more. Did you not love another?

S. Yes, and ever shall most sincerely.

H. Then, *that* is my only hope. If you could feel this sentiment for him, you cannot be what you seem to me of late. But there is another thing I had to say—be what you will, I love you to distraction! You are the only woman that ever made me think she loved me, and that feeling was so new to me, and so delicious, that it "will never from my heart." Thou wert to me a little tender flower, blooming in the wilderness of my life; and though thou should'st turn out a weed, I'll not fling thee from me, while I can help it. Wert thou all that I dread to think—wert thou a wretched wanderer in the street, covered with rags, disease, and infamy, I'd clasp thee to my bosom, and live and die with thee, my love. Kiss me, thou little sorceress!

S. NEVER!

H. Then go: but remember I cannot live without you—nor I will not.

The Reconciliation

H. I HAVE then lost your friendship?

S. Nothing tends more to alienate friendship than insult.

H. The words I uttered hurt me more than they did you.

S. It was not words merely, but actions as well.

H. Nothing I can say or do can ever alter my fondness for you —Ah, Sarah! I am unworthy of your love: I hardly dare ask for your pity; but oh! save me—save me from your scorn: I cannot bear it—it withers me like lightning.

S. I bear no malice, Sir; but my brother, who would scorn to tell a lie for his sister, can bear witness for me that there was no truth in what you were told.

H. I believe it; or there is no truth in woman. It is enough for me to know that you do not return my regard; it would be too much for me to think that you did not deserve it. But cannot you forgive the agony of the moment?

S. I can forgive; but it is not easy to forget some things!

H. Nay, my sweet Sarah (frown if you will, I can bear your resentment for my ill behaviour, it is only your scorn and indifference that harrow up my soul)—but I was going to ask, if you had been engaged to be married to any one, and the day was fixed, and he had heard what I did, whether he could have felt any true regard for the character of his bride, his wife, if he had not been hurt and alarmed as I was?

S. I believe, actual contracts of marriage have sometimes been broken off by unjust suspicions.

H. Or had it been your old friend, what do you think he would have said in my case?

S. He would never have listened to any thing of the sort.

H. He had greater reasons for confidence than I have. But it is your repeated cruel rejection of me that drives me almost to madness. Tell me, love, is there not, besides your attachment to him, a repugnance to me?

S. No, none whatever.

H. I fear there is an original dislike, which no efforts of mine can overcome.

S. It is not you—it is my feelings with respect to another, which are unalterable.

H. And yet you have no hope of ever being his? And yet you accuse me of being romantic in my sentiments.

S. I have indeed long ceased to hope; but yet I sometimes hope against hope.

H. My love! were it in my power, thy hopes should be fulfilled to-morrow. Next to my own, there is nothing that could give me so much satisfaction as to see thine realized! Do I not love thee, when I can feel such an interest in thy love for another? It was that which first wedded my very soul to you. I would give worlds for a share in a heart so rich in pure affection!

S. And yet I did not tell you of the circumstance to raise myself in your opinion.

H. You are a sublime little thing! And yet, as you have no prospects there, I cannot help thinking, the best thing would be to do as I have said.

S. I would never marry a man I did not love beyond all the world.

H. I should be satisfied with less than that—with the love, or regard, or whatever you call it, you have shown me before marriage, if that has only been sincere. You would hardly like me less afterwards.

S. Endearments would, I should think, increase regard, where there was love beforehand; but that is not exactly my case.

H. But I think you would be happier than you are at present. You take pleasure in my conversation, and you say you have an esteem for me; and it is upon this, after the honeymoon, that marriage chiefly turns.

S. Do you think there is no pleasure in a single life?

H. Do you mean on account of its liberty?

S. No, but I feel that forced duty is no duty. I have high ideas of the married state!

H. Higher than of the maiden state?

S. I understand you, Sir.

H. I meant nothing; but you have sometimes spoken of any serious attachment as a tie upon you. It is not that you prefer flirting with "gay young men" to becoming a mere dull domestic wife?

693

S. You have no right to throw out such insinuations: for though I am but a tradesman's daughter, I have as nice a sense of honour as any one can have.

H. Talk of a tradesman's daughter! you would ennoble any family, thou glorious girl, by true nobility of mind.

S. Oh! Sir, you flatter me. I know my own inferiority to most.

H. To none; there is no one above thee, man nor woman either. You are above your situation, which is not fit for you.

S. I am contented with my lot, and do my duty as cheerfully as I can.

H. Have you not told me your spirits grow worse every year?

S. Not on that account: but some disappointments are hard to bear up against.

H. If you talk about that, you'll unman me. But tell me, my love,—I have thought of it as something that might account for some circumstances; that is, as a mere possibility. But tell me, there was not a likeness between me and your old lover that struck you at first sight? Was there?

S. No, Sir, none.

H. Well, I didn't think it likely there should.

S. But there was a likeness.

H. To whom?

S. To that little image! (*looking intently on a small bronze figure of Buonaparte on the mantle-piece.*)

H. What, do you mean to Buonaparte?

S. Yes, all but the nose was just like.

H. And was his figure the same?

S. He was taller!

[I got up and gave her the image, and told her it was hers by every right that was sacred. She refused at first to take so valuable a curiosity, and said she would keep it for me. But I pressed it eagerly, and she took it. She immediately came and sat down, and put her arm round my neck, and kissed me, and I said "Is it not plain we are the best friends in the world since we are always so glad to make it up?" And then I added "How odd it was that the God of my idolatry should turn out to be like her Idol, and said it was no wonder that the same face which awed the world should conquer the sweetest creature in it!" How I loved her at that moment! Is it possible that the wretch who writes this could ever have been so blest! Heavenly delicious creature! Can I live without her?—Oh! no—never—never.

"What is this world? What asken men to have,
Now with his love, now in the cold grave,
Alone withouten any compagnie!"

Let me but see her again! She cannot hate the man who loves her as I do.]

Letters to the Same

Feb. 1822.

—You will scold me for this, and ask me if this is keeping my promise to mind my work. One half of it was to think of Sarah: and besides, I do not neglect my work either, I assure you. I regularly do ten pages a day, which mounts up to thirty guineas' worth a week, so that you see I should grow rich at this rate, if I could keep on so; and I could keep on so, if I had you with me to encourage me with your sweet smiles, and share my lot. The Berwick smacks sail twice a week, and the wind sits fair. When I think of the thousand endearing caresses that have passed between us, I do not wonder at the strong attachment that draws me to you; but I am sorry for my own want of power to please. I hear the wind sigh through the lattice, and keep repeating over and over to myself two lines of Lord Byron's Tragedy—

"So shalt thou find me ever at thy side
Here and hereafter, if the last may be"—

applying them to thee, my love, and thinking whether I shall ever see thee again. Perhaps not—for some years at least—till both thou and I are old—and then, when all else have forsaken thee, I will creep to thee, and die in thine arms. You once made me believe I was not hated by her I loved; and for that sensation, so delicious was it, though but a mockery and a dream, I owe you

695

more than I can ever pay. I thought to have dried up my tears for ever, the day I left you; but as I write this, they stream again. If they did not, I think my heart would burst. I walk out here of an afternoon, and hear the notes of the thrush, that come up from a sheltered valley below, welcome in the spring; but they do not melt my heart as they used: it is grown cold and dead. As you say, it will one day be colder.—Forgive what I have written above; I did not intend it: but you were once my little all, and I cannot bear the thought of having lost you for ever, I fear through my own fault. Has any one called? Do not send any letters that come. I should like you and your mother (if agreeable) to go and see Mr. Kean in *Othello*, and Miss Stephens in *Love in a Village*. If you will, I will write to Mr. T——, to send you tickets. Has Mr. P—— called? I think I must send to him for the picture to kiss and talk to. Kiss me, my best-beloved. Ah! if you can never be mine, still let me be your proud and happy slave.

H.

To the Same

March, 1822.

—You will be glad to learn I have done my work—a volume in less than a month. This is one reason why I am better than when I came, and another is, I have had two letters from Sarah. I am pleased I have got through this job, as I was afraid I might lose reputation by it (which I can little afford to lose)—and besides, I am more anxious to do well now, as I wish you to hear me well spoken of. I walk out of an afternoon, and hear the birds sing as I told you, and think, if I had you hanging on my arm, *and that for life*, how happy I should be—happier than I ever hoped to be, or had any conception of till I knew you. "*But that can never be*"— I hear you answer in a soft, low murmur. Well, let me dream of it sometimes—I am not happy too often, except when that favorite note, the harbinger of spring, recalling the hopes of my youth, whispers thy name and peace together in my ear. I was reading something about Mr. Macready to-day, and this put me in mind of that delicious night, when I went with your mother and you to see *Romeo and Juliet*. Can I forget it for a moment—your sweet modest looks, your infinite propriety of behaviour, all your sweet winning ways—your hesitating about taking my arm as we came out till your mother did—your laughing about nearly losing your cloak—your stepping into the coach without my being able to make the slightest discovery—and oh! my sitting down beside you there, you whom I had loved so long, so well, and your assuring me I had not lessened your pleasure at the play by being with you, and giving me your dear hand to press in mine! I thought I was in heaven—that slender exquisitely turned form contained my all of heaven upon earth; and as I folded you—yes, you, my own best Sarah, to my bosom, there was, as you say, *a tie between us*—you did seem to me, for those few short moments, to be mine in all truth and honour and sacredness—Oh! that we could be always so—Do not mock me, for I am a very child in love. I ought to beg pardon for behaving so ill afterwards, but I hope the *little image* made it up between us, &c.

[*To this letter I have received no answer, not a line. The rolling years of eternity will never fill up that blank. Where shall I be? What am I? Or where have I been?*]

Written in a Blank Leaf of Endymion

I WANT a hand to guide me, an eye to cheer me, a bosom to repose on; all which I shall never have, but shall stagger into my grave, old before my time, unloved and unlovely, unless S. L. keeps her faith with me.

* * * * * * * * * * * * * * * * * * *
* * * * * * * * * * *

—But by her dove's eyes and serpent-shape, I think she does not hate me; by her smooth forehead and her crested hair, I own I love her; by her soft looks and queen-like grace (which men might fall down and worship) I swear to live and die for her!

A Proposal of Love

(Given to her in our early acquaintance)

"Oh! if I thought it could be in a woman
(As, if it can, I will presume in you)
To feed for aye her lamp and flames of love,
To keep her constancy in plight and youth,
Outliving beauties outward with a mind
That doth renew swifter than blood decays:
Or that persuasion could but thus convince me,
That my integrity and truth to you
Might be confronted with the match and weight
Of such a winnowed purity in love—
How were I then uplifted! But, alas,
I am as true as truth's simplicity,
And simpler than the infancy of truth."

TROILUS AND CRESSIDA.

Part II

Letters to C. P.——, Esq.

Bees-Inn.

MY GOOD FRIEND,

Here I am in Scotland (and shall have been here three weeks, next Monday) as I may say, *on my probation.* This is a lone inn, but on a great scale, thirty miles from Edinburgh. It is situated on a rising ground (a mark for all the winds, which blow here incessantly)—there is a woody hill opposite, with a winding valley below, and the London road stretches out on either side. You may guess which way I oftenest walk. I have written two letters to S. L. and got one cold, prudish answer, beginning *Sir,* and ending *From yours truly,* with *Best respects from herself and relations.* I was going to give in, but have returned an answer, which I think is a touch-stone. I send it you on the other side to keep as a curiosity, in case she kills me by her exquisite rejoinder. I am convinced from the profound contemplations I have had on the subject here and coming along, that I am on a wrong scent. We had a famous parting-scene, a complete quarrel and then a reconciliation, in which she did beguile me of my tears, but the deuce a one did she shed. What do you think? She cajoled me out of my little Buonaparte as cleverly as possible, in manner and form following. She was shy the Saturday and Sunday (the day of my departure) so I got in dudgeon, and began to rip up grievances. I asked her how she came to admit me to such extreme familiarities, the first week I entered the house. "If she had no particular regard for me, she must do so (or more) with every one: if she had a liking to me from the first, why refuse me with scorn and wilfulness?" If you had seen how she flounced, and looked, and went to the door, saying "She was obliged to me for letting her know the opinion I had always entertained of her"—then I said, "Sarah!"

699

and she came back and took my hand, and fixed her eyes on the mantle-piece—(she must have been invoking her idol then—if I thought so, I could devour her, the darling—but I doubt her)— So I said "There is one thing that has occurred to me sometimes as possible, to account for your conduct to me at first—there wasn't a likeness, was there to your old friend?" She answered "No, none—but there was a likeness"—I asked, to what? She said "To that little image!" I said, "Do you mean Buonaparte?"—She said, "Yes, all but the nose."—"And the figure?"—"He was taller." —I could not stand this. So I got up and took it, and gave it her, and after some reluctance, she consented to "keep it for me." What will you bet me that it wasn't all a trick? I'll tell you why I suspect it, besides being fairly out of my wits about her. I had told her mother half an hour before, that I should take this image and leave it at Mrs. B.'s, for that I didn't wish to leave anything behind me that must bring me back again. Then up she comes and starts a likeness to her lover: she knew I should give it her on the spot—"No, she would keep it for me!" So I must come back for it. Whether art or nature, it is sublime. I told her I should write and tell you so, and that I parted from her, confiding, ador- ing!—She is beyond me, that's certain. Do go and see her, and desire her not to give my present address to a single soul, and learn if the lodging is let, and to whom. My letter to her is as follows. If she shows the least remorse at it, I'll be hanged, though it might move a stone, I modestly think. (See before, *Part I. page* 695)

N. B. I have begun a book of our conversations (I mean mine and the statue's) which I call LIBER AMORIS. I was detained at Stamford and found myself dull, and could hit upon no other way of employing my time so agreeably.

Letter II

DEAR P———,
Here without loss of time, in order that I may have your opinion upon it, is little YES and No's answer to my last.

"SIR,

"I should not have disregarded your injunction not to send you any more letters that might come to you, had I not promised the Gentleman who left the enclosed to forward it the earliest opportunity, as he said it was of consequence. Mr. P— called the day after you left town. My mother and myself are much obliged by your kind offer of tickets to the play, but must decline accepting it. My family send their best respects, in which they are joined by

Yours truly,

S. L."

The deuce a bit more is there of it. If you can make anything out of it (or any body else) I'll be hanged. You are to understand, this comes in a frank, the second I have received from her, with a name I can't make out, and she won't tell me, though I asked her, where she got franks, as also whether the lodgings were let, to neither of which a word of answer. * * * * is the name on the frank: see if you can decypher it by a Red-book. I suspect her grievously of being an arrant jilt, to say no more—yet I love her dearly. Do you know I'm going to write to the sweet rogue presently, having a whole evening to myself in advance of my work? Now mark, before you set about your exposition of the new Apocalypse of the new Calypso, the only thing to be endured in the above letter is the date. It was written the very day after she received mine. By this she seems willing to lose no time in receiving these letters "of such sweet breath composed." If I thought so—but I wait for your reply. After all, what is there in her but a pretty figure, and that you can't get a word out of her? Hers is the Fabian method of making love and conquests. What do you suppose she said the night before I left her?

"H. Could you not come and live with me as a friend?

S. I don't know: and yet it would be of no use if I did, you would always be hankering after what could never be!"

I asked her if she would do so at once—the very next day? And what do you guess was her answer—"Do you think it would be prudent?" As I didn't proceed to extremities on the spot, she began to look grave, and declare off. "Would she live with me in her own house—to be with me all day as dear friends, if nothing more, to sit and read and talk with me?"—"She would make no promises, but I should find her the same."—"Would she go to the play with me sometimes, and let it be understood that I was paying my addresses to her?"—"She could not, as a habit—her father was rather strict, and would object."—Now what am I to think of all this? Am I mad or a fool? Answer me to that, Master Brook! You are a philosopher.

Letter III

DEAR FRIEND,

I ought to have written to you before; but since I received your letter, I have been in a sort of purgatory, and what is worse, I see no prospect of getting out of it. I would put an end to my torments at once; but I am as great a coward as I have been a dupe. Do you know I have not had a word of answer from her since! What can be the reason? Is she offended at my letting you know she wrote to me, or is it some new affair? I wrote to her in the tenderest, most respectful manner, poured my soul at her feet, and this is the return she makes me! Can you account for it, except on the admission of my worst doubts concerning her? Oh God! can I bear after all to think of her so, or that I am scorned and made a sport of by the creature to whom I had given my whole heart?—Thus has it been with me all my life; and so will it be to the end of it!—If you should learn anything, good or bad, tell me, I conjure you: I can bear anything but this cruel suspense. If I knew she was a mere abandoned creature, I should try to forget her; but till I do know this, nothing can tear me from her. I have drank in poison from her lips too long—alas! mine do not poison again. I sit and indulge my grief by the hour together; my weakness grows upon me; and I have no hope left, unless I could lose my senses quite. Do you know I think I should like this? To forget, ah! to forget—there would be something in that—to change to an idiot for some few years, and then to wake up a poor wretched old man, to recollect my misery as past, and die! Yet, oh! with her, only a little while ago, I had different hopes, forfeited for nothing that I know of! * * * * * * * * If you can give me any consolation on the subject of my tormentor, pray do. The pain I suffer wears me out daily. I write this on the supposition that Mrs. —— may still come here, and that I may be detained some weeks longer. Direct to me at the Postoffice; and if I return to town directly as I fear, I will leave word for them to forward the letter to me in London— not at my old lodgings. I will not go back there: yet how can I breathe away from her? Her hatred of me must be great, since my love of her could not overcome it! I have finished the book of my conversations with her, which I told you of: if I am not mistaken, you will think it very nice reading.

Yours ever.

Have you read Sardanapalus? How like the little Greek slave, Myrrha, is to *her!*

Letter IV

(Written in the Winter)

MY GOOD FRIEND,

I received your letter this morning, and I kiss the rod not only with submission, but gratitude. Your reproofs of me and your defences of her are the only things that save my soul from perdition. She is my heart's idol; and believe me those words of yours applied to the dear saint—"To lip a chaste one and suppose her wanton"— were balm and rapture to me. I have *lipped* her, God knows how often, and oh! is it even possible that she is chaste, and that she has bestowed her loved "endearments" on me (her own sweet word) out of true regard? That thought, out of the lowest depths of despair, would at any time make me strike my forehead against the stars. Could I but think the love "honest," I am proof against all hazards. She by her silence makes my *dark hour*; and you by your encouragements dissipate it for twenty-four hours. Another thing has brought me to life. Mrs. —— is actually on her way here about the divorce. Should this unpleasant business (which has been so long talked of) succeed, and I should become free, do you think S. L. will agree to change her name to ——? If she *will*, she *shall*; and to call her so to you or to hear her called so by

7º3

others, would be music to my ears, such as they never drank in. Do you think if she knew how I love her, my depressions and my altitudes, my wanderings and my constancy, it would not move her? She knows it all; and if she is not an *incorrigible*, she loves me, or regards me with a feeling next to love. I don't believe that any woman was ever courted more passionately than she has been by me. As Rousseau said of Madame d'Houptot (forgive the allusion) my heart has found a tongue in speaking to her, and I have talked to her the divine language of love. Yet she says, she is insensible to it. Am I to believe her or you? You—for I wish it and wish it to madness, now that I am like to be free, and to have it in my power to say to her without a possibility of suspicion, "Sarah, will you be mine?" When I sometimes think of the time I first saw the sweet apparition, August 16, 1820, and that possibly she may be my bride before that day two years, it makes me dizzy with incredible joy and love of her. Write soon.

Letter V

MY DEAR FRIEND,

I read your answer this morning with gratitude. I have felt somewhat easier since. It showed your interest in my vexations, and also that you know nothing worse than I do. I cannot describe the weakness of mind to which she has reduced me. This state of suspense is like hanging in the air by a single thread that exhausts all your strength to keep hold of it; and yet if that fails you, you have nothing in the world else left to trust to. I am come back to Edinburgh about this cursed business, and Mrs. —— is coming from Montrose next week. How it will end, I can't say; and don't care, except as it regards the other affair. I should, I confess, like to have it in my power to make her the offer direct and unequivocal, to see how she'd receive it. It would be worth something at any rate to see her superfine airs upon the occasion; and if she should take it into her head to turn round her sweet neck, drop her eye-lids, and say—"Yes, I will be yours!"—why then, "treason domestic, foreign levy, nothing could touch me further." By Heaven! I doat on her. The truth is, I never had any pleasure, like love, with any one but her. Then how can I bear to part with her? Do you know I like to think of her best in her morning-gown and mob-cap—it is so she has oftenest come into my room and enchanted me! She was once ill, pale, and had lost all her freshness. I only adored her the more for it, and fell in love with the decay of her beauty. I could devour the little witch. If she had a plague-spot on her, I could touch the infection: if she was in a burning fever, I could kiss her, and drink death as I have drank life from her lips. When I press her hand, I enjoy perfect happiness and contentment of soul. It is not what she says or what she does—it is herself that I love. To be with her is to be at peace. I have no other wish or desire. The air about her is serene, blissful; and he who breathes it is like one of the Gods! So that I can but have her with me always, I care for nothing more. I never could tire of her sweetness; I feel that I could grow to her, body and soul! My heart, my heart is hers.

Letter VI

(Written in May)

DEAR P——,

What have I suffered since I parted with you! A raging fire is in my heart and in my brain, that never quits me. The steam-boat (which I foolishly ventured on board) seems a prison-house, a sort of spectre-ship, moving on through an infernal lake, without wind or tide, by some necromantic power—the splashing of the waves, the noise of the engine gives me no rest, night or day—no tree, no natural object varies the scene—but the abyss is before me, and all my peace lies weltering in it! I feel the eternity of punishment in this life; for I see no end of my woes. The people about me are ill, uncomfortable, wretched enough, many of them —but to-morrow or next day, they reach the place of their destination, and all will be new and delightful. To me it will be the same. I can neither escape from her, nor from myself. All is endurable where there is a limit: but I have nothing but the blackness and the fiendishness of scorn around me—mocked by her (the false one) in whom I placed my hope, and who hardens herself against

me!—I believe you thought me quite gay, vain, insolent, half mad,
the night I left the house—no tongue can tell the heaviness of
heart I felt at that moment. No footsteps ever fell more slow, more
sad than mine; for every step bore me farther from her, with
whom my soul and every thought lingered. I had parted with her
in anger, and each had spoken words of high disdain, not soon to
be forgiven. Should I ever behold her again? Where go to live and
die far from her? In her sight there was Elysium; her smile was
heaven; her voice was enchantment; the air of love waved round
her, breathing balm into my heart: for a little while I had sat with
the Gods at their golden tables, I had tasted of all earth's bliss,
"both living and loving!" But now Paradise barred its doors against
me; I was driven from her presence, where rosy blushes and delicious sighs and all soft wishes dwelt, the outcast of nature and
the scoff of love! I thought of the time when I was a little happy
careless child, of my father's house, of my early lessons, of my
brother's picture of me when a boy, of all that had since happened
to me, and of the waste of years to come—I stopped, faltered,
and was going to turn back once more to make a longer truce
with wretchedness and patch up a hollow league with love,
when the recollection of her words—"I always told you I had no
affection for you"—steeled my resolution, and I determined to
proceed. You see by this she always hated me, and only played
with my credulity till she could find some one to supply the place
of her unalterable attachment to *the little image.* * * * * * * I
am a little, a very little better to-day. Would it were quietly over;
and that this misshapen form (made to be mocked) were hid
out of the sight of cold, sullen eyes! The people about me even
take notice of my dumb despair, and pity me. What is to be done?
I cannot forget *her*; and I can find no other like what *she seemed.*
I should wish you to call, if you can make an excuse, and see
whether or no she is quite marble—whether I may go back again
at my return, and whether she will see me and talk to me sometimes as an old friend. Suppose you were to call on M—— from
me, and ask him what his impression is that I ought to do. But
do as you think best. Pardon, pardon.

P. S. I send this from Scarborough, where the vessel stops
for a few minutes. I scarcely know what I should have done, but
for this relief to my feelings.

Letter VII

MY DEAR FRIEND,

The important step is taken, and I am virtually a free man.
* * * What had I better do in these circumstances? I dare not
write to her, I dare not write to her father, or else I would. She
has shot me through with poisoned arrows, and I think another
"winged wound" would finish me. It is a pleasant sort of balm
(as you express it) she has left in my heart! One thing I agree
with you in, it will remain there for ever; but yet not very long.
It festers, and consumes me. If it were not for my little boy,
whose face I see struck blank at the news, looking through the
world for pity and meeting with contempt instead, I should soon,
I fear, settle the question by my death. That recollection is the
only thought that brings my wandering reason to an anchor; that
stirs the smallest interest in me; or gives me fortitude to bear up
against what I am doomed to feel for the *ungrateful*. Otherwise,
I am dead to every thing but the sense of what I have lost. She
was my life—it is gone from me, and I am grown spectral! If I
find myself in a place I am acquainted with, it reminds me of her,
of the way in which I thought of her,

> ——"and carved on every tree
> The soft, the fair, the inexpressive she!"

If it is a place that is new to me, it is desolate, barren of all
interest; for nothing touches me but what has a reference to
her. If the clock strikes, the sound jars me; a million of hours will
not bring back peace to my breast. The light startles me; the
darkness terrifies me. I seem falling into a pit, without a hand
to help me. She has deceived me, and the earth fails from under
my feet: no object in nature is substantial, real, but false and
hollow, like her faith on which I built my trust. She came (I
knew not how) and sat by my side and was folded in my arms,
a vision of love and joy, as if she had dropped from the Heavens
to bless me by some especial dispensation of a favouring Providence, and make me amends for all; and now without any fault
of mine but too much fondness, she has vanished from me, and
I am left to perish. My heart is torn out of me, with every

feeling for which I wished to live. The whole is like a dream, an effect of enchantment; it torments me, and it drives me mad. I lie down with it; I rise up with it; and see no chance of repose. I grasp at a shadow, I try to undo the past, and weep with rage and pity over my own weakness and misery. I spared her again and again (fool that I was) thinking what she allowed from me was love, friendship, sweetness, not wantonness. How could I doubt it, looking in her face, and hearing her words, like sighs breathed from the gentlest of all bosoms? I had hopes, I had prospects to come, the flattery of something like fame, a pleasure in writing, health even would have come back with her smile—she has blighted all, turned all to poison and childish tears. Yet the barbed arrow is in my heart—I can neither endure it, nor draw it out; for with it flows my life's-blood. I had conversed too long with abstracted truth to trust myself with the immortal thoughts of love. *That S. L. might have been mine, and now never can*— these are the two sole propositions that forever stare me in the face, and look ghastly in at my poor brain, I am in some sense proud that I can feel this dreadful passion—it gives me a kind of rank in the kingdom of love—but I could have wished it had been for an object that at least could have understood its value and pitied its excess. You say her not coming to the door when you went is a proof—yes, that her complement is at present full! That is the reason she doesn't want me there, lest I should discover the new affair—wretch that I am! Another has possession of her, oh Hell! I'm satisfied of it from her manner, which had a wanton insolence in it. Well might I run wild when I received no letters from her. I foresaw, I felt my fate. The gates of Paradise were once open to me too, and I blushed to enter but with the golden keys of love! I would die; but her lover—my love of her— ought not to die. When I am dead, who will love her as I have done? If she should be in misfortune, who will comfort her? When she is old, who will look in her face, and bless her? Would there be any harm in calling upon M——, to know confidentially if he thinks it worth my while to make her an offer the instant it is in my power? Let me have an answer, and save me, if possible, for her and *from* myself.

Letter VIII

MY DEAR FRIEND,

Your letter raised me for a moment from the depths of despair; but not hearing from you yesterday or to-day (as I hoped) I have had a relapse. You say I want to get rid of her. I hope you are more right in your conjectures about her than in this about me. Oh no! believe it, I love her as I do my own soul; my very heart is wedded to her (be she what she may) and I would not hesitate a moment between her and "an angel from Heaven." I grant all you say about my self-tormenting folly: but has it been without cause? Has she not refused me again and again with a mixture of scorn and resentment, after going the utmost lengths with a man for whom she now disclaims all affection; and what security can I have for her reserve with others, who will not be restrained by feelings of delicacy towards her, and whom she has probably preferred to me for their want of it? *"She can make no more confidences"*—these words ring for ever in my ears, and will be my death-watch. They can have but one meaning, be sure of it—she always expressed herself with the exactest propriety. That was one of the things for which I loved her—shall I live to hate her for it? My poor fond heart, that brooded over her and the remains of her affections as my only hope of comfort upon earth, cannot brook this new degradation. Who is there so low as me? Who is there besides (I ask) after the homage I have paid her and the caresses she has lavished on me, so vile, so abhorrent to love, to whom such an indignity could have happened? When I think of this (and I think of nothing else) it stifles me. I am pent up in burning, fruitless desires, which can find no vent or object. Am I not hated, repulsed, derided by her whom alone I love or ever did love? I cannot stay in any place, and seek in vain for relief from the sense of her contempt and her ingratitude. I can settle to nothing: what is the use of all I have done? Is it not that very circumstance (my thinking beyond my strength, my feeling more than I need about so many things) that has withered me up, and made me a thing for Love to shrink from and wonder at? Who could ever feel that peace from the touch of her dear hand that I have done; and is it not torn from me for ever? My state is this, that I shall never lie down again at night nor rise up in the morning in peace, nor ever behold my little boy's face with pleasure while I live—unless I am restored to her favour. Instead of that delicious feeling I had when she was heavenly-kind to me, and my heart softened and melted in its own tenderness and her sweetness, I am now inclosed in a dungeon of despair. The sky is marble to my thoughts; nature is dead around me, as hope is within me; no object can give me one gleam of satisfaction now, nor the prospect of it in time to come. I wander by the sea-side; and the eternal ocean and lasting despair and her face are before me. Slighted by her, on whom my heart by its last fibre hung, where shall I turn? I wake with her by my side, not as my sweet bedfellow, but as the corpse of my love, without a heart in her bosom, cold, insensible, or struggling from me; and the worm gnaws me, and the sting of unrequited love, and the canker of a hopeless, endless sorrow. I have lost the taste of my food by feverish anxiety; and my favourite beverage, which used to refresh me when I got up, has no moisture in it. Oh! cold, solitary, sepulchral breakfasts, compared with those which I promised myself with her; or which I made when she had been standing an hour by my side, my guardian-angel, my wife, my sister, my sweet friend, my Eve, my all; and had blest me with her seraph-kisses! Ah! what I suffer at present only shews what I have enjoyed. But "the girl is a good girl, if there is goodness in human nature." I thank you for those words; and I will fall down and worship you, if you can prove them true: and I would not do much less for him that proves her a demon. She is one or the other, that's certain; but I fear the worst. Do let me know if anything has passed: suspense is my greatest punishment. I am going into the country to see if I can work a little in the three weeks I have yet to stay here. Write on the receipt of this, and believe me ever your unspeakably obliged friend.

To Edinburgh

——"Stony-hearted" Edinburgh! What art thou to me? The dust of thy streets mingles with my tears and blinds me. City of palaces, or of tombs—a quarry, rather than the habitation of men! Art thou like London, that populous hive, with its sun-burnt, well-baked, brick-built houses—its public edifices, its theatres, its bridges, its squares, its ladies, and its pomp, its throng of wealth, its outstretched magnitude, and its mighty heart that never lies still? Thy cold grey walls reflect back the leaden melancholy of the soul. The square, hard-edged, unyielding faces of thy inhabitants have no sympathy to impart. What is it to me that I look along the level line of thy tenantless streets, and meet perhaps a lawyer like a grasshopper chirping and skipping, or the daughter of a Highland laird, haughty, fair, and freckled? Or why should I look down your boasted Prince's-street, with the beetle-browed Castle on one side, and the Calton-hill with its proud monument at the further end, and the ridgy steep of Salisbury-Crag, cut off abruptly by Nature's boldest hand, and Arthur's-Seat overlooking all, like a lioness watching her cubs? Or shall I turn to the far-off Pentland-hills, with Craig-Crook nestling beneath them, where lives the prince of critics and the king of men? Or cast my eye unsated over the Firth of Forth, that from my window of an evening (as I read of AMY and her love) glitters like a broad golden mirror in the sun, and kisses the winding shores of kingly Fife? Oh no! But to thee, to thee I turn, North Berwick-Law, with thy blue cone rising out of summer seas; for thou art the beacon of my banished thoughts, and dost point my way to her, who is my heart's true home. The air is too thin for me, that has not the breath of Love in it; that is not embalmed by her sighs!

A Thought

I am not mad, but my heart is so; and raves within me, fierce and untameable, like a panther in its den, and tries to get loose to its lost mate, and fawn on her hand, and bend lowly at her feet.

ANOTHER

Oh! thou dumb heart, lonely, sad, shut up in the prison-house of this rude form, that hast never found a fellow but for an instant, and in very mockery of thy misery, speak, find bleeding words to express thy thoughts, break thy dungeon-gloom, or die pronouncing thy Infelice's name!

ANOTHER

Within my heart is lurking suspicion, and base fear, and shame and hate; but above all, tyrannous love sits throned, crowned with her graces, silent and in tears.

Letter IX

MY DEAR P——

You have been very kind to me in this business; but I fear even your indulgence for my infirmities is beginning to fail. To what a state am I reduced, and for what? For fancying a little artful vixen to be an angel and a saint, because she affected to look like one, to hide her rank thoughts and deadly purposes. Has she not murdered me under the mask of the tenderest friendship? And why? Because I have loved her with unutterable love, and sought to make her my wife. You say it is my own "outrageous conduct" that has estranged her: nay, I have been *too gentle* with her. I ask you first in candour whether the ambiguity of her behaviour with respect to me, sitting and fondling a man (circumstanced as I was) sometimes for half a day together, and then declaring she had no love for him beyond common regard, and professing never to marry, was not enough to excite my suspicions, which the different exposures from the conversations below-stairs were not calculated to allay? I ask you what you yourself would have felt or done, if loving her as I did, you had heard what I did, time after time? Did not her mother own to one of the grossest charges (which I shall not repeat)—and is such indelicacy to be reconciled with her pretended character (that character with which I fell in love, and to which I *made love*) without supposing her to be the greatest hypocrite in the world? My unpardonable offence has been that I took her at her word, and was willing to believe her the precise little puritanical person she set up for. After exciting her wayward desires by the fondest embraces and the purest kisses, as if she had been "made my wedded wife yestreen," or was to become so to-morrow (for that was always my feeling with respect to her)—I did not proceed to gratify them, or to follow up my advantage by any action which

should declare, "I think you a common adventurer, and will see
whether you are so or not!" Yet any one but a credulous fool
like me would have made the experiment, with whatever violence
to himself, as a matter of life and death; for I had every reason
to distrust appearances. Her conduct has been of a piece from
the beginning. In the midst of her closest and falsest endearments,
she has always (with one or two exceptions) disclaimed the
natural inference to be drawn from them, and made a verbal
reservation, by which she might lead me on in a Fool's Paradise,
and make me the tool of her levity, her avarice, and her love of
intrigue as long as she liked, and dismiss me whenever it suited her.
This, you see, she has done, because my intentions grew serious,
and if complied with, would deprive her of *the pleasures of a
single life!* Offer marriage to this "tradesman's daughter, who has
as nice a sense of honour as any one can have"; and like Lady
Bellaston in *Tom Jones*, she *cuts* you immediately in a fit of
abhorrence and alarm. Yet she seemed to be of a different mind
formerly, when struggling from me in the height of our first
intimacy, she exclaimed—"However I might agree to my own
ruin, I never will consent to bring disgrace upon my family!" That
I should have spared the traitress after expressions like this,
astonishes me when I look back upon it. Yet if it were all to do
over again, I know I should act just the same part. Such is her
power over me! I cannot run the least risk of offending her—I
love her so. When I look in her face, I cannot doubt her truth!
Wretched being that I am! I have thrown away my heart and
soul upon an unfeeling girl; and my life (that might have been
so happy, had she been what I thought her) will soon follow either
voluntarily, or by the force of grief, remorse, and disappointment.
I cannot get rid of the reflection for an instant, nor even seek
relief from its galling pressure. Ah! what a heart she has lost! All
the love and affection of my whole life were centered in her, who
alone, I thought, of all women had found out my true character,
and knew how to value my tenderness. Alas! alas! that this, the
only hope, joy, or comfort I ever had, should turn to a mockery,
and hang like an ugly film over the remainder of my days!—I
was at Roslin Castle yesterday. It lies low in a rude, but sheltered
valley, hid from the vulgar gaze, and powerfully reminds one of
the old song. The straggling fragments of the russet ruins, suspended smiling and graceful in the air as if they would linger

713

out another century to please the curious beholder, the green larch-trees trembling between with the blue sky and white silver clouds, the wild mountain plants starting out here and there, the date of the year on an old low door-way, but still more, the beds of flowers in orderly decay, that seem to have no hand to tend them, but keep up a sort of traditional remembrance of civilization in former ages, present altogether a delightful and amiable subject for contemplation. The exquisite beauty of the scene, with the thought of what I should feel, should I ever be restored to her, and have to lead her through such places as my adored, my angel-wife, almost drove me beside myself. For this picture, this ecstatic vision, what have I of late instead as the image of the reality? Demoniacal possessions. I see the young witch seated in another's lap, twining her serpent arms round him, her eye glancing and her cheeks on fire—why does not the hideous thought choke me? Or why do I not go and find out the truth at once? The moonlight streams over the silver waters: the bark is in the bay that might waft me to her, almost with a wish. The mountain-breeze sighs out her name: old ocean with a world of tears murmurs back my woes! Does not my heart yearn to be with her; and shall I not follow its bidding? No, I must wait till I am free; and then I will take my Freedom (a glad prize) and lay it at her feet and tell her my proud love of her that would not brook a rival in her dishonour, and that would have her all or none, and gain her or lose myself for ever!—

You see by this letter the way I am in, and I hope you will excuse it as the picture of a half-disordered mind. The least respite from my uneasiness (such as I had yesterday) only brings the contrary reflection back upon me, like a flood; and by letting me see the happiness I have lost, makes me feel, by contrast, more acutely what I am doomed to bear.

Letter X

DEAR FRIEND,

Here I am at St. Bees once more, amid the scenes which I greeted in their barrenness in winter; but which have now put on their full green attire that shows luxuriant to the eye, but speaks a tale of sadness to this heart widowed of its last, its dearest, its only hope! Oh! lovely Bees-Inn! here I composed a volume of law-cases, here I wrote my enamoured follies to her, thinking her human, and that "all below was not the fiend's"—here I got two cold, sullen answers from the little witch, and here I was ————— and I was damned. I thought the revisiting the old haunts would have soothed me for a time, but it only brings back the sense of what I have suffered for her and of her unkindness the more strongly, till I cannot endure the recollection. I eye the Heavens in dumb despair, or vent my sorrows in the desert air. "To the winds, to the waves, to the rocks I complain"—you may suppose with what effect! I fear I shall be obliged to return. I am tossed about (backwards and forwards) by my passion, so as to become ridiculous. I can now understand how it is that mad people never remain in the same place—they are moving on for ever, *from themselves!*

Do you know, you would have been delighted with the effect of the Northern twilight on this romantic country as I rode along last night? The hills and groves and herds of cattle were seen reposing in the grey dawn of midnight, as in a moonlight without shadow. The whole wide canopy of Heaven shed its reflex light upon them, like a pure crystal mirror. No sharp points, no petty details, no hard contrasts—every object was seen softened yet distinct, in its simple outline and natural tones, transparent with an inward light, breathing its own mild lustre. The landscape altogether was like an airy piece of mosaic-work, or like one of Poussin's broad massy landscapes or Titian's lovely pastoral scenes. Is it not so, that poets see nature, veiled to the sight, but revealed to the soul in visionary grace and grandeur! I confess the sight touched me; and might have removed all sadness except mine. So (I thought) the light of her celestial face once shone into my soul, and wrapt me in a heavenly trance. The sense I have of beauty raises me for a moment above myself, but depresses me the more afterwards, when I recollect how it is thrown away in vain admiration, and that it only makes me more susceptible of pain from the mortifications I meet with. Would I had never seen her! I might then not indeed have been happy, but at least I might have passed my life in peace, and have sunk into forgetful-

715

ness without a pang.—The noble scenery in this country mixes with my passion, and refines, but does not relieve it. I was at Stirling Castle not long ago. It gave me no pleasure. The declivity seemed to me abrupt, not sublime; for in truth I did not shrink back from it with terror. The weather-beaten towers were stiff and formal: the air was damp and chill: the river winded its dull, slimy way like a snake along the marshy grounds: and the dim misty tops of Ben Leddi, and the lovely Highlands (woven fantastically of thin air) mocked my embraces and tempted my longing eyes like her, the sole queen and mistress of my thoughts! I never found my contemplations on this subject so subtilised and at the same time so desponding as on that occasion. I wept myself almost blind, and I gazed at the broad golden sun-set though my tears that fell in showers. As I trod the green mountain turf, oh! how I wished to be laid beneath it—in one grave with her—that I might sleep with her in that cold bed, my hand in hers, and my heart for ever still—while worms should taste her sweet body, that I had never tasted! There was a time when I could bear solitude; but it is too much for me at present. Now I am no sooner left to myself than I am lost in infinite space, and look round me in vain for support or comfort. She was my stay, my hope: without her hand to cling to, I stagger like an infant on the edge of a precipice. The universe without her is one wide, hollow abyss, in which my harassed thoughts can find no resting-place. I must break off here; for the *hysterica passio* comes upon me, and threatens to unhinge my reason.

Letter XI

MY DEAR AND GOOD FRIEND,

I am afraid I trouble you with my querulous epistles, but this is probably the last. To-morrow or the next day decides my fate with respect to the divorce, when I expect to be a free man. In vain! Was it not for her and to lay my freedom at her feet, that I consented to this step which has cost me infinite perplexity, and now to be discarded for the first pretender that came in her way! If so, I hardly think I can survive it. You who have been a favourite with women, do not know what it is to be deprived of one's only hope, and to have it turned to shame and disappointment. There is nothing in the world left that can afford me one drop of comfort—*this* I feel more and more. Every thing is to me a mockery of pleasure, like her love. The breeze does not cool me: the blue sky does not cheer me. I gaze only on her face averted from me—alas! the only face that ever was turned fondly to me! And why am I thus treated? Because I wanted her to be mine for ever in love or friendship, and did not push my gross familiarities as far as I might. "Why can you not go on as we have done, and say nothing about the word, *forever*?" Was it not plain from this that she even then meditated an escape from me to some less sentimental lover? "Do you allow any one else to do so?" I said to her once, as I was toying with her. "No, not now!" was her answer; that is, because there was nobody else in the house to take freedoms with her. I was very well as a stopgap, but I was to be nothing more. While the coast was clear, I had it all my own way: but the instant C—— came, she flung herself at his head in the most barefaced way, ran breathless up stairs before him, blushed when his foot was heard, watched for him in the passage, and was sure to be in close conference with him when he went down again. It was then my mad proceedings commenced. No wonder. Had I not reason to be jealous of every appearance of familiarity with others, knowing how easy she had been with me at first, and that she only grew shy when I did not take farther liberties? What has her character to rest upon but her attachment to me, which she now denies, not modestly, but impudently? Will you yourself say that if she had all along no particular regard for me, she will not do as much or more with other more likely men? "She has had," she says, "enough of my conversation," so it could not be that! Ah! my friend, it was not to be supposed I should ever meet even with the outward demonstrations of regard from any woman but a common trader in the endearments of love! I have tasted the sweets of the well practised illusion, and now feel the bitterness of knowing what a bliss I am deprived of, and must ever be deprived of. Intolerable conviction! Yet I might, I believe, have won her by other methods; but some demon held my hand. How indeed could I offer her the least insult when I worshipped her very footsteps; and even now pay her divine honours from my inmost heart, whenever I think of her, abased and brutalised as I have been by that Circean cup of kisses, of enchantments, of which I have drunk! I am choked, withered, dried up with chagrin, remorse, despair, from which I have not a moment's respite, day or night. I have always some horrid dream about her, and wake wondering what is the matter that "she is no longer the same to me as ever?" I thought at least we should always remain dear friends, if nothing more—did she not talk of coming to live with me only the day before I left her in the winter? But "she's gone, I am abused, and my revenge must be to *love* her!"—Yet she knows that one line, one word would save me, the cruel, heartless destroyer! I see nothing for it but madness, unless Friday brings a change, or unless she is willing to let me go back. You must know I wrote to her to that purpose, but it was a very quiet, sober letter, begging pardon, and professing reform for the future, and all that. What effect it will have, I know not. I was forced to get out of the way of her answer, till Friday came.

Ever yours.

To S. L.

MY DEAR MISS L——,

Evil to them that evil think, is an old saying; and I have found it a true one. I have ruined myself by my unjust suspicions of you. Your sweet friendship was the balm of my life; and I have lost it, I fear for ever, by one fault and folly after another. What would I give to be restored to the place in your esteem, which, you assured me, I held only a few months ago! Yet I was not contented, but did all I could to torment myself and harass you by endless doubts and jealousy. Can you not forget and forgive the past, and judge of me by my conduct in future? Can you not take all my follies in the lump, and say like a good, generous girl, "Well, I'll think no more of them?" In a word, may I come back, and try to behave better? A line to say so would be an additional favour to so many already received by

Your obliged friend,
And sincere well-wisher.

Letter XII to C. P——

I HAVE no answer from her. I'm mad. I wish you to call on M—— in confidence, to say I intend to make her an offer of my hand, and that I will write to her father to that effect the instant I am free, and ask him whether he thinks it will be to any purpose, and what he would advise me to do.

Unaltered Love

"Love is not love that alteration finds:
Oh no! it is an ever-fixed mark,
That looks on tempests and is never shaken."

SHALL I NOT love her for herself alone, in spite of fickleness and folly? To love her for her regard to me, is not to love her, but myself. She has robbed me of herself: shall she also rob me of my love of her? Did I not live on her smile? Is it less sweet because it is withdrawn from me? Did I not adore her every grace? Does she bend less enchantingly, because she has turned from me to another? Is my love then in the power of fortune, or of her caprice? No, I will have it lasting as it is pure; and I will make a Goddess of her, and build a temple to her in my heart, and worship her on indestructible altars, and raise statues to her: and my homage shall be unblemished as her unrivalled symmetry of form; and when that fails, the memory of it shall survive; and my bosom shall be proof to scorn, as hers has been to pity; and I will pursue her with an unrelenting love, and sue to be her slave, and tend her steps without notice and without reward; and serve her living, and mourn for her when dead. And thus my love will have shown itself superior to her hate; and I shall triumph and then die. This is my idea of the only true and heroic love! Such is mine for her.

Perfect Love

PERFECT LOVE HAS this advantage in it, that it leaves the possessor of it nothing farther to desire. There is one object (at least) in which the soul finds absolute content, for which it seeks to live, or dares to die. The heart has as it were filled up the moulds of the imagination. The truth of passion keeps pace with and outvies the extravagance of mere language. There are no words so fine, no flattery so soft, that there is not a sentiment beyond them, that it is impossible to express, at the bottom of the heart where true love is. What idle sounds the common phrases, *adorable creature, angel, divinity,* are! What a proud reflection it is to have a feeling answering to all these, rooted in the breast, unalterable, unutterable, to which all other feelings are light and vain! Perfect love reposes on the object of its choice, like the halcyon on the wave; and the air of heaven is around it.

FROM C. P. ESQ.

London, July 4th, 1822.

I have seen M——! Now, my dear H—, let me entreat and adjure you to take what I have to tell you, *for what it is worth*— neither for less, nor more. In the first place, I have learned nothing decisive from him. This, as you will at once see, is, as far as it goes, good. I am either to hear from him, or see him again in a day or two; but I thought you would like to know what passed inconclusive as it was—so I write without delay, and in great haste to save a post. I found him frank, and even friendly in his manner to me, and in his views respecting you. I think that he is sincerely sorry for your situation; and he feels that the person who has placed you in that situation is not much less awkwardly situated herself; and he professes that he would willingly do what he can for the good of both. But he sees great difficulties attending the affair—which he frankly professes to consider as an altogether unfortunate one. With respect to the marriage, he seems to see the most formidable objections to it, on both sides; but yet he by no means decidedly says that it cannot, or that it ought not to take place. These, mind you, are his own feelings on the subject: but the most important point I learn from him is this, that he is not prepared to use his influence either way—that the rest of the family are of the same way of feeling; and that, in fact, the thing must and does entirely rest with herself. To learn this was, as you see, gaining a great point.—When I then endeavoured to ascertain whether he knew any thing decisive as to what are her views on the subject, I found that he did not. He has an opinion on the subject, and he didn't scruple to tell me what it was; but he has no positive knowledge. In short, he believes, from what he learns from herself (and he had purposely seen her on the subject, in consequence of my application to him) that she is at present indisposed to the marriage; but he is not prepared to say positively that she will not consent to it. Now all this, coming from him in the most frank and unaffected manner, and without any appearance of cant, caution, or reserve, I take to be most important as it respects your views, whatever they may be; and certainly much more favorable to them (I confess it) than I was prepared to expect, supposing them to remain as they were. In fact, as I said before, the affair rests entirely with herself. They are none of them disposed either to further the marriage, or throw any insurmountable obstacles in the way of it; and what is more important than all, they are evidently by no means certain that SHE may not, at some future period, consent to it; or they would, for her sake as well as their own, let you know as much flatly, and put an end to the affair at once.

Seeing in how frank and straitforward a manner he received what I had to say to him, and replied to it, I proceeded to ask him what were *his* views, and what were likely to be *hers* (in case she did not consent) as to whether you should return to live in the house;—but I added, without waiting for his answer, that if she intended to persist in treating you as she had done for some time past, it would be worse than madness for you to think of returning. I added that, in case you did return, all you would expect from her would be that she would treat you with civility and kindness—that she would continue to evince that friendly feeling towards you, that she had done for a great length of time, &c. To this, he said, he could really give no decisive reply, but that he should be most happy if, by any intervention of his, he could conduce to your comfort; but he seemed to think that for you to return on any express understanding that she should behave to you in any particular manner, would be to place her in a most awkward situation. He went somewhat at length into this point, and talked very reasonably about it; the result however was that he would not throw any obstacles in the way of your return, or of her treating you as a friend, &c. nor did it appear that he believed she would refuse to do so. And, finally, we parted on the understanding that he would see them on the subject, and ascertain what could be done for the comfort of all parties: though he was of opinion that if you could make up your mind to break off the acquaintance altogether, it would be the best plan of all. I am to hear from him again in a day or two.—Well, what do you say to all this? Can you turn it to anything but good—comparative good? If you would know what *I* say to it, it is this:—She is still to be won by wise and prudent conduct on your part;—she was always to have been won by such;—and if she is lost, it has been (not, as you sometimes suppose, because you have not carried that unwise, may I not say *unworthy?* conduct still farther, but) because you gave way to it at all. Of course I use the terms "wise" and "prudent" with reference to your object. Whether the pursuit of that object is wise, only yourself can judge. I say she has all along been to be won, and she still is to be won; and all that stands in the way of your views at this moment is your past conduct. They are all of them, every soul, frightened at you; they have seen enough of you to make them so; and they have doubtless heard ten times more than they have seen, or than any one else has seen. They are all of them, including M—— (and particularly she herself) frightened out of their wits, as to what might be your treatment of her if she were yours; and they dare not trust you— they will not trust you, at present. I do not say that they will trust you or rather that *she* will, for it all depends on her, when you have gone through a probation, but I am sure that she will not trust you till you have. You will, I hope, not be angry with me when I say that she would be a fool if she did. If she were to accept you at present, and without knowing more of you, even *I* should begin to suspect that she had an unworthy motive for doing it. Let me not forget to mention what is perhaps as important a point as any, as it regards the marriage. I of course stated to M—— that when you are free, you are prepared to make her a formal offer of your hand; but I begged him, if he was certain that such an offer would be refused, to tell me so plainly at once, that I might endeavour, in that case, to dissuade you from subjecting yourself to the pain of such a refusal. *He would not tell me that he was certain.* He said his opinion was that she would not accept your offer, but still he seemed to think that there would be no harm in making it!—One word more, and a very important one. He once, and without my referring in the slightest manner to that part of the subject, spoke of her as a *good girl,* and *likely to make any man an excellent wife!* Do you think if she were a bad girl (and if she were, he must know her to be so) he would have dared to do this, under these circumstances?—And once, in speaking of *his* not being a fit person to set his face against "marrying for love," he added "I did so myself, and out of that house; and I have had reason to rejoice at it ever since." And mind (for I anticipate your cursed suspicions) I'm certain, at least, if manner can entitle one to be certain of any thing, that he said all this spontaneously, and without any understood motive; and I'm certain, too, that he knows you to be a person that it would not do to play any tricks of this kind with. I believe—(and all this would never have entered my thoughts, but that I know it will enter yours) I believe that even if they thought (as you have sometimes supposed they do) that she needs whitewashing, or making an honest woman of, you would be the last person they would think of using for such a purpose, for they know (as well as I do) that you couldn't fail to find out the trick in a month, and would turn her into the street the next moment, though she were twenty times your wife—and that, as to the consequences of doing so, you would laugh at them, even if you couldn't escape from them.—I shall lose the post if I say more.

Believe me,
Ever truly your friend,
C. P.

Letter XIII

MY DEAR P——,

You have saved my life. If I do not keep friends with her now, I deserve to be hanged, drawn, and quartered. She is an angel from Heaven, and you cannot pretend I ever said a word to the contrary! The little rogue must have liked me from the first, or she never could have stood all these hurricanes without slipping her cable. What could she find in me? "I have mistook my person all this while," &c. Do you know I saw a picture, the very pattern of her, the other day, at Dalkeith Palace (Hope finding Fortune in the Sea) just before this blessed news came, and the resemblance drove me almost out of my senses. Such delicacy, such fulness, such perfect softness, such buoyancy, such grace! If it is not the very image of her, I am no judge.—You have the face to doubt my making the best husband in the world: you might as well doubt it if I was married to one of the Houris of Paradise. She is a saint, an angel, a love. If she deceives me again, she kills me. But I will have such a kiss when I get back, as shall last me twenty years. May God bless her for not utterly disowning and destroying me! What an exquisite little creature it is, and how she holds out to the last in her system of consistent contradictions! Since I wrote to you about making a formal proposal, I have had her face constantly before me, looking so like some faultless marble statue, as cold, as fixed and graceful as ever statue did; the expression (nothing was ever like *that!*) seemed to say—"I wish I could love you better than I do, but still I will be yours." No, I'll never believe again that she will not be mine; for I think she was made on purpose for me. If there's any one else that understands that turn of her head as I do, I'll give her up without scruple. I have made up my mind to this, never to dream of another woman, while she even thinks it worth her while to *refuse to have* me. You see I am not hard to please, after all. Did M—— know of the intimacy that had subsisted between us? Or did you hint at it? I think it would be a *clencher*, if he did. How ought I to behave when I go back? Advise a fool, who had nearly lost a Goddess by his folly. The thing was, I could not think it possible she should ever like *me*. Her taste is singular, but not the worse for that. I'd rather have her love, or liking (call it what you will) than empires. I deserve to call her mine; for nothing else *can* atone for what I've gone through for her. I hope your next letter will not reverse all, and then I shall be happy till I see her—one of the blest when I do see her, if she looks like my own beautiful love. I may perhaps write a line when I come to my right wits.—Farewell at present, and thank you a thousand times for what you have done for your poor friend.

P. S. I like what M—— said about her sister, much. There are good people in the world: I begin to see it, and believe it.

Letter the Last

DEAR P——,

To-morrow is the decisive day that makes me or mars me. I will let you know the result by a line added to this. Yet what signifies it, since either way I have little hope there, "whence alone my hope cometh!" You must know I am strangely in the dumps at this present writing. My reception with her is doubtful, and my fate is then certain. The hearing of your happiness has, I own, made me thoughtful. It is just what I proposed to her to do—to have crossed the Alps with me, to sail on sunny seas, to bask in Italian skies, to have visited Vevai and the rocks of Meillerie, and to have repeated to her on the spot the story of Julia and St. Preux, and to have shown her all that my heart had stored up for her—but on my forehead alone is written—REJECTED! Yet I too could have adored as fervently, and loved as tenderly as others, had I been permitted. You are going abroad, you say, happy in making happy. Where shall I be? In the grave, I hope, or else in her arms. To me, alas! there is no sweetness out of her sight, and that sweetness has turned to bitterness, I fear; that gentleness to sullen scorn! Still I hope for the best. If she will but *have* me, I'll make her *love* me: and I think her not giving a positive answer looks like it, and also shows that there is no one else. Her holding out to the last also, I think, proves that she was never to have been gained but with honour. She's a strange, almost an inscrutable

girl: but if I once win her consent, I shall kill her with kindness.—
Will you let me have a sight of *somebody* before you go? I should
be most proud. I was in hopes to have got away by the Steam-boat
to-morrow, but owing to the business not coming on till then, I
cannot; and may not be in town for another week, unless I come
by the Mail, which I am strongly tempted to do. In the latter
case I shall be *there*, and visible on Saturday evening. Will you look
in and see, about eight o'clock? I wish much to see you and her
and J. H. and my little boy once more; and then, if she is not
what she once was to me, I care not if I die that instant. I will
conclude here till to-morrow, as I am getting into my old melancholy.—

It is all over, and I am my own man, and yours ever—

Part III

Addressed to J. S. K——

MY DEAR K——,

IT IS ALL over, and I know my fate. I told you I would send you word, if any thing decisive happened; but an impenetrable mystery hung over the affair till lately. It is at last (by the merest accident in the world) dissipated; and I keep my promise, both for your satisfaction, and for the ease of my own mind.

You remember the morning when I said "I will go and repose my sorrows at the foot of Ben Lomond"—and when from Dumbarton-bridge its giant-shadow, clad in air and sunshine, appeared in view. We had a pleasant day's walk. We passed Smollett's monument on the road (somehow these poets touch one in reflection more than most military heroes)—talked of old times; you repeated Logan's beautiful verses to the cuckoo,[1] which I wanted to compare with Wordsworth's, but my courage failed me; you then told me some passages of an early attachment which was suddenly broken off; we considered together which was the most to be pitied, a disappointment in love where the attachment was mutual or one where there has been no return, and we both agreed, I think, that the former was best to be endured, and that to have the consciousness of it a companion for life was the least evil of

---

[1] "Sweet bird, thy bower is ever green,
Thy sky is ever clear;
Thou hast no sorrow in thy song,
No winter in thy year."

So they begin. It was the month of May; the cuckoo sang shrouded in some woody copse; the showers fell between whiles; my friend repeated the lines with native enthusiasm in a clear manly voice, still resonant of youth and hope. Mr. Wordsworth will excuse me, if in these circumstances I declined entering the field with his profounder metaphysical strain, and kept my preference to myself.

the two, as there was a secret sweetness that took off the bitterness and the sting of regret, and "the memory of what once had been" atoned, in some measure, and at intervals, for what "never more could be." In the other case, there was nothing to look back to with tender satisfaction, no redeeming trait, not even a possibility of turning it to good. It left behind it not cherished sighs, but stifled pangs. The galling sense of it did not bring moisture into the eyes, but dried up the heart ever after. One had been my fate, the other had been yours!—

You startled me every now and then from my reverie by the robust voice, in which you asked the country people (by no means prodigal of their answers)—"If there was any trout-fishing in those streams?"—and our dinner at Luss set us up for the rest of our day's march. The sky now became overcast; but this, I think, added to the effect of the scene. The road to Tarbet is superb. It is on the very verge of the lake—hard, level, rocky, with low stone-bridges constantly flung across it, and fringed with birch trees, just then budding into spring, behind which, as through a slight veil, you saw the huge shadowy form of Ben Lomond. It lifts its enormous but graceful bulk direct from the edge of the water without any projecting lowlands, and has in this respect much the advantage of Skiddaw. Loch Lomond comes upon you by degrees as you advance, unfolding and then withdrawing its conscious beauties like an accomplished coquet. You are struck with the point of a rock, the arch of a bridge, the Highland huts (like the first rude habitations of men) dug out of the soil, built of turf, and covered with brown heather, a sheep-cote, some straggling cattle feeding half-way down a precipice; but as you advance farther on, the view expands into the perfection of lake scenery. It is nothing (or your eye is caught by nothing) but water, earth, and sky. Ben Lomond waves to the right, in its simple majesty, cloud-capt or bare, and descending to a point at the head of the lake, shows the Trossacs beyond, tumbling about their blue ridges like woods waving; to the left is the Cobler, whose top is like a castle shattered in pieces and nodding to its ruin; and at your side rise the shapes of round pastoral hills, green, fleeced with herds, and retiring into mountainous bays and upland valleys, where solitude and peace might make their lasting home, if peace were to be found in solitude! That it was not always so, I was a sufficient proof; for there was one image that alone haunted me in the midst of all this sublimity and beauty, and turned it to a mockery and a dream!

The snow on the mountain would not let us ascend; and being weary of waiting and of being visited by the guide every two hours to let us know that the weather would not do, we returned, you homewards, and I to London—

"Italiam, Italiam!"

You know the anxious expectations with which I set out:—now hear the result.—

As the vessel sailed up the Thames, the air thickened with the consciousness of being near her, and I "heaved her name pantingly forth." As I approached the house, I could not help thinking of the lines—

"How near am I to a happiness,
That earth exceeds not! Not another like it.
The treasures of the deep are not so precious
As are the conceal'd comforts of a man
Lock'd up in woman's love. I scent the air
Of blessings when I come but near the house.
What a delicious breath true love sends forth!
The violet-beds not sweeter. Now for a welcome
Able to draw men's envies upon man:
A kiss now that will hang upon my lip,
As sweet as morning dew upon a rose,
And full as long!"

I saw her, but I saw at the first glance that there was something amiss. It was with much difficulty and after several pressing in-treaties that she was prevailed on to come up into the room; and when she did, she stood at the door, cold distant, averse; and when at length she was persuaded by my repeated remonstrances to come and take my hand, and I offered to touch her lips, she turned her head and shrunk from my embraces, as if quite alienated or mortally offended. I asked what it could mean? What had I done in her absence to have incurred her displeasure? Why had she not written to me? I could get only short, sullen, disconnected answers, as if there was something labouring in her mind which she either could not or would not impart. I hardly knew how to bear this first reception after so long an absence, and so different from the one my sentiments towards her merited; but I thought it possible it might be prudery (as I had returned without having actually accomplished what I went about) or that she had taken offence at something in my letters. She saw how much I was hurt. I asked her, "If she was altered since I went away?"—"No." "If there was any one else who had been so fortunate as to gain her favourable opinion?"—"No, there was no one else." "What was it then? Was it any thing in my letters? Or had I displeased her by letting Mr. P—— know she wrote to me?"—"No, not at all; but she did not apprehend my last letter required any answer, or she would have replied to it." All this appeared to me very unsatisfactory and evasive; but I could get no more from her, and was obliged to let her go with a heavy, foreboding heart. I however found that C—— was gone, and no one else had been there, of whom I had cause to be jealous.—"Should I see her on the morrow?"—"She believed so, but she could not promise." The next morning she did not appear with the breakfast as usual. At this I grew somewhat uneasy. The little Buonaparte, however, was placed in its old position on the mantle-piece, which I considered as a sort of recognition of old times. I saw her once or twice casually; nothing particular happened till the next day, which was Sunday. I took occasion to go into the parlour for the newspaper, which she gave me with a gracious smile, and seemed tolerably frank and cordial. This of course acted as a spell upon me. I walked out with my little boy, intending to go and dine out at one or two places, but I found that I still contrived to bend my steps towards her, and I went back to take tea at home. While we were out, I talked to William about Sarah, saying that she too was unhappy, and asking him to make it up with her. He said, if she was unhappy, he would not bear her malice any more. When she came up with the tea-things, I said to her, "William has something to say to you—I believe he wants to be friends." On which he said in his abrupt, hearty manner, "Sarah, I'm sorry if I've ever said anything to vex you"—so they shook hands, and she said, smiling affably—"Then I'll think no more of it!" I added— "I see you've brought me back my little Buonaparte"—She answered with tremulous softness—"I told you I'd keep it safe for you!"—as if her pride and pleasure in doing so had been equal, and she had, as it were, thought of nothing during my absence but how to greet me with this proof of her fidelity on my return. I cannot describe her manner. Her words are few and simple; but you can have no idea of the exquisite, unstudied, irresistible graces with which she accompanies them, unless you can suppose a Greek statue to smile, move, and speak. Those lines in Tibullus seem to have been writen on purpose for her—

> Quicquid agit, quoquo vestigià vertit,
> Componit furtim, subsequiturque decor.

Or what do you think of those in a modern play, which might actually have been composed with an eye to this little trifler—

> ——"See with what a waving air she goes
> Along the corridor. How like a fawn!
> Yet statelier. No sound (however soft)
> Nor gentlest echo telleth when she treads,
> But every motion of her shape doth seem
> Hallowed by silence. So did Hebe grow
> Among the Gods a paragon! Away, I'm grown
> The very fool of Love!"

The truth is, I never saw anything like her, nor I never shall again. How then do I console myself for the loss of her? Shall I tell you, but you will not mention it again? I am foolish enough to believe that she and I, in spite of every thing, shall be sitting together over a sea-coal fire, a comfortable good old couple, twenty years hence! But to my narrative.—

I was delighted with the alteration in her manner, and said, referring to the bust—"You know it is not mine, but yours; I gave it you; nay, I have given you all—my heart, and whatever I possess, is yours!" She seemed good-humouredly to decline this *carte blanche* offer, and waved, like a thing of enchantment, out of the room. False calm!—Deceitful smiles!—Short interval of peace, followed by lasting woe! I sought an interview with her that same evening. I could not get her to come any farther than the door. "She was busy—she could hear what I had to say there." "Why do you seem to avoid me as you do? Not one five minutes' conversation, for the sake of old acquaintance? Well, then, for the sake of *the little image!*" The appeal seemed to have lost its efficacy; the charm was broken; she remained immoveable. "Well, then, I must come to you, if you will not run away." I went and sat down in a chair near the door, and took her hand, and talked to her for three quarters of an hour; and she listened patiently, thoughtfully, and seemed a good deal affected by what I said. I told her how much I had felt, how much I had suffered for her in my absence, and how much I had been hurt by her sudden silence, for which I knew not how to account. I could have done nothing to offend her while I was away; and my letters were, I hoped, tender and respectful. I had had but one thought ever present with me; her image never quitted my side, alone or in company, to delight or distract me. Without her I could have no peace, nor ever should again, unless she would behave to me as she had done formerly. There was no abatement of my regard to her; why was she so changed? I said to her, "Ah! Sarah, when I think that it is only a year ago that you were everything to me I could wish, and that now you seem lost to me for ever, the month of May (the name of which ought to be a signal for joy and hope) strikes chill to my heart.—How different is this meeting from that delicious parting, when you seemed never weary of repeating the proofs of your regard and tenderness, and it was with difficulty we tore ourselves asunder at last! I am ten thousand times fonder of you than I was then, and ten thousand times more unhappy." "You have no reason to be so; my feelings towards you are the same as they ever were." I told her "She was my all of hope or comfort: my passion for her grew stronger every time I saw her." She answered, "She was sorry for it; for *that* she never could return." I said something about looking ill: she said in her pretty, mincing, emphatic way, "I despise looks!" So, thought I, it is not that; and she says there's no one else: it must be some strange air she gives herself, in consequence of the approaching change in my circumstances. She has been probably advised not to give up till all is fairly over, and then she will be my own sweet girl again. All this time she was standing just outside the door, my hand in hers (would that they could have grown together!) she was dressed in a loose morning-gown, her hair curled beautifully; she stood with her profile to me, and looked down the whole time. No expression was ever more soft or perfect. Her whole attitude, her whole form, was dignity and bewitching grace. I said to her, "You look like a queen, my love, adorned with your own graces!" I grew idolatrous, and would have kneeled to her. She made a movement, as if she was displeased. I tried to draw her towards me. She wouldn't. I then got up, and offered to kiss her at parting. I found she obstinately refused. This stung me to the quick. It was the first time in her life she had ever done so. There must be some new bar between us to produce these continued denials; and she had not even esteem enough left to tell me so. I followed her half-way down-stairs, but to no purpose, and returned into my room, confirmed in my most dreadful surmises. I could bear it no longer. I gave way to all the fury of disappointed hope and jealous passion. I was made the dupe of trick and cunning, killed with cold, sullen scorn; and, after all the agony I had suffered, could obtain no explanation why I was subjected to it. I was still to be tantalized, tortured, made the cruel sport of one, for whom I would have sacrificed all. I tore the locket which contained her hair (and which I used to wear continually in my bosom, as the precious token of her dear regard) from my neck, and trampled it in pieces. I then dashed the little Buonaparte on the ground, and stamped upon it, as one of her instruments of mockery. I could not stay in the room; I could not leave it; my rage, my despair were uncontrollable. I shrieked curses on her name, and on her false love; and the scream I uttered (so pitiful and so piercing was it, that the sound of it terrified me) instantly brought the whole house, father, mother, lodgers and all, into the room. They thought I was destroying her and myself. I had gone into the bed-room, merely to hide away from myself, and as I came out of it, raging-mad with the new sense of present shame and lasting misery, Mrs. F—— said, "She's in there! He has got her in there!" thinking the cries had proceeded from her, and that I had been offering her violence. "Oh! no," I said, "She's in no danger from me; I am not the person"; and tried to burst from this scene of degradation. The mother endeavoured to stop me, and said, "For God's sake, don't go out, Mr.——! for God's sake, don't!" Her father, who was not, I believe, in the secret, and was therefore justly scandalised at such outrageous conduct, said angrily, "Let him go! Why should he stay?" I however sprang down stairs, and as they called out to me, "What is it?—What has she done to you?" I answered, "She has murdered me!—She has

destroyed me for ever!—She has doomed my soul to perdition!"
I rushed out of the house, thinking to quit it forever; but I was no
sooner in the street, than the desolation and the darkness became
greater, more intolerable; and the eddying violence of my passion
drove me back to the source, from whence it sprung. This unexpected explosion, with the conjectures to which it would give
rise, could not be very agreeable to the *precieuse* or her family;
and when I went back, the father was waiting at the door, as if
anticipating this sudden turn of my feelings, with no friendly
aspect. I said, "I have to beg pardon, Sir; but my mad fit is over,
and I wish to say a few words to you in private." He seemed to
hesitate, but some uneasy forebodings on his own account, probably,
prevailed over his resentment; or perhaps (as philosophers have a
desire to know the cause of thunder) it was a natural curiosity to
know what circumstances of provocation had given rise to such an
extraordinary scene of confusion. When we reached my room, I
requested him to be seated. I said, "It is true, Sir, I have lost my
peace of mind forever, but at present I am quite calm and collected, and I wish to explain to you why I have behaved in so
extravagant a way, and to ask for your advice and intercession." He
appeared satisfied, and I went on. I had no chance either of
exculpating myself, or of probing the question to the bottom,
but by stating the naked truth, and therefore I said at once, "Sarah
told me, Sir (and I never shall forget the way in which she told
me, fixing her dove's eyes upon me, and looking a thousand tender
reproaches for the loss of that good opinion, which she held dearer
than all the world) she told me, Sir, that as you one day passed
the door, which stood a-jar, you saw her in an attitude which a
good deal startled you; I mean sitting in my lap, with her arms
round my neck, and mine twined round her in the fondest manner.
What I wished to ask was, whether this was actually the case, or
whether it was a mere invention of her own, to enhance the sense
of my obligations to her; for I begin to doubt everything?"—"Indeed, it was so; and very much surprised and hurt I was to see it."
"Well, then, Sir, I can only say, that as you saw her sitting then,
so she had been sitting for the last year and a half, almost every
day of her life, by the hour together; and you may judge yourself,
knowing what a nice modest-looking girl she is, whether, after
having been admitted to such intimacy with so sweet a creature,

and for so long a time, it is not enough to make any one frantic to be received by her as I have been since my return, without any provocation given or cause assigned for it." The old man answered very seriously, and, as I think, sincerely, "What you now tell me, Sir, mortifies and shocks me, as much as it can do yourself. I had no idea such a thing was possible. I was much pained at what I saw; but I thought it an accident, and that it would never happen again."—"It was a constant habit; it has happened a hundred times since, and a thousand before. I lived on her caresses as my daily food, nor can I live without them." So I told him the whole story, "what conjurations, and what mighty magic I won his daughter with," to be anything but *mine for life*. Nothing could well exceed his astonishment and apparent mortification. "What I had said," he owned, "had left a weight upon his mind that he should not easily get rid of." I told him, "For myself, I never could recover from the blow I had received. I thought, however, for her own sake, she ought to alter her present behaviour. Her marked neglect and dislike, so far from justifying, left her former intimacies without excuse; for nothing could reconcile them to propriety, or even a pretence to common decency, but either love, or friendship so strong and pure that it could put on the guise of love. She was certainly a singular girl. Did she think it right and becoming to be free with strangers, and strange to old friends?" I frankly declared, "I did not see how it was in human nature for any one who was not rendered callous to such familiarities by bestowing them indiscriminately on every one, to grant the extreme and continued indulgences she had done to me, without either liking the man at first, or coming to like him in the end, in spite of herself. When my addresses had nothing, and could have nothing honourable in them, she gave them every encouragement; when I wished to make them honourable, she treated them with the utmost contempt. The terms we had been all along on were such as if she had been to be my bride next day. It was only when I wished her actually to become so, to ensure her own character and my happiness, that she shrunk back with precipitation and panic-fear. There seemed to me something wrong in all this; a want both of common propriety, and I might say, of natural feeling; yet, with all her faults, I loved her, and ever should, beyond any other human being. I had drank in the poison of her sweetness too long ever to be cured of it; and though I might find it to be poison in the end, it was still in my veins. My only ambition was to be permitted to live with her, and to die in her arms. Be she what she would, treat me how she would, I felt that my soul was wedded to hers; and were she a mere lost creature, I would try to snatch her from perdition, and marry her to-morrow if she would have me. That was the question—"Would she have me, or would she not?" He said he could not tell; but should not attempt to put any constraint upon her inclinations, one way or other. I acquiesced, and added, that "I had brought all this upon myself, by acting contrary to the suggestions of my friend, Mr.——, who had desired me to take no notice whether she came near me or kept away, whether she smiled or frowned, was kind or contemptuous—all you have to do, is to wait patiently for a month till you are your own man, as you will be in all probability; then make her an offer of your hand, and if she refuses, there's an end of the matter." Mr. L. said, "Well, Sir, and I don't think you can follow a better advice!" I took this as at least a sort of negative encouragement, and so we parted.

To the Same (in continuation)

MY DEAR FRIEND,

The next day I felt almost as sailors must do after a violent storm over-night, that has subsided towards day-break. The morning was a dull and stupid calm, and I found she was unwell, in consequence of what had happened. In the evening I grew more uneasy, and determined on going into the country for a week or two. I gathered up the fragments of the locket of her hair, and the little bronze statue, which were strewed about the floor, kissed them, folded them up in a sheet of paper, and sent them to her, with these lines written in pencil on the outside—"*Pieces of a broken heart, to be kept in remembrance of the unhappy. Farewell.*" No notice was taken; nor did I expect any. The following morning I requested Betsey to pack up my box for me, as I should go out of town the next day, and at the same time wrote a note to her sister to say, I should take it as a favour if she would please to accept of the enclosed copies of the Vicar of Wakefield, *The Man of Feeling*, and *Nature and Art*, in lieu of three volumes of my own writings, which I had given her on different occasions, in the course of our acquaintance. I was piqued, in fact, that she should have these to show as proofs of my weakness, and as if I thought the way to win her was by plaguing her with my own performances. She sent me word back that the books I had sent were of no use to her, and that I should have those I wished for in the afternoon; but that she could not before, as she had lent them to her sister, Mrs. M——. I said, "Very well;" but observed (laughing) to Betsey, "It's a bad rule to give and take; so, if Sarah won't have these books, you must; they are very pretty ones, I assure you." She curtsied and took them, according to the family custom. In the afternoon, when I came back to tea, I found the little girl on her knees, busy in packing up my things, and a large paper-parcel on the table, which I could not at first tell what to make of. On opening it, however, I soon found what it was. It contained a number of volumes which I had given her at different times (among others, a little Prayer-Book, bound in crimson velvet, with green silk linings; she kissed it twenty times when she received it, and said it was the prettiest present in the world, and that she would show it to her aunt, who would be proud of it)—and all these she had returned together. Her name in the title-page was cut out of them all. I doubted at the instant whether she had done this before or after I had sent for them back, and I have doubted of it since; but there is no occasion to suppose her *ugly all over with hypocrisy*. Poor little thing! She has enough to answer for, as it is. I asked Betsey if she could carry a message for me, and she said "Yes." "Will you tell your sister, then, that I did not want all these books; and give my love to her, and say that I shall be obliged if she will still keep these that I have sent back, and tell her that it is only those of my own writing that I think unworthy of her." What do you think the little imp made answer? She raised herself on the other side of the table where she stood, as if inspired by the genius of the place, and said—"AND THOSE ARE THE ONES THAT SHE PRIZES THE MOST!" If there were ever words spoken that could revive the dead, those were the words. Let me kiss them, and forget that my ears have heard aught else! I said, "Are you sure of that?" and she said, "Yes, quite sure." I told her, "If I could be, I should be very different from what I was." And I became so that instant, for these casual words carried assurance to my heart of her esteem —that once implied, I had proofs enough of her fondness. Oh! how I felt at that moment! Restored to love, hope, and joy, by a breath which I had caught by the merest accident, and which I might have pined in absence and mute despair for want of hearing! I did not know how to contain myself; I was childish, wanton, drunk with pleasure. I gave Betsey a twenty-shilling note which I happened to have in my hand, and on her asking "What's this for, Sir?" I said, "It's for you. Don't you think it worth that to be made happy? You once made me very wretched by some words I heard you drop, and now you have made me as happy; and all I wish you is, when you grow up, that you may find some one to love you as well as I do your sister, and that you may love better than she does me!" I continued in this state of delirium or dotage all that day and the next, talked incessantly, laughed at every thing, and was so extravagant, nobody could tell what was the matter with me. I murmured her name; I blest her; I folded her to my heart in delicious fondness; I called her by my own name; I worshipped her; I was mad for her. I told P—— I should laugh in her face, if ever she pretended not to like me again. Her mother came in and said, she hoped I should excuse Sarah's coming up. "Oh! Ma'am," I said, "I have no wish to see her; I feel her at my heart; she does not hate me after all, and I wish for nothing. Let her come when she will, she is to me welcomer than light, than life; but let it be in her own sweet time, and at her own dear pleasure." Betsey also told me she was "so glad to get the books back." I, however, sobered and wavered (by degrees) from seeing nothing of her, day after day; and in less than a week I was devoted to the Infernal Gods. I could hold out no longer than the Monday evening following. I sent a message to her; she returned an ambiguous answer; but she came up. Pity me, my friend, for the shame of this recital. Pity me for the pain of having ever had to make it! If the spirits of mortal creatures, purified by faith and hope, can (according to the highest assurances) ever, during thousands of years of smooth-rolling eternity and balmy, sainted repose, forget the pain, the toil, the anguish, the helplessness, and the despair they have suffered here, in this frail being, then may I forget that withering hour, and her, that fair, pale form that entered, my inhuman betrayer, and my only earthly love! She said, "Did you wish to speak to me, Sir?" I said "Yes, may I not speak to you? I wanted to see you and be friends." I rose up, offered her an arm-chair which stood facing, bowed on it, and knelt to her adoring. She said (going) "If that's all, I have nothing to say." I replied, "Why do you treat me thus? What have I done to become thus hateful to you?" Answer, "I always told you I had no affection for you." You may suppose this was a blow, after the imaginary honeymoon in which I had passed the preceding week. I was stunned by it; my heart sunk within me. I contrived to say, "Nay, my dear girl, not always neither; for did you not once (if I might presume to look back to those happy, happy times) when you were sitting on my knee as usual, embracing and embraced, and I asked if you could not love me at last, did you not make answer, in the softest tones that ever man heard, '*I could easily say so, whether I did or not; you should judge by my actions!*' Was I to blame in taking you at your word, when every hope I had depended on your sincerity? And did you not say since I came back, '*Your feelings to me were the same as ever?*' Why then is your behaviour so different?" S. "Is it nothing, your exposing me to the whole house in the way you did the other evening?" H. "Nay, that was the consequence of your cruel reception of me, not the cause of it. I had better have gone away last year, as I proposed to do, unless you would give some pledge of your fidelity; but it was your own offer that I should remain. 'Why should I go?' you said, 'Why could we not go on the same as we had done, and say nothing about the word *forever?*'" S. "And how did you behave when you returned?" H. "That was all forgiven when we last parted, and your last words were, 'I should find you the same as ever' when I came back? Did you not that very day enchant and madden me over again by the purest kisses and embraces, and did I not go from you (as I said) adoring, confiding, with every assurance of mutual esteem and friendship?" S. "Yes, and in your absence I found that you had told my aunt what had passed between us." H. "It was to induce her to extort your real sentiments from you, that you might no longer make a secret of your true regard for me, which your actions (but not your words) confessed." S. "I own I have been guilty of improprieties, which you have gone and repeated, not only in the house, but out of it; so that it has come to my ears from various quarters, as if

I was a light character. And I am determined in future to be guided by the advice of my relations, and particularly of my aunt, whom I consider as my best friend, and keep every lodger at a proper distance." You will find hereafter that her favourite lodger, whom she visits daily, had left the house; so that she might easily make and keep this vow of extraordinary self-denial. Precious little dissembler! Yet her aunt, her best friend, says, "No, Sir, no; Sarah's no hypocrite!" which I was fool enough to believe; and yet my great and unpardonable offence is to have entertained passing doubts on this delicate point. I said, Whatever errors I had committed, arose from my anxiety to have every thing explained to her honour: my conduct showed that I had that at heart, and that I built on the purity of her character as on a rock. My esteem for her amounted to adoration. "She did not want adoration." It was only when any thing happened to imply that I had been mistaken, that I committed any extravagance, because I could not bear to think her short of perfection. "She was far from perfection," she replied, with an air and manner (oh, my God!) as near it as possible. "How could she accuse me of a want of regard to her? It was but the other day, Sarah," I said to her, "when that little circumstance of the books happened, and I fancied the expressions your sister dropped proved the sincerity of all your kindness to me —you don't know how my heart melted within me at the thought, that after all, I might be dear to you. New hopes sprung up in my heart, and I felt as Adam must have done when his Eve was created for him!" "She had heard enough of that sort of conversation," (moving towards the door). This, I own, was the unkindest cut of all. I had, in that case, no hopes whatever. I felt that I had expended words in vain, and that the conversation below stairs (which I told you of when I saw you) had spoiled her taste for mine. If the allusion had been classical I should have been to blame; but it was scriptural, it was a sort of religious courtship, and Miss L. is religious!

> At once he took his Muse and dipt her
> Right in the middle of the Scripture.

It would not do—the lady could make neither head nor tail of it. This is a poor attempt at levity. Alas! I am sad enough. "Would she go and leave me so? If it was only my own behaviour, I still did not doubt of success. I knew the sincerity of my love, and she would be convinced of it in time. If that was all, I did not care: but tell me true, is there not a new attachment that is the real cause of your estrangement? Tell me, my sweet friend, and before you tell me, give me your hand (nay, both hands) that I may have something to support me under the dreadful conviction." She let me take her hands in mine, saying, "She supposed there could be no objection to that," as if she acted on the suggestions of others, instead of following her own will—but still avoided giving me any answer. I conjured her to tell me the worst, and kill me on the spot. Any thing was better than my present state. I said, "Is it Mr. C——?" She smiled, and said with gay indifference. "Mr. C—— was here a very short time." "Well, then, was it Mr.——?" She hesitated, and then replied faintly, "No." This was a mere trick to mislead; one of the profoundnesses of Satan, in which she is an adept. "But," she added hastily, "she could make no more confidences." "Then," said I, "you have something to communicate." "No; but she had once mentioned a thing of the sort, which I had hinted to her mother, though it signified little." All this while I was in tortures. Every word, every half-denial, stabbed me. "Had she any tie?" "No, I have no tie." "You are not going to be married soon?" "I don't intend ever to marry at all!" "Can't you be friends with me as of old?" "She could give no promises." "Would she make her own terms?" "She would make none."—"I was sadly afraid the *little image* was dethroned from her heart, as I had dashed it to the ground the other night."—"She was neither desperate nor violent." I did not answer—"But deliberate and deadly,"—though I might; and so she vanished in this running fight of question and answer, in spite of my vain efforts to detain her. The cockatrice, I said, mocks me: so she has always done. The thought was a dagger to me. My head reeled, my heart recoiled within me. I was stung with scorpions; my flesh crawled; I was choked with rage; her scorn scorched me like flames; her air (her heavenly air) withdrawn from me, stifled me, and left me gasping for breath and being. It was a fable. She started up in her own likeness, a serpent in place of a woman. She had fascinated, she had stung me, and had returned to her proper shape, gliding from me after inflicting the mortal wound, and instilling deadly poison into every pore; but her form lost none of its original brightness by the change of character, but was all glittering, beauteous, voluptuous grace. Seed of the serpent or of the woman, she was divine! I felt that she was a witch, and had bewitched me. Fate had enclosed me round about. *I* was transformed too, no longer human (any more than she, to whom I had knit myself) my feelings were marble; my blood was of molten lead; my thoughts on fire. I was taken out of myself, wrapt into another sphere, far from the light of day, of hope, of love. I had no natural affection left; she had slain me, but no other thing had power over me. Her arms embraced another; but her mock-embrace, the phantom of her love, still bound me, and I had not a wish to escape. So I felt then, and so perhaps shall feel till I grow old and die, nor have any desire that my years should last longer than they are linked in the chain of those amorous folds, or than her enchantments steep my soul in oblivion of all other things! I started to find myself alone—for ever alone, without a creature to love me. I looked round the room for help; I saw the tables, the chairs, the places where she stood or sat, empty, deserted, dead. I could not stay where I was; I had no one to go to but to the parent-mischief, the preternatural hag, that had "drugged this posset" of her daughter's charms and falsehood for me, and I went down and (such was my weakness and helplessness) sat with her for an hour, and talked with her of her daughter, and the sweet days we had passed together, and said I thought her a good girl, and believed that if there was no rival, she still had a regard for me at the bottom of her heart; and how I liked her all the better for her coy, maiden airs: and I received the assurance over and over that there was no one else; and that Sarah (they all knew) never staid five minutes with any other lodger, while with me she would stay by the hour together, in spite of all her father could say to her (what were her motives, was best known to herself!) and while we were talking of her, she came bounding into the room, smiling with smothered delight at the consummation of my folly and her own art; and I asked her mother whether she thought she looked as if she hated me, and I took her wrinkled, withered, cadaverous, clammy hand at parting, and kissed it. Faugh!—

I will make an end of this story; there is something in it discordant to honest ears. I left the house the next day, and returned to Scotland in a state so near to phrenzy, that I take it the shades

sometimes ran into one another. R—— met me the day after I
arrived, and will tell you the way I was in. I was like a person in
a high fever; only mine was in the mind instead of the body. It
had the same irritating uncomfortable effect on the bystanders.
I was incapable of any application, and don't know what I should
have done, had it not been for the kindness of——. I came to see
you, to "bestow some of my tediousness upon you," but you were
gone from home. Every thing went on well as to the law-business;
and as it approached to a conclusion, I wrote to my good friend
P—— to go to M——, who had married her sister, and ask him if
it would be worth my while to make her a formal offer, as soon as
I was free, as, with the least encouragement, I was ready to throw
myself at her feet; and to know, in case of refusal, whether I might
go back there and be treated as an old friend. Not a word of answer
could be got from her on either point, notwithstanding every
importunity and intreaty; but it was the opinion of M—— that
I might go and try my fortune. I did so with joy, with something
like confidence. I thought her giving no positive answer implied
a chance, at least, of the reversion of her favour, in case I behaved
well. All was false, hollow, insidious. The first night after I got
home, I slept on down. In Scotland, the flint had been my pillow.
But now I slept under the same roof with her. What softness, what
balmy repose in the very thought! I saw her that same day and
shook hands with her, and told her how glad I was to see her; and
she was kind and comfortable, though still cold and distant. Her
manner was altered from what it was the last time. She still
absented herself from the room, but was mild and affable when
she did come. She was pale, dejected, evidently uneasy about something, and had been ill. I thought it was perhaps her reluctance to
yield to my wishes, her pity for what I suffered; and that in the
struggle between both, she did not know what to do. How I worshipped her at these moments! We had a long interview the third
day, and I thought all was doing well. I found her sitting at work
in the window-seat of the front parlour; and on my asking if I
might come in, she made no objection. I sat down by her; she let
me take her hand; I talked to her of indifferent things, and of old
times. I asked her if she would put some new frills on my shirts?—
"With the greatest pleasure." If she could get *the little image*
mended? "It was broken in three pieces, and the sword was gone,

but she would try." I then asked her to make up a plaid silk which I had given her in the winter, and which she said would make a pretty summer gown. I so longed to see her in it!—"She had little time to spare, but perhaps might!" Think what I felt, talking peaceably, kindly, tenderly with my love,—not passionately, not violently. I tried to take pattern by her patient meekness, as I thought it, and to subdue my desires to her will. I then sued to her, but respectfully, to be admitted to her friendship—she must know I was as true a friend as ever woman had—or if there was a bar to our intimacy from a dearer attachment, to let me know it frankly, as I showed her all my heart. She drew out her handkerchief and wiped her eyes "of tears which sacred pity had engendered there." Was it so or not? I cannot tell. But so she stood (while I pleaded my cause to her with all the earnestness and fondness in the world) with the tears trickling from her eye-lashes, her head stooping, her attitude fixed, with the finest expression that ever was seen of mixed regret, pity, and stubborn resolution; but without speaking a word, without altering a feature. It was like a petrifaction of a human face in the softest moment of passion. "Ah!" I said, "how you look! I have prayed again and again while I was away from you, in the agony of my spirit, that I might but live to see you look so again, and then breathe my last!" I intreated her to give me some explanation. In vain! At length she said she must go, and disappeared like a spirit. That week she did all the little trifling favours I had asked of her. The frills were put on, and she sent up to know if I wanted any more done. She got the Buonaparte mended. This was like healing old wounds indeed! How? As follows, for thereby hangs the conclusion of my tale. Listen.

I had sent a message one evening to speak to her about some special affairs of the house, and received no answer. I waited an hour expecting her, and then went out in great vexation at my disappointment. I complained to her mother a day or two after, saying I thought it so unlike Sarah's usual propriety of behaviour, that she must mean it as a mark of disrespect. Mrs. L—— said, "La! Sir, you're always fancying things. Why, she was dressing to go out, and she was only going to get the little image you're both so fond of mended; and it's to be done this evening. She has been to two or three places to see about it, before she could get any one to undertake it." My heart, my poor fond heart, almost melted within me at this news. I answered, "Ah! Madame, that's always the way with the dear creature. I am finding fault with her and thinking the hardest things of her; and at that very time she's doing something to show the most delicate attention, and that she has no greater satisfaction than in gratifying my wishes!" On this we had some farther talk, and I took nearly the whole of the lodgings at a hundred guineas a year, that (as I said) she might have a little leisure to sit at her needle of an evening, or to read if she chose, or to walk out when it was fine. She was not in good health, and it would do her good to be less confined. I would be the drudge and she should no longer be the slave. I asked nothing in return. To see her happy, to make her so, was to be so myself. —This was agreed to. I went over to Blackheath that evening, delighted as I could be after all I had suffered, and lay the whole of the next morning on the heath under the open sky, dreaming of my earthly Goddess. This was Sunday. That evening I returned, for I could hardly bear to be for a moment out of the house where she was, and the next morning she tapped at the door—it was opened—it was she—she hesitated and then came forward: she had got the little image in her hand, I took it, and blest her from my heart. She said "They had been obliged to put some new pieces to it." I said "I didn't care how it was done, so that I had it restored to me safe, and by her." I thanked her and begged to shake hands with her. She did so, and as I held the only hand in the world that I never wished to let go, I looked up in her face, and said "Have pity on me, have pity on me, and save me if you can!" Not a word of answer, but she looked full in my eyes, as much as to say, "Well, I'll think of it; and if I can, I will save you!" We talked about the expense of repairing the figure. "Was the man waiting?"—"No, she had fetched it on Saturday evening." I said I'd give her the money in the course of the day, and then shook hands with her again in token of reconciliation; and she went waving out of the room, but at the door turned round and looked full at me, as she did the first time she beguiled me of my heart. This was the last.—

All that day I longed to go down stairs to ask her and her mother to set out with me for Scotland on Wednesday, and on Saturday I would make her my wife. Something withheld me. In the evening, however, I could not rest without seeing her, and I said to her younger sister, "Betsey, if Sarah will come up now, I'll pay her what she laid out for me the other day."—"My sister's gone out, Sir," was the answer. What again! thought I, That's somewhat sudden. I told P——— her sitting in the window-seat of the front parlour boded me no good. It was not in her old character. She did not use to know there were doors or windows in the house— and now she goes out three times in a week. It is to meet some one, I'll lay my life on't. "Where is she gone?"—"To my grand-mother's, Sir." "Where does your grandmother live now?"—"At Somers' Town." I immediately set out to Somers' Town, I passed one or two streets, and at last turned up King-street, thinking it most likely she would return that way home. I passed a house in King-street where I had once lived, and had not proceeded many paces, ruminating on chance and change and old times, when I saw her coming towards me. I felt a strange pang at the sight, but I thought her alone. Some people before me moved on, and I saw another person with her. *The murder was out.* It was a tall, rather well-looking young man, but I did not at first recollect him. We passed at the crossing of the street without speaking. Will you believe it, after all that had passed between us for two years, after what had passed in the last half-year, after what had passed that very morning, she went by me without even changing countenance, without expressing the slightest emotion, without betraying either shame or pity or remorse or any other feeling that any other human being but herself must have shown in the same situation. She had no time to prepare for acting a part, to suppress her feelings—the truth is, she has not one natural feeling in her bosom to suppress. I turned and looked—they also turned and looked—and as if by mutual consent, we both retrod our steps and passed again, in the same way. I went home. I was stifled. I could not stay in the house, walked into the street, and met them coming towards home. As soon as he had left her at the door (I fancy she had prevailed with him to accompany her, dreading some violence) I returned, went up stairs, and requested an interview. Tell her, I said, I'm in ex-cellent temper and good spirits, but I must see her! She came smiling, and I said, "Come in, my dear girl, and sit down, and tell me all about it, how it is and who it is."—"What," she said, "do you mean Mr. C———?" "Oh," said I, "then it is he! Ah! you rogue, I always suspected there was something between you, but you know you denied it lustily: why did you not tell me all about it at the time, instead of letting me suffer as I have done? But however, no reproaches. I only wish it may all end happily and honourably for you, and I am satisfied. But," I said, "you know you used to tell me, you despised looks."—"She didn't think Mr. C—— was so particularly handsome." "No, but he's very well to pass, and a well-grown youth into the bargain." Pshaw! let me put an end to the fulsome detail. I found he had lived over the way, that he had been lured thence, no doubt, almost a year before, that they had first spoken in the street, and that he had never once hinted at marriage, and had gone away, because (as he said) they were too much together, and that it was better for her to meet him occasionally out of doors. "There could be no harm in their walking together." "No, but you may go somewhere afterwards."—"One must trust to one's principle for that." Consummate hypocrite! * I told her Mr. M——, who had married her sister, did not wish to leave the house. I, who would have married her, did not wish to leave it. I told her I hoped I should not live to see her come to shame, after all my love of her; but put her on her guard as well as I could, and said, after the lengths she had permitted herself with me, I could not help being alarmed at the influence of one over her, whom she could hardly herself suppose to have a tenth part of my esteem for her! ! She made no answer to this, but thanked me coldly for my good advice, and rose to go. I begged her to sit a few minutes, that I might try to recollect if there was any thing else I wished to say to her, perhaps for the last time; and then, not finding anything, I bade her good night, and asked for a farewell kiss. Do you know she refused; so little does she understand what is due to friendship, or love, or honour! We parted friends, however, and I felt deep grief, but no enmity against her. I thought C—— had pressed his suit after I went, and had prevailed. There was no harm in that—a little fickleness or so, a little over-pretension to unalterable attachment—but that was all. She liked him better than me—it was my hard hap, but I must bear it. I went out to roam the desert streets, when, turning a corner, whom should I meet but her very lover? I went up to him and asked for a few minutes' conversation on a subject that was highly interesting to me and I believed not indifferent to him: and in the course of four hours' talk, it came out that for three months previous to my quitting London for Scotland, she had been playing the same game with him as with me—that he breakfasted first, and enjoyed an hour of her society, and then I took my turn, so that we never jostled; and this explained why, when he came back sometimes and passed my door, as she was sitting in my lap, she coloured violently, thinking, if her lover looked in, what a *denouement* there would be. He could not help again and again expressing his astonishment at finding that our intimacy had continued unimpaired up to so late a period after he came, and when they were on the most intimate footing. She used to deny positively to him that there was anything between us, just as she used to assure me with impenetrable effrontery that "Mr. C—— was nothing to her, but merely a lodger." All this while she kept up the farce of her romantic attachment to her old lover, vowed that she never could alter in that respect, let me go to Scotland on the solemn and repeated assurance that there was no new flame, that there was no bar between us but this shadowy love—I leave her on this understanding, she becomes more fond or more intimate with her new lover; he quitting the house (whether tired out or not, I can't say)—in revenge she ceases to write to me, keeps me in wretched suspense, treats me like something loathsome to her when I return to inquire the cause, denies it with scorn and impudence, destroys me and shows no pity, no desire to soothe or shorten the pangs she has occasioned by her wantonness and hypocrisy, and wishes to linger the affair on to the last moment, going out to keep an appointment with another while she pretends to be obliging me in the tenderest point (which C—— himself said was too much)......? What do you think of all this? Shall I tell you my opinion? But I must try to do it in another letter.

To the Same (in conclusion)

I did not sleep a wink all that night; nor did I know till the next day the full meaning of what had happened to me. With the morning's light, conviction glared in upon me that I had not only lost her for ever—but every feeling I had ever had towards her—respect, tenderness, pity—all but my fatal passion, was gone. The whole was a mockery, a frightful illusion. I had embraced the false Florimel instead of the true; or was like the man in the Arabian Nights who had married a goul. How different was the idea I once had of her! Was this she,

> —"Who had been beguiled—she who was made
> Within a gentle bosom to be laid—
> To bless and to be blessed—to be heart-bare
> To one who found his bettered likeness there—
> To think for ever with him, like a bride—
> To haunt his eye, like taste personified—
> To double his delight, to share his sorrow,
> And like a morning beam, wake to him every morrow?"

I saw her pale, cold form glide silent by me, dead to shame as to pity. Still I seemed to clasp this piece of witchcraft to my bosom; this lifeless image, which was all that was left of my love, was the only thing to which my sad heart clung. Were she dead, should I not wish to gaze once more upon her pallid features? She is dead to me; but what she once was to me, can never die! The agony, the conflict of hope and fear, of adoration and jealousy is over; or it would, ere long, have ended with my life. I am no more lifted now to Heaven, and then plunged in the abyss; but I seem to have been thrown from the top of a precipice, and to lie groveling, stunned, and stupefied. I am melancholy, lonesome, and weaker than a child. The worst is, I have no prospect of any alteration for the better: she has cut off all possibility of a reconcilement at any future period. Were she even to return to her former pretended fondness and endearments, I could have no pleasure, no confidence in them. I can scarce make out the contradiction to myself. I strive to think she always was what I now know she is; but I have great difficulty in it, and can hardly believe but she still is what she so long seemed. Poor thing! I am afraid she is little better off herself; nor do I see what is to become of her, unless she throws off the mask at once, and runs a-muck at infamy. She is exposed and laid bare to all those whose opinion she set a value upon. Yet she held her head very high, and must feel (if she feels anything) proportionably mortified.—A more complete experiment on character was never made. If I had not met her lover immediately after

I parted with her, it would have been nothing. I might have supposed she had changed her mind in my absence, and had given him the preference as soon as she felt it, and even shown her delicacy in declining any farther intimacy with me. But it comes out that she had gone on in the most forward and familiar way with both at once—(she could not change her mind in passing from one room to another)—told both the same bare-faced and unblushing falsehoods, like the commonest creature; received presents from me to the very last, and wished to keep up the game still longer, either to gratify her humour, her avarice, or her vanity in playing with my passion, or to have me as a *dernier resort*, in case of accidents. Again, it would have been nothing, if she had not come up with her demure, well-composed, wheedling looks that morning, and then met me in the evening in a situation, which (she believed) might kill me on the spot, with no more feeling than a common courtesan shows who *bilks* a customer, and passes him, leering up at her bully, the moment after. If there had been the frailty of passion, it would have been excusable; but it is evident she is a practised, callous jilt, a regular lodging-house decoy, played off by her mother upon the lodgers, one after another, applying them to her different purposes, laughing at them in turns, and herself the probable dupe and victim of some favourite gallant in the end. I know all this; but what do I gain by it, unless I could find some one with her shape and air, to supply the place of the lovely apparition? That a professed wanton should come and sit on a man's knee, and put her arms round his neck, and caress him, and seem fond of him, means nothing, proves nothing, no one concludes anything from it; but that a pretty, reserved, modest, delicate-looking girl should do this, from the first hour to the last of your being in the house, without intending anything by it, is new, and, I think, worth explaining. It was, I confess, out of my calculation, and may be out of that of others. Her unmoved indifference and self-possession all the while, show that it is her constant practice. Her look even, if closely examined, bears this interpretation. It is that of studied hypocrisy or startled guilt, rather than of refined sensibility or conscious innocence. "She defied any one to read her thoughts," she once told me. "Do they then require concealing?" I imprudently asked her. The command over herself is surprising. She never once betrays herself by any momentary forgetfulness, by any appearance of triumph or superiority to the person who is her dupe, by any levity of manner in the plenitude of her success; it is one faultless, undeviating, consistent, consummate piece of acting. Were she a saint on earth, she could not seem more like one. Her hypocritical high-flown pretensions, indeed, make her the worse: but still the ascendancy of her will, her determined perseverance in what she undertakes to do, has something admirable in it, approaching to the heroic. She is certainly an extraordinary girl! Her retired manner, and invariable propriety of behaviour made me think it next to impossible she could grant the same favours indiscriminately to every one that she did to me. Yet this now appears to be the fact. She must have done the very same with C——, invited him into the house to carry on a closer intrigue with her, and then commenced the double game with both together. She always "despised looks." This was a favourite phrase with her, and one of the hooks which she baited for me. Nothing could win her but a man's behaviour and sentiments. Besides, she could never like another—she was a martyr to disappointed affection—and friendship was all she could ever extend to any other man. All the time, she was making signals, playing off her pretty person, and having occasional interviews in the street with this very man, whom she could only have taken so sudden and violent a liking to from his looks, his personal appearance, and what she probably conjectured of his circumstances. Her sister had married a counsellor—the Miss F——'s, who kept the house before, had done so too—and so would she. "There was precedent for it." Yet if she was so desperately enamoured of this new acquaintance, if he had displaced *the little image* from her breast, if he was become her *second* "unalterable attachment" (which I would have given my life to have been) why continue the same unwarrantable familiarities with me to the last, and promise that they should be renewed on my return (if I had not unfortunately stumbled upon the truth to her aunt)—and yet keep up the same refined cant about her old attachment all the time, as if it was that which stood in the way of my pretensions, and not her faithlessness to it? "If one swerves from one, one shall swerve from another"—was her excuse for not returning my regard. Yet that which I thought a prophecy, was I suspect a history. She had swerved twice from her vowed engagements, first to me, and then from me to another. If she made a fool of me, what did she make of her lover? I fancy he has put that question to himself. I said nothing to him about the amount of the presents; which is another damning circumstance, that might have opened my eyes long before; but they were shut by my fond affection, which "turned all to favour and to prettiness." She cannot be supposed to have kept up an appearance of old regard to me, from a fear of hurting my feelings by her desertion; for she not only showed herself indifferent to, but evidently triumphed in my sufferings, and heaped every kind of insult and indignity upon them. I must have incurred her contempt and resentment by my mistaken delicacy at different times; and her manner, when I have hinted at becoming a reformed man in this respect, convinces me of it. "She hated it!" She always hated whatever she liked most. She "hated Mr. C——'s red slippers," when he first came! One more count finishes the indictment. She not only discovered the most hardened indifference to the feelings of others; she has not shown the least regard to her own character, or shame when she was detected. When found out, she seemed to say, "Well, what if I am? I have played the game as long as I could; and if I could keep it up no longer, it was not for want of good will!" Her colouring once or twice is the only sign of grace she has exhibited. Such is the creature on whom I had thrown away my heart and soul—one who was incapable of feeling the commonest emotions of human nature, as they regarded herself or any one else. "She had no feelings with respect to herself," she often said. She in fact knows what she is, and recoils from the good opinion or sympathy of others, which she feels to be founded on a deception; so that my overweening opinion of her must have appeared like irony, or direct insult. My seeing her in the street has gone a good way to satisfy me. Her manner there explains her manner in-doors to be conscious and overdone; and besides, she looks but indifferently. She is diminutive in stature, and her measured step and timid air do not suit these public airings. I am afraid she will soon grow common to my imagination, as well as worthless in herself. Her image seems fast "going into the wastes of time," like a weed that the wave bears farther and farther from me. Alas! thou poor hapless weed, when I entirely lose sight of thee, and forever, no flower will ever bloom on earth to glad my heart again!

Between the Acts

1941

VIRGINIA WOOLF

Virginia Woolf needs no introduction; she has a claim to be the greatest English novelist of the twentieth century, or if we prefer it, to be considered the greatest poet writing in the form of the novel. It is possible to dispute these claims, and they are being disputed, but it is not easy to set up a successful rival. Galsworthy? Maugham? Bennett? Lawrence? Huxley? E. M. Forster? None except Joyce (who was not English) has attempted to do so much with the form of the novel, to alter its relationship with reality, even as the Impressionists altered the relationship of a strip of canvas to the visible world. To the Lighthouse, The Waves, The Years, are three splendid assaults on the Everest of perfection. Some basic provision for the climb was unfortunately lacking, a pair of stout boots or an ice axe, some protection against the treacherous unreality of the exalted atmosphere. She tended to create a series of poetic dreamers who are neither real people nor dreamers of great poetry; her visions and intuitions of love and death and art and madness were superior to the conventional language in which she tried to clothe them, her masculine intelligence was thwarted by an inability to portray the basic human relationships. Mrs. Dalloway is an example of this failure.

What makes Between the Acts so fascinating are the signs of a reversal in technique. It is an astringently written, highly compressed and expertly calculated book. Every epithet, every phrase tells, every detail contributes to the carefully composed picture in which an old lady and her brother whose son is at variance with his beautiful wife watch a mediocre village pageant in the grounds of their manor house throughout a lingering summer day of 1939. Every fact and every hint about this family is as it were telegraphed to the reader, except the pageant itself, about which there hangs a cloud both watery and turgid. It is not quite a parody, it is almost a bore. What

755

did she mean? What was she trying to tell us as she completed this last brief work which she had no time to revise before she was found drowned in her shallow Sussex river? Between the Acts—what is the significance of the title? The pageant is the false drama; the true one is enacted in the family relationship. Of that we can be fairly certain. Remember that we are dealing with the most subtle intelligence in contemporary fiction and with an expert literary critic! The authoress of Orlando could not for a moment have thought her Elizabethan and Restoration pastiches in the Pageant to be anything but grotesque. What is the sloppy poetry, the banal fragments of song in the heads of the characters trying to say? It seems to me that she wishes to tell us, under an allegory, something about England. Written in the gloomiest days of the war, while Spitfires and Messerschmitts fell around her Sussex home in the Battle of Britain, and published before the tide of war had turned, her book is about the eternal England, the beautiful threatened civilisation which she had always loved and which is symbolised by Pointz Hall, the old but not illustrious manor, the ancient garden, and the rather ordinary family who live in it.

Mr. Oliver, the retired Indian civil servant, is the Roman element—reason, justice, books, wine. A serene old pagan like Peacock, he has obligations, memories, a sense of duty, he loves his son and frightens his grandson. His sister, 'Old Flimsy,' is the unicorn to his lion, the mystical, ancient absent-minded wise woman of Celtic tradition. He remembers that the site chosen for the cesspool lies over the Roman road while she daydreams of pre-historic monsters and rhododendron forests in Piccadilly. The book begins with the old couple at breakfast and ends with them going to bed. Even so there is one England which is even more real: the millennial villagers who insouciantly play the part of their ancestors in the Pageant. The England of the present is represented by Mr. Oliver's son Giles, a stockbroker who would have liked to have been a farmer, and his wife Isobel, by the vulgar vital Mrs. Manresa ('all sensation') who fancies Giles and flirts with his father, even as William, her unhappy homosexual protégé, finds peace in the company of Mr. Oliver's aged sister. The quarrel between Isobel, the frustrated natural beauty of England and her commuting husband (its commercial wealth) is the central situation and it takes all day and the Pageant to resolve it.

The Pageant is written and produced by Miss La Trobe, a retired actress who lives alone and sometimes gets drunk at the 'local.' She certainly represents the artist and the Pageant is her attempt to dominate life, an attempt which fails, even as Virginia Woolf may have thought that her own novels had failed, and I think its mediocrity must be a kind of satire on history—perhaps on literature as well. On the one side we have the real England—the villagers, the old couple, Isobel, the garden and the park—and on the other we have history and literature and the Pageant; the dreadful botch that these two recording muses have made of life and the past. After the Victorian episode Isobel asks, "Were they like that?" and the old lady answers, "The Victorians—I don't believe there were ever such people. Only you and me and William dressed differently." " 'You don't believe in history?' said William. The stage remained empty. The cows moved in the field. The shadows were deeper under the trees."

Between the Acts

VIRGINIA WOOLF

IT WAS A summer's night and they were talking, in the big room with the windows open to the garden, about the cesspool. The county council had promised to bring water to the village, but they hadn't.

Mrs. Haines, the wife of the gentleman farmer, a goosefaced woman with eyes protruding as if they saw something to gobble in the gutter, said affectedly: "What a subject to talk about on a night like this!"

Then there was silence; and a cow coughed; and that led her to say how odd it was, as a child, she had never feared cows, only horses. But, then, as a small child in a perambulator, a great cart-horse had brushed within an inch of her face. Her family, she told the old man in the arm-chair, had lived near Liskeard for many centuries. There were the graves in the churchyard to prove it.

A bird chuckled outside. "A nightingale?" asked Mrs. Haines. No, nightingales didn't come so far north. It was a daylight bird, chuckling over the substance and succulence of the day, over worms, snails, grit, even in sleep.

The old man in the arm-chair—Mr. Oliver, of the Indian Civil Service, retired—said that the site they had chosen for the cesspool was, if he had heard aright, on the Roman road. From an aeroplane, he said, you could still see, plainly marked, the scars made by the Britons; by the Romans; by the Elizabethan manor house;

759

and by the plough, when they ploughed the hill to grow wheat in the Napoleonic wars.

"But you don't remember . . ." Mrs. Haines began. No, not that. Still he did remember—— and he was about to tell them what, when there was a sound outside, and Isa, his son's wife, came in with her hair in pigtails; she was wearing a dressing-gown with faded peacocks on it. She came in like a swan swimming its way; then was checked and stopped; was surprised to find people there; and lights burning. She had been sitting with her little boy who wasn't well, she apologized. What had they been saying?

"Discussing the cesspool," said Mr. Oliver.

"What a subject to talk about on a night like this!" Mrs. Haines exclaimed again.

What had *he* said about the cesspool; or indeed about anything? Isa wondered, inclining her head towards the gentleman farmer, Rupert Haines. She had met him at a Bazaar; and at a tennis party. He had handed her a cup and a racquet—that was all. But in his ravaged face she always felt mystery; and in his silence, passion. At the tennis party she had felt this, and at the Bazaar. Now a third time, if anything more strongly, she felt it again.

"I remember," the old man interrupted, "my mother. . . ." Of his mother he remembered that she was very stout; kept her tea-caddy locked; yet had given him in that very room a copy of Byron. It was over sixty years ago, he told them, that his mother had given him the works of Byron in that very room. He paused.

"She walks in beauty like the night," he quoted.

Then again:

"So we'll go no more a-roving by the light of the moon."

Isa raised her head. The words made two rings, perfect rings, that floated them, herself and Haines, like two swans down stream. But his snow-white breast was circled with a tangle of dirty duck-weed; and she too, in her webbed feet was entangled, by her husband, the stockbroker. Sitting on her three-cornered chair she swayed, with her dark pigtails hanging, and her body like a bolster in its faded dressing-gown.

Mrs. Haines was aware of the emotion circling them, excluding her. She waited, as one waits for the strain of an organ to die out before leaving church. In the car going home to the red villa in the cornfields, she would destroy it, as a thrush pecks the wings off a butterfly. Allowing ten seconds to intervene, she rose; paused; and then, as if she had heard the last strain die out, offered Mrs. Giles Oliver her hand.

But Isa, though she should have risen at the same moment that Mrs. Haines rose, sat on. Mrs. Haines glared at her out of goose-like eyes, gobbling, "Please, Mrs. Giles Oliver, do me the kindness to recognize my existence. . . ." which she was forced to do, rising at last from her chair, in her faded dressing-gown, with the pigtails falling over each shoulder.

Pointz Hall was seen in the light of an early summer morning to be a middle-sized house. It did not rank among the houses that are mentioned in guide books. It was too homely. But this whitish house with the grey roof, and the wing thrown out at right angles, lying unfortunately low on the meadow with a fringe of trees on the bank above it so that smoke curled up to the nests of the rooks, was a desirable house to live in. Driving past, people said to each other: "I wonder if that'll ever come into the market?" and to the chauffeur: "Who lives there?"

The chauffeur didn't know. The Olivers, who had bought the place something over a century ago, had no connection with the Warings, the Elveys, the Mannerings or the Burnets; the old families who had all intermarried, and lay in their deaths inter-twisted, like the ivy roots, beneath the churchyard wall.

Only something over a hundred and twenty years the Olivers had been there. Still, on going up the principal staircase—there was another, a mere ladder at the back for the servants—there was a portrait. A length of yellow brocade was visible half-way up; and, as one reached the top, a small powdered face, a great head-dress slung with pearls, came into view; an ancestress of sorts. Six or seven bedrooms opened out of the corridor. The butler had been a soldier; had married a lady's maid; and, under a glass case there was a watch that had stopped a bullet on the field of Waterloo.

It was early morning. The dew was on the grass. The church clock struck eight times. Mrs. Swithin drew the curtain in her bed-room—the faded white chintz that so agreeably from the outside tinged the window with its green lining. There with her old hands on the hasp, jerking it open, she stood: old Oliver's married sister; a widow. She always meant to set up a house of her own; perhaps in Kensington, perhaps at Kew, so that she could have the benefit of the gardens. But she stayed on all through the summer; and when winter wept its damp upon the panes, and choked the gutters with dead leaves, she said: "Why, Bart, did they build the house in the hollow, facing north?" Her brother said, "Obviously to escape from nature. Weren't four horses needed to drag the family coach through the mud?" Then he told her the famous story of the great eighteenth-century winter; when for a whole month the house had been blocked by snow. And the trees had fallen. So every year, when winter came, Mrs. Swithin retired to Hastings.

But it was summer now. She had been waked by the birds. How they sang! attacking the dawn like so many choir boys attacking an iced cake. Forced to listen, she had stretched for her favourite reading—an Outline of History—and had spent the hours between three and five thinking of rhododendron forests in Piccadilly; when the entire continent, not then, she understood, divided by a channel, was all one; populated, she understood, by elephant-bodied, seal-necked, heaving, surging, slowly writhing, and, she supposed, barking monsters; the iguanodon, the mammoth, and the mastodon; from whom presumably, she thought, jerking the window open, we descend.

It took her five seconds in actual time, in mind time ever so much longer, to separate Grace herself, with blue china on a tray, from the leather-covered grunting monster who was about, as the door opened, to demolish a whole tree in the green steaming undergrowth of the primeval forest. Naturally, she jumped, as Grace put the tray down and said: "Good morning, Ma'am." "Batty," Grace called her, as she felt on her face the divided glance that was half meant for a beast in a swamp, half for a maid in a print frock and white apron.

"How those birds sing!" said Mrs. Swithin, at a venture. The window was open now; the birds certainly were singing. An obliging thrush hopped across the lawn; a coil of pinkish rubber twisted in its beak. Tempted by the sight to continue her imaginative reconstruction of the past, Mrs. Swithin paused; she was given to increasing the bounds of the moment by flights into past or future; or sidelong down corridors and alleys; but she remembered her mother—her mother in that very room rebuking her. "Don't stand

gaping, Lucy, or the wind'll change . . ." How often her mother
had rebuked her in that very room—"but in a very different world,"
as her brother would remind her. So she sat down to morning tea,
like any other old lady with a high nose, thin cheeks, a ring on
her finger and the usual trappings of rather shabby but gallant
old age, which included in her case a cross gleaming gold on her
breast.

The nurses after breakfast were trundling the perambulator up
and down the terrace; and as they trundled they were talking—not
shaping pellets of information or handing ideas from one to another, but rolling words, like sweets on their tongues; which, as
they thinned to transparency, gave off pink, green, and sweetness.
This morning that sweetness was: "How cook had told 'im off
about the asparagus; how when she rang I said: how it was a sweet
costume with blouse to match"; and that was leading to something
about a feller as they walked up and down the terrace rolling
sweets, trundling the perambulator.

It was a pity that the man who had built Pointz Hall had
pitched the house in a hollow, when beyond the flower garden
and the vegetables there was this stretch of high ground. Nature
had provided a site for a house; man had built his house in a hollow. Nature had provided a stretch of turf half a mile in length
and level, till it suddenly dipped to the lily pool. The terrace was
broad enough to take the entire shadow of one of the great trees
laid flat. There you could walk up and down, up and down, under
the shade of the trees. Two or three grew close together; then
there were gaps. Their roots broke the turf, and among those
bones were green waterfalls and cushions of grass in which violets
grew in spring or in summer the wild purple orchis.

Amy was saying something about a feller when Mabel, with her
hand on the pram, turned sharply, her sweet swallowed. "Leave
off grubbing," she said sharply. "Come along, George."

The little boy had lagged and was grouting in the grass. Then
the baby, Caro, thrust her fist out over the coverlet and the furry
bear was jerked overboard. Amy had to stoop. George grubbed.
The flower blazed between the angles of the roots. Membrane
after membrane was torn. It blazed a soft yellow, a lambent light
under a film of velvet; it filled the caverns behind the eyes with

light. All that inner darkness became a hall, leaf smelling, earth smelling, of yellow light. And the tree was beyond the flower; the grass, the flower and the tree were entire. Down on his knees grubbing he held the flower complete. Then there was a roar and a hot breath and a stream of coarse grey hair rushed between him and the flower. Up he leapt, toppling in his fright, and saw coming towards him a terrible peaked eyeless monster moving on legs, brandishing arms.

"Good morning, sir," a hollow voice boomed at him from a beak of paper.

The old man had sprung upon him from his hiding-place behind a tree.

"Say good morning, George; say 'Good morning, Grandpa,'" Mabel urged him, giving him a push towards the man. But George stood gaping. George stood gazing. Then Mr. Oliver crumpled the paper which he had cocked into a snout and appeared in person. A very tall old man, with gleaming eyes, wrinkled cheeks, and a head with no hair on it. He turned.

"Heel!" he bawled, "heel, you brute!" And George turned; and the nurses turned holding the furry bear; they all turned to look at Sohrab the Afghan hound bounding and bouncing among the flowers.

"Heel!" the old man bawled, as if he were commanding a regiment. It was impressive, to the nurses, the way an old boy of his age could still bawl and make a brute like that obey him. Back came the Afghan hound, sidling, apologetic. And as he cringed at the old man's feet, a string was slipped over his collar; the noose that old Oliver always carried with him.

"You wild beast . . . you bad beast," he grumbled, stooping. George looked at the dog only. The hairy flanks were sucked in and out; there was a blob of foam on its nostrils. He burst out crying.

Old Oliver raised himself, his veins swollen, his cheeks flushed; he was angry. His little game with the paper hadn't worked. The boy was a cry-baby. He nodded and sauntered on, smoothing out the crumpled paper and muttering, as he tried to find his line in the column, "A cry-baby—a cry-baby." But the breeze blew the great sheet out; and over the edge he surveyed the landscape—flowing fields, heath and woods. Framed, they became a picture.

Had he been a painter, he would have fixed his easel here, where
the country, barred by trees, looked like a picture. Then the
breeze fell.

"M. Daladier," he read, finding his place in the column, "has
been successful in pegging down the franc. . . ."

Mrs. Giles Oliver drew the comb through the thick tangle of
hair which, after giving the matter her best attention, she had
never had shingled or bobbed; and lifted the heavily embossed
silver brush that had been a wedding present and had its uses in
impressing chambermaids in hotels. She lifted it and stood in
front of the three-folded mirror, so that she could see three separate
versions of her rather heavy, yet handsome, face; and also, outside
the glass, a slip of terrace, lawn and tree tops.

Inside the glass, in her eyes, she saw what she had felt overnight
for the ravaged, the silent, the romantic gentleman farmer. "In
love," was in her eyes. But outside, on the washstand, on the
dressing-table, among the silver boxes and tooth-brushes, was the
other love; love for her husband, the stockbroker—"The father
of my children," she added, slipping into the cliché conveniently
provided by fiction. Inner love was in the eyes; outer love on the
dressing-table. But what feeling was it that stirred in her now
when above the looking-glass, out of doors, she saw coming across
the lawn the perambulator; two nurses; and her little boy George,
lagging behind?

She tapped on the window with her embossed hairbrush. They
were too far off to hear. The drone of the trees was in their ears;
the chirp of birds; other incidents of garden life, inaudible, invisible to her in the bedroom, absorbed them. Isolated on a green
island, hedged about with snowdrops, laid with a counterpane of
puckered silk, the innocent island floated under her window. Only
George lagged behind.

She returned to her eyes in the looking-glass. "In love," she
must be; since the presence of his body in the room last night
could so affect her; since the words he said, handing her a teacup,
handing her a tennis racquet, could so attach themselves to a
certain spot in her; and thus lie between them like a wire, tingling,
tangling, vibrating—she groped, in the depths of the looking-
glass, for a word to fit the infinitely quick vibrations of the aero-

plane propeller that she had seen once at dawn at Croydon. Faster, faster, faster, it whizzed, whirred, buzzed, till all the flails became one flail and up soared the plane away and away. . . .

"Where we know not, where we go not, neither know nor care," she hummed. "Flying, rushing through the ambient, incandescent, summer silent . . ."

The rhyme was "air." She put down her brush. She took up the telephone.

"Three, four, eight, Pyecombe," she said.

"Mrs. Oliver speaking. . . . What fish have you this morning? Cod? Halibut? Sole? Plaice?"

"There to lose what binds us here," she murmured. "Soles. Filleted. In time for lunch please," she said aloud. "With a feather, a blue feather . . . flying mounting through the air . . . there to lose what binds us here . . ." The words weren't worth writing in the book bound like an account book in case Giles suspected. "Abortive," was the word that expressed her. She never came out of a shop, for example, with the clothes she admired; nor did her figure, seen against the dark roll of trousering in a shop window, please her. Thick of waist, large of limb, and, save for her hair, fashionable in the tight modern way, she never looked like Sappho, or one of the beautiful young men whose photographs adorned the weekly papers. She looked what she was: Sir Richard's daughter; and niece of the two old ladies at Wimbledon who were so proud, being O'Neils, of their descent from the Kings of Ireland.

A foolish, flattering lady, pausing on the threshold of what she once called "the heart of the house," the threshold of the library, had once said: "Next to the kitchen, the library's always the nicest room in the house." Then she added, stepping across the threshold: "Books are the mirrors of the soul."

In this case a tarnished, a spotted soul. For as the train took over three hours to reach this remote village in the very heart of England, no one ventured so long a journey without staving off possible mind-hunger, without buying a book on a bookstall. Thus the mirror that reflected the soul sublime, reflected also the soul bored. Nobody could pretend, as they looked at the shuffle of shilling shockers that week-enders had dropped, that the looking-glass always reflected the anguish of a Queen or the heroism of King Harry.

At this early hour of a June morning the library was empty. Mrs. Giles had to visit the kitchen. Mr. Oliver still tramped the terrace. And Mrs. Swithin was of course at church. The light but variable breeze, foretold by the weather expert, flapped the yellow curtain, tossing light, then shadow. The first greyed, then glowed, and the tortoiseshell butterfly beat on the lower pane of the window; beat, beat, beat; repeating that if no human being ever came, never, never, never, the books would be mouldy, the fire out and the tortoiseshell butterfly dead on the pane.

Heralded by the impetuosity of the Afghan hound, the old man entered. He had read his paper; he was drowsy; and so sank down into the chintz-covered chair with the dog at his feet—the Afghan hound. His nose on his paws, his haunches drawn up, he looked a stone dog, a crusader's dog, guarding even in the realms of death the sleep of his master. But the master was not dead; only dreaming; drowsily, seeing as in a glass, its lustre spotted, himself, a young man helmeted; and a cascade falling. But no water; and the hills, like grey stuff pleated; and in the sand a hoop of ribs; a bullock maggot-eaten in the sun; and in the shadow of the rock, savages; and in his hand a gun. The dream hand clenched; the real hand lay on the chair arm, the veins swollen but only with a brownish fluid now.

The door opened.

"Am I," Isa apologized, "interrupting?"

Of course she was—destroying youth and India. It was his fault, since she had persisted in stretching his thread of life so fine, so far. Indeed he was grateful to her, watching her as she strolled about the room, for continuing.

Many old men had only their India—old men in clubs, old men in rooms off Jermyn Street. She in her striped dress continued him, murmuring, in front of the book case: "The moor is dark beneath the moon, rapid clouds have drunk the last pale beams of even. . . . I have ordered the fish," she said aloud, turning, "though whether it'll be fresh or not I can't promise. But veal is dear, and everybody in the house is sick of beef and mutton. . . . Sohrab," she said, coming to a standstill in front of them. "What's he been doing?"

His tail never wagged. He never admitted the ties of domesticity. Either he cringed or he bit. Now his wild yellow eyes gazed at her, gazed at him. He could outstare them both. Then Oliver remembered:

"Your little boy's a cry-baby," he said scornfully.

"Oh," she sighed, pegged down on a chair arm, like a captive balloon, by a myriad of hair-thin ties into domesticity. "What's been happening?"

"I took the newspaper," he explained, "so . . ."

He took it and crumpled it into a beak over his nose. "So," he had sprung out from behind a tree on to the children.

"And he howled. He's a coward, your boy is."

She frowned. He was not a coward, her boy wasn't. And she loathed the domestic, the possessive; the maternal. And he knew it and did it on purpose to tease her, the old brute, her father-in-law.

She looked away.

"The library's always the nicest room in the house," she quoted, and ran her eyes along the books. "The mirror of the soul" books were. *The Faerie Queene* and Kinglake's *Crimea*; Keats and the *Kreutzer Sonata*. There they were, reflecting. What? What remedy was there for her at her age—the age of the century, thirty-nine—in books? Book-shy she was, like the rest of her generation; and gun-shy too. Yet as a person with a raging tooth runs her eye in a chemist shop over green bottles with gilt scrolls on them lest one of them may contain a cure, she considered: Keats and Shelley; Yeats and Donne. Or perhaps not a poem; a life. The life of Garibaldi. The life of Lord Palmerston. Or perhaps not a person's life; a county's. *The Antiquities of Durham*; *The Proceedings of the Archaeological Society of Nottingham*. Or not a life at all, but science—Eddington, Darwin, or Jeans.

None of them stopped her toothache. For her generation the newspaper was a book; and, as her father-in-law had dropped the *Times*, she took it and read: "A horse with a green tail . . ." which was fantastic. Next, "The guard at Whitehall . . ." which was romantic and then, building word upon word, she read: "The troopers told her the horse had a green tail; but she found it was just an ordinary horse. And they dragged her up to the barrack room where she was thrown upon a bed. Then one of the troopers removed part of her clothing, and she screamed and hit him about the face. . . ."

That was real; so real that on the mahogany door panels she saw the Arch in Whitehall; through the Arch the barrack room; in the barrack room the bed, and on the bed the girl was screaming and hitting him about the face, when the door (for in fact it was a door) opened and in came Mrs. Swithin carrying a hammer.

She advanced, sidling, as if the floor were fluid under her shabby garden shoes, and, advancing, pursed her lips and smiled, sidelong, at her brother. Not a word passed between them as she went to the cupboard in the corner and replaced the hammer, which she had taken without asking leave; together—she unclosed her fist— with a handful of nails.

"Cindy—Cindy," he growled, as she shut the cupboard door.

Lucy, his sister, was three years younger than he was. The name Cindy, or Sindy, for it could be spelt either way, was short for Lucy. It was by this name that he had called her when they were children; when she had trotted after him as he fished, and had made the meadow flowers into tight little bunches, winding one long grass stalk round and round and round. Once, she remembered, he had made her take the fish off the hook herself. The blood had shocked her—"Oh!" she had cried—for the gills were full of blood. And he had growled: "Cindy!" The ghost of that morning in the meadow was in her mind as she replaced the hammer where it belonged on one shelf; and the nails where they belonged on another; and shut the cupboard about which, for he still kept his fishing tackle there, he was still so very particular.

"I've been nailing the placard on the Barn," she said, giving him a little pat on the shoulder.

The words were like the first peal of a chime of bells. As the first peals, you hear the second; as the second peals, you hear the third. So when Isa heard Mrs. Swithin say: "I've been nailing the placard on the Barn," she knew she would say next:

"For the pageant."

And he would say:

"Today? By Jupiter! I'd forgotten!"

"If it's fine," Mrs. Swithin continued, "they'll act on the terrace . . ."

"And if it's wet," Bartholomew continued, "in the Barn."

"And which will it be?" Mrs. Swithin continued. "Wet or fine?"

Then, for the seventh time in succession, they both looked out of the window.

Every summer, for seven summers now, Isa had heard the same words; about the hammer and the nails; the pageant and the weather. Every year they said, would it be wet or fine; and every year it was—one or the other. The same chime followed the same chime, only this year beneath the chime she heard: "The girl screamed and hit him about the face with a hammer."

"The forecast," said Mr. Oliver, turning the pages till he found it, "says: Variable winds; fair average temperature; rain at times."

He put down the paper, and they all looked at the sky to see whether the sky obeyed the meteorologist. Certainly the weather was variable. It was green in the garden; grey the next. Here came the sun—an illimitable rapture of joy, embracing every flower, every leaf. Then in compassion it withdrew, covering its face, as if it forbore to look on human suffering. There was a fecklessness, a lack of symmetry and order in the clouds, as they thinned and thickened. Was it their own law, or no law, they obeyed? Some were wisps of white hair merely. One, high up, very distant, had hardened to golden alabaster; was made of immortal marble. Beyond that was blue, pure blue, black blue; blue that had never filtered down; that had escaped registration. It never fell as sun, shadow, or rain upon the world, but disregarded the little coloured ball of earth entirely. No flower felt it; no field; no garden.

Mrs. Swithin's eyes glazed as she looked at it. Isa thought her gaze was fixed because she saw God there, God on his throne. But as a shadow fell next moment on the garden Mrs. Swithin loosed and lowered her fixed look and said:

"It's very unsettled. It'll rain, I'm afraid. We can only pray," she added, and fingered her crucifix.

"And provide umbrellas," said her brother.

Lucy flushed. He had struck her faith. When she said "pray," he added "umbrellas." She half covered the cross with her fingers. She shrank; she cowered; but next moment she exclaimed:

"Oh there they are—the darlings!"

The perambulator was passing across the lawn.

Isa looked too. What an angel she was—the old woman! Thus to salute the children; to beat up against those immensities and the old man's irreverences her skinny hands, her laughing eyes! How courageous to defy Bart and the weather!

"He looks blooming," said Mrs. Swithin.

"It's astonishing how they pick up," said Isa.

"He ate his breakfast?" Mrs. Swithin asked.

"Every scrap," said Isa.

"And baby? No sign of measles?"

Isa shook her head. "Touch wood," she added, tapping the table.

"Tell me, Bart," said Mrs. Swithin, turning to her brother, "what's the origin of that? Touch wood . . . Antaeus, didn't he touch earth?"

She would have been, he thought, a very clever woman, had she fixed her gaze. But this led to that; that to the other. What went in at this ear, went out at that. And all were circled, as happens after seventy, by one recurring question. Hers was, should she live at Kensington or at Kew? But every year, when winter came, she did neither. She took lodgings at Hastings.

"Touch wood; touch earth; Antaeus," he muttered, bringing the scattered bits together. Lemprière would settle it; or the Encyclopaedia. But it was not in books the answer to his question— why, in Lucy's skull, shaped so much like his own, there existed a prayable being? She didn't, he supposed, invest it with hair, teeth or toenails. It was, he supposed, more of a force or a radiance, controlling the thrush and the worm; the tulip and the hound; and himself, too, an old man with swollen veins. It got her out of bed on a cold morning and sent her down the muddy path to worship it, whose mouthpiece was Streatfield. A good fellow, who smoked cigars in the vestry. He needed some solace, doling out preachments to asthmatic elders, perpetually repairing the perpetually falling steeple, by means of placards nailed to Barns. The love, he was thinking, that they should give to flesh and blood they give to the church . . . when Lucy, rapping her fingers on the table, said:

"What's the origin—the origin—of that?"

"Superstition," he said.

She flushed, and the little breath too was audible that she drew in as once more he struck a blow at her faith. But, brother and sister, flesh and blood was not a barrier, but a mist. Nothing changed their affection; no argument; no fact; no truth. What she saw he didn't; what he saw she didn't—and so on, ad infinitum. "Cindy," he growled. And the quarrel was over.

The Barn to which Lucy had nailed her placard was a great building in the farmyard. It was as old as the church, and built of the same stone, but it had no steeple. It was raised on cones of grey stone at the corners to protect it from rats and damp. Those who had been to Greece always said it reminded them of a temple. Those who had never been to Greece—the majority—admired it all the same. The roof was weathered red-orange; and inside it was a hollow hall, sun-shafted, brown, smelling of corn, dark when the doors were shut, but splendidly illuminated when the doors at the end stood open, as they did to let the wagons in— the long low wagons, like ships of the sea, breasting the corn, not the sea, returning in the evening shagged with hay. The lanes caught tufts where the wagons had passed.

Now benches were drawn across the floor of the Barn. If it rained, the actors were to act in the Barn; planks had been laid together at one end to form a stage. Wet or fine, the audience would take tea there. Young men and women—Jim, Iris, David, Jessica—were even now busy with garlands of red and white paper roses left over from the Coronation. The seeds and the dust from the sacks made them sneeze. Iris had a handkerchief bound round her forehead; Jessica wore breeches. The young men worked in shirt sleeves. Pale husks had stuck in their hair, and it was easy to run a splinter of wood into the fingers.

"Old Flimsy" (Mrs. Swithin's nickname) had been nailing another placard on the Barn. The first had been blown down, or the village idiot, who always tore down what had been nailed up, had done it, and was chuckling over the placard under the shade of some hedge. The workers were laughing too, as if old Swithin had left a wake of laughter behind her. The old girl with a wisp of white hair flying, knobbed shoes as if she had claws corned like a canary's, and black stockings wrinkled over the ankles, naturally made David cock his eye and Jessica wink back, as she handed him a length of paper roses. Snobs they were; long enough stationed that is in that one corner of the world to have taken indelibly the print of some three hundred years of customary behaviour. So they laughed; but respected. If she wore pearls, pearls they were.

"Old Flimsy on the hop," said David. She would be in and out twenty times, and finally bring them lemonade in a great jug and a plate of sandwiches. Jessie held the garland; he hammered. A hen strayed in; a file of cows passed the door; then a sheep dog; then the cowman, Bond, who stopped.

He contemplated the young people hanging roses from one rafter to another. He thought very little of anybody, simples or gentry. Leaning, silent, sardonic, against the door he was like a withered willow, bent over a stream, all its leaves shed, and in his eyes the whimsical flow of the waters.

"Hi—huh!" he cried suddenly. It was cow language presumably, for the particoloured cow, who had thrust her head in at the door, lowered her horns, lashed her tail and ambled off. Bond followed after.

"That's the problem," said Mrs. Swithin. While Mr. Oliver consulted the Encyclopaedia, searching under Superstition for the origin of the expression "Touch Wood," she and Isa discussed fish: whether, coming from a distance, it would be fresh.

They were so far from the sea. A hundred miles away, Mrs. Swithin said; no, perhaps a hundred and fifty. "But they do say," she continued, "one can hear the waves on a still night. After a storm, they say, you can hear a wave break. . . . I like that story," she reflected. "Hearing the waves in the middle of the night he saddled a horse and rode to the sea. Who was it, Bart, who rode to the sea?"

He was reading.

"You can't expect it brought to your door in a pail of water," said Mrs. Swithin, "as I remember when we were children, living in a house by the sea. Lobsters, fresh from the lobster pots. How they pinched the stick cook gave them! And salmon. You know if they're fresh because they have lice in their scales."

Bartholomew nodded. A fact that was. He remembered, the house by the sea. And the lobster.

They were bringing up nets full of fish from the sea; but Isa was seeing—the garden, variable as the forecast said, in the light breeze. Again, the children passed, and she tapped on the window and blew them a kiss. In the drone of the garden it went unheeded.

"Are we really," she said, turning round, "a hundred miles from the sea?"

"Thirty-five only," her father-in-law said, as if he had whipped a tape measure from his pocket and measured it exactly.

"It seems more," said Isa. "It seems from the terrace as if the land went on for ever and ever."

"Once there was no sea," said Mrs. Swithin. "No sea at all between us and the continent. I was reading that in a book this morning. There were rhododendrons in the Strand; and mammoths in Piccadilly."

"When we were savages," said Isa.

Then she remembered; her dentist had told her that savages could perform very skilful operations on the brain. Savages had false teeth, he said. False teeth were invented, she thought he said, in the time of the Pharaohs.

"At least so my dentist told me," she concluded.

"Which man d'you go to now?" Mrs. Swithin asked her.

"The same old couple; Batty and Bates in Sloane Street."

"And Mr. Batty told you they had false teeth in the time of the Pharaohs?" Mrs. Swithin pondered.

"Batty? Oh not Batty. Bates," Isa corrected her.

Batty, she recalled, only talked about Royalty. Batty, she told Mrs. Swithin, had a patient a Princess.

"So he kept me waiting well over an hour. And you know, when one's a child, how long that seems."

"Marriages with cousins," said Mrs. Swithin, "can't be good for the teeth."

Bart put his finger inside his mouth and projected the upper row outside his lips. They were false. Yet, he said, the Olivers hadn't married cousins. The Olivers couldn't trace their descent for more than two or three hundred years. But the Swithins could. The Swithins were there before the Conquest.

"The Swithins," Mrs. Swithin began. Then she stopped. Bart would crack another joke about Saints, if she gave him the chance. And she had had two jokes cracked at her already; one about an umbrella; another about superstition.

So she stopped and said, "How did we begin this talk?" She counted on her fingers. "The Pharaohs. Dentists. Fish . . . Oh yes, you were saying, Isa, you'd ordered fish; and you were afraid it wouldn't be fresh. And I said, 'That's the problem. . . .' "

The fish had been delivered. Mitchell's boy, holding them in a crook of his arm, jumped off his motor bike. There was no feeding the pony with lumps of sugar at the kitchen door, nor time for gossip, since his round had been increased. He had to deliver right over the hill at Bickley; also go round by Waythorn, Roddam, and Pyeminster, whose names, like his own, were in Domesday Book. But the cook—Mrs. Sands she was called, but by old friends Trixie —had never in all her fifty years been over the hill, nor wanted to.

He dabbed them down on the kitchen table, the filleted soles, the semi-transparent boneless fish. And before Mrs. Sands had time to peel the paper off, he was gone, giving a slap to the very fine yellow cat who rose majestically from the basket chair and advanced superbly to the table, winding the fish.

Were they a bit whiffy? Mrs. Sands held them to her nose. The cat rubbed itself this way, that way against the table legs, against her legs. She would save a slice for Sunny—his drawing-room name Sung-Yen had undergone a kitchen change into Sunny. She took them, the cat attendant, to the larder, and laid them on a plate in that semi-ecclesiastical apartment. For the house before the Reformation, like so many houses in that neighbourhood, had a chapel; and the chapel had become a larder, changing, like the cat's name, as religion changed. The Master (his drawing-room name; in the kitchen they called him Bartie) would bring gentlemen sometimes to see the larder—often when cook wasn't dressed. Not to see the hams that hung from hooks, or the butter on a blue slate, or the joint for tomorrow's dinner, but to see the cellar that opened out of the larder and its carved arch. If you tapped—one gentleman had a hammer—there was a hollow sound; a reverberation; undoubtedly, he said, a concealed passage where once somebody had hid. So it might be. But Mrs. Sands wished they wouldn't come into her kitchen telling stories with the girls about. It put ideas into their silly heads. They heard dead men rolling barrels. They saw a white lady walking under the trees. No one would cross the terrace after dark. If a cat sneezed, "There's the ghost!"

Sunny had his little bit off the fillet. Then Mrs. Sands took an egg from the brown basket full of eggs; some with yellow fluff sticking to the shells; then a pinch of flour to coat those semi-transparent slips; and a crust from the great earthenware crock full of crusts. Then, returning to the kitchen, she made those quick movements at the oven, cinder raking, stoking, damping, which sent strange echoes through the house, so that in the library, the sitting-room, the dining-room, and the nursery, whatever they were doing, thinking, saying, they knew, they all knew, it was getting on for breakfast, lunch, or dinner.

"The sandwiches . . ." said Mrs. Swithin, coming into the kitchen. She refrained from adding "Sands" to "sandwiches," for Sand and sandwiches clashed. "Never play," her mother used to say, "on people's names." And Trixie was not a name that suited, as Sands did, the thin, acid woman, red-haired sharp and clean, who never dashed off masterpieces, it was true; but then never dropped hairpins in the soup. "What in the name of Thunder?" Bart had said, raising a hairpin in his spoon, in the old days, fifteen years ago, before Sands came, in the time of Jessie Pook.

Mrs. Sands fetched bread; Mrs. Swithin fetched ham. One cut the bread; the other the ham. It was soothing, it was consolidating, this handwork together. The cook's hands cut, cut, cut. Whereas Lucy, holding the loaf, held the knife up. Why's stale bread, she mused, easier to cut than fresh? And so skipped, sidelong, from yeast to alcohol; so to fermentation; so to inebriation; so to Bacchus; and lay under purple lamps in a vineyard in Italy, as she had done, often; while Sands heard the clock tick; saw the cat; noted a fly buzz; and registered, as her lips showed, a grudge she mustn't speak against people making work in the kitchen while they had a high old time hanging paper roses in the Barn.

"Will it be fine?" asked Mrs. Swithin, her knife suspended. In the kitchen they humoured old Mother Swithin's fancies.

"Seems like it," said Mrs. Sands, giving her sharp look-out of the kitchen window.

"It wasn't last year," said Mrs. Swithin. "D'you remember what a rush we had—when the rain came—getting in the chairs?" She cut again. Then she asked about Billy, Mrs. Sands's nephew, apprenticed to the butcher.

"He's been doing," Mrs. Sands said, "what boys shouldn't; cheeking the master."

"That'll be all right," said Mrs. Swithin, half meaning the boy, half meaning the sandwich, as it happened a very neat one, trimmed, triangular.

"Mr. Giles may be late," she added, laying it, complacently, on top of the pile.

For Isa's husband, the stockbroker, was coming from London. And the local train, which met the express train, arrived by no means punctually, even if he caught the early train which was by no means certain. In which case it meant—but what it meant to Mrs. Sands, when people missed their trains, and she, whatever she might want to do, must wait, by the oven, keeping meat hot, no one knew.

"There!" said Mrs. Swithin, surveying the sandwiches, some neat, some not, "I'll take 'em to the Barn." As for the lemonade, she assumed, without a flicker of doubt, that Jane the kitchenmaid would follow after.

Candish paused in the dining-room to move a yellow rose. Yellow, white, carnation red—he placed them. He loved flowers, and arranging them, and placing the green sword or heart-shaped leaf that came, fitly, between them. Queerly, he loved them, considering his gambling and drinking. The yellow rose went there. Now all was ready—silver and white, forks and napkins, and in the middle the splashed bowl of variegated roses. So, with one last look, he left the dining-room.

Two pictures hung opposite the window. In real life they had never met, the long lady and the man holding his horse by the rein. The lady was a picture, bought by Oliver because he liked the picture; the man was an ancestor. He had a name. He held the rein in his hand. He had said to the painter:

"If you want my likeness, dang it sir, take it when the leaves are on the trees." There were leaves on the trees. He had said: "Ain't there room for Colin as well as Buster?" Colin was his famous hound. But there was only room for Buster. It was, he seemed to say, addressing the company not the painter, a damned shame to leave out Colin whom he wished buried at his feet, in the same grave, about 1750; but that skunk the Reverend Whatshisname wouldn't allow it.

He was a talk producer, that ancestor. But the lady was a picture.

In her yellow robe, leaning, with a pillar to support her, a silver arrow in her hand, and a feather in her hair, she led the eye up, down, from the curve to the straight, through glades of greenery and shades of silver, dun and rose into silence. The room was empty.

Empty, empty, empty; silent, silent, silent. The room was a shell, singing of what was before time was; a vase stood in the heart of the house, alabaster, smooth, cold, holding the still, distilled essence of emptiness, silence.

Across the hall a door opened. One voice, another voice, a third voice came wimpling and warbling: gruff—Bart's voice; quavering —Lucy's voice; middle-toned—Isa's voice. Their voices impetuously, impatiently, protestingly came across the hall, saying: "The train's late"; saying: "Keep it hot"; saying: "We won't, no, Candish, we won't wait."

Coming out from the library the voices stopped in the hall. They encountered an obstacle evidently; a rock. Utterly impossible was it, even in the heart of the country, to be alone? That was the shock. After that, the rock was raced round, embraced. If it was painful, it was essential. There must be society. Coming out of the library it was painful, but pleasant, to run slap into Mrs. Manresa and an unknown young man with tow-coloured hair and a twisted face. No escape was possible; meeting was inevitable. Uninvited, unexpected, droppers-in, lured off the high road by the very same instinct that caused the sheep and the cows to desire propinquity, they had come. But they had brought a lunch basket. Here it was.

"We couldn't resist when we saw the name on the signpost," Mrs. Manresa began in her rich fluty voice. "And this is a friend— William Dodge. We were going to sit all alone in a field. And I said: 'Why not ask our dear friends,' seeing the signpost, 'to shelter us?' A seat at the table—that's all we want. We have our grub. We have our glasses. We ask nothing but——" society apparently, to be with her kind.

And she waved her hand upon which there was a glove, and under the glove, it seemed, rings, at old Mr. Oliver.

He bowed deep over her hand; a century ago, he would have kissed it. In all this sound of welcome, protestation, apology and again welcome, there was an element of silence, supplied by

Isabella, observing the unknown young man. He was of course a gentleman; witness socks and trousers; brainy—tie spotted, waistcoat undone; urban, professional, that is putty coloured, unwholesome; very nervous, exhibiting a twitch at this sudden introduction, and fundamentally infernally conceited, for he deprecated Mrs. Manresa's effusion, yet was her guest.

Isa felt antagonised, yet curious. But when Mrs. Manresa added, to make all shipshape: "He's an artist," and when William Dodge corrected her: "I'm a clerk in an office"—she thought he said Education or Somerset House—she had her finger on the knot which had tied itself so tightly, almost to the extent of squinting, certainly of twitching, in his face.

Then they went in to lunch, and Mrs. Manresa bubbled up, enjoying her own capacity to surmount, without turning a hair, this minor social crisis—this laying of two more places. For had she not complete faith in flesh and blood? and aren't we all flesh and blood? and how silly to make bones of trifles when we're all flesh and blood under the skin—men and women too! But she preferred men—obviously.

"Or what are your rings for, and your nails, and that really adorable little straw hat?" said Isabella, addressing Mrs. Manresa silently and thereby making silence add its unmistakable contribution to talk. Her hat, her rings, her finger nails red as roses, smooth as shells, were there for all to see. But not her life history. That was only scraps and fragments to all of them, excluding perhaps William Dodge, whom she called "Bill" publicly—a sign perhaps that he knew more than they did. Some of the things that he knew —that she strolled the garden at midnight in silk pyjamas, had the loud speaker playing jazz, and a cocktail bar, of course they knew also. But nothing private; no strict biographical facts.

She had been born, but it was only gossip said so, in Tasmania: her grandfather had been exported for some hanky-panky mid-Victorian scandal; malversation of trusts, was it? But the story got no further the only time Isabella heard it than "exported," for the husband of the communicative lady—Mrs. Blencowe of the Grange—took exception, pedantically, to "exported," said "expatriated" was more like it, but not the right word, which he had on the tip of his tongue, but couldn't get at. And so the story dwindled away. Sometimes she referred to an uncle, a Bishop. But he was thought to have been a Colonial Bishop only. They forgot and forgave very easily in the Colonies. Also it was said her diamonds and rubies had been dug out of the earth with his own hands by a "husband" who was not Ralph Manresa. Ralph, a Jew, got up to look the very spit and image of the landed gentry, supplied from directing City companies—that was certain—tons of money; and they had no child. But surely with George the Sixth on the throne it was old fashioned, dowdy, savoured of moth-eaten furs, bugles, cameos and black-edged notepaper, to go ferreting into people's pasts?

"All I need," said Mrs. Manresa ogling Candish, as if he were a real man, not a stuffed man, "is a corkscrew." She had a bottle of champagne, but no corkscrew.

"Look, Bill," she continued, cocking her thumb—she was opening the bottle—"at the pictures. Didn't I tell you you'd have a treat?"

Vulgar she was in her gestures, in her whole person, over-sexed, over-dressed for a picnic. But what a desirable, at least valuable, quality it was—for everybody felt, directly she spoke, "She's said it, she's done it, not I," and could take advantage of the breach of decorum, of the fresh air that blew in, to follow like leaping dolphins in the wake of an ice-breaking vessel. Did she not restore to old Bartholomew his spice islands, his youth?

"I told him," she went on, ogling Bart now, "that he wouldn't look at our things" (of which they had heaps and mountains) "after yours. And I promised him you'd show him the—the——" here the champagne fizzed up and she insisted upon filling Bart's glass first. "What is it all you learned gentlemen rave about? An arch? Norman? Saxon? Who's the last from school? Mrs. Giles?"

She ogled Isabella now, conferring youth upon her; but always when she spoke to women, she veiled her eyes, for they, being conspirators, saw through it.

So with blow after blow, with champagne and ogling, she staked out her claim to be a wild child of nature, blowing into this—she did give one secret smile—sheltered harbour; which did make her smile, after London; yet it did, too, challenge London. For on she went to offer them a sample of her life; a few gobbets of gossip; mere trash; but she gave it for what it was worth; how last Tuesday she had been sitting next so and so; and she added, very casually a

Christian name; then a nickname; and he'd said—for, as a mere nobody they didn't mind what they said to her—and in "in strict confidence, I needn't tell you," she told them. And they all pricked their ears. And then, with a gesture of her hands as if tossing overboard that odious crackling-under-the-pot London life—so—she exclaimed, "There! . . . And what's the first thing I do when I come down here?" They had only come last night, driving through June lanes, alone with Bill it was understood, leaving London, suddenly become dissolute and dirty, to sit down to dinner. "What do I do? Can I say it aloud? Is it permitted, Mrs. Swithin? Yes, everything can be said in this house. I take off my stays" (here she pressed her hands to her sides—she was stout) "and roll in the grass. Roll—you'll believe that . . ." She laughed wholeheartedly. She had given up dealing with her figure and thus gained freedom.

"That's genuine," Isa thought. Quite genuine. And her love of the country too. Often when Ralph Manresa had to stay in town she came down alone; wore an old garden hat; taught the village women *not* how to pickle and preserve; but how to weave frivolous baskets out of coloured straw. Pleasure's what they want, she said. You often heard her, if you called, yodelling among the hollyhocks "Hoity te doity te ray do . . ."

A thorough good sort she was. She made old Bart feel young. Out of the corner of his eye, as he raised his glass, he saw a flash of white in the garden. Someone passing.

The scullery maid, before the plates came out, was cooling her cheeks by the lily pond.

There had always been lilies there, self-sown from wind-dropped seed, floating red and white on the green plates of their leaves. Water, for hundreds of years, had silted down into the hollow, and lay there four or five feet deep over a black cushion of mud. Under the thick plate of green water, glazed in their self-centred world, fish swam—gold, splashed with white, streaked with black or silver. Silently they manoeuvred in their water world, poised in the blue patch made by the sky, or shot silently to the edge where the grass, trembling, made a fringe of nodding shadow. On the water-pavement spiders printed their delicate feet. A grain fell and spiralled down; a petal fell, filled and sank. At that the fleet of boat-shaped bodies paused; poised; equipped; mailed; then with a waver of undulation off they flashed.

It was in that deep centre, in that black heart, that the lady had drowned herself. Ten years since the pool had been dredged and a thigh bone recovered. Alas, it was a sheep's, not a lady's. And sheep have no ghosts, for sheep have no souls. But, the servants insisted, they must have a ghost; the ghost must be a lady's; who had drowned herself for love. So none of them would walk by the lily pool at night, only now when the sun shone and the gentry still sat at table.

The flower petal sank; the maid returned to the kitchen; Bartholomew sipped his wine. Happy he felt as a boy; yet reckless as an old man; an unusual, an agreeable sensation. Fumbling in his mind for something to say to the adorable lady, he chose the first thing that came handy; the story of the sheep's thigh. "Servants," he said, "must have their ghost." Kitchenmaids must have their drowned lady.

"But so must I!" cried the wild child of nature, Mrs. Manresa. She became, of a sudden, solemn as an owl. She knew, she said, pinching a bit of bread to make this emphatic, that Ralph, when he was at the war, couldn't have been killed without her seeing him—"wherever I was, whatever I was doing," she added, waving her hands so that the diamonds flashed in the sun.

"I don't feel that," said Mrs. Swithin, shaking her head.

"No," Mrs. Manresa laughed. "You wouldn't. None of you would. You see I'm on a level with . . ." she waited till Candish had retired, "the servants. I'm nothing like so grown up as you are."

She preened, approving her adolescence. Rightly or wrongly? A spring of feeling bubbled up through her mud. They had laid theirs with blocks of marble. Sheep's bones were sheep's bones to them, not the relics of the drowned Lady Ermyntrude.

"And which camp," said Bartholomew turning to the unknown guest, "d'you belong to? The grown, or the ungrown?"

Isabella opened her mouth, hoping that Dodge would open his, and so enable her to place him. But he sat staring. "I beg your pardon, sir?" he said. They all looked at him. "I was looking at the pictures."

The picture looked at nobody. The picture drew them down the paths of silence.

Lucy broke it.

"Mrs. Manresa, I'm going to ask you a favour—If it comes to a pinch this afternoon, will you sing?"

This afternoon? Mrs. Manresa was aghast. Was it the pageant? She had never dreamt it was this afternoon. They would never have thrust themselves in—had they known it was this afternoon. And, of course, once more the chime pealed. Isa heard the first chime; and the second; and the third—If it was wet, it would be in the Barn; if it was fine on the terrace. And which would it be, wet or fine? And they all looked out of the window. Then the door opened. Candish said Mr. Giles had come. Mr. Giles would be down in a moment.

Giles had come. He had seen the great silver-plated car at the door with the initials R. M. twisted so as to look at a distance like a coronet. Visitors, he had concluded, as he drew up behind; and had gone to his room to change. The ghost of convention rose to the surface, as a blush or a tear rises to the surface at the pressure of emotion; so the car touched his training. He must change. And he came into the dining-room looking like a cricketer, in flannels, wearing a blue coat with brass buttons; though he was enraged. Had he not read, in the morning paper, in the train, that sixteen men had been shot, others prisoned, just over there, across the gulf, in the flat land which divided them from the continent? Yet he changed. It was Aunt Lucy, waving her hand at him as he came in, who made him change. He hung his grievances on her, as one hangs a coat on a hook, instinctively. Aunt Lucy, foolish, free; always, since he had chosen, after leaving college, to take a job in the city, expressing her amazement, her amusement, at men who spent their lives, buying and selling—ploughs? glass beads was it? or stocks and shares?—to savages who wished most oddly—for were they not beautiful naked?—to dress and live like the English? A frivolous, a malignant statement hers was of a problem which, for he had no special gift, no capital, and had been furiously in love with his wife—he nodded to her across the table—had afflicted him for ten years. Given his choice, he would have chosen to farm. But he was not given his choice. So one thing led to another; and the conglomeration of things pressed you flat; held you fast, like a fish in water. So he came for the week-end, and changed.

"How d'you do?" he said all round; nodded to the unknown guest; took against him; and ate his fillet of sole.

He was the very type of all that Mrs. Manresa adored. His hair curled; far from running away, as many chins did, his was firm; the nose straight, if short; the eyes, of course, with that hair, blue; and finally to make the type complete, there was something fierce, untamed, in the expression which incited her, even at forty-five, to furbish up her ancient batteries.

"He is my husband," Isabella thought, as they nodded across the bunch of many-coloured flowers. "The father of my children." It worked, that old cliché; she felt pride; and affection; then pride again in herself, whom he had chosen. It was a shock to find, after the morning's look in the glass, and the arrow of desire shot through her last night by the gentleman farmer, how much she felt when he came in, not a dapper city gent, but a cricketer, of love; and of hate.

They had met first in Scotland, fishing—she from one rock, he from another. Her line had got tangled; she had given over, and had watched him with the stream rushing between his legs, casting, casting—until, like a thick ingot of silver bent in the middle, the salmon had leapt, had been caught, and she had loved him.

Bartholomew too loved him; and noted his anger—about what? But he remembered his guest. The family was not a family in the presence of strangers. He must, rather laboriously, tell them the story of the pictures at which the unknown guest had been looking when Giles came in.

"That," he indicated the man with a horse, "was my ancestor. He had a dog. The dog was famous. The dog has his place in history. He left it on record that he wished his dog to be buried with him."

They looked at the picture.

"I always feel," Lucy broke the silence, "he's saying: 'Paint my dog.'"

"But what about the horse?" said Mrs. Manresa.

he horse," said Bartholomew, putting on his glasses. He
d at the horse. The hindquarters were not satisfactory.
But William Dodge was still looking at the lady.

h," said Bartholomew who had bought that picture because
d that picture, "you're an artist."

e denied it, for the second time in half an hour, or so

for did a good sort like the woman Manresa bring these
reeds in her trail? Giles asked himself. And his silence made
contribution to talk—Dodge that is, shook his head. "I like
that picture." That was all he could bring himself to say.

"And you're right," said Bartholomew. "A man—I forget his
name—a man connected with some Institute, a man who goes
about giving advice, gratis, to descendants like ourselves, degenerate descendants, said . . . said . . ." He paused. They all
looked at the lady. But she looked over their heads, looking at
nothing. She led them down green glades into the heart of silence.

"Said it was by Sir Joshua?" Mrs. Manresa broke the silence
abruptly.

"No, no," William Dodge said hastily, but under his breath.

"Why's he afraid?" Isabella asked herself. A poor specimen he
was; afraid to stick up for his own beliefs—just as she was afraid,
of her husband. Didn't she write her poetry in a book bound like
an account book lest Giles might suspect? She looked at Giles.

He had finished his fish; he had eaten quickly, not to keep
them waiting. Now there was cherry tart. Mrs. Manresa was counting the stones.

"Tinker, tailor, soldier, sailor, apothecary, ploughboy . . . that's
me!" she cried, delighted to have it confirmed by the cherry stones
that she was a wild child of nature.

"You believe," said the old gentleman, courteously chaffing her,
"in that too?"

"Of course, of course I do!" she cried. Now she was on the rails
again. Now she was a thorough good sort again. And they too were
delighted; now they could follow in her wake and leave the silver
and dun shades that led to the heart of silence.

"I had a father," said Dodge beneath his breath to Isa who sat
next him, "who loved pictures."

"Oh, I too!" she exclaimed. Flurriedly, disconnectedly, she ex-

plained. She used to stay when she was a child, when she ha
whooping cough, with an uncle, a clergyman; who wore a
cap; and never did anything; didn't even preach; but made
poems, walking in his garden, saying them aloud.

"People thought him mad," she said. "I didn't. . . ."
She stopped.

"Tinker, tailor, soldier, sailor, apothecary, ploughboy. . . . It
appears," said old Bartholomew, laying down his spoon, "that I am
a thief. Shall we take our coffee in the garden?" He rose.

Isa dragged her chair across the gravel muttering: "To what
dark antre of the unvisited earth, or windbrushed forest, shall we
go now? Or spin from star to star and dance in the maze of the
moon? Or. . . ."

She held her deck chair at the wrong angle. The frame with
the notches was upside down.

"Songs my uncle taught me?" said William Dodge, hearing her
mutter. He unfolded the chair and fixed the bar into the right
notch.

She flushed, as if she had spoken in an empty room and someone had stepped out from behind a curtain.

"Don't you, if you're doing something with your hands, talk
nonsense?" she stumbled. But what did he do with his hands, the
white, the fine, the shapely?

Giles went back to the house and brought more chairs and
placed them in a semi-circle, so that the view might be shared,
and the shelter of the old wall. For by some lucky chance a wall
had been built continuing the house, it might be with the intention of adding another wing, on the raised ground in the sun. But
funds were lacking; the plan was abandoned, and the wall remained, nothing but a wall. Later, another generation had planted
fruit trees, which in time had spread their arms widely across the
red-orange weathered brick. Mrs. Sands called it a good year if
she could make six pots of apricot jam from them—the fruit was
never sweet enough for dessert. Perhaps three apricots were worth
enclosing in muslin bags. But they were so beautiful, naked, with
one flushed cheek, one green, that Mrs. Swithin left them naked,
and the wasps burrowed holes.

The ground sloped up, so that to quote Figgis's Guide Book

(1833), "it commanded a fine view of the surrounding country.
. . . The spire of Bolney Minster, Rough Norton woods, and on an
eminence rather to the left, Hogben's Folly, so called because. . . ."

The Guide Book still told the truth. 1830 was true in 1939. No
house had been built; no town had sprung up. Hogben's Folly
was still eminent; the very flat, field-parcelled land had changed
only in this—the tractor had to some extent superseded the
plough. The horse had gone; but the cow remained. If Figgis were
here now, Figgis would have said the same. So they always said
when in summer they sat there to drink coffee, if they had guests.
When they were alone, they said nothing. They looked at the
view; they looked at what they knew, to see if what they knew
might perhaps be different today. Most days it was the same.

"That's what makes a view so sad," said Mrs. Swithin, lowering
herself into the deck chair which Giles had brought her. "And so
beautiful. It'll be there," she nodded at the strip of gauze laid upon
the distant fields, "when we're not."

Giles nicked his chair into position with a jerk. Thus only could
he show his irritation, his rage with old fogies who sat and looked
at views over coffee and cream when the whole of Europe—over
there—was bristling like. . . . He had no command of metaphor.
Only the ineffective word "hedgehog" illustrated his vision of
Europe, bristling with guns, poised with planes. At any moment
guns would rake that land into furrows; planes splinter Bolney
Minster into smithereens and blast the Folly. He, too, loved the
view. And blamed Aunt Lucy, looking at views, instead of—doing
what? What she had done was to marry a squire now dead; she
had borne two children, one in Canada, the other, married, in
Birmingham. His father, whom he loved, he exempted from censure; as for himself, one thing followed another; and so he sat,
with old fogies, looking at views.

"Beautiful," said Mrs. Manresa, "beautiful . . ." she mumbled.
She was lighting a cigarette. The breeze blew out her match.
Giles hollowed his hand and lit another. She too was exempted
—why, he could not say.

"Since you're interested in pictures," said Bartholomew, turning to the silent guest, "why, tell me, are we, as a race, so incurious,
irresponsive and insensitive"—the champagne had given him a
flow of unusual three-decker words—"to that noble art, whereas,

Mrs. Manresa, if she'll allow me my old man's liberty, has her Shakespeare by heart?"

"Shakespeare by heart!" Mrs. Manresa protested. She struck an attitude. "To be, or not to be, that is the question. Whether 'tis nobler . . . Go on!" she nudged Giles, who sat next her.

"Fade far away and quite forget what thou amongst the leaves hast never known . . ." Isa supplied the first words that came into her head by way of helping her husband out of his difficulty.

"The weariness, the torture, and the fret . . ." William Dodge added, burying the end of his cigarette in a grave between two stones.

"There!" Bartholomew exclaimed, cocking his forefinger aloft. "That proves it! What springs touched, what secret drawer displays its treasures, if I say"—he raised more fingers—"Reynolds! Constable! Crome!"

"Why called 'Old'?" Mrs. Manresa thrust in.

"We haven't the words—we haven't the words," Mrs. Swithin protested. "Behind the eyes; not on the lips; that's all."

"Thoughts without words," her brother mused. "Can that be?"

"Quite beyond me!" cried Mrs. Manresa, shaking her head. "Much too clever! May I help myself? I know it's wrong. But I've reached the age—and the figure—when I do what I like."

She took the little silver cream jug and let the smooth fluid curl luxuriously into her coffee, to which she added a shovel full of brown sugar candy. Sensuously, rhythmically, she stirred the mixture round and round.

"Take what you like! Help yourself!" Bartholomew exclaimed. He felt the champagne withdrawing and hastened, before the last trace of geniality was withdrawn, to make the most of it, as if he cast one last look into a lit-up chamber before going to bed.

The wild child, afloat once more on the tide of the old man's benignity, looked over her coffee cup at Giles, with whom she felt in conspiracy. A thread united them—visible, invisible, like those threads, now seen, now not, that unite trembling grass blades in autumn before the sun rises. She had met him once only, at a cricket match. And then had been spun between them an early morning thread before the twigs and leaves of real friendship emerge. She looked before she drank. Looking was part of drinking. Why waste sensation, she seemed to ask, why waste a single drop that can be pressed out of this ripe, this melting, this adorable world? Then she drank. And the air round her became threaded with sensation. Bartholomew felt it; Giles felt it. Had he been a horse, the thin brown skin would have twitched, as if a fly had settled. Isabella twitched too. Jealousy, anger, pierced her skin.

"And now," said Mrs. Manresa, putting down her cup, "about this entertainment—this pageant, into which we've gone and butted"—she made it, too, seem ripe like the apricot into which the wasps were burrowing—"Tell me, what's it to be?" She turned. "Don't I hear?" She listened. She heard laughter, down among the bushes, where the terrace dipped to the bushes.

Beyond the lily pool the ground sank again, and in that dip of the ground, bushes and brambles had mobbed themselves together. It was always shady; sun-flecked in summer, dark and damp in winter. In the summer there were always butterflies; fritillaries darting through; Red Admirals feasting and floating; cabbage whites, unambitiously fluttering round a bush, like muslin milkmaids, content to spend a life there. Butterfly catching, for generation after generation, began there; for Bartholomew and Lucy; for Giles; for George it had begun only the day before yesterday, when, in his little green net, he had caught a cabbage white.

It was the very place for a dressing-room, just as, obviously, the terrace was the very place for a play.

"The very place!" Miss La Trobe had exclaimed the first time she came to call and was shown the grounds. It was a winter's day. The trees were leafless then.

"That's the place for a pageant, Mr. Oliver!" she had exclaimed. "Winding in and out between the trees. . . ." She waved her hand at the trees standing bare in the clear light of January.

"There the stage; here the audience; and down there among the bushes a perfect dressing-room for the actors."

She was always all agog to get things up. But where did she spring from? With that name she wasn't presumably pure English. From the Channel Islands perhaps? Only her eyes and something about her always made Mrs. Bingham suspect that she had Rus-

sian blood in her. "Those deep-set eyes; that very square jaw" reminded her—not that she had been to Russia—of the Tartars.
Rumour said that she had kept a tea shop at Winchester; that
had failed. She had been an actress. That had failed. She had
bought a four-roomed cottage and shared it with an actress. They
had quarrelled. Very little was actually known about her. Out-
wardly she was swarthy, sturdy and thick set; strode about the fields
in a smock frock; sometimes with a cigarette in her mouth; often
with a whip in her hand; and used rather strong language—perhaps, then, she wasn't altogether a lady? At any rate, she had a
passion for getting things up.

The laughter died away.
"Are they going to act?" Mrs. Manresa asked.
"Act; dance; sing; a little bit of everything," said Giles.
"Miss La Trobe is a lady of wonderful energy," said Mrs.
Swithin.
"She makes everyone do something," said Isabella.
"Our part," said Bartholomew, "is to be the audience. And a very
important part too."
"Also, we provide the tea," said Mrs. Swithin.
"Shan't we go and help?" said Mrs. Manresa. "Cut up bread
and butter?"
"No, no," said Mr. Oliver. "We are the audience."
"One year we had *Gammer Gurton's Needle*," said Mrs.
Swithin. "One year we wrote the play ourselves. The son of our
blacksmith—Tony? Tommy?—had the loveliest voice. And Elsie
at the Crossways—how she mimicked! Took us all off. Bart; Giles;
Old Flimsy—that's me. People are gifted—very. The question is—
how to bring it out? That's where she's so clever—Miss La Trobe.
Of course, there's the whole of English literature to choose from.
But how can one choose? Often on a wet day I begin counting up;
what I've read; what I haven't read."
"And leaving books on the floor," said her brother. "Like the
pig in the story; or was it a donkey?"
She laughed, tapping him lightly on the knee.
"The donkey who couldn't choose between hay and turnips and
so starved," Isabella explained, interposing—anything—between
her aunt and her husband, who hated this kind of talk this after-

noon. Books open; no conclusion come to; and he sitting in the audience.

"We remain seated"—"We are the audience." Words this afternoon ceased to lie flat in the sentence. They rose, became menacing and shook their fists at you. This afternoon he wasn't Giles Oliver come to see the villagers act their annual pageant; manacled to a rock he was, and forced passively to behold indescribable horror. His face showed it; and Isa, not knowing what to say, abruptly, half purposely, knocked over a coffee cup.

William Dodge caught it as it fell. He held it for a moment. He turned it. From the faint blue mark, as of crossed daggers, in the glaze at the bottom he knew that it was English, made perhaps at Nottingham; date about 1760. His expression, considering the daggers, coming to this conclusion, gave Giles another peg on which to hang his rage as one hangs a coat on a peg, conveniently. A toady; a lickspittle; not a downright plain man of his senses; but a teaser and twitcher; a fingerer of sensations; picking and choosing; dillying and dallying; not a man to have straightforward love for a woman—his head was close to Isa's head—but simply a——— At this word, which he could not speak in public, he pursed his lips; and the signet-ring on his little finger looked redder, for the flesh next it whitened as he gripped the arm of his chair.

"Oh what fun!" cried Mrs. Manresa in her fluty voice. "A little bit of everything. A song; a dance; then a play acted by the villagers themselves. Only," here she turned with her head on one side to Isabella, "I'm sure *she's* written it. Haven't you, Mrs. Giles?"

Isa flushed and denied it.

"For myself," Mrs. Manresa continued, "speaking plainly, I can't put two words together. I don't know how it is—such a chatterbox as I am with my tongue, once I hold a pen———" She made a face, screwed her fingers as if she held a pen in them. But the pen she held thus on the little table absolutely refused to move.

"And my handwriting—so huge—so clumsy—" She made another face and dropped the invisible pen.

Very delicately William Dodge set the cup in its saucer. "Now *he*," said Mrs. Manresa, as if referring to the delicacy with which he did this, and imputing to him the same skill in writing, "writes beautifully. Every letter perfectly formed."

Again they all looked at him. Instantly he put his hands in his pockets.

Isabella guessed the word that Giles had not spoken. Well, was it wrong if he was that word? Why judge each other? Do we know each other? Not here, not now. But somewhere, this cloud, this crust, this doubt, this dust—— She waited for a rhyme, it failed her; but somewhere surely one sun would shine and all, without a doubt, would be clear.

She started. Again, sounds of laughter reached her. "I think I hear them," she said. "They're getting ready. They're dressing up in the bushes."

Miss La Trobe was pacing to and fro between the leaning birch trees. One hand was deep stuck in her jacket pocket; the other held a foolscap sheet. She was reading what was written there. She had the look of a commander pacing his deck. The leaning graceful trees with black bracelets circling the silver bark were distant about a ship's length.

Wet would it be, or fine? Out came the sun; and, shading her eyes in the attitude proper to an Admiral on his quarter-deck, she decided to risk the engagement out of doors. Doubts were over. All stage properties, she commanded, must be moved from the Barn to the bushes. It was done. And the actors, while she paced, taking all responsibility and plumping for fine, not wet, dressed among the brambles. Hence the laughter.

The clothes were strewn on the grass. Cardboard crowns, swords made of silver paper, turbans that were sixpenny dish cloths, lay on the grass or were flung on the bushes. There were pools of red and purple in the shade; flashes of silver in the sun. The dresses attracted the butterflies. Red and silver, blue and yellow gave off warmth and sweetness. Red Admirals gluttonously absorbed richness from dish cloths, cabbage whites drank icy coolness from silver paper. Flitting, tasting, returning, they sampled the colours.

Miss La Trobe stopped her pacing and surveyed the scene. "It has the makings . . ." she murmured. For another play always lay behind the play she had just written. Shading her eyes, she looked. The butterflies circling; the light changing; the children leaping;

the mothers laughing—— "No, I don't get it," she muttered and resumed her pacing.

"Bossy" they called her privately, just as they called Mrs. Swithin "Flimsy." Her abrupt manner and stocky figure; her thick ankles and sturdy shoes; her rapid decisions barked out in guttural accents—all this "got their goat." No one liked to be ordered about singly. But in little troops they appealed to her. Someone must lead. Then too they could put the blame on her. Suppose it poured?

"Miss La Trobe!" they hailed her now. "What's the idea about this?"

She stopped. David and Iris each had a hand on the gramophone. It must be hidden; yet must be close enough to the audience to be heard. Well, hadn't she given orders? Where were the hurdles covered in leaves? Fetch them. Mr. Streatfield had said he would see to it. Where was Mr. Streatfield? No clergyman was visible. Perhaps he's in the Barn? "Tommy, cut along and fetch him." "Tommy's wanted in the first scene." "Beryl then . . ." The mothers disputed. One child had been chosen; another not. Fair hair was unjustly preferred to dark. Mrs. Ebury had forbidden Fanny to act because of the nettle-rash. There was another name in the village for nettle-rash.

Mrs. Ball's cottage was not what you might call clean. In the last war Mrs. Ball lived with another man while her husband was in the trenches. All this Miss La Trobe knew, but refused to be mixed up in it. She splashed into the fine mesh like a great stone into the lily pool. The criss-cross was shattered. Only the roots beneath water were of use to her. Vanity, for example, made them all malleable. The boys wanted the big parts; the girls wanted the fine clothes. Expenses had to be kept down. Ten pounds was the limit. Thus conventions were outraged. Swathed in conventions, they couldn't see, as she could, that a dish cloth wound round a head in the open looked much richer than real silk. So they squabbled; but she kept out of it. Waiting for Mr. Streatfield, she paced between the birch trees.

The other trees were magnificently straight. They were not too regular; but regular enough to suggest columns in a church; in a church without a roof; in an open-air cathedral, a place where swallows darting seemed, by the regularity of the trees, to make a pattern, dancing, like the Russians, only not to music, but to the unheard rhythm of their own wild hearts.

The laughter died away.

"We must possess our souls in patience," said Mrs. Manresa again. "Or could we help?" she suggested, glancing over her shoulder, "with those chairs?"

Candish, a gardener, and a maid were all bringing chairs—for the audience. There was nothing for the audience to do. Mrs. Manresa suppressed a yawn. They were silent. They stared at the view, as if something might happen in one of those fields to relieve them of the intolerable burden of sitting silent, doing nothing, in company. Their minds and bodies were too close, yet not close enough. We aren't free, each one of them felt separately, to feel or think separately, nor yet to fall asleep. We're too close; but not close enough. So they fidgeted.

The heat had increased. The clouds had vanished. All was sun now. The view laid bare by the sun was flattened, silenced, stilled. The cows were motionless; the brick wall, no longer sheltering, beat back grains of heat. Old Mr. Oliver sighed profoundly. His head jerked; his hand fell. It fell within an inch of the dog's head on the grass by his side. Then up he jerked it again on to his knee.

Giles glared. With his hands bound tight round his knees he stared at the flat fields. Staring, glaring, he sat silent.

Isabella felt prisoned. Through the bars of the prison, through the sleep haze that deflected them, blunt arrows bruised her; of love, then of hate. Through other people's bodies she felt neither love nor hate distinctly. Most consciously she felt—she had drunk sweet wine at luncheon—a desire for water. "A beaker of cold water, a beaker of cold water," she repeated, and saw water surrounded by walls of shining glass.

Mrs. Manresa longed to relax and curl in a corner with a cushion, a picture paper, and a bag of sweets.

Mrs. Swithin and William surveyed the view aloofly, and with detachment.

How tempting, how very tempting, to let the view triumph; to reflect its ripple; to let their own minds ripple; to let outlines elongate and pitch over—so—with a sudden jerk.

Mrs. Manresa yielded, pitched, plunged, then pulled herself up.

"What a view!" she exclaimed, pretending to dust the ashes of her cigarette, but in truth concealing her yawn. Then she sighed, pretending to express not her own drowsiness, but something connected with what she felt about views.

Nobody answered her. The flat fields glared green yellow, blue yellow, red yellow, then blue again. The repetition was senseless, hideous, stupefying.

"Then," said Mrs. Swithin, in a low voice, as if the exact moment for speech had come, as if she had promised, and it was time to fulfil her promise, "come, come and I'll show you the house."

She addressed no one in particular. But William Dodge knew she meant him. He rose with a jerk, like a toy suddenly pulled straight by a string.

"What energy!" Mrs. Manresa half sighed, half yawned. "Have I the courage to go too?" Isabella asked herself. They were going; above all things, she desired cold water, a beaker of cold water; but desire petered out, suppressed by the leaden duty she owed to others. She watched them go—Mrs. Swithin tottering yet tripping; and Dodge unfurled and straightened, as he strode beside her along the blazing tiles under the hot wall, till they reached the shade of the house.

A match-box fell—Bartholomew's. His fingers had loosed it; he had dropped it. He gave up the game; he couldn't be bothered. With his head on one side, his hand dangling above the dog's head he slept; he snored.

Mrs. Swithin paused for a moment in the hall among the gilt-clawed tables.

"This," she said, "is the staircase. And now—up we go."

She went up, two stairs ahead of her guest. Lengths of yellow satin unfurled themselves on a cracked canvas as they mounted.

"Not an ancestress," said Mrs. Swithin, as they came level with the head in the picture. "But we claim her because we've known her—O, ever so many years. Who was she?" she gazed. "Who painted her?" She shook her head. She looked lit up, as if for a banquet, with the sun pouring over her.

"But I like her best in the moonlight," Mrs. Swithin reflected, and mounted more stairs.

She panted slightly, going upstairs. Then she ran her hand over the sunk books in the wall on the landing, as if they were pan pipes.

"Here are the poets from whom we descend by way of the mind, Mr. . . ." she murmured. She had forgotten his name. Yet she had singled him out.

"My brother says, they built the house north for shelter, not south for sun. So they're damp in the winter." She paused. "And now what comes next?"

She stopped. There was a door.

"The morning room." She opened the door. "Where my mother received her guests."

Two chairs faced each other on either side of a fine fluted mantelpiece. He looked over her shoulder.

She shut the door.

"Now up, now up again." Again they mounted. "Up and up they went," she panted, seeing, it seemed, an invisible procession, "up and up to bed."

"A bishop; a traveller;—I've forgotten even their names. I ignore. I forget."

She stopped at a window in the passage and held back the curtain. Beneath was the garden, bathed in sun. The grass was sleek and shining. Three white pigeons were flirting and tiptoeing as ornate as ladies in ball dresses. Their elegant bodies swayed as they minced with tiny steps on their little pink feet upon the grass. Suddenly, up they rose in a flutter, circled, and flew away.

"Now," she said, "for the bedrooms." She tapped twice very distinctly on a door. With her head on one side, she listened.

"One never knows," she murmured, "if there's somebody there." Then she flung open the door.

He half expected to see somebody there, naked, or half dressed, or knelt in prayer. But the room was empty. The room was tidy as a pin, not slept in for months, a spare room. Candles stood on the dressing table. The counterpane was straight. Mrs. Swithin stopped by the bed.

"Here," she said, "yes, here," she tapped the counterpane, "I was born. In this bed."

Her voice died away. She sank down on the edge of the bed. She was tired, no doubt, by the stairs, by the heat.

"But we have other lives, I think, I hope," she murmured. "We live in others, Mr. . . . We live in things."

She spoke simply. She spoke with an effort. She spoke as if she must overcome her tiredness out of charity towards a stranger, a guest. She had forgotten his name. Twice she had said "Mr." and stopped.

The furniture was mid-Victorian, bought at Maples, perhaps, in the forties. The carpet was covered with small purple dots. And a white circle marked the place where the slop pail had stood by the washstand.

Could he say "I'm William"? He wished to. Old and frail she had climbed the stairs. She had spoken her thoughts, ignoring, not caring if he thought her, as he had, inconsequent, sentimental, foolish. She had lent him a hand to help him up a steep place. She had guessed his trouble. Sitting on the bed he heard her sing, swinging her little legs, "Come and see my sea weeds, come and see my sea shells, come and see my dicky bird hop upon its perch"—an old child's nursery rhyme to help a child. Standing by the cupboard in the corner he saw her reflected in the glass. Cut off from their bodies, their eyes smiled, their bodiless eyes, at their eyes in the glass.

Then she slipped off the bed.

"Now," she said, "what comes next?" and pattered down the corridor. A door stood open. Everyone was out in the garden. The room was like a ship deserted by its crew. The children had been playing—there was a spotted horse in the middle of the carpet. The nurse had been sewing—there was a piece of linen on the table. The baby had been in the cot. The cot was empty.

"The nursery," said Mrs. Swithin.

Words raised themselves and became symbolical. "The cradle of our race," she seemed to say.

Dodge crossed to the fireplace and looked at the Newfoundland Dog in the Christmas Annual that was pinned to the wall. The room smelt warm and sweet; of clothes drying; of milk; of biscuits and warm water. "Good Friends" the picture was called. A rushing sound came in through the open door. He turned. The old woman had wandered out into the passage and leant against the window.

He left the door open for the crew to come back to and joined her.

Down in the courtyard beneath the window cars were assembling. Their narrow black roofs were laid together like the blocks of a floor. Chauffeurs were jumping down; here old ladies gingerly advanced black legs with silver-buckled shoes; old men striped trousers. Young men in shorts leapt out on one side; girls with skin-coloured legs on the other. There was a purring and a churning of the yellow gravel. The audience was assembling. But they, looking down from the window, were truants, detached. Together they leant half out of the window.

And then a breeze blew and all the muslin blinds fluttered out, as if some majestic goddess, rising from her throne among her peers, had tossed her amber-coloured raiment, and the other gods, seeing her rise and go, laughed, and their laughter floated her on.

Mrs. Swithin put her hands to her hair, for the breeze had ruffled it.

"Mr. . . ." she began.

"I'm William," he interrupted.

At that she smiled a ravishing girl's smile, as if the wind had warmed the wintry blue in her eyes to amber.

"I took you," she apologized, "away from your friends, William, because I felt wound tight here. . . ." She touched her bony forehead upon which a blue vein wriggled like a blue worm. But her eyes in their caves of bone were still lambent. He saw her eyes only. And he wished to kneel before her, to kiss her hand, and to say: "At school they held me under a bucket of dirty water, Mrs. Swithin; when I looked up, the world was dirty, Mrs. Swithin; so I married; but my child's not my child, Mrs. Swithin. I'm a half-man, Mrs. Swithin; a flickering, mind-divided little snake in the grass, Mrs. Swithin; as Giles saw; but you've healed me. . . ." So he wished to say; but said nothing; and the breeze went lolloping along the corridors, blowing the blinds out.

Once more he looked and she looked down on to the yellow gravel that made a crescent round the door. Pendant from her chain her cross swung as she leant out and the sun struck it. How could she weight herself down by that sleek symbol? How stamp

herself, so volatile, so vagrant, with that image? As he looked at
it, they were truants no more. The purring of the wheels became
vocal. "Hurry, hurry, hurry," it seemed to say, "or you'll be late.
Hurry, hurry, hurry, or the best seats'll be taken."

"Oh," cried Mrs. Swithin, "there's Mr. Streatfield!" And they saw
a clergyman, a strapping clergyman, carrying a hurdle, a leafy
hurdle. He was striding through the cars with the air of a person
of authority, who is awaited, expected, and now comes.

"Is it time," said Mrs. Swithin, "to go and join——" She left
the sentence unfinished, as if she were of two minds, and they
fluttered to right and to left, like pigeons rising from the grass.

The audience was assembling. They came streaming along the
paths and spreading across the lawn. Some were old; some were in
the prime of life. There were children among them. Among them,
as Mr. Figgis might have observed, were representatives of our
most respected families—the Dyces of Denton; the Wickhams of
Owlswick; and so on. Some had been there for centuries, never
selling an acre. On the other hand there were new-comers, the
Manresas, bringing the old houses up to date, adding bathrooms.
And a scatter of odds and ends, like Cobbet of Cobbs Corner,
retired, it was understood, on a pension from a tea plantation.
Not an asset. He did his own housework and dug in his garden.
The building of a car factory and of an aerodrome in the neighbourhood had attracted a number of unattached floating residents.
Also there was Mr. Page, the reporter, representing the local paper. Roughly speaking, however, had Figgis been there in person
and called a roll call, half the ladies and gentlemen present would
have said: "*Adsum*; I'm here, in place of my grandfather or great-
grandfather," as the case might be. At this very moment, half-
past three on a June day in 1939 they greeted each other, and as
they took their seats, finding if possible a seat next one another,
they said: "That hideous new house at Pyes Corner! What an
eyesore! And those bungalows!—have you seen 'em?"

Again, had Figgis called the names of the villagers, they too
would have answered. Mrs. Sands was born Iliffe; Candish's mother
was one of the Perrys. The green mounds in the churchyard had
been cast up by their molings, which for centuries had made the
earth friable. True, there were absentees when Mr. Streatfield
called his roll call in the church. The motor bike, the motor bus,

and the movies—when Mr. Streatfield called his roll call, he laid the blame on them.

Rows of chairs, deck chairs, gilt chairs, hired cane chairs, and indigenous garden seats had been drawn up on the terrace. There were plenty of seats for everybody. But some preferred to sit on the ground. Certainly Miss La Trobe had spoken the truth when she said: "The very place for a pageant!" The lawn was as flat as the floor of a theatre. The terrace, rising, made a natural stage. The trees barred the stage like pillars. And the human figure was seen to great advantage against a background of sky. As for the weather, it was turning out, against all expectation, a very fine day. A perfect summer afternoon.

"What luck!" Mrs. Carter was saying. "Last year . . ." Then the play began. Was it, or was it not, the play? Chuff, chuff, chuff sounded from the bushes. It was the noise a machine makes when something has gone wrong. Some sat down hastily; others stopped talking guiltily. All looked at the bushes. For the stage was empty. Chuff, chuff, chuff, the machine buzzed in the bushes. While they looked apprehensively and some finished their sentences, a small girl, like a rosebud in pink, advanced; took her stand on a mat, behind a conch hung with leaves, and piped:

Gentles and simples, I address you all . . .

So it was the play then. Or was it the prologue?

Come hither for our festival (she continued)
This is a pageant, all may see
Drawn from our island history.
England am I. . . .

"She's England," they whispered. "It's begun." "The prologue," they added, looking down at the programme.

"England am I," she piped again; and stopped.

She had forgotten her lines.

"Hear! Hear!" said an old man in a white waistcoat briskly. "Bravo! Bravo!"

"Blast 'em!" cursed Miss La Trobe, hidden behind the tree. She looked along the front row. They glared as if they were exposed to a frost that nipped them and fixed them all at the same level. Only Bond the cowman looked fluid and natural.

"Music!" she signalled. "Music!" But the machine continued: Chuff, chuff, chuff.

"A child new born . . ." she prompted.

"A child new born," Phyllis Jones continued,
Sprung from the sea
Whose billows blown by mighty storm
Cut off from France and Germany
   This isle.

She glanced back over her shoulder. Chuff, chuff, chuff, the machine buzzed. A long line of villagers in shirts made of sacking began passing in and out in single file behind her between the trees. They were singing, but not a word reached the audience.

England am I, Phyllis Jones continued, facing the audience,
Now weak and small
A child, as all may see . . .

Her words peppered the audience as with a shower of hard little stones. Mrs. Manresa in the very centre smiled; but she felt as if her skin cracked when she smiled. There was a vast vacancy between her, the singing villagers and the piping child.

Chuff, chuff, chuff, went the machine like a corn-cutter on a hot day.

The villagers were singing, but half their words were blown away.

Cutting the roads . . . up to the hill top . . . we climbed. Down in the valley . . . sow, wild boar, hog, rhinoceros, reindeer . . . Dug ourselves in to the hill top . . . Ground roots between stones . . . Ground corn . . . till we too . . . lay under g—r—o—u—n—d.

The words petered away. Chuff, chuff, chuff, the machine ticked. Then at last the machine ground out a tune!

Armed against fate
The valiant Rhoderick
Armed and valiant
Bold and blatant

Firm elatant
See the warriors—here they come . . .

The pompous popular tune brayed and blared. Miss La Trobe
watched from behind the tree. Muscles loosened; ice cracked.
The stout lady in the middle began to beat time with her hand
on her chair. Mrs. Manresa was humming:

> My home is at Windsor, close to the Inn.
> Royal George is the name of the pub.
> And boys you'll believe me,
> I don't want no asking . . .

She was afloat on the stream of the melody. Radiating royalty,
complacency, good humour, the wild child was Queen of the
festival. The play had begun.

But there was an interruption. "O," Miss La Trobe growled
behind her tree, "the torture of these interruptions!"

"Sorry I'm so late," said Mrs. Swithin. She pushed her way
through the chairs to a seat beside her brother.

"What's it all about? I've missed the prologue. England? That
little girl? Now she's gone . . ."

Phyllis had slipped off her mat.

"And who's this?" asked Mrs. Swithin.

It was Hilda, the carpenter's daughter. She now stood where
England had stood.

"*O, England's grown . . .*" Miss La Trobe prompted her.

"*O, England's grown a girl now,*" Hilda sang out
("What a lovely voice!" someone exclaimed)
With roses in her hair,
Wild roses, red roses,
She roams the lanes and chooses
A garland for her hair.

"A cushion? Thank you so much," said Mrs. Swithin, stuffing
the cushion behind her back. Then she leant forward.

"That's England in the time of Chaucer, I take it. She's been
maying, nutting. She has flowers in her hair . . . But those passing
behind her——" she pointed. "The Canterbury pilgrims? Look!"

All the time the villagers were passing in and out between the
trees. They were singing; but only a word or two was audible

"... wore ruts in the grass ... built the house in the lane ..."
The wind blew away the connecting words of their chant, and
then, as they reached the tree at the end they sang:

"To the shrine of the Saint ... to the tomb ... lovers ...
believers ... we come ..."

They grouped themselves together.

Then there was a rustle and an interruption. Chairs were drawn
back. Isa looked behind her. Mr. and Mrs. Rupert Haines, detained by a breakdown on the road, had arrived. He was sitting to
the right, several rows back, the man in grey.

Meanwhile the pilgrims, having done their homage to the tomb,
were, it appeared, tossing hay on their rakes.

> I kissed a girl and let her go,
> Another did I tumble,
> In the straw and in the hay ...

—that was what they were singing, as they scooped and tossed the
invisible hay, when she looked round again.

"Scenes from English history," Mrs. Manresa explained to Mrs.
Swithin. She spoke in a loud cheerful voice, as if the old lady
were deaf. "Merry England."

She clapped energetically.

The singers scampered away into the bushes. The tune stopped.
Chuff, chuff, chuff, the machine ticked. Mrs. Manresa looked at
her programme. It would take till midnight unless they skipped.
Early Briton; Plantagenets; Tudors; Stuarts—she ticked them off,
but probably she had forgotten a reign or two.

"Ambitious, ain't it?" she said to Bartholomew, while they
waited. Chuff, chuff, chuff went the machine. Could they talk?
Could they move? No, for the play was going on. Yet the stage
was empty; only the cows moved in the meadows; only the tick
of the gramophone needle was heard. The tick, tick, tick seemed
to hold them together, tranced. Nothing whatsoever appeared on
the stage.

"I'd no notion we looked so nice," Mrs. Swithin whispered to
William. Hadn't she? The children; the pilgrims; behind the pilgrims the trees, and behind them the fields—the beauty of the

visible world took his breath away. Tick, tick, tick the machine continued.

"Marking time," said old Oliver beneath his breath.

"Which don't exist for us," Lucy murmured. "We've only the present."

"Isn't that enough?" William asked himself. Beauty—isn't that enough? But here Isa fidgeted. Her bare brown arms went nervously to her head. She half turned in her seat. "No, not for us, who've the future," she seemed to say. The future disturbing our present. Who was she looking for? William, turning, following her eyes, saw only a man in grey.

The ticking stopped. A dance tune was put on the machine. In time to it, Isa hummed: "What do I ask? To fly away, from night and day, and issue where—no partings are—but eye meets eye—and . . . O," she cried aloud: "Look at her!"

Everyone was clapping and laughing. From behind the bushes issued Queen Elizabeth—Eliza Clark, licensed to sell tobacco. Could she be Mrs. Clark of the village shop? She was splendidly made up. Her head, pearl-hung, rose from a vast ruff. Shiny satins draped her. Sixpenny brooches glared like cats' eyes and tigers' eyes; pearls looked down; her cape was made of cloth of silver—in fact swabs used to scour saucepans. She looked the age in person. And when she mounted the soap box in the centre, representing perhaps a rock in the ocean, her size made her appear gigantic. She could reach a flitch of bacon or haul a tub of oil with one sweep of her arm in the shop. For a moment she stood there, eminent, dominant, on the soap box with the blue and sailing clouds behind her. The breeze had risen.

The Queen of this great land . . .
—those were the first words that could be heard above the roar of laughter and applause.

Mistress of ships and bearded men (she bawled)
Hawkins, Frobisher, Drake,
Tumbling their oranges, ingots of silver,
Cargoes of diamonds, ducats of gold,
Down on the jetty, there in the west land—
(she pointed her fist at the blazing blue sky)
Mistress of pinnacles, spires and palaces—

804

(her arm swept towards the house)
For me Shakespeare sang—
(a cow mooed. A bird twittered)
The throstle, the mavis (she continued)
In the green wood, the wild wood,
Carolled and sang, praising England, the Queen,
Then there was heard too
On granite and cobble
From Windsor to Oxford
Loud laughter, low laughter
Of warrior and lover,
The fighter, the singer.
The ashen haired babe
(she stretched out her swarthy, muscular arm)
Stretched his arm in contentment
As home from the Isles came
The sea faring men. . . .

Here the wind gave a tug at her head dress. Loops of pearls made it top-heavy. She had to steady the ruffle which threatened to blow away.

"Laughter, loud laughter," Giles muttered. The tune on the gramophone reeled from side to side as if drunk with merriment. Mrs. Manresa began beating her foot and humming in time to it.

"Bravo! Bravo!" she cried. "There's life in the old dog yet!" And she trolloped out the words of the song with an abandonment which, if vulgar, was a great help to the Elizabethan age. For the ruff had become unpinned and Great Eliza had forgotten her lines. But the audience laughed so loud that it did not matter.

"I fear I am not in my perfect mind," Giles muttered to the same tune. Words came to the surface—he remembered "a stricken deer in whose lean flank the world's harsh scorn has struck its thorn. . . . Exiled from its festival, the music turned ironical. . . . A churchyard haunter at whom the owl hoots and the ivy mocks tap-tap-tapping on the pane. . . . For they are dead, and I . . . I . . . I," he repeated, forgetting the words, and glaring at his Aunt Lucy who sat craned forward, her mouth gaping, and her bony little hands clapping.

What were they laughing at?

At Albert, the village idiot, apparently. There was no need to dress him up. There he came, acting his part to perfection. He came ambling across the grass, mopping and mowing.

I know where the tit nests, he began
In the hedgerow. I know, I know—
What don't I know?
All your secrets, ladies,
And yours too, gentlemen . . .

He skipped along the front row of the audience, leering at each in turn. Now he was picking and plucking at Great Eliza's skirts. She cuffed him on the ear. He tweaked her back. He was enjoying himself immensely.

"Albert having the time of his life," Bartholomew muttered.

"Hope he don't have a fit," Lucy murmured.

"*I know . . . I know . . .*" Albert tittered, skipping round the soap box.

"The village idiot," whispered a stout black lady—Mrs. Elmhurst—who came from a village ten miles distant where they, too, had an idiot. It wasn't nice. Suppose he suddenly did something dreadful? There he was pinching the Queen's skirts. She half covered her eyes, in case he did do—something dreadful.

Hoppety, jiggety, Albert resumed
In at the window, out at the door,
What does the little bird hear? (he whistled on his fingers)
And see! There's a mouse. . . .
(he made as if chasing it through the grass)
Now the clock strikes!
(he stood erect, puffing out his cheeks as if he were blowing a dandelion clock)
One, two, three, four. . . .

And off he skipped, as if his turn was over.

"Glad that's over," said Mrs. Elmhurst, uncovering her face. "Now what comes next? A tableau . . . ?"

For helpers, issuing swiftly from the bushes, carrying hurdles, had enclosed the Queen's throne with screens papered to represent walls. They had strewn the ground with rushes. And the pilgrims who had continued their march and their chant in the background, now gathered round the figure of Eliza on her soap box as if to form the audience at a play.

Were they about to act a play in the presence of Queen Elizabeth? Was this, perhaps, the Globe theatre?

"What does the programme say?" Mrs. Herbert Winthrop asked, raising her lorgnette.

She mumbled through the blurred carbon sheet. Yes; it was a scene from a play.

"About a false Duke; and a Princess disguised as a boy; then the long lost heir turns out to be the beggar, because of a mole on his cheek; and Ferdinando and Carinthia—that's the Duke's daughter, only she's been lost in a cave—falls in love with Ferdinando who had been put into a basket as a baby by an aged crone. And they marry. That's I think what happens," she said, looking up from the programme.

"*Play out the play*," Great Eliza commanded. An aged crone tottered forward.

("Mrs. Otter of the End House," someone murmured.)

She sat herself on a packing case, and made motions, plucking her dishevelled locks and rocking herself from side to side as if she were an aged beldame in a chimney corner.

("The crone, who saved the rightful heir," Mrs. Winthrop explained.)

'Twas a winter's night (she croaked out)
I mind me that, I to whom all's one now, summer or winter.
You say the sun shines? I believe you, Sir.
'Oh but it's winter, and the fog's abroad.'
All's one to Elsbeth, summer or winter,
By the fireside, in the chimney corner, telling her beads.
I've cause to tell 'em.
Each bead (she held a bead between thumb and finger)
A crime!
'Twas a winter's night, before cockcrow,
Yet the cock did crow ere he left me—
The man with a hood on his face, and the bloody hands
And the babe in the basket.

'Tee hee,' he mewed, as who should say, 'I want my toy.'
Poor witling!
'Tee hee, tee hee!' I could not slay him!
For that, Mary in Heaven forgive me
The sins I've sinned before cockcrow!
Down to the creek i' the dawn I slipped
Where the gull haunts and the heron stands
Like a stake on the edge of the marshes . . .
Who's here?
(Three young men swaggered on to the stage and accosted her)
—Are you come to torture me, Sirs?
There is little blood in this arm,
(she extended her skinny forearm from her ragged shift)
Saints in Heaven preserve me!

She bawled. They bawled. All together they bawled, and so loud that it was difficult to make out what they were saying: apparently it was: *Did she remember concealing a child in a cradle among the rushes some twenty years previously? A babe in a basket, crone! A babe in a basket?* they bawled. *The wind howls and the bittern shrieks,* she replied.

"There is little blood in my arm," Isabella repeated.

That was all she heard. There was such a medley of things going on, what with the beldame's deafness, the bawling of the youths, and the confusion of the plot that she could make nothing of it.

Did the plot matter? She shifted and looked over her right shoulder. The plot was only there to beget emotion. There were only two emotions: love; and hate. There was no need to puzzle out the plot. Perhaps Miss La Trobe meant that when she cut this knot in the centre?

Don't bother about the plot: the plot's nothing.
But what was happening? The Prince had come.

Plucking up his sleeve, the beldame recognized the mole; and, staggering back in her chair, shrieked:
My child! My child!
Recognition followed. The young Prince (Albert Perry) was

almost smothered in the withered arms of the beldame. Then suddenly he started apart.

Look *where she comes! he cried.*

They all looked where she came—Sylvia Edwards in white satin.

Who came? Isa looked. The nightingale's song? The pearl in night's black ear? Love embodied.

All arms were raised; all faces stared.

Hail, sweet Carinthia! said the Prince, sweeping his hat off. And she to him, raising her eyes:

My love! My lord!

"It was enough. Enough. Enough," Isa repeated.

All else was verbiage, repetition.

The beldame meanwhile, because that was enough, had sunk back on her chair, the beads dangling from her fingers.

Look to the beldame there—old Elsbeth's sick!

(They crowded round her)

Dead, Sirs!

She fell back lifeless. The crowd drew away. Peace, let her pass. She to whom all's one now, summer or winter.

Peace was the third emotion. Love. Hate. Peace. Three emotions made the ply of human life. Now the priest, whose cotton wool moustache confused his utterance, stepped forward and pronounced benediction.

From the distaff of life's tangled skein, unloose her hands.

(They unloosed her hands)

Of her frailty, let nothing now remembered be.

Call for the robin redbreast and the wren.

And roses fall your crimson pall.

(Petals were strewn from wicker baskets)

Cover the corpse. Sleep well.

(They covered the corpse)

On you, fair Sirs (he turned to the happy couple)

Let Heaven rain benediction!

Haste ere the envying sun

Night's curtain hath undone. Let music sound

And the free air of Heaven waft you to your slumber!
Lead on the dance!

The gramophone blared. Dukes, priests, shepherds, pilgrims and serving men took hands and danced. The idiot scampered in and out. Hands joined, heads knocking, they danced round the majestic figure of the Elizabethan age personified by Mrs. Clark, licensed to sell tobacco, on her soap box.

It was a mellay; a medley; an entrancing spectacle (to William) of dappled light and shade on half clothed, fantastically coloured, leaping, jerking, swinging legs and arms. He clapped till his palms stung.

Mrs. Manresa applauded loudly. Somehow she was the Queen; and he (Giles) was the surly hero.

"Bravo! Bravo!" she cried, and her enthusiasm made the surly hero squirm on his seat. Then the great lady in the bath chair, the lady whose marriage with the local peer had obliterated in his trashy title a name that had been a name when there were brambles and briars where the Church now stood—so indigenous was she that even her body, crippled by arthritis, resembled an uncouth, nocturnal animal, now nearly extinct—clapped and laughed loud—the sudden laughter of a startled jay.

"Ha, ha, ha!" she laughed and clutched the arms of her chair with ungloved twisted hands.

A-maying, a-maying, they bawled. *In and out and round about, a-maying, a-maying. . . .*

It didn't matter what the words were; or who sang what. Round and round they whirled, intoxicated by the music. Then, at a sign from Miss La Trobe behind the tree, the dance stopped. A procession formed. Great Eliza descended from her soap box. Taking her skirts in her hand, striding with long strides, surrounded by Dukes and Princes, followed by the lovers arm in arm, with Albert the idiot playing in and out, and the corpse on its bier concluding the procession, the Elizabethan age passed from the scene.

"Curse! Blast! Damn 'em!" Miss La Trobe in her rage stubbed her toe against a root. Here was her downfall; here was the Interval. Writing this skimble-skamble stuff in her cottage, she had agreed to cut the play here; a slave to her audience—to Mrs. Sands' grumble—about tea; about dinner—she had gashed the scene here. Just as she had brewed emotion, she spilt it. So she signalled: Phyllis! And, summoned, Phyllis popped up on the mat again in the middle.

> Gentles and simples, I address you all (she piped)
> Our act is done, our scene is over.
> Past is the day of crone and lover.
> The bud has flowered; the flower has fallen.
> But soon will rise another dawning,
> For time whose children small we be
> Hath in his keeping, you shall see,
> You shall see. . . .

Her voice petered out. No one was listening. Heads bent, they read "Interval" on the programme. And, cutting short her words, the megaphone announced in plain English: "An interval." Half an hour's interval, for tea. Then the gramophone blared out:

> Armed against fate,
> The valiant Rhoderick,
> Bold and blatant,
> Firm, elatant, etc., etc.

At that, the audience stirred. Some rose briskly; others stooped, retrieving walking-sticks, hats, bags. And then, as they raised themselves and turned about, the music modulated. The music chanted: *Dispersed are we*. It moaned: *Dispersed are we*. It lamented: *Dispersed are we*, as they streamed, spotting the grass with colour, across the lawns, and down the paths: *Dispersed are we*.

Mrs. Manresa took up the strain. *Dispersed are we*. "Freely, boldly, fearing no one" (she pushed a deck chair out of her way). "Youths and maidens" (she glanced behind her; but Giles had his back turned). "Follow, follow, follow me. . . . Oh Mr. Parker, what a pleasure to see you here! I'm for tea!"

"Dispersed are we," Isabella followed her, humming. "All is over. The wave has broken. Left us stranded, high and dry. Single, separate on the shingle. Broken is the three-fold ply . . . Now I follow" (she pushed her chair back . . . The man in grey was lost in the crowd by the ilex) "that old strumpet" (she invoked Mrs. Manresa's tight, flowered figure in front of her) "to have tea."

Dodge remained behind. "Shall I," he murmured, "go or stay? Slip out some other way? Or follow, follow, follow the dispersing company?"

Dispersed are we, the music wailed; *dispersed are we*. Giles remained like a stake in the tide of the flowing company.

"Follow?" He kicked his chair back. "Whom? Where?" He stubbed his light tennis shoes on the wood. "Nowhere. Anywhere." Stark still he stood.

Here Cobbet of Cobbs Corner, alone under the monkey puzzle tree, rose and muttered: "What was in her mind, eh? What idea lay behind, eh? What made her indue the antique with this glamour—this sham lure, and set 'em climbing, climbing, climbing up the monkey puzzle tree?"

Dispersed are we, the music wailed. *Dispersed are we*. He turned and sauntered slowly after the retreating company.

Now Lucy, retrieving her bag from beneath the seat, chirruped to her brother:

"Bart, my dear, come with me. . . . D'you remember, when we were children, the play we acted in the nursery?"

He remembered. Red Indians the game was; a reed with a note wrapped up in a pebble.

"But for us, my old Cindy"—he picked up his hat— "the game's over." The glare and the stare and the beat of the tom-tom, he meant. He gave her his arm. Off they strolled. And Mr. Page, the reporter, noted, "Mrs. Swithin; Mr. B. Oliver," then turning, added further "Lady Haslip, of Haslip Manor," as he spied that old lady wheeled in her chair by her footman winding up the procession.

To the valediction of the gramophone hid in the bushes the audience departed. *Dispersed*, it wailed, *Dispersed are we*.

Now Miss La Trobe stepped from her hiding. Flowing, and streaming, on the grass, on the gravel, still for one moment she held them together—the dispersing company. Hadn't she, for twenty-five minutes, made them see? A vision imparted was relief from agony . . . for one moment . . . one moment. Then the music petered out on the word *we*. She heard the breeze rustle in

812

the branches. She saw Giles Oliver with his back to the audience. Also Cobbet of Cobbs Corner. She hadn't made them see. It was a failure, another damned failure! As usual. Her vision escaped her. And turning, she strode to the actors, undressing, down in the hollow, where butterflies feasted upon swords of silver paper; where the dish cloths in the shadow made pools of yellow.

Cobbet had out his watch. Three hours till seven, he noted; then water the plants. He turned.

Giles, nicking his chair into its notch, turned too, in the other direction. He took the short cut by the fields to the Barn. This dry summer the path was hard as brick across the fields. This dry summer the path was strewn with stones. He kicked—a flinty yellow stone, a sharp stone, edged as if cut by a savage for an arrow. A barbaric stone; a pre-historic. Stone-kicking was a child's game. He remembered the rules. By the rules of the game, one stone, the same stone, must be kicked to the goal. Say a gate, or a tree. He played it alone. The gate was a goal; to be reached in ten. The first kick was Manresa (lust). The second, Dodge (perversion). The third, himself (coward). And the fourth and the fifth and all the others were the same.

He reached it in ten. There, couched in the grass, curled in an olive green ring, was a snake. Dead? No, choked with a toad in its mouth. The snake was unable to swallow; the toad was unable to die. A spasm made the ribs contract; blood oozed. It was birth the wrong way round—a monstrous inversion. So, raising his foot, he stamped on them. The mass crushed and slithered. The white canvas on his tennis shoes was bloodstained and sticky. But it was action. Action relieved him. He strode to the Barn, with blood on his shoes.

The Barn, the Noble Barn, the barn that had been built over seven hundred years ago and reminded some people of a Greek temple, others of the Middle Ages, most people of an age before their own, scarcely anybody of the present moment, was empty.

The great doors stood open. A shaft of light like a yellow banner sloped from roof to floor. Festoons of paper roses, left over from the Coronation, drooped from the rafters. A long table, on which stood an urn, plates and cups, cakes and bread and butter, stretched across one end. The Barn was empty. Mice slid in and out of holes or stood upright, nibbling. Swallows were busy with straw in pockets of earth in the rafters. Countless beetles and insects of various sorts burrowed in the dry wood. A stray bitch had made the dark corner where the sacks stood a lying-in ground for her puppies. All these eyes, expanding and narrowing, some adapted to light, others to darkness, looked from different angles and edges. Minute nibblings and rustlings broke the silence. Whiffs of sweetness and richness veined the air. A blue-bottle had settled on the cake and stabbed its yellow rock with its short drill. A butterfly sunned itself sensuously on a sunlit yellow plate.

But Mrs. Sands was approaching. She was pushing her way through the crowd. She had turned the corner. She could see the great open door. But butterflies she never saw; mice were only black pellets in kitchen drawers; moths she bundled in her hands and put out of the window. Bitches suggested only servant girls misbehaving. Had there been a cat she would have seen it —any cat, a starved cat with a patch of mange on its rump opened the flood gates of her childless heart. But there was no cat. The barn was empty. And so running, panting, set upon reaching the Barn and taking up her station behind the tea urn before the company came, she reached the Barn. And the butterfly rose and the blue-bottle.

Following her in a scud came the servants and helpers—David, John, Irene, Lois. Water boiled. Steam issued. Cake was sliced. Swallows swooped from rafter to rafter. And the company entered.

"This fine old Barn . . ." said Mrs. Manresa, stopping in the doorway. It was not for her to press ahead of the villagers. It was for her, moved by the beauty of the Barn, to stand still; to draw aside; to gaze; to let other people come first.

"We have one, much like it, at Lathom," said Mrs. Parker, stopping, for the same reasons. "Perhaps," she added, "not quite so large."

The villagers hung back. Then, hesitating, dribbled past.

"And the decorations . . ." said Mrs. Manresa, looking round for someone to congratulate. She stood smiling, waiting. Then old Mrs. Swithin came in. She was gazing up too, but not at the decorations. At the swallows apparently.

"They come every year," she said, "the same birds." Mrs. Manresa smiled benevolently, humouring the old lady's whimsey. It was unlikely, she thought, that the birds were the same.

"The decorations, I suppose, are left over from the Coronation," said Mrs. Parker. "We kept ours too. We built a village hall."

Mrs. Manresa laughed. She remembered. An anecdote was on the tip of her tongue, about a public lavatory built to celebrate the same occasion, and how the Mayor . . . Could she tell it? No. The old lady, gazing at the swallows, looked too refined. "Refeened"—Mrs. Manresa qualified the word to her own advantage, thus confirming her approval of the wild child she was, whose nature was somehow "just human nature." Somehow she could span the old lady's "refeenment," also the boy's fun—Where was that nice fellow Giles? She couldn't see him; nor Bill either. The villagers still hung back. They must have someone to start the ball rolling.

"Well, I'm dying for my tea!" she said in her public voice; and strode forward. She laid hold of a thick china mug. Mrs. Sands giving precedence, of course, to one of the gentry, filled it at once. David gave her cake. She was the first to drink, the first to bite. The villagers still hung back. "It's all my eye about democracy," she concluded. So did Mrs. Parker, taking her mug too. The people looked to them. They led; the rest followed.

"What delicious tea!" each exclaimed, disgusting though it was, like rust boiled in water, and the cake fly-blown. But they had a duty to society.

"They come every year," said Mrs. Swithin, ignoring the fact that she spoke to the empty air. "From Africa." As they had come, she supposed, when the Barn was a swamp.

The Barn filled. Fumes rose. China clattered; voices chattered. Isa pressed her way to the table.

"Dispersed are we," she murmured. And held her cup out to be filled. She took it. "Let me turn away," she murmured, turning, "from the array"—she looked desolately round her—"of china faces, glazed and hard. Down the ride, that leads under the nut tree and the may tree, away, till I come to the wishing well, where the washer-woman's little boy—" she dropped sugar, two lumps, into her tea, "dropped a pin. He got his horse, so they say. But what wish should I drop into the well?" She looked round. She could not see the man in grey, the gentleman farmer; nor anyone known to her. "That the waters should cover me," she added, "of the wishing well."

The noise of china and chatter drowned her murmur. "Sugar for you?" they were saying. "Just a spot of milk? And you?" "Tea without milk or sugar. That's the way I like it." "A bit too strong? Let me add water."

"That's what I wished," Isa added, "when I dropped my pin. Water. Water . . ."

"I must say," the voice said behind her, "it's brave of the King and Queen. They're said to be going to India. She looks such a dear. Someone I know said his hair. . . ."

"There," Isa mused, "would the dead leaf fall, when the leaves fall, on the water. Should I mind not again to see may tree or nut tree? Not again to hear on the trembling spray the thrush sing, or to see, dipping and diving as if he skimmed waves in the air, the yellow woodpecker?"

She was looking at the canary yellow festoons left over from the Coronation.

"I thought they said Canada, not India," the voice said behind her back. To which the other voice answered: "D'you believe what the papers say? For instance, about the Duke of Windsor. He landed on the south coast. Queen Mary met him. She'd been buying furniture—that's a fact. And the papers say she met him . . ."

"Alone, under a tree, the withered tree that keeps all day murmuring of the sea, and hears the Rider gallop . . ."

Isa filled in the phrase. Then she started. William Dodge was by her side.

He smiled. She smiled. They were conspirators; each murmuring some song my uncle taught me.

"It's the play," she said. "The play keeps running in my head."

"Hail, sweet Carinthia. My love. My life," he quoted.

"My lord, my liege," she bowed ironically.

She was handsome. He wanted to see her, not against the tea urn, but with her glass green eyes and thick body, the neck was broad as a pillar, against an arum lily or a vine. He wished she would say: "Come along. I'll show you the green house, the pig sty, or the stable." But she said nothing, and they stood there holding their cups, remembering the play. Then he saw her face change, as if she had got out of one dress and put on another. A small boy battled his way through the crowd, striking against skirts and trousers as if he were swimming blindly.

"Here!" she cried, raising her arm.

He made a bee-line for her. He was her little boy, apparently, her son, her George. She gave him cake; then a mug of milk. Then Nurse came up. Then again she changed her dress. This time, from the expression in her eyes it was apparently something in the nature of a strait waistcoat. Hirsute, handsome, virile, the young man in blue jacket and brass buttons, standing in a beam of dusty light, was her husband. And she his wife. Their relations, as he had noted at lunch, were as people say in novels "strained." As he had noted at the play, her bare arm had raised itself nervously to her shoulder when she turned—looking for whom? But here he was; and the muscular, the hirsute, the virile plunged him into emotions in which the mind had no share. He forgot how she would have looked against vine leaf in a greenhouse. Only at Giles he looked; and looked and looked. Of whom was he thinking as he stood with his face turned? Not of Isa. Of Mrs. Manresa?

Mrs. Manresa half-way down the Barn had gulped her cup of tea. How can I rid myself, she asked, of Mrs. Parker? If they were of her own class, how they bored her—her own sex! Not the class below—cooks, shopkeepers, farmers' wives; nor the class above—peeresses, countesses; it was the woman of her own class that bored her. So she left Mrs. Parker, abruptly.

"Oh Mrs. Moore," she hailed the keeper's wife. "What did you think of it? And what did baby think of it?" Here she pinched baby. "I thought it every bit as good as anything I'd seen in London. . . . But we mustn't be outdone. We'll have a play of our own. In our Barn. We'll show 'em" (here she winked obliquely at the table; so many bought cakes, so few made at home) "how we do it."

Then cracking her jokes, she turned; saw Giles; caught his eye; and swept him in, beckoning. He came. And what—she looked down—had he done with his shoes? They were bloodstained. Vaguely some sense that he had proved his valour for her admiration flattered her. If vague it was sweet. Taking him in tow, she felt: I am the Queen, he my hero, my sulky hero.

"That's Mrs. Neale!" she exclaimed. "A perfect marvel of a woman, aren't you, Mrs. Neale! She runs our post office, Mrs. Neale. She can do sums in her head, can't you, Mrs. Neale?

Twenty-five halfpenny stamps, two packets of stamped envelopes and a packet of post-cards—how much does that come to, Mrs. Neale?"

Mrs. Neale laughed; Mrs. Manresa laughed; Giles too smiled, and looked down at his shoes.

She drew him down the Barn, in and out, from one to another. She knew 'em all. Every one was a thorough good sort. No, she wouldn't allow it, not for a moment—Pinsent's bad leg. "No, no. We're not going to take that for an excuse, Pinsent." If he couldn't bowl, he could bat. Giles agreed. A fish on a line meant the same to him and Pinsent; also jays and magpies. Pinsent stayed on the land; Giles went to an office. That was all. And she was a thorough good sort, making him feel less of an audience, more of an actor, going round the Barn in her wake.

Then, at the end by the door, they came upon the old couple, Lucy and Bartholomew, sitting on their Windsor chairs.

Chairs had been reserved for them. Mrs. Sands had sent them tea. It would have caused more bother than it was worth—asserting the democratic principle; standing in the crowd at the table.

"Swallows," said Lucy, holding her cup, looking at the birds. Excited by the company they were flitting from rafter to rafter. Across Africa, across France they had come to nest here. Year after year they came. Before there was a channel, when the earth, upon which the Windsor chair was planted, was a riot of rhododendrons, and humming birds quivered at the mouths of scarlet trumpets, as she had read that morning in her Outline of History, they had come . . . Here Bart rose from his chair.

But Mrs. Manresa absolutely refused to take his seat. "Go on sitting, go on sitting," she pressed him down again. "I'll squat on the floor." She squatted. The surly knight remained in attendance.

"And what did you think of the play?" she asked.

Bartholomew looked at his son. His son remained silent.

"And you Mrs. Swithin?" Mrs. Manresa pressed the old lady. Lucy mumbled, looking at the swallows.

"I was hoping you'd tell me," said Mrs. Manresa. "Was it an old play? Was it a new play?"

No one answered.

"Look!" Lucy exclaimed.

"The birds?" said Mrs. Manresa, looking up.

There was a bird with a straw in its beak; and the straw dropped.
Lucy clapped her hands. Giles turned away. She was mocking
him as usual, laughing.

"Going?" said Bartholomew. "Time for the next act?"

And he heaved himself up from his chair. Regardless of Mrs.
Manresa and of Lucy, off he strolled too.

"Swallow, my sister, O sister swallow," he muttered, feeling for
his cigar case, following his son.

Mrs. Manresa was nettled. What for had she squatted on the
floor then? Were her charms fading? Both were gone. But, woman
of action as she was, deserted by the male sex, she was not going
to suffer tortures of boredom from the refeened old lady. Up she
scrambled, putting her hands to hair as if it were high time that
she went too, though it was nothing of the kind and her hair was
perfectly tidy. Cobbet in his corner saw through her little game.
He had known human nature in the East. It was the same in the
West. Plants remained—the carnation, the zinnia, and the geranium. Automatically he consulted his watch; noted time to water
at seven; and observed the little game of the woman following
the man to the table in the West as in the East.

William at the table, now attached to Mrs. Parker and Isa,
watched him approach. Armed and valiant, bold and blatant, firm
elatant—the popular march tune rang in his head. And the fingers
of William's left hand closed firmly, surreptitiously, as the hero
approached.

Mrs. Parker was deploring to Isa in a low voice the village idiot.
"Oh that idiot!" she was saying. But Isa was immobile, watching
her husband. She could feel the Manresa in his wake. She could
hear in the dusk in their bedroom the usual explanation. It made
no difference; his infidelity—but hers did.

"The idiot?" William answered Mrs. Parker for her. "He's in
the tradition."

"But surely," said Mrs. Parker, and told Giles how creepy the
idiot—"We have one in our village"—had made her feel. "Surely,
Mr. Oliver, we're more civilized?"

"We?" said Giles. "We?" He looked, once, at William. He
knew not his name; but what his left hand was doing. It was a bit
of luck—that he could despise him, not himself. Also Mrs. Parker.

819

But not Isa—not his wife. She had not spoken to him, not one word. Nor looked at him either.

"Surely," said Mrs. Parker, looking from one to the other. "Surely we are?"

Giles then did what to Isa was his little trick; shut his lips; frowned; and took up the pose of one who bears the burden of the world's woe, making money for her to spend.

"No," said Isa, as plainly as words could say it. "I don't admire you," and looked, not at his face, but at his feet. "Silly little boy, with blood on his boots."

Giles shifted his feet. Whom then did she admire? Not Dodge. That he could take for certain. Who else? Some man he knew. Some man, he was sure, in the Barn. Which man? He looked round him.

Then Mr. Streatfield, the clergyman, interrupted. He was carrying cups.

"So I shake hands with my heart!" he exclaimed, nodding his handsome, grizzled head and depositing his burden safely.

Mrs. Parker took the tribute to herself.

"Mr. Streatfield!" she exclaimed. "Doing all the work! While we stand gossiping!"

"Like to see the greenhouse?" said Isa suddenly, turning to William Dodge.

O not now, he could have cried. But had to follow, leaving Giles to welcome the approaching Manresa, who had him in thrall.

The path was narrow. Isa went ahead. And she was broad; she fairly filled the path, swaying slightly as she walked, and plucking a leaf here and there from the hedge.

"Fly then, follow," she hummed, "the dappled herds in the cedar grove, who, sporting, play, the red with the roe, the stag with the doe. Fly, away. I grieving stay. Alone I linger, I pluck the bitter herb by the ruined wall, the churchyard wall, and press its sour, its sweet, its sour, long grey leaf, so, twixt thumb and finger. . . ."

She threw away the shred of Old Man's Beard that she had picked in passing and kicked open the greenhouse door. Dodge had lagged behind. She waited. She picked up a knife from the plank. He saw her standing against the green glass, the fig tree, and the blue hydrangea, knife in hand.

"She spake," Isa murmured. "And from her bosom's snowy antre drew the gleaming blade. 'Plunge blade!' she said. And struck. 'Faithless!' she cried. Knife, too! It broke. So too my heart," she said.

She was smiling ironically as he came up.

"I wish the play didn't run in my head," she said. Then she sat down on a plank under the vine. And he sat beside her. The little grapes above them were green buds; the leaves thin and yellow as the web between birds' claws.

"Still the play?" he asked. She nodded. "That was your son," he said, "in the Barn?"

She had a daughter too, she told him, in the cradle.

"And you—married?" she asked. From her tone he knew she guessed, as women always guessed, everything. They knew at once they had nothing to fear, nothing to hope. At first they resented— serving as statues in a greenhouse. Then they liked it. For then they could say—as she did—whatever came into their heads. And hand him, as she handed him, a flower.

"There's something for your buttonhole Mr. . . ." she said, handing him a sprig of scented geranium.

"I'm William," he said, taking the furry leaf and pressing it between thumb and finger.

"I'm Isa," she answered. Then they talked as if they had known each other all their lives; which was odd, she said, as they always did, considering she'd known him perhaps one hour. Weren't they, though, conspirators, seekers after hidden faces? That confessed, she paused and wondered, as they always did, why they could speak so plainly to each other. And added: "Perhaps because we've never met before, and never shall again."

"The doom of sudden death hanging over us," he said. "There's no retreating and advancing"—he was thinking of the old lady showing him the house—"for us as for them."

The future shadowed their present, like the sun coming through the many-veined transparent vine leaf; a criss-cross of lines making no pattern.

They had left the greenhouse door open, and now music came through it. A.B.C., A.B.C., A.B.C.—someone was practising scales. C.A.T. C.A.T. C.A.T. . . . Then the separate letters made one word "Cat." Other words followed. It was a simple tune, like a nursery rhyme——

The King is in his counting house
Counting out his money,
The Queen is in her parlour
Eating bread and honey.

They listened. Another voice, a third voice, was saying something simple. And they sat on in the greenhouse, on the plank with the vine over them, listening to Miss La Trobe or whoever it was, practising her scales.

He could not find his son. He had lost him in the crowd. So old Bartholomew left the Barn, and went to his own room, holding his cheroot and murmuring:

"O sister swallow, O sister swallow,
How can thy heart be full of the spring?"

"How can my heart be full of the spring?" he said aloud, standing in front of the book case. Books: the treasured life-blood of immortal spirits. Poets; the legislators of mankind. Doubtless, it was so. But Giles was unhappy. "How can my heart, how can my heart," he repeated, puffing at his cheroot. "Condemned in life's infernal mine, condemned in solitude to pine . . ." Arms akimbo, he stood in front of his country gentleman's library. Garibaldi; Wellington; Irrigation Officers' Reports; and Hibbert on the Diseases of the Horse. A great harvest the mind had reaped; but for all this, compared with his son, he did not care one damn.

"What's the use, what's the use," he sank down into his chair muttering, "O sister swallow, O sister swallow, of singing your song?" The dog, who had followed him, flopped down on to the floor at his feet. Flanks sucked in and out, the long nose resting on his paws, a fleck of foam on the nostril, there he was, his familiar spirit, his Afghan hound.

The door trembled and stood half open. That was Lucy's way of coming in—as if she did not know what she would find. Really! It was her brother! And his dog! She seemed to see them for the first time. Was it that she had no body? Up in the clouds, like an air ball, her mind touched ground now and then with a shock of surprise. There was nothing in her to weigh a man like Giles to the earth.

She perched on the edge of a chair like a bird on a telegraph wire before starting for Africa.

"Swallow, my sister, O sister swallow . . ." he murmured.

From the garden—the window was open—came the sound of someone practising scales. A.B.C. A.B.C. A.B.C. Then the separate letters formed one word "Dog." Then a phrase. It was a simple tune, another voice speaking.

> "Hark, hark, the dogs do bark,
> The beggars are coming to town . . ."

Then it languished and lengthened, and became a waltz. As they listened and looked—out into the garden—the trees tossing and the birds swirling seemed called out of their private lives, out of their separate avocations, and made to take part.

> The lamp of love burns high, over the dark cedar groves,
> The lamp of love shines clear, clear as a star in the sky. . . .

Old Bartholomew tapped his fingers on his knee in time to the tune.

> Leave your casement and come, lady,
> I love till I die,

He looked sardonically at Lucy, perched on her chair. How, he wondered, had she ever borne children?

> For all are dancing, retreating and advancing,
> The moth and the dragon fly. . . .

She was thinking, he supposed, God is peace. God is love. For she belonged to the unifiers; he to the separatists.

Then the tune with its feet always on the same spot, became sugared, insipid; bored a hole with its perpetual invocation to perpetual adoration. Had it—he was ignorant of musical terms—gone into the minor key?

> For this day and this dance and this merry, merry May
> Will be over (he tapped his forefinger on his knee)
> With the cutting of the clover this retreating and advanc-
>   ing—the swifts seemed to have shot beyond their
>   orbits—

Will be over, over, over,
And the ice will dart its splinter, and the winter,
O the winter, will fill the grate with ashes,
And there'll be no glow, no glow on the log.

He knocked the ash off his cheroot and rose.

"So we must," said Lucy; as if he had said aloud, It's time to go."

The audience was assembling. The music was summoning them. Down the paths, across the lawns they were streaming again. There was Mrs. Manresa, with Giles at her side, heading the procession. In taut plump curves her scarf blew round her shoulders. The breeze was rising. She looked, as she crossed the lawn to the strains of the gramophone, goddess-like, buoyant, abundant, her cornucopia running over. Bartholomew, following, blessed the power of the human body to make the earth fruitful. Giles would keep his orbit so long as she weighted him to the earth. She stirred the stagnant pool of his old heart even—where bones lay buried, but the dragon flies shot and the grass trembled as Mrs. Manresa advanced across the lawn to the strains of the gramophone.

Feet crunched the gravel. Voices chattered. The inner voice, the other voice was saying: How can we deny that this brave music, wafted from the bushes, is expressive of some inner harmony? "When we wake" (some were thinking) "the day breaks us with its hard mallet blows." "The office" (some were thinking) "compels disparity. Scattered, shattered, hither thither summoned by the bell. 'Ping-ping-ping' that's the phone. 'Forward!' 'Serving!'— that's the shop." So we answer to the infernal, agelong and eternal order issued from on high. And obey. "Working, serving, pushing, striving, earning wages—to be spent—here? Oh dear no. Now? No, by and by. When ears are deaf and the heart is dry."

Here Cobbet of Cobbs Corner who had stooped—there was a flower—was pressed on by people pushing from behind.

For I hear music, they were saying. Music wakes us. Music makes us see the hidden, join the broken. Look and listen. See the flowers, how they ray their redness, whiteness, silverness and blue. And the trees with their many-tongued much syllabling, their green and yellow leaves hustle us and shuffle us, and bid us, like the starlings, and the rooks, come together, crowd together, to chatter and make merry while the red cow moves forward and the black cow stands still.

The audience had reached their seats. Some sat down; others stood a moment, turned, and looked at the view. The stage was empty; the actors were still dressing up among the bushes. The audience turned to one another and began to talk. Scraps and fragments reached Miss La Trobe where she stood, script in hand, behind the tree.

"They're not ready . . . I hear 'em laughing" (they were saying). ". . . Dressing up. That's the great thing, dressing up. And it's pleasant now, the sun's not so hot . . . That's one good the war brought us—longer days . . . Where did we leave off? D'you remember? The Elizabethans . . . Perhaps she'll reach the present, if she skips. . . . D'you think people change? Their clothes, of course. . . . But I meant ourselves . . . Clearing out a cupboard, I found my father's old top hat. . . . But ourselves—do we change?"

"No, I don't go by politicians. I've a friend who's been to Russia. He says . . . And my daughter, just back from Rome, she says the common people, in the cafés, hate Dictators. . . . Well, different people say different things. . . ."

"Did you see it in the papers—the case about the dog? D'you believe dogs can't have puppies? . . . And Queen Mary and the Duke of Windsor on the south coast? . . . D'you believe what's in the papers? I ask the butcher or the grocer . . . That's Mr. Streatfield, carrying a hurdle. . . . The good clergyman, I say, does more work for less pay than all the lot . . . It's the wives that make the trouble. . . ."

"And what about the Jews? The refugees . . . the Jews . . . People like ourselves, beginning life again . . . But it's always been the same. . . . My old mother, who's over eighty, can remember . . . Yes, she still reads without glasses. . . . How amazing! Well, don't they say, after eighty . . . Now they're coming . . . No, that's nothing. . . . I'd make it penal, leaving litter. But then, who's, my husband says, to collect the fines? . . . Ah there she is, Miss La Trobe, over there, behind that tree . . ."

Over there behind the tree Miss La Trobe gnashed her teeth. She crushed her manuscript. The actors delayed. Every moment the audience slipped the noose; split up into scraps and fragments.

"Music!" she signalled. "Music!"

"What's the origin," said a voice, "of the expression 'with a flea in his ear'?"

Down came her hand peremptorily. "Music, music," she signalled.

And the gramophone began A.B.C., A.B.C.

> The King is in his counting house
> Counting out his money,
> The Queen is in her parlour
> Eating bread and honey. . . .

Miss La Trobe watched them sink down peacefully into the nursery rhyme. She watched them fold their hands and compose their faces. Then she beckoned. And at last, with a final touch to her head dress, which had been giving trouble, Mabel Hopkins strode from the bushes, and took her place on the raised ground facing the audience.

Eyes fed on her as fish rise to a crumb of bread on the water. Who was she? What did she represent? She was beautiful—very. Her cheeks had been powdered; her colour glowed smooth and clear underneath. Her grey satin robe (a bedspread), pinned in stone-like folds, gave her the majesty of a statue. She carried a sceptre and a little round orb. England was she? Queen Anne was she? Who was she? She spoke too low at first; all they heard was

. . . reason holds sway.

Old Bartholomew applauded.

"Hear! Hear!" he cried. "Bravo! Bravo!"

Thus encouraged Reason spoke out.

Time, leaning on his sickle, stands amazed. While Commerce from her Cornucopia pours the mingled tribute of her different ores. In distant mines the savage sweats; and from the reluctant earth the painted pot is shaped. At my behest, the armed warrior lays his shield aside; the heathen leaves the Altar steaming with unholy sacrifice. The violet and the eglantine over the riven earth their flowers entwine. No longer fears the unwary wanderer the poisoned snake. And in the helmet, yellow bees their honey make.

She paused. A long line of villagers in sacking were passing in and out of the trees behind her.

Digging and delving, ploughing and sowing they were singing, but the wind blew their words away.

Beneath the shelter of my flowing robe (she resumed, extending her arms) *the arts arise. Music for me unfolds her heavenly harmony. At my behest the miser leaves his hoard untouched; at peace the mother sees her children play. . . . Her children play . . .* she repeated, and, waving her sceptre, figures advanced from the bushes.

Let swains and nymphs lead on the play, while Zephyr sleeps, and the unruly tribes of Heaven confess my sway.

A merry little old tune was played on the gramophone. Old Bartholomew joined his finger tips; Mrs. Manresa smoothed her skirts about her knees.

> *Young Damon said to Cynthia,*
> *Come out now with the dawn*
> *And don your azure tippet*
> *And cast your cares adown*
> *For peace has come to England,*
> *And reason now holds sway.*
> *What pleasure lies in dreaming*
> *When blue and green's the day?*
> *Now cast your cares behind you.*
> *Night passes: here is Day.*

Digging and delving, the villagers sang passing in single file in and out between the trees, *for the earth is always the same, summer and winter and spring; and spring and winter again; ploughing and sowing, eating and growing; time passes. . . .*

The wind blew the words away.

The dance stopped. The nymphs and swains withdrew. Reason held the centre of the stage alone. Her arms extended, her robes flowing, holding orb and sceptre, Mabel Hopkins stood sublimely looking over the heads of the audience. The audience gazed at her. She ignored the audience. Then while she gazed, helpers from the bushes arranged round her what appeared to be the three sides of a room. In the middle they stood a table. On the table they placed a china tea service. Reason surveyed this domestic scene from her lofty eminence unmoved. There was a pause.

"Another scene from another play, I suppose," said Mrs. Elmhurst, referring to her programme. She read out for the benefit of her husband, who was deaf: "*Where there's a Will there's a Way.* That's the name of the play. And the characters. . . ." She read out: "Lady Harpy Harraden, in love with Sir Spaniel Lilyliver. Deb, her maid. Flavinda, her niece, in love with Valentine. Sir Spaniel Lilyliver, in love with Flavinda. Sir Smirking Peace-be-with-you-all, a clergyman. Lord and Lady Fribble. Valentine, in love with Flavinda. What names for real people! But look—here they come!"

Out they came from the bushes—men in flowered waistcoats, white waistcoats and buckled shoes; women wearing brocades tucked up, hooped and draped; glass stars, blue ribands and imitation pearls made them look the very image of Lords and Ladies.

"The first scene," Mrs. Elmhurst whispered into her husband's ear, "is Lady Harraden's dressing-room. . . . That's her. . . ." She pointed. "Mrs. Otter, I think, from the End House; but she's wonderfully made up. And that's Deb her maid. Who she is, I don't know."

"Hush, hush, hush," someone protested.

Mrs. Elmhurst dropped her programme. The play had begun.

Lady Harpy Harraden entered her dressing-room, followed by Deb her maid.

LADY H. H. . . . *Give me the pounce-box. Then the patch. Hand me the mirror, girl. So. Now my wig. . . . A pox on the girl—she's dreaming!*

DEB . . . *I was thinking, my lady, what the gentleman said when he saw you in the Park.*

LADY H. H. (gazing in the glass). *So, so—what was it? Some silly trash! Cupid's dart—hah, hah! lighting his taper—tush—at my eyes. . . . pooh! That was in milord's time, twenty years since. . . . But now—what'll he say of me now? (She looks in the mirror.) Sir Spaniel Lilyliver, I mean . . . (a rap at the door). Hark! That's his chaise at the door. Run child. Don't stand gaping.*

DEB . . . (going to the door). *Say? He'll rattle his tongue as a gambler rattles dice in a box. He'll find no words to fit you. He'll stand like a pig in a poke. . . . Your servant, Sir Spaniel.*

Enter Sir Spaniel.

Sɪʀ S. L. . . . *Hail, my fair Saint! What, out o' bed so early? Methought, as I came along the Mall the air was something brighter than usual. Here's the reason. . . . Venus, Aphrodite, upon my word a very galaxy, a constellation! As I'm a sinner, a very Aurora Borealis!*

(*He sweeps his hat off.*)

Lᴀᴅʏ H. H. *Oh flatterer, flatterer! I know your ways. But come. Sit down. . . . A glass of Aqua Vitae. Take this seat, Sir Spaniel. I've something very private and particular to say to you. . . . You had my letter, Sir?*

Sɪʀ S. L. . . . *Pinned to my heart!*

(*He strikes his breast.*)

Lᴀᴅʏ H. H. . . . *I have a favour to ask of you, Sir.*

Sɪʀ S. L. . . . (*singing*). *What favour could fair Chloe ask that Damon would not get her? . . . A done with rhymes. Rhymes are still-a-bed. Let's speak prose. What can Asphodilla ask of her plain servant Lilyliver? Speak out, Madam. An ape with a ring in his nose, or a strong young jackanapes to tell tales of us when we're no longer here to tell truth about ourselves?*

Lᴀᴅʏ H. H. (*flirting her fan*). *Fie, fie, Sir Spaniel. You make me blush—you do indeed. But come closer.* (*She shifts her seat nearer to him.*) *We don't want the whole world to hear us.*

Sɪʀ S. L. (*aside*). *Come closer? A pox on my life! The old hag stinks like a red herring that's been stood over head in a tar barrel!* (*Aloud.*) *Your meaning, Madam? You were saying?*

Lᴀᴅʏ H. H. *I have a niece, Sir Spaniel, Flavinda by name.*

Sɪʀ S. L. (*aside*). *Why that's the girl I love, to be sure!* (*Aloud.*) *You have a niece, Madam? I seem to remember hearing so. An only child, left by your brother, so I've heard, in your Ladyship's charge —him that perished at sea.*

Lᴀᴅʏ H. H. *The very same Sir. She's of age now and marriageable. I've kept her close as a weevil, Sir Spaniel, wrapped in the sere cloths of her virginity. Only maids about her, never a man to my knowledge, save Clout the servingman, who has a wart on his nose and a face like a nutgrater. Yet some fool has caught her fancy. Some gilded fly—some Harry, Dick; call him what you will.*

SIR S. L. (aside). *That's young Valentine, I warrant. I caught 'em at the play together.* (Aloud.) *Say you so, Madam?*

LADY H. H. *She's not so ill favoured, Sir Spaniel—there's beauty in our line—but that a gentleman of taste and breeding like yourself now might take pity on her.*

SIR S. L. *Saving your presence, Madam. Eyes that have seen the sun are not so easily dazzled by the lesser lights—the Cassiopeias, Aldebarans, Great Bears and so on—A fig for them when the sun's up!*

LADY H. H. (ogling him). *You praise my hairdresser, Sir, or my ear-rings.* (She shakes her head.)

SIR S. L. (aside). *She jingles like a she-ass at a fair! She's rigged like a barber's pole of a May Day.* (Aloud.) *Your commands, Madam?*

LADY H. H. *Well Sir, 'twas this way Sir. Brother Bob, for my father was a plain country gentleman and would have none of the fancy names the foreigners brought with 'em—Asphodilla I call myself, but my Christian name's plain Sue—Brother Bob, as I was telling you, ran away to sea; and, so they say, became Emperor of the Indies; where the very stones are emeralds and the sheep-crop rubies. Which, for a tenderer-hearted man never lived, he would have brought back with him, Sir, to mend the family fortunes, Sir. But the brig, frigate or what they call it, for I've no head for sea terms, never crossed a ditch without saying the Lord's Prayer backwards, struck a rock. The Whale had him. But the cradle was by the bounty of Heaven washed ashore. With the girl in it; Flavinda here. What's more to the point, with the Will in it; safe and sound; wrapped in parchment. Brother Bob's Will. Deb there! Deb I say! Deb!*

(She holloas for Deb.)

SIR S. L. (aside). *Ah hah! I smell a rat! A will, quotha! Where there's a Will there's a Way.*

LADY H. H. (bawling). *The Will, Deb! The Will! In the ebony box by the right hand of the escritoire opposite the window. . . . A pox on the girl! She's dreaming. It's these romances, Sir Spaniel— these romances. Can't see a candle gutter but it's her heart that's melting, or snuff a wick without reciting all the names in Cupid's Calendar . . .*

(Enter Deb carrying a parchment.)

LADY H. H. *So . . . Give it here. The Will. Brother Bob's Will.* (She mumbles over the Will.)

LADY H. H. *To cut the matter short, Sir, for these lawyers even at the Antipodes are a long-winded race*——

SIR S. L. *To match their ears, Ma'am*——

LADY H. H. *Very true, very true. To cut the matter short, Sir, my Brother Bob left all he died possessed of to his only child Flavinda; with this proviso, mark ye. That she marry to her Aunt's liking. Her Aunt; that's me. Otherwise, mark ye, all—to wit ten bushels of diamonds; item of rubies; item two hundred square miles of fertile territory bounding the River Amazon to the Nor-Nor-East; item his snuff box; item his flageolet—he was always one to love a tune, Sir, Brother Bob; item six Macaws and as many Concubines as he had with him at the time of his decease—all this with other trifles needless to specify he left, mark ye, should she fail to marry to her Aunt's liking—that's me—to found a Chapel, Sir Spaniel, where six poor Virgins should sing hymns in perpetuity for the repose of his soul—which, to speak the truth, Sir Spaniel, poor Brother Bob stands in need of, perambulating the Gulf Stream as he is and consorting with Syrens. But take it; read the Will yourself, Sir.*

SIR S. L. (reading). *"Must marry to her Aunt's liking." That's plain enough.*

LADY H. H. *Her Aunt, Sir. That's me. That's plain enough.*

SIR S. L. (aside). *She speaks the truth there!* (Aloud.) *You would have me understand, Madam. . . .?*

LADY H. H. *Hist! Come closer. Let me whisper in your ear . . . You and I have long entertained a high opinion of one another, Sir Spaniel. Played at ball together. Bound our wrists with daisy chains together. If I mind aright, you called me little bride—'tis fifty years since. We might have made a match of it, Sir Spaniel, had fortune favoured. . . . You take my meaning, Sir?*

SIR S. L. *Had it been written in letters of gold, fifty feet high, visible from Paul's Churchyard to the Goat and Compasses at Peckham, it could have been no plainer. . . . Hist, I'll whisper it. I, Sir Spaniel Lilyliver, do hereby bind myself to take thee—what's the name of the green girl that was cast up in a lobster pot covered*

with seaweed? Flavinda, eh? Flavinda, so—to be my wedded wife
. . . O for a lawyer to have it all in writing!

LADY H. H. On condition, Sir Spaniel.

SIR S. L. On condition, Asphodilla.

(Both speak together.)

That the money is shared between us.

LADY H. H. we want no lawyer to certify that! Your hand on it,
Sir Spaniel!

SIR S. L. Your lips, Madam!

(They embrace.)

SIR S. L. Pah! She stinks!

"Ha! Ha! Ha!" laughed the indigenous old lady in her bathchair.

"Reason, begad! Reason!" exclaimed old Bartholomew, and
looked at his son as if exhorting him to give over these womanish
vapours and be a man, Sir.

Giles sat straight as a dart, his feet tucked under him.

Mrs. Manresa had out her mirror and lipstick and attended to
her lips and nose.

The gramophone, while the scene was removed, gently stated
certain facts which everybody knows to be perfectly true. The
tune said, more or less, how Eve, gathering her robes about her,
stands reluctant still to let her dewy mantle fall. The herded flocks,
the tune continued, in peace repose. The poor man to his cot
returns, and, to the eager ears of wife and child, the simple story
of his toil relates: what yield the furrow bears; and how the team
the plover on the nest has spared; while Wat her courses ran; and
speckled eggs in the warm hollow lay. Meanwhile the good wife
on the table spreads her simple fare; and to the shepherd's flute,
from toil released, the nymphs and swains join hands and foot it
on the green. Then Eve lets down her sombre tresses brown and
spreads her lucent veil o'er hamlet, spire, and mead, etc., etc. And
the tune repeated itself once more.

The view repeated in its own way what the tune was saying.
The sun was sinking; the colours were merging; and the view was
saying how after toil men rest from their labours; how coolness
comes; reason prevails; and having unharnessed the team from the

plough, neighbours dig in cottage gardens and lean over cottage gates.

The cows, making a step forward, then standing still, were saying the same thing to perfection.

Folded in this triple melody, the audience sat gazing; and beheld gently and approvingly without interrogation, for it seemed inevitable, a box tree in a green tub take the place of the ladies' dressing-room; while on what seemed to be a wall, was hung a great clock face; the hands pointing to three minutes to the hour; which was seven.

Mrs. Elmhurst roused herself from her reverie; and looked at her programme.

"Scene Two. The Mall," she read out. "Time; early morning. Enter Flavinda. Here she comes!"

Here came Millie Loder (shop assistant at Messrs. Hunt and Dicksons, drapery emporium), in sprigged satin, representing Flavinda.

FLAV. *Seven he said, and there's the clock's word for it. But Valentine—where's Valentine? La! How my heart beats! Yet it's not the time o' day, for I'm often afoot before the sun's up in the meadows . . . See—the fine folk passing! All a-tiptoeing like peacocks with spread tails! And I in my petticoat that looked so fine by my Aunt's cracked mirror. Why, here it's a dish clout . . . And they heap their hair up like a birthday cake stuck about with candles. . . . That's a diamond—that's a ruby . . . Where's Valentine? The Orange Tree in the Mall, he said. The tree—there. Valentine—nowhere. That's a courtier, I'll warrant, that old fox with his tail between his legs. That's a serving wench out without her master's knowledge. That's a man with a broom to sweep paths for the fine ladies' flounces . . . La! the red in their cheeks! They never got that in the fields, I warrant! O faithless, cruel, hardhearted Valentine. Valentine! Valentine!*

(She wrings her hands, turning from side to side.)

Didn't I leave my bed a-tiptoe and steal like a mouse in the wainscot for fear of waking Aunt? And lard my hair from her powder box? And scrub my cheeks to make 'em shine? And lie awake watching the stars climb the chimney pots? And give my

833

gold guinea that Godfather hid behind the mistletoe last Twelfth Night to Deb so she shouldn't tell on me? And grease the key in the lock so that Aunt shouldn't wake and shriek Flavvy! Flavvy! Val, I say Val——That's him coming. . . . No, I could tell him a mile off the way he strides the waves like what d'you call him in the picture book. . . . That's not Val. . . . That's a cit; that's a fop; raising his glass, prithee, to have his fill of me . . . I'll be home then . . . No, I won't . . . That's to play the green girl again and sew samplers . . . I'm of age, ain't I, come Michaelmas? Only three turns of the moon and I inherit . . . Didn't I read it in the Will the day the ball bounced on top of the old chest where Aunt keeps her furbelows, and the lid opened? . . . "All I die possessed of to my Daughter . . ." So far I'd read when the old lady came tapping down the passage like a blind man in an alley. . . . I'm no castaway, I'd have you know, Sir; no fishtailed mermaid with a robe of sea weed, at your mercy. I'm a match for any of 'em—the chits you dally with, and bid me meet you at the Orange Tree when you're drowsing the night off spent in their arms. . . . Fie upon you, Sir, making sport with a poor girl so. . . . I'll not cry, I swear I won't. I'll not brew a drop of the salt liquid for a man who's served me so. . . . Yet to think on't—how we hid in the dairy the day the cat jumped. And read romances under the holly tree. La! how I cried when the Duke left poor Polly. . . . And my Aunt found me with eyes like red jellies. "What stung, niece?" says she. And cried "Quick Deb, the blue bag." I told ye . . . La, to think I read it all in a book and cried for another! . . . Hist, what's there among the trees? It's come—it's gone. The breeze is it? In the shade now— in the sun now. . . . Valentine on my life! It's he! Quick, I'll hide. Let the tree conceal me!

(Flavinda hides behind the tree.)

He's here . . . He turns . . . He casts about . . . He's lost the scent . . . He gazes—this way, that way. . . . Let him feast his eyes on the fine faces—taste 'em, sample 'em, say: "That's the fine lady I danced with . . . that I lay with . . . that I kissed under the mistletoe . . ." Ha! How he spews 'em out! Brave Valentine! How he casts his eyes upon the ground! How his frowns become him! "Where's Flavinda?" he sighs. "She I love like the heart in my breast." See him pull his watch out! "O faithless wretch!" he sighs. *See how he stamps the earth! Now turns on his heel. . . . He sees me—no, the sun's in his eyes. Tears fill 'em . . . Lord, how he fingers his sword! He'll run it through his breast like the Duke in the story book! . . . Stop, Sir, stop!*

    (She reveals herself.)

VALENTINE. *. . . O Flavinda, O!*
FLAVINDA. *. . . O Valentine, O!*

    (They embrace.)
                The clock strikes nine.

"All that fuss about nothing!" a voice exclaimed. People laughed. The voice stopped. But the voice had seen; the voice had heard. For a moment Miss La Trobe behind her tree glowed with glory. The next, turning to the villagers who were passing in and out between the trees, she barked:
"Louder! Louder!"
For the stage was empty; the emotion must be continued; the only thing to continue the emotion was the song; and the words were inaudible.
"Louder! Louder!" She threatened them with her clenched fists.

Digging and delving (they sang), *hedging and ditching, we pass. . . . Summer and winter, autumn and spring return . . . All passes but we, all changes . . . but we remain forever the same . . .*
(The breeze blew gaps between their words.)

"Louder, louder!" Miss La Trobe vociferated.

Palaces tumble down (they resumed), *Babylon, Nineveh, Troy . . . And Caesar's great house . . . all fallen they lie . . . Where the plover nests was the arch . . . through which the Romans trod . . . Digging and delving we break with the share of the plough the clod . . . Where Clytemnestra watched for her Lord . . . saw the beacons blaze on the hills . . . we see only the clod . . . Digging and delving we pass. . . . and the Queen and the Watch Tower fall . . . for Agamemnon has ridden away. . . . Clytemnestra is nothing but. . . .*

The words died away. Only a few great names—Babylon, Nineveh, Clytemnestra, Agamemnon, Troy—floated across the open

835

space. Then the wind rose, and in the rustle of the leaves even the great words became inaudible; and the audience sat staring at the villagers, whose mouths opened, but no sound came.

And the stage was empty. Miss La Trobe leant against the tree, paralyzed. Her power had left her. Beads of perspiration broke on her forehead. Illusion had failed. "This is death," she murmured, "death."

Then suddenly, as the illusion petered out, the cows took up the burden. One had lost her calf. In the very nick of time she lifted her great moon-eyed head and bellowed. All the great moon-eyed heads laid themselves back. From cow after cow came the same yearning bellow. The whole world was filled with dumb yearning. It was the primeval voice sounding loud in the ear of the present moment. Then the whole herd caught the infection. Lashing their tails, blobbed like pokers, they tossed their heads high, plunged and bellowed, as if Eros had planted his dart in their flanks and goaded them to fury. The cows annihilated the gap; bridged the distance; filled the emptiness and continued the emotion.

Miss La Trobe waved her hand ecstatically at the cows.

"Thank Heaven!" she exclaimed.

Suddenly the cows stopped; lowered their heads, and began browsing. Simultaneously the audience lowered their heads and read their programmes.

"The producer," Mrs. Elmhurst read out for her husband's benefit, "craves the indulgence of the audience. Owing to lack of time a scene has been omitted; and she begs the audience to imagine that in the interval Sir Spaniel Lilyliver has contracted an engagement with Flavinda; who had been about to plight her troth; when Valentine, hidden inside the grandfather's clock, steps forward; claims Flavinda as his bride; reveals the plot to rob her of her inheritance; and, during the confusion that ensues, the lovers fly together, leaving Lady Harpy and Sir Spaniel alone together."

"We're asked to imagine all that," she said, putting down her glasses.

"That's very wise of her," said Mrs. Manresa, addressing Mrs. Swithin. "If she'd put it all in, we should have been here till

836

midnight. So we've got to imagine, Mrs. Swithin." She patted the old lady on the knee.

"Imagine?" said Mrs. Swithin. "How right! Actors show us too much. The Chinese, you know, put a dagger on the table and that's a battle. And so Racine . . ."

"Yes, they bore one stiff," Mrs. Manresa interrupted, scenting culture, resenting the snub to the jolly human heart. "T'other day I took my nephew—such a jolly boy at Sandhurst—to *Pop Goes the Weasel*. Seen it?" She turned to Giles.

"Up and down the City Road," he hummed by way of an answer.

"Did your Nanny sing that!" Mrs. Manresa exclaimed. "Mine did. And when she said 'Pop' she made a noise like a cork being drawn from a ginger-beer bottle. Pop!"

She made the noise.

"Hush, hush," someone whispered.

"Now I'm being naughty and shocking your aunt," she said. "We must be good and attend. This is Scene Three. Lady Harpy Harraden's Closet. The sound of horses' hooves is heard in the distance."

The sound of horses' hooves, energetically represented by Albert the idiot with a wooden spoon on a tray, died away.

LADY H. H. *Half-way to Gretna Green already. O my deceitful niece! You that I rescued from the brine and stood on the hearth-stone dripping! O that the whale had swallowed you whole! Perfidious porpoise, O! Didn't the Horn book teach you Honour thy Great Aunt? How have you misread it and misspelt it, learnt thieving and cheating and reading of wills in old boxes and hiding of rascals in honest time-pieces that have never missed a second since King Charles's day! O Flavinda! O porpoise, O!*

SIR S. L. (trying to pull on his jack boots). *Old—old—old. He called me "old"—"To your bed, old fool, and drink hot posset!"*

LADY H. H. *And she, stopping at the door and pointing the finger of scorn at me said "old," Sir—"woman" Sir—I that am in the prime of life and a lady!*

SIR S. L. (tugging at his boots). *But I'll be even with him. I'll have the law on 'em! I'll run 'em to earth . . .*

(He hobbles up and down, one boot on, one boot off.)

LADY H. H. (laying her hand on his arm). *Have mercy on your gout, Sir Spaniel. Bethink you, Sir—let's not run mad, we that are on the sunny side of fifty. What's this youth they prate on? Nothing but a goose feather blown on a north wind. Sit you down, Sir Spaniel. Rest your leg—so——*

(She pushes a cushion under his leg.)

SIR S. L. *"Old" he called me . . . jumping from the clock like a jack-in-the-box . . . And she, making mock of me, points to my leg and cries "Cupid's darts, Sir Spaniel, Cupid's darts." O that I could braise 'em in a mortar and serve 'em up smoking hot on the altar of—O my gout, O my gout!*

LADY H. H. *This talk, Sir, ill befits a man of sense. Bethink you, Sir, only t'other day you were invoking—ahem—the Constellations. Cassiopeia, Aldebaran; the Aurora Borealis . . . It's not to be denied that one of 'em has left her sphere, has shot, has eloped, to put it plainly, with the entrails of a time-piece, the mere pendulum of a grandfather's clock. But, Sir Spaniel, there are some stars that—ahem—stay fixed; that shine, to put it in a nutshell, never so bright as by a sea-coal fire on a brisk morning.*

SIR S. L. *O that I were five and twenty with a sharp sword at my side!*

LADY H. H. (bridling). *I take your meaning, Sir. Tee hee—To be sure, I regret it as you do. But youth's not all. To let you into a secret, I've passed the meridian myself. Am on t'other side of the Equator too. Sleep sound o' nights without turning. The dog days are over. . . . But bethink you, Sir. Where there's a will there's a way.*

SIR S. L. *God's truth Ma'am . . . ah my foot's like a burning, burning horseshoe on the devil's anvil ah!—What's your meaning?*

LADY H. H. *My meaning, Sir? Must I disrupt my modesty and unquilt that which has been laid in lavender since my lord, peace be to his name—'tis twenty years since—was lapped in lead? In plain words, Sir, Flavinda's flown. The cage is empty. But we that have bound our wrists with cowslips might join 'em with a stouter chain. To have done with fallals and figures. Here am I, Asphodilla —but my plain name Sue. No matter what my name is—Asphodilla or Sue—here am I, hale and hearty, at your service. Now that the plot's out, Brother Bob's bounty must go to the virgins. That's*

plain. Here's Lawyer Quill's word for it. "Virgins . . . in perpetuity
. . . sing for his soul." And I warrant you, he has need of it . . .
But no matter. Though we have thrown that to the fishes that
might have wrapped us in lamb's-wool, I'm no beggar. There's
messuages; tenements; napery; cattle; my dowry; an inventory. I'll
show you; engrossed on parchment; enough I'll warrant you to
keep us handsomely, for what's to run of our time, as husband
and wife.

SIR S. L. Husband and wife! So that's the plain truth of it! Why,
Madam, I'd rather lash myself to a tar barrel, be bound to a thorn
tree in a winter's gale. Faugh!

LADY H. H. . . . A tar barrel, quotha! A thorn tree—quotha! You
that were harping on galaxies and milky ways! You that were swearing I outshone 'em all! A pox on you—you faithless! You shark,
you! You serpent in jack boots, you! So you won't have me? Reject
my hand do you?

(She proffers her hand; he strikes it from him.)

SIR S. L. . . . Hide your chalk stones in a woollen mit! pah! I'll
none of 'em! Were they diamond, pure diamond, and half the
habitable globe and all its concubines strung in string round your
throat I'd none of it . . . none of it. Unhand me, scritch owl, witch,
vampire! Let me go!

LADY H. H. . . . So all your fine words were tinsel wrapped round
a Christmas cracker!

SIR S. L. . . . Bells hung on an ass's neck! Paper roses on a
barber's pole . . . O my foot, my foot . . . Cupid's darts, she
mocked me . . . Old, old, he called me old . . .

(He hobbles away.)

LADY H. H. (left alone). All gone. Following the wind. He's
gone; she's gone; and the old clock that the rascal made himself
into a pendulum for is the only one of 'em all to stop. A pox on
'em—turning an honest woman's house into a brothel. I that was
Aurora Borealis am shrunk to a tar barrel. I that was Cassiopeia
am turned to a she-ass. My head turns. There's no trusting man
nor woman; nor fine speeches; nor fine looks. Off comes the
sheep's skin; out creeps the serpent. Get ye to Gretna Green;
couch on the wet grass and breed vipers. My head spins . . . Tar

barrels, quotha. Cassiopeia . . . Chalk stones . . . Andromeda . . . Thorn trees. . . . Deb, I say, Deb. (She holloas.) Unlace me. I'm fit to burst . . . Bring me my green baize table and set the cards. . . . And my fur lined slippers, Deb. And a dish of chocolate. . . . I'll be even with 'em . . . I'll outlive 'em all . . . Deb, I say! Deb! A pox on the girl! Can't she hear me? Deb, I say, you gipsy's spawn that I snatched from the hedge and taught to sew samplers! Deb! Deb!

(She throws open the door leading to the maid's closet.)

Empty! She's gone too! . . . Hist, what's that on the dresser?

(She picks up a scrap of paper and reads.)

"What care I for your goose-feather bed? I'm off with the raggle-taggle gipsies, O! Signed; Deborah, one time your maid." So! She that I fed on apple parings and crusts from my own table, she that I taught to play cribbage and sew chemises . . . she's gone too. O ingratitude, thy name is Deborah! Who's to wash the dishes now; who's to bring me my posset now, suffer my temper and unlace my stays? . . . All gone. I'm alone then. Sans niece, sans lover; and sans maid.

> And so to end the play, the moral is,
> The God of love is full of tricks;
> Into the foot his dart he sticks,
> But the way of the will is plain to see;
> Let holy virgins hymn perpetually:
> "Where there's a will there's a way."
> Good people all, farewell.

(Dropping a curtsey, Lady H. H. withdrew.)

The scene ended. Reason descended from her plinth. Gathering her robes about her, serenely acknowledging the applause of the audience, she passed across the stage; while Lords and Ladies in stars and garters followed after; Sir Spaniel limping escorted Lady Harraden smirking; and Valentine and Flavinda arm in arm bowed and curtsied.

"God's truth!" cried Bartholomew, catching the infection of the language. "There's a moral for you!"

He threw himself back in his chair and laughed, like a horse whinnying.

A moral. What? Giles supposed it was: Where there's a Will there's a Way. The words rose and pointed a finger of scorn at him. Off to Gretna Green with his girl; the deed done. Damn the consequences.

"Like to see the greenhouse?" he said abruptly, turning to Mrs. Manresa.

"Love to!" she exclaimed, and rose.

Was there an interval? Yes, the programme said so. The machine in the bushes went chuff, chuff, chuff. And the next scene?

"The Victorian Age," Mrs. Elmhurst read out. Presumably there was time then for a stroll round the gardens, even for a look over the house. Yet somehow they felt—how could one put it—a little not quite here or there. As if the play had jerked the ball out of the cup; as if what I call myself was still floating unattached, and didn't settle. Not quite themselves, they felt. Or was it simply that they felt clothes conscious? Skimpy out-of-date voile dresses; flannel trousers; panama hats; hats wreathed with raspberry-coloured net in the style of the Royal Duchess's hat at Ascot seemed flimsy somehow.

"How lovely the clothes were," said someone, casting a last look at Flavinda disappearing. "Most becoming. I wish . . ."

Chuff, chuff, chuff went the machine in the bushes, accurately, insistently.

Clouds were passing across the sky. The weather looked a little unsettled. Hogben's Folly was for a moment ashen white. Then the sun struck the gilt vane of Bolney Minster.

"Looks a little unsettled," said someone.

"Up you get . . . Let's stretch our legs," said another voice. Soon the lawns were floating with little moving islands of coloured dresses. Yet some of the audience remained seated.

"Major and Mrs. Mayhew," Page the reporter noted, licking his pencil. As for the play, he would collar Miss Whatshername and ask for a synopsis. But Miss La Trobe had vanished.

Down among the bushes she worked like a nigger. Flavinda was in her petticoats. Reason had thrown her mantle on a holly hedge. Sir Spaniel was tugging at his jack boots. Miss La Trobe was scattering and foraging.

"The Victorian mantle with the bead fringe . . . Where is the damned thing? Chuck it here . . . Now the whiskers . . ."

Ducking up and down she cast her quick bird's eye over· the bushes at the audience. The audience was on the move. The audience was strolling up and down. They kept their distance from the dressing-room; they respected the conventions. But if they wandered too far, if they began exploring the grounds, going over the house, then. . . . Chuff, chuff, chuff went the machine. Time was passing. How long would time hold them together? It was a gamble; a risk. . . . And she laid about her energetically, flinging clothes on the grass.

Over the tops of the bushes came stray voices, voices without bodies, symbolical voices they seemed to her, half hearing, seeing nothing, but still, over the bushes, feeling invisible threads connecting the bodiless voices.

"It all looks very black."

"No one wants it save those damned Germans."

There was a pause.

"I'd cut down those trees . . ."

"How they get their roses to grow!"

"They say there's been a garden here for five hundred years . . ."

"Why, even old Gladstone, to do him justice . . ."

Then there was silence. The voices passed the bushes. The trees rustled. Many eyes, Miss La Trobe knew, for every cell in her body was absorbent, looked at the view. Out of the corner of her eye she could see Hogben's Folly; then the vane flashed.

"The glass is falling," said a voice.

She could feel them slipping through her fingers, looking at the view.

"Where's that damned woman, Mrs. Rogers? Who's seen Mrs. Rogers?" she cried, snatching up a Victorian mantle.

Then, ignoring the conventions, a head popped up between the trembling sprays: Mrs. Swithin's.

"Oh Miss La Trobe!" she exclaimed; and stopped. Then she began again: "Oh Miss La Trobe, I do congratulate you!"

She hesitated. "You've given me . . ." She skipped, then alighted —"Ever since I was a child I've felt . . ." A film fell over her eyes, shutting off the present. She tried to recall her childhood; then gave it up; and, with a little wave of her hand, as if asking Miss La

Trobe to help her out, continued: "This daily round; this going up and down stairs; this saying 'What am I going for? My specs? I have 'em on my nose.' . . ."

She gazed at Miss La Trobe with a cloudless old-aged stare. Their eyes met in a common effort to bring a common meaning to birth. They failed; and Mrs. Swithin, laying hold desperately of a fraction of her meaning, said: "What a small part I've had to play! But you've made me feel I could have played . . . Cleopatra!"

She nodded between the trembling bushes and ambled off.

The villagers winked. "Batty" was the word for Old Flimsy, breaking through the bushes.

"I might have been—Cleopatra," Miss La Trobe repeated. "You've stirred in me my unacted part," she meant.

"Now for the skirt, Mrs. Rogers," she said.

Mrs. Rogers stood grotesque in her black stockings. Miss La Trobe pulled the voluminous flounces of the Victorian age over her head. She tied the tapes. "You've twitched the invisible strings," was what the old lady meant; and revealed—of all people—Cleopatra! Glory possessed her. Ah, but she was not merely a twitcher of individual strings; she was one who seethes wandering bodies and floating voices in a cauldron, and makes rise up from its amorphous mass a re-created world. Her moment was on her— her glory.

"There!" she said, tying the black ribbons under Mrs. Rogers' chin. "That's done it! Now for the gentleman. Hammond!"

She beckoned Hammond. Sheepishly he came forward, and submitted to the application of black side whiskers. With his eyes half shut, his head leant back, he looked, Miss La Trobe thought, like King Arthur—noble, knightly, thin.

"Where's the Major's old frock coat?" she asked, trusting to the effect of that to transform him.

Tick, tick, tick, the machine continued. Time was passing. The audience was wandering, dispersing. Only the tick, tick of the gramophone held them together. There, sauntering solitary far away by the flower beds was Mrs. Giles escaping.

"The tune!" Miss La Trobe commanded. "Hurry up! The tune! The next tune! Number Ten!"

"Now may I pluck," Isa murmured, picking a rose, "my single

flower. The white or the pink? And press it so, twixt thumb and finger. . . ."

She looked among the passing faces for the face of the man in grey. There he was for one second; but surrounded, inaccessible. And now vanished.

She dropped her flower. What single, separate leaf could she press? None. Nor stray by the beds alone. She must go on; and she turned in the direction of the stable.

"Where do I wander?" she mused. "Down what draughty tunnels? Where the eyeless wind blows? And there grows nothing for the eye. No rose. To issue where? In some harvestless dim field where no evening lets fall her mantle; nor sun rises. All's equal there. Unblowing, ungrowing are the roses there. Change is not; nor the mutable and lovable; nor greetings nor partings; nor furtive findings and feelings, where hand seeks hand and eye seeks shelter from the eye."

She had come into the stable yard where the dogs were chained; where the buckets stood; where the great pear tree spread its ladder of branches against the wall. The tree, whose roots went beneath the flags, was weighted with hard green pears. Fingering one of them she murmured: "How am I burdened with what they drew from the earth; memories; possessions. This is the burden that the past laid on me, last little donkey in the long caravanserai crossing the desert. 'Kneel down,' said the past. 'Fill your pannier from our tree. Rise up, donkey. Go your way till your heels blister and your hoofs crack.' "

The pear was hard as stone. She looked down at the cracked flags beneath which the roots spread. "That was the burden," she mused, "laid on me in the cradle; murmured by waves; breathed by restless elm trees; crooned by singing women; what we must remember: what we would forget."

She looked up. The gilt hands of the stable clock pointed inflexibly at two minutes to the hour. The clock was about to strike.

"Now comes the lightning," she muttered, "from the stone blue sky. The thongs are burst that the dead tied. Loosed are our possessions."

Voices interrupted. People passed the stable yard, talking.

"It's a good day, some say, the day we are stripped naked. Others, it's the end of the day. They see the Inn and the Inn's keeper. But none speaks with a single voice. None with a voice free from the old vibrations. Always I hear corrupt murmurs; the chink of gold and metal. Mad music. . . ."

More voices sounded. The audience was streaming back to the terrace. She roused herself. She encouraged herself. "On, little donkey, patiently stumble. Hear not the frantic cries of the leaders who in that they seek to lead desert us. Nor the chatter of china faces glazed and hard. Hear rather the shepherd, coughing by the farmyard wall; the withered tree that sighs when the Rider gallops; the brawl in the barrack room when they stripped her naked; or the cry which in London when I thrust the window open someone cries . . ." She had come out on to the path that led past the greenhouse. The door was kicked open. Out came Mrs. Manresa and Giles. Unseen, Isa followed them across the lawns to the front row of seats.

The chuff, chuff, chuff of the machine in the bushes had stopped. In obedience to Miss La Trobe's command, another tune had been put on the gramophone. Number Ten. London street cries it was called. "A Pot Pourri."

"Lavender, sweet lavender, who'll buy my sweet lavender," the tune trilled and tinkled, ineffectively shepherding the audience. Some ignored it. Some still wandered. Others stopped, but stood upright. Some, like Colonel and Mrs. Mayhew, who had never left their seats, brooded over the blurred carbon sheet which had been issued for their information.

"The Nineteenth Century." Colonel Mayhew did not dispute the producer's right to skip two hundred years in less than fifteen minutes. But the choice of scenes baffled him.

"Why leave out the British Army? What's history without the Army, eh?" he mused. Inclining her head, Mrs. Mayhew protested after all one mustn't ask too much. Besides, very likely there would be a Grand Ensemble, round the Union Jack, to end with. Meanwhile, there was the view. They looked at the view.

"Sweet lavender . . . sweet lavender. . . ." Humming the tune old Mrs. Lynn Jones (of the Mount) pushed a chair forward. "Here, Etty," she said, and plumped down, with Etty Springett, with whom, since both were widows now, she shared a house.

"I remember . . ." she nodded in time to the tune. "You remember too—how they used to cry it down the streets." They remembered—the curtains blowing, and the men crying: "All a blowing, all a growing," as they came with geraniums, sweet william, in pots, down the street.

"A harp, I remember, and a hansom and a growler. So quiet the street was then. Two for a hansom, was it? One for a growler? And Ellen, in cap and apron, whistling in the street? D'you remember? And the runners, my dear, who followed, all the way from the station, if one had a box."

The tune changed. "Any old iron, any old iron to sell?" "D'you remember? That was what the men shouted in the fog. Seven Dials they came from. Men with red handkerchiefs. Garrotters, did they call them? You couldn't walk—Oh, dear me, no—home from the play. Regent Street. Piccadilly. Hyde Park Corner. The loose women . . . And everywhere loaves of bread in the gutter. The Irish you know round Covent Garden . . . Coming back from a Ball, past the clock at Hyde Park Corner, d'you remember the feel of white gloves? . . . My father remembered the old Duke in the Park. Two fingers like that—he'd touch his hat . . . I've got my mother's album. A lake and two lovers. She'd copied out Byron, I suppose, in what was called then the Italian hand. . . ."

"What's that? 'Knocked 'em in the Old Kent Road.' I remember the bootboy whistled it. Oh, my dear, the servants . . . Old Ellen . . . Sixteen pound a year wages . . . And the cans of hot water! And the crinolines! And the stays! D'you remember the Crystal Palace, and the fireworks, and how Mira's slipper got lost in the mud?"

"That's young Mrs. Giles . . . I remember her mother. She died in India . . . We wore, I suppose, a great many petticoats then. Unhygienic? I dare say . . . Well, look at my daughter. To the right, just behind you. Forty, but slim as a wand. Each flat has its refrigerator . . . It took my mother half the morning to order dinner. . . . We were eleven. Counting servants, eighteen in family. . . . Now they simply ring up the Stores . . . That's Giles coming, with Mrs. Manresa. She's a type I don't myself fancy. I may be wrong . . . And Colonel Mayhew, as spruce as ever . . . And Mr. Cobbet of Cobbs Corner, there, under the monkey puzzle tree. One don't see him often . . . That's what's so nice—it brings people together. These days, when we're all so busy, that's what one wants . . . The programme? Have you got it? Let's see what comes next . . . The Nineteenth Century . . . Look, there's the chorus, the villagers, coming on now, between the trees. First, there's a prologue. . . ."

A great box, draped in red baize festooned with heavy gold tassels, had been moved into the middle of the stage. There was a swish of dresses, a stir of chairs. The audience seated themselves, hastily, guiltily. Miss La Trobe's eye was on them. She gave them ten seconds to settle their faces. Then she flicked her hand. A pompous march tune brayed. "Firm, elatant, bold and blatant," etc. . . . And once more a huge symbolical figure emerged from the bushes. It was Budge the publican; but so disguised that even cronies who drank with him nightly failed to recognize him; and a little titter of enquiry as to his identity ran about among the villagers. He wore a long black many-caped cloak; waterproof; shiny; of the substance of a statue in Parliament Square; a helmet which suggested a policeman; a row of medals crossed his breast; and in his right hand he held extended a special constable's baton (loaned by Mr. Willert of the Hall). It was his voice, husky and rusty, issuing from a thick black cotton-wool beard that gave him away.

"Budge, Budge. That's Mr. Budge," the audience whispered.

Budge extended his truncheon and spoke:

It ain't an easy job, directing the traffic at 'Yde Park Corner. Buses and 'ansom cabs. All a-clatter on the cobbles. Keep to the right, can't you? Hi there, Stop!

(He waved his truncheon.)

There she goes, the old party with the umbrella right under the 'orse's nose.

(The truncheon pointed markedly at Mrs. Swithin.)

She raised her skinny hand as if in truth she had fluttered off the pavement on the impulse of the moment to the just rage of authority. Got her, Giles thought, taking sides with authority against his aunt.

Fog or fine weather, I does my duty (Budge continued). *At Piccadilly Circus; at 'Yde Park Corner, directing the traffic of 'Er Majesty's Empire. The Shah of Persia; Sultan of Morocco; or it may be 'Er Majesty in person; or Cook's tourists; black men; white* men; sailors, soldiers; crossing the ocean; to proclaim her Empire; all of 'em Obey the Rule of my truncheon.

(He flourished it magnificently from right to left.)

But my job don't end there. I take under my protection and direction the purity and security of all Her Majesty's minions; in all parts of her dominions; insist that they obey the laws of God and Man.

The laws of God and man (he repeated and made as if to consult a Statute; engrossed on a sheet of parchment which with great deliberation he now produced from his trouser pocket).

Go to Church on Sunday; on Monday, nine sharp, catch the City Bus. On Tuesday it may be, attend a meeting at the Mansion House for the redemption of the sinner; at dinner on Wednesday attend another—turtle soup. Some bother it may be in Ireland; Famine. Fenians. What not. On Thursday it's the natives of Peru require protection and correction; we give 'em what's due. But mark you, our rule don't end there. It's a Christian country, our Empire; under the White Queen Victoria. Over thought and religion; drink; dress; manners; marriage too, I wield my truncheon. Prosperity and respectability always go, as we know, 'and in 'and. The ruler of an Empire must keep his eye on the cot; spy too in the kitchen; drawing-room; library; wherever one or two, me and you, come together. Purity our watchword; prosperity and respectability. If not, why, let 'em fester in . . .

(He paused—no, he had not forgotten his words.)

Cripplegate; St. Gile's; Whitechapel; the Minories. Let 'em sweat at the mines; cough at the looms; rightly endure their lot. That's the price of Empire; that's the white man's burden. And, I can tell you, to direct the traffic orderly, at 'Yde Park Corner, Piccadilly Circus, is a whole-time, white man's job.

He paused, eminent, dominant, glaring from his pedestal. A very fine figure of a man he was, everyone agreed, his truncheon extended; his waterproof pendant. It only wanted a shower of rain, a flight of pigeons round his head, and the pealing bells of St. Paul's and the Abbey to transform him into the very spit and image of a Victorian constable; and to transport them to a foggy London afternoon, with the muffin bells ringing and the church bells pealing at the very height of Victorian prosperity.

There was a pause. The voices of the pilgrims singing, as they wound in and out between the trees, could be heard; but the words were inaudible. The audience sat waiting.

"Tut-tut-tut," Mrs. Lynn Jones expostulated. "There were grand men among them . . ." Why she did not know, yet somehow she felt that a sneer had been aimed at her father; therefore at herself.

Etty Springett tutted too. Yet, children did draw trucks in mines; there was the basement; yet Papa read Walter Scott aloud after dinner; and divorced ladies were not received at Court. How difficult to come to any conclusion! She wished they would hurry on with the next scene. She liked to leave a theatre knowing exactly what was meant. Of course this was only a village play. . . . They were setting another scene, round the red baize box. She read out from her programme:

"The Picnic Party. About 1860. Scene: A Lake. Characters——"

She stopped. A sheet had been spread on the Terrace. It was a lake apparently. Roughly painted ripples represented water. Those green stakes were bulrushes. Rather prettily, real swallows darted across the sheet.

"Look, Minnie!" she exclaimed. "Those are real swallows!"

"Hush, hush," she was admonished. For the scene had begun. A young man in peg-top trousers and side whiskers carrying a spiked stick appeared by the lake.

EDGAR T. . . . *Let me help you, Miss Hardcastle! There!*

(He helps Miss Eleanor Hardcastle, a young lady in crinoline and mushroom hat, to the top. They stand for a moment panting slightly, looking at the view.)

ELEANOR. *How small the Church looks down among the trees!*
EDGAR. . . . *So this is Wanderer's Well, the trysting place.*
ELEANOR. . . . *Please Mr. Thorold, finish what you were saying before the others come. You were saying, "Our aim in life . . ."*
EDGAR. . . . *Should be to help our fellow men.*
ELEANOR (sighing deeply). *How true—how profoundly true!*
EDGAR. . . . *Why sigh, Miss Hardcastle?—You have nothing to reproach yourself with—you whose whole life is spent in the service*

of others. *It was of myself that I was thinking. I am no longer
young. At twenty-four the best days of life are over. My life has
passed* (he throws a pebble on to the lake) *like a ripple in water.*

ELEANOR. *Oh Mr. Thorold, you do not know me. I am not what
I seem. I too*——

EDGAR. . . . *Do not tell me, Miss Hardcastle—no, I cannot believe
it—You have doubted?*

ELEANOR. *Thank Heaven not that, not that . . . But safe and
sheltered as I am, always at home, protected as you see me, as you
think me. O what am I saying? But yes, I will speak the truth,
before Mama comes. I too have longed to convert the heathen!*

EDGAR. . . . *Miss Hardcastle . . . Eleanor . . . You tempt me!
Dare I ask you? No—so young, so fair, so innocent. Think, I im-
plore you, before you answer.*

ELEANOR. . . . *I have thought—on my knees!*

EDGAR (taking a ring from his pocket). *Then. . . . My mother
with her last breath charged me to give this ring only to one to
whom a lifetime in the African desert among the heathens would
be*——

ELEANOR (taking the ring). *Perfect happiness! But hist!* (She
slips the ring into her pocket.) *Here's Mama!* (They start asunder.)

(Enter Mrs. Hardcastle, a stout lady in black bombazine,
upon a donkey, escorted by an elderly gentleman in a deer-
stalker's cap.)

MRS. H. . . . *So you stole a march upon us, young people. There
was a time, Sir John, when you and I were always first on top,
Now . . .*

(He helps her to alight. Children, young men, young women,
some carrying hampers, others butterfly nets, others spy-glasses,
others tin botanical cases, arrive. A rug is thrown by the lake
and Mrs. H. and Sir John seat themselves on camp stools.)

MRS. H. . . . *Now who'll fill the kettles? Who'll gather the sticks?
Alfred* (to a small boy), *don't run about chasing butterflies or
you'll make yourself sick . . . Sir John and I will unpack the
hampers, here where the grass is burnt, where we had the picnic
last year.*

850

(The young people scatter off in different directions. Mrs. H.
and Sir John begin to unpack the hamper.)

MRS. H. . . . *Last year poor dear Mr. Beach was with us. It was
a blessed release.* (She takes out a black-bordered handkerchief and
wipes her eyes.) *Every year one of us is missing. That's the ham . . .
That's the grouse . . . There in that packet are the game pasties . . .*
(She spreads the eatables on the grass.) *As I was saying poor dear
Mr. Beach . . . I do hope the cream hasn't curdled. Mr. Hardcastle
is bringing the claret. I always leave that to him. Only when Mr.
Hardcastle gets talking with Mr. Pigott about the Romans . . . last
year they quite came to words. . . . But it's nice for gentlemen to
have a hobby, though they do gather the dust—those skulls and
things. . . . But I was saying—— poor dear Mr. Beach. . . . I wanted
to ask you* (she drops her voice) *as a friend of the family, about the
new clergyman—they can't hear us, can they? No, they're picking
up sticks. . . . Last year, such a disappointment. Just got the things
out . . . down came the rain. But I wanted to ask you, about the
new clergyman, the one who's come in place of dear Mr. Beach. I'm
told the name's Sibthorp. To be sure, I hope I'm right, for I had
a cousin who married a girl of that name, and as a friend of the
family, we don't stand on ceremony . . . And when one has daughters—I'm sure I quite envy you, with only one daughter, Sir John,
and I have four! So I was asking you to tell me in confidence, about
this young—if that's-his-name—Sibthorp, for I must tell you the
day before yesterday our Mrs. Potts happened to say, as she passed
the Rectory, bringing our laundry, they were unpacking the furniture; and what did she see on top of the wardrobe? A tea cosy! But
of course she might be mistaken . . . But it occurred to me to ask
you, as a friend of the family, in confidence, has Mr. Sibthorp
a wife?*

Here a chorus composed of villagers in Victorian mantles, side
whiskers and top hats sang in concert:

*O has Mr. Sibthorp a wife? O has Mr. Sibthorp a wife? That is
the hornet, the bee in the bonnet, the screw in the cork and the
drill; that whirling and twirling are for ever unfurling the folds of
the motherly heart; for a mother must ask, if daughters she has,
begot in the feathery billowy fourposter family bed, O did he*

unpack, with his prayer book and bands; his gown and his cane; his rod and his line; and the family album and gun; did he also display the connubial respectable tea-table token, a cosy with honeysuckle embossed. Has Mr. Sibthorp a wife? O has Mr. Sibthorp a wife?

While the chorus was sung, the picnickers assembled. Corks popped. Grouse, ham, chickens were sliced. Lips munched. Glasses were drained. Nothing was heard but the chump of jaws and the chink of glasses.

"They did eat," Mrs. Lynn Jones whispered to Mrs. Springett. "That's true. More than was good for them, I dare say."

MR. HARDCASTLE . . . (brushing flakes of meat from his whiskers). Now . . .

"Now what?" whispered Mrs. Springett, anticipating further travesty.

Now that we have gratified the inner man, let us gratify the desire of the spirit. I call upon one of the young ladies for a song. CHORUS OF YOUNG LADIES . . . O not me . . . not me . . . I really couldn't . . . No, you cruel thing, you know I've lost my voice . . . I can't sing without the instrument . . . etc. etc. CHORUS OF YOUNG MEN. O bosh! Let's have "The Last Rose of Summer." Let's have "I Never Loved a Dear Gazelle." MRS. H. (authoritatively). Eleanor and Mildred will now sing "I'd be a Butterfly."

(Eleanor and Mildred rise obediently and sing a duet: "I'd be a Butterfly.")

MRS. H. Thank you very much, my dears. And now gentlemen, Our Country!

(Arthur and Edgar sing "Rule, Britannia.")

MRS. H. . . . Thank you very much. Mr. Hardcastle——
MR. HARDCASTLE (rising to his feet, clasping his fossil). Let us pray.

(The whole company rise to their feet.)

"This is too much, too much," Mrs. Springett protested.

MR. H. . . . Almighty God, giver of all good things, we thank

852

Thee: for our food and drink; for the beauties of Nature; for the understanding with which Thou hast enlightened us (he fumbled with his fossil). And for thy great gift of Peace. Grant us to be thy servants on earth; grant us to spread the light of thy . . .

Here the hindquarters of the donkey, represented by Albert the idiot, became active. Intentional was it, or accidental? "Look at the donkey! Look at the donkey!" A titter drowned Mr. Hardcastle's prayer; and then he was heard saying:

. . . a happy homecoming with bodies refreshed by thy bounty, and minds inspired by thy wisdom. Amen.

Holding his fossil in front of him, Mr. Hardcastle marched off. The donkey was captured; hampers were loaded; and forming into a procession, the picnickers began to disappear over the hill.

EDGAR (winding up the procession with Eleanor). *To convert the heathen!*

ELEANOR. *To help our fellow men!*

(The actors disappeared into the bushes.)

BUDGE. . . . *It's time, gentlemen, time ladies, time to pack up and be gone. From where I stand, truncheon in hand, guarding respectability, and prosperity, and the purity of Victoria's land, I see before me*—(he pointed: there was Pointz Hall; the rooks cawing; the smoke rising)—

'Ome, Sweet 'Ome.

The gramophone took up the strain: *Through pleasures and palaces, etc. There's no place like Home.*

BUDGE. . . . *Home, gentlemen; home, ladies, it's time to pack up and go home. Don't I see the fire* (he pointed: one window blazed red) *blazing ever higher? In kitchen; and nursery; drawing-room and library? That's the fire of 'Ome. And see! Our Jane has brought the tea. Now children where's the toys? Mama, your knitting, quick. For here* (he swept his truncheon at Cobbet of Cobbs Corner) *comes the bread-winner, home from the city, home from the counter, home from the shop. "Mama, a cup o' tea." "Children, gather round my knee. I will read aloud. Which shall it be? Sindbad the sailor? Or some simple tale from the Scriptures? And show you the pictures? What none of 'em? Then out with the bricks. Let's build: A conservatory? A laboratory? A mechanics' institute? Or shall it be a tower; with our flag on top; where our widowed Queen, after tea, calls the Royal orphans round her knee? For it's 'Ome, ladies, 'Ome, gentlemen. Be it never so humble, there's no place like 'Ome."*

The gramophone warbled Home, Sweet Home, and Budge, swaying slightly, descended from his box and followed the procession off the stage.

There was an interval.

"Oh but it was beautiful," Mrs. Lynn Jones protested. Home she meant; the lamplit room; the ruby curtains; and Papa reading aloud.

They were rolling up the lake and uprooting the bulrushes. Real swallows were skimming over real grass. But she still saw the home.

"It was . . ." she repeated, referring to the home.

"Cheap and nasty, I call it," snapped Etty Springett, referring to the play, and shot a vicious glance at Dodge's green trousers, yellow spotted tie, and unbuttoned waistcoat.

But Mrs. Lynn Jones still saw the home. Was there, she mused, as Budge's red baize pediment was rolled off, something—not impure, that wasn't the word—but perhaps "unhygienic" about the home? Like a bit of meat gone sour, with whiskers, as the servants called it? Or why had it perished? Time went on and on like the hands of the kitchen clock. (The machine chuffed in the bushes.) If they had met with no resistance, she mused, nothing wrong, they'd still be going round and round and round. The Home would have remained; and Papa's beard, she thought, would have grown and grown; and Mama's knitting—what did she do with all her knitting?—Change had to come, she said to herself, or there'd have been yards and yards of Papa's beard, of Mama's knitting. Nowadays her son-in-law was clean shaven. Her daughter had a refrigerator. . . . Dear, how my mind wanders, she checked herself. What she meant was, change had to come, unless things were perfect; in which case she supposed they resisted Time. Heaven was changeless.

"Were they like that?" Isa asked abruptly. She looked at Mrs. Swithin as if she had been a dinosaur or a very diminutive mammoth. Extinct she must be, since she had lived in the reign of Queen Victoria.

854

Tick, tick, tick, went the machine in the bushes.

"The Victorians," Mrs. Swithin mused. "I don't believe," she said with her odd little smile, "that there ever were such people. Only you and me and William dressed differently."

"You don't believe in history," said William.

The stage remained empty. The cows moved in the field. The shadows were deeper under the trees.

Mrs. Swithin caressed her cross. She gazed vaguely at the view. She was off, they guessed, on a circular tour of the imagination—one-making. Sheep, cows, grass, trees, ourselves—all are one. If discordant, producing harmony—if not to us, to a gigantic ear attached to a gigantic head. And thus—she was smiling benignly—the agony of the particular sheep, cow, or human being is necessary; and so—she was beaming seraphically at the gilt vane in the distance—we reach the conclusion that all is harmony, could we hear it. And we shall. Her eyes now rested on the white summit of a cloud. Well, if the thought gave her comfort, William and Isa smiled across her, let her think it.

Tick, tick, tick the machine reiterated.

"D'you get her meaning?" said Mrs. Swithin alighting suddenly. "Miss La Trobe's?"

Isa, whose eyes had been wandering, shook her head.

"But you might say the same of Shakespeare," said Mrs. Swithin.

"Shakespeare and the musical glasses!" Mrs. Manresa intervened. "Dear, what a barbarian you all make me feel!"

She turned to Giles. She invoked his help against this attack upon the jolly human heart.

"Tosh," Giles muttered.

Nothing whatever appeared on the stage.

Darts of red and green light flashed from the rings on Mrs. Manresa's fingers. He looked from them at Aunt Lucy. From her to William Dodge. From him to Isa. She refused to meet his eyes. And he looked down at his blood-stained tennis shoes.

He said (without words), "I'm damnably unhappy."

"So am I," Dodge echoed.

"And I too," Isa thought.

They were all caught and caged; prisoners; watching a spectacle. Nothing happened. The tick of the machine was maddening.

"On, little donkey," Isa murmured, "crossing the desert . . . bearing your burden . . ."

She felt Dodge's eye upon her as her lips moved. Always some cold eye crawled over the surface like a winter blue-bottle! She flicked him off.

"What a time they take!" she exclaimed irritably.

"Another interval," Dodge read out, looking at the programme.

"And after that, what?" asked Lucy.

"Present Time. Ourselves," he read.

"Let's hope to God that's the end," said Giles gruffly.

"Now you're being naughty," Mrs. Manresa reproved her little boy, her surly hero.

No one moved. There they sat, facing the empty stage, the cows, the meadows and the view, while the machine ticked in the bushes.

"What's the object," said Bartholomew, suddenly rousing himself, "of this entertainment?"

"The profits," Isa read out from her blurred carbon copy, "are to go to a fund for installing electric light in the Church."

"All our village festivals," Mr. Oliver snorted turning to Mrs. Manresa, "end with a demand for money."

"Of course, of course," she murmured, deprecating his severity, and the coins in her bead bag jingled.

"Nothing's done for nothing in England," the old man continued. Mrs. Manresa protested. It might be true, perhaps, of the Victorians; but surely not of ourselves? Did she really believe that we were disinterested? Mr. Oliver demanded.

"Oh you don't know my husband!" the wild child exclaimed, striking an attitude.

Admirable woman! You could trust her to crow when the hour struck like an alarm clock; to stop like an old bus horse when the bell rang. Oliver said nothing. Mrs. Manresa had out her mirror and attended to her face.

All their nerves were on edge. They sat exposed. The machine ticked. There was no music. The horns of cars on the high road were heard. And the swish of trees. They were neither one thing nor the other; neither Victorians nor themselves. They were suspended, without being, in limbo. Tick, tick, tick went the machine.

Isa fidgeted; glancing to right and to left over her shoulder.

"Four and twenty blackbirds, strung upon a string," she muttered.

"Down came an Ostrich, an eagle, an executioner,
'Which of you is ripe,' he said, 'to bake in my pie?
Which of you is ripe, which of you is ready,
Come my pretty gentleman,
Come my pretty lady.' . . ."

How long was she going to keep them waiting? "The Present Time. Ourselves." They read it on the programme. Then they read what came next: "The profits are to go to a fund for installing electric light in the Church." Where was the Church? Over there. You could see the spire among the trees.

"Ourselves. . . ." They returned to the programme. But what could she know about ourselves? The Elizabethans, yes; the Victorians, perhaps; but ourselves; sitting here on a June day in 1939—it was ridiculous. "Myself"—it was impossible. Other people, perhaps . . . Cobbet of Cobbs Corner; the Major; old Bartholomew; Mrs. Swithin—them, perhaps. But she won't get me—no, not me. The audience fidgeted. Sounds of laughter came from the bushes. But nothing whatsoever appeared on the stage.

"What's she keeping us waiting for?" Colonel Mayhew asked irritably. "They don't need to dress up if it's present time."

Mrs. Mayhew agreed. Unless of course she was going to end with a Grand Ensemble. Army; Navy; Union Jack; and behind them perhaps—Mrs. Mayhew sketched what she would have done had it been her pageant—the Church. In cardboard. One window, looking east, brilliantly illuminated to symbolize—she could work that out when the time came.

"There she is, behind the tree," she whispered, pointing at Miss La Trobe.

Miss La Trobe stood there with her eye on her script. "After Vic.," she had written, "try ten mins. of present time. Swallows, cows, etc." She wanted to expose them, as it were, to douche them, with present-time reality. But something was going wrong with the experiment. "Reality too strong," she muttered. "Curse 'em!" She felt everything they felt. Audiences were the devil. O to write a play without an audience—*the* play. But here she was fronting her audience. Every second they were slipping the noose. Her little game had gone wrong. If only she'd a back-cloth to hang between the trees—to shut out cows, swallows, present time! But she had nothing. She had forbidden music. Grating her fingers in the bark, she damned the audience. Panic seized her. Blood seemed to pour from her shoes. This is death, death, death, she noted in the margin of her mind; when illusion fails. Unable to lift her hand, she stood facing the audience.

And then the shower fell, sudden, profuse.

No one had seen the cloud coming. There it was, black, swollen, on top of them. Down it poured like all the people in the world weeping. Tears. Tears. Tears.

"O that our human pain could here have ending!" Isa murmured. Looking up she received two great blots of rain full in her face. They trickled down her cheeks as if they were her own tears. But they were all people's tears, weeping for all people. Hands were raised. Here and there a parasol opened. The rain was sudden and universal. Then it stopped. From the grass rose a fresh earthy smell.

"That's done it," sighed Miss La Trobe, wiping away the drops on her cheeks. Nature once more had taken her part. The risk she had run acting in the open air was justified. She brandished her script. Music began—A.B.C.—A.B.C. The tune was as simple as could be. But now that the shower had fallen, it was the other voice speaking, the voice that was no one's voice. And the voice that wept for human pain unending said:

> The King is in his counting house
> Counting out his money,
> The Queen is in her parlour . . .

"O that my life could here have ending," Isa murmured (taking care not to move her lips). Readily would she endow this voice with all her treasure if so be tears could be ended. The little twist of sound could have the whole of her. On the altar of the rain-soaked earth she laid down her sacrifice. . . .

"O look!" she cried aloud.

That was a ladder. And that (a cloth roughly painted) was a wall. And that a man with a hod on his back. Mr. Page the reporter, licking his pencil, noted: "With the very limited means at her disposal, Miss La Trobe conveyed to the audience Civilization (the wall) in ruins; rebuilt (witness man with hod) by human effort; witness also woman handing bricks. Any fool could grasp that. Now issued black man in fuzzy wig; coffee-coloured ditto in silver turban; they signify presumably the League of . . ."

A burst of applause greeted this flattering tribute to ourselves. Crude of course. But then she had to keep expenses down. A painted cloth must convey—what the *Times* and *Telegraph* both said in their leaders that very morning.

The tune hummed:

> The King is in his counting house
> Counting out his money,
> The Queen is in her parlour
> Eating . . .

Suddenly the tune stopped. The tune changed. A waltz, was it? Something half known, half not. The swallows danced it. Round and round, in and out they skimmed. Real swallows. Retreating and advancing. And the trees, O the trees, how gravely and sedately like senators in council, or the spaced pillars of some cathedral church. . . . Yes, they barred the music, and massed and hoarded; and prevented what was fluid from overflowing. The swallows—or martins were they?—The temple-haunting martins who come, have always come . . . Yes, perched on the wall, they seemed to foretell what after all the *Times* was saying yesterday. Homes will be built. Each flat with its refrigerator, in the crannied wall. Each of us a free man; plates washed by machinery; not an aeroplane to vex us; all liberated; made whole. . . .

The tune changed; snapped; broke; jagged. Foxtrot, was it? Jazz? Anyhow the rhythm kicked, reared, snapped short. What a jangle and a jingle! Well, with the means at her disposal, you can't ask too much. What a cackle, a cacophony! Nothing ended. So abrupt. And corrupt. Such an outrage; such an insult; And not plain. Very up to date, all the same. What is her game? To disrupt? Jog and trot? Jerk and smirk? Put the finger to the nose? Squint and pry? Peek and spy? O the irreverence of the generation which is only momentarily—thanks be—"the young." The young, who can't make, but only break; shiver into splinters the old vision; smash to atoms what was whole. What a cackle, what a rattle, what a yaffle—as they call the woodpecker, the laughing bird that flits from tree to tree.

Look! Out they come, from the bushes—the riffraff. Children?
Imps—elves—demons. Holding what? Tin cans? Bedroom candlesticks? Old jars? My dear, that's the cheval glass from the Rectory!
And the mirror—that I lent her. My mother's. Cracked. What's
the notion? Anything that's bright enough to reflect, presumably,
ourselves?

Ourselves! Ourselves!

Out they leapt, jerked, skipped. Flashing, dazzling, dancing,
jumping. Now old Bart . . . he was caught. Now Manresa. Here
a nose . . . There a skirt . . . Then trousers only . . . Now perhaps
a face. . . . Ourselves? But that's cruel. To snap us as we are, before we've had time to assume . . . And only, too, in parts. . . .
That's what's so distorting and upsetting and utterly unfair.

Mopping, mowing, whisking, frisking, the looking-glasses darted,
flashed, exposed. People in the back rows stood up to see the
fun. Down they sat, caught themselves . . . What an awful show-
up! Even for the old who, one might suppose, hadn't any longer
any care about their faces. . . . And Lord! the jangle and the din!
The very cows joined in. Walloping, tail lashing, the reticence of
nature was undone, and the barriers which should divide Man the
Master from the Brute were dissolved. Then the dogs joined in.
Excited by the uproar, scurrying and worrying, here they came!
Look at them! And the hound, the Afghan hound . . . look at him!

Then once more, in the uproar which by this time has passed
quite beyond control, behold Miss Whatshername behind the
tree summoned from the bushes—or was it they who broke away—
Queen Bess; Queen Anne; and the girl in the Mall; and the Age
of Reason; and Budge the policeman. Here they came. And the
Pilgrims. And the lovers. And the grandfather's clock. And the
old man with a beard. They all appeared. What's more, each
declaimed some phrase or fragment from their parts. . . . *I am
not* (said one) *in my perfect mind* . . . Another, *Reason am I* . . .
And I? I'm the old top hat. . . . *Home is the hunter, home from
the hill* . . . *Home? Where the miner sweats, and the maiden
faith is rudely strumpeted. . . . Sweet and low; sweet and low,
wind of the western sea* . . . *Is that a dagger that I see before me?
. . . The owl hoots and the ivy mocks tap-tap-tapping on the
pane. . . . Lady I love till I die, leave thy chamber and come* . . .
Where the worm weaves its winding sheet . . . I'd be a butterfly.

860

I'd be a butterfly. . . . In thy will is our peace. . . . Here, Papa, take your book and read aloud. . . . Hark, hark, the dogs do bark and the beggars . . .

It was the cheval glass that proved too heavy. Young Bonthorp for all his muscle couldn't lug the damned thing about any longer. He stopped. So did they all—hand glasses, tin cans, scraps of scullery glass, harness room glass, and heavily embossed silver mirrors—all stopped. And the audience saw themselves, not whole by any means, but at any rate sitting still.

The hands of the clock had stopped at the present moment. It was now. Ourselves.

So that was her little game! To show us up, as we are, here and now. All shifted, preened, minced; hands were raised, legs shifted. Even Bart, even Lucy, turned away. All evaded or shaded themselves—save Mrs. Manresa who, facing herself in the glass, used it as a glass; had out her mirror; powdered her nose; and moved one curl, disturbed by the breeze, to its place.

"Magnificent!" cried old Bartholomew. Alone she preserved unashamed her identity, and faced without blinking herself. Calmly she reddened her lips.

The mirror bearers squatted; malicious; observant; expectant; expository.

"That's them," the back rows were tittering. "Must we submit passively to this malignant indignity?" the front row demanded. Each turned ostensibly to say—O whatever came handy—to his neighbour. Each tried to shift an inch or two beyond the inquisitive insulting eye. Some made as if to go.

"The play's over, I take it," muttered Colonel Mayhew, retrieving his hat. "It's time . . ."

But before they had come to any common conclusion, a voice asserted itself. Whose voice it was no one knew. It came from the bushes—a megaphonic, anonymous, loud-speaking affirmation. The voice said:

Before we part, ladies and gentlemen, before we go . . . (Those who had risen sat down) *. . . let's talk in words of one syllable, without larding, stuffing or cant. Let's break the rhythm and forget the rhyme. And calmly consider ourselves. Ourselves. Some bony. Some fat.* (The glasses confirmed this.) *Liars most of us. Thieves too.* (The glasses made no comment on that.) *The poor are as bad*

861

as the rich are. Perhaps worse. Don't hide among rags. Or let our cloth protect us. Or for the matter of that book learning; or skilful practice on pianos; or laying on of paint. Or presume there's innocency in childhood. Consider the sheep. Or faith in love. Consider the dogs. Or virtue in those that have grown white hairs. Consider the gun slayers, bomb droppers here or there. They do openly what we do slyly. Take for example (here the megaphone adopted a colloquial, conversational tone) Mr. M's bungalow. A view spoilt for ever. That's murder. . . . Or Mrs. E's lipstick and blood-red nails. . . . A tyrant, remember, is half a slave. Item the vanity of Mr. H. the writer, scraping in the dunghill for sixpenny fame . . . Then there's the amiable condescension of the lady of the manor—the upper class manner. And buying shares in the market to sell 'em. . . . O we're all the same. Take myself now. Do I escape my own reprobation, simulating indignation, in the bush, among the leaves? There's a rhyme, to suggest, in spite of protestation and the desire for immolation, I too have had some, what's called, education . . . Look at ourselves, ladies and gentlemen! Then at the wall; and ask how's this wall, the great wall, which we call, perhaps miscall, civilization, to be built by (here the mirrors flicked and flashed) orts, scraps and fragments like ourselves?

All the same here I change (by way of the rhyme mark ye) to a loftier strain—there's something to be said: for our kindness to the cat; note too in today's paper "Dearly loved by his wife"; and the impulse which leads us—mark you, when no one's looking—to the window at midnight to smell the bean. Or the resolute refusal of some pimpled dirty little scrub in sandals to sell his soul. There is such a thing—you can't deny it. What? You can't descry it? All you can see of yourselves is scraps, orts and fragments? Well then listen to the gramophone affirming. . . .

A hitch occurred here. The records had been mixed. Fox-trot, Sweet Lavender, Home Sweet Home, Rule Britannia—sweating profusely, Jimmy, who had charge of the music, threw them aside and fitted the right one—was it Bach, Handel, Beethoven, Mozart or nobody famous, but merely a traditional tune? Anyhow, thank heaven, it was somebody speaking after the anonymous bray of the infernal megaphone.

Like quicksilver sliding, filings magnetized, the distracted united.

The tune began; the first note meant a second; the second a third. Then down beneath a force was born in opposition; then another. On different levels they diverged. On different levels ourselves went forward; flower gathering some on the surface; others descending to wrestle with the meaning; but all comprehending; all enlisted. The whole population of the mind's immeasurable profundity came flocking; from the unprotected, the unskinned; and dawn rose; and azure; from chaos and cacophony measure; but not the melody of surface sound alone controlled it; but also the warring battle-plumed warriors straining asunder: To part? No. Compelled from the ends of the horizon; recalled from the edge of appalling crevasses; they crashed; solved; united. And some relaxed their fingers; and other uncrossed their legs.

Was that voice ourselves? Scraps, orts and fragments, are we, also, that? The voice died away.

As waves withdrawing uncover; as mist uplifting reveals; so, raising their eyes (Mrs. Manresa's were wet; for an instant tears ravaged her powder) they saw, as waters withdrawing leave visible a tramp's old boot, a man in a clergyman's collar surreptitiously mounting a soap-box.

"The Rev. G. W. Streatfield," the reporter licked his pencil and noted, "then spoke . . ."

All gazed. What an intolerable constriction, contraction, and reduction to simplified absurdity he was to be sure! Of all incongruous sights a clergyman in the livery of his servitude to the summing up was the most grotesque and entire. He opened his mouth. O Lord, protect and preserve us from words the defilers, from words the impure! What need have we of words to remind us? Must I be Thomas, you Jane?

As if a rook had hopped unseen to a prominent bald branch, he touched his collar and hemmed his preliminary croak. One fact mitigated the horror; his forefinger, raised in the customary manner, was stained with tobacco juice. He wasn't such a bad fellow; the Rev. G. W. Streatfield; a piece of traditional church furniture; a corner cupboard; or the top beam of a gate, fashioned by generations of village carpenters after some lost-in-the-mists-of-antiquity model.

He looked at the audience; then up at the sky. The whole lot of them, gentles and simples, felt embarrassed, for him, for themselves. There he stood their representative spokesman; their symbol; themselves; a butt, a clod, laughed at by looking-glasses; ignored by the cows, condemned by the clouds which continued their majestic rearrangement of the celestial landscape; an irrelevant forked stake in the flow and majesty of the summer silent world.

His first words (the breeze had risen; the leaves were rustling) were lost. Then he was heard saying: "What." To that word he added another "Message"; and at last a whole sentence emerged; not comprehensible; say rather audible. "What message," it seemed he was asking, "was our pageant meant to convey?"

They folded their hands in the traditional manner as if they were seated in church.

"I have been asking myself"—the words were repeated—"what meaning, or message, this pageant was meant to convey?"

If he didn't know, calling himself Reverend, also M.A., who after all could?

"As one of the audience," he continued (words now put on meaning), "I will offer, very humbly, for I am not a critic"—and he touched the white gate that enclosed his neck with a yellow forefinger—"my interpretation. No, that is too bold a word. The gifted lady . . ." He looked round. La Trobe was invisible. He continued. "Speaking merely as one of the audience, I confess I was puzzled. For what reason, I asked, were we shown these scenes? Briefly, it is true. The means at our disposal this afternoon were limited. Still we were shown different groups. We were shown, unless I mistake, the effort renewed. A few were chosen; the many passed in the background. That surely we were shown. But again, were we not given to understand—am I too presumptuous? Am I treading, like angels, where as a fool I should absent myself? To me at least it was indicated that we are members one of another. Each is part of the whole. Yes, that occurred to me, sitting among you in the audience. Did I not perceive Mr. Hardcastle here" (he pointed) "at one time a Viking? And in Lady Harridan—excuse me, if I get the names wrong—a Canterbury pilgrim? We act different parts; but are the same. That I leave to you. Then again, as the play or pageant proceeded, my attention was distracted. Perhaps that too was part of the producer's intention? I thought I perceived that nature takes her part. Dare we, I asked myself, limit life to ourselves? May we not hold that there is a spirit that inspires, pervades . . ." (The swallows were sweeping round him. They seemed cognizant of his meaning. Then they swept out of sight.) "I leave that to you. I am not here to explain. That role has not been assigned me. I speak only as one of the audience, one of ourselves. I caught myself too reflected, as it happened in my own mirror . . ." (Laughter) "Scraps, orts and fragments! Surely, we should unite?"

"But" ("but" marked a new paragraph) "I speak also in another capacity. As Treasurer of the Fund. In which capacity" (he consulted a sheet of paper) "I am glad to be able to tell you that a sum of thirty-six pounds ten shillings and eightpence has been raised by this afternoon's entertainment towards our object: the illumination of our dear old church."

"Applause," the reporter reported.

Mr. Streatfield paused. He listened. Did he hear some distant music?

He continued: "But there is still a deficit" (he consulted his paper) "of one hundred and seventy-five pounds odd. So that each of us who has enjoyed this pageant has still an op . . . ." The word was cut in two. A zoom severed it. Twelve aeroplanes in perfect formation like a flight of wild duck came overhead. That was the music. The audience gaped; the audience gazed. Then zoom became drone. The planes had passed.

". . . portunity," Mr. Streatfield continued, "to make a contribution." He signalled. Instantly collecting boxes were in operation. Hidden behind glasses they emerged. Coppers rattled. Silver jingled. But O what a pity—how creepy it made one feel! Here came Albert, the idiot, jingling his collecting box—an aluminium saucepan without a lid. You couldn't very well deny him, poor fellow. Shillings were dropped. He rattled and sniggered; chattered and jibbered. As Mrs. Parker made her contribution—half a crown as it happened—she appealed to Mr. Streatfield to exorcise this evil, to extend the protection of his cloth.

The good man contemplated the idiot benignly. His faith had room, he indicated, for him too. He too, Mr. Streatfield appeared to be saying, is part of ourselves. But not a part we like to recognize, Mrs. Springett added silently, dropping her sixpence.

Contemplating the idiot, Mr. Streatfield had lost the thread of his discourse. His command over words seemed gone. He

865

twiddled the cross on his watchchain. Then his hand sought his trouser pocket. Surreptitiously he extracted a small silver box. It was plain to all that the natural desire of the natural man was overcoming him. He had no further use for words.

"And now," he resumed, cuddling the pipe lighter in the palm of his hand, "for the pleasantest part of my duty. To propose a vote of thanks to the gifted lady . . ." He looked round for an object corresponding to this description. None such was visible. ". . . who wishes it seems to remain anonymous." He paused. "And so . . ." He paused again.

It was an awkward moment. How to make an end? Whom to thank? Every sound in nature was painfully audible; the swish of the trees; the gulp of a cow; even the skim of the swallows over the grass could be heard. But no one spoke. Whom could they make responsible? Whom could they thank for their entertainment? Was there no one?

Then there was a scuffle behind the bush; a preliminary premonitory scratching. A needle scraped a disc; chuff, chuff, chuff; then having found the rut, there was a roll and a flutter which portended God . . . (they all rose to their feet) Save the King.

Standing, the audience faced the actors; who also stood with their collecting boxes quiescent, their looking-glasses hidden, and the robes of their various parts hanging stiff.

> Happy and glorious,
> Long to reign over us,
> God save the King

The notes died away.

Was that the end? The actors were reluctant to go. They lingered; they mingled. There was Budge the policeman talking to old Queen Bess. And the Age of Reason hobnobbed with the foreparts of the donkey. And Mrs. Hardcastle patted out the folds of her crinoline. And little England, still a child, sucked a peppermint drop out of a bag. Each still acted the unacted part conferred on them by their clothes. Beauty was on them. Beauty revealed them. Was it the light that did it?—the tender, the fading, the uninquisitive but searching light of evening that reveals depths in water and makes even the red brick bungalow radiant?

866

"Look," the audience whispered, "O look, look, look—" And once more they applauded; and the actors joined hands and bowed.

Old Mrs. Lynn Jones, fumbling for her bag, sighed, "What a pity—must they change?"

But it was time to pack up and be off.

"Home, gentlemen; home ladies; it's time to pack up and be off," the reporter whistled, snapping the band round his notebook. And Mrs. Parker was stooping.

"I'm afraid I've dropped my glove. I'm so sorry to trouble you. Down there, between the seats. . . ."

The gramophone was affirming in tones there was no denying, triumphant yet valedictory: *Dispersed are we; who have come together. But,* the gramophone asserted, *let us retain whatever made that harmony.*

O let us, the audience echoed (stooping, peering, fumbling), keep together. For there is joy, sweet joy, in company.

Dispersed are we, the gramophone repeated.

And the audience turning saw the flaming windows, each daubed with golden sun; and murmured: "Home, gentlemen; sweet . . ." yet delayed a moment, seeing through the golden glory perhaps a crack in the boiler; perhaps a hole in the carpet; and hearing, perhaps, the daily drop of the daily bill.

Dispersed are we, the gramophone informed them. And dismissed them. So, straightening themselves for the last time, each grasping, it might be a hat, or a stick or a pair of suède gloves, for the last time they applauded Budge and Queen Bess; the trees; the white road; Bolney Minster; and the Folly. One hailed another, and they dispersed, across lawns, down paths, past the house to the gravel-strewn crescent, where cars, push bikes and cycles were crowded together.

Friends hailed each other in passing.

"I do think," someone was saying, "Miss Whatshername should have come forward and not left it to the rector . . . After all, she wrote it. . . . I thought it brilliantly clever . . . O my dear, I thought it utter bosh. Did you understand the meaning? Well, he said she meant we all act all parts. . . . He said, too, if I caught his meaning, Nature takes part. . . . Then there was the idiot. . . . Also, why leave out the Army, as my husband was saying, if it's history? And if one spirit animates the whole, what about the aeroplanes? . . . Ah, but you're being too exacting. After all, remember, it was only a village play. . . . For my part, I think they should have passed a vote of thanks to the owners. When we had our pageant, the grass didn't recover till autumn . . . Then we had tents. . . . That's the man, Cobbet of Cobbs Corner, who wins all the prizes at all the shows. I don't myself admire prize flowers, nor yet prize dogs . . ."

Dispersed are we, the gramophone triumphed, yet lamented,
Dispersed are we. . . .

"But you must remember," the old cronies chatted, "they had to do it on the cheap. You can't get people, at this time o' year, to rehearse. There's the hay, let alone the movies. . . . What we need is a centre. Something to bring us all together . . . The Brookes have gone to Italy, in spite of everything. Rather rash? . . . If the worst should come—let's hope it won't—they'd hire an aeroplane, so they said. . . . What amused me was old Streatfield, feeling for his pouch. I like a man to be natural, not always on a perch. . . . Then those voices from the bushes. . . . Oracles? You're referring to the Greeks? We're the oracles, if I'm not being irreverent, a foretaste of our own religion? Which is what? . . . Crepe soles? That's so sensible . . . They last much longer and protect the feet. . . . But I was saying: can the Christian faith adapt itself? In times like these . . . At Larting no one goes to church . . . There's the dogs, there's the pictures. . . . It's odd that science, so they tell me, is making things (so to speak) more spiritual . . . The very latest notion, so I'm told is, nothing's solid . . . There, you can get a glimpse of the church through the trees. . . .

"Mr. Umphelby! How nice to see you! Do come and dine . . . No, alas, we're going back to town. The House is sitting . . . I was telling them, the Brookes have gone to Italy. They've seen the volcano. Most impressive, so they say—they were lucky—in eruption. I agree—things look worse than ever on the continent. And what's the channel, come to think of it, if they mean to invade us? The aeroplanes, I didn't like to say it, made one think. . . . No, I thought it much too scrappy. Take the idiot. Did she mean, so to speak, something hidden, the unconscious as they call it? But why always drag in sex. . . . It's true, there's a sense

in which we all, I admit, are savages still. Those women with red
nails. And dressing up—what's that? The old savage, I suppose. . . .
That's the bell. Ding dong. Ding . . . Rather a cracked old bell . . .
And the mirrors! Reflecting us . . . I called that cruel. One feels
such a fool, caught unprotected . . . There's Mr. Streatfield,
going, I suppose to take the evening service. He'll have to hurry,
or he won't have time to change. . . . He said she meant we all act.
Yes, but whose play? Ah, that's the question! And if we're left
asking questions, isn't it a failure, as a play? I must say I like to
feel sure if I go to the theatre, that I've grasped the meaning . . .
Or was that, perhaps, what she meant? . . . Ding dong. Ding . . .
that if we don't jump to conclusions, if you think, and I think,
perhaps one day, thinking differently, we shall think the same?

"There's dear old Mr. Carfax . . . Can't we give you a lift, if you
don't mind playing bodkin? We were asking questions, Mr.
Carfax, about the play. The looking-glasses now—did they mean
the reflection is the dream; and the tune—was it Bach, Handel, or
no one in particular—is the truth? Or was it t'other way about?

"Bless my soul, what a dither! Nobody seems to know one car
from another. That's why I have a mascot, a monkey . . . But I
can't see it . . . While we're waiting, tell me, did you feel when
the shower fell, someone wept for us all? There's a poem, *Tears,
tears tears*, it begins. And goes on, *O then the unloosened ocean
. . .* but I can't remember the rest.

"Then when Mr. Streatfield said: One spirit animates the
whole—the aeroplanes interrupted. That's the worst of playing
out of doors. . . . Unless of course she meant that very thing . . .
Dear me, the parking arrangements are not what you might call
adequate . . . I shouldn't have expected either so many Hispano-
Suizas . . . That's a Rolls . . . That's a Bentley . . . That's the
new type of Ford. . . . To return to the meaning—Are machines
the devil, or do they introduce a discord . . . Ding dong, ding . . .
by means of which we reach the final . . . Ding dong. . . . Here's
the car with the monkey . . . Hop in . . . And good-bye, Mrs.
Parker . . . Ring us up. Next time we're down don't forget . . .
Next time . . . Next time . . ."

The wheels scurred on the gravel. The cars drove off.

The gramophone gurgled *Unity—Dispersity*. It gurgled *Un . . .
dis . . .* And ceased.

The little company who had come together at luncheon were left standing on the terrace. The pilgrims had bruised a lane on the grass. Also, the lawn would need a deal of clearing up. Tomorrow the telephone would ring: "Did I leave my handbag? . . . A pair of spectacles in a red leather case? . . . A little old brooch of no value to anyone but me?" Tomorrow the telephone would ring.

Now Mr. Oliver said: "Dear lady," and, taking Mrs. Manresa's gloved hand in his, pressed it, as if to say: "You have given me what you now take from me." He would have liked to hold on for a moment longer to the emeralds and rubies dug up, so people said, by thin Ralph Manresa in his ragamuffin days. But alas, sunset light was unsympathetic to her make-up; plated it looked, not deeply interfused. And he dropped her hand; and she gave him an arch roguish twinkle, as if to say—but the end of that sentence was cut short. For she turned, and Giles stepped forward; and the light breeze which the meteorologist had foretold fluttered her skirts; and she went, like a goddess, buoyant, abundant, with flower-chained captives following in her wake.

All were retreating, withdrawing and dispersing; and he was left with the ash grown cold and no glow, no glow on the log. What word expressed the sag at his heart, the effusion in his veins, as the retreating Manresa, with Giles attendant, admirable woman, all sensation, ripped the rag doll and let the sawdust stream from his heart?

The old man made a guttural sound, and turned to the right. On with the hobble, on with the limp, since the dance was over. He strolled alone past the trees. It was here, early that very morning, that he had destroyed the little boy's world. He had popped out with his newspaper; the child had cried.

Down in the dell, past the lily pool, the actors were undressing. He could see them among the brambles. In vests and trousers; unhooking; buttoning up: on all fours; stuffing clothes into cheap attaché cases; with silver swords, beards and emeralds on the grass. Miss La Trobe in coat and skirt—too short, for her legs were stout—battled with the billows of a crinoline. He must respect the conventions. So he stopped, by the pool. The water was opaque over the mud.

Then, coming up behind him, "Oughtn't we to thank her?" Lucy asked him. She gave him a light pat on the arm.

How imperceptive her religion made her! The fumes of that incense obscured the human heart. Skimming the surface, she ignored the battle in the mud. After La Trobe had been excruciated by the Rector's interpretation, by the maulings and the manglings of the actors . . . "She don't want our thanks, Lucy," he said gruffly. What she wanted, like that carp (something moved in the water) was darkness in the mud; a whisky and soda at the pub; and coarse words descending like maggots through the waters.

"Thank the actors, not the author," he said. "Or ourselves, the audience."

He looked over his shoulder. The old lady, the indigenous, the prehistoric, was being wheeled away by a footman. He rolled her through the arch. Now the lawn was empty. The line of the roof, the upright chimneys, rose hard and red against the blue of the evening. The house emerged; the house that had been obliterated. He was damned glad it was over—the scurry and the scuffle, the rouge and the rings. He stooped and raised a peony that had shed its petals. Solitude had come again. And reason and the lamplit paper. . . . But where was his dog? Chained in a kennel? The little veins swelled with rage on his temples. He whistled. And here, released by Candish, racing across the lawn with a fleck of foam on the nostril, came his dog.

Lucy still gazed at the lily pool. "All gone," she murmured, "under the leaves." Scared by shadows passing, the fish had withdrawn. She gazed at the water. Perfunctorily she caressed her cross. But her eyes went water searching, looking for fish. The lilies were shutting; the red lily, the white lily, each on its plate of leaf. Above, the air rushed; beneath was water. She stood between two fluidities, caressing her cross. Faith required hours of kneeling in the early morning. Often the delight of the roaming eye seduced her—a sunbeam, a shadow. Now the jagged leaf at the corner suggested, by its contours, Europe. There were other leaves. She fluttered her eye over the surface, naming leaves India, Africa, America. Islands of security, glossy and thick.

"Bart . . ." She spoke to him. She had meant to ask him about the dragon-fly—couldn't the blue thread settle, if we destroyed it here, then there? But he had gone into the house.

Then something moved in the water; her favorite fantail. The golden orfe followed. Then she had a glimpse of silver—the great carp himself, who came to the surface so very seldom. They slid on, in and out between the stalks, silver; pink; gold; splashed; streaked; pied.

"Ourselves," she murmured. And retrieving some glint of faith from the grey waters, hopefully, without much help from reason, she followed the fish; the speckled, streaked, and blotched; seeing in that vision beauty, power, and glory in ourselves.

Fish had faith, she reasoned. They trust us because we've never caught 'em. But her brother would reply: "That's greed." "Their beauty!" she protested. "Sex," he would say. "Who makes sex susceptible to beauty?" she would argue. He shrugged who? Why? Silenced, she returned to her private vision; of beauty which is goodness; the sea on which we float. Mostly impervious, but surely every boat sometimes leaks?

He would carry the torch of reason till it went out in the darkness of the cave. For herself, every morning, kneeling, she protected her vision. Every night she opened the window and looked at leaves against the sky. Then slept. Then the random ribbons of birds' voices woke her.

The fish had come to the surface. She had nothing to give them—not a crumb of bread. "Wait, my darlings," she addressed them. She would trot into the house and ask Mrs. Sands for a biscuit. Then a shadow fell. Off they flashed. How vexatious! Who was it? Dear me, the young man whose name she had forgotten; not Jones! nor Hodge . . .

Dodge had left Mrs. Manresa abruptly. All over the garden he had been searching for Mrs. Swithin. Now he found her; and she had forgotten his name.

"I'm William," he said. At that she revived, like a girl in a garden in white, among roses, who came running to meet him—an unacted part.

"I was going to get a biscuit—no, to thank the actors," she stumbled, virginal, blushing. Then she remembered her brother. "My brother," she added, "says one mustn't thank the author, Miss La Trobe."

It was always "my brother . . . my brother" who rose from the depths of her lily pool.

As for the actors, Hammond had detached his whiskers and was now buttoning up his coat. When the chain was inserted between the buttons he was off.

Only Miss La Trobe remained, bending over something in the grass.

"The play's over," he said. "The actors have departed."

"And we mustn't, my brother says, thank the author," Mrs. Swithin repeated, looking in the direction of Miss La Trobe.

"So I thank you," he said. He took her hand and pressed it. Putting one thing with another, it was unlikely that they would ever meet again.

The church bells always stopped, leaving you to ask: Won't there be another note? Isa, half-way across the lawn, listened. . . . Ding, dong, ding . . . There was not going to be another note. The congregation was assembled, on their knees, in the church. The service was beginning. The play was over; swallows skimmed the grass that had been the stage.

There was Dodge, the lip reader, her semblable, her conspirator, a seeker like her after hidden faces. He was hurrying to rejoin Mrs. Manresa who had gone in front with Giles—"the father of my children," she muttered. The flesh poured over her, the hot, nerve wired, now lit up, now dark as the grave physical body. By way of healing the rusty fester of the poisoned dart she sought the face that all day long she had been seeking. Preening and peering, between backs, over shoulders, she had sought the man in grey. He had given her a cup of tea at a tennis party; handed her, once, a racquet. That was all. But, she was crying, had we met before the salmon leapt like a bar of silver . . . had we met, she was crying. And when her little boy came battling through the bodies in the Barn "Had he been his son," she had muttered . . . In passing she stripped the bitter leaf that grew, as it happened, outside the nursery window. Old Man's Beard. Shrivelling the shreds in lieu of words, for no words grow there, nor roses either, she swept past her conspirator, her semblable, the seeker after vanished faces "like Venus" he thought, making a rough translation, "to her prey . . ." and followed after.

Turning the corner, there was Giles attached to Mrs. Manresa. She was standing at the door of her car. Giles had his foot on the edge of the running board. Did they perceive the arrows about to strike them?

"Jump in, Bill," Mrs. Manresa chaffed him.

And the wheels scurred on the gravel, and the car drove off.

At last, Miss La Trobe could raise herself from her stooping position. It had been prolonged to avoid attention. The bells had stopped; the audience had gone; also the actors. She could straighten her back. She could open her arms. She could say to the world, You have taken my gift! Glory possessed her—for one moment. But what had she given? A cloud that melted into the other clouds on the horizon. It was in the giving that the triumph was. And the triumph faded. Her gift meant nothing. If they had understood her meaning; if they had known their parts; if the pearls had been real and the funds illimitable—it would have been a better gift. Now it had gone to join the others.

"A failure," she groaned, and stooped to put away the records.

Then suddenly the starlings attacked the tree behind which she had hidden. In one flock they pelted it like so many winged stones. The whole tree hummed with the whizz they made, as if each bird plucked a wire. A whizz, a buzz rose from the bird-buzzing, bird-vibrant, bird-blackened tree. The tree became a rhapsody, a quivering cacophony, a whizz and vibrant rapture, branches, leaves, birds syllabling discordantly life, life, life, without measure, without stop devouring the tree. Then up! Then off!

What interrupted? It was old Mrs. Chalmers, creeping through the grass with a bunch of flowers—pinks apparently—to fill the vase that stood on her husband's grave. In winter it was holly, or ivy. In summer, a flower. It was she who had scared the starlings. Now she passed.

Miss La Trobe nicked the lock and hoisted the heavy case of gramophone records to her shoulder. She crossed the terrace and stopped by the tree where the starlings had gathered. It was here that she had suffered triumph, humiliation, ecstasy, despair—for nothing. Her heels had ground a hole in the grass.

It was growing dark. Since there were no clouds to trouble the sky, the blue was bluer, the green greener. There was no longer a view—no Folly, no spire of Bolney Minster. It was land merely, no land in particular. She put down her case and stood looking at the land. Then something rose to the surface.

"I should group them," she murmured, "here." It would be midnight; there would be two figures, half concealed by a rock. The curtain would rise. What would the first words be? The words escaped her.

Again she lifted the heavy suit case to her shoulder. She strode off across the lawn. The house was dormant; one thread of smoke thickened against the trees. It was strange that the earth, with all those flowers incandescent—the lilies, the roses, and clumps of white flowers and bushes of burning green—should still be hard. From the earth green waters seemed to rise over her. She took her voyage away from the shore, and, raising her hand, fumbled for the latch of the iron entrance gate.

She would drop her suit case in at the kitchen window, and then go on up to the Inn. Since the row with the actress who had shared her bed and her purse the need of drink had grown on her. And the horror and the terror of being alone. One of these days she would break—which of the village laws? Sobriety? Chastity? Or take something that did not properly belong to her?

At the corner she ran into old Mrs. Chalmers returning from the grave. The old woman looked down at the dead flowers she was carrying and cut her. The women in the cottages with the red geraniums always did that. She was an outcast. Nature had somehow set her apart from her kind. Yet she had scribbled in the margin of her manuscript: "I am the slave of my audience."

She thrust her suit case in at the scullery window and walked on, till at the corner she saw the red curtain at the bar window. There would be shelter; voices; oblivion. She turned the handle of the public house door. The acrid smell of stale beer saluted her; and voices talking. They stopped. They had been talking about Bossy as they called her—it didn't matter. She took her chair and looked through the smoke at a crude glass painting of a cow in a stable; also at a cock and a hen. She raised her glass to her lips. And drank. And listened. Words of one syllable sank down into the mud. She drowsed; she nodded. The mud became fertile. Words rose above the intolerably laden dumb oxen plodding through the mud. Words without meaning—wonderful words.

The cheap clock ticked; smoke obscured the pictures. Smoke became tart on the roof of her mouth. Smoke obscured the earth-coloured jackets. She no longer saw them, yet they upheld her, sitting arms akimbo with her glass before her. There was the high ground at midnight; there the rock; and two scarcely perceptible figures. Suddenly the tree was pelted with starlings. She set down her glass. She heard the first words.

Down in the hollow, at Pointz Hall, beneath the trees, the table was cleared in the dining room. Candish, with his curved brush had swept the crumbs; had spared the petals and finally left the family to dessert. The play was over, the strangers gone, and they were alone—the family.

Still the play hung in the sky of the mind—moving, diminishing, but still there. Dipping her raspberry in sugar, Mrs. Swithin looked at the play. She said, popping the berry into her mouth, "What did it mean?" and added: "The peasants; the kings; the fool and" (she swallowed) "ourselves?"

They all looked at the play; Isa, Giles and Mr. Oliver. Each of course saw something different. In another moment it would be beneath the horizon, gone to join the other plays. Mr. Oliver, holding out his cheroot said: "Too ambitious." And, lighting his cheroot he added: "Considering her means."

It was drifting away to join the other clouds: becoming invisible. Through the smoke Isa saw not the play but the audience dispersing. Some drove; others cycled. A gate swung open. A car swept up the drive to the red villa in the cornfields. Low hanging boughs of acacia brushed the roof. Acacia petalled the car arrived.

"The looking-glasses and the voices in the bushes," she murmured. "What did she mean?"

"When Mr. Streatfield asked her to explain, she wouldn't," said Mrs. Swithin.

Here, with its sheaf sliced in four, exposing a white cone, Giles offered his wife a banana. She refused it. He stubbed his match on the plate. Out it went with a little fizz in the raspberry juice.

"We should be thankful," said Mrs. Swithin, folding her napkin, "for the weather, which was perfect, save for one shower."

Here she rose, Isa followed her across the hall to the big room.

They never pulled the curtains till it was too dark to see, nor shut the windows till it was too cold. Why shut out the day before it was over? The flowers were still bright; the birds chirped. You could see more in the evening often when nothing interrupted, when there was no fish to order, no telephone to answer. Mrs. Swithin stopped by the great picture of Venice—school of Canaletto. Possibly in the hood of the gondola there was a little figure—a woman, veiled; or a man?

Isa, sweeping her sewing from the table, sank, her knee doubled, into the chair by the window. Within the shell of the room she overlooked the summer night. Lucy returned from her voyage into the picture and stood silent. The sun made each pane of her glasses shine red. Silver sparkled on her black shawl. For a moment she looked like a tragic figure from another play.

Then she spoke in her usual voice. "We made more this year than last, he said. But then last year it rained."

"This year, last year, next year, never . . ." Isa murmured. Her hand burnt in the sun on the window sill. Mrs. Swithin took her knitting from the table.

"Did you feel," she asked, "what he said: we act different parts but are the same?"

"Yes," Isa answered. "No," she added. It was Yes, No. Yes, yes, yes, the tide rushed out embracing. No, no, no, it contracted. The old boot appeared on the shingle.

"Orts, scraps and fragments," she quoted what she remembered of the vanishing play.

Lucy had just opened her lips to reply, and had laid her hand on her cross caressingly, when the gentlemen came in. She made her little chirruping sound of welcome. She shuffled her feet to clear a space. But in fact there was more space than was needed, and great hooded chairs.

They sat down, ennobled both of them by the setting sun. Both had changed. Giles now wore the black coat and white tie of the professional classes, which needed—Isa looked down at his feet—patent leather pumps. "Our representative, our spokesman," she sneered. Yet he was extraordinarily handsome. "The father of my children, whom I love and hate." Love and hate—how they tore her asunder! Surely it was time someone invented a new plot, or that the author came out from the bushes . . .

Here Candish came in. He brought the second post on a silver salver. There were letters; bills; and the morning paper—the paper that obliterated the day before. Like a fish rising to a crumb of biscuit, Bartholomew snapped at the paper. Giles slit the flap of an apparently business document. Lucy read a criss-cross from an old friend at Scarborough. Isa had only bills.

The usual sounds reverberated through the shell; Sands making up the fire; Candish stoking the boiler. Isa had done with her bills. Sitting in the shell of the room she watched the pageant fade. The flowers flashed before they faded. She watched them flash.

The paper crackled. The second hand jerked on. M. Daladier had pegged down the franc. The girl had gone skylarking with the troopers. She had screamed. She had hit him. . . . What then?

When Isa looked at the flowers again, the flowers had faded.

Bartholomew flicked on the reading lamp. The circle of the readers, attached to white papers, was lit up. There in that hollow of the sun-baked field were congregated the grasshopper, the ant, and the beetle, rolling pebbles of sun-baked earth through the glistening stubble. In that rosy corner of the sun-baked field Bartholomew, Giles and Lucy polished and nibbled and broke off crumbs. Isa watched them.

Then the newspaper dropped.

"Finished?" said Giles, taking it from his father.

The old man relinquished his paper. He basked. One hand caressing the dog rippled folds of skin towards the collar.

The clock ticked. The house gave little cracks as if it were very brittle, very dry. Isa's hand on the window felt suddenly cold. Shadow had obliterated the garden. Roses had withdrawn for the night.

Mrs. Swithin folding her letter murmured to Isa: "I looked in and saw the babies, sound asleep, under the paper roses."

"Left over from the Coronation," Bartholomew muttered, half asleep.

"But we needn't have been to all that trouble with the decorations," Lucy added, "for it didn't rain this year."

"This year, last year, next year, never," Isa murmured.

"Tinker, tailor, soldier, sailor," Bartholomew echoed. He was talking in his sleep.

Lucy slipped her letter into its envelope. It was time to read now, her Outline of History. But she had lost her place. She turned the pages looking at pictures—mammoths, mastodons, prehistoric birds. Then she found the page where she had stopped.

The darkness increased. The breeze swept round the room. With a little shiver Mrs. Swithin drew her sequin shawl about her shoulders. She was too deep in the story to ask for the window to be shut. "England," she was reading, "was then a swamp. Thick forests covered the land. On the top of their matted branches birds sang . . ."

The great square of the open window showed only sky now. It was drained of light, severe, stone cold. Shadows fell. Shadows crept over Bartholomew's high forehead; over his great nose. He looked leafless, spectral, and his chair monumental. As a dog shudders its skin, his skin shuddered. He rose, shook himself, glared at nothing, and stalked from the room. They heard the dog's paws padding on the carpet behind him.

Lucy turned the page, quickly, guiltily, like a child who will be told to go to bed before the end of the chapter.

"Prehistoric man," she read, "half-human, half-ape, roused himself from his semi-crouching position and raised great stones."

She slipped the letter from Scarborough between the pages to mark the end of the chapter, rose, smiled, and tiptoed silently out of the room.

The old people had gone up to bed. Giles crumpled the newspaper and turned out the light. Left alone together for the first time that day, they were silent. Alone, enmity was bared; also love. Before they slept, they must fight; after they had fought, they would embrace. From that embrace another life might be born. But first they must fight, as the dog fox fights with the vixen, in the heart of darkness, in the fields of night.

Isa let her sewing drop. The great hooded chairs had become enormous. And Giles too. And Isa too against the window. The window was all sky without colour. The house had lost its shelter. It was night before roads were made, or houses. It was the night that dwellers in caves had watched from some high place among rocks.

Then the curtain rose. They spoke.

PERMANENT LIBRARY BOOKS

The Permanent Library makes available to the general reader those works of the world's great writers which have long been out of print, or which are not readily obtainable. They give a better understanding of the wide range of the talents of these masters of literature. The volumes are carefully edited, durably bound and tastefully designed. The average length is in excess of 700 pages.

Printed in the United States of America
by The Haddon Craftsmen, Inc., Scranton, Pa.